The Romance of Leonardo da Vinci

DMITRI MEREJKOWSKI

THE ROMANCE OF LEONARDO DA VINCI

GARDEN CITY PUBLISHING COMPANY, INC.
GARDEN CITY, NEW YORK

THE ROMANCE OF LEONARDO DA VINCI

The Gods Resurgent

Translated by Bernard Guilbert Guerney from the Russian of Dmitri Merejkowski

Printed in the United States of America

RANDOM HOUSE NEW YORK, N. Y.

THIS TRANSLATION OF A
RUSSIAN MASTERPIECE AND A WORLD CLASSIC
IS DEDICATED TO

C. T. REVERE, Esq.,

AS A MARK OF THE TRANSLATOR'S
SINCERE ESTEEM AND REGARD

B. G. G.

FOREWORD AND BIOGRAPHICAL SKETCH

In the introduction to his translation of Merejkowski's *Menace of the Mob*,—a most Sibylline book,—the present writer and translator dealt with Dmitri Sergeivich as Prophet, Publicist, and Practicing Christian. The volume at hand will show the author as an artist in letters.

Dmitri, youngest son of Sergei Ivanovich Merejkowski and Varvara Vasilievna, *née* Chestrokova, was born (ah, the inevitable but inescapable *cliché* of biography!) August 14, 1865. He had three sisters and five brothers, and was his mother's favourite son,—he pays a grateful tribute to her good influence upon him. His father, on the contrary, was most stern,—Dmitri, in speaking of his own education, bluntly proclaims that he owes just as little to his schooling as to his father.

The melancholy pervading the ancestral marish park, with its copses, its pools and its sea view, could not else than affect his childhood. As a schoolboy he was shy and withdrawn; nor must we omit the "holy legends and folk-tales" told him by his old nurse, —such a nurse as Pushkin has immortalized. Even before the first of his teens he was imbued with mysticism, and penned poetry! His first critical effort, as well, was made at about the same age. And it is also significant that the winters of his childhood were spent in an old house builded in the reign of Peter the Great,—and within sight of the great Czar's palace, his hut, and his church.

The future author of *Peter and Alexis* was educated at the end of the eighties and the commencement of the nineties,—the era of severest classicism. Graduating from the gymnasia, in 1884, he matriculated at the University of St. Petersburg, taking the Historical-Philosophical course. Here he had his initiatory experience with the government: he formed a Molière club, which as a matter of course underwent an *obisk*—"raid" conveys but mildly the meaning of this word—by the political police; exile was averted only through his father's influence. Later, toward the end of the nineties, he was to found a religious and philosophical society, under the impetus of his wife, Zinaida Hippius, the famous poetess. Needless to add, this society also was promptly suppressed.

At the University he went in for Positivism in earnest, studying

Comte, Spencer, Mill and Darwin. "But, since I was religious, I perceived, dimly, the instability of the Positivistic Philosophy. Ponder as I might, I could discover no way out, and was beset by pains and doubts." The "way out"—Christianity—is indicated most clearly in *The Menace of the Mob*,—but is also shown, to varying extents, in practically all his other works. But this revelation was to come later; the "dim perception" haunted him for years.

Merejkowski first appeared in print in 1882, when a poem of his was published in the *Illustrated Survey*—under the editorship of Schiller-Mikhailov. His subsequent efforts were printed in *Notes of the Fatherland*. To the *Northern Messenger* he contributed a "ponderous dramatic poem, *Sylvia*," and an essay on Chekhov, when the latter was just beginning, and had not yet won recognition. The trilogy of *Christ and Antichrist* was begun in 1893,—and took twelve years to complete. *The Death of the Gods: Julian the Apostate* was everywhere rejected, but finally accepted by the *Sievernyi Viestnik* —*The Northern Messenger*—"And there the novel was taken only through pity." We are told further: "I received an especially poor welcome in Russian literature, and, to this day, have to contend with a certain attitude of animosity. I can by now celebrate my twenty-fifth anniversary of unfair persecution at the hands of Russian critics."

At present Merejkowski, like many other Russian literary giants, including Kuprin and Bunin, lives in Paris.

As for the work at hand,—I am fully familiar with the effectiveness of quotation; but, since space forbids, I shall have to content myself by merely hinting at the excellencies of *Leonardo da Vinci*. There is but one other book which can be compared with it in the magic power of evoking startlingly vivid pictures of the Middle Ages,—I refer, of course, to *Contes Drolatiques*. What a gorgeous pageant, full of pomp and magnificence, is *Leonardo!* Yet it is not devoid, here and there, of the necessary and skillfully timed peeps behind the *coulisses*,—into the mortal and the humble frailties and exigencies behind the grandeur. . . . To me, although it must be said that the novel is not entirely free from certain time-honoured devices and *impedimenta* of the historical novel, it is, odd as it may sound, chock-full of a sly, crisp humour,—a comparison with *Romola* (which, as the reader will doubtlessly recall, treats of much the same period, personages and places) will clearly demonstrate the point; also, that while Eliot has succeeded to some extent in giving us a capable study in the deterioration of a moral structure, she has not, to any corresponding extent, galvanized that character's era into any perceptible semblance of life; whereas Merejkowski is veritably a necromancer,—using the term in its precise meaning. The reader comes away not only with the memory of a full-length, throbbingly living depiction of one of the world's most remarkable true genuises,—but of an entire era, as remarkable as the geniuses it has produced—or been produced by. . . .

Hardened as I am, by daily higgling and chaffering, I have yet, during the past few months felt myself daily—or, rather, nightly—hobnobbing with the great, grand and curious ones of this world: with prelates, popes, princes; with meretrices, mercenaries and martyrs; with alchemists, wizards and witches; with Machiavelli, Michelangelo, and the Borgias. . . . How odd it was to be Englishing—at four in the morning!—the passages dealing with the nocturnal habits of Cæsar Borgia, whose wont it was to turn night into day. . . . One of New York's main arteries lying with its pulse well-nigh still; the moonlight upon it seemed the moonlight of Florence; the policeman trying the shop door was in mediæval trappings, and his club was a halberd. . . . Dawn would break; sleep had long since been subdued, and one was in a half-dazed, yet strangely alert mood, when one's perceptions are of a peculiar keenness, when one sees the most curious of analogies in everyday objects, when one's mind is thronged with unbelievably quaint and droll conceits,—a mood, I imagine, similar to that induced by hashish-eating. . . . The fumes which swirled out of the opened shop door on such mornings did not seem those of night-long stale tobacco smoke, but of an alchemical furnace. . . . If any of my patrons have, of such a morning, found me at all up-stage, or my speech of an archaic turn, I trust they will bear in mind the lofty company I had spent the night with, and accept the apologies now extended.

One or two things more, and I am ready to release the eager reader to the delectable pages that follow. *Leonardo* contains portions which are veritable poems in prose—such as Cassandra's visit to the deserted isle temple of an unknown god; curiously read as I am, I can recall no other bit, in any language, that even approximates Merejkowski's stark description of Walpurgis night,—a sheer *tour de force* of the *macabre*. . . . "Great" and "greatest" have been so bandied about by criticasters as to have lost practically all meaning; nevertheless, I must apply the term of great to *Leonardo* among the world's best historical novels; and, even as *The Cloister and the Hearth* ranks as greatest of such novels in English, I would rank *Leonardo* as the greatest of the *genre* in Russian. As to whether it be the greatest historical romance in any language, I shall let the truest of all critics and the ultimate arbiter—the gentle *purchaser*—decide.

A word as to the translation: whatever its merits,—or possible defects,—the *purchaser* will find it more complete than any other in English,—this translation has, moreover, the distinct advantage of being absolutely unbowdlerized—and the only version in English, I firmly believe, done directly from the original Russian, and not re-translated from the French. . . . I have also taken full advantage of the opportunity afforded by this new edition to revise the slips and errors that seem inevitable . . . Should the *purchaser*—or even the reader—derive half as much pleasure from the perusal of *Leonardo* as I have from the Englishing, he will be amply rewarded.

BERNARD GUILBERT GUERNEY.

At the Sign of the Blue Faun,
Autumn of 1927.
Revised, Spring of 1930.

BOOK ONE

The White She-Demon

I

N FLORENCE, THE WAREHOUSES OF THE GUILD of Dyers were situated side by side with the Canonica of Or San Michele.

The clumsy additions, coops, uneven abutments on rickety props, clung to the houses, their tiled roofs meeting so closely up above that all that was left of the sky was a narrow crack, and, even in the daytime, it was dark in the street. Near the entrances to the shops, upon cross-pieces, hung samples of foreign woollen stuffs, dyed in Florence. In the gutter in the middle of the street, which was paved with flat cobbles, swirled multicoloured liquids, poured out of the dyeing vats. Over the doors of the more important *fondachi*, or mercers' shops, could be seen shields with the coat of arms of the Calimala, the Guild of the Dyers: on a field scarlet an eagle of gold upon a round bale of white wool.

Messer Cipriano Buonaccorsi, a rich Florentine merchant and a Consul of the noble art of the Calimala, was sitting in one of the *fondachi* surrounded by commercial records and thick account books.

In the cold light of a March day, amid the exhalations of dampness wafted up from the cellars cumbered up with goods, the old man shivered and wrapped himself closely in his coat of squirrel fur,—much worn and out-at-the-elbows. A goose quill was stuck behind his ear, and with his weak, near-sighted, but all-seeing eyes, he was looking over, with seeming negligence but in reality with attentiveness, the parchment leaves of an enormous book, its pages divided lengthwise and across into sections; *Credit* to the left, *Debit* to the right. The entries of goods were made in an even, round hand, all in capitals, without any dots or commas, with Roman numerals,—by no means Arabic, which were deemed a flighty innovation, unseemly for business records. On the first page, in large letters, was written:

IN THE NAME OF OUR LORD JESUS CHRIST AND THE EVER VIRGIN MARY THIS ACCOMPT BOOK IS BEGUN IN THE YEAR OF OUR LORD MCCCCXCIV.

Having finished checking the latest entries, and after painstakingly correcting an error in the number of measures of long cayenne peppers, ginger from Mecca, and bundles of chicory, taken as security for woollen goods, Messer Cipriano with a tired air leaned back in his chair, closed his eyes, and fell to planning a business letter, which he had to despatch to his chief clerk at the wool fair in Montpellier, in France.

Someone entered the shop. The old man, opening his eyes, saw a tenant farmer of his, Grillo, who rented some tilth and vineyards from him at his villa of San Gervasio, at the foot of the mountains, in the valley of Mugnone.

Grillo was bowing, holding a basket of eggs, neatly nested in straw. Dangling at his belt, with their small combs downward, and their legs trussed, were two live cockerels.

"Ah, Grillo!" said Buonaccorsi, with his wonted amiability, which he used both for the great and the humble alike. "How doth the Lord treat thee? 'Twould seem this will be a friendly spring."

"Even the spring bringeth no joy to us who are old, Messer Cipriano: our bones ache grievously—a-crying for the grave.—Here be some eggs and cockerels for your lordship against the radiant holiday," he added, after a short silence.

Grillo, with a sly kindliness, puckered up his greenish eyes, the fine sunburned wrinkles gathering about them,—such wrinkles as are to be seen in people used to sun and wind. Buonaccorsi, having thanked the old man, fell to business.

"Well, now, are the labourers ready on the farm? Will we succeed in finishing before daylight?"

Grillo sighed heavily and became lost in thought, leaning on his stick.

"All is in readiness, and there are labourers enough. Only here is something of which I would inform you, messer,—would it not be better to bide our time?"

"Thou thyself, old man, didst say but the other day that it was impossible to wait,—someone might get wind of it before us."

"That may be so, well enough, but still, a body is afraid. 'Tis a sin! These be holy days, and lenten, whereas our business is none of the cleanest. . . ."

"Ah, well, I shall take the sin upon my soul. Have no fear, I shall not give thee away. The only thing is,—shall we find aught?"

"How else! There be all the favourable omens. Our sires and grandsires knew of the mound behind the mill at the Wet Glen. Little phantom-fires run at night over San Giovanni. Then, too, it must be said,—we have a lot of this here rubbish. They do say, now, that when they were digging a well the other day in the vineyard at Marignola, they dragged a whole devil out of the clay. . . ."

"Whatever are you saying? A whole devil?"

"Of copper, with horns. His legs were rough, like a goat's—with hoofs at the ends of them. And his little muzzle was gay,—just like he was a-laughing; a-dancing on one leg, he was, and a-snapping of his fingers. Grown all green from age, he was, and all over with moss."

"What was done with him?"

"They melted him into a bell for the new chapel of the Archangel Michele."

Messer Cipriano became well-nigh wroth.

"Why hast thou told me naught of this before, Grillo?"

"You were going away to Siena on business."

"Well, thou couldst have written me. I would have sent someone. I would have come myself,—nor would I have spared any sum; ten bells would I have moulded for them. Fools! A bell,—out of a dancing Faun; mayhap the work of the ancient Hellenic sculptor Scopas. . . ."

"Yea, verily,—they were fools. Only, may it please you, be not wroth, Messer Cipriano. For punished they are, even as it is,—ever since the time of the hanging of the new bell, for two years running, the worms have been eating the apples and cherries in the orchards, and the olives have failed. And the sound of the bell is ill."

"But wherein is it ill?"

"How shall I tell you? It hath no real sound. It doth not gladden the heart. It just simply gibbers somewhat or other, that hath no meaning. You know how it is yourself,—what sort of a bell can a body expect to get out of a devil! Messer, I say it not to anger your lordship,—but the priest may, after all, be in the right: out of all these unclean things that are dug up no good can come. Here a body must carry the matter out with care, and keep his eyes open,—guarding himself with the cross and with prayer, for strong is the devil and cunning, the son of a dog,—he will crawl in at one ear and out th' other! Take, for instance, even this marble hand that Zacciello dug up last year at the Mill Mound,—the Foul One did lead us astray, and we did but gain misfortune from it,—God forbid, 'tis frightful even to recall it. . . ."

"Tell me Grillo,—how did you find it?"

"The matter fell out in autumn, on the eve of St. Martin's Day. We had sat down to supper, and the housewife had just put on the table a dish of bread mash, when a farm hand runs into the room,—my gossip's nephew, Zacciello. Now, I must tell you, I had left him that night in the field, by the Mill Mound, to uproot an olive stump,—I wanted to plant that place with hemp. 'Master, eh master!' mumbles Zacciello, all out of his wits; he's all shivering, and his teeth all a-chatter, 'The Lord be with thee, lad!' 'There's an ill hap,' says he, 'going on in the field, there's a dead man clambering out from under the stump. If ye believe it not, go, look for yourselves.' We took lanthorns and went.

"It had grown dark. The crescent moon had come up from behind the grove. Then we see the stump,—alongside there is upturned earth, and something white glimmering in it. I bend down and look, —there's a hand sticking up out of the earth, white, and the fingers beautiful, slender, like those of city maids. 'Ah, a fit take thee,' thinks I, 'what devil's doings be these?' I lower the lanthorn into the pit, so as to have a better look all around it,—when the hand starts stirring, beckoning me with its dainty fingers. After that I could not hold out any more; I began shouting, and my legs gave way from under me. But Monna Bonda, the gammer,—we count her a knowing one, a sorceress and a midwife, a spry old woman, even though an ancient,—she up and says: 'Whatever are ye feared of, ye fools, can ye not see the hand is nor living nor dead, but of stone?' She grabbed hold of it, gave a jerk, and pulled it out of the ground, like a turnip. At the joint, above the wrist, the hand was broken off. 'Granny,' I yell to her, 'oh, granny, leave it be, touch it not, let us bury it in the ground, fast as we can, or else, like as not, we may but gain misfortune with it.' 'No,' says she, 'that would not be right; the best thing, now, is to bring it first to the church, to the priest, that he may read an exorcism over it.' She fooled me, did the old woman: she never took the hand to the priest, but put it in her chest which she kept in a corner, where she had all sorts of odds and ends, —bits of rag, ointments, herbs and vials. I railed at her to give the hand up, but Monna Bonda had gotten her back up. And since that time gammer has taken to working wonder cures. If someone gets a toothache,—she will but touch the cheek with the idol's hand, and the swelling goes down. It has helped in fever, in belly-ache, in the falling sickness. If a cow be in torment, and can not drop her calf, gammer will put the stone hand upon her belly; the cow will let out a moo, and, lo and behold ye,—there's the little calf, already stirring in the straw.

"The fame of it started going around the neighbouring settlements. The old woman took in a lot of money at that time. Only no good came of it. The priest, Father Faustino, would give me no peace: if I went to church, he would reproach me at sermon before everybody, calling me a son of perdition, a servant of the devil; threatening to complain to the bishop, and deprive me of the Holy Sacrament. The urchins ran after me on the street, pointing their fingers at me: 'There goes Grillo; Grillo himself is a sorcerer, and his gammer is a witch; both sold their souls to the devil.' Would you believe it, even at night I had no rest: I dreamt of the marble hand all the time—it seemed to steal up on me, taking me softly, oh, so softly by the neck, as though it were caressing me, with its long, clammy fingers and then, suddenly, it would seize me so hard, squeezing my gullet and choking me,—I'd want to cry out and could not.

"Eh, thinks I, 'tis an evil jest. One morning I got up before it was light, and when gammer went out over the dew in the meadows to pick grasses, I broke the lock of the chest, took the hand, and carried it off to you,—though the rag-picker Lotto was giving me ten *soldi*, whereas from you I got but eight. But we would not spare even our life for your lordship, let alone two *soldi*,—may the Lord send you good days, and to Madonna Angelica, and your little children, and your grandchildren."

"Yes, judging by all thou tellest me, Grillo, we shall find somewhat at the Mill Mound," Cipriano pronounced meditatively.

"We will, never fear," continued the old man, again sighing deeply, "only what if Father Faustino gets wind of it? If he but should, he would rake me over the coals good and plenty, as well as interfere with you,—he'd stir up the country-folk, nor let us finish the work. Ah, well, God is gracious. Only do you not also forsake me, my benefactor,—put in a word for me before the judge."

"Dost thou mean the piece of land that the miller would get away from thee?"

"Just so, messer. The miller is a skinflint and a cheat. He knows where the devil has his tail. I had made the judge the gift of a heifer, d'you see, and so had he,—but one that was heavy with calf. During the litigation she ups and drops her calf. He had gone me one better, the scoundrel. So I fear me the judge may somehow decide in his favour, because the heifer, for my sins, calved a bullock. Do you now defend me, father of mine! 'Tis only for your lordship that I am trying so hard at the Mound of the Mill,—nor would I take such a sin upon my soul for anyone else. . . ."

"Set your mind at ease, Grillo. The judge is a crony of mine, and I shall take care of thee. And now go. They shall feed thee and treat thee to wine in the kitchen. This night we shall both ride to San Gervasio."

The old man, making a low bow, thanked him and departed, while Messer Cipriano withdrew to his little workroom next the shop, where none had permission to enter.

Here, as in a museum, marbles and bronzes were set and hung about the wall. Ancient coins and medals were set off to their best advantage on cloth-covered boards. Fragments of statues, as yet unassorted, were lying in boxes. Through his multitudinous mercantile agencies he acquired antiquities from every source where they could be found,—from Athens, Smyrna, and Halicarnassus; from Cyprus, Leukosia, and Rhodes; from the depths of Egypt and of Asia Minor.

Having surveyed his treasures, the Consul of Calimala again plunged into austere, weighty thoughts about customs duties on wool, and, having considered everything thoroughly, he began composing the letter to his trusted agent in Montpellier.

II

At the same time, in the depth of the warehouse, where the bales of goods, piled up to the ceiling, were seen even during the day only by a small hanging lamp glimmering before a Madonna, three young men were conversing: Doffo, Antonio, and Giovanni. Doffo, a clerk of Messer Buonaccorsi, red-haired, pug-nosed, and good-naturedly gay, was inscribing in a book the number of ells of measured cloth. Antonio da Vinci, a youth of elderly looks, with glassy, ichthyal eyes, with stubbornly unruly strands of thin black hair, was dexterously measuring the stuffs with the *canna*,—a Florentine linear measure. Giovanni Beltraffio—a timid and retiring Milanese youth of nineteen, a student of painting, whose big grey eyes were innocent and mournful, and whose face bore an expression of vacillation —was seated cross-legged on a bale already checked, attentively listening.

"There, brethren, that's what we have come to," Antonio was saying, in a low and malevolent voice; "they have taken to digging up pagan deities out of the ground!

"Scotch wool, with nap, brown, thirty ells, six palms, eight inches," he added, turning to Doffo, who entered the figures in the stock record. Then, having folded the measured bolt, Antonio threw it, angrily but deftly, so that it fell exactly in the place intended, and, elevating his index finger with the air of a prophet, imitating Fra Girolamo Savonarola, he exclaimed:

"*Gladius Dei super terram cito et velociter!* To St. John at Patmos came a vision: an Angel 'laid hold on the dragon, that old serpent, which is the Devil,' and bound him a thousand years, and cast him into the bottomless pit, and shut him up, and set a seal upon him, that he should deceive the nations no more till the thousand years should be fulfilled;[1] to the full time, and over. Now Satan is getting free from his dungeon. The thousand years have come to an end. False gods, forerunners, and the servants of Antichrist are coming out of the ground, out from under the seal of the Angel, that they may seduce the nations. Woe to them that dwell on the earth and on the sea! . . . Yellow Brabant wool, smooth—seventeen ells, four palms, nine inches."

"How think ye, then, Antonio," asked Giovanni with a timid and avid curiosity, "do all these portents bear witness?"

"Yea, yea,—not otherwise. Be on your guard! The time is near. And now they dig up not only the ancient gods, but create new ones in the image of the ancient. The sculptors and painters of today serve Moloch,—the Devil, that is. Out of the Church of the Lord they make the Temple of Satan. Upon the holy images, in the guise of martyrs and saints, they depict unclean gods, before whom they prostrate themselves: instead of John the Precursor,—Bacchus; instead of the Mother of God,—Venus the wanton Whore. Such pictures ought to be burned and their ashes cast to the winds!"

In the dull eyes of the pious clerk a malevolent fire sprang up.

Giovanni kept his peace, not daring to contradict, contracting his thin, childlike eyebrows in a helpless effort of thought.

"Antonio," he spoke at last, "I have heard that your cousin, Leonardo da Vinci, accepts pupils in his atelier occasionally. I have been wanting for a long time . . ."

"If you would," Antonio cut him short, "if you would send your soul to perdition,—go to Messer Leonardo."

"How? Why?"

"Even though he be my cousin, and older than I by twenty years, still the Scripture sayeth: Thou shalt turn away from a heretic, after a first admonition, and a second. Messer Leonardo is a heretic and a godless man. His mind is darkened by a Satanic pride. Through the medium of mathematics and black magic he thinks to penetrate the mysteries of nature. . . ."

And, lifting up his eyes to heaven, he quoted the words of Savonarola's latest sermon:

"'The wisdom of this age is madness before the Lord. Full well we know these learned men: they shall all come to the dwelling-place of Satan!'"

"But have you heard, Antonio," continued Giovanni, still more timidly, "that Messer Leonardo is now here, in Florence? He has just arrived from Milan."

"What for?"

"The Duke has sent him, to find out if it be not possible to purchase certain of the pictures which belonged to the late Lorenzo the Magnificent."

"If he be here, then he here be,—'tis all one to me," Antonio cut him short, applying himself with still greater assiduity to measuring the cloth with the *canna*.

The churches began their evensong. Doffo stretched himself with pleasure and slammed the book shut. Work was over; the shops were closing up. Giovanni went out into the street. Between the wet roofs was a grey sky with the barely perceptible pink shading of evening. A fine drizzle was falling through the windless air.

Suddenly from an open window in a neighbouring alley came a song:

> *O vaghe montanine e pastorelle.*
> Oh mountain maids, oh lovely shepherd girls.

The voice was a young and a resonant one. Giovanni surmised, by the even sound of a pedal, that it was a spinster singing at her spinning wheel.

He lost himself in listening, recalled that it was the time of spring, and felt his heart beat from inexplicable emotion and pensiveness.

"Nanna! Nanna! Wherever art thou at, thou devil's wench? Art thou grown deaf, or what? Come to supper! The macaroni will grow cold."

Wooden shoon,—*zoccoli*,—clattered sprightlily over a brick floor, —and everything grew quiet.

Giovanni continued standing for a long while, gazing at the empty window, and in his ears rang the vernal refrain like the trills of a distant shepherd's pipe:

O vaghe montanine e pastorelle.

Then, sighing softly, he entered the house of the Consul of Calimala, and by a steep staircase with rotted, shaky railings, bored through and through by worms, went up into a large room which served as a library, where, bent over a writing stand, sat one Giorgio Merulla, the court chronicler of the Duke of Milan.

III

MERULLA had come to Florence at the order of his lord, for the purchase of rare works from the library of Lorenzo de Medici, and, as always, had stopped at the house of his friend, as great a lover of antiquities as himself,—Messer Cipriano Buonaccorsi. With Giovanni Beltraffio the learned historian had become acquainted by chance at a hostelry on the road from Milan, and, under the pretence that he, Merulla, stood in need of a good scribe, and that Giovanni wrote a beautiful and clear hand, had taken him along into Cipriano's house.

When Giovanni entered the room, Merulla was painstakingly looking over a tattered book, which looked like a church missal or psalter. He was carefully passing a moist sponge over its thin parchment, of the finest, made from the skin of a still-born Hibernian lamb; some of the lines he erased with a pumice stone, smoothing them down with a knife blade and a polishing iron, then inspected them again, lifting them up to the light.

"Ye little darlings!" he was muttering under his breath, spluttering in his joyous emotion. "Come, come now, ye poor little things.

—come out into God's daylight. . . . But,—how long you are, how beautiful!"

He snapped two fingers and, momentarily desisting from his labours, lifted up his little bald head, with its bloated face, its gentle, mobile wrinkles, its purple livid nose, and little leaden eyes, full of life and irrepressible gaiety. Alongside, on the window sill, stood a clay pitcher and a mug. The scholar poured out some wine for himself, drained it, grunted, and was about to plunge once more into his work, when he caught sight of Giovanni.

"Good day, my little friar!" the old man greeted him jocosely—he dubbed Giovanni thus for his modesty. "I have grown weary for thee. 'Wherever did he go to?' thinks I. What if, of all things, he hath fallen in love? There be fine little girls in Florence, now. 'Tis no sin to fall in love. But then, I am not losing time in vain, either. Thou hast never seen such an amusing thing in all thy born days, probably. Wouldst have me show it to thee? Or better not,—for thou mayst blab of it. For I have bought it from a Jew, an old-clothes-man, for a copper,—found it among rubbish. Oh, well, come what may,—to thee alone!"

He beckoned to him with his finger:

"Here, here, to the light!"

And he pointed to the page, covered with crowded, angular letters of church script. These were acathisti, prayers, psalms, with enormous, clumsy notes for singing.

Then he took the book from him, opened it at another page, raised it up to the light almost on a level with his eyes,—and Giovanni noted that wherever Merulla had scraped off the churchly letters, other lines had appeared, almost imperceptible, the colourless impressions of ancient writing, depressions in the parchment,—not letters, but mere wraiths of long vanished letters, wan and gentle.

"What? See, see,—dost see them?" Merulla reiterated with exultation. "There they are, the darlings! I told thee, little friar, 'twas a pleasant thing!"

"What is this? From what work?" asked Giovanni.

"I know not myself, as yet. Fragments from an old anthology, 'twould seem. And mayhap they are even new, as yet unknown to the world, treasures of the Hellenic muse. But then, if it were not for me, they would never have even seen God's daylight! They would lie to the end of time under antiphonies and penitential psalms. . . ."

And Merulla explained to him, how some mediæval monkish transcriber, desirous of utilizing the precious parchment, had scraped off the ancient pagan lines and had inscribed new ones over them.

The sun, without rending the rain-veil, but merely glimmering through, filled the room with its fading rosy reflection, and caused the intensified impressions, the shadows of the ancient letters, to stand out still more clearly.

"See, see,—the dead are coming out of their graves!" Merulla was repeating, enraptured. "A hymn to the Olympians, 'twould seem. Here, look, one can read the first lines!"

And he translated for him from the Greek:

Glory to thee, Bacchus, benignant, splendidly crowned with clusters,
Glory, to thee, far-darting Phœbus, silver-crescented, awesome,
God of the beautiful locks, slayer of the sons of Niobe.

"And here, too, is a hymn to Venus, whom thou dost dread so, little friar! Only 'tis difficult to make it out. . . ."

Glory to thee, golden-limbed mother, Aphrodite,
Joyance of gods and of mortals. . . .

The stanza ended abruptly, disappearing under the church script.

Giovanni lowered the book, and the impressions of the letters paled, the depressions became effaced, sunk in the even yellowness of the parchment,—the shadows had disappeared. Only the distinct, fat, black letters of the monastery missal were visible, and the enormous, clumsy pothooks of the notes of the penitential psalm:

Give ear to my prayer, O God; attend unto me and hear me: I mourn in my complaint, and make a noise; my heart is sore pained within me; and the terrors of death are fallen upon me.[2]

The rosy glow expired, and the room began to grow dark. Merulla poured some wine out of the pitcher, drained it, and offered some to his companion.

"Well, brother, here is to my health. *Vinum super omnia bonum diligamus!*"

Giovanni declined.

"Well, then, God be with thee. I shall drink for thee. But why art thou so cast down to-day, little friar,—just as though someone had dowsed thee? Or has that holier-than-thou Antonio again scared thee with prophecies? Out upon them, Giovanni,—really, now—out upon them! And why do they croak so, the bigots?—be damned to them! Confess,—didst speak with Antonio?"

"I did."

"Whereof?"

"Of Antichrist and Messer Leonardo da Vinci. . . ."

"Well, there it is! Why, that is all thou dost rave about, this Leonardo. Has he bewitched thee, or what? Listen, brother, throw all that nonsense out of thy head. Do thou stay as my secretary,— I shall quickly make a man of mark of thee; I shall teach thee Latin, make thee a jurist, an orator, or a poet laureate; thou shalt wax rich, and become renowned. Well, now, what is painting? Even the philosopher Seneca dubbed it a trade, unworthy of a freeman. Look upon the painters,—all ignorant folk and uncouth. . . ."

"I have heard," retorted Giovanni, "that Messer Leonardo is a great man of learning."

"Man of learning? Guess again! Why, he can not even read Latin; he confuses Cicero with Quintilian; and as for Greek,—he hath not as much as a sniff of it. What a man of learning thou hast found! 'Tis enough to make anyone laugh."

"They do say," Beltraffio would not be downed, "that he is inventing wondrous machines, and that his observations of nature . . ."

"Machines, observations! Well, brother, thou wilt not go far with that. In my *Beauties of the Latin Tongue* there be gathered more than two thousand of new, most elegant turns of speech. And dost thou know what that has cost me? . . . But to fit intricate little wheels in mechanical thingamajigs, to watch how the birds fly in the sky, how the grasses in the field grow,—that is not learning, but pastime and play for children! . . ."

The old man was silent for a space; his face became sterner. Taking his companion by the hand, he uttered with quiet solemnity:

"Listen, Giovanni, and store it up in thy mind. Our masters are the ancient Greeks and Romans. They have accomplished all that man can accomplish on this earth. As for us, all that is left us is to follow in their footsteps, and emulate them. For it is said: no pupil is greater than his master."

He took a sip of wine, looked straight into Giovanni's eyes with a merry slyness, and suddenly his soft wrinkles spread into a broad smile:

"Eh, youth, youth! I look upon thee, little friar, and am filled with envy. A spring bud,—that's what thou art! He drinketh not wine; he runneth away from women. A quiet fellow and a peaceful one,—but there is an imp within. For I see right through thee. Bide a while, my fine fellow, and the imp will out. Thou art a sad dog thyself, but one feels gay in thy company. Thou art now, Giovanni, like unto this book. See—on the surface there be psalms of repentance, but under them a hymn to Aphrodite!"

"It has grown dark, Messer Giorgio. Is it not time to light a light?"

"Wait—it does not matter. I love to wag my tongue a bit in the twilight,—to recall my youth. . . ."

His tongue was growing heavier, his speech was becoming disjointed.

"I know, my dear friend," he continued, "that thou art looking at me and thinking: He has gotten drunk, the old dotard, and is grinding out nonsense. But still, I have somewhat here, after all!"

He pointed with his finger to his bald forehead, with self-satisfaction.

"I make no boast; but then, do thou ask the first-met scholar: he shall tell thee if any has ever surpassed Merulla in the elegancies of Latin speech. Who discovered Martial?" He went on, becoming still more absorbed: "Who deciphered the famous inscription on the ruins of the Tiburtian gates? You used to clamber so high that your head grew dizzy; a stone flew downward from under your foot,—you scarce had time to catch hold of a bush in order not to fall off yourself. For days at a time you suffered under the baking sun, making out the ancient inscriptions and transcribing them. Pretty little village girls would pass by and go off into gales of laughter: 'Look ye, lasses,—that's a funny kind of quail perching up there! Look where he has climbed up to, the ninny,—he must be looking for a treasure trove.' You would bandy a few pleasant words with them; they would go on,—and then again to work. Where the stones had fallen down, under the ivy and the bramble bushes one might find but two words: *Gloria Romanorum.*"

And, as though hearkening to the sound of the great words, long since stilled, he repeated in a low and solemn voice:

"*Gloria Romanorum!*"

"Eh, but what avails recollection,—the past can never be called back!"

He made a despondent gesture, and raising his goblet, began in a hoarse, long-drawn-out voice a students' drinking song:

I will never miss a line,
Though my stomach may fast;
Life-long loved I inns and wine,
And dying would see casks last.
Just like wine love songs I,
And the Latin gracious;
I may drink, but still sing I,
Better than Horatius.
In my heart's a drunken rout,
Dum vinum potamus,—
Brethren, unto Bacchus shout:
Te Deum laudamus!

He went off into a coughing spell and did not finish.

It was dark in the room by now. Giovanni could make out the face of his companion only with difficulty. The rain was falling harder, and one could hear the frequent drops from the water-spout falling into a puddle.

"So that is how things stand, little friar," muttered Merulla with a tongue of which he had lost control. "What was I talking of, now? My wife is a beauty. . . . No, not that. Wait a while. Yes, yes. . . . Remember the line:

Tu regere imperio populos, Romane, memento.

Mark my words, there were titans in those days,—the lords of the universe! . . ."

His voice quavered, and Giovanni imagined that tears glistened in the eyes of Messer Giorgio.

"Yea—titans! But now,—'tis a shame to talk of such. . . . Take even this Duke of Milan of ours, for instance, this Ludovico Moro. Of course I am in his pay; I am writing a history on the style of Titus Livius; with Pompey and Cæsar do I liken this cowardly jack-rabbit, this upstart. But in my soul, Giovanni, in my soul. . . ."

Through the habit of an old courtier he cast a suspicious glance at the door, lest someone be eavesdropping,—and, leaning toward his companion, he whispered in his ear:

"In the soul of old Merulla has never burned out, nor ever will burn out, a passion for liberty. But tell no one of this. These be evil times, never have there been worse. And what homunculi,—'tis nauseating to look at them; they be mildew, not to be told apart from the earth. And yet they strut about with their noses up in the air, comparing themselves with the ancients! And wherein, thinkest thou, does their point of superiority lie; what do they rejoice about? There is a certain friend of mine writes me from Greece, now: not so long ago, on the Island of Chios, some washerwomen from the convent, when they were rinsing clothes one dawn, did find on the seashore a veritable ancient god,—a triton with a fish-tail, with fins, all in scales. The fool women became frightened,—they thought it was a devil and ran away. But then they see that he is old, feeble, in all probability ill, lying flat on the sand, all a-shiver and warming his back—green, scaly—in the sun. His head was grey; his eyes were glazed like those of suckling babes. They gathered courage, the low-down scum, surrounding him with their Christian prayers, and then up and started beating him with their rollers. They beat him to death, like a dog,—this ancient god, the last of the mighty gods of Ocean, mayhap the grandson of Poseidon. . . ."

The old man fell silent, despondently hanging his head, and two maudlin tears coursed down his cheeks in pity for this wonder from the sea. A servant brought lights and closed the shutters. The pagan phantoms flew away. Supper was announced; but Merulla had grown so heavy with wine that they had to lead him off to bed, supporting him under his arms.

Beltraffio could not fall asleep for a long time that night, and, listening to the care-free snoring of Messer Giorgio, thought of that which latterly engrossed him most of all—of Leonardo da Vinci.

IV

GIOVANNI had come to Florence from Milan, at the behest of an uncle of his, Oswald Ingrim, a master glazier, in order to buy certain pigments of especial brilliancy and transparency, such as could be procured nowhere save in Florence.

This glazier-painter, a native of Gratz, and pupil of the celebrated Strassburg master Johannes Kirchheim, was at work on the windows of the northern sacristy of the Milan Cathedral. Giovanni, an orphan, the illegitimate son of Oswald's brother, Reynold, a stonemason, received his name of Beltraffio from his mother, a native of Lombardy, who, according to the words of his uncle, was a loose woman and had brought Giovanni's father to ruin. In the house of his gloomy uncle he had grown up, a lonely child. Oswald's endless stories about all sorts of unclean powers, fiends, witches, wizards and changelings darkened his soul. An especial terror was inspired in the boy by the legend, made up by the northern people of pagan Italy, about a demon in the form of a woman—the so-called Flaxen-Fair Mother or the White She-Demon.

Even in his early childhood, when Giovanni used to cry in bed of nights, Uncle Ingrim would frighten him with the White She-Demon, and the child would immediately grow quiet, hiding his head under the pillow; but beneath the quivering of his terror he felt a curiosity, a desire, sometime to behold the Flaxen-Fair One face to face.

Oswald gave his nephew in apprenticeship to Fra Benedetto, a painter of holy pictures.

This was a simple-hearted and a kindly old man. He taught that, upon approaching painting, one ought to call for aid upon the almighty God; the Virgin Mary, the beloved intercessor of sinners; St. Luke the Evangelist, the first Christian painter; and all the saints of Paradise; then to array oneself in the raiment of love, fear, humility, and patience; finally, to fix the tempera for the colours with the yolk of an egg and the milky sap of young branches of the fig tree, mixed with water and wine; to prepare the small panels for the pictures from old fig- or beech-wood, rubbing them through and through with a powder made out of burned bones,—preferably of the rib- and wing-bones of hens and capons, or the rib- and shoulder-bones of a ram.

These were inexhaustible precepts. Giovanni knew beforehand with what a supercilious air Fra Benedetto would elevate his eyebrows when the conversation would turn upon the colour styled Dragon's Blood, and would inevitably say: "Leave it be, and grieve not too much over it; it can not bring thee much credit." He surmised that the same words had been spoken by the master of Fra Benedetto, and by his master's master. Just as unchanging was the smile of quiet pride with which Fra Benedetto imparted to him the mysteries of craftsmanship, which seemed to the monk the pinnacle of all human artifices and cunning devices: such, for instance, as taking for the preparation of a fixative in painting young faces, the eggs of city hens, because the yolks of such eggs are lighter than those of eggs laid by country hens,—the yolks of the latter sort of eggs, in consequence of their reddish colour, being more fit in the painting of old, swarthy flesh.

Despite all these refinements, Fra Benedetto remained an artist as guileless as a babe. He prepared himself for his work by fasts and vigils; when beginning, he would prostrate himself face downward and pray, imploring the Lord for strength and wisdom. Whenever he depicted the Crucifixion his face would be inundated with tears.

Giovanni loved his master and deemed him of the greatest. But of late doubt would come upon the pupil when, explaining his sole rule in anatomy,—that the length of the male body must be considered to consist of eight and three-quarter faces,—Fra Benedetto would add with the same supercilious air as in speaking of the Dragon's Blood: "As concerning the body of a woman, let us best set it aside, for it has nothing in it of the proportional." He was convinced of this just as incontrovertibly as that fish—as well as all unreasoning animals in general—were of a dark colour above, and of a light below; or that man has one rib less than woman, since God had taken a rib out of Adam to create Eve.

It once befell him to portray the four elements by means of allegories, designating each one by some animal. Fra Benedetto chose the mole for the earth, a fish for the water, a salamander for fire, and a chameleon for air. But, thinking that the word chameleon was the augmented form of *cammello*, which means a camel, the monk, in the simplicity of his heart, represented the element of air in the guise of a camel, its jaws gaping the better to breathe. But when younger artists began laughing at him, pointing out the error, he bore their jeers with Christian meekness, retaining his conviction that there is no difference between a camel and a chameleon. And the rest of the devout master's knowledge of nature was of the same sort. Long since doubts,—a new spirit of mutiny, "the devil of worldly philosophy," as the monk put it,—had penetrated into Giovanni's heart. But when it befell the pupil of Fra Benedetto, shortly before his journey to Florence, to see certain of the drawings of Leonardo da Vinci, these doubts flooded his soul with such force that he could no longer resist them.

On this night, lying next to the peacefully snoring Messer Giorgio, for the thousandth time he mentally went over these thoughts, but the deeper he got into them, the more entangled did he become.

Finally, he resolved upon having recourse to heavenly aid, and, fixing his gaze, filled with hope, into the darkness of the night, he made this prayer:

"Lord, come Thou to my aid and forsake me not! If Messer Leonardo be verily a godless man, and if there be sin and temptation in his learning, do Thou so that I may no longer think of him, and that I may forget his drawings. Deliver me from temptation, for I fain would not sin before Thee. But, if, still pleasing Thee and glorifying Thy name through the noble art of painting, it be possible to know all that which Fra Benedetto knoweth not, and which I so greatly desire to know,—not only anatomy, but, as well, perspective and the most beautiful laws of light and shade,—then, O Lord, grant me a firm will; enlighten my soul, that I may no longer doubt; do Thou so that Messer Leonardo may take me into his atelier, and that Fra Benedetto—who is so good a man—may also forgive me, and understand that I am in no wise guilty before Thee."

After his prayer Giovanni felt comforted and at peace. His thoughts became indistinct: he recalled how in the hands of the glass-blower the iron point of the emery, made white-hot, sinks into the glass, and cuts it with a pleasant susurrant tinkling; he saw how from under the drawing-knife come out, twisting, the sinuous strips of lead, by means of which the separate pieces of coloured glass are joined in their frames. Some voice resembling his uncle's uttered: "A notch, a bigger notch at the edges,—then the glass will hold faster,"—and everything disappeared. He turned over on the other side and fell asleep.

Giovanni had a dream, which subsequently he frequently recalled: it seemed to him that he was standing in the gloom of an enormous cathedral before a window of varicoloured pieces of glass, on which was depicted the grape harvest of the Mystic Vine, of which it is said in the Scripture: "I am the true vine, and my Father is the husbandman."[3] The naked body of the Crucified is lying in a wine-press, with blood pouring from His wounds. Popes, cardinals, emperors are gathering it, filling casks and rolling them away. Apostles bring the clusters; St. Peter treads them. In the background prophets and patriarchs are digging around the vines, or cutting down the grapes. And a chariot with a tun rides by, harnessed with the evangelical beasts—a lion, a bull, and an eagle—and guided by the angel of St. Matthew. Giovanni had come across windows with such representations in the workshop of his uncle. But nowhere had he seen such pigments,—dark and vivid, like precious stones. The greatest pleasure of all he derived from the scarlet colour of the Lord's blood. And from the depths of the cathedral there reached him the faint, tender sounds of his favourite chant:

O fior di castitate,
Odorifìero giglio,
Con gran soavitate
Sei di color vermiglio.

Chastity's flower,
Languid and tender;
Lily most fragrant
With thy vermeil splendour.

The chant died away, the glass grew darker,—the voice of Antonio da Vinci the clerk spoke in his ear: "Flee, Giovanni, flee! *She* is here!" He wanted to ask "Who?" but surmised that the Flaxen-Fair One was at his back. There was a wave of cold, and suddenly a heavy hand seized his neck from behind and began to strangle him. It seemed to him that he was dying.

He cried out, awoke, and beheld Messer Giorgio, who was standing over him and pulling off his blanket:

"Get up, get up, or else they will ride off without us. 'Tis high time."

"Where to? What is up?" muttered Giovanni, half asleep.

"Why, hast forgotten? To the villa at San Gervasio, to dig at the Mound of the Mill."

"I shall not go. . . ."

"What meanest thou by refusing? Have I aroused thee for naught, then? I have purposely ordered a black mule to be saddled, that it might be more convenient for two to ride. Well, now, do get up, as a favour,—be not obdurate! What art thou afraid of, little friar?"

"I am not afraid; I simply lack the desire. . . ."

"Listen, Giovanni: thy much-praised master, Leonardo da Vinci, will be there."

Giovanni jumped up, and, without any further objections, began to dress.

They went out into the yard.

All was ready for the departure. The active Grillo was giving directions, running about and bustling. They started off.

Several men, the acquaintances of Messer Cipriano, with Leonardo da Vinci among their number, were to come later, by another road, directly to San Gervasio.

V

THE rain ceased. A north wind had dispersed the clouds. The stars glimmered in the moonless sky, like the lights of little lamps before holy images, blown upon by the wind. The pitch torches smoked and crackled, scattering sparks.

Over the Ricasoli Street, past San Marco, they rode up to the crenellated turret of the San Gallo Gate. The guards disputed for a long while, and cursed, not understanding in their half-awake state what the matter was, and, thanks only to a goodly bribe, did they consent to let them out of the city.

The road lay along a deep, narrow valley, the course of the Mugnone. After passing several poor hamlets, with streets just as cramped as those of Florence, with high houses resembling fortresses, built of roughly hewn stones, the travellers rode into an olive grove, belonging to the inhabitants of San Gervasio; they dismounted at the crossing of two roads, and through the vineyard of Messer Cipriano approached the Mound of the Mill, where labourers with spades and pickaxes were awaiting them.

Beyond the Mound, on the farther side of the marsh, called the Wet Gully, was the indistinct white glimmer, through the darkness, of the walls of the Buonaccorsi villa, among its trees. Below, on the Mugnone, stood the water mill. The graceful cypresses showed black on the summit of the Mound.

Grillo indicated where, according to his opinion, they should dig; Merulla was pointing out another place, near the foot of the Mound, where the marble hand had been found; whereas the head of the workmen, Strocco the gardener, affirmed that they ought to dig lower, down near the Wet Gully, since, as he put it, "Uncleanness always dwells nearest the bog." Messer Cipriano gave orders to dig at the spot counselled by Grillo. The noise of the spades began; there came the odour of new-turned earth.

A bat almost touched Giovanni's face with its wing. He gave a shudder.

"Fear not, little friar, fear not!" Merulla patted his shoulder to give him heart. "Ne'er a devil will we find! If only it were not for this ass Grillo. . . . Glory be to God, this is nothing to the excavations we have taken part in! Take, for instance, the one at Rome, on the four hundred and fiftieth Olympiad,"—Merulla, disdaining Christian chronology, used that of ancient Greece,—"during the reign of Pope Innocent VIII, on the Appian Way, near the monument of Cæcilia Metella, in an ancient Roman sarcophagus with the inscription: *Iulia, daughter of Claudius,*—the diggers found the body of a fifteen-year-old girl, covered with wax,—seemingly sleeping. The glow of life had not departed from her face. A throng beyond computing never left her coffin. From far lands did they come to gaze upon her, inasmuch as Julia was so beautiful that, even if it were possible to describe her loveliness, those who had not beheld her would never believe. The Pope grew frightened on learning that the people were adoring the dead pagan woman, and gave orders to have her buried secretly in the night at the Pincian Gates. There, brother, that is what one may call an excavation!"

Merulla looked down with disdain at the rapidly deepening pit.

Suddenly the spade of one of the workers gave forth a ringing sound. All leaned over.

"Bones!" pronounced the gardener. "The cemetery came up to here in the olden times."

A dreary prolonged canine howl came from San Gervasio.

"They have defiled a grave," went through Giovanni's mind. "The devil take them all! One ought to shun sin. . . ."

"A horse's skeleton," added Strocco, with malignant joy, and threw out of the pit a half-rotted elongated skull.

"In truth, Grillo, thou seemest to have made a mistake," said Messer Cipriano. "Ought we not try another spot?"

"Of course! Wherein is the good of listening to a fool?" answered Merulla, and, taking two labourers, went off to dig down farther, near the foot of the Mound. Strocco, also to spite the stubborn Grillo, led off a few people, desiring to begin the search in the Wet Gully.

After a certain time Messer Giorgio exclaimed, in triumph:

"Here, here,—I knew where to dig!"

Everybody made a dash toward him. But the find did not prove an interesting one,—the chip of marble was of unquarried stone.

Nevertheless, no one returned to Grillo, and, feeling himself disgraced, standing at the bottom of the pit, he, with the light of a broken lanthorn, continued scratching at the ground, stubbornly and despondently.

The wind died down; the air grew warmer. Mist arose over the Wet Gully. There came an odour of stagnant water, of vernal yellow flowers and of violets. The sky became more translucent. The cocks crowed for the second time. Night was on the wane.

Suddenly, from the depths of the pit where Grillo was, sounded a desperate cry.

"Help! help! Hold me.—I fall!"

At first they could distinguish nothing in the darkness, since Grillo's lanthorn had gone out. All they could hear was his scrambling, his oh'ing and groaning.

They brought other lanthorns and beheld a brick arch, half covered with the earth which had slid upon it,—apparently the roof of a carefully constructed underground cellar, which had failed to sustain Grillo's weight and had fallen through. Two labourers, young and strong, crawled cautiously down into the pit.

"Wherever art thou at, Grillo? Let's have thy hand! Or art thou entirely done for, poor fellow?"

Grillo had grown deadly still; forgetting the acute pain in his arm,—he thought it broken, though it was only dislocated,—he was at work on something, crawling about and queerly fossicking in the cellar.

At last he began to shout, joyously:

"An idol! An idol! Messer Cipriano,—a most excellent idol!"

"There, there, what art thou yelling about?" grumbled Strocco, mistrustfully. "It is some ass's skull, again."

"Nay, nay! Only its arm is knocked off. . . . But its legs, its trunk, its breast,—everything is as whole as whole can be," Grillo was muttering, gasping from delight.

Having tied ropes under their armpits and around their torsos, lest the vault fall through, the labourers lowered themselves into the pit, and commenced to take apart carefully the brittle, mildew-covered bricks. Giovanni, half-lying on the ground, looked on between the bent backs of the labourers into the depth of the cellar, from whence were wafted up a stuffy dampness and a graveyard chill. When the vault had been almost taken apart, Messer Cipriano spoke:

"Stand aside,—let me see."

And Giovanni beheld at the bottom of the pit, between the brick walls, a white nude body. It lay like a coffined dead body, yet had not the appearance of death, but seemed rosy, alive and warm in the flickering reflection of the torches.

"Venus!" Messer Giorgio whispered in veneration. "The Venus of Praxiteles! Well, I felicitate you, Messer Cipriano. If you were to be presented with the Duchy of Milan, and with Genoa to boot, you could not deem yourself more fortunate! . . ."

Grillo climbed out with an effort, and although blood was running from a scrape on his forehead over his earth-stained face, and he could not stir his dislocated arm,—there was a victor's pride shining in his eyes.

Merulla ran up to him.

"Grillo, thou dearest friend of mine, thou benefactor! And here I was berating thee, calling thee a fool,—thee, the wisest of men!"

And, confining him in his embraces, he tenderly bussed him.

"One time Filippo Brunelleschi, a Florentine architect," Merulla talked on, "found beneath his house, in just such a cellar, a marble statue of the god Mercury; it must have been that at the time when the Christians, having vanquished the pagans, were exterminating idols, the last adorants of the gods, beholding the perfection of the ancient statues and desirous of saving them from destruction, had hidden the sculptures in subterranean crypts of brick."

Grillo listened with a beatific smile, and noted neither a shepherd's syrinx playing in the field, nor the bleating of the sheep on the common, nor that the sky was paling between the hummocks to an aqueous colour, nor the pealing to each other in tender tones of the morning bells.

"Easy, easy,—more to the right,—so. Farther away from the wall," Cipriano was giving orders to the workmen. "I shall give five silver *grossi* to each man of you, if you pull it out without breakage."

The goddess was slowly rising.

With the same serene smile as of yore, when she had risen from the foam of the sea waves, she was emerging from the murk of the earth, out of her grave of a thousand years.

> "Glory to thee, golden-limbed mother, Aphrodite,
> Joyance of gods and of mortals,"

Merulla greeted her.

All the stars expired, save the star of Venus, which was playing like a jewel in the radiance of the dawn. And, in salutation to it, the head of the goddess rose over the edge of her grave.

Giovanni glanced at her face, illuminated by the morning, and, paling from terror, uttered in a whisper:

"The White She-Demon!"

He jumped up and was seized with a desire to flee. But curiosity vanquished fear. And though he were to be told that he was committing a mortal sin, for which he would be condemned to eternal perdition, he would not have been able to tear his gaze away from her stark, pure body, from her splendid countenance.

In the days when Aphrodite had been sovereign of the universe, none had ever gazed upon her with such reverent awe.

VI

THE bell was set ringing in the little communal church of San Gervasio. All looked around involuntarily and froze to the spot. In the stillness of morning this sound resembled a wrathful and piteous cry. At times the high, quivering sound would die away, as though the bell had strained itself; but immediately it would go off into new, ever louder peals of abrupt, despairing ringing.

"Jesus, have mercy upon us!" exclaimed Grillo, clutching his head. "Why, 'tis Father Faustino, the priest! Look,—there is a crowd on the highway, yelling,—they see us, and are waving their arms. They are running hither. . . . I am lost, unlucky that I am! . . ."

New mounted arrivals rode up to the Mound of the Mill. These were the rest of those invited to the excavation, tardy because they had lost their way. Beltraffio cast a casual glance—and, even as engrossed as he was in contemplation of the goddess, he noted the face of one of them. The expression of cold, calm attentiveness and penetrating curiosity with which the stranger was surveying the Venus, and which was in such contrast to the excitement and confusion of Giovanni himself, struck him forcibly. Without lifting his eyes, which he could not avert from the statue, Giovanni all the time sensed behind him the presence of this man of the unusual face.

"Here,—" spoke Messer Cipriano after some pondering, "the villa is but a step or so away. The gates are stout,—they will bear any siege. . . ."

"True enough!" exclaimed Grillo, taking heart. "Come, men, lively, —lift her up!"

His solicitude for the preservation of the idol was paternal in its tenderness. The statue was carried safely through the Wet Gully. Scarce had they crossed the threshold of the house when the awesome visage of Father Faustino appeared at the summit of the Mound of the Mill, with his arms uplifted to heaven.

The lower part of the villa was untenanted. The enormous hall, with whitewashed walls and arches, served as a depository for agricultural implements and large earthen vessels for olive oil. Wheaten straw, thrown down in a corner, towered up to the ceiling in an aureate pile. Upon this straw, this humble rustic couch, they carefully laid the goddess. They had barely entered and locked the gates, when there were heard shouts, curses, and loud knocking at the gates.

"Open, open!" Father Faustino was shouting in a high, cracked voice. "In the name of the living God I adjure you—open!"

Messer Cipriano ascended by an inner stone staircase to a narrow barred window which was located very high above the floor, and looked over the crowd; he convinced himself that it was not numerous, and with that smile which was part of the refined urbanity natural to him, began negotiations.

The priest would not be pacified, and demanded the surrender of the idol, which, so he claimed, had been dug up on cemetery ground.

The Consul of Calimala, resolving on resorting to military strategy, uttered in a voice firm and calm:

"Take heed! A special messenger has been sent to Florence to the chief of the guard, and in two hours there will be a division of cavalry here,—none shall force an entry into my house unpunished."

"Break down the gates!" stormed the priest. "Have no fear! God is with us! Use axes!"

And, snatching an axe from the hands of a purblind pock-marked little ancient, meek and weary of visage, and with his cheek tied up, he struck the gates as hard as he could.

The mob did not follow his example.

"Don Faustino, eh, Don Faustino," lisped the meek little old man, barely touching him by the elbow, "we be poor folk, we dig not money out of the ground with a mattock. If they law us, they will ruin us! . . ."

Many in the throng, catching wind of the city guards, were pondering on how they might slip away unnoticed.

"Of course, had it been on our own parochial land, 'twould be another matter," reasoned others.

"But where does the boundary line pass? For, according to law, brethren . . ."

"Well, what is law? 'Tis but a web,—a fly will get stuck in it, a hornet will fly out. Law is never written for the high-born," others retorted.

"'Tis the truth, that! A man's house is his castle."

Meanwhile Giovanni kept on gazing at the rescued Venus. A ray of the morning sun penetrated the side window. The marble body, as yet not entirely clean of earth, sparkled in the sun, as though it were luxuriating and warming itself after the long underground darkness and cold. The slender yellow stalks of wheat straw seemed to catch fire, surrounding the goddess with a demure yet gorgeous aureole of gold.

And again Giovanni turned his attention to the stranger.

On his knees alongside of the goddess, he took out a pair of compasses, a goniometer, a semicircular arc of copper, on the style of those which were used in mathematical sets, and with the same expression of determined calm and penetrating curiosity in his cold, light-blue eyes and his thin, firmly pressed lips, began measuring different parts of the beautiful body, bending his head, so that the long fair beard touched the marble.

"What is he doing? Who is he?" Giovanni wondered, with growing amazement, almost with fear, following the quick, bold fingers which glided over the limbs of the goddess, penetrating all the mysteries of beauty, feeling by touch and investigating convexities on the marble imperceptible to the eye.

At the gates of the villa the crowd of villagers was thinning out and melting away with every moment.

"Halt, halt, ye good-for-naughts, ye betrayers of Christ! Of the city guards have ye become scared, but of the might of Antichrist ye are not afraid!" clamoured the priest, beseeching with his arms. "*Ipse vero Antichristus opes malorum effodiet et exponet.* Thus spake the great teacher, Anselm of Canterbury. *Effodiet,*—do ye hear?—Antichrist shall dig the ancient gods up out of the earth and show them to the world anew. . . ."

But none would listen to him.

"What a hot-headed fellow we have in Father Faustino!" The prudent miller was shaking his head. "He hath scarce enough flesh to keep his soul in, and yet, look ye, how riled he is! If it were treasure trove they had found, now . . ."

"'Tis a biggish idol, they say, of silver."

"What silver! I saw it myself: she's of marble, all naked, the shameless creature. . . . With such filth, the Lord forgive me, 'tis not worth while even to soil one's hands!"

"Whither art thou bound, Zacciello?"

"'Tis time I was in the field."

"Well, God be with thee; as for me, I am going to the vineyard."

The priest's entire wrath was turned on the parishioners:

"Ah, so that is your way, ye unbelieving dogs, ye low-down spawn! Abandon your pastor, will ye? But do ye know, ye progeny of Satan, that were I not praying for ye day and night, beating my breast, weeping and fasting, your accursed village would long since have sunk through the ground? I wash my hands of ye! I shall leave ye, and shake the dust of your village from my feet! Let your herds and your children and your grandchildren be accursed! No longer am I father to ye, nor your pastor. Anathema!"

VII

In the quiet depth of the hall, where the goddess lay on her couch of aureate straw, Giorgio Merulla approached the stranger measuring the statue.

"Are you seeking divine proportion?" asked the scholar with a patronizing smile. "Would you reduce beauty to mathematics?"

The other looked at him in silence, as though he had not heard the question, and again concentrated on his work.

The legs of the compasses folded and parted describing regular geometrical figures. With a calm, firm movement he applied the goniometer to the beauteous lips of Aphrodite,—the smile of these lips filled the heart of Giovanni with terror,—counted the divisions, and noted them down in his book.

"Pardon my curiosity," persisted Merulla, "how many divisions are there?"

"The implement is inexact," the stranger replied unwillingly. "Usually for the measurement of proportions I divide the human face in degrees, minutes, seconds and thirds. Each division is a twelfth part of the preceding one."

"Really!" exclaimed Merulla. "It seems to me that the last division is smaller than the width of the finest hair. Five times the twelfth part . . ."

"Equals a third," the other explained with the same indifference;

"one forty-eight-thousand-eight-hundred-and-twenty-third part of the entire face."

Merulla elevated his eyebrows and smiled mockingly:

"As we live, we learn, all life long. Never did I think it possible to attain such exactitude!"

"The more exact, the better," remarked the other.

"Oh, of course! . . . Although, do you know, in art, in beauty, all these mathematical calculations, these degrees, these seconds . . . I, to confess, can not believe that any artist, in his transport of rapture, of vehement inspiration, under the influence of God, so to speak . . ."

"Yes, yes, you are right," the stranger concurred, with a weary air, "but still one is curious to know. . . ."

And, bending down, he computed by the goniometer the number of divisions between the beginning of the hair and the chin.

"To know!" reflected Giovanni. "Why, can one know and measure in a case like this? What madness! Or does he not feel, does he not understand? . . ."

Merulla, evidently desiring to flick his opponent on the raw and entice him into dispute, began to speak of the perfection of the ancients,—that one ought to imitate them. But the other kept quiet, and when Merulla had concluded, smiling into his long beard, with refined mockery, he uttered:

"Whosoever can quaff from the source will not drink from a vessel."

"Pardon me!" exclaimed the scholar. "If you esteem the ancients water in a vessel, then what is the well-spring?"

"Nature," the stranger answered with simplicity.

And when Merulla again began speaking pompously and irritatingly, he no longer disputed, but concurred with evasive urbanity. But the wearied gaze of his cold eyes was becoming more and more indifferent.

Finally Giorgio became silent, having exhausted his arguments. Thereupon his companion pointed out certain depressions in the marble: in no light, either faint or strong, could they be seen by the naked eye,—only by touch, gliding the hand over the smooth surface, could one feel these infinite refinements of craftsmanship. And with a single profound, searching glance, devoid of rapture, the stranger surveyed the entire body of the goddess.

"And I thought that he has no emotion!" wondered Giovanni. "But, if he has emotion, then how can he measure it, put it to the test, divide it into numbers? Who is he?"

"Messer," Giovanni whispered in the old man's ear, "hearken, Messer Giorgio,—what is this man's name?"

"Ah, thou art here, little friar," said Merulla, turning around; "I had e'en forgot about thee. Why, 'tis none other than thy favourite himself. How is it thou hast not recognized him? 'Tis Messer Leonardo da Vinci."

VIII

THEY were returning to Florence. Leonardo rode his horse at a pace. Beltraffio walked by his side. They were alone.

Between the black roots of the olive-trees, soaking in moisture, the grass showed green, with blue irises motionless on their thin stalks. It was as quiet as only an early morn in early spring can be.

"Can it really be he?" Giovanni reflected, observing, and finding interesting, every trifle about him.

Da Vinci was past forty. When silent and meditative, his keen, light-blue eyes under their frowning brows had a cold and piercing look. But during conversation they would become kindly. His long fair beard, and thick wavy hair of the same light shade, gave him an august air. His face was full of a fine, almost feminine charm, and his voice, despite his great stature and mighty physique, was thin, strangely high-pitched, very pleasant, but not virile. His fine-looking hand—by his manner of directing his steed, Giovanni surmised that it was possessed of great strength—was soft, with long fingers, just like a woman's.

They were approaching the walls of the city. Through the smoky haze of the morning sun they could see the cupola of the Cathedral and the tower of the Palazzo Vecchio.

"Now or never," Beltraffio was thinking. "I must decide and tell him that I want to enter his atelier."

In the meanwhile Leonardo, having brought his steed to a halt, was observing the flight of a young gerfalcon, which, on the watch for prey—some duck or crane in the marsh reeds of the Mugnone—was circling in the heavens, statelily and leisurely; then falling headlong, just like a stone thrown down from a height, with a short, feral cry, it disappeared behind the tops of the trees. Leonardo followed it with his eyes, without missing a single turn, motion, or beat of its wings; opening the memorandum book attached to his belt, he began writing in it,—probably his observations of the flight of the bird.

Beltraffio noticed that he held his pencil not in his right hand, but in his left, and reflected: "He is left-handed," and recalled the strange rumours which were current about him,—Leonardo was reputed to write his compositions in a reverse script, which could be read only in a mirror,—not from left to right, as all do, but from right to left, as they write in the Orient. People said that he did this to conceal his criminal, heretical thoughts about nature and God.

"Now or never!" Giovanni repeated to himself, and suddenly recalled the harsh words of Antonio da Vinci:

"Go to him, if thou art desirous of sending thy soul to perdition: he is a heretic and an atheist."

Leonardo with a smile pointed out to him an almond sapling,—diminutive, puny, lonely, it grew on the summit of the hillock, and, still almost bare, and chilled, it had already trustingly and festally bedecked itself in rosy-white blossoms, which were radiant, shot through and through with the sun, and was luxuriating against the blue skies. But Beltraffio could not admire. His heart was heavy and confused. Whereupon Leonardo, as though he had surmised his sadness, with a kindly, calm gaze, uttered the words which subsequently Giovanni often recalled.

"If thou wouldst be an artist, forsake all sadness and care, save for thy art. Let thy soul be as a mirror, which reflects all objects, all movements and colours, remaining itself unmoved and clear."

They entered the city gates of Florence.

IX

Beltraffio went to the Cathedral, where Brother Girolamo Savonarola was to preach that morning.

The last sounds of the organ were dying away under the reverberating vaults of Maria del Fiore. The throng filled the church with stifling warmth, with subdued rustling. Men, women and children were divided off from each other by hangings. Under the ogival arches, retreating upward, it was murky and mysterious, as in a dense, slumbrous forest; whereas below, here and there, the rays of the sun, refracting in the darkly-vivid windows, fell in a rain of iridescent reflections upon the living waves of the throng, upon the grey stones of the pillars. Above the altar, through the murk, the flames of the seven-branched candelabra glowed redly.

The mass was over; the throng awaited the preacher. All eyes were turned upon the high wooden cathedra with its spiral staircase, built against one of the columns in the centre of the Cathedral.

Giovanni, standing in the midst of the throng, listened attentively to the quiet conversations of his neighbours.

"Will he come soon?" a squat man, with a pallid, sweaty face, whose hair, tied with a thin strap, was stuck to his forehead,—evidently a carpenter,—was asking in a despondent voice, as he stifled in the crush.

"God alone knows," answered a tinker, an asthmatic giant, with wide cheek-bones and a red face. "He hath in San Marco a certain little friar, a stammerer and a natural. Whenever he sayeth 'tis time, Fra Girolamo ups and goes. The other day we waited four hours on end, thinking he would not come at all, but come he did, after all."

"O Lord, Lord!" the carpenter heaved a sigh. "Why, I am waiting since midnight. I have grown famished,—'tis growing dark before my eyes. Never a sup or bite has passed my lips. If I could but squat on my heels, now . . ."

"I told thee, Damiano, that one must come betimes,—do but see how far away the pulpit is now. We shall hear nary a thing."

"Oh, well, brother,—hear we shall, never fret. When he begins to shout, to thunder,—thou wilt have not only the deaf hearing, but the very dead!"

"I have heard he will prophesy to-day?"

"No,—not till he finishes building Noah's ark. . . ."

"Why, have ye not heard? Everything is finished, to the last plank. And a mystic interpretation has been given forth—the length of it is Faith; the width thereof, Charity; the height, Hope. Hasten, he proclaims, hasten into the Ark of Salvation, whilst yet the doors are open! The time is nigh; the gates shall be closed, and many shall wail, inasmuch as they repented not, neither did they enter. . . ."

"To-day, brethren, 'tis about the flood,—seventeenth verse of the sixth chapter of Genesis."

"He has had, so they say, a new vision of Famine, Pestilence and War."

"A farrier of Vallombrosa was telling how there had been over his settlement, at night, countless hordes battling in the sky; there was heard the clashing of swords and armour. . . ."

"But is it true, now, good people, that a bloody sweat has stood out on the face of the Most Holy Virgin, which is at the 'Nunziata dei Servi?"

"How else! And the eyes of the Madonna on the Bridge of Rubaconte shed tears every night. Aunt Lucia has seen it herself."

"This bodes no good,—oh, it bodes no good! Lord, have mercy upon us sinners. . . ."

There was a commotion in the women's half: a little old woman, in the press of the throng, had fallen in a faint. An attempt was made to lift her and bring her to.

"Will he come soon? There is no more strength in me!" The puny carpenter well-nigh wept, wiping the sweat from his face. And all the throng as well was languishing in interminable expectation.

Suddenly the sea of heads undulated, amid whispering.

"He comes, he comes, he comes!—No, 'tis not he. 'Tis Fra Domenico da Pescia.—It is he, it is!—He comes!"

Giovanni beheld a man in the black and white raiment of the Dominicans, girded with a rope, slowly mount the pulpit and throw his cowl back; his face was emaciated and as yellow as wax, with thick lips, a hooked nose and a low brow.

His left hand, as though in exhaustion, he dropped on the pulpit; his right he lifted up and extended, grasping a crucifix. And in silence, with a slow gaze of his flaming eyes, he surveyed the throng. There came a silence wherein one could hear one's heart beat.

The unmoving eyes of the monk blazed more and more vividly, like coals. He kept silence—and the suspense was becoming unbearable. One more moment, it seemed, and the throng would irresistibly cry out in terror. But the quiet grew still more intense, still more appalling. And suddenly in this dead silence resounded the deafening, rending, inhuman cry of Savonarola:

"*Ecce ego adduco aquas super terram!* I, even I, do bring a flood of waters upon the earth!"[4]

A breath of shivering terror was wafted over the crowd.

Giovanni blanched,—it appeared to him that the earth was quaking, that the vaults of the Cathedral would momently collapse and crush him. The stout boilermaker next him began to quiver like a leaf, his teeth a-chatter. The carpenter was all huddled up, his head tucked in between his shoulders, as though shrinking from a blow, his face all in wrinkles, and his eyes closed.

This was no sermon, but a delirium, which had suddenly seized upon all these thousands of people, and whirled them off before it, even as a hurricane whirls off dry leaves. Giovanni listened, scarcely comprehending. Detached words would occasionally reach him:

"Behold, behold, the heavens are already darkened. The sun is a deep purple, like clotted blood. Flee! There shall be a rain of fire and sulphur, there shall be a hail of red-hot stones and whole crags! . . . *Fuge, o Sion, quæ habitas apud filiam Babulonis!* . . .[5]

"O Italia, there shall come scourges upon scourges! The scourge of War after Famine; the scourge of Pestilence after War! There shall be scourges everywhere ye turn! . . .

"Ye shall not have enough of the quick to bury the dead! They shall be so great in number in all the houses that the grave-diggers shall go about the streets, and shall cry: 'Who hath any dead?'—and shall pile them up in their carts till the bodies touch the very horses, and, having heaped them up in whole mountains, shall burn them up. And again shall they go through the streets, crying: 'Who hath any dead? Who hath any dead?' And ye shall go out to them, and say: 'Here is my son; here is my brother; here is my husband.' And they will go on farther, and will cry: 'Be there any more dead men?'

"O Florence, O Rome, O Italia! The time of songs and festivals is past. Ye are all sick,—yea, even unto death.—Lord, Thou art witness, that I was fain to prop up this heap of ruins with my word. But I no longer can. . . . My strength is at an end! . . . I have no desire to say more, nor know I what more to say. There is left me but to wail, to waste away in tears. . . . Have mercy, have mercy, Lord! . . . O my poor people, O my Florence! . . ."

He opened his arms, and uttered the last words in a barely audible whisper. They floated over the throng, and died away, like the rustling of wind among leaves, like the sigh of an infinite compassion.

And, pressing his deadened lips to the crucifix, he sank to his knees in exhaustion and burst into sobs.

The slow, ponderous sounds of the organ pealed forth, spreading more and more, becoming more and more unencompassable,—constantly increasing in exultation and awesomeness, like to the roar of the ocean at night.

Someone in the crowd of women cried out in a piercing voice:

"*Misericordia!*"

And thousands of voices answered, called to one another. Like to ears of grain under the wind in a field,—wave upon wave, row upon row,—huddling, crushing one another, as sheep do in a frightened flock under a thunder-storm,—they fell down on their knees. And, blending with the many-voiced roar and reverberation of the organ, making the earth to quake, as well as the stone pillars and vaults of the Cathedral, there arose the pentecostal wail of the people: the cry of a perishing people to their God:

"*Misericordia! Misericordia!*"

Giovanni sank down, sobbing. He felt on his back the weight, and on his neck the hot breath of the stout tinker, also sobbing, who had fallen on him in the crush. The puny carpenter alongside was also sniveling, queerly and helplessly, as though he had the hiccups; chokingly spluttering, as little children do, he was screaming piercingly:

"Mercy! Mercy!"

Beltraffio recalled his own pride and worldly love of wisdom, his desire to leave Fra Benedetto and to give himself up to the dangerous, perhaps ungodly, science of Leonardo; he recalled, as well, the last night on the Mound of the Mill,—a most terrible night; the resurrected Venus; his sinful delight before the beauty of the White She-Demon,—and, stretching his arms toward heaven, in the same despairing voice as all the others, he lifted up his voice in anguish:

"Have mercy upon me, Lord! I have sinned before Thee,—forgive and have compassion!"

And at that same moment, having raised his tear-stained face, he saw Leonardo da Vinci at a short distance. The artist was standing, with one shoulder leaning against a column; in his right hand he held his inevitable note-book, and was drawing in it with his left, occasionally throwing a glance at the pulpit, evidently hoping for another glimpse of the preacher's head.

Aloof from all, alone in the terror-possessed crowd, Leonardo preserved an absolute calm. In his cold eyes of a pale blue, in his thin, firmly pressed lips,—the eyes and lips of a man habituated in attentiveness and precision,—there was no scoffing, but that same curiosity as when he had measured the body of Aphrodite with his mathematical instruments.

The tears dried in Giovanni's eyes; prayer died away on his lips.

Having come out of the church, he approached Leonardo and begged permission to look at his sketch. The artist would not consent, at first; but Giovanni insisted with an imploring air, and, finally, Leonardo took him aside and handed him the note-book.

Giovanni beheld a horrible caricature.

This was not the face of Savonarola, but of an old hideous devil in a monk's robe, resembling a Savonarola exhausted with self-tortures, yet not victorious over his pride and lust. His lower jaw jutted out; wrinkles furrowed his cheeks and neck,—the latter loose-skinned, black, like that of a mummified corpse; the upturned eyebrows bristled, and the inhuman gaze, filled with obstinate, almost malevolent supplication, was directed toward Heaven. All that was dark, awful, and insane within him, which gave Brother Girolamo up into the power of the idiotic, stammering clairvoyant Maruffi, was brought out in this drawing, exposed without wrath or pity, with the imperturbable clarity of knowledge.

And Giovanni recalled the words of Leonardo:

"The soul of the artist must be like unto a mirror, which reflects all objects, all movements and colours, remaining itself unmoved and clear."

The pupil of Fra Benedetto lifted his eyes up to Leonardo, and felt that even if eternal perdition were to threaten him, Giovanni,—that, even if he were to become convinced that Leonardo was in very truth a servant of Antichrist,—he could not go away from him, and that an insuperable power was drawing him to this man: he must come to know him to the utmost.

X

Two days later Grillo came running with grievous tidings to Florence, to the house of Messer Cipriano Buonaccorsi, who was at this time taken up with an unexpected influx of business matters, and had for that reason been unable to transfer the Venus to the city. The parochial priest, Father Faustino, abandoning San Gervasio, had set out for the neighbouring mountain settlement of San Maurizio; inspiring the populace with fear of heavenly punishments, he had gathered a division of the villagers in the night-time, had laid siege to the Villa Buonaccorsi, broken down the door, beaten up Strocco the gardener, and tied up hand and foot the guards set to watch the Venus; a prayer composed in ancient time was said over the goddess,—*oratio super effigies vasaque in loco antiquo reperta* (in this prayer over sculptures and vessels found in ancient burying places the servant of the church implores God to cleanse from pagan uncleanness the objects, dug up from the earth, turning them to the benefit of Christian souls, to the glory of the Father, the Son, and the Holy Ghost)—*ut omnii munditia depulsa sint fidelibus tuis utenda per Christum dominum nostrum.* After this the marble statue was broken, the fragments cast into an oven and burned; lime was prepared therefrom, which was used in daubing the recently erected wall of the village burying ground.

From this tale of old Grillo, who well-nigh wept in pity for the idol, Giovanni derived resolution. On that very same day he went to Leonardo and begged that the artist accept him as a pupil in his atelier. And accept him Leonardo did.

A short time afterward the news came to Florence that Charles VIII, the Most Christian King of France, at the head of an innumerable force, had set out on an expedition for the conquest of Naples and Sicily,—mayhap even Rome and Florence.

The burghers were in terror, for they saw the prophecies of Brother Girolamo Savonarola being fulfilled,—the coming of the scourges, and the sword of God descending upon Italy.

BOOK TWO

Ecce Deus—Ecce Homo

I

INCE THE HEAVY EAGLE ON HIS WINGS stays up in the rarefied air, since large ships under sail move over the sea,—why can not man also, cleaving the air with wings, master the wind and rise up, a conqueror on high?" Leonardo read these words in one of his old note-books, written five years before. Next to them was a drawing: a shaft, with a round iron spindle fastened thereto, supporting wings which were brought in motion by cords. Now this machine seemed to him unwieldy and hideous.

His new apparatus resembled a bat. The structure of the wing consisted of five fingers, as in the hand of a skeleton, multiarticulated, bending at the joints. A tendon of straps made out of tanned leather and small cords of raw silk, with a lever and a piston, on the manner of a muscle, joined the fingers. The wing lifted up by means of a movable pin and a connecting rod. Starched taffeta, which did not let the air through, like the web on the foot of a goose, contracted and expanded. The four wings worked crosswise, like the legs of a horse. Their length was forty ells; the height of their sweep, eight ells. They drew back, giving a forward motion, and sank downward, lifting the machine upward. A man, standing, put his feet into stirrups, which caused the wings to move by means of cords, blocks, and levers. The head was steered by means of a large rudder with feathers, in the semblance of a bird's tail.

A bird, before taking off from the ground, must, for the first sweep of its wings, stand up on its legs: a swift, whose legs are short, put on the ground, beats about and can not fly upward. Two short ladders of rushes took the place of the bird's feet in the apparatus.

Leonardo knew by experience that perfect construction in a machine is accompanied by elegance and proportion of all its parts;—the uncouth appearance of the necessary ladders perturbed the inventor.

He plunged into mathematical calculations: he sought for the error and could not find it. Suddenly, in anger, he crossed out the page filled with small, cramped ranks of figures, wrote "Incorrect!" on the margins, and added an oath on one side, in large furious characters: "The devil take it!"

The calculations became more and more involved; the elusive error grew apace.

The flame of the candle flickered unevenly, irritating the eyes. A tom-cat, which had managed to have its full sleep, jumped up on the work-table, stretched itself, arched its back and its little paw began playing with a moth-eaten stuffed bird, hung up on a whip-cord to a transversal wooden beam,—the bird was an appliance for determining the centre of gravity in the study of flight. Leonardo pushed the tom-cat so that it almost fell off the table and gave a piteous meow.

"Well, God be with thee, lie down where thou wilt,—only be not in the way."

Caressingly he passed his hand over the black fur, causing crackling sparks. The tom-cat tucked in its little velvet paws, laid down with dignity, began to purr, and directed upon its master its greenish pupils, filled with languor and mystery.

Again there was the procession of figures, parentheses, fractions, equations, cube and square roots. The second sleepless night was flying by imperceptibly. Ever since his return from Florence to Milan, Leonardo had spent a whole month, going almost nowhere, in work on the flying machine.

Branches of white acacia peeped in at the open window, at times dropping on the table their tender, sweetly fragrant blossoms. The moonlight, softened by the haze of tawny clouds, nacre-shaded, fell into the room, blending with the red light of the guttered candle,—a room cumbered up with machines and appliances for astronomy, physics, chemistry, mechanics, anatomy. Wheels, levers, springs, screws, pipes, rods, shafts, pistons, and other parts of machines,—copper, steel, iron, glass—like the members of monsters or of enormous insects, stood out of the murk, entwining and merging with one another. One could see a diving bell; the glimmering crystal of an optical apparatus, which represented an eye in large proportions; the skeleton of a horse; a stuffed crocodile; a jar with a human fœtus in alcohol, resembling an enormous white pupa; pointed boat-shaped skis for walking over water; and, next to it, probably from the workshop of the artist,—the small clay head of a girl or an angel, with a sly and pensive smile. In the depth of the room, within the dark maw of a smelting furnace with its blacksmith's bellows, embers glowed pinkly under the ashes.

And over all this, from floor to ceiling, spread out the wings of the machine,—one still uncovered, the other with a web drawn over it. Between them, on the floor, a man was sprawled out, with his head thrown back,—he must have been overtaken by sleep while at work. In his right hand was the handle of a sooty ladle, from which the molten pewter had poured out on the floor. One of the wings touched the breast of the sleeper with the nether tip of its light reed framework and would occasionally move quiveringly, as though alive, its pointed upper tip swishing against the ceiling.

In the uncertain glow of the moon and the candle, the machine with the man between its outspread wings had the appearance of a gigantic noctule, ready to rise and fly off.

II

THE moon sank. From the truck gardens surrounding the house of Leonardo in an outskirt of Milan, between the fortress and the monastery of Maria delle Grazie, there was wafted the scent of vegetables and herbs,—*melissa*, mint, fennel. Swallows began twittering in their nest over the window. The ducks in the fish-pond were splashing and joyously quacking. The flame of the candle paled. From the adjacent workshop came the voices of the pupils.

There were two of them,—Giovanni Beltraffio and Andrea Salaino. Giovanni was drawing from an anatomical cast, seated before an appliance for the study of perspective,—a quadrangular wooden frame with a cord network, which corresponded to a similar network of transversal lines on the draughtsman's paper. Salaino was applying alabaster to a panel of linden-wood, intended for a picture. He was a handsome lad with innocent eyes and fair curls, the spoilt favourite of the master, who used him as a model for his angels.

"How think you, Andrea," asked Beltraffio, "will Messer Leonardo finish his machine soon?"

"Why, God knoweth," answered Salaino, whistling a phrase and adjusting the silken, silver-embroidered facings of his new shoes. "Last year he sat two months through and naught came of it,—'twas enough to make one laugh. This bandy-legged bear Zoroastro was seized with the desire to fly, no matter at what cost. The master dissuaded him from it, but the fellow became stubborn. And just imagine, the queer chap did clamber up on the roof, after all, wound his entire body with bull-and-pig-bladders, tied together like a rosary, in order not to smash to smithereens if he should fall; he flapped his wings and at first rose upward, the wind or something carrying him along,—but then he lost his footing, flew down, feet up,—right into a pile of manure. 'Twas soft, and he was not hurt,—but all the bladders on him burst at the same time, and there was thundering as if from a cannon-shot,—even the rooks on a nearby belfry became frightened and flew away. But this new Icarus of ours jiggles his legs in the air, unable to climb out of the manure pile!"

Into the workshop entered a third pupil, Cesare da Sesto, a man no longer young, with a sickly jaundiced face, with clever and malignant eyes. In one hand he held a piece of bread and a slice of ham; in the other, a glass of wine.

"Faugh, what sour stuff!" He spat, making a wry face. "And the ham is like a shoe-sole. I am amazed,—a salary of two thousand ducats a year,—yet he feeds people with such stuff!"

"You might try the other small cask, the one under the staircase, in the lumber-room," Salaino spoke up.

"I have tried it,—still worse.—What hast thou there,—again some new bedizenment?" Cesare was looking at Salaino's dashing *berretta* of crimson velvet. "Well, ours is a fine household, I must say. 'Tis a dog's life! 'Tis the second month that we can not buy a fresh ham for the kitchen,—Marco swears that the master himself has never a groat,—he sinks his all in these accursed wings, keeping us all on a niggardly footing,—yet here is where the money actually is! Showering his little pets with presents, with little velvet caps! And how is it thou art not ashamed, Andrea, to accept presents from strangers? For Leonardo is neither thy father, nor thy brother, and thou art no longer a small child . . ."

"Cesare," said Giovanni, in order to change the conversation, "the other day you promised me to explain a certain rule of perspective, —do you recall? Evidently we shall wait for the master in vain. He is so taken up with the machine . . ."

"Yea, mates, bide a while,—we shall all go up the chimney with this machine yet,—the devil take it! However, if it be not one thing, 'tis another. I remember once, in the midst of his work on The Last Supper, the master became suddenly engrossed with the invention of a new machine for the preparation of *cervellata*,—a white sausage of

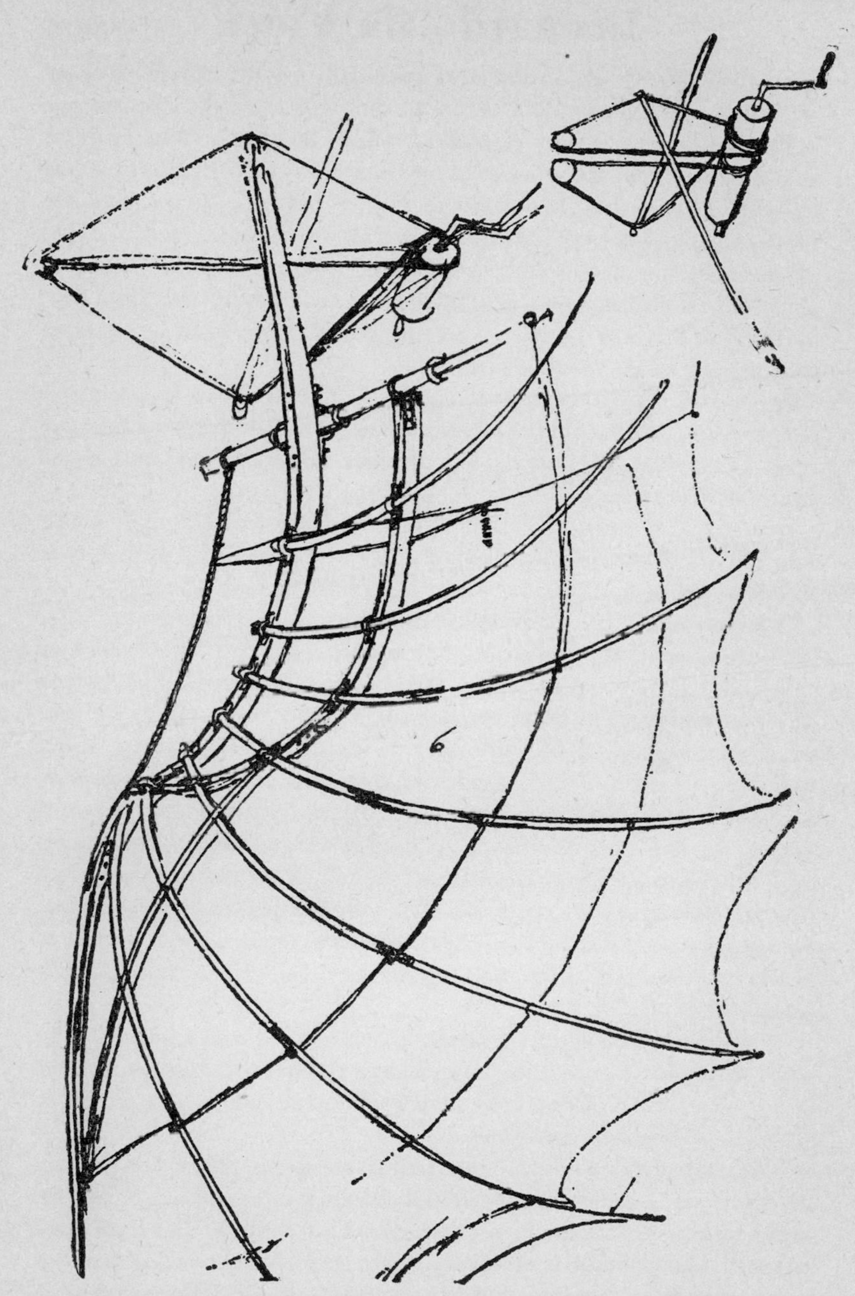
6

brains. And the head of the apostle James the Elder remained as unfinished as ever, awaiting the perfecting of a sausage chopper. The best of his Madonnas he has cast into a corner, while inventing self-turning spits, so that capons and suckling pigs might be evenly roasted. And then this great discovery of extracting washing lye from the droppings of hens! Believe it or not,—there is never a folly that Messer Leonardo would not give himself up to with delight, that he might but shun painting!"

A convulsion ran over Cesare's face; his thin lips formed into a smile of evil mockery.

"And wherefore does God bestow talent on such people?" he added, quietly and ferociously.

III

BUT Leonardo sat on, bent over his work-table.

A swallow flew in at the open window and began flying around and around the room, hitting against the ceiling and walls; finally it got into a wing of the flying apparatus, as into a snare, and its little, living wings became entangled in the net of the cord sinews. Leonardo approached, freed the captive, cautiously, so as not to cause it any pain, took it in his hand, kissed its silky-black little head, and let it out of the window. The swallow soared up and plunged into the sky with a joyous cry.

"How easy, how simple!" he reflected, following it with a wistful, pensive gaze. Then, with a feeling of aversion, he glanced at his machine, at the sombre framework of the gigantic bat.

The man sleeping on the floor woke up. He was an assistant of Leonardo's, a skilled Florentine mechanic and blacksmith, by the name of Zoroastro, or Astro da Peretola. He sprang up, rubbing his only eye,—the other had come out because of a spark which had flown into it from a flaming forge during work. The uncouth giant, with a child-like, simple face, perpetually covered with soot and grime, resembled a Cyclop.

"I have overslept!" exclaimed the blacksmith, clutching his head in despair. "May the devil take me! Eh, how is it you did not awaken me? I hurried, thinking I would finish the left wing toward evening, so as to start flying on the morrow. . . ."

"Thou didst well to have thy full sleep," uttered Leonardo. "The wings can not be used, anyway."

"What? Again? Oh, no, master,—do as you will, but I shall make this machine over. What money, what work have gone into it! And to have everything again go for naught! What else is needed? Not to be able to fly on such wings as these! They would lift not only a man, but an elephant! You will see yet, master! Grant me but one trial,—well, over water, say, so that if I fall I shall have but a ducking; for I swim like a fish, and would never drown!"

He clasped his hands with an imploring mien. Leonardo shook his head.

"Havepatience,friend.Everythingwillcomeinitstime. Later . . ."

"Later!" groaned the blacksmith, well-nigh weeping. "But why not now? In good sooth, messer, I shall fly,—I shall, by the holy God!"

"Thou shalt not, Astro. 'Tis a matter of mathematics."

"I knew that was it! May all the fiends fly away with these mathematics of yours! They do but confound. How many years are we puttering! My soul is weary; every silly midge, every moth, every fly, be it ever so noisome,—the Lord forgive me,—be it even born in manure, still even it can fly; but men crawl, like worms. Is it not a shame? What must we wait for? For there they are,—the wings! Everything is set,—seems to me I'd up, with a blessing, flap them, and away,—and that would be the last you would see of me!"

Suddenly he recalled something, and his face cleared.

"Master, eh, master,—how shall I tell thee? What an amazing dream I had this day!"

"Didst thou fly again?"

"Aye. And oh, if you knew but how! Do you but listen. It seems I was standing amidst a crowd in an unfamiliar chamber, with everybody looking and pointing their fingers at me, and laughing. Well, thinks I, if I fly not now, 'twill go ill with me. I jumped upward, took to waving my arms with all my might, and began to soar upward. At first it was hard, as though there were a mountain on my shoulders. But then it became easier and easier,—I floated upward, almost hitting my head against the ceiling. And everybody cried out: 'Look, look,—he has started flying!' I headed straight through the windows, and ever higher and higher, to the very sky; there was but the wind whistling in my ears, and I felt gay, and laughed,—why, thinks I, have I not been able to fly before? Have I forgotten how, or what? For it is so simple. . . . And there is never a machine needed!"

IV

THERE came sounds of screaming, of cursing, of quick steps tramping on the stairs. The door was flung open, and a man with a stiff, bristly mop of fiery red hair, with a red freckle-covered face ran in. This was Marco d'Oggione, a pupil of Leonardo's. He was cursing, beating and dragging by the ear a thin urchin of some ten years.

"May the Lord send thee an ill Easter, thou good-for-naught! I shall turn thee inside out, that I shall, thou scoundrel!"

"What hast thou against him, Marco?" asked Leonardo.

"Why, messer! He filched two silver buckles, at ten florins each. He managed to pledge one and diced the money away; the other he sewed in his clothes, inside the lining,—and 'twas there I found it. I wanted to pull his mop as he deserves, but he ups and bites my hand till the blood came,—the little imp!"

And with new fury he seized the boy's hair. Leonardo interceded and took the child away from him. Whereupon Marco snatched a bundle of keys out of his pouch,—he filled the post of steward,—and shouted:

"Here are the keys, messer! I've had my fill! I will not live in the same house with scamps and thieves! 'Tis either he or I!"

"Now, now, be calm, Marco, be calm. . . . I shall punish him properly."

The apprentices were peeping out of the workroom. A stout woman pushed her way through,—Maturina, the cook. She had but just returned from market, and was holding a basket with onions, fish, scarlet plump tomatoes, and sprigs of woolly *finocchio*, or fennel. On seeing the small culprit, she took to waving her arms and unloosed a veritable logorrhœa,—just as if dried pease were pouring out of a sack with holes.

Cesare spoke as well, expressing his amazement at Leonardo's keeping in the house this "heathen," for there was no mischief, however wanton and cruel, that Giacopo was incapable of,—the other day he had broken with a stone the leg of sick old Fagianno, the watch-dog; had demolished the swallows' nest over the stable; and everybody knew that his favourite pastime consisted of tearing the wings off butterflies, gloating over their torments.

Giacopo would not leave the master, glowering at his foes from underneath his eyebrows, like a wolf cub at bay. His handsome pale face was immobile. He did not cry, but, when his glance met Leonardo's, his malevolent eyes expressed a timid supplication. Maturina vociferated, demanding that this little fiend be birched at last,—otherwise he would ride roughshod over everybody, and there would be no living with him.

"Quiet, quiet! Be silent, for God's sake!" Leonardo managed to put in, and on his face appeared an expression of a strange pusillanimity, of a helpless weakness before this domestic uprising.

Cesare was smiling and whispering, maliciously rejoicing:

"'Tis nauseating to look at! The weakling! He can not manage to dispose of a boy's case. . . ."

When, finally, everybody had had his or her fill of shouting and had gradually dispersed, Leonardo, having beckoned Beltraffio to him, spoke to him kindly:

"Giovanni, thou hast not yet seen The Last Supper. I am going thither. Wouldst go with me?"

The pupil flushed with pleasure.

V

THEY entered a small courtyard, with a well in the middle, where Leonardo washed himself. Despite two sleepless nights, he felt fresh and wide awake.

The day was hazy, windless, with a pallid, seemingly subaqueous light; the artist loved such days for his work.

While they were standing near the well, Giacopo approached. In his hands he held a small box which he had made himself out of bark.

"Messer Leonardo," uttered the boy, timidly, "this is for you. . . ."

He carefully lifted the lid,—at the bottom of the box was an enormous spider.

"I could hardly catch him," explained Giacopo. "He got into a crack between two stones, held out for three days, he did. The varmint!"

The urchin's face suddenly became animated.

"Just see how he devours flies!"

He caught a fly and threw it into the box. The spider pounced at the prey, caught it with his shaggy paws, and the victim began to thresh about; its buzzing, constantly weakening, came fainter and fainter.

"He is sucking it, he is sucking it! Look," the boy was whispering, languishing with enjoyment. His eyes were ablaze with a cruel curiosity, and a vague smile hovered on his lips. Leonardo also bent over, gazing at the monstrous insect. And suddenly it seemed to Giovanni that in the faces of both there flickered the same expression, as though, despite the abyss which separated the child from the artist, they were on common ground in this curiosity toward the horrible.

When the fly had been eaten up, Giacopo carefully covered the little box and said:

"I shall bring it over to your table, Messer Leonardo,—mayhap you will look at it some more. He fights amusingly with other spiders. . . ."

The boy wanted to go away, but stopped and lifted up his eyes with a pleading air. The corners of his lips drooped and quivered.

"Messer," he uttered, quietly and gravely, "be not wroth at me! So be it then,—I shall go away, even of my own accord; I have been thinking for a long while that I must go away,—only not for their sakes,—'tis all one to me what they say,—but for yours. For I know that you have grown weary of me. You alone are kind,—whereas they are evil, just the same as I; only they pretend, whereas I can not . . . I shall go away and live alone. 'Tis best so. But still, you had best forgive me. . . ."

Tears glistened on the boy's long eyelashes. He repeated in a still lower voice, with his eyes cast down:

"Forgive me, Messer Leonardo! As for the little box, I shall carry it into the house. Let it remain to remind you of me,—the spider will live for a long while. I shall ask Astro to feed him."

Leonardo laid his hand on the youngster's head:

"Where wilt thou go, boy? Stay on. Marco will forgive thee,—and as for me, I am not wroth. Go, and henceforth try to work ill to none."

Giacopo looked at him in silence with great, uncomprehending eyes, in which shone not gratitude, but amazement,—almost fear.

Leonardo answered him with a quiet, kindly smile, and patted his head with tenderness, as though surmising the eternal secret of this heart, created by nature both evil and guiltless of evil.

"'Tis time," said the master, "let us go, Giovanni."

They went through the little swinging gate and, over the deserted street, between the fences of gardens, truck farms and vineyards, set out in the direction of the monastery of Maria delle Grazie.

VI

Of late Beltraffio had been grieved over the fact that he could not bring the master the stipulated monthly payment of six florins. His uncle had quarrelled with him and would not give him a copper. Giovanni had taken money from Fra Benedetto for two months' payment. But the monk had no more,—he had given him his last. Giovanni wanted to apologize to the master.

"Messer," he began timidly, stammering and turning red, "to-day is the fourteenth, and I pay on the tenth, according to the agreement. I feel greatly conscience-stricken. . . . But all I have here is only three florins. Perhaps you will agree to wait,—I shall get money soon. Merulla promised me some transcription. . . ."

Leonardo looked at him with amazement:

"Whatever art thou about, Giovanni? The Lord be with thee! How is it thou art not ashamed to speak of this?"

By the confused face of his pupil, by the clumsy, pitiful and shame-inspired patches on his old shoes, with their yarn stitches rubbed through, by his worn clothes,—he surmised that Giovanni was in sore need. Leonardo frowned and began speaking of something else. But in a little while, with a careless and seemingly absent-minded air, he felt in his pocket, took out a gold coin, and said:

"Giovanni, I would ask thee to drop in later at a shop, to buy me some blue drawing paper—some twenty sheets; a packet of red chalk, and also some fitch-brushes. Here, take this."

"You have a ducat here. Ten *soldi* will suffice for the purchase. I shall bring you the change. . . ."

"Thou wilt bring naught. Thou hast time to give it back. Dare not even to think of the money again,—dost thou hear?"

He turned away and said, pointing to the hazy morning outlines of the larches, stretching away into the distance in a long row on either bank of the Naviglio Grande,—a canal as straight as an arrow:

"Hast thou noticed, Giovanni, how in a light haze the verdure of the trees becomes an æthereal blue, and a pale grey in a thick haze?"

He made several more observations about the differentiation of the shadows cast by clouds on mountains in summer, when they are covered with leafage, and in winter, when they are entirely denuded. Then he turned to the pupil and said:

"But I know why thou didst deem me a niggard. I am ready to make a wager I have guessed aright. When we discussed the monthly stipend, thou hast most probably noted how I interrogated thee in every small particular, and entered everything in a memorandum book,—the amount, the date, the debtor. Only—dost see?—thou must know, my friend, 'tis a habit I have, probably from my father, the notary Pietro da Vinci, the most precise and prudent of men. It has proven of no use to me, nor does it benefit me in any way in business matters. Believe it or not, but at times it makes even me laugh to read the book over—such trifles do I jot down! I can tell exactly how many *denari* the plume and the velvet for Andrea Salaino's new hat cost, but where the thousands of ducats go to, I know not. Mind, now, Giovanni,—in the future pay no attention to this foolish habit. If thou hast need of money, take it, and believe that I give it thee as a father to a son. . . ."

Leonardo looked at him with such a smile as made the pupil's heart lighter and happier.

Pointing out to his companion the strange form of a certain squat mulberry-tree in a garden they were passing, the master remarked that not only every tree, but every leaf, has its own, unique form, never anywhere duplicated, just as every man has an individual countenance.

Giovanni reflected that he discoursed of the trees with the same kindliness with which he had but now discoursed of his, Giovanni's, trouble,—as though this attentiveness to everything animated, when turned upon nature, gave to the gaze of the master the penetration of a clairvoyant.

On the low, fertile plain, from behind the dark-green mulberry-trees, appeared the church of the Dominican hostel of Maria delle Grazie,—of brick, rosy and gay against the white cloud-flecked sky, with a broad Lombardian cupola, resembling a tent, with relief ornaments of fired clay,—a building which was a creation of the young Bramante.

They entered the monastery refectory.

VII

THIS was an unassuming long hall with bare whitewashed walls, with the dark wooden ceiling beams receding into the distance. There was an odour of warm humidity, of church incense and the ancient stale fumes of lenten dishes. Near a partition wall, nearest the entrance, stood the small dining table of the Father Abbot. On both sides of it were long, narrow tables for the monks.

It was so still that one could hear the buzzing of a fly in the window with its dusty-yellow panes of glass. From the monastery kitchen floated in voices and the rattling of iron pots and pans.

At the farthest point of the refectory, opposite the prior's table, near a wall curtained over with coarse grey cloth, was reared a scaffolding of boards. Giovanni surmised that under this cloth was the creation over which the master had already been at work for over twelve years,—The Last Supper.

Leonardo mounted the scaffolding, unlocked a wooden box wherein were kept the preliminary cartoons, as well as card-board, brushes, and colours, got out a small, tattered Latin book, its margining scrawled all over with notes, handed it to his pupil, and said:

"Read the thirteenth chapter of John."

And he threw back the covering.

When Giovanni looked at it, at the first moment it seemed to him that this was no mural painting before him, but an actual æthereal depth, a continuation of the monastery refectory,—just as though another room had opened beyond the drawn curtain, so that the longitudinal and transversal beams of the ceiling entered it, narrowing in the distance, and the light of day blended with the peaceful light of evening over the blue summits of Sion, which could be seen in the three windows of this new refectory, almost as simple as the one of the monks, save that it was covered with rugs, and was more cozy and mysterious. The long table in the picture resembled those at which the monks ate,—with precisely the same sort of table-cloth ornamented with narrow stripes, its ends knotted, and with quadrangular folds still not flattened out, as though a trifle damp yet, just this moment taken from the monastery storeroom; with the very same sort of tumblers, plates, knives, glass vessels filled with wine.

And Giovanni read in the Scripture:

> Now before the feast of the passover, when Jesus knew that his hour was come that he should depart out of this world unto the Father, having loved his own which were in the world, he loved them unto the end.
>
> And supper being ended, the devil having now put into the heart of Judas Iscariot, Simon's *son*, to betray him . . .

. . . He was troubled in spirit, and testified, and said, Verily, verily, I say unto you, That one of you shall betray me.

Then the disciples looked one on another, doubting of whom he spake.

Now there was leaning on Jesus' bosom one of his disciples, whom Jesus loved.

Simon Peter therefore beckoned to him, that he should ask who it should be of whom he spake.

He then lying on Jesus' breast, saith unto him, Lord, who is it?

Jesus answered, He it is to whom I shall give a sop, when I have dipped *it.* And when he had dipped the sop, he gave *it* to Judas Iscariot, *the son* of Simon.

And after the sop Satan entered into him.[6]

Giovanni raised his eyes to the picture.

The faces of the apostles were imbued with such life that he seemed to hear their voices, seemed to look into the very depths of their hearts, which were abashed by the most incomprehensible and fearful thing that had ever come to pass in the universe,—the birth of the evil from which God must die.

Especially was Giovanni struck by Judas, John, and Peter. The head of Judas had not yet been drawn,—only his body, thrown back, was slightly sketched in: clutching in his convulsive fingers the bag with the pieces of silver, with a chance movement of his arm he had overturned the salt cellar,—and the salt had spilt.

Peter, in a fit of wrath, had impetuously risen from behind him, his right hand had seized a knife, his left had fallen on John's shoulder, as though questioning the favourite disciple of Jesus: "Who is the betrayer?"—and the aged, silvery grey, radiantly wrathful head shone with that fiery zeal, that thirst for a great deed, with which in time to come he was to exclaim, having comprehended the inevitability of the sufferings and death of the Master: "Lord, why can not I follow thee now? I will lay down my life for thy sake."[7]

Nearest of all to Christ was John,—his hair, soft as silk, smooth at the roots, curling toward the tips; his lowered eyelids, heavy with the languor of sleep; his submissively folded hands; his face, roundly oblong in outline,—everything in him breathed of heavenly calm and serenity. He alone of all the disciples no longer suffered, nor feared, nor was wrathful. In him was fulfilled the word of the Master: "That they all may be one; as thou, Father, *art* in me, and I in thee. . . ."[8]

Giovanni gazed and thought:

"So that is the real Leonardo! And yet I doubted, well-nigh believing slander. Can the man who created this be an atheist? Who among men is nearer to Christ than he! . . ."

Having finished with gentle touches of his brush the face of John, the master, taking a piece of charcoal from the box, tried to outline the head of Jesus, but without any result. After ten years' pondering over this head, he still could not sketch in even a first outline. And now, as always, before the even white spot in the picture where the Lord's face was to appear, yet could not, the artist felt impotence and perplexity.

Throwing aside the charcoal, he wiped off with a sponge its light mark and sank into one of those meditations before the picture which lasted at times for hours at a stretch.

Giovanni ascended the scaffolding, very quietly approached him, and saw that the gloomy face of Leonardo, which appeared aged, bore an expression of an obstinate effort of thought, resembling despair. But, meeting the gaze of his pupil, he uttered amiably:

"What sayest thou, friend?"

"What can I say, master? This is splendid,—the most splendid thing in all the world. And none among men has grasped this, save you. But it is best to say naught. I can not. . . ."

Tears quivered in his voice. And he added quietly, as though with fear:

"And here is somewhat else I ponder on and comprehend not: what must the face of Judas be like amid such faces?"

The master took out of the box a drawing on a fragment of paper and showed it to him. A frightful face it was, yet not repellent, not even malevolent,—only filled with infinite sorrow and the bitterness of realization. Giovanni compared it with the face of John.

"Yes," he pronounced in a whisper, "this is he! He, of whom it is said: 'Satan entered into him.' He, probably, knew more than all of them, but did not accept the word: 'That they all may be one.' He himself wanted to be One. . . ."

Cesare da Sesto entered the refectory with a man in the livery of the court stokers.

"At last we have found you!" exclaimed Cesare. "We are seeking you everywhere. . . . We are from the Duchess, on important business, master."

"Would it please your lordship to repair to the palace?" added the stoker respectfully.

"What has happened?"

"Trouble, Messer Leonardo! The pipes in the baths will not work, and also, as though for our sins, this morning, just as the Duchess was pleased to sit down in the bath, and the maid-servant with the linen had gone into an adjacent chamber, the handle of the hot water faucet broke, so that Her Excellency could in no way stop the flow of water. 'Tis a good thing that she managed to jump out of the bath, —being almost scalded with the hot water. She is pleased to be very wroth; Messer Ambrogio da Ferrari, the chamberlain, complains, saying he has forewarned your lordship more than once about the trouble with the pipes . . ."

"Nonsense!" said Leonardo. "Thou seest I am busy. Betake thyself to Zoroastro,—he will fix all the pipes in half an hour."

"By no manner of means, messer! I am ordered not to come without you. . . ."

Paying no attention to him, Leonardo wanted to resume his work. But, having glanced at the blank space for the head of Jesus, he made a wry face of vexation; with a gesture of despair, as though suddenly comprehending that this time, too, there would be no result, he closed the box of colours, and descended from the scaffolding.

"Well, let us go, 'tis all one! Come after me in the grand court of the castle, Giovanni. Cesare will show thee the way. I shall await you near the steed."

The steed referred to was a monument of the late Duke Francesco Sforza.

And, to the amazement of Giovanni, without turning around to look at The Last Supper, as though glad of an excuse to get away from his labour, the master went off with the stoker to repair the waste pipes in the ducal baths.

"What? Canst thou not get thy fill of gazing?" Cesare turned to Beltraffio. "It is, I grant, truly amazing, until one catches on to the trick . . ."

"What wouldst thou say?"

"Nothing, just so. . . . I shall not try to shake thy faith. Thou mayest even perceive for thyself. Well, and in the meantime have thy joyance of it . . ."

"I implore thee, Cesare, say outright all that thou hast in mind. . . ."

"If thou wilt have it so. . . . Only, now, be not thou angry later, and rebuke me not for the truth. However, I know all that thou wouldst say, and shall not dispute. Naturally, this is a great creation. Never a one of the masters ever had such a knowledge of anatomy, of perspective, of the laws of light and shade. How else should it be! . . . Everything is copied from nature,—every little wrinkle in the faces, every fold on the table-cloth. But the living spirit is not there. There is no God, nor will there ever be. Everything is dead,—dead within, in the heart! Do thou but look closely, Giovanni,—what geometrical regularity, what triangles: two contemplative, two active, the central point in Christ. There, to the right side, the contemplative: absolute good in John; absolute evil in Judas; the differentiation between good and evil,—that is, justice,—in Peter; and alongside, thou hast the active triangle: Andrew, James the Younger, Bartholomew. And to the left of the centre,—again a contemplative one: the love of Philip, the faith of James the Elder, the reasoning of Thomas,—and, once more, an active triangle. Geometry instead of inspiration, mathematics instead of beauty. Everything has been thought out, calculated, masticated by reason to the point of nausea, tested out to the point of revulsion, weighed in the scales, measured with the compasses. Under the holy of holies,—blasphemy!"

"O Cesare!" uttered Giovanni with quiet reproach. "How little thou knowest the master! And what is the reason thou dost . . . hate him so? . . ."

"But dost thou know him, and dost thou love him?" enquired Cesare with a caustic smile, quickly facing him. There was such unlooked-for malevolence flashing in his eyes that Giovanni was suddenly abashed.

"Thou art unjust, Cesare," added he, after a silence. "The picture is not completed: there is as yet no Christ."

"There is no Christ. And art thou sure, Giovanni, that there will ever be? Well, now, we shall see! Only mark my words: Messer Leonardo shall never finish The Last Supper,—neither Christ nor Judas will he ever paint. For, dost see, my friend, through mathematics, knowledge, experience, one can attain a great deal, but not all. Here something else is needed. Here we have a limit which, with all his learning, he never can surmount!"

They went out of the monastery and set out in the direction of the castle,—the Castello di Porta Giovia.

"Thou art surely mistaken in one thing at least, Cesare," said Beltraffio. "There is a Judas . . ."

"There is? Where?"

"I have seen him myself."

"When?"

"Just now, in the monastery. Leonardo showed me the sketch."

"Showed it to thee? Well, well!" Cesare gave him a look and uttered slowly, as though with an effort:

"Well, now, is it good?"

Giovanni nodded his head in silence. Cesare made no reply and during their entire journey did not again venture speaking, plunged as he was in deep thought.

VIII

THEY approached the gates of the castle, and over the Battiponte, a drawbridge, entered into the tower of the southern wall,—the Torre di Filarete, surrounded on all sides by the water of the deep moats. In here everything was gloomy, stuffy, with odours of the barracks, of bread and of manure. The echo under the reverberating vaults repeated the polyglot talk, the laughter and curses of the mercenaries.

Cesare had a pass. But Giovanni, as a stranger, had to undergo a suspicious examination, and his name was written down in the guard book. By a second drawbridge, where they underwent a new examination, they entered the deserted inner square of the castle, the Piazza d'Armi,—the Field of Mars.

Straight before them, above the Dead Moat,—the Fossato Morto,—the crenellated tower of the Bonna of Savoy loomed darkly. To the right was the entrance to the court of honour, the Corte Ducale; to the left, the entrance to the most impregnable part of the castle, the Rocchetta fortalice, a veritable eagle's eyrie.

In the middle of the square could be seen wooden scaffolding surrounded by small additional structures, fences, and sheds of boards, put together slap-dash, but already grown dark with age, and covered in spots with yellow-grey lichens. Above these fences and scaffoldings reared the clay equestrian statue, twelve ells in height, known as the Colossus,—the work of Leonardo.

The gigantic steed, of dark-green clay, stood out against the cloudy sky: it was rearing, trampling a warrior under its hoofs; the conqueror upon it was extending the ducal sceptre. This was the great *condottiere*, Francesco Sforza, a seeker after adventures, selling his blood for money,—half-soldier, half-brigand. The son of a poor tiller of the soil in Romagnola, he had sprung from the people, as strong as a lion, as cunning as a fox; had attained the pinnacle of power through evil deeds, through great exploits, through wisdom, and had died on the throne of the Dukes of Milan.

A ray of the pallid, humid sun fell on the Colossus.

Giovanni read in the obese wrinkles of the double chin, in the frightful eyes, full of a feral keenness, the good-humoured calm of a satiated beast. And on the pediment of the monument, imprinted on the soft clay by the hand of Leonardo himself, he saw the distich:

Expectant animi molemque futuram
Suspiciunt; fluat aes; vox erit: Ecce deus!

He was struck by the last two words: *Ecce deus!*—Behold the god!

"A god," repeated Giovanni, having looked at the clay Colossus and at the human sacrifice, spurned by the steed of the Triumphator, Sforza, the Usurper, and recalled the silent refectory in the Hostel of Mary the Bestower of Good, the blue summits of Sion, the heavenly beauty of St. John's face, and the quiet of the Last Supper of that God of Whom it was said: *Ecce homo!*—Behold the man!

Leonardo approached Giovanni.

"I have finished my work. Let us go, or else they will again summon us to the palace,—it seems the kitchen chimneys are smoking there; we must slip away before 'tis noticed."

Giovanni stood in silence, his eyes downcast; his face was pale.

"Forgive me, master! . . . I ponder, and understand not, how you could create this Colossus and The Last Supper, both at one and the same time?"

Leonardo looked at him with simple-hearted wonder:

"What is it, then, that thou dost not understand?"

"Oh, Messer Leonardo, do you really not perceive yourself? It must not be—these two together. . . ."

"On the contrary, Giovanni. I think that one helps the other: the best thoughts about the Mystic Supper come to me precisely here, when I am working on the Colossus; and, on the other hand, there, in the monastery, I am fond of mulling over the monument. These two are twins. I have begun them together,—together shall I finish them."

"Together! This man—and Christ? Nay, master, it can not be! . . ." exclaimed Beltraffio, and, not being able to express his thoughts better, but feeling his heart wax indignant at the unbearable contradiction, he kept on repeating:

"It can not be! . . ."

"Why can it not?" questioned the master.

Giovanni was just about to speak; but, meeting the gaze of Leonardo's calm, wondering eyes, understood that it was impossible to say anything; he would not understand, anyway.

"When I was looking at the Mystic Supper," Beltraffio pondered, "it seemed to me that I had come to know him. And now I again know naught. Who is he? To which of these twain has he said in his heart: 'Behold the God'? Or is Cesare right, and there is no God in the heart of Leonardo?"

IX

At night, when everyone in the house had lain down to sleep, Giovanni, tortured by sleeplessness, went out into the yard, and sat down by the front steps, on a bench under an arbour of grape-vines.

The yard was quadrangular, with a well in the centre. The side at Giovanni's back was taken up with the wall of the house; opposite him was the stable; to the left a stone enclosure with a small gate, leading out on the highway to the Porta Vercellina; to the right, the wall of a small garden, with a small door, always padlocked, because in the depth of the garden was a separate building, to which the master of the house never admitted anyone, save Astro, and where he frequently worked in complete isolation.

The night was still warm, and humid; the stifling mist was saturated with the opaque moonlight. There came a knock at the small locked gate leading out on the highway. The shutter of one of the lower windows opened; a man leaned out and asked:

"Monna Cassandra?"

"'Tis I. Open."

Astro came out of the house and unlocked the gate. A woman stepped into the courtyard, clad in a white dress, which, under the moon, seemed greenish, like the mist.

At first they talked a bit at the small gate; then passed by Giovanni; without noticing him, enveloped as he was by the black shadow cast by the projection of the front steps and the grape-vines. The girl sat down on the low edge of the well.

Hers was a strange face, passive and immobile, like those of ancient carvings: a low forehead, straight eyebrows, a chin too small, and eyes a transparent yellow, like amber. But most of all was Giovanni struck by her hair,—crisp, downy, æthereal, as though possessed of a distinct life of its own,—like the snakes of Medusa it surrounded her head with an aureole of black, that made her face seem still paler, her crimson lips still more vivid, her yellow eyes still more transparent.

"Astro, hast thou also heard about Brother Angelo?"

"Ay, Monna Cassandra. They say he is sent by the Pope for the extirpation of sorcery and of all heresies. When one hears e'en a bit of what good folks say about these Fathers Inquisitors, 'tis enough to make the chills run down one's back. God save us from falling into their clutches! Be more careful. Forewarn your aunt. . . ."

"She is no aunt of mine!"

"Well, 'tis all one,—this Monna Sidonia with whom you live."

"But dost think, blacksmith, that we be witches?"

"I think naught! Messer Leonardo explained and proved to me in detail that there is no such thing as sorcery, nor can there be, by the laws of nature. Messer Leonardo knoweth everything and believeth nothing. . . ."

"Believeth nothing?" repeated Monna Cassandra, "believeth not in the devil? But what of God?"

"Mock not! He is a righteous man."

"I am not mocking. Only, dost thou know, Astro, what amusing things befall? I have been told that the Fathers Inquisitors found in the possession of a certain great atheist a compact with the Devil, in which this man bound himself to deny, on the basis of logic and natural laws, the existence of witches, and the powers of the Devil, in order that, having rid the servants of Satan from the persecutions of the Most Holy Inquisition, he might by that very means fortify and increase the reign of the Devil on earth. That is why the fathers say: to be a wizard is heresy; but not to believe in wizardry is heresy twice over. Look thou, then, blacksmith, betray not thy master,—tell no one that he believeth not in black magic."

At first Zoroastro was abashed with surprise; but recovering, he began to contradict, vindicating Leonardo. But the girl cut him short:

"Well, now, how is your flying machine coming along? Will it be ready soon?"

The blacksmith made a despondent gesture.

"Ready! Have another guess! We have to make everything over anew."

"Ah, Astro, Astro! And yet thou wilt go on believing in nonsense! Dost not understand, then, that all these machines are but to throw dust into one's eyes? Messer Leonardo, methinks, has already been flying long ere this. . . ."

"Flying? What mean you?"

"Why, even as I do."

He looked at her, meditatively.

"Perhaps you do but dream this, Monna Cassandra?"

"But then, how is it that others see me? Or hast thou not heard of it?"

The blacksmith scratched the back of his ear in indecision.

"However, I had forgot," she continued, with mockery, "for ye are all men of learning here; ye believe not in wonders of any sort,—'tis all mechanics with you!"

"The devil take mechanics! Here is where I am up to in mechanics!" the blacksmith indicated the nape of his neck.

Then, clasping his hands imploringly, he exclaimed:

"Monna Cassandra! You know I am a man to be trusted. And, besides, it would not profit me to blab. First thing I know, Brother Angelo will draw his net tight. Do tell me, then,—do me that kindness, —tell me everything, exactly! . . ."

"Tell thee what?"

"How do you fly?"

"So that is what thou hast a hankering after! Well, no,—that I shall not tell thee. If thou wilt know a great deal, thou wilt grow old early."

She was silent for a space. Then, with a long, steady stare into his eyes, she added quietly:

"Wherein is the good of talk? We must act!"

"What is necessary, then?" he asked, paling a little, with a voice that quivered.

"To know the word; then there is a certain herb, to smear the body withal."

"Have you got it?"

"I have."

"And know you the word?"

The girl nodded her head.

"And will I fly?"

"Try it. Thou shalt see,—'tis more certain than mechanics!"

The blacksmith's sole eye flared up with the fire of an insane desire.

"Monna Cassandra, give me of your herb!"

She burst into quiet, queer laughter.

"Oh, what a strange fellow thou art, Astro! But just now thou thyself didst call the secrets of magic foolish ravings, yet now thou hast suddenly come to believe. . . ."

Astro was abashed, his face took on a despondent, obstinate expression.

"I fain would try. For to me 'tis all one,—by miracle or mechanics, only to fly! I can wait no longer. . . ."

The girl laid her hand on his shoulder.

"Well, God be with thee! I feel sorry for thee. In good sooth, thou mayst really go off thy mind, save thou fly. So be it, then,—I shall give thee the herb and tell thee the word. Only thou too, Astro, must do that which I shall ask of thee."

"I shall, Monna Cassandra,—I shall do all! Speak!"

The girl pointed to the wet roof of tiles, glistening beyond the garden wall in the haze of the moon.

"Let me in there."

Astro frowned and shook his head.

"Nay, nay. . . . All that you will, save only this!"

"Why?"

"I gave my word to let none in."

"And hast been there thyself?"

"I have."

"What have ye there, then?"

"Why, no mysteries of any sort. Really, now, Monna Cassandra, there is naught curious,—machines, instruments, books, manuscripts; there are, also, rare flowers, animals, insects,—travellers bring them to the master from distant lands. And also a certain tree, poisonous. . . ."

"Poisonous? How meanest thou?"

"Why,—for experiments. He envenomed it, studying the action of poisons on plants."

"I beg thee, Astro, tell me all thou knowest of this tree."

"Why, there is nothing to tell. In the early spring, when it was in sap, he drilled an opening in the trunk to its very core, and with a hollow, long syringe squirted in some sort of liquid."

"Strange experiments! What sort of tree is it, then?"

"Peach."

"Well, and what then? Were the fruits swollen with poison?"

"They will be, when they ripen."

"And can one see that they are poisoned?"

"Nay, 'tis not perceptible. That is why he lets none in: one might be tempted by the beauty of the fruit, eat it, and die."

"Hast thou the key upon thee?"

"I have."

"Give me the key, Astro!"

"Nay, nay! Whatever are you about, Monna Cassandra! I have given him my oath. . . ."

"Give me the key!" repeated Cassandra. "I shall compass it so that thou shalt fly this very night: dost hear,—this very night! Look, here is the herb."

She took out of her bosom and showed him a small glass vial, filled with a dark liquid, which faintly glistened in the moonlight; and, drawing her face near his, whispered insinuatingly:

"Whatever art thou afraid of, thou silly little fellow! Thou thyself sayest that there are no mysteries of any sort. We shall but enter and have a look. . . . Well, now, do give me the key!"

"Leave me be!" he spoke up. "I shall not let you through, no matter what happens; nor have I any need of your herb. Get you gone!"

"Coward!" uttered the girl with contempt. "Thou couldst know the secret, but durst not. Now I see that thy master is a wizard and hoodwinks thee as one would a babe. . . ."

Keeping a morose silence, he turned away. The girl again drew near him.

"Very well, then, Astro,—there is no need for it. I shan't go in. Do thou but ope the door and let me peep in. . . ."

"You will not enter?"

"No,—do but open and let me look."

He took out the key and opened the door.

Giovanni, having risen very cautiously, saw in the depth of the little walled-in garden a common peach-tree. But in the pallid mist, under the turbidly-green light of the moon, it appeared to him ominous and phantasmal.

Standing at the threshold with widely open eyes, the girl gazed with avid curiosity,—then made a step forward, in an attempt to enter. The blacksmith held her back; she struggled, writhing in his arms like a snake. He pushed her away so that she almost fell. But she immediately straightened up and looked at him point-blank. Her pallid face, like that of a corpse, was malevolent and awful: at that moment she did, in reality, resemble a witch.

The blacksmith locked the door to the garden and, without bidding good-bye to Monna Cassandra, entered the house. She followed him with her eyes. Then, going rapidly past Giovanni, she slipped out of the small gate to the highway leading to Porta Vercellina. There fell a silence. The mist became still more dense. All things evanished and dissolved within it.

Giovanni shut his eyes. Before him arose, as in a vision, the fearful tree with heavy drops on its wet leaves, with its poisonous fruit in the turbidly-green light of the moon,—and the words of the Scripture came to his recollection:

> And the Lord God commanded the man, saying, Of every tree of the garden thou mayest freely eat.
>
> But of the tree of the knowledge of good and evil, thou shalt not eat of it: for in the day that thou eatest thereof thou shalt surely die.[9]

BOOK THREE

Poisoned Fruits

I

HE DUCHESS BEATRICE USED TO WASH HER hair every Friday, and tint it with gold. After the tinting it was necessary to dry it in the sun. For this purpose small elevations, surrounded with railings, were built on the roofs of houses.

The Duchess was seated on an elevation of this sort atop the enormous suburban Villa Sforzesca, patiently enduring the scorching blaze, at a time when even labourers and their oxen withdrew into the shade. She was enveloped in a voluminous sleeveless mantelet. On her head was a straw hat,—a sunshade for the protection of the face from sunburn. The gold-stained hair, let through the round aperture of the hat, was spread out over the broad brim of the hat. A xanthochroous Circassian slave wetted the hair with a sponge affixed to the sharp point of a spindle; a Tartar woman, with narrow, oblique eye-slits, combed it with an ivory comb.

The tincture for gilding of the hair was prepared from the juice of hickory roots, gathered in May; from saffron, ox-gall, droppings of swallows, grey succinum, burnt bear-claws, and lizard-tallow. Alongside, under the personal supervision of the Duchess herself—on a tripod, over a flame made pale and almost invisible by the sun, in a retort with a long spout like those in use by alchemists—boiled Muscat rose-water, together with precious *viverra*, or civet,—also Adragantian resin and levisticum, or lorage.

Both of the waiting women were bathed in sweat. Even the Duchess's lapdog, a bitch, could not find a spot for herself on the baking elevation, reproachfully gazing at her mistress with puckered eyes, breathing heavily with tongue lolling,—not even growling as was her wont, in answer to the playful overtures of a nimble marmoset. The monkey, however, found the heat just as much to his taste as did a little blackamoor who was holding the mirror, set in pearls and nacre.

Despite the fact that Beatrice always endeavoured to impart austerity to her face, and stateliness to her every motion, as befitted her rank, it was hard to believe that she numbered but nineteen years, that she had had two children, and was now married three years. In the urchin-like fullness of her sun-browned cheeks, in the innocent fold on her slender neck below the too-rounded and plump chin, in her thick lips, sternly compressed, seeming always pouting and capricious, in her narrow shoulders, her flat bosom, her abrupt, impulsive, sometimes almost boyish movements, one could perceive a schoolgirl,—spoiled, self-willed, unrestrainedly lively, and egotistical. And yet, in the firm eyes of brown, as clear as ice, there shone a calculating brain. The most penetrating of the statesmen of that time, the Ambassador of Venice, Marino Sanuto, in his secret letters assured the Signoria that this little girl was veritably as hard as flint in politics, that she was far more sure of herself mentally than the Duke Ludovico, her husband, who did exceedingly well in listening to his wife in everything.

The lap dog broke into angry and hoarse barking. Up the steep little ladder connecting the elevation with the tiring and wardrobe chambers, ascended a beldam in dark widow's weeds, grunting and oh'ing. With one hand she was telling beads; the other held a crutch. The wrinkles of her face would have seemed venerable, were it not for the mawkish sweetness of her smile, and the mouselike shiftiness of her eyes.

"O-ho-ho, old age is no joyance! 'Twas all I could do to clamber up. May the Lord send Your Grace health!" She slavishly lifted from the floor the edge of the Duchess's bathing mantelet and applied it to her lips.

"Ah, Monna Sidonia! Well, now, is it ready?"

The crone took out of her wallet a carefully wrapped and stoppered vial with a turbid, whitish liquid,—the milk of a she-ass and a red she-goat, infused in wild anise, asparagus roots, and the bulbs of white lilies.

"It should have been kept for about two days more in warm horse-manure. Oh, well, it matters not,—methinks 'tis ready even now. Only before washing yourself with it, order it to be filtered through a felt strainer. Wet some soft sweet bread in it and be pleased to rub your lovely little face for as long as it takes to say the Credo thrice. In five weeks 'twill take all the tan off. And it also helps against black-heads."

"Hearken, crone," spoke Beatrice. "Mayhap there is again in this wash some nastiness or other, such as witches use in black magic,—on the nature of snake-grease, the blood of a hoopoe, and powder of frogs, dried out on a pan, as in that ointment for extirpating hair from birth-marks, which thou wert bringing me the other day. If there be, thou hadst better say so right off."

"Nay, nay, Your Grace! Believe not idle chatter. I work conscientiously, without deception. Everyone to their taste. But then, too, it must be said that at times one can not do without filth: here, for instance, was the most worthy Madonna Angelica washing her head all last summer with dog urine, that she might not become bald, and thanked the Lord to boot because it helped."

Then, bending down to the Duchess's ear, she commenced to tell her the latest talk of the town,—of how the youthful wife of the chief Consul of the Salt Traders, the captivating Madonna Filiberta, was betraying her husband and amusing herself with a newly-arrived Spanish knight.

"Oh, thou old go-between!" Beatrice half-jestingly threatened with her finger, evidently enjoying the gossip. "Thou thyself hast seduced the poor wretch. . . ."

"Oh, nothing of the sort, Your Grace,—wherein is she unhappy? She singeth like a very bird,—rejoicing, thanking me every day. 'Verily,' saith she, ''tis only now that I have come to know what a great difference there is between the kisses of a husband and a lover.'"

"And what of the sin? Can it be that her conscience doth not bother her?"

"Conscience? You see, Your Grace,—though monks and popes may assert the contrary, I still think that the sin of love is the most natural of all sins. A few drops of holy water suffice to wash it away. And on top of that, in betraying her husband, Madonna Filiberta, by that very same token, is but paying him tit for tat, as they say; and even if she does not blot his sins out entirely she does, at the very least, considerably lighten them before God."

"But then, does her husband also? . . ."

"I know not for a certainty. But they are all of one cut, for methinks there is not in all the world a husband who would not liefer consent to having but one hand rather than but one wife."

The Duchess burst into laughter.

"Ah, Monna Sidonia, one can not even be wroth at thee! Wherever dost thou get such clever things from?"

"Do you but believe an old woman,—all that I say is the holy truth! For I, too, can tell a straw from a beam in matters of conscience. . . .

Everything in its season. Any of our sisterhood, if she have not her fill of love in youth, is in the winter of her years tortured by such remorse that it brings her into the very claws of the Devil."

"Thou dost discourse like a Magister of Theology!"

"I am an unlettered woman, but I speak with all my heart, Your Grace! Blossoming youth is given us but once in this life, for,—the Lord forgive me,—what the devil are we poor women good for, having grown old? But to watch the ashes on the little embers, perhaps, or, driven off to the kitchen, to purr with the cats and tell over the pots and the dripping pans. Not in vain is it said: Young women shall stuff; old women shall choke and cough. Beauty without love is like a mass without a Paternoster, while the caresses of a husband are as dreary as the games of nuns."

The Duchess again went off into laughter.

"How? How? Repeat that!"

The old woman looked at her attentively; probably deciding that she had amused the Duchess sufficiently with trifles, she again bent down to her ear and fell to whispering. Beatrice ceased laughing, and made a sign. The female slaves withdrew to a distance. The little blackamoor alone remained on the elevation,—he did not understand Italian. Around them was only the still sky, as pallid as though it had become deadened from the scorching heat.

"Mayhap 'tis but nonsense?" said the Duchess, at last. "If one were to believe all the chatter . . ."

"Nay, Signora. I have seen and heard, myself. Others, too, will tell you."

"Were there many people?"

"Some ten thousand,—the entire square before the Castle of Pavia was filled."

"What didst thou hear, then?"

"When Madonna Isabella came forth on the balcony with the little Francesco, all started waving their arms and caps; many wept. 'Long live Isabella of Aragon,' they shouted, 'and Gian Galeazzo, the lawful sovereign of Milan, and their heir Francesco! Death to the usurpers of their throne! . . .'"

Beatrice frowned.

"In those very words?"

"Ay,—and even worse. . . ."

"What were they? Tell all,—have no fear."

"They cried,—my tongue, Signora, refuses to budge,—they cried: 'Death to the thieves!'"

Beatrice shivered; but, immediately mastering herself, asked quietly: "What else didst thou hear?"

"Really, I know not how I may even put it to Your Grace. . . ."

"Come, come, now,—be quick about it! I would know all."

"Would you believe it, Signora, the talk of the mob ran that the Most Illustrious Duke, Ludovico Moro, the guardian and benefactor of Gian Galeazzo, did immure his nephew in the fortalice of Pavia, surrounding him with hired assassins and spies. After that they began a great outcry, demanding that the Duke Gian Galeazzo himself come out to them. But Monna Isabella replied that he was ill abed. . . ."

And Monna Sidonia again fell to whispering mysteriously in the ear of the Duchess. At first Beatrice listened attentively; then she turned around wrathfully and cried out:

"Art thou gone off thy mind, old witch? How durst thou! Why, I shall immediately order thee to be cast down off this height, so that even a crow will not be able to gather thy bones! . . ."

The threat did not frighten Monna Sidonia. Beatrice, also, soon regained her composure.

"I do not as much as believe it," she uttered, looking at the crone from underneath her eyebrows. The latter shrugged her shoulders:

"As you will,—but 'tis impossible not to believe. . . . If 'twill please you to observe,—this is the manner of working it,—" she continued insinuatingly: "a little effigy is moulded out of wax; in its right side is put the heart, and in its left the liver, of a swallow; stick it through with a needle, uttering an incantation; and he whom the effigy resembleth dieth a slow death,—here no leeches can in the least avail. . . ."

"Be still," the Duchess cut her short. "Never dare speak to me of this! . . ."

The old woman again reverently kissed the hem of the Duchess's bathing garment.

"Your Magnificence! My little radiant sun! I love you too much,—therein lies all my fault. Believe me, I pray to God in tears to grant you health whenever the Magnificat is sung on the eve of St. Francis' Day. Folks do say that I am a witch, now; but, even if I were to sell my soul to the Devil, as God is my witness, 'twould be only to do some service to Your Excellency!" And, meditatively, she added: "It can be done without witchcraft also."

The Duchess looked at her in silence, with curiosity.

"When I was coming here through the castle garden," Monna Sidonia went on in a care-free tone, "the gardener was gathering into a basket some most excellent peaches; a present for Gian Galeazzo, perchance?" And, after a silence, she added: "Why, in the garden of Leonardo da Vinci, the Florentine master, there also grow peaches of amazing beauty,—so they say; save that they are poisonous. . . ."

"Poisonous? How meanest thou?"

"Ay, ay. Monna Cassandra, my niece, has seen them. . . ."

The beldam again fell to whispering in Beatrice's ear. The Duchess made no reply; the expression of her eyes remained impenetrable. Her hair was already dry. She arose, threw the mantelet off her shoulders, and descended into the tiring-rooms. These contained three enormous closets. In the first, resembling a magnificent sacristy, were hung in order the four-and-eighty dresses she had managed to make during her three years of married life. Some literally stood out, in consequence of their plenitude of gold and precious stones, which gave them such solidity that they could remain upright on the floor, without support; others were as diaphanous and light as cobwebs. In the second closet were kept equipment for falconry and horse-harness. In the third were perfumes, waters, washes, unguents, dentifrices made out of white coral and pearls; countless little jars, cucurbits, rectifiers, calabashes,—a whole laboratory of feminine alchemy. The room also held boxes of wrought iron, and splendid chests, covered with paintings. A waiting woman opened one of them, in order to take out a fresh shift,—and there was wafted forth the pleasant odour of fine cambric linen, interlaid with bunches of lavender and silken sachets of Levant irises and Damascus roses, dried in the shade.

Dressing, Beatrice conversed with a sempstress about the pattern for a new dress, just now received by runner from her sister, Marchesa of Mantua, Isabella d'Este, also a great lady of fashion; the sisters were rivals in attire. Beatrice envied the taste of Isabella and imitated her,—one of the ambassadors of the Duchess of Milan informed her secretly of all the novelties of the Mantuan wardrobe.

Beatrice donned a dress with a design especially beloved by her because it disguised her small stature,—the weave consisting of longitudinal alternating stripes of green velvet and cloth of gold. The sleeves, tied with ribbands of grey silk, were tight, with modish French slits —*finestrelli*, or "windows"—through which could be glimpsed the snowy white linen of the shift, all in small, showy pleats. The hair, done in a braid, was ornamented with a large-meshed net of gold, as light as smoke; the head was encircled with the thin thread of a *ferroniera* with a little ruby scorpion fastened thereto.

II

SHE was accustomed to spending so much time at her toilette, that to use an expression of the Duke's, one could in the same time outfit an entire merchant vessel for India. But, hearing in the distance the sound of horns and the baying of greyhounds, she recalled that she had ordered a hunt, and began to hurry. Still, when she was all ready, on her way out she stepped into the chambers of her dwarfs, jocosely styled "The Dwelling of the Giants," and constructed in imitation of just such toy chambers in the castle of Isabella d'Este.

The chairs, beds, utensils; the stairs with broad, low steps; even the chapel with a doll's altar, behind which the learned dwarf Ianachi said mass, in an archbishop's chasuble and mitre, especially tailored for him,—everything was done with an eye to the stature of the pigmies. In "The Dwelling of the Giants" there was always hubbub, laughter, weeping, a babel of varied,—at times of frightful,—voices, as in a menagerie or a madhouse, for here swarmed, from the day of their birth to the day of their death, in stuffy, slovenly crowding, marmosets, hunchbacks, parrots, female blackamoors, female zanies, female jesters, hares, dwarfs, and other amusing creatures, in whose midst the young Duchess not infrequently passed whole days, having as much fun as a little girl.

This time, hurrying to the hunt, she dropped in for just one tiny minute, to find out about the health of the little blackamoor Nannino, recently sent from Venice. The skin of Nannino was of such a blackness that, to use an expression of his former owner's, "it were impossible to wish for anything better." The Duchess played with him as with a living doll. The little blackamoor had fallen ill. And the vaunted blackness proved to be not entirely natural, for the paint, a sort of lacquer, which gave to his body a glistening black sheen, began little by little to come off, much to the grief of Beatrice. Last night he had grown worse; there was fear of his dying. On learning this, the Duchess was quite saddened, for she loved him, for old memory's sake, even when he had grown paler. She ordered the little negro to be baptized as soon as possible, that, at the least, he might not die a pagan.

Descending, she met on the staircase her favourite little fool Morgantina, still young, a pretty little thing, and so amusing, that, to use Beatrice's words, she could have made a dead man laugh. Morgantina was fond of pilfering: she would steal something, hiding it in a corner, in a mouse hole, under a broken floor-board, and then strut about, satisfied; but when asked with kindness: "Be a good girl, tell us where thou didst hide it,"—she would take one's hand, with a sly face, leading to and showing the place. Or else, if someone called out, "Come, now,—ford the river!"—Morgantina, unashamed, would lift her dress up as high as she could.

At times a crazy fit would come upon her; then, for whole days on end, she mourned for a non-existent little baby,—she had never had any children,—and would become such a nuisance to everybody that she would be locked up in a cubby-hole. And now, she was sitting in a corner of the staircase, embracing her knees with her arms and rocking to and fro, bathed in bitter tears. Beatrice walked up to her and patted her head.

"Do stop,—like a clever little girl!"

The little fool, raising her childish blue eyes up to her, began to howl still more piteously.

"Oh, oh, oh! They have taken him away,—my own little one! And wherefore, Lord? He never did anyone any harm. I had my joyance of him in peace. . . ."

The Duchess descended into the court, where the huntsmen were awaiting her.

III

Surrounded by outriders, falconers, whippers-in, equerries, pages, and ladies, the Duchess held herself erect and boldly on a wiry, dark bay Barbary stallion, from the Gonzaga stud,—not like a woman, but like an expert equestrian. "A veritable queen of the Amazons!" proudly reflected Duke Moro, who had stepped out on the covered entrance of the castle, in order to admire the departure of his spouse.

On the back of the Duchess's saddle sat a hunting leopard in trappings broidered with knightly coats of arms in gold. On her left hand a Cyprian falcon, white as snow,—the gift of the Sultan,—sparkled with its little hood of gold, scattered over with emeralds. Little bells, giving forth different sounds in little trilling peals, jingled on its talons,—if lost in a fog, or in swamp grass, the sounds would assist in recovering the bird.

The Duchess was in a merry mood, and felt mischievous; she wanted to laugh, to gallop off at a breakneck pace. Looking back with a smile at her husband, who had only time to call out: "Be careful,—the horse is spirited!" she made a sign to her female companions, and rushed off in a race with them, at first over the road, then into a field,—over ditches, ruts, ravines, and wicker-fences.

Her followers fell behind. Ahead of them all rode Beatrice with her enormous wolf-hound, and, by her side, on a black Spanish mare, the merriest and most fearless of her maids-of-honour, Madonna Lucrezia Crivelli. The Duke was, secretly, not indifferent to Lucrezia. Now, admiring both her and Beatrice, he could not decide which one of them pleased him more. But any alarm he experienced was for his wife. When the horses jumped over pits, he puckered his eyes not to see,—nor could he catch his breath. He scolded the Duchess for these pranks, but could not be really angry; suspecting in himself a deficiency of physical courage, of daring, he was secretly proud of his wife's bravery.

The hunters disappeared in a thicket and the dense growths of reeds on the low shore of the Ticino, where geese and cranes abounded.

The Duke returned to his small workroom,—the *studiolo*. Here his chief secretary, Messer Bartolomeo Calco, a dignitary who took charge of foreign affairs, was awaiting him to continue the interrupted work.

IV

Sitting in a high-backed armchair, Moro was gently stroking his smoothly shaven cheeks and rounded chin, with a white, well-cared-for hand. His benign visage bore that imprint of open-hearted frankness, which only the faces of politicians perfect in duplicity acquire. His large, aquiline nose with a hump, as though it were sharpened, his prominent, subtly sinuous lips, that seemed like razor-edges, recalled his father, the great *condottiere*, Francesco Sforza. But if Francesco, to quote the poets, had been at one and the same time both a lion and a fox, the son had inherited from his father and had augmented only the vulpine cunning without the leonine courage.

Moro wore a simple, elegant garment of pale-blue silk with floral designs; his hair was combed in the current style,—smoothly, hair to hair, covering the ears and forehead almost to the eyebrows, in the semblance of a wig. A flat chain of gold dangled on his breast. His demeanour, in its refined urbanity, was alike to all.

"Have you any exact data, Messer Bartolomeo, about the setting out of the French troops from Lyons?"

"None, Your Excellency. Every evening they say 'To-morrow'; every morning they put it off. 'Tis not with military pastimes that the King is infatuated."

"What is the name of his premier mistress?"

"Her name is legion. The tastes of His Majesty are capricious and inconstant."

"Write Count Belgioiso," commanded the Duke, "that I am sending thirty. . . . nay, 'tis too little,—forty. . . . fifty thousand ducats for new presents. Let him not be niggardly. We shall drag the King out of Lyons with chains of gold! And, dost know, Bartolomeo,—of course, this is just between the two of us,—'twould not be amiss to send His Majesty portraits of certain local beauties.—By the way, is the letter ready?"

"'Tis ready, Signor."

"Let me see it."

Moro rubbed his soft, white hands in pleasure. Every time he surveyed the enormous spider's-web of his politics, he experienced a familiar delicious swooning of his heart, as before a complicated and dangerous game. He did not deem himself culpable before his conscience for summoning foreigners, northern barbarians, against Italy, for he was being impelled to this extremity by his enemies, among whom the most malevolent was Isabella of Aragon, the spouse of Gian Galeazzo, who accused Ludovico before all nations of usurping his nephew's throne. But it was not until Alfonso, King of Naples, and father of Isabella, had taken to threatening Moro with war and dethronement, to avenge the wrong done his daughter and son-in-law, that Ludovico, abandoned of all, had turned for help to Charles VIII, King of France.

"Inscrutable are Thy ways, O Lord!" mused the Duke, as the secretary was getting the rough draft of the letter out of a pile of papers. "The salvation of my empire, of Italy,—perhaps of all Europe,—is in the hands of this pitiful marasmus, this lewd and weak-witted infant,—this Most Christian King of France, before whom we, heirs of the great

Sforzas, must squirm, snakelike; crawling cringingly and well-nigh playing the pimp! But such be politics,—when one hunts with the wolf-pack, one must howl like a wolf."

He read the letter over; it seemed eloquent to him,—especially if one were to take into reckoning the fifty thousand ducats, despatched to Count Belgioiso for the bribing of those near to His Majesty, and the accompanying seductive portraits of Italian beauties.

"May the Lord bless thy crusading host, Most Christian One," said this missive, among many other things; "the gates of Ausonia stand open before thee. Delay not, then; enter them, a Triumphator, O thou new Hannibal! The peoples of Italy thirst to accept thy most sweet yoke, thou anointed of God, awaiting thee, as of yore, at the resurrection of the Lord, the patriarchs did await His descent into Hell. With the help of God and of thy renowned artillery, thou shalt conquer not only Naples and Sicily, but the lands of the Grand Turk as well; thou shalt turn the infidels to Christianity; penetrate into the depths of the Holy Land; liberate Jerusalem and the Lord's Sepulchre from the unclean Hagarenes and fill the universe with the glory of thy name."

A bald, hunchbacked little ancient with a long red nose, peeped through the door of the *studiolo*. The Duke smiled amiably at him, ordering him with a sign to wait. The door shut discreetly, and the head vanished. The secretary commenced speaking of another government matter, but Moro listened with his mind elsewhere, glancing at the door from time to time. Messer Bartolomeo finally surmised that the Duke was occupied with extraneous thoughts; he concluded his report and went away. Cautiously looking about him, the Duke approached the door on tiptoe.

"Bernardo, oh, Bernardo?"

"'Tis I, Your Excellency!"

And the court bard, Bernardo Bellincioni, with a mysterious and fawning air, jumped up and was about to fall down on his knees, in order to kiss the hand of his ruler, but was restrained by the latter.

"Well, how do matters stand?"

"All is well."

"Has she given birth?"

"They were pleased to be confined this very night."

"Doth she well? Mayhap a leech should be sent?"

"She doth exceeding well."

"Glory be to God!" The Duke crossed himself. "Didst see the child?"

"Of course! A most beautiful little one."

"Boy or girl?"

"A boy. A very brawler,—and what lusty lungs! His darling hair is light, just like his mother's, while his little eyes simply burn, and always on the go,—black, clever, altogether like those of Your Grace. One can see the kingly blood at a glance! Young Hercules in his cradle, truly! Madonna Cecilia can not have her fill of joy of him. She bade me ask what name would be pleasing to you."

"I have already given it thought," said the Duke. "I say, Bernardo,—let us call him Cæsar. How likest thou the name?"

"Cæsar? Truly, 'tis a splendid name,—sonorous and ancient! Ay, ay,—Cæsar Sforza,—a name worthy a hero!"

"And, by the bye,—what of the husband?"

"The most illustrious Count Bergamini is as kind and amiable as ever."

"An excellent man!" remarked the Duke with conviction.

"Most excellent!" chimed in Bellincioni. "A man of rare virtues, if I may take the liberty of saying so,—such men are hard to find! If his gout permit, the Count desires to come to the supper, to testify his respect for Your Excellency."

The Countess Cecilia Bergamini, the subject of their conversation, had long been a mistress of Moro's. Beatrice, finding out about this *liaison* of the Duke's very shortly after her marriage, waxed jealous, threatening to return to the house of her father, Ercole d'Este, the Duke of Ferrara, and Moro was compelled to give a solemn oath, in the presence of envoys, not to violate his marital fidelity, in confirmation of which he bestowed Cecilia in marriage on the old, bankrupted Count Bergamini, a man amenable to reason and ready for all sorts of services.

Bellincioni, taking a bit of paper out of his pouch, handed it to the Duke,—a *sonetto* in honour of the newly-born; a little dialogue, wherein the poet questioned the sun why it covered itself with clouds; the sun replied, with a courtier's amiability, that it hid itself from chagrin and envy, because of the new sun,—the son of Moro and Cecilia.

The Duke benevolently accepted the sonnet, took a gold piece out of his purse, and handed it to the rhyme-maker.

"By the way, Bernardo, thou hast not forgot that Saturday is the birthday of the Duchess?"

Bellincioni hastily rummaged within a gap of his suit, half-courtly, half-beggarly—a gap which served him for a pouch,—drawing therefrom a whole sheaf of soiled little bits of paper; and, amid such high-soaring odes as those on the death of the hunting falcon of Madonna Angelica, and on the sickness of Signor Pallavicini's dappled grey Hungarian mare, he managed to find the required verses.

"No less than three, for Your Excellency's choosing. I swear by Pegasus, you will rest content!"

The sovereigns of those times used their poets laureate as musical instruments, to sing serenades not only to their inamorati, but their wives as well; worldly fashion demanded in such verses the premise of the same unearthly love of husband and wife as that of Laura and Petrarca.

Moro glanced through the verses with interest,—he deemed himself an exquisite connoisseur of poesy,—a poet in spirit, even though he had not the knack of rhyming. In the first sonnet three lines struck his fancy,—the husband addresses his spouse:

Wherever on earth thou mayest spit
Flowers are sudden born on it,—
As violets bloom in early spring.

In the second the poet, comparing Madonna Beatrice with the Goddess Diana, affirmed that the boars and stags experience bliss in dying by the hand of so beautiful a huntress.

But most of all was His Highness pleased by the third sonnet, wherein Dante addressed a request to God to grant him leave to revisit earth, to which Beatrice, it seemed, had returned in the image of the Duchess of Milan. "O, Jupiter!" exclaimed Alighieri. "Since thou hast again bestowed her to the universe, grant me to be with her as well, that I may behold him upon whom Beatrice bestows bliss,"—to wit, the Duke Ludovico.

Moro graciously patted the poet's shoulder, and promised him cloth for a great-coat,—at which Bernardo contrived to beg some fox-fur for a collar as well, asserting with plaintive and merry-andrew whimsies that his old great-coat had become as draughty and transparent as "vermicelli drying in the sun."

"Last winter," he continued to importune, "for lack of fire-wood, I was ready to burn not only my staircase, but the wooden shoes of St. Francis himself!"

The Duke burst into laughter and promised him fire-wood. Whereupon, in an outburst of gratitude, the poet instantly composed and declaimed a laudatory quatrain:

> When thou dost promise bread unto thy slaves,
> Like God bestowest thou heavenly manna;
> Wherefore the muse Divine, and Phœbus, in sweet staves,
> Oh, noble Moor, do sing to thee Hosanna!

"Meseems thou art in an inspired mood, Bernardo? Hearken, now, I have need of one more poem."

"A love poem?"

"Ay. And a passionate one."

"To the Duchess?"

"Nay. But, look thou to it, and mark me,—blab not of it!"

"O, Signor, you hurt me! For have I ever—"

"Well, well, now,—see thou to it."

"I am mute,—as mute as any fish!"

Bernardo mysteriously and respectfully began to blink his eyes.

"Passionate? 'Tis well,—but the manner of it? In supplication or in gratitude?"

"In supplication."

The poet contracted his eyebrows in deep thought:

"Is she married?"

"She is a maid."

"So. I ought to have her name."

"There, now! Wherefore her name?"

"If it be in supplication, 'twould not do without her name."

"Madonna Lucrezia. But hast thou naught on hand?"

"I have; but 'tis best to have something of the freshest. Allow me to withdraw into the next chamber for but a moment. For I can already feel that 'twill not be at all bad,—the rhymes are simply crowding into my head!"

A page entered and announced:

"Messer Leonardo da Vinci."

Taking quill and paper along, Bellincioni darted out of one door as Leonardo entered through another.

V

After the first greetings, the Duke began discussing with the artist the enormous new canal, Naviglio Sforzesca, which was to join the Sesia with the Ticino, and, branching out into a network of smaller canals, was to irrigate the meadows, fields, and pasture-lands of Lomellina. Leonardo directed the work of construction of the Naviglio, although he did not have the title of the Ducal Architect,—nor even that of Court Painter; retaining, for old times' sake (on account of a certain musical instrument he had invented long ago), the title of Court Musician, which rank was but little higher than the calling of such Court Poets as Bellincioni.

Having explained the plans and estimates in full detail, the artist asked to have an order issued for an appropriation of money for further work.

"How much?" asked the Duke.

"Five hundred and sixty-six ducats for each mile,—fifteen thousand, one hundred and eighty-seven ducats in all," answered Leonardo.

Ludovico made a wry face, recalling the fifty thousand just set aside for bribing and corrupting the French nobles.

"'Tis dear, Messer Leonardo! Really, now, thou art ruining me,—always wanting the impossible. Here is Bramante, now,—also a builder of note, yet he never demands any such moneys."

Leonardo shrugged his shoulders.

"As you please, Signor,—entrust the work to Bramante."

"Well, well, now, be not angry. Thou knowest I'll let none do thee harm!"

They fell to higgling.

"'Tis well,—we shall have time for the business on the morrow," concluded the Duke, trying, as was his wont, to procrastinate the decision in the matter, and began turning the pages of Leonardo's notebooks, filled with unfinished sketches, and architectural plans and projects.

One drawing depicted a titanic mausoleum,—an entire artificial mountain, crowned by a many-columned temple with a round aperture in its cupola, as in the Roman Pantheon, for the lighting of the inner chambers of the tomb, surpassing in splendour the Egyptian pyramids. Alongside were exact figures and a detailed plan of the disposition of the staircases, passages, and halls, calculated for five hundred urns.

"Whatever is this?" asked the Duke. "When, and for whom hast thou conceived this?"

"Just so,—for no one in particular. These be but fancies."

Moro looked at him in wonder and shook his head.

"Strange fancies! A mausoleum for Olympians or for Titans,—just as in a dream or a fairy-tale. . . . And yet thou art a mathematician!"

He glimpsed another drawing: the plan of a city with two-tiered streets,—the upper for the masters, the lower for slaves, draught-animals, and refuse, cleansed with water from a multitude of pipes and canals,—a city built in accordance with an exact knowledge of the laws of nature, but for beings whose conscience would not be perturbed by inequality, by the division into the chosen and the rejected.

"Why, this is not at all bad!" exclaimed the Duke. "And dost thou suppose its erection feasible?"

"Oh, yes!" answered Leonardo, and his face became animated. "I have long dreamed of Your Excellency's being pleased to make an experiment, even if only with one of the suburbs of Milan. Five thousand houses,—for thirty thousand inmates; and the great numbers who now are huddling one atop another, in filthy and miasmic squalor, spreading the seeds of infection and death, would be dispersed. If you were to carry out my plan, Signor, this would be the finest city in the world! . . ."

The artist stopped, noting that the Duke was laughing.

"What a queer fellow thou art, and a droll one, Messer Leonardo! Meseems, give thee but a free hand, and thou wouldst turn everything topsy-turvy; what mischief wouldst thou not wreak in the kingdom! Dost thou not really perceive that the most submissive of slaves would mutiny against thy two-tiered streets; would spit on thy vaunted cleanliness, on the water-spouts and canals of the finest city in the world,—they would fly to the old cities: 'Let us be in filth, now, in squalor,—anything save humiliation'?

"Well, and what have we here?" he asked, indicating another plan. Leonardo was forced to explain this drawing as well; it proved to be a plan for a house of ill fame. Separate rooms, doors and passages were so disposed that visitors could rely on secrecy, without any fear of meeting one another.

"Now there thou hast something real!" the Duke became enraptured. "Really, thou wouldst not believe how bored I have become with complaints about robberies and murders in these dens. But with such an arrangement of rooms there would be order and safety. I shall most certainly build such a house in accordance with your plan!

"I must say," added he, with a sly smile, "I have in thee a master of all trades; thou despisest naught; we have a mausoleum fit for the gods side by side with a house of ill fame!

"Incidentally," he continued, "I have read once in a book by some ancient historian about the so-called Ear of Dionysius the Tyrant, a sound pipe, hid in the thickness of the walls and constructed so that the sovereign might hear in one chamber what is being said in another. What thinkest thou,—could the Ear of Dionysius be built in my palace?"

The Duke was at first a trifle uneasy in conscience; but he immediately regained his ease, sensing that there was no need of being ashamed before the artist. Without confusion, without even considering whether the Ear of Dionysius were good or evil, Leonardo conversed about it as though it were a new scientific appliance, glad of the pretext to investigate, during the construction of these pipes, the laws of the motion of sound waves.

Bellincioni, with his sonnet finished, peeped in at the door. As Leonardo said good-bye, Moro invited him to supper. When the artist had taken his departure, the Duke bade the poet approach and read his verses.

"The Salamander," ran the sonnet, "dwells in fire; yet is it not a greater wonder that within my flaming heart,

Dwells a madonna who is cold as ice
Nor all love-fires to melt this virgin ice suffice?"

Especially tender did the last four lines seem to the Duke:

A swan, I sing; I sing and die;
Love I implore: Have pity, in flames I!
But the Love God doth fan my soul's flame,
And, laughing, saith: With tears put out the same!

VI

Before supper, while waiting for his spouse, who was expected to return soon from the chase, the Duke went walking over his estate.

He looked into the stable, which resembled a Grecian temple with its colonnades and porticoes; into the new magnificent dairy, where he sampled some *giuncata*,—a fresh cream cheese. Past endless hay-lofts and cellars he made his way to the farmstead and cattle yard. Here every detail made the heart of the husbandman rejoice: the sound of the stream of milk squirting from the udder of his favourite, a tawny pied Languedoc cow, and the maternal grunting of an enormous sow, just littered and resembling a mountain of fat, and the yellow foam of cream in the pails of the ash-wood butter-churns, and the overflowing granaries, redolent of honey.

A smile of quiet happiness appeared on the face of Moro,—verily was his house a cup overflowing! He returned to the palace and sat down to rest in a gallery. Evening was coming on, but it was still a long time to sunset. A spicy freshness was wafted up from the inundated meadows of the Ticino. The Duke cast an eye over his possessions: pasturages, fallow-lands, fields, irrigated by a network of canals and trenches, with regularly planted rows of apple-, pear-, and mulberry-trees, joined by hanging garlands of vines. From Mortara to Abbiategrasso, and farther, to the very edge of the sky, where in the distance the snows of Monte Rosa glimmered whitely, the great champaign of Lombardy was a-bloom, like God's Paradise.

"Lord!" he sighed with emotion, raising his eyes to heaven, "I thank Thee for all! What else have I need of? At one time this was a desert; Leonardo and I have laid these canals, have watered the ground, and now every ear of grain, every blade of grass, renders thanks unto me, even as I do unto Thee, O Lord!"

The baying of the greyhounds was heard, and the shouts of the hunters; and, over the bushes of the vineyard, flashed a red hawk's lure, —a stuffed bird with the wings of a partridge for decoying the hawks back. The host with his chief majordomo made the round of the set board, to oversee if all were in order. The Duchess and the guests bidden to the supper entered the hall; among them Leonardo, who would stay the night in the villa.

Grace was said and all sat down at table.

Fresh artichokes, sent in wattling baskets by special post direct from Genoa, were served; as well as fat morays and a carp from the Mantuan fish-ponds,—a present from Isabella d'Este,—and a jelly of capon breasts. Three fingers and a knife were used in eating, but no forks, which were considered an impermissible luxury,—of gold, with handles made of rock crystal, they were served only to ladies for berries and jams.

The heartily hospitable host regaled them assiduously. Everyone ate and drank heavily, almost to the point of incapacitation. The most exquisite of maids and ladies were not ashamed of hunger.

Beatrice sat alongside of Lucrezia. The Duke was again lost in admiration of both,—he felt pleasure in their being together, and in his wife's attentiveness to his inamorata, as she put tid-bits on the latter's plate, whispering something in her ear, and squeezing her hand with an outburst of that sudden tenderness, resembling infatuation, which at times takes possession of young women. The conversation dealt with the chase. Beatrice narrated how a deer had well-nigh knocked her out of her saddle, leaping out of the forest and striking her horse with its horns.

They laughed at the little fool Dioda, a braggart and a bully, who, taking it for a boar, had just stuck a domesticated pig, purposely taken by the hunters into the forest and let out under the feet of the buffoon. Dioda told of his feat and was as proud of it as if he had killed the Erymanthian wild boar. They teased him, and, in order to expose his boasting, brought in the carcass of the stuck pig. He pretended to be infuriated. In reality this was a most cunning knave, who played the profitable rôle of a fool; with his lynx eyes he could have distinguished not merely a domesticated pig from a wild one, but also a stupid jest from a clever one.

The laughter was becoming noisier and noisier, and the faces animated and flushed from copious imbibitions. After the fourth course the younger women stealthily loosened, under cover of the table, their tightly drawn stay-laces. The cup-bearers carried about light white wine; and red wine of Cyprus, thick, warmed, mulled with pistachios, cinnamon and cloves. Whenever His Highness called for wine, the stewards solemnly called to one another, as though officiating at a mass; the goblet was taken off the sideboard, and the chief seneschal would dip thrice into the cup a talisman of unicorn horn on a golden chain: were the wine envenomed the horn would undergo denigration and become bedewed with blood. Similar preventive talismans,—of toad-stone and snake's tongue,—were set in the salt-cellar.

Count Bergamini, the husband of Cecilia, seated by the host in a place of honour, and especially gay on this evening, seemingly even frolicsome, despite his age and gout,—uttered, indicating the unicorn:

"Methinks, Your Excellency, that the King of France himself hath not such a horn. 'Tis of an amazing size!"

"*Ke-he-ke! Ke-he-ka!*" burst out the hunchback Ianachi, the favourite jester of the Duke, thundering with his rattle,—a pig's bladder, filled with pease,—and jangling the little bells of his motley cap with its asses' ears. "Nuncle,—eh, nuncle!" he turned to Moro, pointing to Count Bergamini, "do thou believe him: he knoweth a thing or two about all sorts of horns,—not only those of beasts, but even human ones! . . . *Ke-he-ke, ke-he-ka!* He that hath a she-goat, hath horns also!"

The Duke threatened the jester with his finger.

Silver horns blared forth from the galleries, greeting the roast course, —an enormous boar's head, stuffed with chestnuts; a peacock with an especial little mechanical contrivance inside, making it spread its tail on the salver and beat its wings; and, finally, a majestic tort, in the shape of a fortress, from which at first issued the sounds of a war-trumpet,—and when the well-browned crust was cut there jumped out a dwarf in the feathers of a parrot, who began running over the table; he was caught, and put into a golden cage, where, imitating the celebrated parrot of Cardinal Ascanio Sforza, he began yelling the Paternoster with excruciating drollness.

"Messer," the Duchess addressed her spouse, "to what joyous occasion do we owe so unexpected and magnificent a feast?"

Moro made no reply, merely exchanging pleasant glances by stealth with Count Bergamini,—the happy husband of Cecilia comprehended that the feast was arranged in honour of the newly-born Cæsar. They sat for a trifle less than an hour over the boar's head, nor begrudged time for eating, bearing in mind the proverb: One doth not grow old at table.

Toward the end of the supper a stout friar, by the name of Talpone,— The Rat,—aroused universal merriment. Not without cunning subterfuges and deceptions had the Duke of Milan contrived to entice out of Urbino this famous glutton, over whom sovereigns disputed, and who, so the story ran, had once in Rome, to the no small pleasure of His Holiness, devoured a whole third of a camelot episcopal under-cassock, cut up into pieces and saturated with sauce. At a sign from the Duke there was set before Fra Talpone an enormous bowl of *bu-*

secchio,—gut stuffed with apples of the quince. Making the sign of the cross and rolling up his sleeves, the friar began putting away the greasy fare with a rapidity and a greed unbelievable.

"If a goodly fellow like that had been present at the feeding of the multitude with five loaves of bread and two fishes, the leavings would not have sufficed for even two hounds!" exclaimed Bellincioni.

The guests went off into laughter. All these people were loaded with laughter, which from every jest, as from a spark, was ready to go off in a deafening explosion. Only the face of the lonely and taciturn Leonardo preserved an expression of resigned ennui,—he had, however, long since grown accustomed to the amusements of his patrons.

When gilded oranges, saturated with fragrant Malvasia, had been served on silver saucers, the court poet, Antonio Camelli da Pistoia, a rival of Bellincioni, declaimed an ode, wherein the Arts and Sciences addressed the Duke: "We were slaves; thou didst come and liberate us,—long live Moro!" The four Elements,—Earth, Water, Fire, and Air,—sang forth: "Long live he who, first after God, steers the rudder of the Universe, the wheel of Fortune!" There were also celebrated the domestic love and amity between Moro the uncle and Gian Galeazzo the nephew, the poet taking the occasion to compare the magnanimous guardian with the pelican, which nourisheth its offspring with its own flesh and blood.

VII

After supper the hosts and the guests adjourned to the garden called the Paradise,—Paradiso; formal, laid out in a geometrical design, with alleys of clipped box, laurel, and myrtle; with covered ways, labyrinths, loggias, and arbours of ivy. Upon the green lawn, over which the freshness of the fountain was wafted, rugs and silken pillows were thrown; the ladies and cavaliers disposed themselves in careless ease before a little private theatre. One act of the *Miles Gloriosus* of Plautus was acted. The Latin verses induced boredom, although the auditors, from a superstitious respect for antiquity, dissembled attentiveness. When the performance was ended, the younger people set off for a larger lawn to play ball, primitive tennis, and hoodman-blind,—running and catching one another, laughing like children, amid the bushes of blooming roses and the orange-trees. Their elders played dice, trictrac and chess. The damozels, ladies, and signori who took no part in the games, having gathered in a close circle on the marble steps of the fountain, narrated *novelle* by turns, as did the damozels and signori in the *Decameron* of Boccaccio.

On a small adjacent lawn a dancing ring was formed, to a song of which Lorenzo de Medici,[10] who had died while still young, had been very fond:

Quant'è bella giovenezza.
Ma si fugge tuttavia;
Chi voul esser lieto, sio:
Di doman non c'è certezza.

Youth is wondrous but how fleeting!
Sing, and laugh, and banish sorrow;
Give to happiness good greeting,—
Place thy hopes not on the morrow. . . .

After the dance Donzella Diana, pale and gentle of face, began, to the soft strains of a viol, a despondent plaint, wherein it was proclaimed what great sorrow it was to love without being loved in requital. The games and the laughter ceased. All listened in deep pensiveness. And, when she had ended, for a long space none would break the quiet; naught was heard save the murmur of the fountain. The last rays of the sun poured a rosy light upon the black flat summits of the pines and the high flung spray of the fountain. But shortly talk, and laughter, began anew, and till late in the evening, until the *lucciole*—fire-flies—began to glow in the dark laurels, and the thin sickle of the moon followed their suit in the dark sky, the strains of the song they had danced to would not die away over the happy Paradiso, in the breathless gloaming permeated with the fragrance of orange blossoms:

Give to happiness good greeting,—
Place thy hopes not on the morrow.

VIII

On one of the four towers of the palace, Moro saw a small light: Messer Ambrogio da Rosate, the chief court astrologer of the Duke of Milan, as well as a Senator and a member of the Privy Council, had lit his lonely little lamp over his astronomical instruments, watching the forthcoming conjunction of Mars, Jupiter, and Saturn under the sign of Aquarius, which conjunction was fraught with great significance for the House of Sforza.

The Duke, recalling something, bade farewell to Madonna Lucrezia, with whom he had been holding tender discourse in a snug arbour; he returned to the palace; looking at his watch, he waited for the minute and the seconds designated by the astrologue for taking the pills of rhapontic; and, having swallowed the medicine, glanced at his pocket calendar, in which he read the following notation:

"5th of August, at 8 minutes after 10,—pray most earnestly, on bended knees, with hands folded and eyes raised to heaven."

The Duke hurried to the chapel, in order not to let slip the instant, since otherwise the astrological prayer would lose its efficacy.

In the half-dark chapel a little lamp burned before an image; the Duke loved this icon, painted by Leonardo da Vinci, which represented Cecilia Bergamini under the guise of the Madonna, blessing a centifolious rose.

Moro counted off eight minutes by the small sand clock, sank to his knees, folded his hands, and told the Confiteor. Long was his prayer, and delectable.

"O Mother of God," he whispered, lifting up his enraptured gaze; "protect, save, and have mercy upon me, my son Maximilian, and the newly-born babe Cæsar; my spouse Beatrice and Madonna Cecilia, as well as my nephew, Messer Gian Galeazzo, for,—as thou seest my heart, O Most Pure Virgin,—I wish no hurt to my nephew; I pray for him, albeit his death would rid not only my domain, but all Italy as well, from fearful and irreparable misfortunes."

At this point he called to mind the proof of his title to the throne of Milan, invented by the juris-consults: it would seem his elder brother, the father of Gian Galeazzo, was the son not of the *Duke*, but of the *Commandant*, Francesco Sforza, inasmuch as he had been born before Francesco had mounted the throne; whereas he, Ludovico, had been born subsequent to the accession, and consequently was sole heir, with full rights. But now, before the countenance of the Madonna, this proof appeared to him dubious, and he concluded his prayer thus:

"But if I have sinned in some fashion, or if I should sin before thee, thou knowest, Queen of Heaven, that I do not so for myself, but for the good of my domain, for the good of all Italy. Be thou therefore my intercessor before God,—and I shall glorify thy name by building magnificently the Cathedral of Milan, and the Certosa at Pavia, and by many other good works!"

Having concluded his prayer, he took up a candle and went off in the direction of his chamber through the dark apartments of the slumbering palace. In one of them he came upon Lucrezia.

"The God of love himself doth favour me," reflected the Duke.

"Sire! . . ." exclaimed the girl, approaching him. But her voice broke. She was about to fall down on her knees before him; he barely managed to restrain her.

"Have mercy, Sire!"

She confided to him how her brother, Matteo Crivelli, the Chief Financial Secretary of the Mint, a dissolute man but one she loved tenderly, had gambled away at cards large sums of official moneys.

"Be calm, madonna! I shall get your brother out of his scrape. . . ."

After a short silence he added with a heavy sigh:

"But will you also agree not to be cruel? . . ."

She looked at him with her timid eyes, as limpid and innocent as a child's.

"I understand not, Signor. . . ." Her chaste wonder made her still more beautiful.

"This means, my dearling," he babbled passionately, suddenly embracing her waist with a powerful, almost brutal gesture,—"it means . . . But, seest thou not, Lucrezia, that I love thee? . . ."

"Let me go, let me go! O Signor,—whatever are you doing! Madonna Beatrice. . . ."

"Fear not, she will never find out,—I can guard a secret. . . ."

"Nay, nay, Sire,—she is so magnanimous, so kind to me. . . . For God's sake, leave me! . . ."

"I shall save thy brother,—I shall do all thou mayest desire,—I shall be thy slave,—do thou but have pity on me! . . ."

And half-sincere tears began to quaver in his voice as he fell to whispering the verses of Bellincioni:

"A swan, I sing; I sing and die;
Love I implore: Have pity, in flames I!
But the Love God doth fan my soul's flame,
And, laughing, saith: With tears put out the same!"

"Let me go, let me go!" the girl kept on repeating in despair.

He bent toward her, feeling the freshness of her breath, the odour of her perfume,—violets mixed with musk,—and avidly kissed her lips.

For one instant Lucrezia swooned in his embraces. Then she cried out, tore herself away, and ran off.

IX

ENTERING the dortoir, he saw that Beatrice had already put out the light and lain down in bed,—an enormous couch, resembling a mausoleum standing upon a dais in the middle of the room, under a canopy of azure silk and with hangings of silver.

He disrobed, lifted up the edge of the resplendent coverlet—like a sacerdotal chasuble, woven with gold and pearls, the wedding gift of the Duke of Ferrara,—and laid down in his place, beside his wife.

"Bice," he uttered in a caressing whisper, "Bice, art thou asleep?"

He wanted to embrace her, but she repulsed him.

"What is that for?"

"Do leave me alone! I fain would sleep. . . ."

"But why,—do but tell me why? Bice, my dear one! If thou didst but know how I love thee. . . ."

"Ay, ay,—I know you love all of us,—not only me, but Cecilia as well, and even,—not that it would surprise me,—this slave from Muscovy, this red-haired fool, whom you were embracing but the other day in a corner of my wardrobe. . . ."

"I did it but for a jest. . . ."

"Thank you for such jests!"

"Really, now, Bice, for the last few days thou art so cold to me, so severe! Of course I am at fault, I confess,—'twas an unworthy whim. . ."

"Of whims you have plenty, Signor!"

She turned toward him in wrath:

"How is it thou art not ashamed? Well, now, why, why dost thou lie? For do I not know thee, do I not see thee through and through? Please, deem me not jealous. But I do not want to,—dost hear?—I do not want to be merely one of thy mistresses! . . ."

"'Tis not true, Bice,—I swear to thee by the salvation of my soul—never have I loved anybody in this world as I love thee!"

She became silent, listening in wonder not to his words, but to the sound of his voice. And, truly, he was not lying; or, at the least, not altogether lying: the more he deceived her, the more he loved her;

his tenderness seemed to be fanned by shame, by fear, by the gnawings of his conscience, by pity and by repentance.

"Forgive me, Bice, forgive me all, for that I love thee so! . . ."

And they made their peace.

Embracing, yet not seeing her in the dark, his mind called forth timid, innocent eyes, and the odour of violets mixed with musk; called forth another, whom he embraced; he made love to both of them together,—this was criminal and intoxicating.

"Really, to-day thou art truly like one enamoured," said she in a whisper,—this time with a secret pride.

"Ay, ay, my dear one; believe me, I am still as enamoured of thee as in the first days! . . ."

"What nonsense!" she mocked. "Doth not thy conscience bother thee? 'T would be better to think of business; for *he* is getting well. . . ."

"Luigi Marliani was telling me but the other day, that he would die," said the Duke. "He is better now, but 'twill not be for long; certes,—he will die."

"Who knows?" retorted Beatrice. "They look after him so. . . . Mark thou, Moro; I am amazed at thy freedom from care; thou bearest insults like a sheep; thou sayest: 'Power is in our hands.' But is it not better to renounce power entirely, than tremble for it night and day, like thieves; to crawl cringingly before this mongrel, the King of France; to be dependent on the magnanimity of brazen Alfonso; to fawn on the evil witch of Aragon! They do say she is with child again,—a new young viper in the accursed nest! And so all life long, Moro; do but think upon it,—all life long! And of this state thou sayest: 'Power is in our hands! . . .'"

"But the leeches all agree," pronounced the Duke, "that the ailment is incurable: sooner or later. . . ."

"Ay, bide thy time: 'tis already ten years that he is a-dying!"

They became silent. Suddenly she entwined him with her arms, clinging to him with all her body, and whispered something in his ear. He started with a shiver.

"Bice! . . . May Christ and the Most Pure Mother preserve thee! Never,—dost hear?—never speak to me of this. . . ."

"If thou art afraid,—wouldst have me do it myself?"

He made no reply; but, a little later, asked:

"What art thou thinking of?"

"Of the peaches. . . ."

"Ay. I ordered the gardener to send him of the ripest for a present. . . ."

"Nay, not of those. I was thinking of the peaches of Messer Leonardo da Vinci. Or hast thou not heard?"

"What about them?"

"They are poisonous. . . ."

"Poisonous,—how?"

"Very simply. He envenomed them,—for some experiment or other. It may be witchcraft,—Monna Sidonia was telling me. Even though they be poisoned, they are of an amazing beauty. . . ."

Again they both lapsed into silence and lay thus for a long while, embracing, in the stillness, in the dark; both thinking of one and the same thing, each listening intently to the constantly accelerating heart-beats of the other.

Finally Moro with a fatherly tenderness kissed her forehead and made the sign of the cross over her:

"Sleep, my dearest one, sleep, and God be with thee!"

On that night the Duchess saw in a dream some beautiful peaches on a golden platter. She was tempted by their beauty, took one of them, and tasted of it,—it was succulent and fragrant. Suddenly someone's voice said in a whisper: "Poison, poison, poison!" She became frightened, but could no longer stop, continuing to eat the fruits, one after another, and it seemed to her that she was dying, yet that her heart grew more and more lissome and gay.

The Duke, too, dreamed a strange dream: he was, it seemed, strolling over a little green lawn near the fountain of Paradiso, and beheld in the distance three women, all dressed alike in white garments, sitting and embracing one another in sisterly fashion. On approaching he recognized in one Madonna Beatrice, in another Madonna Lucrezia, in the third Madonna Cecilia; and, with profound peace of mind, he reflected: "Well, glory be to God, they have finally made truce with one another,—which they should have done long ago!"

X

THE tower clock struck midnight; the whole place was in slumber, save that aloft, high above the roof, on the wooden scaffolding for drying the hair, the she-dwarf Morgantina, who had escaped from the cubby-hole wherein they had locked her, sat and bewailed her non-existent babe:

"They have taken my own little one, they have killed the little babe. And wherefore, wherefore, O Lord? He did ill to none, and quietly did I have my solace in him. . . ."

The night was clear; the air so transparent that one could distinguish at the rim of the heavens the icy summits of Monte Rosa, resembling eternal crystals.

And throughout the castle, sunk in slumber, long clamoured the piercing, piteous wailing of the half-witted she-dwarf, like the screaming of a bird of ill omen.

Suddenly she sighed, raised up her head, looked at the sky, and immediately grew quiet.

Silence fell.

The she-dwarf was smiling; and the blue stars glimmered above,—just as incomprehensible and innocent as her eyes.

BOOK FOUR

The Witches' Sabbath

I

AR OUT IN THE DESOLATE ENVIRONS OF MILAN, on the outskirts of the Vercellina Gates, near the dam and the river customs house of the Catarana Canal, stood a solitary, decrepit little house, with a great, sooty chimney all awry, from which the smoke belched night and day.

The little house belonged to Monna Sidonia, the midwife. The upper chambers she rented out to Messer Galeotto Sacrobosco, the alchemist; in the lower she dwelt with Cassandra, the daughter of Galeotto's brother, the merchant Luigi, a celebrated traveller, who had thoroughly covered Greece, the Islands of the Archipelago, Syria, Asia Minor, and Egypt, in an unceasing pursuit of antiquities.

He collected all that came to his hand: a beautiful statue,—and a piece of tree-amber with a fly congealed within it; a counterfeit inscription from the grave of Homer,—and an authentic tragedy of Euripides,—or else the clavicle of Demosthenes.

Some deemed him demented; others, a braggart and a cheat; a third group, a great man. His imagination was so imbued with paganism that remaining till his last days a good Christian, Luigi in all seriousness prayed to the "Most Sacred Genius Mercury," and believed Wednesday (*Mercoledì*), dedicated to the winged messenger of the Olympians, to be a day especially lucky for commercial transactions. He stopped at no deprivations or labours in his seekings: once, having boarded a ship and already gone ten miles out to sea, he found out about a curious Greek inscription he had not read over, and immediately returned to shore to transcribe it. Having lost during a shipwreck a precious collection of manuscripts, he turned grey from grief. When they questioned him why he was ruining himself, enduring all his life such great labours and dangers, his reply was always couched in the same unvarying words:

"I fain would resurrect the dead."

In Peloponnesus, near the desolate ruins of Lacedæmon, in the environs of the little city of Mistra, he encountered a girl who resembled a carving of the ancient goddess Artemis; this girl was the daughter of the deacon of a hamlet, who was poor and drank to excess; marrying her, he carried her off to Italy, together with a new transcription of the *Iliad*, the fragments of a marble Hecate, and the shards of terra-cotta amphoræ. To the daughter born to them Luigi gave the name of Cassandra, in glory of the great heroine of Æschylos, since he was at that time infatuated with the fair captive of Agamemnon.

His wife died shortly. Setting out on one of his numerous wanderings, he left his little orphan girl to the care of his old friend, a learned Greek from Constantinople, who had been invited to Milan by the Dukes of Sforza,—the philosopher Demetrios Chalcondylos.

The seventy-year-old ancient, Janus-faced, sly and secretive, while pretending to be an ardent zealot of the Christian church, was in reality, like many learned Greeks in Italy, with Cardinal Bessarion at their head, a follower of one of the last masters of ancient wisdom—the neo-Platonic Gemistos Pletho, who had died forty years ago in Peloponnesus, in that same city of Mistra of which the mother of Cassandra was a native. His pupils believed that the soul of the great Plato had, for the propagation of wisdom, come down to earth from Olympus and become incarnate in Pletho. The Christian masters affirmed that this philosopher was desirous of renewing the Antichrist heresy of Emperor Julian the Apostate,—the worship of ancient Olympian gods,—and that it was not at all the thing to resort to learned arguments and logomachies in contention, but, rather, to the Holy Inquisition and the flame of bonfires. The precise words of Pletho were adduced: three years before his death he had, it seemed, said to his disciples: "But a few years after my demise, over all the tribes and the nations of the earth there shall shine forth a single truth, and all men shall turn with a single spirit to a single faith,—*unam eandemque religionem universum orbem esse suscepturum.*" But when they questioned him: "Which faith,—Christian or Mahomedan?"—he made answer: "Neither one nor the other, but a faith indistinguishable from the ancient Pagan one,—*neutram, sed a gentilitate non differentem.*"

In the house of Demetrios Chalcondylos the little Cassandra was educated in a strict, even though a hypocritical, devoutness. But from conversations overheard the child, without understanding the philosophical refinements of the Platonic ideas, spun for herself a magic fairy-tale of how the dead gods of Olympus would come to life again.

The little girl wore on her breast her father's gift, a talisman against fever,—a seal cut with an image of the god Dionysos. At times, when left alone, she would take out by stealth the ancient gem, and look through it at the sun,—and in the dark-lilac radiance of the translucent amethyst there stood out before her, like a vision, the nude youth Bacchus, holding a thyrsus in one hand, a cluster of grapes in the other; a leaping pard strove to lick this cluster with its tongue. And the heart of the child was filled with love toward this beauteous god. . . .

Messer Luigi, having become ruined through antiquities, died in beggary, in the hut of a shepherd, from putrid fever, amid the ruins of a Phœnician temple he had just discovered. At this juncture, after many years' wanderings in pursuit of the secret of the Philosopher's Stone, the alchemist Galeotto Sacrobosco, the uncle of Cassandra, returned to Milan, and, settling down in the little house near the Vercellina Gates, took the niece to himself.

Giovanni Beltraffio remembered the conversation he had overheard between Monna Cassandra and the mechanic Zoroastro, about the poisonous tree. Later he was wont to meet her at the house of Demetrios Chalcondylos, where Merulla had gotten some transcription work for him. He heard from many people that she was a witch; but the enigmatic charm of the young girl drew him to her.

Almost every evening, having finished his work in the atelier of Leonardo, Giovanni would bend his steps in the direction of the isolated little house beyond the Vercellina Gates, to see Cassandra. They would seat themselves on the little hillock over the water of the still and dark canal, not far from the dam and near the half-ruined wall of the Convent of Santa Redegonda, and would hold long converse. A barely perceptible path, grown over with burdock, elders, and nettles, led up to the little hillock, which was but seldom visited.

II

THE evening was sultry. At times a whirlwind would arise, lift the white dust on the highway, rustle the leaves on the trees, and die away, —and it would become stiller than ever, save that one heard the muffled growling of distant thunder, seeming to come from underground. And against this threateningly exultant rumbling stood out the high-pitched sounds of a strumming lute, of the drunken songs of the customs soldiery in a neighbouring little tavern,—since it was Sunday.

At times pallid heat lightning would flare up in the sky, and then for an instant there would stand out from the darkness the decrepit little house on yonder shore, with its brick chimney, swirls of black smoke belching out of the smelting furnace of the alchemist; the lanky, spare sacristan with his fishing line on the mossy dam; the strait canal with its two rows of larches and common white willows receding into the distance; flat-bottomed barques from Lago Maggiore with blocks of white marble for the Cathedral, drawn by galled nags, and the long whip-lash, striking the water,—then again everything, like a vision, would vanish in the darkness. Only on yonder shore glimmered redly the fire of the alchemist, reflected in the dark waters of the Catarana. From the dam was wafted the odour of warm water, wilted bracken, pitch, and rotting wood.

Giovanni and Cassandra were sitting at their usual spot, above the canal.

"How dreary!" uttered the girl; she stretched herself, crackling her slender white fingers over her head. "Every day is always the same. To-day is like yesterday; to-morrow will be like to-day: the same old stupid, lanky sacristan fishing on the dam,—and never able to catch anything; the same old smoke pouring from the chimney of the laboratory, where Messer Galeotto is seeking for gold,—and never able to find anything; the same old boats drawn by galled nags; the same old lugubrious lute strummed in the same cracked way in the little tavern. If only there would be something new! If only the French would come and devastate Milan, or the sacristan would catch a fish, or my uncle find gold. . . . My God, what dreariness!"

"Ay, I know," retorted Giovanni. "At times I myself am so weary that I want to die. But Fra Benedetto has taught me an excellent prayer for the riddance of the fiend of despondence. Do you want me to tell it to you?"

The girl shook her head.

"Nay, Giovanni. At times I am even fain to, but I have long since forgot how to pray to your God."

"Our God? But is there any other God, save ours,—save the one God?"

The fleeting flame of the heat lightning illumined her face: never yet had it seemed to him so enigmatic, so despondent and beautiful. She fell silent for a space and passed her hand over her black downy hair.

"Hearken, friend. This happened a long while ago,—there, in my native land. I was a child. One day my father took me with him on a journey. We visited the ruins of an ancient temple, rearing up on a promontory, with the sea all around. The gulls moaned; the waves broke noisily against the black stones, sharp-pointed, like needles, gnawed clean by the briny spume. The foam flew upward and fell, running down the needles of the stones in a hissing stream. My father was reading a half-obliterated inscription on a fragment of marble. For a long while I sat alone on the steps before the temple, hearkening to the sea and breathing in its freshness, mingled with the bitter fragrance of wormwood. Then I entered the forsaken temple. The columns of yellowed marble still stood, almost untouched by time, and between them the sky appeared dark; there, up on high, out of the cracks in the stones, poppies were growing. All was still,—save for the muffled thunder of the surf that filled the holy place, as though with a supplicating chant. I hearkened to it closely—and suddenly my heart quivered. I fell down on my knees and began to pray to the god, unknown and desecrated, who had at one time made this place his habitation. I kissed the marble flag-stones; I wept, and loved him for that none on earth any longer loves him or prays to him,—I wept for that he had died. Since that time I have never prayed to anyone as I prayed then. It was a temple of Dionysos."

"Whatever are you saying,—whatever are you saying, Cassandra!" said Giovanni. "'Tis sin and blasphemy! There is no god Dionysos nor ever has been. . . ."

"Nor ever has been?" the girl repeated with a smile of scorn. "But how is it the holy fathers, whom you believe, teach that the exiled gods, at the time of Christ's victory, did transform themselves into mighty demons? How is it that in the book of the famous astrologue Giorgio da Novara there is a prophecy, founded on exact observation of the luminaries of heaven: that the conjunction of the planet Jupiter with Saturn gave birth to the Mosaic teaching; with Mars, the Chaldæan; with the Sun, the Ægyptian; with Venus, the Mahomedan; with Mercury, the Christian,—while this planet's forthcoming conjunction with Luna must bring forth the teaching of Antichrist, —and then shall the gods now dead be resurgent!"

The rumbling of nearing thunder broke forth. The heat lightnings blazed up more and more vividly, illuminating an enormous, heavy cloud, slowly crawling along. The annoying sounds of the lute strummed on as before in the stifling, ominous silence.

"O Cassandra!" exclaimed Beltraffio, clasping his hands in a sorrowing supplication. "How is it you see not that the devil is tempting you, in order to draw you into perdition? May he be damned, the accursed one! . . ."

The girl turned around quickly, put both her hands on his shoulders, and uttered in a whisper:

"But then, has he never tempted thee? If thou art so righteous, Giovanni,—wherefore hast thou left thy teacher Fra Benedetto; why hast thou entered the studio of Leonardo da Vinci, the godless one? Why dost thou come hither, to me? Or knowest thou not that I am a witch,—and that witches be evil, more evil than the devil himself? How is it that thou art not afraid, then, to send thy soul to perdition along with me?"

"The power of the Lord be with us! . . ." he mumbled, as a shudder ran through him. In silence she drew near him, fixing him with her eyes, yellow and translucent, like tree-amber. By now it was no longer heat lightning but real that clave the cloud and lit up her face,—pallid like the face of that marble goddess who had erstwhile risen before Giovanni out of her grave of a thousand years.

"'Tis she!" he thought with horror. "The White She-Demon!"

He made an effort to jump up, and could not; he felt a hot breath on his cheek and listened intently to her whispering:

"Dost want me to, Giovanni? Shall I tell thee all,—all to the very end? If thou dost wish it, dearest, you and I shall fly away,—there, to where *He* is. . . . There it is good, there it is never dreary. And nothing is shameful there, even as in a dream, even as in Paradise,—all things are permitted there! Wouldst go there? . . ."

A chill sweat stood out on his forehead; but with a curiosity that overpowered horror he asked:

"Whither?"

Almost grazing his cheek with her lips, she answered in a barely audible voice, as though she had sighed in passion and in languor.

"To the Sabbath!"

A stroke of thunder, already near, shaking heaven and earth, filled with an ominous joy that resembled the laughter of unseen subterranean giants, reverberated triumphantly, and died away slowly in the breathless quiet. Not a single leaf stirred on the trees. The sounds of the strumming lute ceased abruptly. And at that very moment the despondent, measured ringing of the monastery bell pealed forth the evening Angelus. Giovanni made the sign of the cross. The girl arose and uttered:

"Time for home. 'Tis late. Dost see the torches? 'Tis Duke Moro going to Messer Galeotto. For I had forgot that to-day uncle must perform an experiment,—the transmutation of lead into gold."

The tramping of horses' hoofs was heard. The equestrians along the banks of the canal, from the Vercellina Gates, were going in the direction of the alchemist's house, who, in expectation of the Duke, was concluding in his laboratory the last preparations for the forthcoming experiment.

III

MESSER GALEOTTO had passed all his life in seeking after the Philosopher's Stone.

Having concluded the medical course at the University of Bologna, he had entered as a pupil, or *famulus*, the service of Count Bernardo Trevisano, at that time celebrated as an adept of the occult sciences. Subsequently, during the course of fifteen years, he sought the transmutative Mercury in all possible substances,—in kitchen salt and ammonia; in divers metals; in virgin bismuth and arsenic; in human blood, spleen, and hair; in animals and vegetables. Six thousand ducats of his patrimony had flown up the flue of the smelting furnace. Having spent his own money, he had taken to that of others. His creditors had put him in jail. He had escaped, and during the following eight years made experiments with eggs, wasting twenty thousand of them. Next he worked with Maestro Enrico, the Papal Prothonotary, upon different sorts of copperas, had become ill from their poisonous vapours, had lain ill for fourteen months, abandoned of all, and had almost died. Enduring beggary, humiliations, persecutions, he had visited, as an itinerant laboratorian, Spain, France, Austria, Holland, Northern Africa, Greece, Palestine, and Persia. At the court of the King of Hungary they had tortured him, hoping to find out the secret of transmutation. Finally, already aged, wearied, but not disillusioned, he had returned to Italy, at the invitation of Duke Moro, and had received the title of Court Alchemist.

The middle of the laboratory was taken up by an unwieldy oven of fire-clay with a multiplicity of compartments, fire-doors, sumps, and bellows. In one corner, under a layer of dust, flung down in disorder, were sooty scoria, resembling cooled lava.

Intricate appliances—alembics, stills, chemical receivers, retorts, funnels, mortars, cucurbits with glass vials, long-necked, serpent-shaped pipes, enormous bottles, and the tiniest of jars—encumbered the work-table. Poisonous salts, lyes, and acids exuded a pungent odour. An entire mystical universe of gods lay imprisoned in the metals,—seven gods of Olympus, seven heavenly bodies: in gold, the Sun; Luna in silver; in copper, Venus; in iron, Mars; in lead, Saturn; in pewter, Jupiter; while in the living, glistening quicksilver,—the ever-mobile Mercury. Here were substances with names barbaric, inspiring terror in the uninitiate: Cinnabar Crescent; Wolf's Milk; Brazen Achilles; asterite; androdama; anagallis; panopticum; aristolochia. A precious drop of Lion's Blood, which cureth all ills and bestoweth youth eternal,—gotten through many-yeared toil,—glowed redly, like a ruby.

The alchemist was seated at his work-table. Spare, small, as wrinkled as an old mushroom, but still irrepressibly spry, Messer Galeotto, propping his head with both hands, was attentively watching a cucurbit, which with a low ringing sound was bubbling and coming to a boil over a rarefied bluish flame. This was the Oil of Venus—*Oleum Veneris*,—of a translucent green colour, like a smaragd. A candle, burning beside it, cast an emerald reflection through the cucurbit upon the parchment of an open ancient folio, the work of the Arabic alchemist Jabir Abdalla.

Hearing steps and voices upon the stairs, Galeotto arose, cast a glance about the laboratory, to see if all were in order, made a sign to the servant, a taciturn *famulus*, that he put additional coals in the smelting furnace, and went to meet his guests.

IV

The company was in a merry mood, just after supper and Malvasia. Among the retinue of the Duke were the chief Court Leech, Marliani, a man of great acquirements in alchemy, and Leonardo da Vinci. The ladies entered—and the quiet cell of the man of learning became filled with the fragrance of perfumes, the silken rustling of dresses, frivolous feminine chatter and laughter,—as if with the jargoning of birds. One of them caught with her sleeve a glass retort, sending it to the floor.

"'Tis naught, Signora,—be not perturbed!" spake Galeotto pleas-

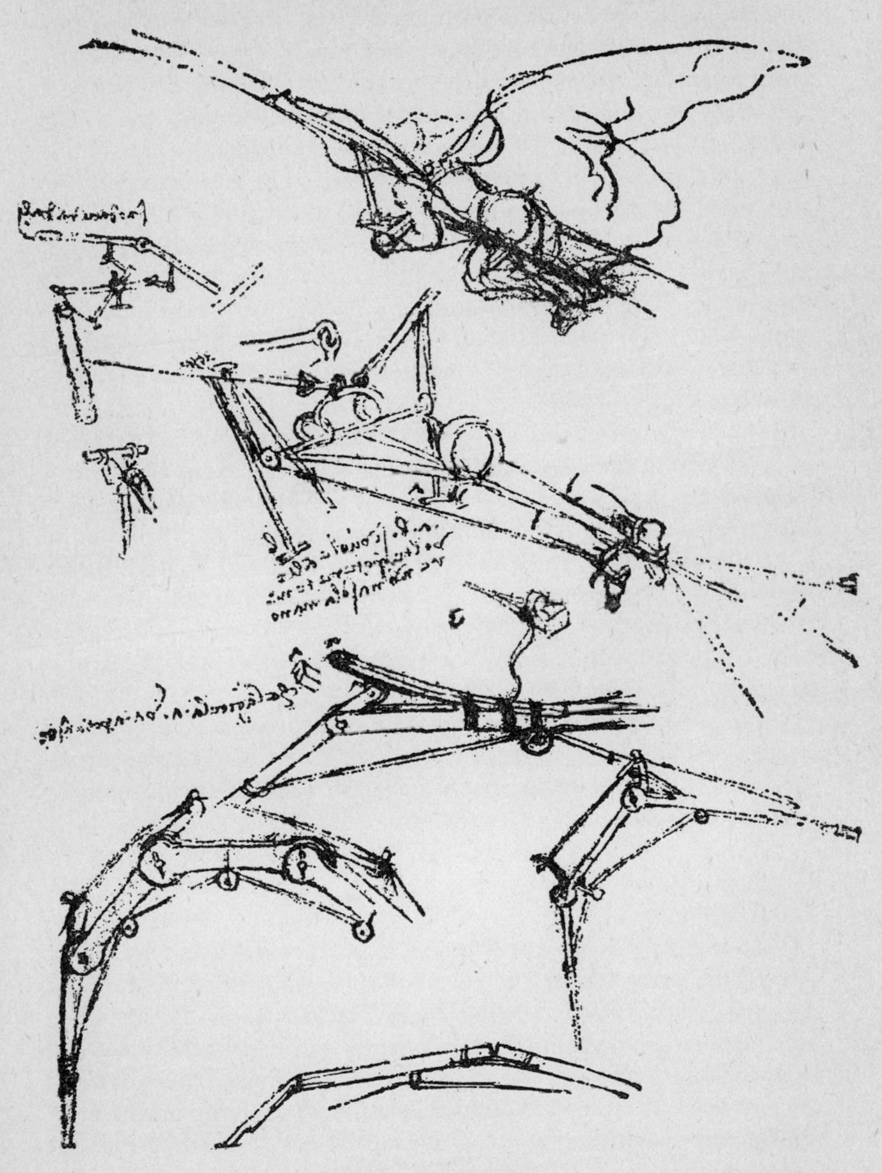

antly. "Allow me to pick up the fragments, lest you cut your dainty foot."

Another took in her hand a sooty piece of iron slag, soiling her light glove, scented with violets, and an adroit cavalier, squeezing her hand on the sly, tried to clean off the stain with a lace handkerchief. The fair-haired, mischievous Donzella Diana, well-nigh swooning from pleasant apprehension, touched a cup filled with quicksilver, spilling two or three drops on the table, and, when they started rolling in shining globules, cried out:

"Look, look, Signori, here be miracles: liquid silver, running of itself, and alive!" And she almost jumped for joy, clapping her palms.

"Is it true that we shall behold the devil in the alchemic fire, when the lead is turning into gold?" asked the pretty little roguish Filiberta, wife of the old Consul of the Salt Industry. "What think you, messer,—is it not a sin to be present at such experiments?"

Filiberta was exceedingly devout, and it was told of her that she permitted everything to her lover save a kiss on the lips, holding that continence was not entirely violated whilst the lips with which she had sworn at the altar to marital fidelity remained innocent.

The alchemist approached Leonardo and whispered in his ear:

"Messer, I assure you I can appreciate the visit of such a man as you. . . ." He pressed his hand hard.

Leonardo was about to protest, but the old man interrupted him and took to nodding his head:

"Oh, of course! . . . 'Tis all a mystery to them,—but surely you and I understand one another? . . ."

Then, with an affable smile, he turned to his guests:

"With the permission of my patron, the Most Illustrious Duke, and also of the ladies, my fair sovereigns, I begin the experiment of divine metamorphosis. Attention, signori!"

In order that no doubts might arise about the genuineness of the experiment, he showed the crucible,—a melting pot with thick sides of fire-clay,—requesting that everyone present look it over, touch it, tap its bottom, and become convinced that there was no deception of any sort about it, during which he explained that alchemists at times secrete gold in melting pots with double bottoms, of which the upper one, cracking from intense heat, reveals the gold. The chunks of pewter and of coal, the bellows, the sticks for stirring the cooling slag of the metal, and the rest of the objects, in which any gold could be concealed,—and even those in which, evidently, there was altogether no chance of concealment,—were also subjected to close scrutiny.

He next cut up the pewter into small pieces, laid it in the crucible, and put it in the maw of the oven upon the flaming coals. The taciturn, cross-eyed *famulus*—with a face so pale and gloomy that one lady well-nigh fell into a swoon, taking him in the darkness for a devil—began to work the enormous bellows. The coals burned more intensely under the noisy stream of air.

Galeotto entertained his guests with patter. Incidentally, he aroused general merriment, by styling alchemy *casta meretrix*,—a chaste-strumpet, that hath many admirers, yet deceiveth all, and, while she seemeth accessible to all, had up to that time been in the embraces of none,—*nullos unquam pervenit amplexus*.

The Court Leech Marliani, a man corpulent and ungainly, with a bloated, clever and pompous face, frowned angrily as he listened to the alchemist's chatter, and wiped his forehead; finally, unable to endure it, he spoke:

"Messer, is it not time for business? The pewter is boiling."

Galeotto reached a blue bit of paper and unwrapped it carefully. It proved to contain a powder, of the light yellow of a lemon, unctuous, glistening, like roughly ground glass, giving off an odour of burnt sea salt,—this was the much sought tincture, the priceless treasure of the alchemists, the wonder-working Stone of Wise Men, *lapis philosophorum*.

With the sharp edge of a knife he separated a barely perceptible grain, no larger than a rape-seed; he rolled it into a pellet with white beeswax, and cast it into the seething pewter.

"What do you suppose the potency of the tincture to be?" asked Marliani.

"One part to two thousand eight hundred and twenty parts of the metal to be transmuted," replied Galeotto. "Of course, the tincture is as yet not perfected, but I think that in a short while I shall attain the magnitude of a unit to the million. 'Twill suffice to take a grain of powder the weight of a millet seed, to dissolve it in a barrel of water, dip up a nutshell full, and sprinkle it on a vine, in order to have ripe clusters appear as early as May! *Mara tingerem, si Mercurius esset!* I would turn the sea into gold, if there be quicksilver enough!"

Marliani shrugged his shoulders: the boasting of Messer Galeotto maddened him. He began proving the impossibility of the transmutation by deductions in scholastics and the syllogisms of Aristotle. The alchemist smiled.

"Bide a while, *domine magister*,—I shall right soon present a syllogism which you will not find it easy to controvert."

He threw on the coals a handful of white powder. Clouds of smoke filled the laboratory. With hissing and crackling the flame leapt up, multicoloured, like a rainbow,—now blue, now green, now red. Confusion arose in the crowd of spectators. Subsequently Madonna Filiberta told that in the purple flame she had seen a devil's phiz. With a long cast-iron hook the alchemist lifted up the lid of the crucible, now at white-heat,—the pewter was boiling, foaming, and gurgling. The crucible was covered again. The bellows whistled, snorted,—and when ten minutes later a thin iron rod was plunged into the pewter, all saw a yellow drop appear on its tip.

"'Tis ready!" uttered the alchemist.

The clay smelter was taken out of the oven, allowed to cool, and broken,—and, ringing and sparkling, an ingot of gold fell out before the gathering which became struck dumb with astonishment.

The alchemist pointed to it, and, turning to Marliani, uttered triumphantly:

"*Solve mihi hunc syllogismum!* Solve me this syllogism!"

"'Tis unheard of. . . . Unbelievable. . . . 'Tis against all laws of nature and logic!" mumbled Marliani, spreading his arms out in confusion.

The face of Messer Galeotto was pale; his eyes flaming. He raised them to heaven and exclaimed:

"*Laudetur Deus in æternum, qui partem suæ infinitæ potentiæ nobis, suis abjectissimis creaturis communicavit. Amen.* Glory to God on high, Who doth bestow upon us, the least worthy of His creatures, a moiety of His infinite power. Amen."

Upon testing of the gold on a touchstone moistened with nitric acid, a yellow glistening streak was left,—it proved purer than the very finest Hungarian or Arabian. All surrounded the old man, felicitating him, wringing his hands. Duke Moro led him aside:

"Wilt thou serve me, truly and faithfully?"

"I fain would have more than one life, in order to dedicate them all to the service of Your Excellency!" replied the alchemist.

"Look thou, then, Galeotto, that none of the other rulers . . ."

"Your Highness, should any find it out, give orders to hang me like a dog!" And, after a short silence, with a fawning obeisance he added:

"If only I might receive—"

"What? Again?"

"Oh, for the last time, as God is my witness,—for the last time. . . ."

"How much?"

"Five thousand ducats."

The Duke after cogitating a while, beat him down by a thousand, and agreed.

The hour was late; Madonna Beatrice might be alarmed. They got ready to depart. The host, escorting his guests, offered a piece of the virgin gold to each one as a memento. Leonardo stayed behind.

V

WHEN the guests had departed, Galeotto approached him and said:

"Master, how did the experiment please you?"

"The gold was in the rods," Leonardo answered calmly.

"What rods? What would you say, Messer?"

"In the rods wherewith you stirred the pewter,—I saw all."

"You yourself inspected them. . . ."

"Nay, not those."

"Not those? What mean you, an it please you . . ."

"Why, I tell you I saw all," Leonardo repeated with a smile. "Persist not in your denial, Galeotto. The gold was hidden inside the hollowed-out rods, and when their wooden ends had burned off it fell into the crucible."

The old man's legs gave way beneath him; on his face was an expression both submissive and piteous, like that of a caught thief.

Leonardo approached and laid his hand upon the alchemist's shoulder.

"Fear not; none shall find out. I shall not tell."

Galeotto seized his hand and uttered with an effort:

"Truly,—you will not? . . ."

"Nay,—I wish you no ill. Only why do you do this? . . ."

"O, Messer Leonardo!" exclaimed Galeotto, and immediately after his immeasurable despair a hope just as immeasurable began to gleam in his eyes. "I swear by God that even if appearances were against me, remember that my deception is but temporary, for the weal of the Duke and for the triumph of science, for I have really found it,—I have really found the stone of the mystagogues! As yet, of course, I do not actually possess it, but to all intents and purposes it can be said to exist, inasmuch as I have found the path,—and as you know the chief thing in this matter is the path. Some three or four experiments more, and 'tis accomplished! What else was I to do, master? Can it be that the discovery of the greatest truth does not warrant such a petty lie? . . ."

"What are you and I about, Messer Galeotto,—just as if we were playing hoodman-blind?" exclaimed Leonardo, shrugging his shoulders. "You know as well as I do that the transmutation of metals is nonsense; there is no Philosopher's Stone, nor can there be. Alchemy, necromancy, black magic, as well as all other sciences not founded on exact experience and mathematics, are either deception or madness,—a wind-bellied banner of charlatans, bellied by the wind, after which banner the foolish rabble flocks. . . ."

The alchemist continued to gaze at Leonardo with clear and wondering eyes. Suddenly he bent his head to one side, slyly closed one eye, and began to laugh:

"Well, now, that is not at all nice, master,—not at all nice, really! For am I not of the initiate, eh? As though we do not know that you are the greatest of the alchemists, the possessor of the most hidden secrets of nature, a new Hermes Trismegistus and a new Prometheus!"

"I?"

"Why, yes,—you, of course."

"You are a jocose fellow, Messer Galeotto!"

"Nay, it is you who are jocose, Messer Leonardo! *Ai*, *ai*, *ai*, what a dissembler you are! I have in my time seen alchemists jealous of the mystery of their science, but never yet to such a degree as yourself!"

Leonardo looked at him attentively, was about to become angry, but could not.

"So,—you really do," he said with an involuntary smile, "you really do believe in such things? . . ."

"Do I believe!" exclaimed Galeotto. "Why, do you know, Messer, that if God himself were to come down to me right now and say: 'Galeotto, there is no Philosopher's Stone,' I would reply to Him: 'Lord, even as it is true that Thou hast created me, so is it true that the Stone exists, and that I shall find it!"

Leonardo no longer contradicted, nor grew indignant; he listened with curiosity.

When the conversation touched on the aid of the Devil in the cryptic sciences, the alchemist with a smile of conquest remarked that the Devil was the poorest creature in all nature, and that there was not a single being in the universe more weak than he. The old man believed only in the might of the human reason, and asserted that all was possible to science.

Then suddenly, as though recalling something amusing and charming, he asked if Leonardo saw frequently the spirits of the elements: but when his companion confessed that he had not seen them once as yet, Galeotto was again incredulous, and, with relish, explained in detail that a Salamander has an elongated body, a finger and a half in length, spotted, thin, and rough; while the Sylphide's is translucently blue, like the sky, and æthereal. He told about nymphs,—Undines, living in the water; of underground Gnomes and Pygmies; of Durdallas, who inhabit plants, and the rare Diameias, dwellers in precious stones.

"I could not even convey to you," he finished his narration, "how benevolent they are!"

"But wherefore do the elemental spirits appear not to all, but only to the elect?"

"How could it be possible for them to appear to all? They fear coarse people,—libertines, drunkards, gluttons. They are to be found only where malice and cunning are not. Otherwise they become timid like the beasts of the forest, and hide from human gaze in their native elements."

The old man's face became illumined with a tender smile.

"What a strange, pitiful and endearing fellow!" reflected Leonardo, no longer feeling indignation against his alchemical ravings, endeavouring to speak with him cautiously, as with a child, ready to pretend the possession of any secret desired, that he might not hurt the feelings of Messer Galeotto.

They parted friends.

VI

WHILE all this was taking place above, Monna Sidonia, the landlady, and Cassandra were sitting before the hearth in the lower chamber, situated underneath the laboratory.

Over a faggot of flaming brushwood hung a cast-iron pot, in which was cooking a porridge of garlic and rape for their supper. With a monotonous movement of her wrinkled fingers the old woman pulled out the thread from a distaff-ful and twisted it, now raising, now lowering the rapidly turning spindle. Cassandra was contemplating the spinner and reflecting,—again the same old state of things: to-day the same as yesterday; to-morrow the same as to-day; the cricket singing, the mouse scratching, the spindle humming; the dry stalks of pearl-wort crackling; the smell of garlic and rape; the old woman again reproaching with the same words,—like the sawing of a dull saw: She, Monna Sidonia is a poor woman; although folks gossip about a jug of money buried in her vineyard, 'tis but nonsense. Messer Galeotto is ruining her. Uncle and niece, both, hang upon her neck, the Lord forgive her! She keep and feeds them only out of the goodness of her heart. But Cassandra is no longer little,—'tis time to think of the future. Her uncle will die and leave her a beggar. Why not marry the rich horse-trader from Abbiategrasso, who has been a-courting for so long? True, he is no longer young, but then he is a sober-minded man, and a pious; he has a flour-shop, a mill, an olive grove with a new press. The Lord sendeth him good-fortune. What, then, is amiss? What-ever can she want?

Monna Cassandra listened, and a heavy ennui welled up in her throat, like a lump; the ennui choked her and pressed her temples, so that she was fain to weep, to cry out from it as from pain.

The old woman took out of the small pot a smoking radish, stuck it through with a pointed little wooden stick, pared it with a knife, poured some thick, soured grape-juice over it, and fell to eating, smacking her toothless mouth. The young girl with an accustomed gesture, with an air of submissive despair, stretched herself, crackling her slender pale fingers over her head.

When, after supper, the sleepy spinner, like a dismal Parca, began to nod her head, as her eyes took to blinking, the while her rasping voice became listless and her chatter about the horse-trader disconnected,—Cassandra took out from under her clothing the gift of her father, Messer Luigi: the talisman hung on a thin cord, its precious stone warmed by her body; she raised it up to her eyes, so that the flame from the hearth might shine through it, and fell to gazing at the image of Bacchus: in the dark-lilac radiance of the translucent amethyst there stood out before her, like a vision, the nude youth Bacchus, holding a thyrsus in one hand, a cluster of grapes in the other; a leaping pard strove to lick this cluster with its tongue. And the heart of Cassandra was filled with love toward this beauteous god. . . .

She sighed heavily, hid the talisman, and uttered hesitatingly:

"Monna Sidonia, they are gathering this night at Barco di Ferrara and at Benevento. . . . Good aunt! Dear, kind aunt! We shan't even dance,—we shall give but one look, and then right back. I shall do all you wish; I shall e'en wheedle a present out of the trader,—only let us fly, let us fly this night, this minute! . . ."

Insane desire sparkled in her eyes. The old woman bestowed a look upon her, and suddenly her bluish, wrinkled lips spread in a wide grin, revealing a solitary yellow tooth that resembled a fang; her face became frightful and gay.

"Dost want it?" she uttered. "Very much, eh? Hast gotten into the taste of it? Look ye, what a hellion maid! She would fly every night,—there is no holding her! Remember, then, Cassandra: the sin is upon thy soul. I did not e'en have as much as a thought of it in my mind to-day. 'Tis but for thee I do it. . . ."

Leisurely she went around the chamber, closed all the shutters tightly, stuffed the cracks with bits of rags, turned the key in the door, locking it, doused the embers on the hearth with water, lit the candle-end of black magic tallow, and took out of a small iron casket an earthern pot of a pungently smelling unguent. She put on a pretence of protraction and prudence. But her hands trembled, like a drunkard's; her little eyes from lecherous longing by turns became dull and dazed, or blazed up like coals. Cassandra dragged out into the middle of the chamber two large troughs, used for the leavening of dough.

Having concluded her preparations, Monna Sidonia stripped herself to the skin, put the pot between the troughs, sat down in one of them, astride a scovel, and commenced to rub her entire body with the greasy greenish unguent from the pot. The penetrating odour filled the chamber. This magic concoction to make witches fly was compounded from poisonous lactuca, swamp smallage, hemlock, banewort, henbane, roots of mandragora, serpents' blood, and the fat of unchristened infants, tortured to death by the sorceresses.

Cassandra turned away, in order not to see the hideousness of the old woman's body. At the last moment, when that which she so much desired was imminent and inevitable, a loathing arose in the depth of her heart.

"Well, now,—what are you dawdling about?" grumbled the old witch, squatting on her heels in the trough. "Thou wast hurrying me thyself, yet now thou art at thy whims. I shan't fly alone. Take thy clothes off!"

"Right away. Do you put out the light, Monna Sidonia. I can do naught in the light. . . ."

"Look ye, what a modest body! But on the Mount, now, never fear, thou art not ashamed? . . ."

She blew out the candle-end, making, to please the Devil, the sacrilegious, left-handed sign of the cross, customary to witches. The young girl undressed, save for her under shift; then she got down on her knees in the trough, and began hurriedly anointing herself with the unguent.

In the darkness the old woman could be heard muttering, senseless, fragmentary words of incantations:

"*Emen Hatan, eman hetan* . . . Pallud, Baalberith, Astharoth, come to our aid! *Agora, agora, Patrica*,—come to our aid!"

Avidly Cassandra breathed in the strong odour of the magical preparation. The skin of her body burned; her head swam; a delectable chill ran down her back. Red and green circles, blending, began to float before her eyes, and, as though from afar, there suddenly reached her the piercing, triumphant cry of Monna Sidonia:

"*Garr! Garr!* Up from below,—and steer clear! . . ."

VII

Out of the hearth-chimney flew Cassandra, sitting astride a black goat whose soft wool felt pleasant against her bare legs. Rapture filled her soul, and, gasping for breath, she shouted and screamed, like a swallow plunging into the sky:

"*Garr! Garr!* Up from below,—and steer clear! . . . We fly! We fly!"

Naked, dishevelled, hideous Aunt Sidonia was rushing beside her, astride her scovel. They flew at such speed that the air they clave whistled in their ears like a hurricane.

"To the North! To the North!" shouted the old woman, guiding her scovel like an obedient steed. Cassandra gave herself up to the intoxication of flight.

"But this mechanician of ours, now,—this poor Leonardo da Vinci with his flying machines!" she recalled suddenly,—and became still merrier.

Now she would rise upwards,—black clouds piled up beneath her, blue lightnings quivering in their heart. Up above was a clear sky with a full moon,—enormous, dazzling, round as a millstone, and so near that it seemed one could touch it with one's hand. Then she would direct the goat downward anew, seizing him by his twisted horns, and flew headlong, like a loosened stone, into the bottomless abyss.

"Whither goest thou? Whither goest thou? Thou wilt break thy neck! Hast become mad, thou devil's wench?" vociferated Aunt Sidonia, barely keeping up with her.

And now they were rushing so near the ground that they heard the slumbrous grasses in the swamp rustling; the night-fires lit their way, and the bluish rotted logs glimmered; the tawny owl, the bittern, and the goat-sucking whippoorwill called plaintively to one another within the dreamy forest.

They flew over the summits of the Alps, sparkling under the moon with their transparent bowlders of ice, and descended to the surface of the sea. Cassandra, having scooped up some water in her hand, flung it upward, admiring the sapphire drops. With every moment their flight grew faster. More and more frequently did they come upon fellow wayfarers: a grey, shaggy wizard in a tub; a merry prebendary pot-bellied, rosy-faced, like Silenus, on a poker; a fair-haired girl of some ten years, innocent of face, blue-eyed, on a bath-broom; a young, naked, rufous anthropophagite witch, on a grunting boar; and a multitude of others.

"Whence come ye, little sisters?" Aunt Sidonia hailed them.

"Out of Ellada, from the Island of Candia!"

Other voices replied:

"From Valencia. . . . Off the Brocken. . . . From Salaguzzi. . . . Mirandola. . . . From Benevento. . . . Out of Norcia."

"Whither go ye?"

"To Biterne! To Biterne! There the Great Goat celebrates his espousal,—*el Boch de Biterne*. Fly, fly! Gather to the supper!"

Now in a whole flock, like crows, they sped over the dismal plain. In the fog the moon seemed blood-red. In the distance the cross of a lonely village chapel took on a warm glow. The rufous one,—she who was galloping astride a hog,—with a squeal flew up to the church, tore off the big bell, cast it with all her force into a bog, and, as it splashed into a pool with a plaintive clang, burst into laughter, just as if she were barking. The fair-haired girl on the bath-broom began to clap her hands with mischievous playfulness.

VIII

THE moon hid behind the clouds. In the light of the twisted green torches of wax, their blaze vivid and blue, like lightning, upon the snow-white, chalky upland, the enormous coal-black shadows of the dancing witches ran, intertwined, and separated.

"*Garr! Garr!* The Sabbath, the Sabbath! Right to left, right to left!"

Around the Goat of the Night, *Hyrcus Nocturnus*, enthroned in state on a crag, thousands upon thousands whirled by, like black rotted leaves of autumn,—sans beginning, sans end.

"*Garr! Garr!* Glorify the Goat of the Night! *El Boch de Biterne! El Boch de Biterne!* Ended are all our tribulations! Rejoice!"

High and hoarse skirled the bag-pipes, made of hollowed dead men's bones; and the drum, drawn over with the skin of men who had met their end on the gallows, thumped with a wolf's tail, throbbed and rumbled, muffled and even: *toop, toop, toop*. In gigantic cauldrons a horrible mess was coming to a boil, unutterably delectable, even though unsalted, for the Host of this place detested salt.

In modest little nooks love-jinks were starting up,—of daughters with their fathers, of brothers with their sisters; of a black were-cat, a tom, dainty-mannered and green-eyed, with a submissive little girl, slender, and as pale as a lily; of a visageless, shaggy incubus, as gray as a spider, with a nun who bared her teeth in a shameless smile. Everywhere were loathsome couplings, squirming in their abominations.

A white-fleshed, fat witch-giantess, with a maternal smile on her foolish and kindly face, was feeding two new-born imps,—the gluttonous sucklings had attached themselves greedily to her pendulous breasts, and, with loud smacking, gulped down the milk.

Three-year-old infants, who had never yet participated in the Sabbath, were modestly tending, on the edge of the field, a herd of knobby toads with little bells, tricked out in caparisons of cardinals' purple, and fatted on the Holy Eucharist.

"Let us dance!" Aunt Sidonia was impatiently tugging Cassandra.

"The horse-trader might see us!" exclaimed the girl, laughing.

"May he be food for the dogs, this horse-trader!" answered the old woman.

They both dashed off, and the dance carried them off like a gale, with din, howling, squealing, roaring and laughter:

"*Garr! Garr!* Right to left. Right to left!"

Someone's long, wet moustaches, just like those of a walrus, were pricking Cassandra's neck from behind: someone's thin, hard tail was tickling her in front; someone or other pinched her painfully and shamelessly; someone or other bit her, having whispered in her ear a monstrous caress. But she did not resist: the worse,—the better; the more awful,—the more intoxicating.

Suddenly they all stopped, instantaneously, rooted to the spot; they turned to stone and grew deathly still.

From the black throne, where the Unknown sat in state, surrounded with horror, resounded a stifled voice that was like to the rumble of an earthquake:

"Accept ye my gifts,—the humble, my strength; the meek, my pride; the poor in spirit, my knowledge; the grieving at heart, my joyousness,—accept ye them!"

A greybeard dotard, benignant of visage, one of the higher members of the Most Holy Inquisition, a patriarch of the wizards, performing the black mass, solemnly proclaimed:

"*Sanctificetur nomen tuum per universum mundum, et libera nos ab omni malo*. Fall prostrate, ye faithful!"

All prostrated themselves, and, mimicking churchly chanting, the sacrilegious choir burst forth:

"*Credo in Deum patrem Luciferum, qui creavit cœlum et terram. Et in filium ejus Beelzebub.*"

When the last sounds had died away, and silence again fell, the former voice that was like to the rumble of an earthquake again resounded:

"Bring me my spouse unespoused,—my dove undefiled!"

The high priest interrogated:

"What is the name of thy spouse, of thy dove undefiled?"

"Madonna Cassandra! Madonna Cassandra!" the answer rumbled forth.

Hearing her name, the witch felt her blood turning to ice in her veins, felt the hair on her head stand up on end.

"Madonna Cassandra! Madonna Cassandra!" the cry floated over the horde. "Where is she? Where is our sovereign mistress? *Ave, archisponsa Cassandra!*"

She covered her face with her hands, and was fain to flee,—but bony fingers, claws, tentacles, proboscides, and shaggy spiders' paws stretched forth, seized her, tore off her shift, and drew her toward the throne stark-naked and shivering.

A goatish stench and the chill of death were wafted in her face. She cast down her eyes in order not to see.

Then He that sate upon the throne spake, saying:

"Come!"

She bent her head still lower and saw at her very feet a fiery cross, shining in the dark. Making a supreme effort, she overcame her loathing, made a step, and lifted up her eyes to Him who rose up before her.

And the miracle was wrought.

The goat's hide fell from Him, even as the shed skin sloughs from a snake, and the ancient Olympic god Dionysos appeared before Monna Cassandra, with a smile of eternal rejoicing on his lips, holding a thyrsus uplifted in one hand, a cluster of grapes in the other; a leaping panther strove to lick this cluster with its tongue.

And at the very same instant the Devil's Sabbath was transformed into the divine orgy of Bacchus; the old witches into youthful mænads; the monstrous demons into ægipedal satyrs; and there, where the dead bowlders of the chalky cliffs were, sprang up colonnades of white marble, illuminated by the sun; between them, in the distance, the azure sea began to sparkle, and Cassandra beheld in the clouds the entire sun-clad throng of the gods of Hellas.

The satyrs, the bacchantes,—striking tympani, stabbing their nipples with knives, squeezing out the scarlet juice of grapes into kratcræ of gold and mixing it with their own blood,—danced, whirled, and chanted:

"Glory, glory to Dionysos! The great gods have arisen from the dead! Glory to the gods arisen!"

The nude youth Bacchus opened his embraces to Cassandra, and his voice was like unto thunder, shaking heaven and earth:

"Come, come, my spouse, my dove undefiled!"

Cassandra sank into the embraces of the god.

IX

THE morning crowing of a rooster was heard. There came the odour of mist, and of a biting smoky dampness. From somewhere, from an infinite distance, there reached them the summons of a church bell. Great confusion sprang up on the mountain from this sound: the bacchantes again turned into monstrous witches; the ægipedal fauns into misshapen devils, and the God Dionysos into the Goat of the Night,—into the malodorous *Hyrcus Nocturnus*.

"Away, away! Homewards! Flee, save yourselves!"

"They have stolen my poker!" vociferated the pot-bellied prebendary-Silenus, with despair, and darted hither and yon, like one asphyxiated.

"My boar, my boar, come to me!" called the rufous one, naked, shivering from the morning dampness, and coughing.

The sinking moon swam out from behind the clouds, and in its purple reflected light, soaring up swarm upon swarm, the thoroughly frightened witches, like black flies, took flight in all directions from the Chalk Mount.

"*Garr! Garr!* Up from below,—and steer clear! Save yourselves,—flee!"

The Goat of the Night began to bleat piteously and fell through the ground, disseminating the evil odour of stifling sulphur.

The summons of the church bell pealed on.

X

Cassandra came to herself on the floor of the dark chamber in the little house near the Vercellina Gates. She felt nauseated, as after heavy drinking. Her head felt just as if it were filled with lead. Her body was prostrated with fatigue.

The bell of Santa Redegonda was ringing dismally. Through this ringing resounded a persistent knocking at the outer door, which had probably been going on for a long while. Cassandra listened closely and recognized the voice of her bridegroom, the horse-trader from Abbiategrasso.

"Open! Open! Monna Sidonia! Monna Cassandra! Have ye grown deaf, or what? I have gotten soaked through and through like a dog. Am I to go back, then, over this devil's slush?"

The girl got up with an effort, drew near the tightly shuttered window, and took out the packing with which Aunt Sidonia had so painstakingly stuffed up the cracks. The light of the mournful morning fell in a small bluish streak, lighting up the naked old witch, sleeping the sleep of the dead on the floor alongside the overturned bread-trough. Cassandra peeped through a crack.

The day was a nasty one, the rain pouring as if out of a bucket. Before the door of the house, behind the opaque veil of the rain, she could see the enamoured horse-trader. Beside him, with its head drooping low in despond, stood a flap-eared, diminutive burro, harnessed to a cart, out of which a hobbled calf had stuck its head, lowing.

The trader, without abatement, kept knocking on the door. Cassandra waited to see how all this would culminate. Finally a shutter above, in one of the windows of the laboratory, crashed open. The old alchemist looked out,—he had not had his full sleep; his hair was rumpled, and his face morose and malevolent as usual at those moments when, awaking from his dream visions, he began to realize that lead could not be transmuted into gold.

"Who is knocking?" he called out, leaning out of the window. "What dost thou want? Hast gone out of thy head, old duffer, or what? May the Lord send thee an untimely death! Canst thou not see that everyone is asleep in this house? Betake thyself off!"

"Messer Galeotto! Do be reasonable,—whatever are you scolding me for? I am come on important business, about your niece. And here is a milk-fed calf as a little present. . . ."

"The devil take thee!" Galeotto began to shout in fury. "Take thyself, thou good-for-naught, with thy calf, under the devil's tail!"

And the shutter slammed to. The trader, in a quandary, quieted down for a minute. But at once, recollecting himself, he began knocking with his fists with redoubled strength, as though he wanted to break down the door. The burro drooped its head still lower; little streams of rain ran down his hopelessly hanging wet ears.

"Lord, what boredom!" said Monna Cassandra in a whisper, and closed her eyes.

She recalled the merriment of the Sabbath, the transformation of the Goat of the Night into Dionysos, the resurrection of the great gods, and reflected:

"Was this in a dream, or in reality? Probably, in a dream. But that which is taking place now,—*that* is reality. After Sunday comes Monday. . . ."

"Open up! Open up!" vociferated the trader, by now in a voice grown hoarse and desperate.

The heavy drops from the water-spout splashed monotonously into a dirty puddle. The calf lowed piteously. The monastery bell dismally tolled on.

BOOK FIVE

Thy Will Be Done

I

ORBOLLO THE COBBLER, CITIZEN OF MILAN, having returned home at night in an alcoholically jolly mood, had gotten from his wife, to use his own expression, more blows than it would take to make a lazy ass go from Milan to Rome. Early in the morning, when she had set out to her neighbour, a rag-picker woman, to partake of *milliacci*,—a jelly of pig's blood,—Còrbollo, having felt in his wallet several coins secreted from his spouse, left his wretched little shop under the guardianship of his apprentice, and went off for a hair of the dog that bit him.

His hands shoved into the pockets of his worn breeches, he perambulated at a lazy pace through the winding dark alley, so cramped that an equestrian, upon meeting a pedestrian, must needs catch the latter with toe or spur. It smelt of the cooking fumes of olive oil, of rotten eggs, sour wine, and the mould of cellars. Whistling a snatch, casting a glance now and then at the narrow strip of dark blue sky between the tall houses, or at the motley tatters hung out by the housewives on ropes stretching across the street, and now transpierced by the morning sun, Còrbollo consoled himself with a wise saw,—which, however, he never put to practice:

"Every woman, good or bad, hath need of a stick."

To shorten the way, he passed through the Cathedral. Here was an eternal bustle, as on a mart. In one door and out another, despite the toll, passed a multitude of people, even with mules and horses.

The padres were singing *Te Deums* in snuffling voices; one could hear the whispers in the offertories; the holy lamps burned on the altars. And, alongside, the street gamins were playing at leap-frog; dogs were sniffing one another, amid the jostling of tattered beggars. Còrbollo paused for a moment in a crowd of gaping loungers to listen, with sly and good-natured amusement, to the squabbling of two monks.

Brother Cippolo, a barefooted Franciscan, exceedingly squat, redhaired, with a jolly face as round and oily as a pancake, was proving to his opponent, Brother Timoteo, a Dominican, that Francis, being like unto Christ in forty particulars, had taken the place left vacant in heaven upon the fall of Lucifer, and that the Mother of God herself would not be able to distinguish his stigmata from the wounds Jesus had gotten on the Cross.

The morose, tall, and pale-faced Brother Timoteo set up against the wounds of the Seraphic Martyr the wounds of St. Catherine, who had upon her forehead the bloody mark of the crown of thorns, which St. Francis lacked.

Còrbollo was forced to pucker up his eyes from the sun as he came out of the shade of the Cathedral on to the Piazza Arengo, the liveliest spot in Milan, cluttered up with the shops of petty merchants, fishmongers, rag-pickers, and huckstresses of greens,—such a multiplicity of boxes, sheds, and troughs that scarcely a passageway, even of the narrowest, was left between them. From times immemorable had these traders made their nests on this piazza before the Cathedral, and no laws or mulcts could drive them away from here.

"Salad of Valtellina! Lemons! Oranges! Asparagus,—good asparagus!" cried the huckstresses, enticing purchasers. Female rag-pickers drove their trade, clucking like setting hens. A stubborn little burro, disappearing beneath a load of yellow and blue grapes, of oranges, rutabaga, beets, red cabbage, *finocchio* and onions, was braying in a rending voice: *Io, io, io!* His driver was thwacking him resoundingly from the rear with a cudgel on his galled flanks, and urging him on with an abrupt, guttural cry: *Arri! Arri!* A string of blind men, with staffs and a leader, was chanting a piteous *Intemerata.* . . . A street charlatan, a tooth-jerker, with a carcanet of teeth on his otter cap, with the rapid and dexterous movements of a prestidigitateur, standing behind a man sitting on the ground and squeezing his head with his knees, was drawing his tooth with enormous pincers. . . . Urchins were showing a sow's ear to a Jew, and letting a *trottola*, or humming-top, under the feet of the passers-by. The most abandoned of these mischief-makers, the swarthy, pug-nosed Farfanicchio, brought a mouse-trap, let out the mouse, and besom in hand, began a hunt, with whistling and a piercing battle-cry: "There she goes, there she goes!" Running away from pursuit, the mouse darted headlong under the amplest of skirts, those of the fat-breasted, plump huckstress of greens, Barbaccia, peacefully knitting a stocking. She jumped up, setting up screeching, as though she had been scalded, and, amid the general laughter, raised up her dress, trying to shake out the mouse.

"Wait, I'll take a cobble-stone and smash in thy monkey's pate, thou good-for-naught!" she bawled, infuriated. Farfanicchio, from a distance, showed his tongue and hopped enraptured.

A porter with an enormous carcass of a swine on his head turned around to the hubbub. The horse of Messer Gabbadeo, the leech, became frightened, shied to one side, and dashed off, catching and knocking down a whole mound of kitchen ware in the miserable little shop of a trader in old iron. Skimmers, frying pans, graters, pots, poured down with a deafening din. The thoroughly scared Messer Gabbadeo galloped off, with loosed reins, and vociferated:

"Whoa, whoa, thou devil's pepper-pot!"

Dogs barked. Faces full of curiosity were thrust out of the windows. Laughter, cursing, squealing, whistling, human shouting and asinine braying, rose over the piazza. Admiring this spectacle, the cobbler reflected with a meek smile:

"What a fine thing 'twould be to be living in this world, were it not for wives, who consume their husbands, even as rust consumeth iron!"

Cupping his hand over his eyes, to shield them from the sun, he cast a glance upward at a gigantic, unfinished edifice, surrounded by the carpenters' scaffoldings. This was the Cathedral, in the process of erection by the people, for the glory of the Birth of Her Who Bore a God. Small and great took part in the building-up of this temple. The Queen of Cyprus had sent precious palls, woven with gold; the poor little old woman Caterina, a rag-picker, had laid down on the altar, as her gift-offering to Virgin Mary, without thinking of the cold of the coming winter, her ancient and only warm short jacket, twenty *soldi* in value. Còrbollo, used since childhood to watching the process of building, on this morning noticed a new turret, and rejoiced over it.

The stone-masons were noisy with their mallets. From the unloading wharf of Lagetto at San Stefano, not far from the Ospedale Maggiore, where the barques hove to, were brought up enormous, sparkling bowlders of white marble from the Lago Maggiore stone quarries. The crane chains creaked and grated; the iron saws screeched as they sawed the marble. Workmen clambered over the scaffolding, like ants.

And the great edifice grew, rearing on high its countless multitude of arrowy, stalactite-like pinnacles, belfries, and towers of pure white marble against the blue heavens,—the eternal praise of the people to Mariæ Nascenti.

FIVE

Leonardo da Vinci

II

Còrbollo descended the steep steps into the cellar of Tibaldo, the German taverner,—a cellar cool, vaulted, with wine casks set all about it. He courteously greeted the guests, sat down next to Scarabullo, a tinker, whom he knew, requested a mug of wine for himself and hot *offeletti*,—Milan patties with cumin,—leisurely took a sip and a bite, and said:

"If thou wouldst be wise, Scarabullo, never marry!"

"Wherefore?"

"Well, dost thou see, friend," continued the cobbler profoundly, "marrying is just the same as letting one's hand into a bag of snakes, on the chance of drawing out an eel. 'Tis better to have the gout than a wife, Scarabullo!"

At a little table alongside, Mascarello, an embroiderer in gold, a fine talker and a droll fellow, was dilating to hungry tatterdemalions on the wonders of the uncharted land of Berlintzona,—a blessed region, called Live-High, where the grape-vines are tied up with sausages, and a goose fetches but a groat, with a suckling pig thrown in. In that country stands a mountain of grated cheese, and the people living thereon busy themselves with naught but the preparation of *macaroni* and *ravioli*, cooking them in a broth of capons, and throwing them downward. He that catcheth most hath the most. And right nearby there flows a river of *vernaccio*,—none hath ever drunk a better wine, and there is nary a drop of water in it.

A little man, scrofulous, with purblind eyes, like those of a puppy that has not yet gotten the full use of them, ran into the cellar,—Gorgoglio, the glass-blower, a great gossip and lover of news.

"Signori," he solemnly announced, raising his hat, dusty and full of holes, and wiping the sweat from his face, "signori, I am just come from the Frenchmen!"

"Whatever art thou saying, Gorgoglio? Why, are they already here?"

"Aye, even so,—in Pavia. . . . Phew,—let me catch my breath! I ran at a breakneck pace. . . . What if, thinks I, someone should get ahead of me . . ."

"Here is a mug for thee, drink and tell us,—what sort of people be these Frenchmen?"

"They are a mischievous people, maties,—never thrust a finger in their mouths. They are a boisterous folk, savage, outlandish, ungodly, bestial,—in one word, barbarians! They have culverins and arquebuses eight ells long; brazen mortars, bombards of cast iron that shoot stones; steeds like sea monsters, with clipped ears and tails."

"And are there many of them?" queried one, Maso by name.

"Hosts upon hosts! Like locusts, they have covered all the plain around with never an end in sight. The Lord hath sent us this black plague, these devils of the north for our sins!"

"But wherefore art thou reviling them, Gorgoglio?" remarked Mascarello. "For are they not our friends and allies?"

"Allies! Thou hast another guess coming! A friend like that is worse than a foe,—give him an inch and he will take an ell."

"Well, well, now, do not spin out thy nonsense, but talk sense: wherein are the French our foes?" Maso persisted in his questioning.

"Why, they be foes inasmuch as they trample down our fields of grain, chop down our trees, drive off our cattle, rape our womenfolk. The King of the French, now, is a miserable-looking knave,—'tis a wonder what keeps the life in him,—yet is he a great hand for women. He hath a book of portraits of naked Italian beauties. 'If,' say they, 'God will aid us, we shall not leave a single innocent maid between Milan and Naples!'"

"The scoundrels!" exclaimed Scarabullo, pounding his fist against the table with all his might, so that the bottles and tumblers were set a-ringing.

"Our Moro, now, dances on his hind paws to the French fife," continued Gorgoglio. "The French do not hold us for human beings, even. 'All of you,' say they, 'are thieves and murderers. Ye did away with your own lawful Duke by means of poison; an innocent lad was done to death by you. God is punishing you for it, and is giving your land over to us.'—Maties, we regale them with all our heart, but they give our offerings to the horses to taste,—there may be in the food, now, some of the poison with which we have poisoned the Duke."

"Thou liest, Gorgoglio!"

"Strike me blind,—may my tongue wither! And hearken, signori, how else they boast: 'We shall vanquish,' say they, 'all the peoples of Italy, all the seas and lands shall we subdue, and capture the Great Turk; take Constantinople; rear up the cross on the Mount of Olives in Jerusalem, and after that return to you again. And then the judgment of God shall be fulfilled upon you. And if ye shall not submit to us, we shall wipe out your very name from the face of the earth!'"

"'Tis an evil pass, maties," uttered Mascarello, the embroiderer in gold, "oh, but 'tis an evil pass! Such things have never yet befallen us. . . ."

All grew quiet.

Brother Timoteo, the same monk who had disputed with Brother Cippolo in the Cathedral, exclaimed triumphantly, raising his hands up to heaven:

"The word of the great prophet of God, Girolamo Savonarola: 'There shall come a man, that shall vanquish Italy, without taking his sword out of his scabbard. O Florence, O Rome, O Milan,—the time of songs and festivals is past. Repent! Repent! The blood of Duke Gian Galeazzo, the blood of Abel slain by Cain, crieth out for vengeance to the Lord!'"

III

"The French! The French! Look!" Gorgoglio was pointing to two soldiers, entering the cellar.

One, a Gascon, a well-built young man with small red moustaches, with a handsome and brazen face, by the name of Bonnivard, was sergeant in the French cavalry. His comrade was a Picardian, the cannoneer Gros-Guillioche,—a stout, squat old man with a bull's neck, with a face bloated with blood, with protuberant lobster's eyes, and a copper ear-ring in one ear. Both were inebriatedly jolly.

"Will we finally find, in this thrice-accursed town, a mug of good wine?" asked the sergeant, slapping Gros-Guillioche on the shoulder. "This sour and wretched Lombardian stuff makes the throat raw, like vinegar!"

Bonnivard, with a squeamish, bored air, slumped sprawlingly at one of the little tables, casting supercilious glances at the other guests, rapped with a pewter cup, and called out in broken Italian:

"White, dry, of the very oldest! Salt *cervellata* as a snack."

"Yes, brother," sighed Gros-Guillioche, "when one recalls one's native Burgundian, or the precious Beaune, as golden-tinted as the hair of my Lizon,—the heart contracts from longing for home! And it also must be said: like people, like wine. Let us drink, matey, to beloved France!

"Du grand Dieu soit mauldit à outrance.
Qui mal voudrait au royaume de France!"

"What are they gabbling about?" Scarabullo whispered in Gorgoglio's ear.

"They are pleased to be dainty, blackguarding our wines, praising their own."

"Look ye, how they strut it, the French roosters!" grumbled the tinker, frowning. "My hand itcheth,—oh, how it itcheth,—to teach them a fitting lesson!"

Tibaldo, their German host,—pot-bellied, spindle-shanked, with an enormous bunch of keys stuck in his broad leathern girdle,—looking askance at his foreign guests, drew from a cask half a *brente* and served it to the Frenchmen in a clay jug sweating from the cold.

Bonnivard drained at one draught his mug of wine, but, although it struck him as excellent, he spat, and his face assumed an expression of revulsion.

Lotta, the daughter of the host, a fair-haired girl of charming appearance, with the same kindly blue eyes as Tibaldo's, walked past him. The Gascon winked slyly at his comrade and with bravado twirled his red moustache; then, taking another sip, began a soldiers' ditty about Charles VIII, Gros-Guillioche chiming in in a hoarse voice:

"*Charles fera si grandes batailles,*
Qu'il conquerra les Itailles,
En Jerusalem entrera
Et mont Olivet montera."

When Lotta, on her way back, was again passing by them, her eyes modestly cast down, the sergeant embraced her waist, desiring to seat the girl on his lap. Pushing him away, she extricated herself, and ran away. He jumped up, caught her, and kissed her cheek with lips wet from wine. The girl cried out, dropped to the floor a clay jug, which was shattered to smithereens, and, turning around, struck the Frenchman's face with all her force, so that for a moment he was dazed. The guests burst into laughter.

"There's a wench for you!" exclaimed the embroiderer in gold, "I swear by San Gervasio that never, in all my born days, have I seen such a sturdy slap in the face! What a goodie he got that time!"

"Let her go,—do not start up." Gros-Guillioche was restraining Bonnivard. The Gascon would not listen. The drink had immediately gone to his head. He burst out into forced laughter and cried out:

"Bide a while, my beauty; it shan't be the cheek this time, but the very lips!"

He darted after her, upset a table, caught up with her, and was about to kiss her. But the mighty arm of the tinker Scarabullo seized him from behind by his coat collar.

"Ah, thou son of a dog, thou shameless French phiz!" Scarabullo was yelling, shaking Bonnivard and squeezing his neck harder and harder. "Bide a while, I shall buffet thy sides so that thou wilt long remember what it means to insult the girls of Milan!"

"Away, scoundrel! Long live France!" the infuriated Gros-Guillioche set up a scream in his turn. He swung his sword and would have plunged it into the tinker's back, had not Mascarello, Gorgoglio, Maso and their other bottle-companions jumped up and pinioned his arms. And, amid the overturned tables, benches, shards of broken jugs and pools of wine, a rough-and-tumble fight was on. Beholding blood, and the unsheathed swords and knives, the frightened Tibaldo jumped out of his cellar and began yelling all over the piazza:

"Death and murder! The French are robbing us!"

The market bell was rung. Another, in Broletto, responded to it. Cautious merchants began locking up their shops. The rag-wives and the huckstresses of greens carried away the bins with their goods.

"The saints in heaven be our intercessors,—Protasio, Gervasio!" vociferated Barbaccia.

"What's up there? A fire, or what?"

"Kill, kill the French!"

Little Farfanicchio was hopping about in rapture, and squealing piercingly:

"Kill them! Kill them!"

The city guards appeared,—*berrovieri* with arquebuses and halberds. They came up in time to prevent murder and to snatch Gros-Guillioche and Bonnivard out of the hands of the rabble. Taking along all whom they could lay their hands on, they seized Còrbollo the cobbler as well. His wife, who had come running at the noise, wrung her hands and set up a howl:

"Have pity,—do let my dear husband go; give him up to me! I shall deal with him in my own fashion, now,—never again will he go thrusting his nose into any street brawls! Really, now, signori, this fool is not even worth the rope to hang him with!"

Còrbollo sadly and shamefacedly cast down his eyes, pretending that he did not hear his wife's words, and hid from her behind the backs of the city guards.

IV

OVER the scaffolding of the unfinished Cathedral, up a narrow rope ladder, a young stone-mason was climbing up one of the slender belfries, not far from the main cupola, bearing in his hands a small carving of the great martyr Catherine, which was to be fastened on the very tip of the arrowy tower.

All around him reared up, as though they were soaring, sharp-pointed towers and spires, like stalactites, flowing arches, stone lacework of flowers, shoots, and leaves, whose counterparts were not to be found in nature; innumerable prophets, martyrs, angels, with laughing masks of devils, monstrous birds, sirens, harpies, and dragons with prickly wings, with gaping maws, at the terminations of the water-spouts. All these, of virgin marble, blindingly white, with shadows blue, like smoke, resembled an enormous winter forest, covered with sparkling hoar-frost.

It was quiet. Only swallows, with their cries, winged past over the head of the stone-mason. The hum of the crowd on the piazza floated up to him, like the faint susurration of an ant-heap. On the horizon of illimitable, green Lombardy the snowy masses of the Alps shone radiantly,—just as pointed, as white, as the summits of the Cathedral. At times he thought he heard below the echoes of the organ, like the sighs of prayer coming from the interior of the temple, from the depths of its heart of stone,—and at such times the edifice seemed alive, breathing, growing, and rearing itself up to the sky, like eternal praise to Mariæ Nascenti, like a joyous hymn of all ages and all peoples to the Most Pure Virgin, the Woman Clad in the Sun.

Suddenly the noise on the piazza increased. The tocsin sounded. The stone-mason stopped, looked downward,—and his head began to spin around, everything growing black before his eyes; the gigantic edifice appeared to topple under him, the slender turret up which he was clambering to bend, like a reed.

"'Tis the end,—I am falling!" he reflected, with horror.

With a last desperate effort he clutched the rope step, shut his eyes, and whispered:

"*Ave, dolce Maria, di grazia piena!*"

He felt relief. A cool breeze blew down lightly from up on high. He took a breathing spell, gathered his strength, and continued his climb, no longer heeding the earthly voices, as he rose higher and higher, toward the serene, pure sky, repeating with great joyousness:

"*Ave, dolce Maria, di grazia piena!*"

Simultaneously, walking over the broad marble roof of the Cathedral, almost flat, came the members of the Building Council, Italian and foreign architects, invited by the Duke for a consultation about the *tiburio*,—the central turret over the cupola of the temple. Leonardo da Vinci was of their number. He had offered his project, but the members of the Council had rejected it as too daring, unusual, and latitudinarian, inconsistent with the traditions of church architecture. They disputed, nor could come to any agreement. Some asserted that the interior pillars were not sufficiently firm. "If," they maintained, "the *tiburio* and other towers were now ready, then the structure would soon collapse, inasmuch as the erection has been begun by ignorami." According to the opinion of others, the Cathedral would stand through eternity. Leonardo, according to his wont, stood at one side, solitary and silent, without taking part in the dispute.

One of the workmen approached and handed him a letter.

"Messer, a mounted messenger from Pavia awaits your worship below on the piazza."

The artist unsealed the letter and read:

> Leonardo, come quickly—I must see thee,
> DUKE GIAN GALEAZZO.
> October 14th.

He made his excuses to the members of the Council, descended to the piazza, mounted, and set out for the Castello di Pavia,—a castle at a few hours' ride from Milan.

V

THE chestnuts, elms, and maples of the enormous park glowed in the sun with the gold and purple of autumn. Fluttering, like butterflies, the dead leaves fell. No water rose and fell in the fountains grown over with grass; the asters were wilting in the neglected flower-beds.

As he drew near the castle, Leonardo caught sight of a dwarf,—the old jester of Gian Galeazzo, who had remained faithful to his master when all the other servants had abandoned the dying Duke. Recognizing Leonardo, hobbling and hopping, the dwarf ran to meet him.

"How is the Duke's health?" asked the artist.

The other made no answer, save for a hopeless gesture with his hand. Leonardo was about to walk up the main garden-path.

"Nay, nay, not that way!" the dwarf stopped him. "They can see you here. His Excellence requested that it be in secret. . . . For if the Duchess Isabella were to find out, she might e'en hinder you. We had best go in a roundabout way, by the little side path. . . ."

Entering the corner turret, they ascended some stairs and passed several sombre chambers which must at one time have been magnificent but now uninhabitable. The hangings of Cordovan leather, gold-pressed, were torn down from the walls; the ducal seat under a canopy of silks was woven over with cobwebs. Through the windows with broken glass the wind of the autumn nights had carried in yellow leaves from the park.

"The miscreants, the robbers!" muttered the dwarf under his nose, indicating the traces of neglect to his companion. "Would you believe it, my eyes would fain not look on what is being wrought here! I would run away to the end of the world, were it not for the Duke, whom there is none to look after, save me, an old monster. . . . This way, this way, an you please."

Opening the door, he admitted Leonardo into a stuffy, dark room permeated with the smell of medicines.

VI

The phlebotomy, in accordance with the precepts of the healing art, was performed by candle-light, with closed shutters. The barber's assistant held the brazen basin into which the blood ran. The tonsorialist himself—a modest little ancient, with his sleeves rolled back,—performed the incision of the vein. The leech, "Master of Physicks," with a profoundly grave face, in spectacles, with a doctor's cape of dark-lilac velvet lined with squirrel-fur, without participating in the work of the barber,—touching the instruments of chirurgery was deemed debasing to the dignity of a leech,—was merely a spectator.

"Before night please phlebotomize anew," said he, commandingly, after the arm had been bandaged, and the invalid had been placed on the pillows.

"*Domine magister*," answered the tonsor, respectfully and timidly, "would it not be better to wait,—lest the loss of blood prove excessive? . . ."

The leech looked at him with a contemptuous smile.

"Shame on you, my dear fellow! 'Tis time for you to know that out of the four and twenty pounds of blood in the human body, twenty can be let out, without any danger to life and health. The more corrupted water you take out of a well, the more of the fresh is left. I have let blood from infants at the breast, without compunction, and thanks to God, it always helped."

Leonardo, listening to this conversation attentively, wanted to contradict, but reflected that arguing with leeches was just as bootless as arguing with alchemists.

The doctor and the barber withdrew. The dwarf adjusted the pillows, and tucked the blanket about the invalid's feet. Leonardo looked around the room. Over the bed hung a cage with a little green parrakeet. On a little round table were scattered cards and dice; a glass vessel, filled with water, with gold-fish therein, also stood upon it. At the feet of the Duke slept a little white dog, curled up. All these were the last amusements, which the faithful servant devised for the diversion of his master.

"Hast thou sent the letter off?" murmured the Duke, without opening his eyes.

"Ah, Your Excellency," the dwarf began to bustle, "why, we are biding your pleasure, thinking you asleep. For Messer Leonardo is here . . ."

"Here?"

The invalid with a smile of joy made an effort to raise himself up.

"Master, at last! I was afraid thou wouldst not come. . . ."

He took the artist by the hand, and the splendid, altogether young face of Gian Galeazzo—he was but twenty-four,—became animated with a pallid flush. The dwarf left the room, in order to guard the door.

"My friend," the invalid continued, "thou hast heard, of course? . . ."

"What, Your Excellency?"

"Thou dost not know? Well, if it be so, then there is no need of even recalling it. However, I shall tell thee,—so be it; we shall have a laugh over it together. They do say . . ."

He paused, looked straight into Leonardo's eyes and concluded with a quiet smile:

"They say that thou art—my murderer."

Leonardo thought that the sick man was in delirium.

"Yes, yes, what madness,—is it not so? Thou,—my murderer! . . ." repeated the Duke. "Three weeks ago, my Uncle Moro and Beatrice sent me a basket of peaches as a present. Madonna Isabella is confident that since my tasting those fruits I have grown worse; that I am dying from slow poison; and that, 'twould seem, thou hast a certain tree in thy garden. . . ."

"'Tis true," uttered Leonardo, "I have such a tree."

"Whatever art thou saying? . . . Can it be possible? . . ."

"Nay, God hath saved me,—if the fruits be really from my garden. Now I can understand whence these rumours sprang,—investigating the action of poisons, I wanted to envenom a peach tree. I told my pupil, Zoroastro da Peretola, that the peaches were poisoned. But the experiment did not succeed,—the fruits are harmless. Probably, my pupil was hasty and imparted the idea to someone. . . ."

"I knew 'twas so!" exclaimed the Duke joyously. "None is guilty of my death! But in the meanwhile they all suspect, hate, and fear one another. . . . Oh, if it were but possible to inform them all, even as simply as you and I are speaking now! My uncle deems himself my murderer, yet I know that he is kind, but weak and timorous. Wherefore, then, should he seek to slay me? I myself am ready to give my sovereignty over to him. I have no need of anything. . . . I would have gone away from all, living in freedom, in retirement, with my friends. I would have turned monk or become thy pupil, Leonardo. But none wanted to believe that I really do not long for power. . . . And wherefore, my God,—wherefore have they done this? It is not I, but themselves, that they have poisoned with the innocent fruits of thy innocent tree,—poor, blind creatures! . . . I have hitherto thought myself miserable because I must die. But now I have comprehended everything, master. I no longer desire aught, or fear aught. I feel well, at peace, and as joyous as though on a sultry day I had cast off my dusty raiment and were entering pure, cool water. Oh, my friend, I cannot voice it,—but thou surely understandest whereof I speak? Thou thyself art of the same nature. . . ."

Leonardo, in silence, with a serene smile, pressed his hand.

"I knew," continued the sick man with still greater joy, "I knew that thou wouldst understand me. . . . Dost remember, thou hast told me on a time, that the contemplation of the eternal laws of mechanics, of natural necessity, teaches people a great humility and peacefulness? At that time I did not comprehend. But now, in my illness, in solitude, in delirium, how often have I recalled thee, thy face, thy voice, thy every word, master! Dost know,—it seems to me at times that by different ways thou and I have come to the same conclusion: thou, in life; I, in death. . . ."

The doors opened; the dwarf ran in with a frightened face and announced:

"Monna Druda!"

Leonardo was about to go away, but the Duke held him back. Into the room entered the old nurse of Gian Galeazzo, holding a small vial with a yellowish turbid liquid,—scorpion ointment. In the middle of summer, when the sun is in conjunction with Sirius, the dog-star,—during the dog-days,—the scorpions were caught, immersed alive in olive oil a century old, with staurolite, mithridate, and serpentine; the mixture was infused in the sun for the duration of fifty days; it was smeared every day into the patient's armpits, over his temples, belly, and on the breast, in the vicinity of the heart. Old women knowing in leechcraft affirmed that there was no better remedy not only against all poisons, but also against witchcraft, bewitchment, and evil spells.

The crone, seeing Leonardo, who was sitting on the edge of the bed, stopped short, turned pale, and her hands began shaking so that she almost let the vial drop.

"The power of the Lord be with us! . . . Most Holy Mother of God! . . ."

Crossing herself, mumbling prayers, she backed toward the door, and, having made her way out, started running with all the haste her old legs would allow to her mistress, Madonna Isabella, to impart to her the dreadful news.

Monna Druda was convinced that the evil-doer Moro and his tool Leonardo had done away with the Duke, if not by poison then by the evil eye, by spells, by working on an effigy, or by some other fiendish charms.

The Duchess was praying in the oratory, kneeling before a holy image. When Monna Druda had informed her that Leonardo was with the Duke, she jumped up and exclaimed:

"It can not be! Who let him in? . . ."

"Who let him in?" the old woman mumbled, shaking her head.

"Would you believe, Your Excellency, I rack my mind in vain to think whence he bobbed up from, the accursed one! 'Tis as if he had sprung up from the earth, or flown in through a chimney,—the Lord forgive us! 'Tis an ill affair, to be sure. I have long since been telling Your Excellency. . . ."

A page entered the oratory and respectfully bent his knee:

"Most Illustrious Madonna, will it please you and your spouse to receive His Majesty, the Most Christian King of France?"

VII

CHARLES VIII was stopping in the lower chambers of the Castle of Pavia, luxuriously fitted out for him by the Duke Ludovico Moro.

Resting after the dinner, the king listened to the reading of a rather illiterate work,—*The Wonders of the City of Rome*,—*Mirabilia Urbis Romæ*—translated shortly before from the Latin into French by his command.

Charles, a solitary, sickly child, made timid by his father, passing dreary years in the desolate Castle of Amboise, had been brought up on romances of chivalry, which had completely turned his head, already weak enough without that. Finding himself on the throne of France, and having imagined himself the hero of legendary exploits on the manner of those told of the Knights Errant of the Table Round, of Launcelot and Tristram, the lad of twenty, inexperienced and shy, kindly and full of crotchets, had gotten it into his head to carry out in reality that which he had read out of books. "Son of the God Mars, Scion of Julius Cæsar," to use the terms of the court chroniclers, he had descended upon Lombardy at the head of an enormous army, for the conquest of Naples, Sicily, Constantinople, Jerusalem; for the overthrow of the Great Turk, the complete extirpation of the Mahomedan heresy, and the liberation of the Sepulchre of Our Lord from the yoke of the infidels.

Listening to the *Wonders of the City of Rome* with simple-hearted trust, the king tasted beforehand the glory he would acquire by vanquishing such a great city. His thoughts were confused. He felt a pain in the pit of his stomach, and his head felt heavy, all from yesterday's exceedingly merry supper with the ladies of Milan. The face of one of them, Lucrezia Crivelli, had appeared to him in his dreams all night long.

FIVE · Leonardo da Vinci

Charles VIII was small of stature and hideous of face. He was bandy-legged and spindle-shanked; he had narrow shoulders, one higher than the other; a sunken chest; an enormously hooked nose; thin hair, of a pallid red; a strange yellowish down instead of moustache and beard; his face and hands betrayed a nervous tic. His thick lips, constantly open, as with little children, his up-turned eyebrows, his huge, whitish and myopic eyes, bulging out, all gave him an expression of despondence, absent-mindedness, and, at the same time, of straining,—such an expression as one finds in persons of weak mentality. His speech was indistinct and disjointed. There were tales to the effect that the King had been born with six toes, and that, in order to conceal this, he had introduced at the court the hideous fashion of rounded soft slippers of black velvet, resembling horses' hoofs.

"Thibaud, eh, Thibaud?" he addressed the court *valet de chambre*, interrupting the reading, with his customary air of absent-mindedness, stammering and at a loss for the necessary words; "I, dear fellow, now . . . Methinks I would drink. . . . Eh? . . . Is it heart-burn, now, or what? . . . Do fetch some wine, Thibaud. . . ."

Cardinal Brissonet entered and announced that the Duke awaited the King's pleasure.

"Eh? Eh? What is it? . . . The Duke? . . . Well, right away. I will but take a drink. . . ."

Charles took the goblet proffered by a courtier.

Brissonet stopped the King and asked Thibaud:

"Ours?"

"*Non*, Monseigneur,—from a local cellar. Ours is all exhausted."

The cardinal threw out the wine.

"Forgive me, Your Majesty. The local wines may be injurious to your health. Thibaud, order the cup-bearer to run over to the camp and fetch a small cask from the field-cellar."

"Wherefore? Eh? What is it? . . ." mumbled the King, uncomprehending.

The cardinal whispered in his ear that he was afraid of poisoning, inasmuch as one might expect any treachery from people who had done to death their own lawful sovereign; and, although there were no visible proofs, caution was not amiss.

"Eh, nonsense! Why so? I would drink," said Charles, shrugging one shoulder with vexation, but submitting.

The heralds ran on ahead. Four pages lifted over the King a magnificent baldaquin of blue silk, worked with the silver lilies of France; the seneschal threw over his shoulders a mantle with ermine edging, with bees of gold embroidered on red velvet and the knightly device: The King of the Bees hath no Sting,—*le roi des abeilles n'a pas d'aiguillon;* and through the sombre, neglected chambers of the Castle of Pavia, the procession set out for the dying man's room.

Going past the oratory, Charles beheld the Duchess. He doffed his *berretta* respectfully, desiring to approach, and, in accordance with the anciently ordained custom of France, to kiss the lady's lips, styling her "Beloved Little Sister." But the Duchess approached him herself and cast herself down at his feet.

"Sire," she began the previously prepared speech, "take pity upon us! God shall reward thee. Protect the innocent, O magnanimous knight! Moro hath taken all from us, hath usurped our throne, hath poisoned my spouse, the lawful Duke of Milan, Gian Galeazzo. In our own house are we surrounded with assassins. . . ."

Charles understood but ill and scarcely listened to what she was saying.

"Eh? Eh? What is it?" he babbled, as though half-awake, nervously jerking one shoulder and stammering. "Well, well,—there is no need of that. . . . I beg of you. . . . There is really no need of that, little sister. . . . Arise, arise!"

But rise she would not, catching his hands and kissing them; she wanted to embrace his knees, and, finally, bursting into tears, exclaimed with unsimulated despair:

"If you, too, abandon me, Sire, I shall lay hands on myself! . . ."

The King lost his head entirely, and his face puckered up painfully, as though he himself were ready to burst out crying.

"There, there, now! . . . My God. . . . I can not. . . . Brissonet. . . . If you please. . . . I do not know. . . . Tell her. . . ."

He longed to run away; she aroused no compassion in him whatsoever, inasmuch as even in her very abasement, in her despair, she was too haughty and beauteous, resembling a grandiose heroine of tragedy.

"*Madonna illustrissima,* calm yourself. His Majesty will do all that is possible for you and your spouse, Messer Jean Galeasseau," said the cardinal, in a manner polite and chill, with a shade of patronage, pronouncing the Duke's name in the French manner.

The Duchess turned around to look at the cardinal, looked the King intently in the face, and abruptly, as though but now comprehending with whom she was speaking, grew silent. Misshapen, laughable and pitiful, he stood before her with his thick lips gaping, like a little child's, with a meaningless, strained and confused smile, his enormous whitish eyes bulging out.

"I,—at the feet of this marasmus, this half-wit; I, the granddaughter of Ferdinand of Aragon!"

She arose; her pallid cheeks flared up. The King felt that the occasion demanded some utterance, some way out of this oppressive silence. He made a desperate effort, took to jerking his shoulder and blinking his eyes, and, having babbled out only his usual: "Eh? Eh? What is it?" began to stammer, made a hopeless gesture with his hand, and fell silent. The Duchess measured him with her eyes in unconcealed disdain. Charles lowered his head.

"Brissonet, let us go, let us go. . . . What say you? . . . Eh? . . ."

When the pages had flung the doors open, Charles entered the sick man's room. The shutters were open. The serene light of the autumn evening fell in the window across the tall aureate summits of the trees in the park. The King approached the invalid's couch, calling him "Dear Cousin,"—*mon cousin*,—and enquired about his health. Gian Galeazzo replied with such a cordial smile that Charles at once began to feel better; his confusion passed, and little by little he regained his composure.

"Sire, may the Lord send victory to Your Majesty!" said the Duke, among other things. "When you shall be in Jerusalem, at the Sepulchre of Our Lord, say a prayer for my poor soul also, for toward that time I . . ."

"Ah, nay, nay, cousin, how can that be? Wherefore say you this?" the King interrupted him. "God is merciful. You and I shall yet take the field together, and war with the impious Turk,—mark my word, now! Eh? What? . . ."

Gian Galeazzo shook his head:

"Nay, 'tis no longer possible for me."

And, having looked straight into the eyes of the King with a deep, searching gaze, he added:

"When I shall die, Sire, forsake not my boy, Francesco, and also Isabella; she is unhappy,—for she hath no one in this world. . . ."

"Oh, Lord, Lord!" exclaimed Charles with unexpected, violent agitation; his thick lips quivered, their corners drooped, and, as though with a sudden inner light, his face was illumined by an extraordinary kindliness.

He quickly bent over the sick man, and, embracing him with impulsive tenderness, lisped out:

"Dearest cousin of mine! . . . My poor fellow,—oh, so poor! . . ."

They smiled to one another, like pitiful sick children,—and their lips were joined in a brotherly kiss.

Having come out of the Duke's room, the King beckoned for the cardinal to approach.

"Brissonet, eh, Brissonet. . . . Dost know, we must somehow . . . now . . . intercede with our protection. . . . It must not be so,—it must not. . . . I am a knight. . . . They must be protected. . . . Dost hear?"

"Your Majesty," answered the Cardinal evasively, "he is bound to die anyway. Besides, of what help could we be? We shall only wreak harm to ourselves,—Duke Moro is our ally. . . ."

"Duke Moro is a miscreant, no more, no less,—yes, a murderer!" exclaimed the King, and his eyes flashed with a reasoning wrath.

"What is to be done, then?" asked the Cardinal, with a refined, condescending smile, shrugging his shoulders. "Duke Moro is neither better nor worse than the others. Politics, my Liege Lord! We are all human. . . ."

The cup-bearer brought up to the King a goblet of French wine. Charles drained it avidly. The wine animated him and put to rout his sombre thoughts. Together with the cup-bearer entered one of Moro's grandees with an invitation to supper. The King declined. The envoy implored; but, seeing that his requests had no effect, he walked up to Thibaud, and whispered something in his ear. The latter nodded his head as a sign of assent, and, in his turn, whispered to the King:

"Your Majesty, Madonna Lucrezia. . . ."

"Eh? What? What is it? . . . What Lucrezia?"

"The same with whom you were pleased to dance at yesterday's ball."

"Ah, yes, of course, of course. . . . I remember. . . . Madonna Lucrezia. . . . A most pretty little thing! . . . She will be at the supper, thou sayest?"

"She positively will, and imploreth Your Majesty. . . ."

"She imploreth. . . . So that is how things stand! Well, then, Thibaud? Eh? How thinkest thou? I might, of course. . . . 'Tis all one. . . . Come what may! . . . To-morrow we take to the field. . . . This will be the last time. . . . Thank the Duke, messer," he turned to the envoy, "and say that I, now . . . eh? . . . why not? . . ."

The King led Thibaud to one side:

"Listen, who is this Madonna Lucrezia?"

"Moro's mistress, Your Majesty."

"Moro's mistress,—so that is how things stand! 'Tis a pity. . . ."

"Sire, but one little word,—and we shall arrange everything in an instant. To-day, an it please you."

"Nay, nay! How is it possible? . . . I am a guest. . . ."

"Moro will be flattered, Liege Lord. You know not the manikins hereabouts. . . ."

"Well, it is all one, it is all one. As thou wilt. 'Tis thy affair. . . ."

"Do you be assured, Your Majesty. But one little word. . . ."

"Ask not. . . . I like it not. . . . I told thee,—'tis thy affair. . . . I know naught. . . . As thou wilt. . . ."

Thibaud, silently, made a low obeisance.

Descending the staircase, the King again frowned and with a helpless effort of thought rubbed his forehead:

"Brissonet, eh, Brissonet. . . . How thinkest thou? . . . What was it I wanted to say, now? . . . Ah, yes, yes. . . . To intercede. . . . An innocent man. . . . A grievous wrong. . . . Such things must not be. I am a knight!"

"Sire, leave this care,—we have no time for that now. Better later, when we shall return from the campaign, having vanquished the Turks, having conquered Jerusalem."

"Aye, aye, Jerusalem! . . ." muttered the King, and his eyes grew wider; on his lips appeared a pallid, vague and, dreamy smile.

"The hand of the Lord leads Your Majesty to victories," continued Brissonet, "the finger of God points the way to the crusading army."

"The finger of God! The finger of God!" Charles VIII repeated solemnly, lifting his eyes up to heaven.

VIII

EIGHT days later the young Duke expired.

Before death he implored his wife for an interview with Leonardo.

She denied him this,—Monna Druda had convinced Isabella that those bewitched always experience an insuperable and fatal desire to behold the one who had cast the spell upon them. The old crone zealously smeared the invalid with the scorpion ointment; the leeches tortured him to the last with their phlebotomizations.

He died peacefully.

"Thy will be done!" were his last words.

Moro ordered the body of the deceased to be carried over from Pavia to Milan, and to be laid in state in the Cathedral.

The grandees gathered in the castle at Milan. Ludovico, asserting that the untimely death of his nephew was causing him unbelievable grief, proposed that the legitimate heir to the throne, little Francesco, son of Gian Galeazzo, be proclaimed Duke. All opposed this, and, asserting that such great power ought not to be entrusted to one not yet of age, in the name of the people begged Moro to accept the ducal sceptre. Hypocritically, he refused; finally, seemingly against his will, he gave in to their supplications.

A splendid raiment of cloth of gold was brought; the new Duke donned it, mounted a steed, and set out for the church of Sant' Ambrogio, surrounded by a horde of adherents, rending the air with their cries of: "Long live Moro, long live the Duke!"—to the sound of trumpets, cannon-shots, the ringing of bells,—and amid the silence of the people.

On the Piazza of Commerce, from the Loggia degli Osii, on the south side of the castellar Town Hall, in the presence of the elders, consuls, eminent burghers, and syndics, the *Privilege* granted to Duke Moro by the Perpetual August of the Holy Roman Empire, Maximilian, was read out by a herald:

"*Maximilianus divina favente clementia Romanorum Rex semper Augustus*—all domains, lands, cities, hamlets, castles and fortresses, mountains, pasture-lands and plains, forests, meadows, waste-lands, rivers, lakes, hunting grounds, fishing ponds, salt-marshes, ores, the possessions of vassals, marquises, counts, barons; monasteries, churches, parishes,—all and several do We grant to thee, Ludovico Sforza, and to thy heirs; We affirm, designate, elevate, and choose thee and thy sons, and thy grandsons, and thy great-grandsons, to be the sovereign rulers of Lombardy to the end of time."

After several days announcement was made of the solemn transfer to the Cathedral of Milan's greatest relic,—one of the nails wherewith the Lord had been crucified.

Moro had hopes of pleasing the people, and strengthening his power through this festival.

IX

At night, on the Piazza Arengo, a crowd gathered in front of Tibaldo's wine-cellar. Here were present Scarabullo the tinker, Mascarello the embroiderer in gold, Maso the skin-dresser, the cobbler Còrbollo, and the glass-blower Gorgoglio. In the midst of the crowd, standing on a cask, Fra Timoteo the Dominican was holding forth:

"Brethren, when St. Helena, under the idol temple of the goddess Venus, did obtain the life-bearing Wood of the Cross and the other instruments of the Lord's Passion, buried in the ground by pagans,—the Emperor Constantine, taking a single one of these most holy and awesome Nails, did order his smiths to fasten it within the bridle-bit of his war-steed, that the words of the Prophet Zechariah might be fulfilled: 'In that day shall there be upon the bells of the horses, HOLINESS UNTO THE LORD.'[11] And this ineffable holiness did bestow upon him victory over the foes and adversaries of the Roman Empire. After the death of the Cæsar the Nail was lost, and a long while later found by the great prelate, Ambrogio of Mediolanum, in the city of Rome, in the shop of a certain Paolino, a dealer in old iron; 'twas carried off to Milan, and since that time has our city been in possession of the Most Precious and Most Holy of Nails,—the one wherewith was transpierced the right palm of the Almighty God on the Tree of Salvation. Five inches and a half is the exact measure of the length of this Nail. Being longer and thicker than the Nail at Rome, it hath also a sharp point, whereas the one at Rome is blunted. For the duration of three hours was this our Nail in the palm of the Saviour, as is proven by the learned padre Alexio by many most refined syllogisms."

Fra Timoteo paused for an instant, then exclaimed in a loud voice, raising his arms up to heaven:

"But now, my beloved ones, a great dissoluteness is being wrought: Moro, the miscreant, the murderer, the usurper of the throne, tempteth the people with godless festivals, and doth use the Most Holy Nails but to prop up his tottering throne!"

The crowd began to buzz.

"And know ye, my brethren," continued the monk, "to whom he hath entrusted the construction of a machine for the elevation of the Nail to the main cupola of the Cathedral, over the altar?"

"To whom?"

"To the Florentine, Leonardo da Vinci!"

"Leonardo? Who is he?" asked some.

"We know," they were answered by others, "the very same that hath poisoned the young Duke with fruits. . . ."

"A sorcerer, a heretic, an atheist!"

"But then, maties, how is it I have heard," Còrbollo timidly interceded, "that this Messer Leonardo seems a kindly man? He doth harm to none, and is good not only to men, but to every creature. . . ."

"Be still, Còrbollo! What art thou jabbering nonsense for?"

"Why, how can a sorcerer be good?"

"Oh, my children," Fra Timoteo expounded, "in the time to come people will say also of the Great Seducer, of Him that Cometh in Darkness: 'He is good, he is benevolent, he is perfect,' inasmuch as his face shall be like unto the face of Christ, and he will be given a voice persuasive, delectable, like the sound of a reed-pipe. And many shall he corrupt with his cunning mercifulness. And he shall summon together from the four winds of heaven tribes and peoples, even as a partridge calls to her nest with a deceitful call a brood from another nest. Be ye vigilant, therefore, my brethren! This angel of darkness, the prince of this world, called Antichrist, shall come in human shape: the Florentine Leonardo is a servant and a forerunner of Antichrist!"

The glass-blower Gorgoglio, who had never hitherto heard anything about Leonardo, uttered with conviction:

"'Tis verily so! He hath sold his soul to the Devil, and signed the compact with blood."

"Most Pure Mother, defend thou us and have mercy!" whimpered the huckstress Barbaccia. "The wench Stamma was saying but the other day,—she is a scullion with the hangman at the gaol,—that this same Leonardo, it seems—though one shouldn't name him toward nightfall,—thieves dead bodies from the gallows, cuts them up with knives, disembowels them, pulls their guts out. . . ."

"Well, that is a matter beyond thy mind, Barbaccia," Còrbollo remarked ostentatiously, "this is a science, styled anatomy. . . ."

"He has invented a machine, they say, that he might fly on birds' wings," the gold-embroiderer Mascarello volunteered the information.

"The winged serpent Beliar of old is rising up against God," Fra

Timoteo explained again. "Simon the Magus also did rise up into the air, but was cast down by the Apostle Paul."

"He walks over the sea as over dry land," announced Scarabullo. "'Our Lord, now, did walk upon the water, and I shall walk also!'—that is how he blasphemes."

"He goes down to the bottom of the sea in a glass bell," added Maso the skin-dresser.

"Eh, maties, believe it not! What need hath he of a bell? He turneth into a fish, and swims; he turneth into a bird, and flies!" decided Gorgoglio.

"Look ye, what an accursed warlock it is,—may he drop dead!"

"And wherever are the eyes of the Fathers Inquisitors? To the burning stake with him, now!"

"An aspen stake ought to be driven down his throat!"

"Alas, alas! Woe to us, my beloved ones!" Fra Timoteo again raised up his voice. "The Most Holy Nail,—the Most Holy Nail,—in the hands of Leonardo!"

"It shall never be!" Scarabullo commenced to yell, clinching his fists. "We shall die, rather than give up holy things to profanation. We shall take the Nail away from the atheist!"

"Let us avenge the Nail! Let us avenge the murdered Duke!"

"Whither are ye bound, maties?" the cobbler wrung his hands. "The night watch will be making their round right away. The Captain of the Giustizia . . ."

"To the devil with the Captain of the Giustizia! Get under thy wife's petticoat, Còrbollo, if thou art afraid!"

Armed with sticks, stakes, axes and stones, yelling and cursing, the crowd surged through the streets. At its head walked the monk, a crucifix in his hands, and chanted a psalm:

"Let God arise, let his enemies be scattered: let them also that hate him flee before him. As smoke is driven away, so drive them away: as wax melteth before the fire, so let the wicked perish at the presence of God." [12]

The pitch links smoked and crackled. In their dark-red reflection the inverted sickle of the solitary moon grew pallid. The serene stars glimmered.

X

LEONARDO was working in his atelier on the machine for the elevation of the Most Holy Nail. Zoroastro was making a round case with panes and golden rays, in which the sacred relic was to be kept. In a dark corner Giovanni Beltraffio was seated, at rare intervals glancing at the master.

Plunged in his study of the problem of transmission of power by means of blocks and levers, Leonardo had forgotten the machine. He had just finished the complicated calculation. The inner necessity of nature, *i.e.*, the law of mathematics, justified the outer necessity of reason, *i.e.*, the law of mechanics: two great secrets blended into a single one, and a still greater.

"Never will men invent," he reflected, with a quiet smile, "anything still simpler or more beautiful than a manifestation of nature. Divine necessity by its laws compels the effect to flow out of the cause by the shortest path."

In his soul was that familiar emotion of reverent amazement before the abyss into which he was peering,—an emotion which has no similarity with any of the other emotions within the ken of man. On the margins, alongside of the plan for the machine for elevating the Most Holy Nail, alongside of the figures and calculations, he wrote down the words which resounded in his heart like a prayer:

"O, Thy wondrous justice, Thou First Mover! Thou didst not desire to deprive any force of the order and ability of its necessary actions; inasmuch as, if it be supposed to move a body for an hundred ells, and it meet an obstacle in its path, Thou hast ordained that the force of the blow produce new motion, receiving as compensation for the untraversed distance divers jolts and shocks,—oh, Thy divine necessity, Thou First Mover!"

A loud knocking resounded at the outer door, together with the chanting of psalms, the cursing and outcries of an infuriated mob. Giovanni and Zoroastro ran down to see what the matter was.

Maturina, the cook, who had but this moment jumped out of bed, half-dressed, dishevelled, darted into the room, yelling:

"Robbers! Robbers! Help! Most Holy Mother, have mercy upon us!"

Marco d'Oggione came in, with arquebus in hand, and hurriedly locked the shutters on the windows.

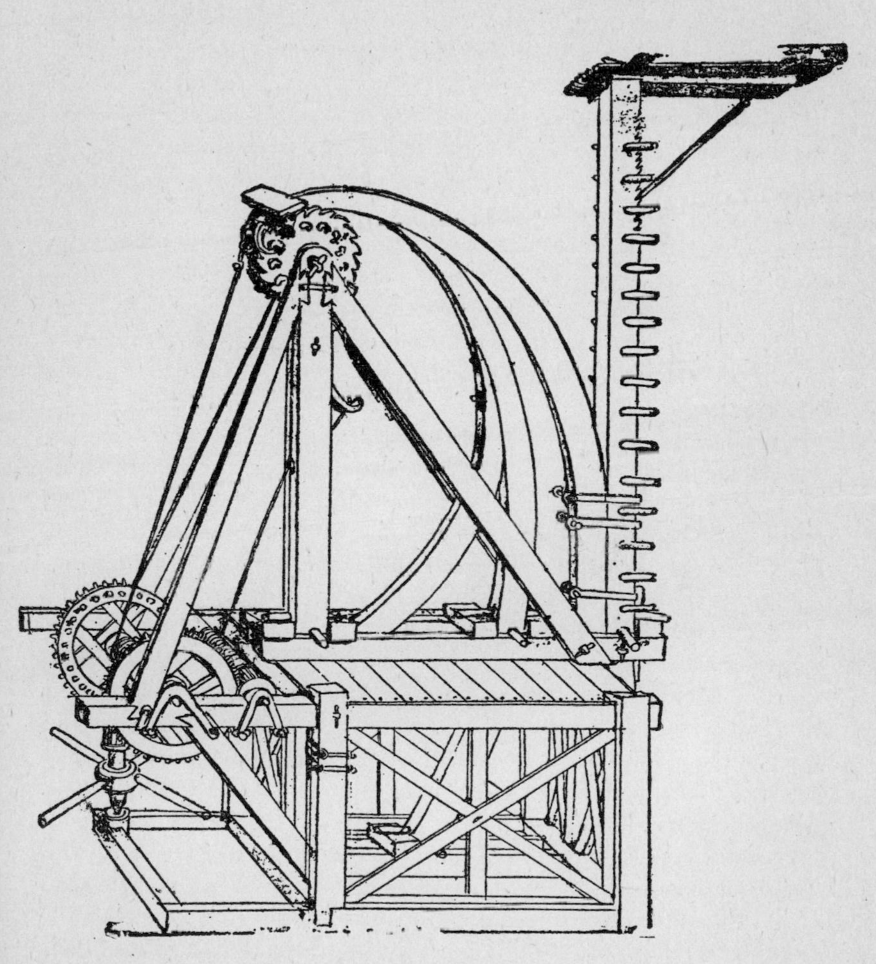

"What is it, Marco?" inquired Leonardo.

"I know not. Some scoundrels or other are breaking into the house. Probably the monks have stirred up the rabble."

"What is it they want?"

"The devil only can make them out, the half-witted scum! They demand the Most Holy Nail."

"I have it not,—it is in the sacristy of the Archbishop Archimboldo."

"That is the very thing I tell them, but they will not listen, and carry on as though they were possessed. They call Your Grace the poisoner of the Duke Gian Galeazzo; a wizard, and an atheist."

The shouts out in the street were gaining in power:

"Open! Open! Or we shall burn your damned nest down! Bide a while, we shall get at thy hide, Leonardo, thou accursed Antichrist!"

" 'Let God arise, let his enemies be scattered!' " proclaimed Fra Timoteo, and with his chanting was mingled the piercing whistle of the mischief-maker Farfanicchio.

Into the room ran the little servant Giacopo; he sprang up on the window-ledge, and would have jumped out into the yard, had not Leonardo held him back by the hem of his garment.

"Whither art thou bound?"

"For the *berrovieri*,—the guard of the Captain of the Giustizia passes at a short distance from here at this time."

"What art thou saying? God be with thee, Giacopo,—thou shalt be caught and killed."

"They'll never catch me! I shall get over the wall into Aunt Trulla's truck-garden, then into the ditch with the burdocks, and then through back ways. . . . And even if they kill me, 'tis better that it be me!"

Looking back at Leonardo with a tender and brave smile, the boy tore himself out of his hands, jumped out of the window, called from the yard: "I shall deliver you, never fear!" and clapped the shutter to.

"A mischief-maker, a little imp," Maturina shook her head, "and yet he came in handy in an evil plight."

There came the tinkling of broken glass from one of the upper windows. The cook emitted a piteous cry, wrung her hands, ran out of the room, felt in the dark for the steep ladder to the cellar, rolled down it, and, as she subsequently retold it herself, crawled into an empty wine-cask, where she would have sat right through till morning, had she not been dragged out.

Marco ran upstairs to lock up the shutters.

Giovanni returned into the workroom, was about to sit down again in his corner, with a face pale, downcast, and indifferent to everything; but, after a look at Leonardo, he approached and suddenly fell down on his knees before him.

"What is the matter with thee? What preys upon thee, Giovanni?"

"They say, master. . . . I know it is not true. . . . I do not believe it. . . . But tell me . . . for God's sake, tell me yourself! . . ."

And he could not finish, gasping from emotion.

"Thou hast thy doubts," Leonardo said with a sad smile, "whether they tell the truth in saying I am a murderer?"

"One word, but one word, master, from your lips! . . ."

"What can I tell thee, my friend? And wherein would be the use? Thou wouldst not believe, anyway. . . ."

"Oh, Messer Leonardo!" exclaimed Giovanni. "I have become so tortured,—unto exhaustion; I know not what is the matter with me. . . . I am going out of my mind, master. . . . Help me! Have pity! I can no longer bear it. . . . Say that it is not true! . . ."

Leonardo kept silent. Then, turning away, he uttered in a voice that shook:

"And thou, too, art with them; and thou, too, art against me! . . ."

There came the sound of such blows as made the whole house tremble: the tinker Scarabullo was chopping the door down with an axe. Leonardo hearkened closely to the screams of the rabble, and his heart contracted from a familiar quiet melancholy, from a feeling of an illimitable loneliness. He let his head drop,—and his eyes fell upon the lines he had just written down:

"O, Thy wondrous justice, Thou First Mover!"

"So," he reflected, "all good, all things, come from Thee!"

He smiled, and with great resignation repeated the words of the dying Duke Galeazzo:

"Thy will be done on earth as it is in heaven."

BOOK SIX

The Diary of Giovanni Beltraffio

N THE 25TH OF MARCH, IN THE YEAR 1494, I became a pupil of the Florentine master, Leonardo da Vinci.

Here is the curriculum: perspective, the dimensions and proportions of the human body; drawing after the examples of good masters; drawing from nature.

* * *

To-day my comrade Marco d'Oggione gave me a book on perspective, written down from the words of the master. It beginneth thus: "The light of the sun gives its greatest joy to the body; the clarity of mathematical verity gives its greatest joy to the spirit. That is why the science of perspective (in which the contemplation of the radiant line,—the greatest joyance to the eyes, is joined with the clarity of mathematics,—the greatest joyance of the mind) must be preferred to all the rest of human researches and sciences. Therefore, may He who hath said of Himself: 'I am the light of the world'[13] enlighten me, and may He also help me to expound the science of perspective, the Science of Light. And I divide this book into three parts,—the First: of the diminution in the distance of the size of objects; the Second: of the diminution of the distinctness of colours; the Third: of the diminution of the distinctness of outlines."

* * *

The master is as concerned in me as though I were one of his kin: having found out that I am poor, he did not want to accept the monthly stipend.

* * *

The master has said:

"When thou shalt master perspective, and shalt know by heart the proportions of the human body, observe diligently during thy strolls the movements of people,—how they stand and walk, how they talk and argue, laugh and fight; what their faces are on such occasions, as well as the faces of those spectators who would separate them, and of those who are silent standers-by; mark all this off and draw it, in pencil, as soon as possible, in a small book of coloured paper, which thou shouldst have inseparably by thee; but when it shall be full, replace it with another, while the old one thou shouldst put away and preserve. Remember, that these old drawings should not be destroyed nor rubbed out, but treasured, for the motions of bodies are so endless in nature, that no human memory is able to retain them. Therefore do thou look upon these rough sketches as thy best preceptors and teachers."

I have begun such a book for myself and every evening I write in it the memorable words of the master that I may have heard during the course of the day.

* * *

To-day, in the alley of the rag-wives, not far from the Cathedral, I met my uncle, Oswald Ingrim, the master glazier. He told me that he disowns me, that I have sent my soul to perdition, having taken up my domicile in the house of Leonardo, the atheist and the heretic. Now am I absolutely alone,—I have none near or dear in the world,—nor relatives, nor friends,—none save the master. I repeat the splendid prayer of the master: "May the Lord, the Light of the Universe, enlighten me, and may He help me to master perspective, the science of His light." Can these be the words of an atheist?

* * *

No matter how oppressed I may feel, I have but to glance at his face,—and my soul grows lighter and more joyous. What eyes he hath,—clear, pale-blue, and cold, like ice; what a quiet, pleasant voice, what a smile! The most malevolent, obstinate of people can not resist his ingratiating words, whether he wants to influence them *pro* or *con*. I frequently gaze at him for long, as he sits at his work-table, plunged in meditation, and with an accustomed, leisurely movement runs his slender fingers through his aureate beard and smooths it,—'tis as twining and soft as the silk of a maiden's curls. When conversing with anyone, he usually puckers up one eye, with a somewhat sly, mischievously mocking and good-natured expression; on such occasions the gaze from underneath his thick, overhanging eyebrows seems to penetrate to one's very soul.

* * *

He is simple in his dress; he can not bear loud colours in attire, nor the new fashions; nor does he like perfumes of any sort. But his linen is always of fine Rhenish weave, always white, like snow. His *berretta* of black velvet is devoid of all ornaments, medals, or feathers. A-top a black short jacket he wears a dark-red cape of an ancient Florentine cut, falling in straight folds to the knee. His movements are stately and calm. Despite his modest garb, always, no matter where he be, among grandees or a crowd of common folk, his appearance is such that none can help but notice him,—he does not resemble anyone else.

* * *

All things can he do, he knows all things; he is an excellent marksman with the bow and the arbalest, an excellent horseman, swimmer, and master of fencing. On one occasion I saw him in a contest with the first strong men among the people; the game consisted of tossing up a small coin so that it touch the very centre of the cupola of the church they were in. Messer Leonardo vanquished all with his dexterity and strength.

He is left-handed. But with this left hand of his, in appearance as soft and slender as that of a young woman, he can bend iron horseshoes and twist the tongue of a brazen bell; yet, drawing the face of a beautiful girl with the very same hand, he applies transparent shades, in charcoal or pencil, with touches as light as the quiverings of a butterfly's wings.

* * *

To-day, after dinner, he was finishing a drawing depicting the drooping head of the Virgin Mary, hearkening to the glad tidings of the Archangel. From underneath her headband, ornamented with pearls and two wings of a dove, shyly fluttering in the breeze wafted from the angelic wings, locks of hair struggled out, braided after the fashion of the Florentine maids into a hairdress apparently negligent, but in reality done with great art. The beauty of these tendrillar locks captivates one like strange music. And the mystery of her eyes, that seem to shine through the lowered eyelids, with a dense shadow from the eyelashes, resembles the mystery of underwater flowers, seen through transparent waters, yet unattainable.

Suddenly the little servant Giacopo ran into the room, and, hopping and clapping his hands, began to shout:

"Monsters! Monsters! Messer Leonardo, go to the kitchen as fast as you can! I have brought you such little beauties as are bound to please you!"

"Where didst thou get them?" asked the master.

"From the porch of Sant' Ambrogio. Beggars out of Bergamo. I told them you would treat them to supper, if they would allow their portraits to be done."

"Let them wait a while. I shall finish this drawing right away."

"Nay, master, they will not wait: they are hurrying back to Bergamo before nightfall. Do but give a look, now,—you will ne'er regret it! 'Tis worth the while, truly, 'tis worth the while! You can not imagine what monstrosities these be!"

Abandoning the unfinished drawing of the Virgin Mary, the master went to the kitchen. I followed him. We saw two old men, brothers, sitting decorously on a bench,—corpulent, as if they were bloated with the dropsy, with the repulsive, pendulous swellings of enormous goitres on their necks,—a disorder common among the inhabitants of the Bergamo mountains; and the wife of one of them,—a wrinkled, spare little old crone, by the name of She-spider, and fully meriting her name.

Giacopo's face beamed with pride:

"There, now, you see," he whispered, "did I not tell you that they would please you! For I know what you want. . . ."

Leonardo sat down near them, ordered some wine to be given them, began to regale them, to question them amiably, to make them laugh with silly little stories. At first they were like creatures of the wild, looking askance, not understanding, probably, why they had been brought hither. But when he had told them the *novella* going the round of the piazzas,—about the dead Jew, cut up into little pieces by a co-religionist of his, in order to avoid the law forbidding the burial of Jews in the ground of the city of Bologna, and pickled in a barrel with honey and spices, sent off to Venice together with goods on a ship, and inadvertently eaten up by a certain Florentine traveller, a Christian,—the She-spider began to be overpowered with laughter. Soon all three, having grown tipsy, burst out laughing with repellent mannerisms. In confusion, I dropped my eyes and turned away, in order not to see. But Leonardo was looking at them with a profound, avid curiosity, like a man of science performing an experiment. When their hideousness had attained its apogee, he took paper and began drawing these abominable grotesques, with the very same pencil, and with the very same love, with which he had but a little while back been drawing the divine smile on the Virgin Mary.

In the evening he showed me a multitude of caricatures, not only of human beings, but of animals as well,—fearful faces, resembling those that haunt sick men in delirium, something of the human gleaming through the bestial; something of the bestial, through the human; each blending into the other easily and naturally, until one felt horror. I carried off in my memory the snout of a porcupine, with prickly bristling quills, with its nether lip pendent,—dangling, soft, and thin, like a rag, exposing the elongated white teeth, like almonds, in a vile human smile. Also, never shall I forget the face of a hag, with her hair pulled upward into a wild, insane arrangement, with a scanty little braid behind, with a gigantic bald brow, with a flattened-out nose, diminutive, like a wart, and with lips monstrously thick, reminding one of those flabby, slimy mushrooms that grow on rotten stumps. And the most horrible of all was the fact that these monsters seemed familiar, as though one had already seen them somewhere; there is also in them something seductive, which repels and at the same time draws one on, like an abyss. One looks, is horrified,—and can not take one's eyes off it, just as in the case of the divine smile of the Virgin Mary.

Both in the one case and in the other, one feels amazement, as before a miracle.

Cesare da Sesto tells how Leonardo, upon meeting somewhere in a crowd, on the street, a curious monster, is capable of tracking him for a whole day, like one enamoured, and of observing him, trying to memorize his face. Great hideousness in people, says the master, is just as rare and unusual as great beauty; only the mediocre is usual.

* * *

He has invented a strange means of remembering the faces of people. His premise is that people have three sorts of noses: either straight, or with a little hump, or with a little scoop. The straight ones can be either short or long, with tips obtuse or sharp. The hump is found either above, at the end, or in the middle of the nose,—and so on, for every portion of the face. All these innumerable subdivisions, species, kinds, marked off with figures, are entered in a specially ruled book. When the artist somewhere on his ramble meets a face which he wants to remember, all he has to do is to mark off with a small sign the corresponding species of nose, forehead, eyes, chin, and in this manner, by means of a row of figures, there is retained firmly in his mind a sort of instantaneous picture of the living face. At his leisure, upon returning home, he unites these parts into a single image.

He has also conceived the idea of a little spoon, for the impeccably exact, mathematical measurement of the quantity of colours needed to depict the gradual transitions, barely perceptible to the eye, of light to shade, and of shade to light. If, for instance, one desires to get a given density of shade, one has but to take ten spoonfuls of black pigment; then to get the following degree, eleven; then twelve, thirteen, and so on. Every time, having dipped up the pigment, the top is taken off, levelled by a glass bevel,—as in the market-place they make even a measure filled with grain.

* * *

Marco d'Oggione is the most diligent and conscientious of all the pupils of Leonardo. He works like an ox, he carries out with exactitude all of the master's rules; but the more he works, the less he succeeds. Marco is obstinate: whatever he gets into his head you could not drive out with a stake. He is convinced that "patience and labour will all things conquer,"—and does not lose hope of becoming a great artist. More than all of us does he rejoice over those inventions of the master which reduce art to mechanics. The other day, having taken along the little book with figures for remembering faces, he set off for the Piazza Broletto, chose some faces in the crowd, and noted them down with the marks corresponding to those of the tables. But when he returned home, no matter how much he struggled, he could not, in any way, unite the separate parts into a living face. He came to similar grief with the little spoon for measuring the black pigment; despite the fact that in his work he observes mathematical exactitude, the shadings remain untransparent and unnatural, just as his faces are wooden and devoid of all beauty. Marco explains this by his not having carried out all of the master's rules, and redoubles his effort. Meanwhile Cesare da Sesto malignantly rejoices.

"The most worthy Marco is a true martyr of art! His example proves that all these lauded rules and little spoons, and the tables for the noses, are not worth sending to the devil. 'Tis not enough to know how children are born, in order to give birth. Leonardo is merely deceiving himself and others,—he says one thing, and does another. When he paints, he does not mind any rules, but simply follows inspiration. But it does not suffice him to be a great painter,—he would also be a great man of science,—he wants to reconcile art and science, inspiration and mathematics. I fear me, however, that having started in pursuit of two hares, he will not catch a one."

Perhaps there is a moiety of truth in the words of Cesare. But wherefore does he dislike the master so? Leonardo forgives him everything, willingly hears his malicious, scoffing tirades through, values his intellect, and never gets angry.

* * *

I observe how he works on The Last Supper. Early in the morning, just as soon as the sun has risen, he leaves the house, sets out for the monastery refectory, and for the duration of the whole day, until it grows dark, he paints, without letting the brush out of his hands, forgetting about food and drink. Or else a week will pass, and another, —he does not even touch the brushes; but every day he stands for two or three hours at a stretch on the scaffolding before the picture, looking over and considering that which has been done; sometimes at noon, in the greatest heat, abandoning any work he may have begun, he runs to the monastery over the deserted streets, without choosing the shady side, as though drawn by an unseen force, climbs up on the scaffolding, makes two or three dabs, and immediately leaves.

* * *

All these days he has been working on the head of the Apostle John. To-day he was to finish it. But, to my astonishment, he stayed at home, and, from the very morning, with little Giacopo, busied himself with the observation of the flight of bumblebees, wasps, and flies. He is as deeply plunged in the study of their bodies and wings as if the fate of the universe depended on them. He was filled with joy, as over God knows what, when he found that their hind legs serve the flies in lieu of rudders. In the opinion of the master, this is exceedingly useful and important for the invention of a flying machine. Mayhap. But still it hurts to have the head of the Apostle John abandoned for the legs of flies.

* * *

To-day there is new grief. The flies are forgotten, as well as The Last Supper. He is creating an intricate, fine design for the coat-of-arms of the non-existent Academy of Painting of Milan,—a mere project of the Duke's. This device consists of a quadrangle of intertwining knots of rope, interwoven into one another, sans beginning, sans end, and surrounding the Latin inscription: *Leonardi Vinci Accademia.* So swallowed up is he with the working up of this pattern, that nothing else seems to exist in the universe, save this difficult and useless game; apparently, no efforts could tear him away from it. I could not endure it longer, and decided to remind him of the unfinished head of the Apostle John. He shrugged his shoulders, and, without lifting his eyes from the knots of rope, drawled out through his teeth:

"'Twill not fly away,—there is time enough."

At times I understand Cesare's malice.

* * *

Duke Moro has entrusted to him the construction of listening pipes in the castle, concealed in the thickness of the walls,—the Ear of Dionysius, so-called, which allows the ruler to hear from one chamber all that goes on in another. With great enthusiasm at first, the master undertook the laying of these pipes. But soon, as is his wont, he cooled, and began to put things off under different pretexts. This morning men were sent here several times from the castle. But the master is taken up with a new matter, which seems to him no less important than the construction of the Ear of Dionysius,—experiments with plants: cutting off the roots of a gourd, and leaving but one rootlet, he nourishes it copiously with water. To his no small joy, the gourd did not dry up, and the mother, as he puts it, has successfully nurtured all of her children,—sixty long gourds. With what patience, with what love, did he follow the life of this plant! To-day he sat until the evening glow on a plat in the truck-garden, observing its broad leaves drinking in the night dew. "The earth," says he, "quenches the plants with moisture, and the heavens do so with dew,—whereas the sun bestows a soul upon them," for he supposes that not only man, but that animals, even plants, each possess a soul,—an opinion which Fra Benedetto deems quite heretical.

* * *

He loves all animals. At times, for whole days at a stretch, he observes and draws cats, studying their ways and habits, how they play, fight, sleep, wash their mouths with their little paws, catch mice, arch their backs, and bristle up at dogs. Or else with the same curiosity he contemplates, through the walls of a big glass vessel, fishes, molluscs, hair-worms, scuttle-fish, and all sorts of other aquatic animals. His face expresses a deep, serene satisfaction as they fight and devour one another.

* * *

He carries on thousands of enterprises at once. Without concluding one, he takes up another. However, each one of these enterprises resembles a game,—and every game, an enterprise. He is versatile and inconstant. Cesare says there is a greater possibility of rivers flowing up-hill than of Leonardo's ever concentrating on some one project and carrying it through to the end. He styles the master the greatest of all shiftless people, asserting that of all his unencompassable works nothing useful will ever result. Leonardo, 'twould seem, has written an hundred and twenty books, styled *On Nature—Delle Cose Naturali*. But all these are chance fragments, isolated notes, unmatched bits of paper,—more than five thousand small sheets in such frightful disorder that he himself can not at times make head or tail of them, seeking some necessary note or other and not being able to find it.

* * *

What an insatiable curiosity is his, what a kindly, prophetic eye for nature! How he can perceive the imperceptible! He is joyously and avidly amazed at everything, as children are, as the first men in Paradise were.

Sometimes he will make some such remark about the most everyday thing that afterward, all lifelong, though you live to be a hundred, you will not forget it,—'twill stick to your memory and never leave you.

The other day, entering my cubicle, the master said: "Giovanni, have you ever noticed that small rooms make the mind concentrate, whereas large ones arouse it to action?"

Or else: "In a shadowy rain the outlines of objects seem clearer than in a sunny one."

And here is something from yesterday's business conversation with the master founder, about some war ordnance ordered by the Duke: "The explosion of the powder between the breech of the bombard and the shot acts like a man who, propping his behind against a wall, pushes a weight in front of him, exerting his arms to their utmost."

Once, in speaking of abstract mechanics, he said: "Force is always desirous of overcoming its cause, and, having overcome it, to die. The Blow is the son of Motion and the Grandson of Force, while their mutual ancestor is Weight."

In an argument with a certain architect he exclaimed with impatience: "How is it that you do not understand, messer? 'Tis as clear as day. Well, what is an arc? An arc is nothing else save force, born of two united and opposed weaknesses." The architect simply gaped from astonishment. As for me, everything in their conversation became clear, as though a candle had been brought into a dark room.

* * *

Again two days of work on the head of the Apostle John. But, alas, something has been lost in the endless fuss with the flies' wings, the gourd, the cats, the Ear of Dionysius, the design of Gordian knots, and the like important matters. Again he did not finish, abandoning it, and, filled with revulsion toward painting, plunged himself wholly into geometry,—like a snail into its shell, to use an expression of Cesare's. He says that, apparently, the very smell of paints, the sight of the brushes and canvas, are repugnant to him.

And that is how we live, at the whim of chance, from day to day. Having surrendered ourselves to the will of God, we sit on the shore and bide fair weather. 'Tis a good thing that he had not come to the flying machine, for then we might as well give up,—he would burrow himself so deeply into mechanics that that would be the last we saw of him!

* * *

I have noticed that every time when, after prolonged excuses, doubts and vacillations, he does, finally, attack his work, does pick up his brush, a feeling akin to fear seems to possess him. He is always dissatisfied with that which he has already done. In creations which to others seem the limit of perfection, he notices errors. He is ever striving toward the highest, toward the unattainable, toward that to which the hand of man, no matter how infinite its cunning, can not give expression. That is why he almost never completes his works.

* * *

To-day a Jew trader came selling horses. The master wanted to buy a bay stallion. The Jew fell to talking him into buying a mare along with the stallion, and implored, insisted, fidgeted and vowed so much that Leonardo, who loves horses and knows good horseflesh, finally burst out laughing, gave up the struggle, took the mare and allowed himself to be duped, just so as to be rid of the Jew. I watched, listened, and wondered.

"What art thou astounded at?" Cesare explained to me later. "'Tis always thus,—the first comer can get around him. There is nothing in which he may be relied upon, nor is there anything he can come to a firm decision about. Everything is two ways with him—*meum* and *teum*, yea and nay. He goeth where the wind bloweth. No firmness, no manliness. He is all soft, vacillating, yielding, just as if he had no backbone, as though he were enfeebled, despite all his strength. He bends iron horseshoes, he thinks up levers to lift the Baptistry of San Giovanni up into the air like a sparrow's nest,—and all this in play; but when it comes to something real, where will-power is required,—nary a straw will he lift, nary a lady-bug will he durst to wrong! . . ."

Cesare kept up his tirade for a long while, palpably exaggerating, and even slandering. But I felt that, mixed with the untruth, there was also truth in his words.

* * *

Andrea Salaino took sick. The master nurses him, does not sleep of nights, as he sits at the head of Andrea's bed. But he will not hear of medicines. Marco d'Oggione brought the sick man some sort of pills. Leonardo found them and threw them out the window.

But when Andrea himself merely ventured to suggest that it might be a good thing to let blood,—he knows a certain barber who is an excellent hand at opening veins,—the master waxed wroth in downright earnest, reviling all doctors in unseemly language, and saying, among other things:

"I advise thee to think not of how to cure thyself, but of how thou mayest keep thy health, which last thou shalt the better attain the more thou art on thy guard against doctors, whose medicines are akin to the absurd compounds of the alchemists."

And he added, with a gay, simple-heartedly sly smile:

"Why should they not be getting rich, the cheats, when everyone is but trying to hoard up as much money as possible, in order to give it to the doctors, the destroyers of human life!"

* * *

The master amuses the sick man with funny stories, fables and riddles, of which Salaino is exceedingly fond. I watch, listen, and am amazed at the master. How merry he is!

Here, for example, are some of these riddles:

"Men shall flay cruelly that which is the cause of their living.—The threshing of grain.

"The forests shall bring forth into the world offspring that are fated to destroy their parents.—Axe-handles.

"The hides of beasts shall make men forsake quiet, to swear and to shout.—Playing with small balls of leather."

After long hours passed in inventing of war engines, in mathematical calculations, or work at the Mystic Supper, he consoles himself with these riddles, like a child, He writes them down in his work-books, side by side with sketches of future great productions, or with laws of nature he may have just discovered.

* * *

He has conceived and drawn, in eulogy of the Duke's generosity, a strange, intricate allegory, on which he has spent not a little labour: in the guise of Fortune, Moro is taking under his protection a youth running away from the fearful Parca, Poverty, whose face is the face of the She-spider; he covers the youth with his mantle, and threatens the monstrous divinity with his golden sceptre. Leonardo has executed it in colours on one of the walls of the castle. These allegories have become the vogue at court. It seems that they enjoy a greater popularity than all of the master's other creations. Ladies, knights, grandees, all importune him, striving to get some small picture with an involved allegorical conceit.

For one of the two chief concubines of the Duke, Countess Cecilia Bergamini, he has composed an Allegory of Envy: a decrepit old woman with pendulous paps, clad in a leopard skin, with a quiver of envenomed tongues slung over her shoulders, holding in her hand a goblet filled with snakes, and riding astride a human skeleton.

He had occasion to compose another allegory as well, also of Envy, for the Duke's other concubine, Lucrezia Crivelli, in order that she might not take offence: the branch of a filbert-tree being beaten with sticks, and shaken—since 'tis thus treated only at the very time of having brought its fruit to perfect maturity. Alongside is an inscription: *For Good Deeds*.

Finally, for the spouse of the Duke as well, the Most Illustrious Madonna Beatrice, he found it necessary to think up an Allegory of Ingratitude: a man, as the sun rises, extinguishing a candle, which had served him all through the night.

Now poor master hath no peace, day or night: commissions, requests, little notes from the ladies, pour down upon him: he knoweth not how to escape them. Cesare is all of a pother: "All these silly chivalric devices and sweetish allegories befit rather some court toady, but scarcely such an artist as Leonardo. 'Tis a shame!" I do not think he is right. The master does not at all think of honour. He amuses himself with the allegories, just as with a game of riddles, or with mathematical verities, or else the divine smile of the Virgin Mary and the design made of rope-knots.

* * *

He has conceived and already commenced, long ago,—but, as is his wont, has not yet finished, and God knows when he will finish,—*A Book About Painting—Trattato della Pittura.* Of late, being engaged a great deal in instructing me in aerial and lineal perspective, and light and shade, he has applied citations and isolated truths about art from that book. I am writing down here what I have remembered.

May the Lord reward the master for the love and wisdom with which he guides me on all the high paths of this most noble science. Therefore let them into whose hands these leaves may fall, remember in their prayers the soul of the humble servant of God, his unworthy pupil, Giovanni Beltraffio, and the soul of the great master, Leonardo da Vinci, the Florentine.

* * *

The master saith:

"All that is beautiful dies in man, but not in art."

"He that despiseth painting, despiseth the philosophical and refined contemplation of the universe, inasmuch as painting is the lawful Daughter, or, to put it better, Granddaughter of Nature. All that is, has been born of nature, and has in its turn given birth to painting. Therefore do I say that painting is the Granddaughter of Nature and related to God. Whosoever blasphemes against painting, blasphemes against God."

"The painter must be all-embracing. O thou artist, may thy variety be even as infinite as the phenomena of Nature. Carrying on that which God has begun, strive to multiply not the works of man's hands, but the eternal creations of God. Never imitate anyone. Let thy every production be like to a new phenomenon of Nature."

"For him who is master of the first, general laws of natural phenomena, for him who *knoweth*,—it is easy to be all-embracing, inasmuch as in their structure all bodies, of animals as well as men, have a resemblance."

"Beware, lest greed for the acquisition of gold stifle in thee love for art. Remember, that the acquisition of fame is something greater than the fame of acquisition. The remembrance of the rich perisheth with them; remembrance of the wise shall never disappear, inasmuch as wisdom and learning are truly the legitimate offspring of their parents, and not those begotten on the wrong side of the blanket, such as riches are. Cherish fame and fear not poverty. Reflect how many great philosophers, born to riches, did condemn themselves to voluntary beggary, so that they might not defile their souls with riches."

"Learning maketh the soul young: it decreaseth the bitterness of old age. Gather, then, wisdom; gather sweet fare for thy old age."

"I know such painters as will, devoid of all shame, for the amusement of the rabble, bedaub pictures with gold and azure, asserting with supercilious brazenness that they could do work in no way inferior to that of other masters, were they to be paid more. Oh, men of folly! Who, then, interferes with their making something beautiful, and proclaim,—this picture is of such and such a price; that one is cheaper; as for that other one 'tis altogether of the market-place,—proving in this manner that they can do work at every price."

"Not infrequently greed for money degrades even good masters to the level of artisans. Thus, my fellow countryman and comrade, Perugino, the Florentine, has attained such speed in executing commissions that once he made answer to his wife from the scaffolding: 'Do thou serve the soup, and in the meanwhile I shall paint another saint!'"

"The artist who does not doubt attains but little. 'Tis a good thing for thee if thy creation be above the value thou dost set by it; 'tis bad if it be equal; but the greatest misfortune of all is for it to be below it,—which is the case with those who wonder how it was that God helped them to make anything so excellently."

"Hearken in patience to the opinions of all about thy picture, weigh and consider if they be right that do reproach thee and find faults;

if they be right,—make corrections; if not, pretend that thou hast not heard, and prove their error only to those people who are worthy of attention."

"The judgment of an enemy is not infrequently of more truth and benefit than the judgment of a friend. Hatred in men is almost always deeper than love. The gaze of one who hates is more penetrating than the gaze of one who loves. A true friend is like to thyself. An enemy does not resemble thee,—therein is his strength. Hatred illumines much that is hidden from love. Remember this, and do not contemn the censure of enemies."

"Vivid colours captivate the mob. But the true artist caters not to the mob, but to the chosen ones. His pride and aim are not in glistening colours, but that there should take place in the picture that which is like to a miracle: that light and shade make the flat surfaces appear convex. He that scorns shading, sacrificing it for colours, resembles the chatter-box who sacrifices the meaning of speech for empty and resonant words."

"Most of all beware of coarse outlines. May the edges of thy shadows on young and tender flesh be neither dead, nor petrified, but light, imperceptible, and translucent, like air, inasmuch as the body of man itself is translucent, of which thou canst convince thyself, shouldst thou look at the sun through thy fingers. Too bright a light does not result in beautiful shades. Shun bright light. In twilight, or on misty days, when the sun is beclouded, remark what tenderness and beauty there is in the faces of the men and women passing through shady streets between the dark walls of the houses. This is the most perfect light. Let thy shading, therefore, as it vanishes little by little in the light, melt away, like smoke, like the sounds of soft music. Remember: betwixt light and murk there is something intermediate, dual, belonging equally to the one and the other, a light shade, as it were, or dark light. Seek it, O artist: in it lies the secret of captivating beauty!"

Thus saith he, and, having raised his hand, as though desiring to impress these words on our memories, repeated with an expression beyond conveying:

"Beware of the coarse and the abrupt. Let your shadings melt away, like smoke, like the sounds of distant music!"

Cesare, who had been intently listening, smiled scoffingly, raised his eyes to Leonardo, and wanted to say something in contradiction, but let it pass in silence.

* * *

A little time after, speaking now of something else, the master said: "Untruth is so despicable, that, exalting the greatness of God, it debases Him; truth is so beautiful, that, praising the very least of things, it ennobles them. Betwixt truth and untruth there is the same difference as between darkness and light."

Cesare, having recalled something, looked at him with a searching gaze.

"The same difference as betwixt darkness and light?" he repeated. "But have you not just now asserted yourself, master, that betwixt darkness and light there is something intermediate, dual, belonging equally to one and the other,—a light shadow, as it were, or a dark light? Therefore, is there not a similar something betwixt truth and untruth? . . . But no, this can not be. . . . Really, master, your comparison engenders in my mind a great temptation, inasmuch as an artist seeking the mystery of the captivating beauty in the mingling of light and shade, may, the first thing one knows, ask whether truth and untruth do not mingle as well as light with shade. . . ."

Leonardo at first frowned, as though he were struck,—even angered, —by the words of his pupil; but then, bursting into laughter, he replied: "Tempt me not. Get thee behind me, Satan!"

I expected an answer of another sort, and I think that the words of Cesare were worthy of more than a flippant jest. At any rate, they aroused many torturing thoughts within me.

* * *

This evening I saw him, standing under the rain in a narrow, dirty and stinking alley, attentively contemplating a wall of stone, with spots of dampness,—apparently one with nothing curious about it. This lasted for a long while. Urchins were pointing their fingers at him and laughing. I asked what he had found in this wall.

"Look, Giovanni, what a splendid monster,—a chimæra with gaping maw; while here, alongside, is an angel with a gentle face and waving locks, who is fleeing from the monster. The whim of chance has here created images worthy of a great master."

He drew the outlines of the spots with his fingers, and, to my amazement, I did actually perceive in them that of which he spake.

"It may be that many would consider such power of invention absurd," the master went on, "but I, by my own experience, know how useful it is for arousing the mind to discoveries and projects. Not infrequently on walls, in the confusion of different stones, in cracks, in the designs made by scum on stagnant water, in dying embers, covered over with a thin layer of ashes, in the outlines of clouds,—it has happed to me to find a likeness of the most beautiful localities, with mountains, crags, rivers, plains, and trees; also splendid battles, strange faces, full of inexplicable beauty; curious devils, monsters, and many other astounding images. I chose from them what I needed, and supplied the rest. Thus, in listening closely to the distant ringing of bells, thou canst find in their mingled pealing, at thy wish, every name and word that thou mayst be thinking of."

* * *

He compared the facial wrinkles in weeping and laughter. In conclusion he said:

"Try to be a calm spectator of how people laugh and weep, hate and love, blanch from horror and cry out in pain; look, learn, investigate, observe, in order that thou mayst come to know the expression of all human emotions."

Cesare was telling me that the master loves to escort those sentenced to death, observing in their faces all the degrees of torture and horror; he arouses astonishment in the very headsmen with his curiosity, watching narrowly the last quivers of their muscles as the unfortunates expire.

"Thou canst not even imagine, Giovanni, what a man this is!" added Cesare with a bitter smile. "He will lift a worm from the road and set it on a leaf, in order not to squash it underfoot,—but when the fit comes upon him, 'twould seem that if his own mother were crying, he would but observe how her eyebrows contract, how the skin on her forehead wrinkles, and how the corners of her lips droop."

* * *

The master saith:

"Learn expressive movements from the deaf-mutes."

"When thou observest people, try not to have them notice that thou art looking at them; their movements, their laughter and weeping, are more natural then."

"The variety of human motions is just as infinite as the variety of human emotions. The highest aim of the artist consists of expressing in the face and in the movements of the body the passion of the soul."

"Remember, in the faces of those thou portrayest there must be such power of emotion that it must seem to the spectator that thy picture can compel the dead to laugh and weep."

"When the artist depicts something fearful, grievous, or laugh-provoking, the emotion which the spectator is going through must incite him to such movements of the body as will make him seem to be himself taking part in the actions depicted; but if this be not attained,—know, O artist, that all thy efforts are in vain."

"The master artist whose hands are knotty and bony, willingly depicts people with the same sort of knotty, bony hands, and this is repeated with every part of the body, inasmuch as to every man those faces and bodies are pleasing which resemble his own face and body. That is why, if the artist be homely, he will choose for his depictions faces which are also homely, and *vice versa*. Be on thy guard lest the men and women thou dost depict seem thy brethren and sisters, thy doubles, either in their beauty or their hideousness,—a shortcoming common to many Italian artists. For in painting there is no more dangerous and treacherous error than imitating one's own body. I think this happens because the soul is the artist of its body: at one time it had created and moulded it in its image and likeness, and now, when it is again necessary, with the aid of brushes and pigments, to create a new body, it doth all the more willingly repeat the image in which it had once before become incarnate."

"Take care that thy creation repulse not the spectator, even as the cold air of winter doth repulse a man just gotten out of bed; but rather that it attract and captivate his soul, like as the sleeper is decoyed out of bed by the pleasant freshness of the summer morn."

* * *

Here is a history of painting, told by the master in a few words:

"After the Romans, when painters commenced to imitate one another, art fell into a decline lasting for many ages. But there appeared Giotto, a Florentine, who was not content to imitate his master, Cimabue; Giotto, having been born among mountains and deserts, inhabited only by goats and the like animals, and, being incited to art by nature, began to draw on stones the movements of the goats, which he herded, and of all the animals that dwelt in his country; and, finally, through long study, surpassed not only all the teachers of his time, but of ages past as well. After Giotto the art of painting again fell into a decline, because everyone commenced to imitate the example ready to hand.

This lasted for whole centuries, until Tommaso, a Florentine, yclept Masaccio, did prove with his perfect creations to what degree those who take for an example anything at all save nature itself do spend their time in vain,—he was the teacher of all teachers."

* * *

"The first production of painting was a line drawn around the shadow of a man, cast by the sun upon a wall."

* * *

Discoursing of how an artist ought to compose the ideas for pictures, the master told us, by way of an example, of a representation of the deluge that he had conceived.

"Abysses and maelstroms, lit up by lightnings. Branches of enormous oaks, with people clinging to them, carried along by a water-spout. Waters, strewn with fragments of household furniture, upon which people seek to save themselves. Herds of quadrupeds, surrounded by water, on high table-lands,—some with their legs on the backs of others, crushing and trampling one another. A horde of people, defending, with arms in hand, the last patch of ground from feral beasts. Some are wringing their hands, gnawing them so that the blood runs; others stuff their ears so as not to hear the rumble of the thunder-shocks; or else, not content with having shut their eyes, place one hand a-top the other, pressing them to their eyelids, in order not to see their impending death. Some commit suicide,—suffocating, strangling themselves, impaling themselves upon swords, casting themselves into the raging deep from cliffs; and mothers, cursing God, seize their children to smash their heads against stones. Decomposed corpses float up to the surface, colliding with and striking one another, and rebounding like little balls inflated with air. Birds perch on them; or, sinking down from exhaustion, descend on the living men and animals, finding no other place to rest."

From Marco and Salaino I found out that Leonardo during many years has been questioning travellers and all who had ever seen any water-spouts, floods, hurricanes, avalanches, earthquakes,—finding out exact details, and patiently, like a man of science, gathering feature after feature, observation after observation, in order to construct the project of a picture which, perhaps, he will never execute. I remember that listening to him as he told of the flood, I experienced the same sensation as upon beholding the sight of the devils' faces and of monsters in his drawings,—a horror which attracted.

And here is somewhat else that did astound me: while narrating his fearful conception, the artist seemed calm and impassive.

Speaking of the flashes of lightning, reflected by water, he remarked: "There ought to be more of them on the waves the farthest from the spectator, less on those nearest him, as is demanded by the law of the reflection of light on flat surfaces."

Speaking of the dead bodies colliding in the whirlpools, he added: "In depicting these blows and collisions, forget not the law in mechanics, according to which the angle of descent is equal to the angle of refraction."

I smiled involuntarily, and reflected: "There he is,—full-length,—in that admonition!"

* * *

The master saith:

"It is not experience, the father of all arts and sciences, that deceiveth people, but imagination, which promiseth them that which experience can not give. Experience is guiltless,—'tis our vain and insane desires that are criminal. Distinguishing untruth from truth, experience teaches us to strive toward the possible and not to hope, through ignorance, for that which it is impossible to attain, in order that we may not be compelled, being deceived in hope, to give ourselves up to despair."

When we were left alone, Cesare recalled these words to me and said, with a squeamish pucker:

"Again, lying and hypocrisy!"

"Wherein has he lied now, Cesare?" asked I with amazement. "Meseems the master . . ."

"Not to strive toward the impossible, not to desire the unattainable!" continued he, without listening to me. "First thing thou knowest, someone will take him at his word. Nay, but he hath not come upon such fools here: 'tis not for him to speak, nor for me to listen! I can see him through and through. . . ."

"What is it thou seest, then, Cesare?"

"Why, this,—that all his life long he has striven only for the impossible, has longed only for the unattainable. Well, tell me, as a favour: to invent such machines as would enable men to fly through the air, like birds, to enable them to swim under water, like fish,—does it not mean to strive for the impossible? And the horror of the flood, and the non-existent monsters in spots of dampness and in clouds, the non-existent beauty of divine faces, resembling angelic visions,—whence does he get all this? Can it be from experience, from the mathematical table of noses, and the little spoon for measuring off pigments? . . . Wherefore, then, does he deceive himself and others, wherefore does he lie? He hath need of mechanics for a miracle,—in order to soar up to the skies on wings; in order, being in possession of natural forces, to direct them to that which is above and against the nature of humanity, above and against the laws of nature,—'tis all one to him if he be headed toward God or the devil, if it be but toward the untried, toward the impossible! For, perhaps, believe he does not; yet is he inquisitive,—the less he believeth, the more curious he is,—this leaning of his is like inextinguishable lust, like a coal at white heat, which naught can slake,—neither knowledge nor experience of any sort! . . ."

Cesare's words have filled me with confusion and fear. All these days, of late, I think of them, longing to forget them, yet unable to.

To-day, as though in answer to my doubts, the master said:

"Little knowledge imparts to people pride; great knowledge imparts humility. Thus, ears empty of grain disdainfully lift up their heads to heaven, whereas those full bend theirs low, toward the earth, their mother."

"But how is it then, master," retorted Cesare, with his usual caustically-probing smile, "how is it they say, that it was the great knowledge—so 'twould seem—of which the most radiant of cherubim, Lucifer, was possessed, which instilled within him not resignation, but pride, for which he was e'en cast down into the lower depths?"

Leonardo made no reply, but, after a short silence, told us a fable:

"Once on a time a drop of water conceived the idea of rising to the sky. With the aid of fire it flew up in fine steam. But, having attained to a height, it met with rarefied, cold air; it condensed, grew heavier,—and its pride was transformed into horror. The drop fell as rain. The dry earth drank it up. And for a long while the drop of water, confined in its dark underground prison, was compelled to repent of its sin."

* * *

'Twould seem that the longer one lives with him, the less one knows him.

To-day he again amused himself like an urchin. And what pranks his are! I was sitting upstairs in my room, toward evening, reading before sleep my favourite book, *The Little Flowers of Saint Francis*. Suddenly there sounded through the whole house the screaming of our cook, Maturina:

"Fire! Fire! Help! The house is afire! . . ."

I rushed headlong downstairs and became frightened, seeing the thick smoke which filled the workroom. Lit up by the reflection of a blue flame, that resembled lightning, the master was standing in the midst of the clouds of smoke, like some magus of old, and with a jolly grin was looking at Maturina, pale from terror, waving her arms about, and at Marco, who had come running with two pails of water and would have thrown their contents upon the table, sparing neither drawings nor manuscripts, had not the master halted him, by crying out that all this was but a jest. Thereupon we saw that the smoke and flame rose up from a white powder made of frankincense and rosin, on a brazen pan at white-heat,—a compound invented by him for making mock fires. I know not who was more enraptured from the prank,—the inevitable companion of all his games, the little imp Giacopo, or Leonardo himself. How he did laugh over the fright of Maturina and over the rescuing buckets of Marco! God knoweth that he who can laugh in such wise can not be a man of evil.

But, in the midst of his merriment and laughter, he did not let pass the opportunity of noting down the observation he had made of Maturina's face,—about the folds of the skin and the wrinkles which horror evokes on human faces.

* * *

He almost never speaks about women. Only once did he do so, saying that men act toward them just as lawlessly as toward animals. However, he laughs over the Platonic Love now in vogue. To one enamoured youth, who was declaiming a tearful sonnet in the style of Petrarca,—he retorted with three lines,—probably the sole verses ever composed by him, inasmuch as he is rather a poor versificator:

S'el Petrarca amo si forte il lauro,—
E perchè gli è bon fralla salsiccia e tordo.
I'non posso di lor ciancie far tesauro.

"If Petrarca was so exceedingly fond of Laurel (Laura), it was probably because laurel leaves are a goodly condiment for sausages and roasted blackbirds. As for me, I can not go into transports over such silly things."

Cesare asserts that, apparently, Leonardo has been so taken up with mechanics and geometry during his whole life that he has had no time to love; but, however, his chastity can hardly be perfect, for, of course, even if only once, he must have coupled with a woman,—not for enjoyment, as common mortals do, but out of curiosity, for scientific observations in anatomy, investigating the mystery of love just as dispassionately, with mathematical exactitude, as other phenomena of nature.

* * *

It seems to me at times that I ought never to discuss him with Cesare. It appears just as if we were eavesdropping, peeping, like spies. Cesare experiences an evil joy every time that he succeeds in putting the master in the shade anew. And whatever does he want of me, wherefore doth he poison my soul? We now frequently go to a vile little inn, near the customs house on the Catarana River, beyond the Vercellina Gates. For whole hours through, over half a *brenta* of cheap sour wine, we converse to the sound of the boatmen playing with greasy cards, and conspire, like traitors.

To-day Cesare has asked me whether I know that in Florence Leonardo had been accused of sodomy. I could not believe my ears; I thought Cesare was drunk or raving. But he explained everything to me, in detail and exactly.

In the year 1476,—Leonardo was at that time twenty-four, whereas his master, the famous Florentine artist, Andrea Verrocchio, was forty, —an anonymous complaint accusing Leonardo and Verrocchio of pæderasty was dropped into one of those round wooden boxes, styled "drums"—*tamburi*,—which are hung on the columns of the main Florentine churches, chiefly in the Cathedral of Maria del Fiore. On the 9th of April of the same year the Night and Monastery Officials, —*Ufficiale di notte e monasteri*,—sifted the matter and exonerated the accused, but on the condition that the accusation be repeated,—*assoluti cum conditione, ut retamburentur;* and, after a new accusation, on the 9th of June, Leonardo and Verrocchio were entirely exonerated. Nothing more than that is known to anyone. Shortly thereafter Leonardo, having left Verrocchio's atelier and Florence, made his home in Milan.

"Oh, of course, 'tis a vile libel!" added Cesare with a mocking sparkle in his eyes. "Although thou knowest not, as yet, with what contradictions his heart is filled. 'Tis, dost thou see, a labyrinth wherein the Devil himself would break a leg. Of riddles and mysteries thou shalt find no end! On the one hand he does, I admit, appear a virgin man; but on the other hand, now . . ."

I suddenly felt all my blood rush to my heart; I jumped up and cried out:

"How durst thou, thou vile fellow! . . ."

"Whatever is the matter with thee? Forgive me. . . . Well, well, I will desist! Calm thyself! Really, I did not think that thou didst attach so much importance to all this. . . ."

"Attach importance to what? To what? Come out with it,—come out with all of it! Do not equivocate,—do not shilly-shally! . . ."

"Eh, nonsense! Wherefore grow heated? Is it worth while for two such friends as thou and I to quarrel over trifles? Let us drink to thy health! *In vino veritas*. . . ."

And we drank, and continued the talk.

Nay, nay, 'tis enough! 'Tis at an end. I shall never again talk with him about the master. He is an enemy not only of his, but of mine as well. He is a man of evil. I feel abominably,—I know not if from the wine drunk in the accursed little tavern, or else from what we spoke of in there. 'Tis shameful to think what a base joy people can find in degrading a great man.

* * *

The master saith:

"Artist, thy strength lies in solitude. When thou art alone, thou belongest to thyself entirely; but when thou art even with one companion, thou belongest but half to thyself, or even less, depending on the indiscretion of thy friend. Having several friends, thou shalt fall still deeper into the same misfortune. But shouldst thou say: 'I shall draw apart from them, and be alone, that I may give myself up more freely to the contemplation of nature,—' I say unto thee, 'twill scarce succeed, for thou shalt not have fortitude to refrain from distractions, and not hearken to their chitter-chatter. Thou shalt be a bad comrade, and a worse worker, inasmuch as no man can serve two masters. And if thou shouldst retort: 'I shall draw off to such a distance that I may not hear their converse altogether,—' I shall tell thee: they shall deem thee a madman,—but still thou shalt scarce be left entirely to thyself. But, if thou must needs have friends, let them be painters, and the pupils of thy workroom. Any other friendship is dangerous. Remember, O artist, thy strength lies in solitude."

Now do I understand why Leonardo withdraws from women,—for great contemplation great leisure is needed.

* * *

Andrea Salaino at times complains bitterly of boredom, of our monotonous and withdrawn life, asserting that, apparently, the pupils of other masters live far more merrily. He loves new things to wear, just like a young girl, and grieves because there is none to show them off to. He would have festivals, noise, glitter, crowds, and enamoured glances.

To-day the master, having heard to the end the reproaches and complaints of his favourite, with a wonted movement of his hand began to stroke Andrea's long, soft curls, and answered him with a kindly smile:

"Grieve not, lad: I promise to take thee the next gala-day to the Castle. But now, dost want me to tell thee a story?"

"Tell it to me, master!" Andrea became joyous, and sat down at Leonardo's feet.

"On a high place, over the highway, at a spot where a fence marked the limit of a garden, there once lay a stone, surrounded by trees, moss, flowers, and grasses. Once, when it beheld a large number of stones below, on the highway, it felt a longing to be with them, and said to itself: 'What joyance have I of these most gentle, short-lived flowers and grasses? I would fain live among those who are my kinsmen and my brethren, among other stones that are like unto me!' And it rolled downward to the highway, toward those it had styled its kinsmen and its brethren. But here the wheels of heavy carriages began to crush it; the hoofs of asses and of mules, the hobnail boots of passers-by began to trample upon it. But when at times it would succeed in raising itself a trifle, and dream of drawing a freer breath, sticky mud or the excrement of animals would cover it. Sadly did it gaze at its former place, the retired sanctuary of the garden, and it did appear a paradise. Thus is it with those, Andrea, who forsake quiet contemplation and plunge into the passions of the crowd, which is filled with eternal evil."

* * *

The master does not allow any harm to be wrought to any living creatures,—even plants. The mechanic Zoroastro da Peretola has told me that Leonardo ever since his youthful years does not eat meat, and says that there will come a time when all men, like him, will be content with vegetarian fare, deeming the killing of animals just as criminal as the killing of men.

Once, in passing a butcher-shop on the Mercato Nuovo, and pointing with disgust to the carcasses of calves, sheep, steers, and swine on the stretchers, he said to me:

"Yea, verily, man is the king of animals,—or, to put it better, the king of beasts, inasmuch as his bestiality is of the greatest."

And, after a silence, he added with a quiet sorrow:

"We create our life out of the deaths of others! Men and beasts are but the eternal resting-places of the dead, the graves for one another. . . ."

"Such is the law of nature, whose benevolence and wisdom you yourself glorify so, master," retorted Cesare. "I am amazed why you, by refraining from meat, disturb this natural law, which commands all creatures to devour one another."

Leonardo looked at him and answered calmly:

"Nature, finding endless joy in the invention of new forms, in the building of new lives, and creating them with a greater speed than time can exterminate, has contrived so that certain creatures, nourishing themselves on others, may clear the space for coming generations. That is why she not infrequently sends plagues and miasmas wherever creatures have multiplied excessively, especially men, with whom the excess of births is not balanced by deaths, inasmuch as the other beasts do not devour them."

Thus does Leonardo,—though with the great calmness of reason,—explain natural laws, without waxing indignant or lamenting; but he himself acts in accordance with another law, abstaining from using as food anything that hath life.

Last night I read for long in a book with which I never part,—*The Little Flowers of Saint Francis*. Francis, just like Leonardo, was compassionate to all creatures. At times, in lieu of prayers, praising the wisdom of God, he would observe in an apiary, for whole hours at a stretch, how the bees mould their wax cells and fill them with honey. Once, on a desert mountain, he preached the word of God to the birds; they sat in rows at his feet and hearkened; but when he had concluded, they shook themselves, took to fluttering their wings, burst into jargoning, and, opening their beaks, began to rub their heads caressingly against the garments of St. Francis, as though desirous of telling him that they had understood his sermon; he did bless them, and they flew away with joyous cries.

I read for a long while. Later I fell asleep. It seemed to me that my slumber was filled with the gentle wind of the wings of doves.

I awoke early. The sun had just risen. Everyone in the house was yet asleep. I went out into the yard, in order to wash myself with the chill water from the well. Everything was quiet. The ringing of distant bells resembled the droning of bees. There was an odour of freshness, with something of smoke about it. Suddenly I heard behind me, as though it were out of my dream, the fluttering of countless wings. I raised my eyes and beheld Messer Leonardo on the ladder of the high dove-cote.

With his hair shot through by the sun, surrounding his head like a halo, he stood in the heavens, alone and joyous. A flock of white pigeons, cooing, was crowding at his feet. They fluttered about him, trustingly perching on his shoulders, on his arms, on his head. He caressed them, and fed them from his mouth. Then he waved his arms, just as though he had bestowed a benediction,—and the pigeons soared upward, with silken rustle of their wings, flying away, like white flakes of snow, melting into the azure of the heavens. He followed them with a tender gaze.

And I reflected that Leonardo resembles St. Francis, the friend of all living creatures, who did call the wind his brother, and the water his sister, and the earth his mother.

* * *

May God e'en forgive me; again I could not hold out; again did Cesare and I go to the accursed little inn. I began speaking of the master's kindness of heart.

"Is it not of Messer Leonardo's abstinence from meat that thou wouldst speak, Giovanni,—of his nourishing himself on God's little grasses?"

"And what if I were speaking of that, Cesare? I know . . ."

"Thou knowest naught! Messer Leonardo doth this not at all out of goodness, but merely amusing himself with it, as with everything else,—playing the natural. . . ."

"How,—playing the natural? What art thou saying? . . ."

He burst out laughing with assumed gaiety.

"Now, now,—very well! We shall not dispute over it. But thou hadst better wait; when we come home, then I shall show thee certain curious little drawings of our master's."

Having returned, we most quietly, like very thieves, did make our way stealthily into the master's workshop. He was not there. Cesare rummaged, took a note-book out from beneath a pile of books on the work-table, and began showing me the drawings. I knew that what I was doing was evil, but had not the strength to resist, and looked on with curiosity.

These were pictures of enormous bombards, explosive shells, many-barrelled cannon and other military engines,—drawings executed with the same æthereal tenderness of shades and light as the faces of the most beautiful of his Madonnas. I remember one bomb, half an ell in length, styled *fragilica*, whose construction Cesare explained to me; it is moulded out of bronze; the inner cavity is stuffed with oakum mixed with gypsum and fish-glue, with wool clippings, tar, and sulphur; and, on the manner of a labyrinth, brazen pipes are interwoven within it, wound about with the strongest of ox-sinews,—the pipes, in their turn, stuffed with gunpowder and bullets. The openings of the pipes are placed screw-fashion on the surface of the bomb. Through them the fire flies out at the explosion, and the *fragilica* whirls and hops with incredible speed, like a gigantic top, hawking forth sheaves of fire. Alongside, on the margins, was written in Leonardo's hand: "This is a bomb of a most beautiful and useful construction. It ignites after discharge from the cannon within as short a space of time as would take to say an *Ave Maria*."

"*Ave Maria!* How does that please thee, my friend? And what an enterprising fellow is this Messer Leonardo! *Ave Maria*—alongside a monstrosity like this! And, by the by,—dost thou know how he styles war?"

"How?"

"'*Pazzia bestialissima*. Most bestial madness.' Truly, not a bad little saying from the lips of the inventor of such machines?"

He turned the leaf over and showed me a representation of a war chariot with enormous scythes of iron. At full tilt it cuts into the enemy's ranks. The enormous scythe-shaped blades of steel, as sharp as razors, resembling the paws of an enormous spider, must revolve in the air with piercing whistling, screeching and creaking of the notched wheels, scattering shreds of meat and spurts of blood, as they cleave men in half. All around are strewn severed legs, arms, heads, cloven torsos.

I also remember another drawing: rows of stripped workers, resembling demons, who are raising an enormous cannon with an ominously yawning muzzle, in the yard of an arsenal; straining their mighty sinews in an unbelievable effort, clinging to and using as a point of resistance for their legs and arms the levers of a gigantic gate, joined by ropes with an elevating machine. Others are wheeling up an axle on two wheels. A horror was wafted upon me from these clusters of nude bodies, pendent in the air. It resembled an armoury of devils a smithy of hell.

"Well, now? Did I tell thee the truth?" said Cesare. "Most curious little drawings, are they not? Here he is, the blessed man that hath mercy on all creatures, that tasteth not of meat, that lifteth a worm up from the path lest the passers-by trample upon it! This, and the other,—together. To-day a creature of dark hell; to-morrow a saint fit for heaven. A Janus two-faced: one face toward Christ, one toward Antichrist. Go thou and distinguish which is the true face and which is the false. Or are they both true? . . . And yet all this is done with a light heart, with the mysticism of a captivating grace, as though but in jest and in play!"

I listened in silence; a chill, like unto the chill of death, was darting through my heart.

"What is the matter with thee, Giovanni?" remarked Cesare. "Thou art scarcely recognizable,—poor little fellow! Thou dost take all this too near to heart, my friend. . . . Bide a while,—use will create love. When thou hast grown accustomed, thou shalt wonder at naught, even as I.—But now let us return to the cellar of The Golden Turtle and drink anew.

Dum vinum, potamus.
To god Bacchus let us sing:
Te Deum laudamus."

I made no reply, covering my face with my hands, and ran away.

* * *

How can it be? The same man,—he that bestoweth his benediction, with a guiltless smile, upon the pigeons, like to St. Francis; and he, of the smithy of hell, the inventor of the iron monster with the ensanguined spiders' paws,—the same man? Nay, this can not be; this is past bearing! Anything is better than this! 'Tis better to be an atheist, than a servant both of God and of the Devil,—both the visage of Christ and of Sforza the Usurper!

* * *

To-day Marco d'Oggione said:

"Messer Leonardo, many accuse thee, and us, thy pupils, of going to church but rarely, and of working on holidays even as on weekdays."

"Let the bigots say what they will," Leonardo made answer. "Let not your hearts be confused, my friends! To study the manifestations of nature is work pleasing to God. 'Tis verily the same as praying. Coming to know the natural laws, we do by that very thing glorify the First Inventor, the Artist of the Universe, and learn to love Him, inasmuch as great love toward God flows out of great knowledge. He that hath small understanding hath small love. But if thou lovest the Creator for the temporal favours which thou dost expect from Him, and not for His eternal loving-kindness and might,—thou art like to a hound, that doth wag its tail and lick its master's hand in the hope of a tid-bit being thrown to it. Reflect, how much more the hound would love its master were it to fathom his soul and reason. Remember then, my children: love is the daughter of understanding; love is the more vehement the more the understanding is exact. Even in the Scripture it is said: 'Be ye therefore wise as serpents, and harmless as doves.'"[14]

"Is it possible to unite the wisdom of the serpent with the harmlessness of the dove?" retorted Cesare. "Meseems we must choose one of the two. . . ."

"Nay, both together!" answered Leonardo. "Together,—one is impossible without the other: perfect knowledge and perfect love are one and the same."

To-day, reading the Apostle Paul, I found in the eighth chapter of the First Epistle to the Corinthians the following words: "Knowledge puffeth up, but charity edifieth. And if any man think that he knoweth anything, he knoweth nothing yet as he ought to know. But if any man love God, the same is known of him."

The Apostle asserts that knowledge comes from charity; whereas Leonardo, that charity comes from knowledge. Which is right? I can not decide this,—nor can I live on without deciding.

* * *

Meseems I have lost my way in the windings of a fearful labyrinth. I shout, I call aloud,—and there is no answering cry. The farther I go, the more confused I become. Where am I? What will become of me if Thou, too, dost forsake me, O Lord?

* * *

O Fra Benedetto, how I long to return to thy peaceful cell, to tell thee of my torment, to fall on thy breast, that thou mayst take pity on me, take from my soul this burden, my most beloved father, my most meek lamb, who hast fulfilled Christ's behest: Blessed are the poor in spirit!

To-day, a new misfortune.

The court chronicler, Messer Giorgio Merulla and his old friend, the poet Bernardo Bellincioni, were holding converse alone in an empty hall of the Castle. The matter took place after supper. Merulla was gaily tipsy, and, after his wont, in boasting of his free-thinking dreams, his contempt of the insignificant rulers of our age, did make disrespectful remarks about Duke Moro, and, in taking to pieces one of the sonnets of Bellincioni, in which were exalted the would-be services rendered by the Duke to Gian Galeazzo, he called Moro a murderer, the poisoner of the legitimate Duke. Thanks to the artifice with which the tubes of the Ear of Dionysius had been constructed, the Duke, overhearing the conversation from a distant chamber, ordered Merulla to be seized and placed in a cellar prison under the main moat of the fortress, the Redefosso, which surrounds the Castle.

What are Leonardo's thoughts about this,—Leonardo, who constructed the Ear of Dionysius, thinking neither of good nor evil, studying curious laws, "in jest and in play," to use Cesare's expression, —just as he does everything: inventing monstrous war engines, explosive bombs, spiders of iron that cleave with each sweep of their enormous paws some half-hundred people?

* * *

The Apostle saith: "And through thy knowledge shall the weak brother perish, for whom Christ died?"[15]

Is it out of such knowledge that love flows forth? Or are not knowledge and love one and the same?

* * *

At times the face of the master is so radiant and innocent, filled with a purity so dovelike, that I am ready to forgive all, to believe all,—and to give my soul up to him anew. But suddenly in the impenetrable folds of his thin lips there will flash an expression which frightens me, as if I were peering through a transparent depth into underwater abysses. And again it seems to me that there is a mystery within his soul, and I recall one of his enigmas:

"The greatest rivers flow underground."

* * *

Duke Gian Galeazzo has died.

They say,—O God sees, I scarce can lift my hand to write this word, nor do I believe it!—they say that Leonardo is a murderer: he, 'twould seem, has poisoned the Duke with fruits from an envenomed tree.

I remember how the mechanic Zoroastro da Peretola was showing Monna Cassandra this accursed tree. 'Twere better had I never seen it! Even at this moment I imagine I see it, as it was on that night, in the turbidly-green mist of the moon, with drops of venom on its wet leaves, with its quietly burgeoning fruits, surrounded by death and horror. And again resound in my ears the words of the Scripture: "But of the tree of the knowledge of good and evil, thou shalt not eat of it: for in the day that thou eatest thereof thou shalt surely die."[16]

O woe, woe is me, who am accursed! Erstwhile, in the delectable cell of my father Benedetto, in my innocent simplicity, I was like unto the first man, in Paradise. But I have sinned, have given my soul up to the temptations of the Wise Serpent, have tasted of the Tree of Knowledge,—and lo, my eyes were opened, and I perceived good and evil, light and shade, God and the Devil; and also perceived I that I am naked, orphaned, and poor,—and my soul is dying its death.

* * *

Out of the depths of hell do I cry out to Thee, Lord; attend unto the voice of my supplication; hearken unto me and have compassion! Like the robber on the cross do I call Thy name: remember me, Lord, when Thou comest into Thy Kingdom!

* * *

Leonardo has begun limning the face of Christ anew.

* * *

The Duke has entrusted him with the construction of a machine for the elevation of the Most Holy Nail. With mathematical exactness will he weigh on the scales the instrument of the Lord's Passion, like a fragment of old iron,—so many ounces, so many grains,—and the holy relic is but a numeral among numerals to him, only a part among the parts of the elevating mechanism,—among ropes, wheels, levers and pulleys!

* * *

The Apostle saith: "Little children, it is the last time: and as ye have heard that antichrist shall come, even now are there many antichrists; whereby we know that it is the last time." [17]

* * *

At night a mob of people surrounded our house, demanding the Most Holy Nail, and yelling: "Sorcerer! atheist, poisoner of the Duke, Antichrist!"

Leonardo heard the outcries of the rabble without anger. When Marco would have shot his arquebus, he forbade him. The master's face was calm and impenetrable, as ever.

I fell down at his feet, imploring him to tell me but one word, that my doubts might be dispelled. As the living God is my witness, I would have believed him! But he did not want to, or could not, tell me anything.

Little Giacopo slipped out of the house, made a circuit around the crowd, a few blocks farther came across the patrol of the mounted guard of the Captain of the Giustizia, brought them to the house,—and at the very moment when the shattered doors were already falling down under the press of the crowd, the soldiers attacked it from the rear. The rioters ran away. Giacopo is wounded in the head by a stone,—almost killed.

* * *

To-day I was in the Cathedral, at the festival of the Most Holy Nail. It was elevated at the instant determined upon by the astrologers. Leonardo's machine could not have worked better. Neither the ropes nor the pulleys could be seen. It appeared as if the round vessel with its crystal sides and golden rays, within which the Nail was confined, was going up of itself, in the clouds of incense, like to the rising sun. This was the miracle of mechanics. The choir burst forth:

Confixa Clavis viscera,
Tendens manus vestigia,
Redemptionis gratia
Hic immolata est Hostia.

And the ark came to a rest in the dark arch, over the main altar of the Cathedral, surrounded by five inextinguishable holy lamps.

The archbishop proclaimed:

"*O Crux benedicta, quæ sola fuisti digna portare Regem cœlorum et Dominum. Alleluia!*"

The people fell down on their knees, repeating after him:

"*Alleluia!*"

And the usurper of the throne, the murderer Moro, in tears, raised his arms up to the Most Holy Nail.

After that they regaled the people with wine, with carcasses of steers, five thousand measures of pease, and over seven thousand pounds of lard. The rabble, having forgotten the murdered Duke, glutting itself and guzzling, kept shouting "Long live Moro! Long live the Nail!"

Bellincioni composed hexameters, which proclaim that under the moderate rule of Augustus, of Moro, beloved of the Gods, there shall shine forth for the universe from the ancient Nail of Iron a new Age of Gold.

Coming out of the Cathedral, the Duke approached Leonardo, embraced him, kissed him, calling him his own Archimedes, thanked him for the wondrous construction of the elevating machine, and promised to bestow upon him a pure-blooded Barbary mare from his own stud on the Villa Sforzesca, together with two thousand imperial ducats; after that, having condescendingly patted his shoulder, he said that now the master could, at his leisure, finish the visage of Christ in the Mystic Supper.

* * *

I have comprehended the words of the Scripture: "A double minded man *is* unstable in all his ways."[18]

I can no longer bear it! I perish, I am going out of my mind, because of these double-minded thoughts, from the visage of Antichrist peering through the visage of Christ. Wherefore hast Thou forsaken me, O Lord?

* * *

I must flee, ere it be too late.

* * *

I arose in the night, tied up my clothes, linen and books into a bundle for travelling, took a walking staff, descended in the darkness, groping my way downstairs to the workshop, laid down thirty florins on the table,—the stipend for the last six months of tuition (in order to obtain them I had sold a ring with an emerald, my mother's gift), and, without saying farewell to anyone,—everybody being still asleep—went away from the house of Leonardo forever.

* * *

Fra Benedetto told me that ever since I had forsaken him, he prayed every night for me, and that he had a vision of God's turning me back to the path of salvation.

Fra Benedetto is going on a journey to Florence to see his sick brother, a Dominican in the Monastery of San Marco, where Girolamo Savonarola is father-superior.

* * *

Praise and thanksgiving be unto Thee, O Lord! Thou hast drawn me out from the shadow of death, out from the jaws of hell.

Now do I renounce the wisdom of this age, sealed with the seal of the Seven-Headed Serpent, the Beast coming in the darkness, yclept the Antichrist.

I renounce the fruits of the poisoned Tree of Knowledge; the pride of vain reason; ungodly science, whose father is the Devil.

I renounce all temptation of pagan beauty.

I renounce all that is not Thy will, Thy glory, Thy wisdom, my God Christ!

Enlighten my soul with Thy sole light; deliver my soul from accursed double-minded thoughts; strengthen my steps in Thy ways, that my feet may not waver: shelter me under the shadow of Thy wings!

Praise the Lord, my soul! I shall sing the praise of the Lord all the days of my life; I shall chant unto my God all the days that I am!

* * *

In two days from now Fra Benedetto and I are going to Florence. With the blessing of my spiritual father I would become a novice in the cloister of San Marco, under the great chosen one of God, Fra Girolamo Savonarola.—God hath saved me.

* * *

[With these words the diary of Giovanni Beltraffio ends.]

BOOK SEVEN

The Holocaust of Vanities

I

ORE THAN A YEAR HAD PASSED SINCE BELTRAFFIO had entered the cloister of San Marco as a novice.

One day, after noon, at the end of the carnival of the year fourteen hundred and ninety-six, Girolamo Savonarola, sitting at his work-table in his cell, was writing down the vision he had recently had from God about the Two Crosses over the city of Rome,—one, black, in a death-laden whirlwind, with the inscription: The Cross of the Wrath of The Lord; and one, shining in the azure, with the inscription: The Cross of the Compassion of The Lord.

He felt fatigue and a fever ague. Putting by his pen, he let his head drop on his arms, shut his eyes, and began to recall the things he had heard that morning concerning the life of Pope Alexander VI, one of the Borgias, told him by the humble Fra Pagolo, a monk sent to Rome for reconnaissance, and but now returned to Florence.

Like the visions of the Apocalypse, monstrous images whirled past him: the Scarlet Bull from the hereditary shield of the Borgias, a likeness of the ancient Egyptian Apis, the Golden Calf offered up to the Roman pontiff, instead of the meek Lamb of the Lord; the shameless sports at night, after the feasting in the halls of the Vatican, before the Most Holy Father, his own daughter, and a throng of cardinals; the most beautiful Giulia Farnese, the youthful concubine of the sexagenarian Pope, depicted upon holy icons in the guise of the Mother of God; the two elder sons of Alexander,—Don Cæsar, Cardinal of Valentino, and Don Giovanni, the colour-bearer of the Roman Church,—both hating one another to the verge of Cain-like fratricide out of their unclean lust toward their sister, Lucrezia.

And a shiver ran through Girolamo, as he recalled that of which Fra Pagolo had scarce durst whisper in his ear,—the incestuous lust of the father toward his daughter,—of the old Pope toward Madonna Lucrezia.

"Nay, nay, God sees I believe it not,—'tis a slander. . . . 'Tis impossible!" he kept on repeating, yet secretly felt that all things were possible in the fearful nest of the Borgias. A cold sweat stood out on the forehead of the monk. He threw himself on his knees before the crucifix.

A quiet knocking sounded on the door of the cell.

"Who is there?"

"I, father!"

Girolamo recognized, by his voice, his right-hand man and faithful friend, Brother Domenico Buonvicini.

"The most worthy Ricciardo Becchi, the legate of the Pope, begs permission to speak with thee."

"'Tis well; let him wait a while. Send Brother Silvestro to me."

Silvestro Maruffi was a weak-minded monk, suffering with the falling sickness. Girolamo deemed him the chosen vessel of God's blessing; he loved and feared him, explained the visions of Silvestro according to all the rules of the most refined scholastics of the Great Angel of the Schola, Thomas Aquinas, by the aid of crafty deductions, logical premises, enthymemes, apothegms and syllogisms, and finding a prophetic meaning in that which seemed the meaningless babbling of an innocent. Maruffi did not evince any respect toward his father-superior; not infrequently he reviled him, cursed him out before all, even beating him. Girolamo accepted these contumelies with resignation and submitted to him in all things. If the people of Florence were in the power of Girolamo,—then he, in his turn, was in the hands of the weak-minded Maruffi.

Upon entering the cell, Brother Silvestro seated himself on the floor, in a corner, and, scratching his red, bare legs, commenced purring a monotonous little song. There was a dull and woebegone expression on his freckled face, with its little nose, as pointed as an awl, its pendulous nether lip, and its rheumy eyes, a turbid bottle-green in colour.

"Brother," said Girolamo, "out of Rome has come an envoy from the Pope. Tell me, shall I receive him, and what reply shall I make to him? Has no vision or voice been vouchsafed thee?"

Maruffi contrived a clownish grimace, and fell to barking like a dog and grunting like a pig,—he had the gift of mimicking to perfection the voices of animals.

"Dear little brother," Savonarola beseeched him, "utter but one little word, like a good soul! My soul doth sicken unto death. Pray to God, that He may send down upon thee the spirit of prophecy. . . ."

The innocent stuck out his tongue; his face became distorted.

"Well, now, why, why dost thou press me so, thou accursed windbag, thou brainless quail, thou sheep's head! Ugh, may the rats gnaw off thy nose!" he cried out, with unexpected malevolence. "Thou hast made thy bed, now lie in it. I am no prophet for thee, nor thy counsellor!"

Then he looked up at Savonarola from underneath his eyebrows, and continued in another voice, quieter and more kindly:

"I feel sorry for thee, little brother,—oh, how sorry, thou foolish little one! . . . And how dost thou know that my visions are from God, and not from the Devil?"

He lapsed into silence, narrowed his eyelids, and his face became immobile, as though dead. Savonarola, thinking this a vision, grew deathly still in reverent expectation. But Maruffi opened his eyes, turned his head slowly, as though he were trying to hear something, looked out the window, and with a kind, radiant, almost intelligent smile, he uttered:

"Little birds,—dost hear them?—little birds! There is grass in the field now, have no fear, and little yellow flowerets. Eh, brother Girolamo, thou hast made confusion enough here, hast humoured thy pride, made the fiend rejoice,—and enough! One must think of God also. Let thee and me go from this accursed world into the dear desert!"

And he began singing in a pleasing, low voice, as he rocked himself:

"Let us to green woods wander,
Seek shelter yet unknown;
Where chilly springs meander,
'Midst orioles' sweet moan."

Suddenly jumping up,—his iron fetters emitting a clank,—he ran up to Savonarola, seized him by the hand, and said in a whisper, as though gasping from ferocity:

"I had a vision, I had a vision, I had a vision! Ugh, thou son of a devil, thou head of an ass, may the rats gnaw off thy nose,—I had a vision! . . ."

"Tell me, little brother, tell me, then, quickly. . . ."

"Flame! Flame!" exclaimed Maruffi.

"Well, well,—what else?"

"A flame about a stake," continued Silvestro, "and a man thereon! . . ."

"Who?" asked Girolamo.

Maruffi nodded his head, but did not reply at once: at first he fixed Savonarola with his piercing, green little eyes, and burst into low laughter, like a madman; then he bent over and whispered in his ear:

"Thee!"

A shudder ran through Girolamo, and he staggered back.

Maruffi arose and withdrew from the cell, clanking his fetters from time to time, humming the snatch:

"Let us to green woods wander,
Seek shelter yet unknown;
Where chilly springs meander,
'Midst orioles' sweet moan."

Regaining his composure, Girolamo ordered the Pope's legate, Ricciardo Becchi, to be summoned to him.

II

RUSTLING in his long, silken raiment, resembling a cassock, of the shade of March violets,—a shade much in vogue,—with Venetian sleeves thrown back, with a border of dark-brown fox fur, disseminating a zephyr of musk amber all about him, the Scriptor of the Most Holy Apostolic Chancery entered the cell of Savonarola. Messer Ricciardo Becchi was possessed of a certain unctuousness in his movements, in his clever and grandly-kind smile, in his clear, almost ingenuous eyes, in the amiable, laughing dimples of his fresh, smooth-shaven cheeks,—that unctuousness so habitual to the grandees of the Court of Rome.

He asked for a blessing, bending his back with a semi-courtly dexterity, kissed the gaunt hand of the Prior of San Marco, and began speaking in Latin, with elegant Ciceronian turns of speech, with lengthy, statelily developed periods. Beginning in a roundabout way, with that which in the rules of the art of oratory is termed ingratiation, he mentioned the fame of the Florentine preacher; then he passed on to the matter on hand: the Most Holy Father, righteously incensed by the obdurate refusals of Brother Girolamo to appear in Rome, yet being ardent in his zeal toward the weal of the Church, toward perfect unity of those faithful in Christ, toward the peace of all the world, and desiring not the death, but the salvation of a sinner, showed a fatherly readiness, in the event of Savonarola's repentance, to restore him to his good graces.

The monk lifted his eyes and said in a low voice:

"Messer, what think ye,—doth the Most Holy Father believe in God?"

Ricciardo made no reply, as though he had not heard, or had purposely let pass the unseemly question, and again reverting to the matter at hand, hinted that the highest rank of the spiritual hierarchy,—the red hat of a cardinal,—was awaiting Brother Girolamo in the event of submission, and, bending quickly toward the monk, tapping his hand with a finger, added with an insinuating smile:

"One little word, Father Girolamo, but one little word,— and the red hat is yours!"

Savonarola fixed his companion with his steadfast eyes and spoke:

"And what, messer, if I submit not,—if I hold not my peace? What if the unreasoning monk spurn the honour of the Roman purple, will not be tempted by the red hat, will not cease to bark, guarding the house of his Lord, like a faithful hound, whose mouth you can not stuff with any sop?"

Ricciardo looked at him with curiosity, wrinkled his brow a trifle, elevated his eyebrows, meditatively admired his nails, smooth and elongated, like almonds, and adjusted his rings. Then, leisurely, he took out of his pocket, unrolled, and handed to the Prior the excommunication from the Church of one Brother Girolamo Savonarola, ready for the signature and the application of the Great Seal of the Fisher, wherein, among other things, the Pope styled him the son of perdition and the most despicable of insects,—*nequissimus omniredo.*

"Do you await an answer?" asked the monk, having read it.

The Scriptor silently bowed his head.

Savonarola raised himself to his full height and threw the Pope's bull at the feet of the envoy.

"There is my answer! Go to Rome, and say that I accept the challenge to a duel with Pope Antichrist. We shall see whether he shall excommunicate me from the Church, or I him!"

The door of the cell opened with the utmost caution, and Brother Domenico peered in. Hearing the loud voice of the Prior, he had come running to find out what had occurred. The monks had huddled in a knot near the entrance.

Ricciardo had already looked around at the door several times, and, finally, remarked politely:

"I am taking the liberty of reminding you that I am empowered to hold only a confidential meeting. . . ."

Savonarola walked up to the door and flung it ajar.

"Hearken!" he exclaimed. "Hearken all, for not only to you alone, brethren, but to all the people of Florence do I proclaim the base barter, —the choice between excommunication from the Church and the cardinal's purple!"

His sunken eyes beneath the low forehead glowed like embers; his hideous lower jaw was quiveringly thrust forward.

"The time is come! I shall go forth against ye, ye cardinals and prelates of Rome, as against pagans! I shall turn the key in the lock, open the coffer of abominations,—and there shall come forth such an evil odour out of your Rome that the people shall be stifled. I shall utter words such as will cause ye to blanch, and the universe shall quake to its foundations, and the Church of God, slain of ye, shall hear my voice: 'Lazarus, come forth!'—and it shall arise and come forth out of its grave. . . . Neither of your mitres have I any need, nor of your cardinals' hats! The red hat of death alone, the bloody crown of Thy martyrs, bestow Thou upon me, O Lord!"

He fell down on his knees, sobbing, stretching forth his bloodless hands toward the Crucifix.

Ricciardo, taking advantage of the confusion of the minute, nimbly slipped out of the cell and hurriedly made his escape.

III

In the crowd of monks who had been listening attentively to Savonarola was the novice Giovanni Beltraffio.

When the brethren had begun to disperse, he, too, descended the staircase to the main courtyard of the monastery and sat down at his favourite place, in the long covered passageway, where at this time of the day it was always cool and deserted.

Between the white walls of the cloister grew laurels, cypresses, and bushes of damask roses, under whose shade Brother Girolamo was fond of preaching: the legend saith that the angels watered these roses at night.

The novice opened at the First Epistle of Paul to the Corinthians, and read:

"Ye can not drink the cup of the Lord, and the cup of devils: ye can not be partakers of the Lord's table, and of the table of devils."[19]

He arose and took to pacing the gallery, recalling his thoughts and emotions during the last year, passed in the cloister of San Marco.

At first he had tasted great spiritual delectation among the disciples of Savonarola. Sometimes, of a morning, Father Girolamo would lead them off beyond the walls of the city. By a steep little path, which seemed to lead straight up to heaven, they would rise to the summit of Fiesole, from whence, between its knolls, they could see Florence, lying in the valley of the Arno. On a little green meadow, where there were throngs of violets, lilies-of-the-valley, and irises, and where the trunks of the young cypresses, warmed up by the sun, exuded rosin, the Prior would sit down. The monks would lie down at his feet on the grass; they wove garlands, held converse, danced, romped like children, the while others played on violins, altos and violas, resembling those with which Fra Beato depicts his choirs of angels.

Savonarola instructed them not, neither did he preach; he did but make kindly discourses for them; he played himself and laughed, like a child. Giovanni contemplated the smile which irradiated his face, —and it seemed to him that in the deserted grove, filled with music and singing, upon the summit of Fiesole, surrounded by the blue heavens, they resembled God's angels in Paradise.

Savonarola would approach the precipice and with love gaze upon Florence, wrapped around with the slight haze of morning, as a mother would upon a slumbering babe. Up from below floated the first ringing of bells, just like the sleepy babbling of children.

While on summer nights when the fireflies flitted about like the serene candles of invisible angels, under the sweet-scented thicket of damask roses in the courtyard of San Marco, he would tell the brethren of the sanguinary stigmata, of the wounds of heavenly love on the body of St. Catherine of Siena, which resembled the wounds of the Lord, and gave forth a sweet odour, like roses.

"With the pain of wounds let me be sated,
With the torture of the cross elated,—
With the torture of Thy Son!"

chanted the monks, and Giovanni desired that in this case also might be repeated the miracle of which Savonarola spoke,—that the fiery rays coming out of the cup with the Holy Sacrament might sear in his body, like iron at white-heat, with the wounds of the Cross.

"Gesù, Gesù, amore!"

he would sigh, languishing from delectation.

On one occasion Savonarola had sent him, as he also did other novices, to tend a very ill man in the Villa Carreggi, situated some two miles from Florence, on the southern slope of the Uccelatoio Knolls,—the very same villa where Lorenzo de Medici used to live for long periods of time, and where he had died. In one of the chambers of the castle, desolate and silent, lighted by a feeble light, like that of the grave, through the chinks of the closed shutters, Giovanni beheld a picture of Sandro Botticelli's,—the birth of the goddess Venus,—*Venus Anadyomene*. Stark naked, white, just like a water lily,—humid, as though fragrant with the briny freshness of the sea,—she glided over the waves, standing on a pearl shell. The golden, heavy strands of her hair twined like serpents. With a demure gesture of her right hand she pressed them against her loins, covering her nudity, and her beauteous body breathed with the seductiveness of sin, while her innocent lips, her childlike eyes, were full of a holy pensiveness.

The face of the goddess seemed familiar to Giovanni. He gazed at her for long, and suddenly recalled that just such a face, just such childlike eyes, that seemed to be tear-stained, just such innocent eyes, with an expression of unearthly sadness, he had seen in another picture of the same Sandro Botticelli,—the Lord's Mother. Inexpressible confusion filled his soul. With eyes cast down he left the villa.

Going down-hill to Florence, by a narrow lane, he noticed in a wall-niche an ancient Crucifix, fell on his knees before it, and began praying, to drive away temptation. From behind the wall in the garden, probably beneath the shade of the same roses that overhung the niche, came the sound of a mandolin,—someone cried out, someone's voice uttered in a frightened whisper:

"Nay, nay, let me be. . . ."

"Dearest," another voice replied, "O love, my love! *Amore!*"

The lute fell down, its strings quivering resonantly,—and the sound of a kiss was heard.

Giovanni jumped up, repeating: "*Gesù! Gesù!*"—without daring to add: "*Amore!*"

"Here, too," he reflected, "here, too,—*she* is. In the face of the Madonna, in the words of a sacred hymn, in the pleasant odour of roses shading the Crucifix! . . ."

He covered his face with his hands and started away, as though fleeing from invisible pursuit.

Having returned to the cloister, he went to Savonarola and told him all. The Prior gave him the usual advice about combating the devil with the weapons of fasting and prayer. But when the novice would have explained that it was not the devil of fleshly desire tempting him, but the demon of spiritual pagan beauty,—the monk did not understand; at first he was amazed, then remarked sternly that the false gods held naught save unclean lust and pride, which are always hideous, inasmuch as beauty consists only of Christian virtues.

Giovanni went away from him, unconsoled. From that day on the fiend of despondency and sedition attacked him.

Once he happened to hear Brother Girolamo, in speaking of painting, demand that every picture bring benefit,—instructing and edifying men by thoughts of saving their souls: were they to destroy by the hand of the headsman all seductive depictions, the Florentines would be doing a deed pleasing to God.

In the same way did the monk judge of science. "A man of folly is he," he would say, "who imagines that logic and philosophy confirm the truths of faith. For doth a strong light have need of a faint one, —the wisdom of the Lord of human wisdom? Were the apostles and martyrs versed in logic and philosophy? An illiterate old crone, praying zealously before an icon, is nearer to a knowledge of God than all the wiseacres and men of learning. Nor logic nor philosophy shall save them on the day of the Last Judgment! Homer and Virgil, Plato and Aristotle,—they are all bound for the dwelling place of Satan! Like unto the sirens—

> With artful songs charming ears to submission,
> While leading souls to eternal perdition.

Science giveth men a stone instead of bread. Behold them that follow the teachings of this world,—their hearts are of stone."

"He that knoweth little, loveth little. Great love is the daughter of great knowledge,"—only now did Giovanni feel the entire profundity of these words, and, listening to the anathemas of the monk against the temptations of art and science, recalled the intelligent discourses of Leonardo; his calm face; his eyes, as chill as the heavens; his smile, filled with a captivating wisdom. He had not forgotten about the fearful fruits of the envenomed tree, about the iron spider, about the Ear of Dionysius, about the machine for the elevation of the Most Holy Nail, about the visage of Antichrist beneath the visage of Christ. But it seemed that he had not come to an ultimate understanding of the master, had not solved the final mystery of his heart; had not disentangled that primary knot in which all threads meet, in which all contradictions are resolved.

Thus did Giovanni recall the past year of his life in the cloister of San Marco. And the while he was pacing back and forth over the darkened gallery, in deep meditation,—evening came on, the quiet ringing of the *Ave Maria* resounded, and the monks in a black file passed through to the church. Giovanni did not follow after them; he sat down at the same spot, again opened the book of the Epistles of the Apostle Paul, and, beclouded by the crafty instigations of the Devil, the great Logician, altered the words of the Scripture in his mind thus:

"Ye can not *but* drink the cup of the Lord, and the cup of the devils: ye can not *but* be partakers of the Lord's table, and of the table of devils."

With a bitter smile, he raised his eyes to heaven, where he beheld the Evening Star, which was like to the light of the most beautiful of the angels of darkness,—Lucifer the Light Bearer.

And there came to his memory a legend he had heard from a certain learned monk,—a legend accepted of the great Origen, and retold anew by Matteo Palmieri the Florentine in his poem *The City of Life*. 'Twould seem that in the times of the Devil's contention with God, among the denizens of heaven had been some who would join neither the host of the Devil, nor the host of God, holding aloof both from the one and the other,—the lone spectators of the contest; 'twas of them that Dante has said:

Angeli che non furon ribelli,
Ne pur fideli a Dio, ma per sè foro.

Angels, that were neither rebels,
Nor faithful to God,—but were for themselves alone.

These free and sad spirits,—neither evil, nor good, nor dark, nor radiant, partaking of evil and good, of darkness and light, had been banished by the All Highest Justice to the earthly vale, midway 'tween heaven and hell,—into the vale of twilight, a twilight that was like to them,—and there they had become men.

"And how is one to know," Giovanni continued his sinful thoughts aloud,—"how is one to know,—perhaps there is no evil in this, per-

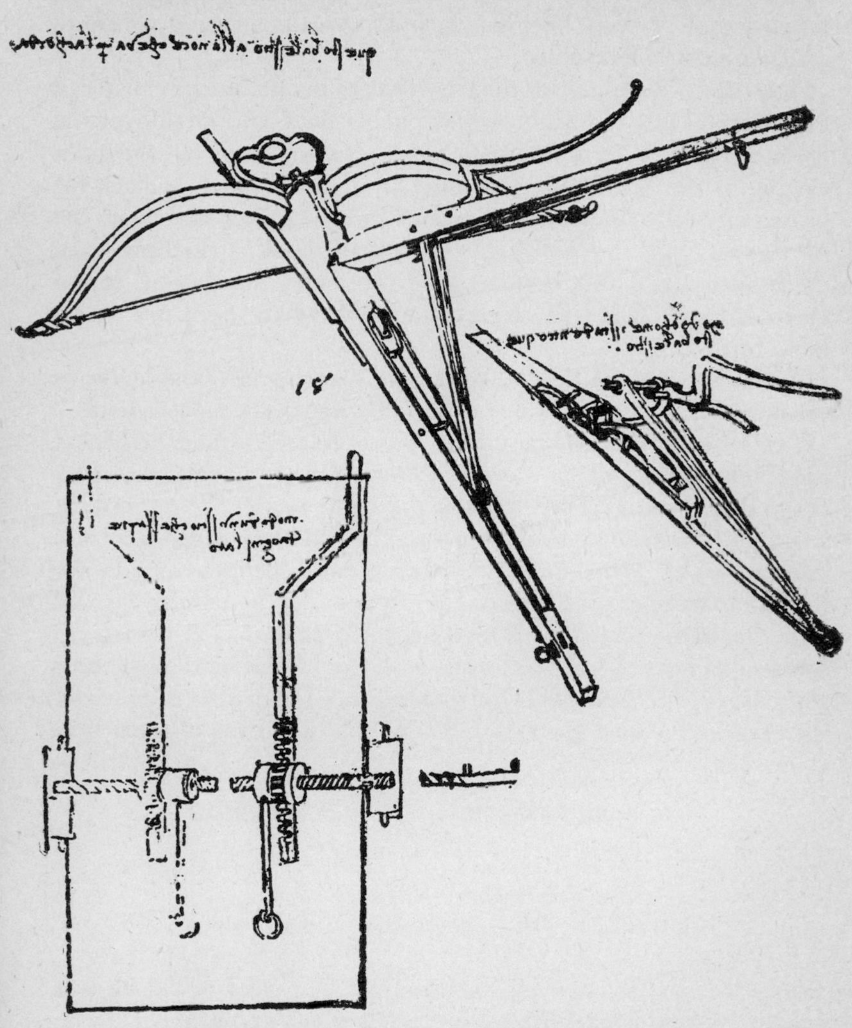

haps one ought to drink to the glory of the Only One out of both cups together?"

And it appeared to him that it was not he that had spoken thus, but that some other, who was bending over and breathing upon him from the back with a cool, caressing breath, had whispered in his ear: "Together, together!"

He jumped up in horror, looked around, and, although there was no one in the deserted gallery, woven over with the cobweb of the twilight, he began to cross himself, trembling and blenching; then he started running precipitately out of the covered way, through the yard, and only within the church, where the candles were burning and the monks were chanting vespers, did he stop and draw his breath; falling on the stone flags, he began praying:

"Lord, save me,—deliver me from these double-minded thoughts! I want not two cups! Thy sole cup, Thy sole truth doth my soul thirst after, Lord!"

But the blessing of God, like to the dew that refresheth dusty grasses, did not soften his heart.

Having returned to his cell, he lay down. Toward morning he dreamt a dream: it seemed that he, with Monna Cassandra, both astride a black goat, were flying through the air. "To the Sabbath! To the Sabbath!" whispered the witch, turning around toward him her face, pale as marble, with lips as scarlet as blood, with eyes as transparent as amber. And he recognized the goddess of earthly love with the unearthly pensiveness in her eyes,—the White She-Demon. The full moon illumined her stark body, so delectably and eerily fragrant that his teeth chattered; he embraced her, and clove to her. "*Amore! Amore!*" she lisped, and laughed,—and the black wool of the goat yielded beneath them, like a soft, sultry couch. And it seemed to him that this —was death.

IV

GIOVANNI awoke from the sun, the ringing of bells, and the voices of children. He descended to the courtyard, and beheld a throng, all in uniform white garments, with olive branches and little scarlet crosses. This was the Holy Army of Infant Inquisitors, established by Savonarola to regulate the purity of morals in Florence.

Giovanni made his way into the throng, and listened to the conversations.

"A complaint, eh?" with an importance conferred upon him by his rank the "captain,"—a thin lad of fourteen was asking another,—impish, spry, red-haired and cross-eyed, with ears sticking out.

"Just that, Messer Federigo,—a complaint!" the other answered, standing stiffly erect, like a soldier, with an occasional respectful glance at the captain.

"I know. Your aunt was dicing?"

"By no means, Your Grace,—not my aunt, but my stepmother, and not dicing, but . . ."

"Ah, yes," Federigo corrected himself, "it was Lippina's aunt who was casting dice last Saturday and blaspheming. What is it, then?"

"I have a stepmother. . . . May God punish her. . . ."

"Do not shilly-shally, dear fellow! There is no time for that. I am up to my neck in business. . . ."

"I hear you, messer. So, if it please you,—my stepmother, with her dearest friend, a monk, did drink up the forbidden little cask of red wine out of my father's cellar, what time my father was going to the fair at Marignola. And the monk advised her to go to the Madonna which is at the Rubaconte bridge, to put up a candle and to pray, that my father might not recall the forbidden cask. She did just that, and when my father, on his return, did not notice anything, in her rejoicing she did hang on the carving of the Holy Virgin a little cask made out of wax, every whit like the wine-cask out of which she had regaled the monk,—in gratitude for that the Mother of God helped her to hoodwink her husband."

"'Tis a sin, a great sin!" declared Federigo, frowning. "But how didst thou get wind of it, Pippo?"

"I got it out of the hostler, while the hostler was told it by my stepmother's wench, a Tartar, whilst the Tartar wench was told it . . ."

"Place of residence?" the captain sternly cut him short.

"The harness shop of Loroncetto, near the Sacra Annunziata."

"'Tis well," concluded Federigo. "We shall have an investigation this very day."

An exceedingly pretty little boy, altogether a mite, of some six years, was sobbing bitterly, leaning against a wall in a corner of the courtyard.

"What art thou crying about?" another, somewhat older, asked him.

"They have shorn me! . . . They have shorn me! . . . I would never have gone had I known that they shear one! . . ."

He passed his hand over his flaxen hair, made hideous by the shears of the monastery barber, who clipped short the hair of all the new recruits joining the Most Holy Army.

"Ah, Luca, Luca," the elder lad shook his head reproachfully, "what sinful thoughts thou hast! If thou wouldst but think of the holy martyrs! When the paynim did chop off their legs and arms, they rendered praise unto God. But thou dost begrudge even thy hair!"

Luca ceased crying, struck by the example of the holy martyrs. But suddenly his face became distorted by terror, and he began howling still more lustily, probably imagining that the monks would chop off his legs and arms also to the glory of God.

"Listen," an old, stout burgher's wife, red from excitement, addressed Giovanni, "could you point out to me a certain boy here, a little dark fellow, with little blue eyes?"

"What is his name?"

"Dino,—Dino de Garbo. . . ."

"What division is he in?"

"Ah, my God, I really do not know! . . . The whole day am I seeking him, running around, questioning, nor can I get anyone to talk sense. My head is spinning around. . . ."

"Your son?"

"My nephew. A quiet, modest lad, an excellent scholar. . . . And suddenly some hellions decoyed him into this horrible Army. Just think of it,—he is a tender child, frail,—whereas, so they say, they fight with stones here. . . ."

And the aunt again took to groaning and oh'ing.

"You yourself are to blame," a dignified elderly citizen, clad in raiment of an old-fashioned cut, turned to her. "Whale the urchins properly,—all this flightiness would not go to their heads! For,—has anyone ever seen the like?—monks and children have gotten the notion of running the government. 'Tis a matter of eggs teaching the hen. Truly, never has there been such folly in the world!"

"Exactly, exactly,—eggs teaching the hen!" the aunt chimed in. "The monks say there will be a paradise on earth. I do not know what may be, but meanwhile we have the darkest hell. In every house there are tears, quarrels, screaming. . . ."

"Have ye heard?" she went on, bending down toward her companion's ear with a mysterious air; "the other day in the Cathedral Brother Girolamo ups before all the people; 'Fathers and Mothers,' says he, 'send your sons and daughters even to the end of the world,—they shall return to me just the same; they are mine! . . .'"

The elderly burgher dived into the throng of children.

"Ah, thou little fiend, thou art caught!" he cried out, seizing a lad by the ear. "Well, just thou bide a while, I shall show thee how to run away from home,—to tie up with riff-raff,—not to obey thy father! . . ."

"We must obey our Heavenly Father more than our earthly," answered the boy in a quiet, firm tone.

"Oh, have a care, Doffo! Better not make me lose my patience. . . . Go on, go on home,—why art thou obstinate!"

"Leave me be, father. I shall not go. . . ."

"Thou shalt not?"

"No."

"Then take that!"

The father struck him in the face.

Doffo did not budge,—even his blanched lips did not quiver. He merely raised his eyes to heaven.

"Quieter, quieter, messer! You must not hurt the children," cried the city guards, who had been assigned by the Signoria for the protection of the children.

"Get ye gone, ye scoundrels!" the old man was yelling, infuriated.

The soldiers were taking the boy away from him; the father was cursing and would not let him go.

"Dino! Dino!" the aunt squealed out, recognizing her nephew in the distance, and darting toward him. But the guards held her back.

"Let me go, let me go! Lord, what is all this!" she was vociferating. "Dino! My boy! Dino!"

At this moment a movement ran through the ranks of the Most Holy Army. Countless little hands began to wave the scarlet crosses and the branches of olive, and, greeting Savonarola, who was coming out into the courtyard, the ringing childish voices began to chant:

> "*Lumen ad revelationem gentium et gloriam plebis Israel.*"
> "A light to lighten the Gentiles, and the glory of thy people Israel."[20]

Little girls surrounded the monk, showering him with yellow spring flowers, pink snowdrops, and dark violets; getting down on their knees, they embraced and kissed his feet.

Inundated by the rays of the sun, silently, with a tender smile, he bestowed his blessing upon the children.

"Long live Christ, the King of Florence! Long live the Virgin Mary, our Queen!" cried the children.

"Get in line! Forward march!" the little military leaders issued their commands.

The music blared forth, the banners rustled, and the regiments moved off.

On the Piazza of the Signoria, before the Palazzo Vecchio, the Burning of the Vanities,—*Bruciamento delle vanità*,—was scheduled to take place. The Holy Army was to go around Florence once more, on a tour of inspection, for the gathering of the "vanities and anathemas."

V

WHEN the courtyard had become deserted, Giovanni saw Messer Cipriano Buonaccorsi, Consul of the art of the Calimala, owner of the *fondachi* near Or San Michele; the lover of antiquities, in whose ground, at San Gervasio, on the Miller's Mound, the ancient sculpture of Venus had been found.

Giovanni walked up to him. They fell to chatting. Messer Cipriano told of how Leonardo da Vinci had recently come to Florence from Milan, with instructions from the Duke to buy up works of art out of palaces devastated by the Holy Army. With the same purpose had come Giorgio Merulla, who had sat two months through in a prison, and had been liberated and pardoned by the Duke, partly through the intervention of Leonardo.

The merchant requested Giovanni to lead him to the prior, and they set out together for the cell of Savonarola.

Standing in the doorway, Beltraffio heard the conversation of the Consul of Calimala with the prior of San Marco.

Messer Cipriano proposed to purchase for two and twenty thousand florins all the books, pictures, statues, and other treasures of art, which were this day destined to perish in the bonfire. The prior refused. The merchant pondered; pondered some more, and threw in eight thousand more.

The monk did not even answer this time. Thereupon Cipriano moved his sunken, toothless mouth, as though he were chewing; tucked the skirts of his worn, wretched pelisse of fox fur over his chilled knees, sighed, puckered up his weak eyes, and spoke in his pleasant and quiet voice:

"Father Girolamo, I shall ruin myself, I shall give all I possess,—forty thousand florins."

Savonarola raised his eyes toward him and asked:

"If you are ruining yourself, and are not moved by covetousness in this matter, why do you exert yourself?"

"I was born in Florence, and love this land," answered the merchant with simplicity, "I would not want men from other lands to be able to say that we, like barbarians, are burning the blameless productions of sages and artists."

"Oh, my son, if thou wouldst but love thy fatherland in heaven as thou lovest thy earthly one! But be consoled: in the bonfire will perish only that which deserves perishing, inasmuch as the evil and the corrupt can not be beautiful, according to the evidence of your lauded sages themselves."

"Are you convinced, father," said Cipriano, "that children are always able to distinguish unerringly the good from the evil in works of art and learning?"

"'Out of the mouths of babes and sucklings. . . .'"[21] retorted the monk. "'Except ye be converted, and become as little children, ye shall not enter into the kingdom of heaven.[22] . . . I will destroy the wisdom of the wise, and will bring to nothing the understanding of the prudent,'[23] saith the Lord. By day and by night do I pray for these little ones that what they may not understand in the vanities of art and learning may be revealed unto them from above, through the blessing of the Holy Ghost."

"I implore you, ponder upon it," concluded the Consul, arising. "Perhaps a certain part . . ."

"Do not waste your words in vain, messer!" Brother Girolamo stopped him. "My decision is unalterable."

Cipriano, champing his bloodless lips, like those of an old crone, mumbled something under his breath. Savonarola caught only the last word:

". . . madness."

"Madness!" he caught him up, and his eyes blazed forth. "Well, but is the Golden Calf of the Borgias, offered up to the Pope in blasphemous revels, not madness? Is not the raising of the Most Holy Nail, to the glory of the Lord, on a devilish machine by the usurper of the throne, the murderer Moro, not madness? Ye dance about the Golden Calf, wax insane to the glory of your god Mammon. Let us, the poor-witted ones, wax insane, play the natural, to the glory of our God, the Christ Crucified! Ye mock the monks dancing before the Cross in the Piazza. Bide a while, there will be more than that! We shall see what ye, the prudent ones, shall say when I shall compel not merely the monks, but all the people of Florence, children and adults, old men and women, in a frenzy pleasing to God, to dance around the mystic Tree of Salvation, as David danced of yore before the Ark of the Covenant, in the ancient Tabernacle of the All-Highest God!"

VI

GIOVANNI, having come out of the cell of Savonarola, set out for the Piazza of the Signoria. On the Via Larga he came upon the Holy Army. The children had halted two black slaves with a palanquin, in which a gorgeously accoutred woman was reclining. A little white dog dozed on her knees; a green parrot and a marmoset were sitting on a perch. Servants and bodyguards brought up the rear of the litter.

This was a courtesan, recently arrived from Venice,—Lena Griffa, from the rank of those whom the rulers of the Most Radiant Republic dubbed with a respectful politeness "*puttana onesta*," "*meretrix onesta*,"—"noble, honest harlot"; or, with a kindly jocosity, "*mammola*,"— "darling." In the famous "*Catologo di tutte le puttane dell bordello con il lor prezzo*,"—"Catalogue of All Harlots in Bordellos, with Their Prices,"—issued for the convenience of travellers, there stood, opposite the name of Lena Griffa, printed in large letters, separately from the others, in the place of the greatest honour, her price, —four ducats; whereas for holy nights, nights before holidays, the price was double,—"In reverence for the Mother of God."

A-sprawl on her cushions, with the air of Cleopatra or the Queen of Sheba, Monna Lena was perusing the *billet doux* of a young bishop who was enamoured of her, with an attached sonnet, which ended in the following lines:

> Whene'er to thy captivating discourse I listen,
> Oh, wonderful Lena, the earth to leave I hasten;
> To beauties of Plato's divine thoughts my spirit soars,
> Straight off, and toward the eternal heavenly shores.

The courtesan was cogitating over a sonnet in reply. She was a perfect mistress of rhymes, and it was not for nothing she was wont to say, that, if it depended on her, she would, of course, spend all her time in "the academies of illustrious men."

The Holy Army surrounded the litter. Doffo, the commander of one of the divisions, stepped forward, raised the scarlet cross over his head, and exclaimed solemnly:

"In the name of Jesus, King of Florence, and the Virgin Mary, our Queen, we command thee to take off these sinful ornaments, vanities, and anathemas. If thou dost not this, may sickness strike thee!"

The little dog woke up and began to bark; the marmoset took to hissing; the parrot flapped its wings, screaming out a verse taught it by its mistress.

Amore a nullo amato amar perdona.

Lena was getting ready to make a sign to the bodyguards to disperse the crowd, when her glance fell upon Doffo. She beckoned him with her finger.

The boy approached, his eyes downcast.

"Away, away with gay raiments!" the children were clamouring. "Away with vanities and anathemas!"

"What a pretty little fellow!" murmured Lena in a low voice, paying no attention to the shouts of the crowd. "Listen, my little Adonis, I would, of course, give these rags up gladly, in order to afford you pleasure,—but here is the rub: they are not mine, but taken out on hire from a Jew. The property of such an unbelieving dog can hardly be an offering pleasing to Jesus and the Virgin Mary."

Doffo raised his eyes to see her. Monna Lena, with a hardly perceptible smile of mockery, having nodded her head, as though confirming his secret thought, uttered in another voice, with the canorous and tender Venetian manner of speech:

"In the Alley of the Coopers, near Santa Trinità. Ask for the courtesan Lena from Venice. I shall await thee. . . ."

Doffo looked around and saw that his comrades were no longer paying any attention to the courtesan, being taken up with throwing stones and exchanging curses with a gang of Savonarola's antagonists, the so-called "madmen"—*arrabbiati*,—who had just come out from behind a corner. He wanted to shout to them to fall upon her, but suddenly became confused and blushed.

Lena began laughing, showing the sharp white teeth between her red lips. Through the image of Cleopatra and the Queen of Sheba one caught a flash of the Venetian *mammola* within,—a mischievous and perky little street girl.

The negroes lifted up the litter, and the courtesan continued on her insouciant way. The little dog again fell to dozing on her knees, the parrot puffed up its crest, and only the irrepressible marmoset, making excruciatingly funny faces, strove to catch with its paw the pencil with which the grand harlot was writing the first line of the sonnet in response to her bishop:

My love is as pure as the sighings of seraphim.

Doffo, by now without any of his former cockiness, was at the head of his division, mounting the staircase of the Medici mansion.

VII

WITHIN the dark chambers, where everything breathed of the grandeur of the past, the children were seized by timidity. But they opened the shutters. The trumpets blared forth; drums were beaten. And with a joyous shout, with laughter and chanting of psalms, the little inquisitors scattered over the halls, wreaking God's justice upon the temptations of art and learning, searching out and seizing "vanities and anathemas" as the Holy Ghost moved them.

Giovanni watched their labours. Wrinkling their brows, their hands clasped behind their backs, with leisurely importance, like judges, the children perambulated among the carvings of great men, philosophers, and heroes of pagan antiquity.

"Pythagoras, Anaximenes, Heraclitus, Plato, Marcus Aurelius, Epictetus," one of the lads was spelling out the Latin inscriptions on the pediments of the marble and copper sculptures.

"Epictetus!" Federigo stopped him, contracting his brows with the air of a savant. "This is that very heretic who asserted that all enjoyments are permissible, and that there is no god. There is one body that ought to be burned! What a pity he is of marble. . . ."

"'Tis naught," shouted the spry, cross-eyed Pippo, "we shall fix him just the same!"

"That is not the one!" cried out Giovanni. "You have Epictetus confused with Epicurus. . . ."

But it was too late; Pippo had swung back, struck the sage with a hammer, and knocked his nose off so dexterously that the boys burst out laughing.

"Eh, what is the difference,—Epictetus, Epicurus; 'tis six of one and half a dozen of the other. 'All shall go to the dwelling place of the devil!'" He repeated Savonarola's favourite saying.

A dispute sprang up before a picture of Botticelli's,—Doffo asserted that it was seductive, since it depicted the naked youth, Bacchus, pierced with the arrows of the god of love; but Federigo, who was contending with Doffo in his ability of distinguishing "vanities and anathemas," approached it, cast a glance at it, and announced that this was not Bacchus at all.

"Well, who is it then, according to thee?" asked Doffo.

"Who! How canst thou ask? How is it you can not see, brethren? The Protomartyr, San Stefano!"

The children stood in wonder before the enigmatic picture: if this were really a saint, then why did his nude body breathe forth such pagan beauty, why did the expression of torture on his face resemble the languor of voluptuousness?

"Do not listen to him, fellows," Doffo began to shout, "this is the vile Bacchus!"

"Thou liest, blasphemer!" exclaimed Federigo, raising his cross, like a weapon.

The boys threw themselves at one another; their comrades barely succeeded in separating them. The picture was left under suspicion.

Meanwhile the irrepressible Pippo, together with Luca, who had long since become consoled and had ceased snivelling over his shorn locks,—for never as yet, it seemed to him, had he taken part in such merry pranks,—had gotten into a small, dark chamber. Here, by a window, on a high pedestal, stood one of those vases which are made by the Venetian glass factories at Murano. Touched by a ray coming through a crack in the closed shutters, it was all a-sparkle in the darkness with the fires of varicoloured glass, like precious stones, and resembled an enormous magic flower.

Pippo scrambled up on a table, most quietly, on his tiptoes,—as if the vase were alive and able to flee,—stole up to it, impishly stuck out the tip of his tongue, elevated the brows above his squint eyes, and pushed it with his finger. The vase swayed, like a tender flower, fell, in a shower of sparkles, emitted a piteous ring, shattered,—and was extinguished. Pippo jumped about, like a little fiend, dexterously throwing up and catching the scarlet cross in the air. Luca, his eyes wide open, burning with the delight of destruction, was also hopping, squealing, and clapping his palms.

Hearing in the distance the joyous shouts of their comrades, they returned to the big hall.

Here Federigo had found a cubby-hole with a multitude of boxes, filled with such vanities as even the most sophisticated of the children had never yet seen. These were masks and costumes for those carnival processions, those allegorical triumphs, which Lorenzo the Magnificent had been so fond of contriving. The children had crowded about the entrance to the cubby-hole. In the light of a tallow candle-end there came out before them *papier-mâché* monstrous faces of fauns, the glass grapes of bacchantes, the quiver and wings of Cupid, the caduceus of Mercury, the trident of Neptune, and, finally, to the explosion of general laughter, appeared the wooden, gilded cobweb-covered lightnings of the Thunder-Bearer and the pitiful, moth-eaten stuffed effigy of the Olympian eagle, with plucked tail, with tatters of padding sticking out of his punctured belly.

Suddenly from the gorgeous flaxen-haired wig, which probably had served Venus, there jumped out a rat. The little girls began to squeal. The smallest one of all, having jumped up on a chair, squeamishly raised her little dress above her knees.

Over the crowd was wafted a breath of the chill of horror, and of a revulsion toward these pagan trappings, toward the graveyard dust of dead gods. The shadows of the bats, frightened by the noise and light, beating against the ceiling, seemed unclean spirits.

Doffo ran up and announced that there was another locked room above,—with a little old man, red-nosed and bald, standing angrily on guard near its door, cursing and letting no one in.

They set off on a reconnaissance. In the little old man guarding the portals of the mysterious room, Giovanni recognized his friend, Messer Giorgio Merulla, the great bibliophile.

"Give us the key!" Doffo shouted to him.

"But whoever told you that I have the key?"

"The watchman of the castle told us that."

"Go your way, go your way,—and God be with ye!"

"Oh, take care, old man! We shall pull the last of thy hair out!"

Doffo gave the signal. Messer Giorgio took his stand before the door, prepared to protect it with his body. The children fell upon him, threw him down, beat him up with their crosses, ransacked his pockets, sought out the key, and opened the door. This was a small study, with a precious treasury of books.

"Here, right here," Merulla was pointing out, "everything you want is right in this corner. Do not climb up on the upper shelves,—there is nothing there. . . ."

But the inquisitors would not listen to him. Everything that fell into their hands,—especially books in magnificent bindings,—they threw into a heap. Next they opened wide the windows, in order to throw the thick folios directly into the street, where a cart, loaded with "vanities and anathemas," was standing. Tibullus, Horace, Ovid, Apuleius, Aristophanes,—rare transcripts, unique editions,—whizzed past Merulla's eyes.

Giovanni noted that the old man had managed to fish out of the heap, and dexterously hide in his bosom, a tiny tome; this was the book of Marcellinus, chronicling the life of Emperor Julian, the Apostate.

Seeing on the floor a transcript of the tragedies of Sophocles, on silk-like parchment, with the most exquisite of illuminated headings, he pounced upon it with avidity, seized it, and fell to frantic supplication:

"Little ones! Darlings! Spare Sophocles! This is the most guileless of poets! Touch him not, touch him not! . . ."

In despair he hugged the book to his bosom; but, feeling the tender, almost living leaves being torn, he burst into tears, took to moaning, as though from pain,—released it, and began screaming in impotent rage:

"But do ye know, ye vile puppies, that every line of this poet is a greater sanctity before God than all the prophecies of your halfwitted Girolamo! . . ."

"Be still, old man, if thou dost not want us to throw thee out the window together with thy poets!"

And, falling anew upon the old man, they jostled him out of the library.

Merulla fell upon Giovanni's bosom:

"Let us go away, let us go away as fast as we can! I do not want to witness this crime! . . ."

They went out of the castle, and, past Maria del Fiore, set out in the direction of the Piazza of the Signoria.

VIII

BEFORE the dark, stately campanile of the Palazzo Vecchio, beside the Loggia Orcani, was prepared a bonfire, thirty ells in height, one hundred and twenty in breadth,—an octagonal pyramid of fifteen steps, knocked together from boards.

On the first step, at the bottom, were gathered the merry-andrew masks, raiments, wigs, false beards, and many other appurtenances of the carnival; on the next three,—free-thinking books, beginning with Anacreon and Ovid, and terminating with the *Decameron* of Boccaccio and the *Morgante* of Pulci; above the books were feminine bedizenments, unguents, perfumes, mirrors, powder-puffs, nail-files, curling-irons, hair-tweezers; still higher,—notes for music, lutes, mandolins, cards, chess-sets, nine-pins, small balls,—all the games wherewith men make the fiend rejoice; next,—seductive pictures, drawings, portraits of handsome women; finally, at the very summit of the pyramid,—the images of pagan gods, of heroes and philosophers, in coloured wax and in wood. Above all reared an enormous effigy,—an image of the Devil, the first progenitor of "vanities and anathemas,"—stuffed with sulphur and gunpowder; monstrously bedaubed, shaggy, ægipedal, resembling the ancient god Pan.

Evening was coming on. The air was chilly, pure, and bestowing resonance to every sound. The first stars began to glimmer warmly in the sky. The throng on the Piazza was a-rustle and swaying with reverent whispering, as though in church. The spiritual hymns,—*laudi spirituali*,—of Savonarola's disciples, the so-called "snivellers," filled the air. The rhymes, tune and measure had remained unchanged,—of the carnival; but the words had been done over on a new style. Giovanni hearkened closely,—and the contradiction of the dreary meaning and the gay tunes seemed savage to him:

To tre once almen di speme,
Tre di fede e sei d'amore. . . .

Take three ounces of love,
Three of faith, and six of hope,
Of repentance, two; then mix them,
Place them in the fire of prayer;
In the fire for three hours hold all;
Add to it spiritual sorrow,

Add contrition, resignation,
In a quantity to make them
Blend into God's own wisdom.

Beneath the Shelter of the Pisans, a man in iron spectacles, with a leathern apron, with a small strap around his sparse, straight strands of hair, smeared with butter, with gnarled, calloused hands, was sermonizing to a crowd of artisans, evidently of the same "sniveller" stamp as himself.

"I am Roberto,—neither ser nor messer, but simply a Florentine tailor," he was saying, thumping his breast with his fist, "I declare unto ye, my brethren, that Jesus, the King of Florence, has, in many visions, expounded to me the new government and law, pleasing to God. Do ye wish that there be neither poor nor rich, neither small nor great,—that all be equal?"

"We do, we do! Tell us, Roberto, how it is to be done."

"If ye have faith, 'tis easily done. One, two,—and 'tis done! Firstly, —" he bent back his left thumb with his right index finger,—"an income impost, to be called a graduated tithe. Secondly,—" he bent back his left index finger,—"a heaven-inspired Parliamento of all the people. . . ."

Then he paused, took off his spectacles, wiped them, put them on, coughed leisurely, and in a monotonous, thick voice, with an obstinate and meek self-satisfaction on his dull face, began to expound whereof the graduated tithe and the God-inspired Parliamento consisted.

Giovanni listened, and kept on listening,—and was overcome by sadness. He walked away to the other end of the Piazza.

Here, in the evening twilight, the monks were moving like shadows, occupied with the final preparations. Toward Brother Domenico Buonvicini, the chief director, there walked up a man on crutches, not yet old, but, evidently, shattered by paralysis, with trembling arms and legs, with eyelids that he could not raise; a convulsive tic ran over his face,—a tic resembling the quivering of a winged bird. He gave to the monk a large bundle.

"What is this?" asked Domenico. "Drawings again?"

"Anatomy. I had e'en forgot about them. But yesterday in my sleep I hear a voice: Over thy workshop, Sandro, in the attic, in thy chests, thou still hast vanities and anathemas.—I arose, went up, and found these very drawings of nude bodies."

The monk took the bundle, and spoke with a gay, almost playful smile:

"But what a fine little fire we shall ignite, Messer Filipepi!"

The latter threw a glance at the pyramid of vanities and anathemas.

"Oh, Lord, Lord, have mercy upon us sinners!" he sighed. "Were it not for Brother Girolamo, we would have died, even without repentance, and unshrived. And, even now, who knows,—will we save ourselves, will we have time to obtain pardon through prayer? . . ."

He made the sign of the cross and took to muttering prayers, as he told his beads.

"Who is that?" Giovanni asked of a monk standing alongside.

"Sandro Botticelli, son of Mariano Filipepi, the tanner," answered the latter.

IX

WHEN it had grown entirely dark, a whisper floated over the crowd: "They come! They come!"

In silence, in the twilight, without hymns, without torches, in long white garments, the child-inquisitors came on, carrying in their hands a carving of the Infant Jesus; with one hand He was pointing to the crown of thorns on His head, with the other He was blessing the people. The children were followed by monks, the clergy, the *gonfalonieri*, the members of the Council of Eighty, canons, doctors and magisters of theology, the knights of the Captain of the Bargello, trumpeters and mace-bearers.

It became as quiet on the Piazza as if before an execution.

Savonarola mounted the Ringhiera,—a stone elevation before the Old Castle; he raised on high the Crucifix, and uttered in a triumphant, loud voice:

"In the name of the Father, the Son, and the Holy Ghost,—ignite it!"

Four monks approached the pyramid, with flaming pitch torches, and set fire to it from the four corners. The flame began to crackle; the smoke swirled up,—at first grey, then black. The trumpeters began blaring. The monks pealed forth: "We praise Thee, God!" The children caught up with ringing voices:

"*Lumen ad revelationem gentium et gloriam plebis Israel.*"

On the tower of the Old Castle the bell started ringing, and to its mighty brazen rumble replied the bells of all the churches in Florence.

The flames were flaring up in a brighter and brighter blaze. The tender, seemingly living leaves of ancient parchment books buckled up and were turned to ashes. From the bottom step, where lay the carnival masks, a false beard whirled upward and flew in a fiery column. The crowd let out a joyous grunt and burst into horselike laughter.

Some prayed, others wept; some others laughed, as they leaped, waving their arms and hats; others still were prophesying.

"Sing, sing the new song to the Lord!" a lame cobbler, with half-crazed eyes, was shouting. "Everything shall collapse; brothers of mine, 'twill all burn up, burn up to ashes, like these vanities and anathemas in the purifying fire,—all, all, all,—the church, laws, governments, powers, arts, sciences,—no stone shall be left upon another stone; and there shall be a new heaven, and a new earth! And God shall wipe every tear from these our eyes, and there shall be no death,—nor weeping, nor sorrow, nor disease! Verily, come Thou, Lord Jesus!"

A young pregnant woman with a thin, suffering face, probably the wife of some poor artisan, fell on her knees, and, stretching forth her arms toward the flame of the bonfire,—as though she were seeing Christ Himself within it,—straining herself, sobbing, like one possessed, was shouting:

"Verily, come Thou, Lord Jesus! Amen! Amen! Come Thou!"

X

GIOVANNI was gazing at a picture, lit up by the flames, but as yet untouched by them,—a creation of Leonardo da Vinci's.

Above the evening waters of mountain lakes stood naked Leda; a gigantic swan had embraced her waist with his wing, arching his long neck, filling the empty sky and earth with the cry of triumphant love; at her feet, among aquatic plants, animals and insects, among the germinating seeds, larvæ and embryos, in the warm murk, in the sultry dankness, were stirring the newly-born twins, Castor and Pollux,—half-gods, half-beasts,—just hatched from the broken shell of an enormous egg. And all of Leda, to the last hidden fold of her body, stark naked, was filled with loving admiration for her children, as she embraced the neck of the swan, and smiled with a chaste and voluptuous smile.

Giovanni watched the flames draw nearer and nearer to her,—and his heart froze within him from horror.

In the meanwhile the monks had erected a black cross in the middle of the Piazza; then, taking each other by the hand, they formed three rings,—in honour of the Trinity,—and, celebrating the spiritual gaiety of the faithful in the burning of the vanities and anathemas, began a dance; slowly, at first, then constantly faster and faster, and, finally, started off at a breakneck pace, with the song:

Ognun gridi, com' io grido,
Sempre pazzo, pazzo, pazzo!

Before the Lord bow low,
Dance long and dance enow,—
E'en as King David did;
Our cassocks we raise up,
Let no one ever stop,
Nor laggards let be hid.
With love are we made drunken,
For God's Son in blood sunken,
In blood upon the cross;
Noisy and wild our gladness,
In madness, yea, in madness,—
Christ's madness is in us!

The heads of those who were watching reeled, their legs and arms jerked of themselves,—and suddenly, dashing from their places, children, old men, women, would dash off, dancing. A bald-headed, stout monk, with a face in blackheads, and resembling an old faun, made a clumsy leap, slipped, fell, and broke his head so that blood came; they barely managed to drag him out of the crowd,—or else they would have trampled him to death.

The purple, flickering reflection of the fire illumined the distorted faces. The Crucifix threw an enormous shadow—the immovable central point of the turning rings.

Our crosses wave like lances,
As each one prances, prances, prances,
E'en as King David did.
After each other whirling,
All circling, circling, circling,
Our carnival amid.
This age's wisdom we deride,
And trample on man's pride;

With babes' simplicity,
God's jesters' motley wear,
And innocents appear,—
Christ's innocents are we!

The flame, encompassing Leda, licked with its red tongue the naked white body, which became rosy, as though alive,—and still more beautiful and mysterious.

Giovanni gazed upon it, a-tremble and blanching. Leda smiled upon him with a last smile, flared up, melted within the fire, like a cloud in the rays of sunset,—and vanished forever.

The enormous effigy of the fiend on the summit of the bonfire burst into flame. His belly, stuffed with gunpowder, burst with deafening crackling. A pillar of fire soared up to the heavens. The monster swayed slowly on its throne of flames, drooped, collapsed, and disintegrated into the ashen heat of embers.

The trumpets and kettle-drums blared anew. All the bells pealed forth. And the mob began to howl in an unearthly, victorious yowl, as though the Devil himself had perished in the flame of the holy bonfire together with falsehood, with suffering, and the evil of the whole universe.

Giovanni clutched his head and wanted to flee. Someone's hand descended on his shoulder, and, turning about, he beheld the calm face of the master.

Leonardo took him by the hand and led him out of the crowd.

XI

FROM the Piazza, covered with swirls of malodorous smoke, illumined by the glow of the dying bonfire, they passed through a dark alley to the shore of the Arno.

Here it was quiet and deserted; one heard only the murmur of the waves. The scythe of the moon lit up the serene summits of the knolls, silvered over with hoar-frost; the stars glimmered, their rays austere and gentle.

"Why didst thou go away from me, Giovanni?" said Leonardo.

The pupil raised his eyes, was about to say something, but his voice broke, his lips quivered, and he burst into tears.

"Forgive me, master! . . ."

"Thou art guilty of naught before me," retorted the master.

"I did not know myself what I was doing," continued Beltraffio. "How could I, O Lord,—how could I go away from you? . . ."

He was about to tell him his madness, his torture, his fearful double-minded thoughts about the cup of the Lord and the cup of the devils, about Christ and Antichrist; but sensed again, as he had done when before the monument to Sforza, that Leonardo would not understand him,—and with a hopeless supplication merely looked into his eyes, —radiant, quiet, and alien, like the stars.

The master did not interrogate him, as though he had surmised all, and, with a smile of infinite pity, placing his hand on Giovanni's head, he said:

"May the Lord help thee, my poor boy! Thou knowest that I have always loved thee like my own son. If thou wouldst again be my pupil, I would accept thee with joy."

And as though to himself, with that peculiar enigmatic and shy brevity with which he usually expressed his secret thoughts, he added, in a barely audible voice:

"The more feeling there is, the more torture. 'Tis a great martyrdom!"

The pealing of bells, the songs of the monks, the cries of the insane mob, could be heard behind them,—but they no longer disturbed the silence which surrounded the master and the pupil.

BOOK EIGHT

The Age of Gold

I

HEN THE YEAR OF FOURTEEN HUNDRED AND ninety-six was drawing to an end, Beatrice, the Duchess of Milan, wrote to her sister Isabella, spouse to the Marquis Francesco Gonzaga, Sovereign of Mantua: "Most illustrious madonna, our most beloved little sister, I and my husband, Signor Ludovico, wish long life to you and to the Most Illustrious Signor Francesco.

"In accordance with your request, I am sending you a portrait of my son Maximiliano. Only, please do not think that he is so very little. We wanted to take exact measurements, in order to send them to you, but were afraid,—the nurse said 'tis prejudicial to his growth. But grow he doth, amazingly,—if I see him not for but a few days, when I do look at him again, he seems to have grown so much that I remain exceedingly pleased and solaced.

"But we also have a great grief,—the little fool Nannino has died. You knew him and also loved him, and therefore will understand that, had I lost any other possession, I would have had hopes of replacing it, but in the place of our Nannino nothing else could have been created by Nature herself, that did exhaust all her powers, having united in one being, for the diversion of sovereigns, most rare folly with most beautiful monstrosity. Bellincioni in his epigraph saith that if his soul be in heaven, then he maketh all paradise to laugh; but if he be in Hades, then Cerberus 'keepeth silent and rejoiceth.' We buried him in our vault in the Maria delle Grazie, by the side of my beloved hunting falcon and the unforgettable bitch Puttina, in order that, even after our death, we may not part with such a pleasant thing. I cried for two nights, and Signor Ludovico, in order to console me, promised to present me at Christmas with a magnificent close-stool of silver for the easement of the stomach, with a depiction of the Battle of the Centaurs and Lapithæ. Inside the vessel is of virgin gold, whereas the baldaquin is of Cramoisie velvet with broidered ducal coats-of-arms, and all of this is every little bit like the one of the Grand Duchess of Lorraine. Such a close-stool, they say, is not owned by any one of the Italian queens,—not even by the Pope, the Emperor, or the Grand Turk. 'Tis more beautiful than the celebrated close-stool of Bassus, described in the Epigrams of Martial.[24] Merulla has composed hexameters, which begin thus:

> *Quis cameram hanc supero aignam neget esse tonante Principe.*
> This throne is worthy the highest, thundering deity in heaven.

"Signor Ludovico desired the Florentine artist Leonardo da Vinci to construct in this close-stool a machine with music, on the manner of a little organ, but Leonardo declined, with the pretence that he was too much occupied with the Colossus and The Last Supper.

"You request, dearest little sister, that I send you this master for a time. I would with pleasure fulfill your request, and would send him to you forever, not merely for a time. But Signor Ludovico, I know not why, is exceedingly well-disposed toward him, and does not wish to part with him under any circumstances. However, do not regret his absence too greatly, inasmuch as this Leonardo is much devoted to alchemy, magick, mechanics, and other such phantasmas, far more than to painting, and is noted for such dilatoriness in filling commissions as would make an angel lose patience. He is, to boot, as I have heard, an heretic and an atheist.

"Recently we had a wolf hunt. I am not allowed to mount a horse, since I am already in the fifth month of pregnancy. I watched the hunt, standing on the high footboards at the back of the carriage, especially built for me,—something like a church cathedra. However, this was no diversion, but torture, rather; when the wolf escaped into the forest I almost burst into tears. Oh, had I been on a horse myself, I would never have let him give us the slip,—I would have broken my neck, but caught the beast!

"Do you remember, little sister, how you and I used to gallop? Why, Donzella Penthesilea fell into a ditch, and broke her head, almost fatally. And what of the wild boar hunt in Cusnago? And the ball-play? And the angling? What a fine time that was!

"Now we divert ourselves as best we can. We play cards. We skate. This diversion was taught us by a young grandee from Flanders. There is a cruel winter holding us in its spell,—not only all the ponds, even the rivers have frozen over. On the skating rink of the palace park Leonardo has moulded a most beautiful Leda with a swan, out of snow as white and hard as marble. What a pity 'twill melt with the spring!

"Well, and how do you spend your days, amiable sister? Has the breed of long-haired cats proven a success? If there will be a red kitten with blue eyes,—a tom,—send it to me together with the female blackamoor you have promised me. As for me, I shall present you with puppies from my bitch, Silky Thread.

"Forget not,—please forget not, Madonna,—to send me the pattern of your blue atlas quilted jacket,—the one with the oblique collar and the border of sables. I asked for it in my last letter. Send it off as quickly as you can,—best of all, on the very morrow, at dawn, with a mounted messenger.

"Send me, also, a vial of your most excellent wash for little pimples, and some of the sandalwood for polishing nails which comes from overseas.

"What of the monument to Virgil, this sweet-sounding swan of the Mantuan lakes? Should you not have enough bronze, we shall send you two old bombards of the finest copper.

"Our astrologers foretell war and a hot summer: dogs will become rabid, and kings wrathful. What sayeth your astrologer? One believeth a stranger always more than one's own.

"I send for your most excellent spouse, Signor Francesco, a recipe against the French sickness, made up by our court physician, Luigi Marliani. It helps,—so they say. The mercury anointments must be made of mornings, on an empty stomach, on the odd days of the month, after the new moon. I have heard that this disease is occasioned by nothing else save the malignant conjunction of certain planets, especially of Mercury with Venus.

"I and Signor Ludovico entrust ourselves to your gracious remembrance, my beloved little sister, and to that of your spouse, the Most Illustrious Marquis Francesco.

"Beatrice Sforza."

II

Despite the seeming ingenuousness, dissimulation and politics were by no means missing in this letter. The Duchess was concealing from her sister her domestic worries. The peace and harmony which might have been deduced from the letter did not exist between the royal couple. Leonardo she hated not because of his heresy and atheism, but because he had, on a time, at the behest of the Duke, drawn a portrait of Cecilia Bergamini, her most bitter rival, the famous concubine of Moro. Latterly she also suspected another love *liaison* of her husband's—with one of the court damozelles, Madonna Lucrezia.

In those days the Duke of Milan had attained the height of his power. The son of Francesco Sforza, the doughty mercenary from Romagnola, half-soldier, half-brigand, he had dreams of becoming the sole sovereign of a united Italy.

"I shall have the Pope for my father-confessor, the Emperor for the leader of my army; the city of Venice as my treasurer, the French King as my runner," Moro was wont to boast.

Ludovicus Maria Sfortia Anglus dux Mediolani,—did he sign his name, tracing his descent from the glorious hero, the companion of Æneas, Anglus of Troy. The Colossus, carved out by Leonardo, the monument to his father, with the inscription: *Ecce Deus!*—Behold the God! —also testified to the divine greatness of the Sforzas.

But, contrary to outward well-being, secret uneasiness and fear tormented the Duke. He knew that his people disliked him, and considered him a usurper of the throne. Once on the Piazza Arengo, beholding in the distance the widow of Gian Galeazzo, with her first-born, Francesco, the crowd began shouting: "Long live the lawful Duke Francesco!"

He was eight years old, and distinguished for his mind and beauty. In the words of the Venetian envoy, Marino Sanuto, "The people yearned to have him for ruler Duke as they yearned for God."

Beatrice and Moro perceived that the death of Gian Galeazzo had tricked them,—it had not made them the lawful sovereigns. And in this child the shade of the dead Duke rose up from out the grave.

In Milan they talked of mysterious portents. The rumour ran that of nights, over the towers of the castle, lights appeared, resembling the glow of a conflagration, and that fearful groans burst out in the chambers of the palace. It was recalled how the left eye of Gian Galeazzo, when he was lying in his grave, would not close, which forefended an impending demise of one of his near relatives. The eyelids of the Madonna dell' Albieri took to quivering. A cow, belonging to a certain little old crone beyond the Ticine Gates, had dropped a two-headed calf. The Duchess fell in a swoon in the empty Hall of the Rocchetta, frightened by an apparition, and afterwards would not speak of it with anyone,—not even her husband.

For some time she had practically lost all her mischievous sprightliness, which characteristic of hers appealed so to the Duke, and with ill forebodings she awaited her confinement.

III

Once, of a December evening, when the flakes of snow were carpeting the streets of the city, intensifying the silence of the twilight, Moro was sitting in a small palazzo, which he had presented to his new mistress, Madonna Lucrezia Crivelli.

The fire blazed in the hearth, lighting up the leaves of the lacquered doors, with their mosaic design depicting perspectives of ancient Roman buildings; lighting up the bas-relief reticulation of the ceiling, ornamented with gold, the walls, covered with gold-pressed Cordovan leather hangings, the high armchairs and the chests of ebony, the round table covered with a cloth of dark green velvet, with a romance of Boyardo open thereon, and rolls of notes, a nacre mandolin, and a cut-glass pitcher of Balnea Aponitana,—a medicinal water, coming into vogue with genteel ladies. On the wall hung a portrait of Lucrezia, from the brush of Leonardo.

Over the fireplace, in the clay carvings of Caradosso, fluttering birds pecked at grapes, and winged, nude children,—with something of Christian cherubim about them, and something of pagan cupids,—danced, playing with the most holy implements of the Lord's Passion: the nails, the spear, the rods, the sponge, and the thorns; they seemed alive in the rosy reflected glow of the flames.

The storm howled in the hearth-chimney, but in the exquisite workchamber,—the *studiolo*,—everything breathed of a cozy languor.

Madonna Lucrezia was seated on a velvet cushion at the feet of Moro. Her countenance was sad. He was tenderly chiding her for not having visited the Duchess Beatrice for a long period.

"Your Grace," answered the girl, casting down her eyes, "I implore you, do not compel me,—I can not lie."

"But think,—does this really mean lying?" Moro expressed his wonder. "We are but resorting to concealment. Did not the Thunderer himself keep hidden his love secrets from his jealous spouse? And what of Theseus, and of Phædra, and Medæa,—and all heroes, all gods of old? Can we, weak mortals that we be, oppose the might of the god of love? Then, too, is not secret evil better than evil evident? Inasmuch as, in concealing evil, we do deliver our near ones from temptation, as is required by Christian compassion. And if there be temptation, so long as there is compassion therewith, then there is no evil,—or well-nigh none. . . ."

He smiled his crafty smile. Lucrezia shook her head and looked straight into his eyes, somewhat from under her brows,—her eyes, stern, grave, like those of children, and innocent.

"You know, liege lord, how happy I am in your love. But at times I am fain to die rather than deceive Madonna Beatrice, who loves me like her own kin. . . ."

"Enough, enough, my child!" said the Duke, and drew her on to his knees, entwining her waist with one hand, while with the other he caressed her glossy black hair, combed smoothly over her ears, and encircled by the thread of a *ferroniera*, upon which a diamond spark hung in the middle of her forehead. Lowering her long, downy lashes,—without rapture, without passion, all cold and pure,—she surrendered to his caresses.

"Oh, if thou didst but know how I love thee, my quiet one, my meek one,—thee alone!" he was whispering, avidly inhaling the familiar aroma of violets and musk.

The door opened, and, before the Duke had time to release the girl from his embraces, a frightened maid-servant ran into the room.

"Madonna, madonna," she mumbled, gasping, "there, below, at the gate. . . . O Lord, have mercy upon us sinners! . . ."

"Well, now, do talk sense," the Duke spoke sharply, "who is at the gate?"

"The Duchess Beatrice!"

Moro blenched.

"The key! The key from the other door! The backstairs,—through the courtyard. . . . Where is the key, now? Quick! . . ."

"The cavaliers of the illustrious madonna are stationed at the back way also!" the maid-servant wrung her hands in despair. "The entire house is surrounded. . . ."

"An ambuscade!" exclaimed the Duke, clutching his head. "And whence did she find out? Who could have told her?"

"None else save Monna Sidonia!" the maid-servant chimed in. "'Tis not for naught that the old witch comes traipsing around us with her mixtures and her ointments. I told you, signora, to be careful. . . ."

"What is to be done,—my God, what is to be done?" babbled the Duke, growing still paler.

From the street came a loud knocking at the outer doors of the house. The maid-servant darted to the staircase.

"Hide me, hide me, Lucrezia!"

"Your Grace," retorted the girl, "Madonna Beatrice, if she suspects, will order the whole house to be searched. Would it not be better for you to come out to meet her openly?"

"Nay, nay, God forfend,—whatever art thou saying, Lucrezia! Come out to meet her? Thou knowest not what a woman this is! Oh, Lord, 'tis a fearful thing to think of the possible outcome of all this! Why, she is pregnant! . . . But do thou hide me,—hide me! . . ."

"Really, I know not where. . . ."

"'Tis all one, wherever thou wilt,—but with all speed!"

The Duke was all a-tremble, and at this moment resembled a caught thief rather than a scion of the legendary hero, Anglus of Troy, companion of Æneas.

Lucrezia led him through the bedroom into the tiring room, and hid him in one of those large closets, let into the wall,—white, with fine designs in gold, in the ancient taste, which served as *garde-robe*,—ambries for the raiment of noble ladies.

He huddled up in a corner among dresses.

"How foolish!" he reflected. "My God, how foolish! Just as in the funny little stories of Franco Sacchetti or Boccaccio."

But he felt far from laughing. He took out of his bosom a small scapular, with the relics of St. Christopher, and another, exactly like the first, containing a talisman in vogue at that time,—a piece of an Ægyptian mummy. The scapulars resembled each other so much that in his haste and in the dark he could not distinguish the one from the other, and, to play safe, fell to kissing both together, crossing himself and rendering up prayers.

Suddenly, hearing the voices of his wife and his mistress as they entered the tiring room, he froze from horror. They were chatting pleasantly, as if nothing were amiss. He conjectured that Lucrezia was showing the Duchess over her new house, at the latter's insistence. Probably Beatrice had no palpable proofs, and did not want to reveal her suspicions.

It was a duel of feminine guile.

"Are there dresses here also?" asked Beatrice in an indifferent tone, approaching the closet in which Moro crouched, more dead than alive.

"Just old ones, to wear around the house. Would Your Grace care to have a look?" said Lucrezia.

And she opened the doors.

"But listen, my dearest," continued the Duchess, "wherever is the one which,—you remember,—I liked so much? You wore it at the summer ball given by Pallavicini. All those little worms, little worms without end, you know,—gold, over dark-blue morello,—glistening like glow-worms at night."

"I can not recall it, somehow," answered Lucrezia calmly. "Ah, yes, yes, right here," she recalled suddenly. "It must be in this closet over here."

And, without closing the doors of the closet which held Moro, she walked away with the Duchess to an adjoining wardrobe.

"And yet she said that she could not lie!" he reflected with admiration. "What presence of mind! Women,—it is from them we rulers ought to learn politics!"

Beatrice and Lucrezia withdrew from the tiring room.

Moro drew a free breath, although he was still clutching convulsively in his palm both scapulars,—the relics and the mummy flesh.

"Two hundred ducats to the cloister of Maria delle Grazie, the Most Pure Intercessor,—for holy oil and for candles, if the upshot of all this be fortuitous!" he was whispering with vehement faith.

The maid-servant came running; with a respectfully-sly mien she let out the Duke, and announced that the danger had passed,—the Most Illustrious Duchess had been pleased to go away, having graciously said farewell to Madonna Lucrezia.

He crossed himself piously, returned to the *studiolo*, drained a glass of Balnea Aponitana to fortify himself, cast a glance at Lucrezia, who sat, as before, in front of the hearth, her head downcast, her face covered with her hands,—and smiled.

Then with quiet, almost vulpine steps, he stole up to her from behind, stooped, and kissed her.

The girl shivered.

"Leave me, leave me,—go away! Oh, how can you, after what has taken place!"

But the Duke, without listening to her, was silently covering her face, her neck and hair, with avid kisses. Never yet had she appeared so beautiful: it seemed as if the feminine deceptiveness, which he had just beheld in her, had surrounded her with a new charm.

She struggled, but weakened by degrees, and, finally, having closed her eyes, with a helpless smile, surrendered her lips up to him.

A December snow-storm howled in the hearth-chimney, while, in the meanwhile, in the rosy reflected glow of the flames, the procession of laughing naked children under the thicket of the grapes of Bacchus danced, playing with the most holy implements of the Lord's Passion.

IV

A BALL was set for the first day of the new year of fourteen hundred and ninety-seven. For three months there had been preparations, in which Bramante, Caradosso, and Leonardo da Vinci had participated.

Toward five o'clock in the afternoon the guests began to drive up to the palace. More than two thousand had been invited.

The snow-storm had covered over all the roads and streets. Against the gloomy sky, under their mounds of snow, the crenellated walls, the barbicans, and the stone embrasures for the cannons' mouths shone whitely. In the courtyard, near flaming bonfires, the hostlers, fast runners, equerries, horsemen, and the palanquin bearers were warming themselves, with merry din. At the entrance to the Palazzo Ducale, and farther, near the iron portcullis leading to the inner courtyard of the little Rocchetta castle, gilded, unwieldy carts, antediluvian travelling carriages and equipages, harnessed to teams of six horses, were crowded together, unloading signors and cavaliers, wrapt up in precious furs from Muscovy. The frosted windows glowed with festal lights.

Entering the front hall, the guests followed each other through two ranks of the ducal bodyguards,—Turkish *mamelukes*, Greek *stradioti*, Scotch cross-bowmen, and Swiss *lands-knechte*, girt in cuirasses, with heavy halberds. To the front stood graceful pages, as charmingly handsome as girls, in uniform, two-coloured liveries, trimmed with swan's-down,—the right side of pink velvet, the left, of blue satin, with the heraldic marks of the house of Sforza Visconti worked in silver on the breast; the raiment clung so closely to the body that it revealed all its curves; only in front, from underneath the belt, did it protrude in short, close, rolled pleats. In their hands they held lit candles,—long, on the style of churchly ones, of red and yellow wax.

When a guest would enter the reception hall, a herald with two trumpeters would call out his name.

A vista of enormous, blindingly illuminated halls, one after another, was revealed: "The Hall of White Doves, on a Field of Red"; "The Field of Gold,"—with a depiction of a ducal hunt; "The Hall of Vermeil,"—from ceiling to floor drawn over with satin, embroidered in gold with flaming firebrands and with buckets, signifying the sovereign might of the Dukes of Milan, who, at their wish, could fan the flame of war or extinguish it with the water of peace. In the exquisite little "Black Hall," built by Bramante, serving as a dressing room for the ladies, upon the vaults and walls could be seen the unfinished frescoes of Leonardo.

The throng in gala attire was a-hum, like a swarm of bees. The dresses were distinguished for their multicoloured vividness, and unbounded, —sometimes tasteless,—luxury. In this riot of colours, in this confusion of a Babel of modes, lacking in respect for the customs of their ancestors,—even, at times, modes buffoonesque and freakish,—one satirist beheld "A portent of an invasion of outlanders,—the coming serfdom of Italy."

The stuffs of the feminine dresses, with stiff, heavy folds, which would not bend in consequence of the copiousness of gold and precious stones, resembled church vestments, and were so well-made that they were passed on as heirlooms from great-grandmothers to great-granddaughters. Deep incisions exposed the shoulders and bosom. The hair, covered in front with a golden net, was plaited, in accordance with the custom of Lombardy, into a tight braid, lengthened to the floor with artificial hair and with ribbons,—in the case of matrons as well as of maidens. Fashion demanded that the eyebrows be barely defined, —women endowed of thick eyebrows plucked them out with special steel tweezers. To do without rouge and white enamel was considered unseemly. The perfumes used were strong, heavy,—musk, amber, viverra, powder of chypre with its penetrating, overpowering odour.

In the throng one came upon young girls and women of especial charm, which is nowhere else to be met with save in Lombardy, with those æthereal shadows, melting away like smoke, upon their skin of an even pallor, upon the tender, soft contours of their faces,—which Leonardo da Vinci was so fond of depicting.

Madonna Violanta Borromeo, black of eye, black of curls, with a vanquishing beauty patent to all, was styled the queen of the ball. Moths, singeing their wings against the flame of a candle,—a warning to those enamoured,—were worked in gold on the dark-purple velvet of her dress.

But it was not Madonna Violanta that drew the eyes of the elect, but Donzella Diana Pallavicini, with eyes as cold and transparent as ice, with hair as grey as ashes, with a smile of indifference and speech as languid as the sound of a viol. She was enveloped in a simple dress of white striped damask, with long silk ribbons, of the dull-green of hydrophytes. Surrounded by glitter and noise, she seemed aloof from everything, alone and pensive, like pale water flowers, that slumber under the moon in forgotten pools.

The trumpets and the kettle-drums burst forth,—and the guests started for the great "Hall of Ball-Play," situated in the Rocchetta. Under the blue, star-sprinkled vault, cruciform joists with waxen candles flared in fiery clusters. From the balcony, serving as a gallery, hung down silken rugs with garlands of laurel, ivy, and juniper.

At the hour, minute, and second designated by the astrologers,—inasmuch as the Duke would not stir a single step, to use the words of one envoy, nor change his shirt, nor kiss his wife, without first taking the position of the stars into consideration,—Moro and Beatrice entered the hall, in regal mantles of cloth of gold, lined with ermine, with long trains which were borne by barons, knights of honour, *splendittori*, and chamberlains. On the bosom of the Duke, in a buckle, shone a ruby of unbelievable size, purloined by him from Gian Galeazzo.

Beatrice had grown thinner and had lost some of her good looks. It was strange to see the abdomen of a pregnant woman on this girl, who seemed almost a child,—with flat bosom and the impulsive movements of a boy.

Moro gave the signal. The chief seneschal raised his staff, the music struck in the gallery,—and the guests settled themselves at the festal boards.

V

A MISUNDERSTANDING arose. The ambassador of the Grand Prince of Muscovy, Danilo Mamyrov, did not choose to sit below the ambassador of the Most Radiant Republic of San Marco. They began to expostulate with Mamyrov. But the stubborn old man, who would listen to none, insisted on having his way: "I shall not sit down,—'tis an ignominy upon me!"

Curious and mocking glances were turned upon him from all quarters.

"What is it? Again unpleasantnesses with the Muscovites? An uncivilized people! They clamber for the highest place,—there is no arguing with them. 'Tis impossible to invite them anywhere. Barbarians! And their language, now,—do you hear it? Altogether like a Turk's. A ferocious tribe! . . ."

The lively and nimble Boccalino, the interpreter, a Mantuan, darted up to Mamyrov:

"Messer Daniele, Messer Daniele," he began to lisp in broken Russian, with fawning manners and much scraping, "you must not, you must not! You should sit down. 'Tis a custom in Milan. 'Tis not good manners to dispute. The Dúk-a is wroth."

The young companion of the old man, the secretary of the Imperial Embassy, Nikita Karachiyarov, also approached Mamyrov.

"Danilo Kusmich, father of mine, be you not wroth! One does not go into a strange monastery with one's own rules. They be foreign folk, they know not our customs. Will it take much more to be disgraced? They may e'en show us the door! We will gain naught but shame. . . ."

"Be still, Nikita, be still! Thou art too young to teach me, an old man. I know what I am about. It shall never be! I shall not sit below the ambassador from Venice. This is a great slight upon our ambassadorial honour. 'Tis said: Every ambassador beareth the face and speaketh the speech of his king. And our king is of the true faith, the Sovereign of All the Russias. . . ."

"Messer Daniele, oh, Messer Daniele!" fidgeted and coaxed the interpreter Boccalino.

"Leave me be! What art thou jabbering about, thou paynim monkey-face? I told thee I shall not sit down,—and I shall not!"

Under his contracted brows Mamyrov's small ursine eyes sparkled with wrath, pride, and unconquerable stubbornness. The emerald-studded head of his staff trembled in his strongly clenched fingers. It was evident that no power would compel him to yield.

Moro called to him the ambassador from Venice; with a captivating amiability, of which he was master, promised him his good graces, and requested him, as a personal favour, to take another seat, in order to avoid disputes and recriminations, asserting that none attributed any significance to the absurd greed for honours of these barbarians. In reality, the Duke valued exceedingly the favour of the "Rozian Grand Duke,"—*gran duca di Rozia*, hoping, with his assistance, to conclude an advantageous treaty with the Turkish Sultan.

The Venetian, having glanced at Mamyrov with a smile of refined mockery and with a contemptuous shrug of his shoulders, remarked that His Grace was right,—disputes of this nature about places were unworthy of people enlightened by the light of "humanism," and sat down at the place indicated.

Danilo Kusmich had not understood the speech of his rival. But, even if he had understood it, he would not have been abashed, and would have continued deeming himself in the right, inasmuch as he knew that, ten years ago, in the year of fourteen hundred and eighty-seven, at the triumphal appearance of Pope Innocent VIII, the Muscovian ambassadors, Dimitri and Manuil Ralev, had, on the steps of the apostolic throne, taken places the most honourable after the Roman Senators, the representatives of the ancient, universe-governing city. It was not in vain that, in the epistle of Sabba Spiridon, the erstwhile Metropolitan of Kiev, the Grand Prince of Muscovy had already been declared sole heir of the two-headed eagle of Byzantium, uniting under its wings East and West, inasmuch as the Lord Omnipotent,—so saith the epistle,—having cast down for their heresies both Romes, the old and the new, had erected a third mystic city, in order to pour out upon it all His glory, all His power and beneficence,—a third, mid-night Rome: Moscow of the Orthodox Faith; as for a fourth Rome,—there never would be any, through all the ages.

Paying no heed to hostile glances, with self-satisfaction stroking his long grey beard, adjusting his sable-lined coat of vermeil velvet, and the girdle about his fat paunch, ponderously and importantly grunting, Danilo Kusmich sank on the place he had gained through battle. A feeling vague and heady, like to tipsiness, filled his soul.

Nikita, together with the interpreter Boccalino, sat down at the lower end of the table, next to Leonardo da Vinci. The bragging Mantuan was telling of the wonders he had seen in Muscovy, mingling fact with impossible fancy. The artist, desirous of getting more exact details from Karachiyarov himself, addressed him through the interpreter and began to interrogate him about the far-away land, which aroused Leonardo's curiosity as did all things immeasurable and enigmatic,

—about her endless plains, raging frosts, mighty rivers and forests; about the flood-tide in the Hyperborean Ocean and the Hyrcanean Sea; about the northern lights; as well as about his friends, who had settled down in Moscow,—the Lombardian artist Pietro Antoni Solario, who had participated in the erection of the Granite Palace, and the architect, Aristotle Fioraventi, of Bologna, who had adorned the Kremlin Square with magnificent edifices.

"Messer," the sprightly, curious, and mischievous Donzella Ermellina, who was seated beside him, addressed the interpreter, "I have heard that,—so it seems,—they style this amazing land Rozia, on account of the great number of roses growing there. Is that true?"

Boccalino began to laugh, and assured the donzella that, despite its name, there were fewer roses there than in any other country, and as proof cited an Italian *novella* about Russian cold.

Certain merchants from the city of Florence had come to Poland. Farther into Rozia they would not let them go, inasmuch as at that time the King of Poland was waging war with the Grand Duke of Muscovy. The Florentines, being desirous of purchasing some sables, invited the Russian merchants to the shore of the Boristhene, separating the two countries. Fearing capture, the Muscovites stood on one shore, the Italians on the other, and began to shout to each other across the river, chaffering. But the frost was so intense that their words, instead of reaching the opposite shore, froze in the air. Whereupon the resourceful Poles built a large fire in the middle of the river on the spot which the words, according to calculation, reached as yet unfrozen. The ice, as hard as marble, could bear any fire at all. And so, when the fire had been lit, the words, which, turned to ice, for the duration of a whole hour had remained in the air without moving, now began to melt, to run down in little runnels, with a low murmur, resembling the thawing dripping of spring, and, finally, were heard by the Florentines distinctly, despite the fact that the Muscovites had long since withdrawn from the opposite shore. [[24a]]

The story was to the taste of all. The glances of the ladies, filled with a compassionate curiosity, were turned upon Nikita Karachiyarov, the inhabitant of such an ill-fated, God-accursed land.

Meanwhile Nikita himself, frozen with amazement, was gazing at an unbelievable sight,—an enormous salver with a naked Andromeda, made out of capon-breasts, chained to a rock of cheese curds, with her deliverer, the winged Perseus, made out of veal.

During the meat courses of the feast everything was of purple, of gold; during the fish courses it turned to silver, to correspond with the watery element. Silvered loaves of bread, silvered lemons in cups as salad, were served; and, finally, on a platter between gigantic sturgeons, lamprons, and sterlets appeared an Amphitrite of the white meat of eels in a nacre chariot, drawn by dolphins over quivering jelly, bluish-green, like sea waves, and lighted up from within.

After that there was a procession of sweets without end,—carvings of marzipan, pistachios, cedar nuts, almonds and burnt sugar, executed after drawings by Bramante, Caradosso, and Leonardo,—Hercules, obtaining the golden apples of the Hesperides; the fables of Hippolytus and Phædra, of Bacchus and Ariadne, of Jupiter and Danaë, —the entire Olympus of the resurrected gods.

Nikita with a childlike curiosity gazed upon these wonders, while Danilo Kusmich, in the meantime, losing all appetite for the viands at the sight of the naked, shameless goddesses, grumbled under his nose:

"Abominations of Antichrist! Pagan vileness!"

VI

THE ball commenced. The dances of that day,—*Venus and Zephyr*, *Cruel Fate*, *Cupidon*,—were distinguished for their slow tempo, since the dresses of the ladies, long and heavy, did not permit of rapid figures. The ladies and the cavaliers came together and drew apart, with leisurely dignity, with exquisite bows, languishing sighs, and sweet smiles. The women were supposed to step out like peahens, to float like swans. And the music was low, tender, almost despondent, filled with voluptuous longing, like the songs of Petrarca.

The chief military leader of Moro, the youthful Signor Galeazzo Sanseverino, an exquisite of the exquisites, all in white, with drawn-back sleeves lined with pink, with diamonds on his white slippers, with a handsome, slothful, dissipated and effeminate face, enchanted the ladies. A whisper of approval ran through the crowd when, during the dance of *Cruel Fate*, dropping, as though accidentally, but really on purpose, a slipper off his foot, or the cape from his shoulder, he would continue to glide and circle over the hall with that "*insouciance d'ennui*" which was deemed a mark of the highest elegance.

Danilo Mamyrov looked upon him, looked again, and spat aside:

"Oh, thou damned clown!"

The Duchess loved dances. But on this evening she was heavy and perturbed at heart. Only the habit of dissimulation, long ingrained, helped her to play the rôle of the hospitable mistress of the house,—to respond to the good wishes for the New Year, to the fulsome pleasantries of the grandees. At times it seemed to her that she would not be able to bear up,—that she would run away, or else burst into tears.

Without being able to find a place for herself, wandering over the densely peopled halls, she stepped into the distant little chamber where, by the cheerily blazing fireplace, young damozels and cavaliers were conversing in a close circle.

She asked the subject of their conversation.

"Of Platonic love, Your Grace," answered one of the ladies. "Messer Antoniotto Fregoso is contending that a woman may kiss a man's lips, without violating chastity, if he doth love her with a celestial love."

"What then, is your contention, Messer Antoniotto?" questioned the Duchess, absent-mindedly puckering up her eyes.

"With the permission of Your Grace, I assert that the lips,—the implement of speech,—serve as the gates of the soul, and when they be united in a Platonic osculation, the souls of the lovers do rush toward the lips, as it were toward their natural exit. That is why Plato doth not inveigh against the kiss, and King Solomon, in his Canticle of Canticles, figuring forth the mystic mingling of the human soul with God, saith: Kiss me with the kisses of thy mouth."

"Pardon me, messer," one of his audience interrupted him,—an old baron, a rural squire with an honest and coarse face,—"it may be that I do not understand these fine points, but do you really maintain that a husband, finding his wife in the embraces of her lover, must endure it? . . ."

"Of course," retorted the court philosopher, "in accordance with the wisdom of spiritual love. . . ."

"But what of marriage, then? . . ."

"Oh, my God! Why, we are speaking of love, not of marriage!" the pretty little Madonna Fiordaliza cut him short, impatiently shrugging her dazzlingly white shoulders.

"But then, marriage also, madonna, according to all human laws . . ." the knight was about to begin.

"Laws!" Fiordaliza contemptuously wrinkled up her tiny scarlet lips. "How can you, messer, in such an exalted conversation, bring up the mention of human laws,—the pitiful creations of the rabble, transforming the sacred names of lover and beloved into such coarse words as husband and wife?"

The baron, with a hopeless gesture, gave up the struggle.

As for Messer Fregoso,—he, without paying any attention to him, continued his discourse upon the mysteries of celestial love. Yet Beatrice knew that there was in great vogue at court a most indecent sonnet of this same Messer Antoniotto Fregoso, dedicated to a handsome youth, and beginning thus:

The king of gods did err, in raping Ganymede.

Ennui fell upon the Duchess. She withdrew very quietly and passed on into an adjacent hall. Here a famous versificator, come from Rome, Serafino d'Aquila, dubbed the Unique,—*Unico*,—was declaiming his verses; a little, spare, scrupulously bathed, shaved, and curled homunculus, with a pink, infantile little face, a languishing smile, vile teeth, and little oleaginous eyes, in which through the eternal tear of transport there glimmered at times a knavish cunning.

Beholding Lucrezia among the ladies surrounding the poet, Beatrice became confused, paling the least trifle, but at once regained her bearing, approached her with customary kindliness, and kissed her.

At this juncture there appeared at the entrance a stout, gaily bedizened, much berouged woman, homely and no longer young, holding a handkerchief to her nose.

"What is it, Madonna Dionysia? Have you hurt yourself, perchance?" Donzella Ermellina asked her with crafty commiseration.

Dionysia explained that during the dances, probably from the heat and fatigue, she had gotten a nose-bleed.

"Here is an occasion upon which even Messer Unico would scarce be able to compose verses," remarked one of the courtiers.

Unico jumped up, put one foot forward, meditatively passed his hand over his hair, and cast his eyes toward the ceiling.

"Quiet, quiet!" the ladies began to *ssh-ssh* reverently, "Messer Unico is composing! Your Grace, be pleased to step this way, one can hear better here."

Donzella Ermellina, picking up a lute, most softly plucked its strings, at random, and to these sounds the poet, in the solemnly muffled, swooning voice of a ventriloquist, declaimed a *sonetto:*

Amour, touched by the prayers of a lover, had aimed an arrow at the heart of the cruel one; but, inasmuch as the eyes of the god are blindfolded, he missed, and, instead of the heart,—

> The arrow pierced the minim nose,
> And into the snowy kerchief flows,
> Like scarlet dew, the blood.

The ladies began to clap their hands.

"Exquisite, exquisite, inimitable! What rapidity! What facility! Oh, our Bellincioni, who sweats whole days over a sonnet, is no match for him! Oh, my dear, would you believe that when he raised his eyes up to heaven, I felt something supernatural pass over my face,—like a wind, as it were; I even grew afraid. . . ."

"Messer Unico, do you want any Rhenish?" one of them bustled.

"Messer Unico,—some cooling pastilles with mint?" offered another.

They seated him comfortably in a chair, and fanned him.

He was in the seventh heaven, melting with ecstasy, and blinked his eyes, like a satiated tom-cat.

Then he declaimed another sonnet, in honour of the Duchess, to the effect that the snow, put to shame by the candour of her skin, had conceived a treacherous revenge, by turning to ice, and that was why, when she had recently gone for a stroll in the courtyard of the castle, she had slipped and almost fallen.

He also read stanzas, dedicated to a beauty who lacked a front tooth: this was a crafty device of Amour, who, dwelling within her mouth, utilizes the opening as an embrasure whence to dart his arrows.

"A genius!" squealed out one of the ladies. "The name of Unico shall, to posterity, stand side by side with Dante!"

"Above that of Dante!" another one chimed in. "Why, can one possibly learn from Dante such refinements of love as from our Unico?"

"Madonne," protested the poet with diffidence, "you exaggerate. Dante, also, has great merits. However, every one to his taste. As far as I am concerned, I would, for your plaudits, give up all the fame of Dante!"

"Unico! Unico!" sighed his admirers, languishing in rapture.

When Serafino began a new sonnet, which described how, during a fire in the home of his inamorata, the folks who had come at a run could not extinguish the conflagration, inasmuch as they had to pour water over the flame of their own hearts, ignited by the glances of the beauty,—Beatrice, at last, could stand it no more and withdrew.

She returned to the larger halls, ordered her page Ricciardetto, a boy loyal and enamoured of her, to go upstairs, and wait for her with a torch at the door of her bedroom, and, hastily traversing several brightly-lit, crowded rooms, stepped into the deserted, remote gallery, where only the guards were drowsing, leaning on their spears. Opening a small iron door, she ascended a dark spiral staircase to an enormous vaulted hall, which served as the ducal chamber, situated in the quadrangular northern tower of the Castle; candle in hand, she approached a small oaken casket, let into the thickness of the stone wall, where the important papers and secret letters of the Duke were kept, inserted the key she had purloined from her husband into the keyhole, and tried to turn it, but found that the lock was broken. Throwing open the folding lid of copper, she beheld the empty shelves, and surmised that Moro, having noticed the disappearance of the key, had secreted the letters in another place. She paused in indecision.

Snow-flakes fluttered outside the window, like white phantoms. The wind was turbulent,—now howling, now wailing. And these voices of the night wind brought remembrances of ancient things, fearfully, eternally familiar to the heart.

The eyes of the Duchess fell upon the cast-iron cover over the round opening of the Ear of Dionysius,—the listening tube laid by Leonardo from the lower chambers of the palace to the ducal chamber. She approached the opening, and, taking the heavy lid off, listened intently. The waves of sound floated up to her, like to the beating of a distant sea, such as one hears in sea-shells; with the hum and the rustling of the festal crowd, with the tender sighs of the music, was blended the howling and the whistling of the night wind.

Suddenly it appeared to her that, not there, below, but at her very ear, someone said in a whisper:

"Bellincioni. . . . Bellincioni. . . ."

A cry escaped her and she paled.

"Bellincioni! . . . How is it I did not surmise it myself? Yes, yes, of course! He is the one I will find out everything from. . . . I must go to him! Only, what if they notice me? . . . They will seek me. . . . But what matters it! I want to know,—I can no longer endure this falsity!"

She recalled that Bellincioni, having given illness as an excuse, had not come to the ball. She conjectured that at this hour he would almost certainly be at home, alone, and called out for her page Ricciardetto, who was standing at the door.

"Order two runners with a litter to wait for me below, in the park, near the secret gate of the Castle. Only, look thou, if thou wouldst please me, let no one know of this,—dost hear?—no one!"

She gave him her hand to kiss. The boy dashed off to carry out her behest.

Beatrice returned to the room, threw a fur cloak over her shoulders, donned a black silk mask, and within a few minutes was seated in the litter, borne in the direction of the Ticine Gates, where Bellincioni lived.

VII

THE poet styled his decrepit, half-ruined little house "the frog's hollow." He received a considerable number of gifts, but led a dissolute life, drinking or gaming away all he had, and therefore poverty, to use Bernardo's own expression, dogged him "like an unloved but faithful wife."

Lying down on a broken bed with but three legs, and a billet of wood in lieu of a fourth, with a mattress torn and as flat as a pancake, he was composing a funerary inscription for the favourite dog of Madonna Cecilia, the while he finished a third pot of wretched sour wine. The poet was watching the last embers dying in the fireplace; vainly trying to warm himself, he pulled over his thin, cranelike legs his sorry, moth-eaten squirrel coat which served him for a blanket, and listened to the prolonged howling of the wind as he anticipated the cold of the night ahead.

He had not gone to the court ball, where his allegory, *Paradise*, which he had composed in honour of the Duchess, was to be presented, not at all on account of his illness,—although he had, in reality, been ailing a long time, and was so thin that, to use his own words, "it was possible, by inspecting his body, to study the anatomy of all human muscles, sinews, and bones!" Even if he had been at his last gasp, he would nevertheless have dragged himself to the festival. The real reason of his absence was envy: he would much liefer have agreed to freeze to death in his kennel, than to behold the triumph of his rival, the brazen knave and charlatan, Messer Unico, who with his absurd versicles had succeeded in turning the heads of the silly court ladies. At the mere thought of Unico, all his bile would rise toward the heart of Bellincioni. He would clench his hands and jump out of bed. But it was so cold in the room that he would at once prudently get into bed again, shivering, coughing, and huddling.

"Scoundrels!" he fumed. "Four sonnets about fire-wood, and with such rhymes, to boot,—and nary a bit of kindling! . . . The ink may freeze, likely enough,—and there will be naught to write with. Should I start a fire with the stair railings, perhaps? What difference would it make,—decent folk do not come to me, and if the Jew usurer should dislocate his neck, it would be no great loss."

But he spared the stairs. His glances turned toward the thick billet which served as a fourth leg for his lame couch. He paused in meditation for a minute: would it be better to shiver all night from cold, or to sleep on a rickety couch?

The snow-storm began to howl through the crack in the window; it began to keen, to laugh in the hearth-chimney, like a witch. With a desperate resolve Bernardo snatched out the billet from under his bed, split it into kindling, and took to casting it into the fireplace. The flame flared up, illuminating the sorry cell. He squatted on his heels and stretched out his hands, which had turned blue, toward the fire, the last friend of lonely poets.

"'Tis a dog's life!" pondered Bellincioni. "But, just to think of it, —wherein am I inferior to others? Was it not of my great-great-great-grandfather, the famous Florentine, at a time when there was not even a thought of the house of Sforza, that the divine Dante composed this verse:

Bellincion Berti vid' io andar cinto
Di cuojo e d' osso?

Bellincion Berti I did see begirt
With hide and bone. [24b]

Never fear, when I came to Milan the court lick-spittles could not tell a *strambotto* from a *sonetto*. Who but I taught them the elegancies of the new poesy? Was it not through my fine hand that the Hippocrene has spread into a whole sea, and now threatens inundation? Now, 'twould seem, the Castalian waters flow e'en in the Grand Canal. . . . And behold my reward! I shall die like a dog on the straw of a kennel! None recognizes a poet fallen to penury, just as though his face were hidden by a mask, or made hideous by smallpox. . . ."

He read over some verses from his epistle to Moro:

> All life long have I heard but one unvaried burden:
> "Go hence, God keep thee,—my posts are all bespoken!"
> What, then, am I to do? My little song is sung, then?
> No more I seek e'en a jester's baubled token;
> But, Most Generous Sire!—thy poet would be beholden
> Placed in some mill, e'en as a beast load-broken. . . .

And, with a bitter smile, he bowed his bald head. Lanky, spare, with a long red nose, squatting on his heels before the fire, he resembled an ailing, shivering bird.

A knocking was heard below at the door; then the sleepy scolding of the quarrelsome, dropsy-bloated crone, his sole servitor, and the clacking of her wooden shoes over the brick floor.

"Who the devil can that be?" wondered Bernardo. "Can it possibly be the Jew coming again for his interest? Ugh, the accursed infidels! They will give one no rest even at night. . . ."

The treads of the staircase creaked. The door opened, and into the room walked a woman in a sable coat, in a mask of black silk.

Bernardo jumped up and fixed his eyes upon her. She approached a chair in silence.

"Be careful, madonna," warned the host. "The back is broken."

And, with a worldly grace he added:

"To what kind genius am I indebted for beholding the most illustrious madonna in my humble abode?"

"Probably, a patroness. Some sort of an amatory madrigalette," he reflected. "Well, what of it,—that, too, means bread. Or, at least, enough for fire-wood. Only 'tis strange,—alone, at such an hour? . . . But, however, my name must mean something, too, evidently. Are there not plenty of unknown fair admirers!"

He became animated, ran up to the hearth, and magnanimously threw his last bit of kindling on the fire. The lady took off her mask.

"'Tis I, Bernardo."

He cried out, took a step backward, and, in order not to fall, had to seize the door-jamb.

"Gesù! Most Pure Virgin!" he babbled, his eyes popping out. "Your Grace. . . . The Most Illustrious Duchess. . . ."

"Bernardo, thou canst do me a great service," said Beatrice; and then asked, looking around, "Can anyone hear us?"

"Be at rest, Your Highness, no one,—save rats and mice!"

"Hearken," continued Beatrice slowly, fixing him with a penetrating glance, "I know that you have written love poems to Madonna Lucrezia. Thou surely hast letters of the Duke's, with instructions and commissions."

He blenched and looked at her in silence, his eyes wide-open, in a trance.

"Fear not," she added, "none shall find out. I give thee my word, —I shall be able to reward thee, if thou shalt fulfill my request. I shall make thee to roll in gold, Bernardo!"

"Your Highness," he uttered with an effort, and a tongue benumbed, "believe it not. . . . 'Tis a slander. . . . There are no letters of any sort. . . . Before God! . . ."

Her eyes flashed with wrath; her thin eyebrows contracted. She arose, and, without taking her oppressive, penetrating gaze off him walked up to him.

"Do not lie! I know all. Give up to me the Duke's letters, if life be dear to thee,—dost hear? Give them up! Beware, Bernardo! My men wait below. I have not come to jest with thee! . . ."

He fell down on his knees before her.

"Your will be done, Signora! I have no letters of any sort. . . ."

"Thou hast not?" she repeated, bending down and peering into his eyes, "Thou hast not, thou sayest? . . ."

"I have not. . . ."

"Wait, then, thou accursed go-between, I shall compel thee to tell me the whole truth! I shall strangle thee with my own hands, thou abominable scoundrel! . . ." she cried out in a frenzy, and really did, with her delicate fingers, seize his throat with such force that he gasped and the veins on his forehead became swollen. Offering no resistance, his arms hanging down, merely blinking his eyes helplessly, he resembled more than ever a pitiful, ailing bird.

"She will kill me," thought Bernardo. "Well, then, let her. . . . But I shall not betray the Duke."

Bellincioni had been all life long a court jester, a shiftless vagabond, a prostituting poetaster, but never had he been a traitor. In his veins flowed noble blood, purer than that of the Romagnola mercenaries, the upstart Sforzas, and at this juncture he was ready to prove it:

His title from the famed Bellincion ta'en

he recalled another verse of Alighieri's anent his great ancestor. [24c]

The Duchess recovered herself; with aversion she released the poet's throat from her hands, pushed him away, walked up to the table, and, seizing the small pewter lamp, with dented sides and burnt wick, went in the direction of an adjacent room. She had noticed it before, and surmised that this was the *studiolo*, the workroom of the poet.

Bernardo jumped up, and, taking his stand before the door, wanted to bar her ingress. But the Duchess measured him in silence with such a look that he shrivelled, hunched up, and let her through.

She entered the habitation of the penurious muse. Here was an odour of the mould of books. Upon the bare walls with their peeling plastering spots of dampness showed darkly. A broken pane in the frost-covered window was stuffed up with a rag. Upon an inclined writing stand, ink-spattered, with goose-quills, plucked and gnawed in the pursuit of elusive rhymes, papers were scattered, probably rough draughts of poems.

Putting the lamp on a shelf, and paying no attention to her host, Beatrice began to rummage through the leaves of paper. Here was a multitude of sonnets to court treasurers, butlers, dapifers, cup-bearers, with merry-andrew complaints, with supplications for money, for firewood, for wine, for warm clothing, for victuals. In one of them the poet importuned Messer Pallavicini for a roast goose, stuffed with quinces, for All Saints' Day. In another, entitled *From Moro to Cecilia*, comparing the Duke with Jupiter, the Duchess with Juno, he related how Moro once, having set out for an assignation with his mistress, and being overtaken on his way by a storm, had been compelled to return home, inasmuch as "jealous Juno, surmising the infidelity of her spouse, had torn the diadem off her head and had scattered the pearls from the heavens, in the form of tempestuous rain and hail."

Suddenly, underneath a pile of papers she noticed an exquisite casket of ebony, opened it,—and beheld a bundle of letters, carefully tied together.

Bernardo, who was watching her, wrung his hands in horror. The Duchess glanced at him, then at the letters, read the name of Lucrezia, recognized the handwriting of Moro, and understood that here, at last, was that which she was seeking,—the letters of Moro, the rough draughts of love poems, ordered by him for Lucrezia; she seized the packet, thrust it within the bosom of her dress, and, silently, having thrown to the poet a purse of gold-pieces, as one would a sop to a dog, went out.

He heard her descending the stairs; heard the door slam; and stood for long in the middle of the room, like one thunder-struck. The floor, it seemed to him, was rocking, like a deck during a swell.

At last, in exhaustion, he tumbled down on his three-legged, lame couch.

VIII

THE Duchess returned to the Castle.

Noting her absence, the guests were exchanging whispers, asking what had happened. The Duke was alarmed.

Entering the hall, she approached her husband with a slightly pale face, and said that, having felt fatigue after the feast, she had withdrawn into the inner chambers, in order to rest.

"Bice," murmured the Duke, taking her by her hand,—cold, and with the slightest of tremors running through it as it touched his,—"if thou art unwell, say so, for God's sake! Forget not that thou art pregnant. Dost want to,—we shall postpone till to-morrow the second part of the festival? For I have begun the whole thing only for thee, dearest. . . ."

"Nay; 'tis not necessary," objected the Duchess. "Please, do not trouble thyself, Vico. I have not felt as well as I do to-day for a long time past. . . . So gay. . . . I want to see *Paradise*. I shall even dance some more! . . ."

"Well, thank God, my dear,—thank God!"—Moro became reassured, kissing with respectful tenderness his wife's hand. The guests again passed on into the large Hall for the Play of Ball, where for the representation of Bellincioni's *Paradise* there had been erected a contrivance invented by the court mechanician, Leonardo da Vinci.

When everybody had settled down, and the lights had been extinguished, Leonardo's voice was heard:

"Ready!"

A powder fuse flared up, and in the darkness, like transparent icy suns, there shone forth globes of crystal, disposed in a circle, filled with water and illuminated from within by a multitude of bright lights, playing like a rainbow.

"Look," the Donzella Ermellina pointed the artist out to a fair neighbour, "do but look; what a face,—a veritable magician! First thing you know, he will lift the whole castle up into the air, as in a fairy-tale!"

"One ought not to play with fire! It does not take long to have a conflagration," declared her neighbour.

In the contrivance, behind the crystal globes, were hidden black, round boxes. Out of one box appeared an angel with white wings, who proclaimed the beginning of the piece, and, while speaking one of the stanzas of the prologue:

The Great Lord makes His spheres revolve—

he pointed to the Duke, giving to understand that Moro ruled his subjects with the same wisdom with which God did His heavenly spheres.

And at the same moment the globes began to move, revolving around the axis of the machine to strange, soft, extraordinarily pleasant sounds, as though the crystal spheres, impinging upon one another, were ringing with that mystic music of which Pythagoreans speak. Special bells of glass, invented by Leonardo, struck by keys, produced these sounds.

The planets came to a stop, and over each one, in his or her turn, began to appear the corresponding deities: Jupiter, Apollo, Mercury, Mars, Diana, Venus, Saturn,—addressing a greeting to Beatrice.

Mercury declaimed:

Thou that didst all ancient luminaries extinguish,
O Sun for all that live, O mirror of heavenly heights,
Thy beauty caused the sire of all the gods to languish,—
Thou miracle of miracles, and light of lights!

Venus made a genuflection before the Duchess:

All of my erstwhile charms hast thou turned to ashes;
To flaunt my olden name of Venus now I would quail
And I, a vanquished star when thy radiance flashes,—
O, thou new solar orb!—from jealousy I wax pale.

Diana supplicated Jupiter:

Bestow me as hand-maiden, sire, in thy gracious plan,
To the goddess of goddesses, the Duchess of Milan.

Saturn, breaking his death-dealing scythe, exclaimed:

May all thy life blessèd be, midst stormless skies azurn,
And thy age golden, like the ancient age of Saturn!

In conclusion, Jupiter presented to Her Highness the Three Hellenic Graces, the Seven Christian Virtues, and all this Olympus, or Paradise, under the shelter of the white angels' wings and the Cross, covered over with the lights of green holy lamps,—symbols of hope,—began to turn anew, accompanied by all the gods and goddesses chanting a hymn in praise of Beatrice, to the music of the crystal spheres and the plaudits of the spectators.

"I say," said the Duchess to Gaspare Visconti, a noble seated next to her, "how is it Juno is not here,—the jealous spouse of Jupiter, who 'tears the head-dress off her curls, that she may scatter the pearls upon earth, like to rain and hail'?"

Hearing these words, the Duke turned around quickly and glanced at her. She burst into such strange, forced laughter that a chill ran momently through the heart of Moro. But, immediately controlling herself, she began speaking of something else, merely pressing closer the packet of letters in her bosom, under her dress.

The anticipated revenge intoxicated her, making her strong, calm, almost gay.

The guests passed on to another hall, where a new spectacle awaited them: the triumphal chariots of Numa Pompilius, Cæsar, Augustus, Trajan, drawn by negroes, leopards, griffons, centaurs, and dragons harnessed thereto, with allegorical pictures and inscriptions, proclaiming that all these heroes were forerunners of Moro; as a finale, there appeared a chariot drawn by unicorns, with an enormous globus, the effigy of a stellar sphere, upon which reclined a warrior in rusty iron armour. A naked golden child, with a branch of the silk-producing mulberry (*moro* in Italian) in its hand was coming out of a crack in the cuirass of the warrior, thereby signifying the death of the old Age of Iron, and the birth of the new Age of Gold, thanks to the wise rule of Moro. To the amazement of all, the gold sculpture proved to be a living child. The boy, as a consequence of the thick coating of gold covering his body, was not feeling well. Tears glistened in his frightened eyes.

In a tremulous, despondent voice, he commenced his greeting to the Duke, with an ever-recurring, monotonous, well-nigh ominous refrain:

Soon, to you, O my people, soon,
With renewed beauty rare,
I will return, as Moro's boon,—
The Age of Gold, without a care.

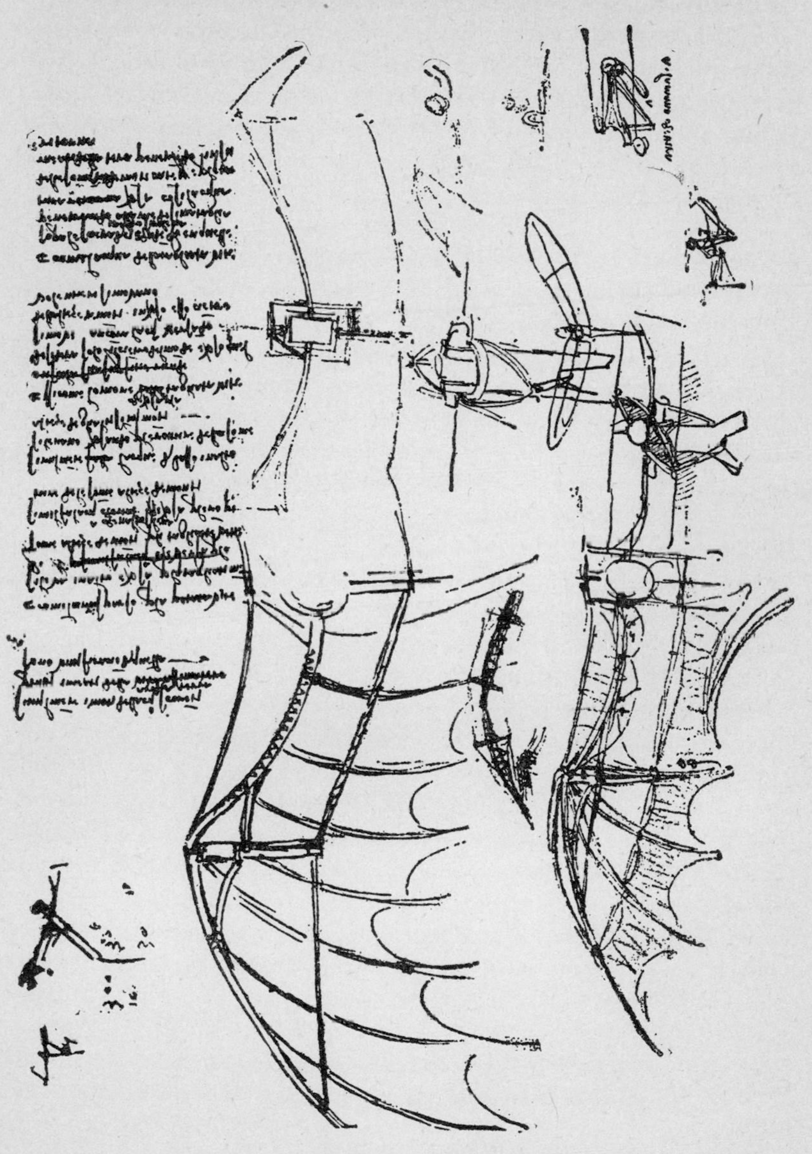

Around the chariot of the Golden Age the dancing was renewed. The endless greeting had become a universal bore. All ceased paying any attention to it. But the boy, standing on his elevation, still babbled on with his golden limbs growing benumbed, with a hopeless and submissive air:

I will return, as Moro's boon,—
The Age of Gold, without a care.

Beatrice was dancing with Gaspare Visconti. At times a convulsion of laughter and sobbing would make her throat contract. With unbearable pain the blood throbbed at her temples,—everything would grow dark before her eyes. But her face seemed to be without a care. She was smiling.

Having finished the dance, she went out of the gala throng and again withdrew, unnoticed.

IX

THE Duchess passed through to the isolated Tower of the Treasury. None ever entered here, save she and the Duke.

Taking a candle from the page Ricciardetto, she ordered him to wait near the entrance, and stepped into the high-ceilinged hall, where it was dark and chill, as in a cellar; she sat down, took out the packet of letters, untied them, and was about to read them,—when suddenly with a piercing screeching, whistling, and rumbling the wind tore in through the chimney of the hearth, and whirled through the whole tower; it howled and swished, and almost extinguished the candle. Then an abrupt silence fell. And it seemed to her that she could distinguish the sounds of the distant music of the ball, as well as other sounds,—barely audible voices, the clanking of iron gyves,—below, in the underground chambers, where the prison was.

And at the same instant she felt someone was standing behind her, in a dark corner. A familiar terror seized her. She knew that she must not look, but could not contain herself and looked around. In the corner stood one whom she had already seen once,—elongated, black,—blacker than darkness itself,—shrouded with head downcast, with a monk's cowl lowered so that his face could not be seen. She wanted to cry out, to summon Ricciardetto, but her voice died away. She jumped up, fain to run away,—but her legs crumpled up under her. She fell down on her knees and whispered:

"Thou. . . . Thou again. . . . Wherefore?"

He slowly raised his head.

And she beheld the face, neither dead nor frightful, of the late Duke Gian Galeazzo, and heard his voice:

"Forgive me. . . . my poor, poor dear. . . ."

He made a step toward her, and upon her face was wafted a cold not of this world. She cried out in a piercing, inhuman scream, and lost consciousness.

Ricciardetto, hearing this scream, came running, and beheld her lying on the floor unconscious. He started running headlong over the dark corridors, lighted up here and there by the dull lanthorns of the sentries, then over the brightly lighted, densely peopled halls, seeking the Duke, with a scream of insane horror:

"Help! Help!"

It was midnight. An enticing gaiety reigned at the ball. A fashionable dance had just been begun, during which the cavaliers and ladies passed in a file under the Arch of Faithful Lovers. A man, who represented the Genius of Love, with a long trumpet, was placed at the top of the Arch; at its foot were the judges. When "Faithful Lovers" approached, the genius would greet them with tender music, the judges would receive them with joy. The faithless ones, however, tried in vain to pass through the magic Arch: the trumpet deafened them with frightful sounds; the judges met them with a storm of confetti, and the unfortunate ones were forced to turn to flight under a hail of mockery.

The Duke had just passed through underneath the Arch, escorted by the softest, most delectable sounds of the trumpet, resembling a shepherd's syrinx or the cooing of doves, as the most faithful of all faithful lovers.

At this moment the crowd parted. Ricciardetto ran into the hall, with a scream of desperation:

"Help! Help!"

Seeing the Duke, he dashed toward him:

"Your Highness, the Duchess doth not feel well. . . . Quick. . . . Help!"

"Not feel well? . . . Again! . . ."

The Duke clutched his head.

"Where is she? Where is she?"

"In the Tower of the Treasury. . . ."

Moro began running so fast that the chain of gold scales upon his breast clinked, his gorgeous, smooth *zazzera*,—hair dressed so as to resemble a wig,—jumped oddly on his head.

The Genius on the Arch of Faithful Lovers, who still kept on trumpeting, finally noticed that something was amiss down below, and grew still. Many ran after the Duke, and suddenly the entire scintillating crowd stirred, dashing toward the doors, like a flock of rams, seized with horror. The Arch was overturned and trampled to bits. The trumpeter, who had barely managed to jump off, dislocated his leg. Someone cried out:

"Fire!"

"There, now, I was saying that one should not play with fire!" exclaimed the woman who had not approved of Leonardo's crystal spheres, wringing her hands.

Another squealed, getting ready to fall in a faint.

"Calm yourselves,—there is no fire," reassured certain guards.

"What is it, then?" asked others.

"The Duchess is ill! . . ."

"She is dying! They have poisoned her!" someone of the courtiers decided, through sudden intuition, and immediately believed his own invention.

"It can not be! The Duchess was here but now. . . . She was dancing. . . ."

"Have you not heard? The widow of the late Duke Gian Galeazzo, Isabella of Aragon, to avenge her husband. . . . Slow poison. . . ."

"The power of the Lord be with us!"

From an adjacent hall sounds of music reached them. There nothing was known of what was going on. In the dance of *Venus and the Zephyr* the ladies, with an amiable smile, led their cavaliers about on chains of gold, as captives,—and when each of the latter, with languishing sighs, would fall prostrate, his partner would place her foot on his back, like a veritable conculatrix.

The chamberlain ran in, waving his arms and shouting to the musicians:

"Quiet, quiet! The Duchess is ill. . . ."

All present turned around at the shout. The music died away. Only a single viola, played by a little old man, purblind and hard of hearing, continued to trill in the silence for a long while with its plaintively tremulous sound.

The servitors hastily brought in a litter,—narrow, long, with a rough mattress, with two cross-beams for the head, two rests on both sides for the arms, and a cross-piece for the feet of the one to be confined, —a piece of furniture preserved from times immemorial in the wardrobe ambries of the palace, and doing duty for the deliveries of all the royal ladies of the House of Sforza. Strange and ominous, in the midst of the ball, in the glitter of gala lights, over a throng of gaily arrayed ladies, did this couch of confinement seem.

All exchanged glances, and understood.

"If it be from fright or a fall," remarked an elderly dame, "she ought to swallow, without any delay, the white of a raw egg, with pieces of scarlet silk, cut small."

Another asserted that red silk had nothing to do with it, but that the embryos of seven hens' eggs should be beaten in the yolk of an eighth.

At this moment Ricciardetto, having entered one of the upper halls, heard behind the doors of a neighbouring room such a fearful scream as made him halt in wonder, and pointing to the door he asked one of the women passing by with baskets of linen, warming pans, and vessels of hot water:

"What is it?"

The other made no reply.

Another, an old woman, probably a midwife, gave him a stern look and pronounced:

"Go thy ways, and God be with thee! Whatever art thou blocking up the way for,—thou art but a nuisance. This be no place for little lads."

The door opened for an instant, and Ricciardetto glimpsed in the depth of the room, in the midst of the disorder of clothes and linen hastily torn off, the face of her whom he loved with a hopeless childish love,—red, sweaty, with locks of hair stuck to her forehead, with mouth gaping, whence issued the unceasing screaming. The lad paled and covered his face with his hands.

Alongside of him sundry gossips, nurses, self-taught doctor-women, women reputed to have supernatural knowledge, and midwives, were discoursing in whispers. Each had her own remedy. One proposed wrapping up the right leg of the confined woman with a snake's skin; another, to sit her down on a cast-iron pot with boiling water; a third, to tie her husband's cap to her abdomen; a fourth, to give her ardent spirits, infused on the stubs of deers' antlers and cochineal.

"The eagle-stone under the right armpit; the lodestone under the left," mumbled an ancient, wrinkled little crone, fussing about more than all the others, "that, mother o' mine, is the first thing to be done! The eagle-stone,—or an emerald, now. . . ."

The Duke came dashing out of the door, and sank on a chair, clutching his head, blubbering like a child:

"Lord, Lord! I can not stand it any more. . . . I can not. . . . Bice, Bice. . . . All because of me,—accursed that I am!"

He was recalling how, but now, the Duchess had, upon beholding him, cried out with frenzied wrath:

"Out! Out! Go to thy Lucrezia! . . ."

The bustling little crone approached him with a little pewter plate:

"Be pleased to taste of this, Your Highness."

"What is it?"

"Wolf's meat. 'Tis an omen: when the husband partaketh of wolf's meat, she who is giving birth will feel better. Wolf's meat, father o' mine,—that is the first thing to be done!"

The Duke, with a submissive and wandering air, tried to swallow the small piece of tough, black meat, which had stuck in his throat.

The old woman, bending over him, was muttering:

"Our Father, which art in Heaven,
In the earth and in the skies;
One she-wolf, and male wolves seven;
Let a whirling wind arise
And our evil carry off.

"Holy, Holy, Holy,—in the name of the Trinity, the one and indivisible, without beginning. Strong be our word. Amen!"

Out of the patient's room come the chief court medicus, Luigi Marliani, in the company of other doctors.

The Duke darted toward him.

"Well, what is the news?"

The men of medicine kept silent.

"Your Highness," Luigi finally uttered, "all measures have been taken. Let us hope that the Lord in His mercy . . ."

The Duke seized his hand:

"Nay, nay. . . . There must be some means or other. . . . It can not be left so. . . . For God's sake. . . . Well, now, do something,—do something! . . ."

The physicians exchanged looks, like augurs, feeling that he must be calmed.

Marliani, contracting his eyebrows sternly, said in Latin to a young doctor, rosy and brazen of face:

"Three ounces of river snails, with muscat nuts and red brayed coral."

"Phlebotomy, perhaps?" remarked a little old man, with a timid and kindly face.

"Phlebotomy? I have already thought of it," continued Marliani, "but unfortunately, Mars is in the constellation of Cancer, in the fourth house of the Sun. In addition to that the influence of the odd day . . ."

The little old man sighed resignedly and lapsed into silence.

"What think ye, master," Marliani was addressed by another physician, red-cheeked, self-assured, with inconquerably gay and hardened eyes, "should we not add to the snail concoction some cow's dung dropped in March?"

"Yes," meditatively agreed Luigi, rubbing the bridge of his nose, "some cow's dung,—yes, yes, of course!"

"Oh, Lord, Lord!" groaned the Duke.

"Your Highness," Marliani addressed him, "calm yourself,—I can assure you that everything prescribed by science . . ."

"The devil take your science!" Suddenly, unable to contain himself, the Duke flew at him, clenching his fists in fury. "She is dying, —dying, do you hear? And here you go puttering about with a decoction of snails, with cow's dung! . . . Scoundrels! . . . You ought to be all strung up! . . ."

And in a deathly sorrow, he took to dashing around the room, as he hearkened to the unceasing screaming.

Suddenly his gaze fell upon Leonardo. He led the latter aside:

"Listen," the Duke began to mutter, as though he were in delirium, evidently not realizing himself what he was saying; "listen, Leonardo, —thou art worth more than all of them put together. I know that thou art master of great secrets. . . . Nay, nay, do not contradict. . . . I know. . . . Ah, my God, my God,—that cry! . . . What was it I wanted to say? Ay,—help me, my friend, help me,—do something! . . . I would give my soul away, only to help her, even if for a brief space,—only not to hear that cry! . . ."

Leonardo was about to reply; but the Duke, having already forgotten about him, had darted off to meet the chaplains and monks entering the room.

"At last! Glory be to God! What have ye?"

"Parts of the body of the most holy Ambrogio, the Ceinture of St. Margherita, who helpeth in child-birth, a most authentic Tooth of San Cristoforo, a Hair of the Virgin Mary. . . ."

"Good, good; go, pray!"

Moro was about to enter the room with them, but at this moment the scream changed into such squealing and roaring that, putting his fingers in his ears, he took to his heels. Passing several darkened halls, he came to a stop in a chapel, feebly lighted by holy lamps, and fell on his knees before an icon.

"I have sinned, Mother of God,—I have sinned, accursed that I am; an innocent youth have I done away with, my lawful liege lord, Gian Galeazzo! But do thou, Merciful One, thou sole Interceder, hearken to my prayer and have compassion! I shall give away all my goods, I shall pray forgiveness for all,—do thou but save her, do thou take my soul instead!"

Fragments of absurd thoughts thronged his head, hindering him from praying; he recalled a story over which he had been laughing recently,—of how a certain mariner, perishing during a storm, had promised the Virgin Mary a candle the size of a ship's mast; but when his comrade asked him whence he would get wax for such a candle, he made answer: "Be still, let us but be saved now, and afterwards we shall have time to consider ways and means; besides, I have hopes that the Madonna will rest content with a candle of a smaller size."

"My God, what am I thinking of!" the Duke checked himself. "Am I going out of my mind, or what? . . ."

He made an effort to marshal his thoughts, and began to pray anew. But the vivid crystal spheres, resembling icy, transparent suns, began to float, to spin before him; he heard low music, together with the annoying refrain of the golden boy:

> Soon, to you, O my people, soon,
> I will return, as Moro's boon.

Then everything vanished.

When he came to, it seemed to him that no more than two or three minutes had elapsed; but, upon walking out of the chapel, he saw in the windows, buried under by the snow-storm, the grey light of a winter morn.

X

Moro returned to the Hall of the Rocchetta. Here was universal quiet. He came upon a woman carrying a hamper with swaddling clothes. She approached him and said:

"Her Grace is pleased to be delivered."

"Is she alive?" he managed to lisp, paling.

"Yes, glory be to God! But the little baby died. Her Grace hath grown very weak,—she desireth to see you,—please step this way."

He entered the room, and beheld on the pillows a diminutive face, like that of a little girl, with enormous eye-hollows, which seemed to be spun over with cobwebs,—a face calm, oddly familiar, and yet that of a stranger. He approached her and bent down.

"Send for Isabella. . . . As quickly as possible," she whispered.

The Duke issued an order. Within a few minutes a tall, stately woman, sad and austere of face,—the Duchess Isabella of Aragon, widow of Gian Galeazzo,—entered the room and approached the dying woman. All withdrew, save the priest and Moro, who took their stand at a short distance.

For some time both women conversed in whispers. Next, Isabella kissed Beatrice with words of final forgiveness, and, getting down on her knees, covering her face with her hands, she began to pray.

Beatrice called her husband toward her once more.

"Vico, forgive me. Weep not. Remember. . . . I am always with thee. . . . I know that it was I alone. . . ."

She did not finish, but he understood what she had wanted to say: "It was I alone whom you loved."

She looked at him with a serene gaze, that seemed infinitely distant, and said in a whisper:

"Kiss me."

Moro touched her forehead with his lips. She wanted to say something, could not, and succeeded only in uttering in a barely audible sigh:

"On the lips. . . ."

A monk commenced reciting the prayer for the dying. Those close to the ducal couple returned to the room.

The Duke, without tearing his lips away from the farewell kiss, felt her lips growing chill,—and in this last kiss received the last breath of his mate.

"She hath expired," said Marliani.

All made the sign of the cross and got down on their knees. Moro arose slowly. His face was immobile. It was not grief that it expressed, but an appalling, unbelievable effort. He breathed heavily and rapidly, as though he were overtaxing his strength in an up-hill climb. Suddenly, unnaturally and queerly, he waved both his arms at once, cried out: "Bice!"—and sank on the dead body.

Of all those present, Leonardo alone had preserved his calm. With a deep, penetrating glance he watched the Duke.

At such times the curiosity of the artist surmounted all else within him. The expression of great suffering in human faces, in the movements of the body, he observed in the light of a rare, unusual experiment, like a new, resplendent manifestation of nature. Not a single wrinkle, not a single quiver of a muscle, escaped his dispassionate, all-seeing eye.

He wanted to draw as soon as possible in his note-book the face of Moro, distorted with despair. He descended to the deserted lower chambers of the palace.

Here the candle-ends were smoking, drops of wax guttering to the floor. In one of the halls he stepped over the overturned, crumpled Arch of Faithful Lovers. Sinister and pitiful did the gorgeous allegories in praise of Moro and Beatrice seem, in the cold light of morning—the triumphal chariots of Numa Pompilius, of Augustus, of Trajan, and the Golden Age.

He approached the extinguished hearth, looked about him, and, making sure there was no one in the hall, took out his note-book and pencil, and had begun to draw, when suddenly he noticed in a corner of the fireplace the boy who had served as a statue of the Golden Age. He slept, benumbed with cold, huddled into a ball, grasping his arms about his knees, on which his head rested. The last breath of the cooling ashes could not warm up his naked, golden body.

Leonardo, with exceeding gentleness, touched his shoulder. The infant did not raise his head,—he merely gave a dull and piteous moan. The artist took him up in his arms.

The boy opened his large, frightened eyes, dark-blue, like violets, and began weeping:

"Home, home!"

"Where dost thou live? What is thy name?" asked Leonardo.

"Lippi," answered the boy. "Home, home! Oh, I feel qualmish, and cold. . . ."

His eyelids closed; he began to lisp in delirium:

Soon, to you, O my people, soon,
With renewed beauty rare,
Shall I return, as Moro's boon,
The Age of Gold, without a care.

Taking his cape off his shoulders, Leonardo wrapped up the child in it, laid him on a chair, went into the foyer, shook the servants, who had managed to get drunk during the hubbub, and were now snoring on the floor, and found out from one of them that Lippi was the son of a poor old widower, a baker on the street of Broletto Nuovo, who for twenty *scudi* had given the boy for the presentation of the Triumph, although good folk had warned the father that the boy might die from the gilt.

The artist, after a search, got his warm winter cloak, put it on, returned to Lippi, carefully wrapped him up in a thick coat, and walked out of the palace, intending to drop in at an apothecary's to buy the ingredients necessary to wash off the gilt from the body of the child, and then take him home.

Suddenly he recalled the drawing he had begun; recalled the curious expression of despair on the face of Moro.

"It matters not," he reflected, "I shall not forget. Mainly, the wrinkles over the eyebrows,—the latter lifted high; and the strange, radiant, almost triumphant smile on his lips,—the same smile that makes so similar the human facial expressions of the greatest suffering and the greatest joy,—two universes that are, as Plato witnesseth, divided at the foundation, but growing into one at the summits."

He felt the boy shivering from a chill.

"Our Golden Age," reflected the artist, with a sad smile.

"My poor little fledgling!" he whispered with infinite pity; and, wrapping him up more warmly, pressed him to his breast so tenderly and with such kindliness that the sick child had a dream of his departed mother caressing and singing him to sleep.

XI

THE Duchess Beatrice died on Tuesday, the second of January, in the year fourteen hundred and ninety-seven, at six in the morning.

The Duke passed more than a day and a night near the body of his wife, without paying heed to any consolations, refusing sleep and food. Those near him feared he would lose his mind.

On Thursday, in the morning, he demanded paper and ink, and indited a letter to Isabella d'Este, sister of the late Duchess, in which, informing her of the death of Beatrice, he said *in passim:*

"'Twould be easier had we died ourselves. We beseech you, send no one to console us, lest our grief be renewed."

On the same day, toward noon, acceding to the supplications of those close to him, he consented to take a little food; but would not sit at table, and ate from a bare board, which Ricciardetto held before him.

At first he relegated the cares anent the funeral to his chief secretary, Bartolomeo Calco. But in designating the order of the procession, which none save he could do, he became engrossed, little by little, and, with the same love which he had bestowed a short while ago on the New Year festival of the Golden Age, he began to arrange the funeral. He took pains, he entered into all the petty details; he specified the exact weight of the enormous candles of white and yellow wax, the exact number of ells of cloth of gold, of black and cremosin velvet for each one of the altar palls, the exact quantity of small coins and of pease and white bacon to be doled out to the poor, in remembrance of the soul of her who had passed away. Choosing the cloth for the mourning habits of the court servitors, he did not disdain to feel the weave and to hold it up to the light, that he might be assured of its good quality. He ordered for himself, as well, out of a coarse, shaggy cloth, a special solemn raiment of "great mourning," with specially made rents, which had the appearance of clothing rent in a paroxysm of despair.

The funeral was set for Friday, late at night. At the head of the funerary procession stepped outrunners, mace-bearers, heralds trumpeting on long silver clarions, with banners suspended therefrom, of black silk; drummers, who beat the tattoo of the burial march; knights with lowered visors, with mourning trappings, upon steeds enveloped in caparisons of black velvet with white crosses; monks from all the monasteries, and the Canon of Milan, all bearing lit six-pound tapers; the Archbishop of Milan with his retinue and clergy. Behind the enormous chariot with its catafalque of cloth of silver, with four angels of silver and the ducal crown, walked Moro, accompanied by his brother, the Cardinal Ascanio, the ambassadors of His Cæsaric Majesty, and those of Spain, Naples, Venice, Florence; farther on, there were members of the Privy Council; Doctors and Magisters of the University of Pavia; prominent merchants; twelve chosen burghers from each one of the gates of Milan, and a countless multitude of the common folk.

The procession was so long that its tail was but leaving the fortress when the head was already entering the Church of Maria delle Grazie.

Within a few days the Duke had adorned the grave of the still-born infant Leone with a magniloquent inscription. He had himself composed it in Italian,—Merulla had translated it into Latin:

> I, unhappy infant, died before beholding the light of day; more unhappy in that, in dying, I have taken her life from my mother,—from my father, his spouse. In such a bitter fate my only consolation is that I was brought into the world by godlike parents,—Ludovicus and Beatrix, Duke and Duchess of Mediolania, in the year 1497, in the third of the Nones of January.

Long did Moro admire this inscription, cut in gold letters on a plate of black marble, over the little sepulchre of Leone, located in the same Monastery of Maria delle Grazie where Beatrice was at rest. He shared the simple-hearted exultation of the stone-mason, who, having finished his work, had stepped back, looked at it from a distance, with head cocked to one side and one eye shut, and had clicked his tongue with delectation:

"'Tis no little tomb,—'tis a little jewel!"

It was a frosty, sunny morning. The snow on the roofs of the houses glistened in its whiteness against the blue heavens. In the crystalline air one could sense that freshness, resembling the fragrance of lilies-of-the-valley, which seems the fragrance of the snow.

Straight from the frost and the snow Leonardo walked, as if into a crypt, into a dark, stuffy, black-taffeta-lined room, with closed shutters and funeral candles. During the first few days after the funeral of the Duchess, the Duke would never leave this gloomy cell.

Having conversed with the artist about The Last Supper, which was to make famous the spot of the eternal rest of Beatrice, he said to him:

"I have heard, Leonardo, that thou hast taken under thy care the boy who represented the birth of the Golden Age on that ill-fated holiday. How is his health?"

"Your Highness, he died on the very day of the funeral of Her Grace."

"He died!" The Duke was amazed,—yet, at the same time, seemed to be glad. "He died. . . . How odd! . . ."

He let his head drop and heaved a profound sigh. Then he suddenly embraced Leonardo:

"Yea,—that is verily the way it should have happened. Our Golden Age has died, died together with my dear one, whom I could never get my fill of gazing upon! We have buried him at the same time with Beatrice, inasmuch as he did not want to, nor could, survive her! Is it not true, my friend? What a prophetic coincidence,—what a splendid allegory!"

XII

A WHOLE year passed in heavy mourning. The Duke would not doff the black apparel with especially made rents, and, without sitting down at table, ate at a board which was held before him by courtiers.

"After the death of the Duchess," wrote in one of his secret despatches Marino Sanuto, the ambassador of Venice, "Moro has waxed devout; he attends all church services, he fasts, he dwells in continence,—so, at least, runs the gossip,—and hath the fear of God in all his thoughts."

During the day, in the affairs of government, the Duke would at times forget his grief, although he missed Beatrice even in these matters. But then, at nights a yearning would consume him. Frequently did he see her in his dreams,—a sixteen-year-old girl, as she had married him,—self-willed, as boisterous as a schoolgirl, a thin little thing, swarthy, resembling a boy; so untamed that she used to hide in wardrobe closets, in order not to appear at affairs of state; so virginal, that during the three months after marriage she still warded off his love advances with tooth and nail, like an Amazon.

Five nights before the first anniversary of her death, Beatrice appeared to him in a dream, as he had once seen her during an angling expedition on the shore of a large, still pond, in her favourite estate at Cusnago. The haul had been a lucky one; the pails were filled with fish to the top. She invented a game: rolling up her sleeves, she would take the fish out of the wet nets and throw them in handfuls back into the water, laughing and rejoicing at the happiness of the freed captives, and their gliding, scaly sheen in the translucent wave. Slippery perch, roach and bream quivered in her bare hands; water-drops glowed in the sun like brilliants; glowed, too, the eyes and the cheeks of this charming girl.

Awakening, he felt that his pillow was wet with tears.

In the morning he set out for the monastery of Maria delle Grazie; prayed over the grave of his wife; had a bite with the prior, and conversed with him for a long while over the question which was at that time agitating the theologians of Italy,—the Immaculate Conception of the Virgin Mary. At dusk he set out straight from the monastery to Madonna Lucrezia.

Despite his sorrow over his wife and the "fear of God," not only had he not forsaken his two mistresses, but had become attached to them more than ever. Of late, Madonna Lucrezia and the Countess Cecilia had become drawn to each other. Having the reputation of a "Heroine of Learning," of a "New Sappho," Cecilia was a simple and a kindly woman, although somewhat given to emotionalizing. After the death of Beatrice there had risen for her a convenient occasion for one of those long-dreamt-of deeds of love she had read of in romances of chivalry. She decided to unite her love with that of her youthful rival, in order to console the Duke. Lucrezia at first fought shy and was jealous of the Duke, but the "Heroine of Learning" disarmed her with her magnanimity. Willy-nilly, Lucrezia was forced to submit to this strange feminine friendship.

In the summer of the year of fourteen hundred and ninety-seven, she gave birth to a son of Moro's. The Countess Cecilia desired to be godmother and, with exaggerated tenderness,—even though she had children of her own sired by the Duke,—began to nurse and fondle the baby, "her little grandson," as she called him. Thus was the coveted dream of Moro fulfilled: his mistresses had become dear friends to each other. He ordered a sonnet from the poet laureate, wherein Lucrezia and Cecilia were likened to the glow at morn and the glow at even, while he himself, the inconsolable widower, was likened to the dark night, between the two radiant goddesses, yet eternally distant from the sun,—*i.e.*, Beatrice.

Entering the familiar cozy chamber of the Palazzo Crivelli, he beheld both women sitting side by side near the hearth. Just as the ladies at court, they were in mourning.

"How is Your Highness's health?" Cecilia turned to him,—she who was "the glow at even," dissimilar from the "glow at morn," although just as beautiful, with her dully-pale skin, her fiery-rufous tint of hair, her tender, green eyes, translucent as the still waters of mountain lakes.

Of late the Duke had gotten in the habit of complaining about his health. On that evening he felt himself no worse than usual, but, as was his wont, he assumed a languid air, heaved a profound sigh, and said:

"Judge for yourself, madonna, what my state of health can be! There is but one thing I ever think on,—to lie down in the grave as soon as I may, side by side with my turtle-dove. . . ."

"Ah, nay, nay, Your Highness, speak not thus!" exclaimed Cecilia, wringing her hands. "'Tis a great sin. How can you? If but Madonna Beatrice could hear you! . . . Every affliction is from God, and we must accept it with gratitude. . . ."

"Certes," agreed Moro. "I complain not, God forfend! I know that God hath greater concern over us than we ourselves have. Blessed are they that weep, for they shall be consoled."

And, squeezing hard with both his hands the hands of his mistresses, he turned his eyes up to the ceiling.

"Yea, may the Lord reward ye, my dears, for that ye have not abandoned an unhappy widower!"

He wiped his eyes with a kerchief, and took two papers out of a pocket of his mourning apparel. One of them was a deed of gift, whereby the Duke bequeathed the enormous lands of the Villa Sforzesca Vigevano to the Pavian Monastery of Maria delle Grazie.

"Your Highness," the Countess was amazed, "'twould seem you were very fond of this region?"

"This region!" smiled Moro bitterly. "Alas, madonna, I have grown out of love not with this region alone. But then, does any man need much ground? . . ."

Seeing that he was again about to speak of death, the Countess with a kindly reproach laid her rosy palm against his lips.

"And what is in the other paper?" she asked with curiosity.

His face cleared up; his former smile, gay and sly, began to play on his lips.

He read out the other document to them,—also a deed of gift with an enumeration of lands, meadows, groves, hamlets, game preserves, fish-ponds, farm buildings, and other estates, which the Duke did bestow upon Madonna Lucrezia Crivelli and his natural son, Gian-Paolo. Here was mentioned as well the Villa Cusnago, beloved of the late Beatrice, and celebrated for its fishing. In a voice trembling with pleasant emotion, Moro read the concluding words of the document:

"This woman, in the wondrous and rare ties of love, hath shown us perfect fidelity, and has evinced such lofty feelings, that frequently in our pleasant communion with her have we obtained infinite delectation and a great surcease from our cares."

Cecilia joyously began to clap her hands, and threw herself at her friend's neck, with tears of maternal tenderness:

"Dost thou see now, little sister,—I have told thee that his heart was of gold! Now my little grandson Paolo is the richest of all the heirs of Milan."

"What date is this?" asked Moro.

"The twenty-eighth of December, Your Grace," answered Cecilia.

"The twenty-eighth!" he repeated meditatively.

This was the very day, the very hour, on which, exactly one year ago, the late Duchess had appeared in the Palazzo Crivelli, and had almost caught the Duke red-handed with his mistress.

He looked about him. Everything in this room was as of yore,—just as bright and cozy; the winter wind howled in the chimney, in just the same way; the fire blazed just as cheerily in the fireplace, and above it danced the procession of clay amours, playing with the implements of the Lord's Passion. And, upon the little round table, covered with a green cloth, stood the same pitcher of Balnea Aponitana, and lay the same notes and mandolin. The doors to the bed-chamber were open in the same way, and, farther on, those which led into the tiring room, where one could see the identical closet in which the Duke had hidden from his wife.

What (so it seemed to him) would he not give to hear at that moment once more the frightful clatter of the knocker at the house-portal below, to have the frightened maid-servant come running in with the cry: "Madonna Beatrice!" to stay, if but for one little minute, as then, and shiver in the wardrobe closet for a space, just like a caught thief, as he heard in the distance the wrathful voice of his never-to-be-looked-at-enough lass.

Moro let his head sink, and tears coursed down his cheeks.

"Ah, my God! There, canst thou see he is weeping again!" The Countess Cecilia began to bustle. "There, now, do thou caress him,—kiss him, and console him. Art thou not ashamed?"

She was most gently pushing her rival into the embraces of her own lover.

Lucrezia had for a long time past been experiencing from this unnatural friendship an emotion akin to nausea, as if from oppressively sweet perfume. She felt like getting up and leaving; she cast down her eyes and blushed. Nevertheless, she was constrained to take the Duke by the hand. He smiled at her through his tears and laid her hand against his heart.

Cecilia, taking up the mandolin from the little round table, and, assuming the same attitude in which Leonardo had depicted her twelve years ago in his famous portrait as the New Sappho, struck up a song, *To Madonna Forze*, by one Ghilberto Carico of Tuscany, balladmonger and mountebank, also called the Satyr:

> The heart, madonna, will not be denied;
> It is not ruled, but rules, the soul, the mind,—
> Moralities, philosophies, I find
> Crumble before it. Its memories abide
> Undimmed: remembrances of candid flesh,
> Of laughing joy, of love-caressing eyes,
> Of red sweet lips, whose taste was paradise,
> Of tresses fine-spun as a spider's mesh. . . .
> Time is a quack. Years can not bring surcease;
> Still the heart's ache, or my poor thoughts withhold
> From winging home, like swallows to their nests,
> To thy dear arms, as in the days of old
> When they found strength, and sanctuaried peace
> In the fair valley of thy dawn-tipped breasts. . . .

The Duke took out his kerchief and, languishing in revery, rolled up his eyes. Several times did he repeat the last line, sobbing and stretching forth his arms, as though to a vision flying by:

> In the fair valley of thy dawn-tipped breasts. . . .

"My little dove! . . . Verily, verily,—'sanctuaried peace!' . . . Do you know, madonne, meseems that she is gazing down from heaven and blessing us three. . . . Oh, Bice, Bice! . . ."

He softly leaned upon Lucrezia's shoulder, burst into sobs, and at the same time embraced her waist and would have drawn her toward him. She resisted, feeling ashamed. He kissed her neck by stealth. Noting this with her keen maternal eye, Cecilia arose, pointing Moro out to Lucrezia, like a sister, who entrusts a brother seriously ill to a friend; walked out on her tiptoes,—not into the bed-chamber, but into a chamber opposite it,—and locked the door after her. The "glow at even" felt no jealousy toward the "glow at morn," inasmuch as she knew by her experience of old that her turn was next, and that to the Duke, after dark hair, the fiery-rufous would seem still more beautiful.

Moro looked about him, embraced Lucrezia with a strong, almost rough movement, and seated her on his knees. The tears for his dead wife had not yet dried on his face, and yet upon his thin, sinuous lips was already flitting a mischievous, ingenuous smile.

"Just like a little nun,—all in black!" he laughed, covering her neck with kisses. "There, now, 'tis but a simple little dress, and yet how it doth become thee. Is it because of the black that thy little neck seemeth so white?"

He was unfastening the agate buttons upon her breast, and suddenly her nakedness flashed forth, still more blindingly dazzling between the folds of the mourning dress. Lucrezia covered her face with her hands.

And over the blazing fireplace, in the clay sculptures of Caradosso, the naked amours—or angels—continued their eternal dance, playing with the implements of the Lord's Passion,—the nails, the mallet, the pincers, the spear,—and in the reflected rosy glow of the flame they seemed to be exchanging sly winks, whispering to each other, peeping out from beneath the arbour of the grapes of Bacchus at Duke Moro and Madonna Lucrezia, while their plump, rounded cherubic cheeks seemed on the point of bursting from laughter.

And from afar floated in the languid sighs of the mandolin and the singing of Countess Cecilia:

> The heart, madonna, will not be denied;
> It is not ruled, but rules, the soul, the mind . . .

And the little ancient gods, hearing the verses of Carico—the song of the new celestial love,—laughed as though they were mad.

BOOK NINE

The Doubles

I

E PLEASED TO LOOK,—HERE, ON THE MAP, IN the Indian Ocean, to the south of the Island of Taprobana, is the inscription: *The Syrens —Wonders of the Sea.* Cristoforo Colombo was telling me that he was quite astonished, having come to this spot and not finding the Syrens. . . . Why do you smile?"

"Nay, nay Guido. Go on,—I am listening."

"Oh, I know, I know. . . . You suppose, Messer Leonardo, that there are no Syrens at all. Well, and what would you say of the Skiapodes, who shelter themselves from the sun under their own soles, as under an umbrella; or of the Pygmies, with such enormous ears that one serveth them for bedding, and the other for a blanket? Or of the tree that beareth, instead of fruit, eggs which hatch out little fowls with yellow down, on the manner of ducklings,—their flesh hath a fishy taste, so that it may be used even on fast-days?[25] Or of the island upon which some ship's men landed, made a fire, cooked their supper, and then perceived that this was no island, but a whale,—which matter was told me by a certain old seaman in Lisbon;—a man most sober, who, swore by the blood and flesh of the Lord as to the truth of his words?"

This conversation took place five years after the discovery of the New World, during Shrove Week, on the sixth of April, in the year fourteen hundred and ninety-eight—at a short distance from the Old Market, Florence, in the Street of the Furriers, in a room above the ware store-rooms of the trading house of Pompeo Berardi, who, having warehouses in Seville, superintended the building of the ships setting out for the lands discovered by Colombo. Messer Guido Berardi, nephew of Pompeo, had since childhood nurtured a great passion for navigation, and intended to take part in the voyage of Vasco da Gama, when he contracted the fearful sickness which appeared at that time, dubbed by Italians the French sickness, and, by the French, the Italian sickness; by the Poles, the German sickness, by the Muscovites the Polish sickness, and, by the Turks, the Christian sickness.[26] He vainly treated himself at all the doctors, and hung up little waxen priapi at all the wonder-working shrines. Shattered by paralysis, condemned to eternal immobility, he preserved his active liveliness of mind, and listening to the stories of seamen, sitting up nights over books and maps, in his reveries he traversed oceans, and discovered unknown lands.

Seagoing impedimenta,—copper equatorial rings, quadrants, sextants, astrolabes, compasses, stellar spheres,—made the room resemble the cabin of a ship. Through the doors opening on the balcony,—a Florentine *loggia*,—the limpid sky of an April evening showed darkly. The flame of the lamp at times wavered from the wind. From below, from the ambries piled with wares, floated up the odour of spicy condiments from other lands,—of Indian pepper and ginger, of chicory, muscat nuts, and cloves.

"So that is how matters stand, Messer Leonardo!" concluded Guido, rubbing with his hand his ailing, bandaged legs. "Not in vain is it said: Faith can remove mountains. Had Colombo doubted, even as you do, he would have accomplished naught. But you will agree that 'tis worth getting grey at thirty from infinite sufferings, in order to consummate a great discovery,—that of the location of the earthly Paradise!"

"Paradise?" Leonardo showed his amazement. "What mean you, Guido?"

"How? Do you not know that, also? Can it be possible that you have not heard of the observations of the Polar Star made by Messer Colombo near the Azores Islands, whereby he proved that the earth hath not the shape of a sphere, of an apple, as has been supposed up to now, but that of a pear, with a sprout or swelling, on the manner of a woman's nipple? On this nipple-mountain, so high that its summit leaneth against the lunar sphere of the heavens, is Paradise situated. . . ."

"But, Guido, this contradicts all the deductions of science. . . ."

"Science!" his companion interrupted him, contemptuously shrugging his shoulders. "Do you know, messer, what Colombo saith of science? I shall cite you his own words from his *Book of Prophecies*, —*Libro de la profezie:* 'It was by no means mathematics, nor the charts of the geographers, nor the deductions of reason, which helped me to accomplish that which I did accomplish; but, solely, the prophecy of Isaiah about a new heaven and a new earth.'"

Guido lapsed into silence. His usual pain in the joints was beginning. At the request of his host, Leonardo called in the servants, who carried the sick man into his bedroom.

Left alone, the artist fell to checking the mathematical results of Colombo in his investigations of the movements of the Polar Star near the Azores Islands, and found in them such glaring errors that he could not believe his eyes.

"What ignorance!" he voiced his astonishment. "It is as though he had stumbled in the darkness, by chance, upon a new world, and can not himself perceive, like a man blind,—he knoweth not what he has discovered; he thinks it is China, or the Ophir of Solomon, or the Earthly Paradise. He will die without finding out."

He read over again that first letter of the twenty-ninth of April, in the year of fourteen hundred and ninety-three, in which Colombo announced his discovery to Europe: *The Letter of Cristoforo Colombo, to whom Our Age is much indebted, anent the Recently Discovered Indian Isles, above Ganges.*

All night through Leonardo sat over the calculations and charts. At times he would walk out on the open *loggia*, and contemplate the stars; and, as he pondered upon the prophet of the New Earth and the New Heaven,—this strange dreamer, with the mind and heart of a child,—he involuntarily compared the latter's destiny with his own:

"How little he knew,—how much he accomplished! But I, with all my knowledge, am at a standstill, just like this Berardi, who is stricken with paralysis,—all life long do I strain toward unknown worlds, yet have not made one step toward them. Faith, say they. But then, are not perfect faith and perfect knowledge one and the same? Do not my eyes see farther than the eyes of Colombo, the blind prophet? . . . Or is such the lot of man: that one must be a seer in order to know, and blind in order to do?"

II

LEONARDO did not notice the passing of the night. The stars were extinguished; a rosy light lit up the tiled projections of roofs, and the slanting wooden beams in the walls of ancient brick houses. On the street one could hear the noise and hum of the crowd.

There was a knock at the door. He opened it. Giovanni entered and reminded the master that an ordeal of fire, or "fiery duel," was scheduled for this day,—Shrove Sabbath.

"What is it all about?" asked Leonardo.

"Fra Domenico, representing Brother Girolamo Savonarola, and

Fra Giuliano Rondinelli, representing Girolamo's foes, shall enter the flames of a bonfire; he that shall be left unscathed shall prove himself in the right before God."

"Well, what matters it? Go, Giovanni. I hope thou mayst see an interesting spectacle."

"But are you not coming?"

"Nay,—as thou canst see, I am busy."

The pupil was about to tell him good-bye, but, making an effort, he said:

"On the way hither I met Paolo Somenzi. He promised to drop in for us and lead us to the very best spot, whence we can see everything. 'Tis a pity you have not the time. But I thought . . . perhaps . . . if I may suggest it, master? . . . The ordeal is set for noon. If you were to get through with your work by then, could we not manage to see it? . . ."

Leonardo smiled.

"But dost thou want so very much to have me see this miracle?"

Giovanni cast down his eyes.

"Well, then, 'tis no use resisting,—I shall go, and God be with thee!"

At the time designated Beltraffio returned for the master together with Paolo Somenzi, a mobile, adroit man, who seemed to be filled with quicksilver. He was the chief Florentine spy of Moro, the bitterest foe of Savonarola.

"What do I hear, Messer Leonardo? Is it true that you wish to accompany us?" Paolo began in a shrill, unpleasant voice, with buffoonesque mannerisms and tricks. "Certes! Who, if not you, the lover of the natural sciences, should be present at this experiment in physics?"

"Will they really allow them to enter the fire?"

"What shall I say? Should matters reach such a pass,—Fra Domenico will not, of course, draw back even from a fire. Nor is he the only one. Two and a half thousand burghers, rich and poor, learned and ignorant, women and children, have announced yesterday in the cloister of San Marco, that they were desirous of taking part in the ordeal. . . . This folly, I must inform you, is at such a pitch that it turns the heads of even the intelligent. These philosophers of ours, these free-thinkers,—why, even they have their fears: well, and what if one of these monks ups and does not burn? Nay, messer, do you but picture to yourself the faces of the pious 'snivellers' when both shall burn up!"

"'Tis impossible that Savonarola really believes," murmured Leonardo meditatively, as though to himself.

"He, I grant you, may not believe," retorted Somenzi, "or, at the least, may not believe entirely. And glad enough would he be to back out of it, but 'tis too late. He has cultivated a sweet tooth in the rabble to his own downfall. They all have their mouths watering now,—serve up a miracle to them, and that is all there is to it! For here, messer, are also mathematics, and no less curious than yours: if there be a God, then wherefore should He not perform a miracle, so that two times two may be not four, but five, in response to the prayer of the faithful, and to the ignominy of the godless atheists,—such as you and I?"

"Well, now, let us go,—'tis time, meseems?" said Leonardo.

"'Tis time, 'tis time!" Paolo began to bustle. "One little word more. Who do you think engineered all these mechanics for the miracle? I! Therefore do I wish, Messer Leonardo, that you may appraise it,—for if not you, who else can? . . ."

"Why I, precisely?" asked the artist with aversion.

"As though you did not understand! I am a simple fellow, as you can see for yourself,—I wear my heart on my sleeve. And, if you will, being also a bit of a philosopher, I know the true worth of the phantasms with which the monks terrify us. You and I, Messer Leonardo, are accomplices in this matter. That is why I say that it is our turn to rejoice. Long live reason, long live science, for if there be a God, or He be not,—two times two is still four!"

The three of them walked out together. A crowd was moving through the streets. On their faces was that festal expectation and curiosity, which Leonardo had already remarked on Giovanni's face.

On the Street of the Hosemakers, before Or San Michele, where, in a niche in a wall, stood the bronze statue by Andrea del Verrocchio,—the apostle Thomas inserting his fingers in the wounds of the Lord,—there was an especial crush. Some were spelling out, while others were listening and discussing, the eight theological theses, printed in large red letters and hung out on the walls, the truth or falsity of which theses the ordeal of fire was to confirm or controvert:

I. The Church of the Lord was to be made over again.
II. God would chastise it.
III. God would make it over again.

IV. After the chastisement, Florence also would be made over again, and be made great over all nations.
V. The unbelievers shall be converted.
VI. All this shall be fulfilled forthwith.
VII. The excommunication of Savonarola by Pope Alexander VI is invalid.
VIII. Those not accepting this excommunication are not in sin.

Pressed by the crowd, Leonardo, Giovanni, and Paolo came to a stop, as they listened to the sundry comments.

"That may all very well be, but still 'tis a frightsome thing," an old artisan was saying. "What if sin be the upshot on't?"

"But what sin can there be, Filippo?" contradicted a young apprentice, with a light-minded and self-satisfied scoffing smile. "Methinks there is no possibility of any sin here. . . ."

"'Tis a temptation, my friend," insisted Filippo. "We beg for a miracle,—but are we worthy of a miracle? It is said: 'Ye shall not tempt the Lord your God.'"[27]

"Be still, greybeard. What art thou croaking for? 'If ye have faith as a grain of mustard-seed, ye shall say unto this mountain, Remove hence to yonder place; and it shall remove.'[28] God can not do otherwise save perform a miracle, if we believe!"

"He can not! He can not!" voices in the crowd caught up.

"But, maties, who shall be the first to enter the fire,—Fra Domenico or Fra Girolamo?"

"They shall both enter together."

"Nay, Fra Girolamo will merely pray, but enter he will not."

"What mean you,—he will not enter? Who else should go in if not he? Fra Domenico will enter first, then Girolamo also; well, and after that, we sinners too, may be deemed worthy,—all those of us who have entered our names at the Monastery of San Marco."

"But is it true what they say,—that Father Girolamo will bring a dead man to life?"

"True it is! The fiery miracle first, and then the resurrection of the dead man. I myself have read his letter to the Pope. Let an opponent, says he, be appointed; both of us shall walk up to the grave and say in turn: Arise! He at whose command the dead man shall arise,—he is the prophet; while the other is but a cheat."

"Bide ye a while; 'tis naught compared to that which is going to be! Have faith, and ye shall see, in the flesh, 'the Son of man coming in the clouds.'[29] There shall be a succession of such portents, of such miracles, as have never been, even of old!"

"Amen! Amen!" came from the crowd,—and there were faces paling, and eyes flaring up with the fire of insanity.

The crowd started off, drawing them along. For the last time Giovanni looked back at Verrocchio's carving. And in the tender, sly, and fearsomely-curious smile of Thomas the Doubter, inserting his fingers in the wounds of the Lord, he imagined he saw a resemblance to the smile of Leonardo.

III

APPROACHING the Piazza of the Signoria, they got into such a crush that Paolo was forced to address an appeal to a passing horseman of the city military to escort them to the Ringhiera,—the stone rostrum before the City Hall, where the places for the ambassadors and the noted burghers were reserved.

Never, so it seemed to Giovanni, had he seen such a throng. Not only the entire square, but even the loggias, turrets, windows, house-tops, were swarming with people. Clinging to iron torch-holders driven into the walls, to gratings, to abutments of roofs and to rain-spouts, the people hung at a vertiginous height, just as though they were bees swarming. They fought for places. Someone fell and was mortally injured.

The streets were barred with *chevaux de frise* and chains,—with the exception of three, where the city guard stood, letting through, one by one, only men,—who had to be adults and unarmed.

Paolo, pointing out the bonfire to his companions, explained the arrangement of the "machine." From the pediment of the Ringhiera, where stood the Marzocco, the heraldic bronze lion of Florence, in the direction of a tiled shed,—the Shelter of the Pisans,—a fire was laid; narrow, long, with a passageway for those about to undergo the ordeal,—a path, paved with stone, clay, and sand, between two walls of fire-wood, smeared over with pitch and strewn over with gunpowder.

Out of the Strada Vecherecchia came the Franciscans, the enemies of Savonarola; the Dominicans came next. Fra Girolamo, in a cassock of white silk, holding a ciborium that flashed in the sun, and Fra Domenico in a garment of flaming red velvet, brought up the procession.

"Ascribe ye strength unto God," chanted the Dominicans, "His excellency is over Israel, and his strength is in the clouds. O God, thou art terrible out of thy holy places."[30]

And, catching up the chant of the monks, the crowd responded in a rending shout:

"Hosanna! Hosanna! Blessed is he that cometh in the name of the Lord!"[31]

The enemies of Savonarola took up the half next to the Town Hall; his disciples, the other half of the Loggia Orcania, divided for this occasion with a partition of boards.

Everything was in readiness; there remained but to light the fire and enter it.

Whenever the commissaries who had arranged the ordeal came out of the Palazzo Vecchio, the crowd would grow deathly still. But, after running up to Fra Domenico and holding a whispered consultation with him, the officials would return to the Palace. Fra Giuliano Rondinelli had disappeared.

The uncertainty, the strain, were becoming unbearable. Some stood up on their tiptoes, stretching out their necks, in order to see better; some, crossing themselves and telling their beads, prayed a simple-hearted, childlike prayer, always reiterating one and the same strain: "Work a miracle, work a miracle, work a miracle, Lord!"

It was still and stifling. The peals of thunder, heard since morning, were drawing nearer. The sun was baking. Out on the Ringhiera, from the Palazzo Vecchio, appeared several eminent burghers, members of the Council, in long garments of dark-red cloth, resembling the togas of ancient Rome.

"Signori! Signori!" cried a little old man in round spectacles, with a goose-quill behind his ear,—probably a secretary of the Council. "The meeting is not ended yet. Please enter,—they are collecting votes. . . ."

"The devil take them,—may they sink with their accursed votes!" exclaimed one of the burghers. "I have had my fill! I have an earache from their nonsense!"

"Whatever are they waiting for, now?" remarked another. "If they are so desirous of burning, let them be allowed into the fire,—and end the matter!"

"Whatever are you saying,—why, that would be murder. . . ."

"'Tis naught! Certes, 'twould be small loss, even if there were two fools less on earth!"

"They will burn up, you say. But 'tis necessary that they burn up according to all the rules of the Church, according to all its canons,—therein is the whole gist of the matter! 'Tis a delicate matter, and a theological one. . . ."

"Well, if it be theological,—send them off to the Pope. . . ."

"Pope or no Pope, monks or no monks,—what has that got to do with it? We must think of the people, signori. Were it possible to establish quiet in this city through such a measure, then, of course, all the Popes and all the monks should be despatched not only into fire, but even into water, air, and earth!"

"Water would suffice. My advice is to prepare a tun with water and to plunge both monks within it. He that will come out dry from the water is in the right. At least, there is no danger!"

"Have ye heard, signori?" Paolo put in his oar, snickering fawningly. "Our poor fellow, Fra Giuliano Rondinelli has had such a bad attack of poltroonery that his stomach has become upset. They have let his blood, that he might not die of fright."

"You are forever jesting, signori," said a grave old man, with an intelligent and sad face, "but I, when I hear such discourses coming from the foremost men of my people, do not know whether 'tis better to live or to die. For verily, our ancestors, the founders of our city, would have let their arms drop in despond if they could have foreseen that their descendants would reach such ignominy! . . ."

The commissaries scurried from the Town Hall to the Loggia, from the Loggia to the Town Hall, and it seemed that there would be no end to their parleys. The Franciscans asserted that Savonarola had bewitched the cassock of Domenico. The monk took it off. But the spells could be upon his underclothing as well. He went to the Palace, and, stripping himself to the skin, donned the garments of another monk. He was forbidden to draw nigh Brother Girolamo, lest the latter bewitch him anew. It was demanded that he leave behind the cross he was holding. Domenico consented, but said that he would enter the fire not otherwise than with the Holy Sacrament. Thereupon the Franciscans proclaimed that the disciples of Savonarola wanted to burn up the Flesh and Blood of the Lord. In vain did Domenico and Girolamo prove that the Holy Eucharist could not burn, that in the fire would perish only the transubstantial *modus*, but not the eternal *substantia*. A scholastic dispute sprang up.

A murmur ran through the crowd. The heavens, meanwhile, became covered over with clouds. Suddenly, from behind the Palazzo Vecchio, from the Street of the Lions,—Via dei Leoni,—where, in a stone den, lions, the heraldic beasts of Florence were kept,—there sounded prolonged roars of hunger. Probably on this day, in the hubbub of the preparations, their feeding had been forgotten. But it appeared as if the bronze Marzocco, made indignant by the disgrace of his people, were roaring in ire.

And in answer to the roaring of the beasts the mob responded in a still more appalling human roar of hunger:

"Hasten, hasten! Into the fire! Fra Girolamo! Give us a miracle! A miracle! A miracle!"

Savonarola, who was praying before the Chalice of the Sacrament, seemed to awaken; he walked up to the very edge of the Loggia, and with his old-time imperious gesture raised his arms, commanded the people to be still. But become still the people would not.

In the rear ranks, under the Shelter of the Pisans, among the band of "the madmen," someone cried out:

"Thou hast lost heart!"

And the cry swept over all the mob.

The iron-clad cavalry of the *arrabbiati* was pressing against the rear ranks. Their desire was, after pushing their way toward the Loggia, to fall upon Savonarola and to assassinate him in the mêlée.

"Kill, kill, kill the accursed bigots!" frenzied cries arose.

Bestial faces began to flicker before Giovanni. He closed his eyes, in order not to see, thinking that Brother Girolamo would be seized forthwith and torn to pieces. But at this moment the thunder pealed forth, the sky flashed with lightning, and the rain beat down,—a rain whose like Florence had not seen in a long while.

It was of brief duration. But, when it had ceased, the ordeal was out of the question,—from the passageway between the two walls of firewood, as out of a rain-spout, a brawling torrent was pouring.

"Eh, these monks!" the crowd was laughing. "They set out to go through fire and fell into water. There is a miracle for you!"

A division of the soldiery escorted Savonarola through the infuriated mob. The storm was succeeded by mildly inclement weather.

The heart of Beltraffio contracted when he saw, in the slow, grey drizzle, Brother Girolamo walking with a hurried, faltering step, his cowl lowered over his eyes, his white garment bespattered with the mire of the streets. Leonardo, after a glance at Giovanni's pale face, took him by the hand, and again, as at the time of the Burning of the Vanities, led him out of the crowd.

IV

On the following day, in the same room, resembling the cabin of a ship, in the house of Berardi, the artist was demonstrating to Messer Guido the incongruities of Colombo's opinion anent the position of Paradise upon the nipple of the pear-shaped earth. The latter at first listened attentively, objecting and disputing; then he suddenly grew quiet and fell into a despondent mood. A little later, complaining of the ache in his legs, Guido gave orders to be carried into his bedroom.

"Wherefore have I caused him pain?" reflected the artist. "'Tis not truth that he, as well as the disciples of Savonarola, stands in need of, but a miracle."

In one of his own working note-books, the leaves of which he was turning, his eyes fell upon the lines he had written on the memorable day when the rabble had been trying to break into his house, demanding the Most Holy Nail:

"O, Thy wondrous justice, Thou First Mover! That hadst desired to deprive no force of the order and quality of its inevitable actions; inasmuch, if it have to move a body an hundred ells, and in its path it meet an obstacle, Thou hast decreed that the force of the blow create a new movement, receiving in exchange for the untraversed distance sundry jolts and shakes. O, Thy divine necessity, Thou First Mover,—thus dost Thou compel with Thy laws all effects to flow out of the cause in the shortest way. *There* is a miracle!"

And, recalling The Last Supper, recalling the countenance of Christ, which he still sought and found not, the artist felt that there must be a connecting tie between these words anent the First Mover, anent divine necessity,—and the perfect wisdom of Him who has said: "One of ye shall betray me."

In the evening Giovanni came to him and told him of the events of the day.

The Signoria had commanded Brother Girolamo and Brother Domenico to leave town. Finding out that they were lingering, "the madmen," with arms and cannons, had, in an innumerable mob, surrounded the cloister of San Marco, and had burst their way into the church, where the monks were holding vespers. The latter defended themselves, dealing blows with flaming candles, with candelabra, with crucifixes of wood and copper. In the swirls of gunpowder smoke, in the glow of the conflagration, they seemed as amusing as enraged doves, as fearful as devils. One had clambered up on the roof and thence threw down stones. Another had jumped up on an altar, and, standing before the Crucifix, kept firing from an arquebus, crying out after each shot: "Glory be to God!"

The monastery was taken by attack. The brethren implored Savonarola to flee. But he gave himself up to the hands of his enemies, together with Brother Domenico. They were led off to prison.

The Guards of the Signoria tried in vain to guard them from the insults of the mob,—or rather pretended a desire to guard them.

Some, from behind, smote Brother Girolamo on the cheeks, imitating the snuffling churchly chanting of the "snivellers."

"Prophesy,—well, now, prophesy, thou man of God, who it was that smote thee,—prophesy!"

Others crawled about at his feet, on all fours, as though they were searching for something, and imitated the grunting of a pig: "The little key, the little key! Has anyone beheld Girolamo's little key?" —hinting at the "little key" so frequently mentioned in his sermons, with which key he had threatened to unlock the secret places of Romish abominations.

The children, quondam soldiers of the Holy Army of little inquisitors, pelted him with rotten apples, with putrid eggs.

Those who had not been successful in making their way through the mob, vociferated from a distance, repeating ever the same words of abuse, as though they could not be sated with them:

"Coward! Coward! Coward! Judas the Betrayer! Sodomite! Wizard! Antichrist!"

Giovanni saw him to the doors of the prison in the Palazzo Vecchio. In farewell, as Brother Girolamo was crossing the threshold of the dark prison cell, out of which he was to come only to his execution, one droll fellow helped him with his knee in his posterior and cried out:

"There is where his prophecies came out of!"

On the next morning Leonardo and Giovanni departed from Florence.

Immediately upon his arrival in Milan, the artist plunged into work which he had been putting off for the duration of eighteen years,—work upon the countenance of the Lord, in The Last Supper.

V

On the very day of the *fiasco* of the ordeal of fire, on the eve of Shrove Sunday, on the seventh of April, in the year fourteen hundred and ninety-eight, Charles VIII, King of France, died a sudden death.

The news of his death horrified Moro, since the Duke of Orleans, the bitterest foe of the House of Sforza, would mount the throne, under the name of Louis XII. The grandson of Valentina Visconti, the daughter of the first Duke of Milan, he deemed himself the sole lawful successor to the rule of Lombardy, and intended to regain the land by conquest, demolishing to ashes the "robbers' nest of Sforza."

Even before the death of Charles VIII, there had taken place in Milan, at the court of Moro, "the Duel of Learning," which had so pleased the Duke that a second had been set for two months later. Many supposed that he would postpone this contest in view of the impending war, but they erred, inasmuch as Moro, skilled in dissimulation, deemed it advantageous to him to show his foes that he recked but little of them, and that under the peaceful sovereignty of the Sforzas the revived arts and sciences, "the fruits of the golden peace," were flourishing in Lombardy more gloriously than ever; that his throne was safeguarded not only by arms, but as well by the glory of the most enlightened of all the rulers of Italy, the patron of the muses.

In the Rocchetta, the "large hall for the play of ball," had gathered sundry doctors, deans, and magisters of the University of Pavia, in quadrangular red caps, in scarlet silk capes, lined with ermine, in gloves of violet chamois, and with gold-embroidered pouches at their belts. The ladies of the court were in gorgeous ball apparel. At Moro's feet, on either side of his throne, sat Madonna Lucrezia and Countess Cecilia.

The meeting was opened by a speech of Giorgio Merulla, who, comparing the Duke with Pericles, Epaminondas, Scipio, Cato, Augustus, Mæcenas, Trajan, Titus, and a multitude of other great people, demonstrated that Milan, the New Athens, had surpassed the Old.

Thereafter commenced a theological dispute of the Immaculate Conception of the Virgin Mary; and then a medical one, on the following questions:

Are handsome women more prolific than homely ones?
Was the healing of Tobith with fish-gall natural?
Is woman an imperfect creation of nature?

In which inner part did the water originate which flowed out of the Lord's wound when He had been pierced by a spear?
Is woman more voluptuous than man?

A philosophical contest followed, as to whether the very first matter of all were multiform or unique.

"What is the signification of this apothegm?" queried a little old man with a venomous, toothless smile, with turbid eyes, like those of infants at breast,—a great doctor of scholastics, confusing his opponents and establishing such a fine distinction between *quidditas* and *habitus*, that none could comprehend him.

"The very first matter of all," demonstrated another, "is neither substance nor accident. But, as long as under each act there is understood either accident or substance, so long is the very first matter of all not an act."

"I assert," a third ejaculated, "that every created substance, spiritual or corporeal, is relative to matter."

The old doctor of scholastics merely kept on shaking his head, as though he knew beforehand all the arguments his opponents would produce and would be able to demolish their sophisms like a cobweb with a single breath.

"Let us put it this way," a fourth expounded, "the universe is the tree: the roots are first matter; the leaves, accidents; the branches, substances; the blossom, the reasoning soul; the fruit, the angelic nature; God, the gardener."

"The very first matter of all is unique," yelled a fifth, deaf to all others, "the secondary-first is double, the tertiary-first is multiple. And all of them strive for uniqueness. *Omnia unitatem appetunt.*"

Leonardo listened, silent and solitary, as always; a slight, scoffing smile would at times flit across his lips.

After the intermission, Fra Luca Paccioli, a Franciscan monk and a mathematician, exhibited crystal exemplifications of many-angled forms, or polyhedrons, expounding the Pythagorean teaching of the five first-created regular bodies, out of which, it would seem, the universe sprang up; and declaimed some verses, wherein these bodies sang their own praises:

> The fruit of Science, most delectably fair
> Did urge all sages, in the days of old,
> The solution of our Unknown Cause to snare.
> With uncorporeal beauty do we flare;

NINE · # Leonardo da Vinci

As all worlds' first beginning are we held;
Our wondrous harmony, past all compare,
Charmed Plato, Pythagoras, and Euclid.
Fillers of the Primordeal Sphere are we;
So perfect is our form that our look did
Unto all bodies the Law and Size decree.

VI

THE Countess Cecilia, indicating Leonardo, whispered something to the Duke. The latter called him over and asked him to take part in the tourney.

"Messer," the Countess herself importuned him, "be so gracious . . ."

"There, thou seest, the ladies beseech thee," interrupted the Duke. "Be not so modest. Well, now, what does it mean for thee? Tell us something that will be as amusing as possible. For I know that thy mind is aye filled with the most wondrous of excellent chimæras. . . ."

"Your Highness, let me off. Gladly would I do it, Madonna Cecilia, but truly, I can not nor know I how. . . ."

Leonardo was not pretending. He, in reality, did not like, and did not know how, to speak before a gathering. In his case there was an eternal barrier between the word and the thought. It seemed to him that every word exaggerated or minimized, or altered and prevaricated. Noting down his observations in his diaries, he constantly changed, crossed out, and corrected. Even in conversation did he speak haltingly, become entangled, and stop short,—he sought for words and found them not. Orators and writers he styled chatterboxes and scribblers, but, with all that, envied them in secret. The rounded, even flow of speech, at times possessed by the most insignificant people, aroused vexation within him, mixed with a simple-hearted rapturous admiration: "There, God doth bestow an art like that on some people!"

But, the more earnestly he declined, the more did the ladies insist.

"Messer," they piped in chorus, surrounding him, "Please! We all,—do you see?—we all implore you. There, now, tell us somewhat,—tell us! . . ."

"Of how men shall fly," proposed Donzella Fiordaliza.

"Of magic would be better," Donzella Ermellina chimed in, "of black magic. That is so curious! Of necromancy,—of how the dead are summoned from the grave. . . ."

"An it please you, madonna, I can assure you that I have never summoned any dead. . . ."

"Well, 'tis all one,—tell us of something else. Only something as *awful* as possible,—and no mathematics! . . ."

Leonardo was never able to refuse, no matter what was asked, or by whom.

"Really, madonne, I know not. . . ." he uttered in confusion.

"He agrees! He agrees!" Ermellina began to clap her hands. "Messer Leonardo will speak. Lend ear!"

"What is it? Eh? Who is it?" a dean of the theological faculty, hard of hearing, and feeble-minded from age, was asking.

"Leonardo!" a young neighbour of his, a magister of medicine, shouted to him.

"About Leonardo Pisano, the mathematician,—is that it?"

"Nay,—Leonardo da Vinci himself."

"Da Vinci? Doctor or magister?"

"Neither a doctor nor a magister,—not even a baccalaureate, but just simply the artist Leonardo,—the one who painted The Last Supper."

"An artist? Is he going to speak of painting?"

"Of natural sciences, 'twould seem. . . ."

"Of natural sciences? Why, have artists become men of science nowadays? Leonardo? Have heard naught of him, somehow. . . . What works has he written?"

"None. He does not publish them."

"Does not publish them?"

"They say he always writes with his left hand," another neighbour interposed, "in a secret script, so that it may not be deciphered."

"So that it might not be deciphered? With his left hand?" with growing perplexity the dean kept on repeating. "Why, signori, this must be something amusing. Eh? By way of a relaxation from serious studies, I take it,—for the diversion of the Duke and the most beautiful signore?"

"It may even be amusing. We shall see, now. . . ."

"There, there,—that is better. You should have said so. Of course, these be court folk: they must needs amuse themselves. But then, what amusing folk these artists be,—they know full well how to make one merry. There was Buffomalco, now, they say; a very tom-fool, and as droll a fellow as you ever saw. . . . Well, we shall hear what sort of a fellow this Leonardo is,—we shall hear!"

He wiped his glasses, the better to see the forthcoming spectacle.

With a last supplication Leonardo looked at the Duke. The latter, although smiling, was frowning. The Countess Cecilia was threatening with a tiny finger.

"For all I know, they may be angered," reflected the artist. "Soon I must ask for bronze for the steed. . . . Eh, what is the odds, let come what may,—I shall tell them the first thing that bobs into my head,—only to get rid of the whole mess."

With desperate resolve he mounted the cathedra and looked over the learned gathering.

"I must forewarn your graces," he began, haltingly and turning red, like a schoolboy. "This has come to me unexpectedly. . . . Only at the insistence of the Duke . . . That is, I want to say . . . It seems to me. . . . Well, to make it short,—I shall speak of sea-shells."

He began telling them of the petrified marine animals, the imprints of seaweeds and corals, found in caves and mountains, at a distance from the sea,—witnesses of how, since times immemorially ancient, the face of the earth has changed; how there, where now are dry land and mountains, had been the bottom of the ocean. Water, the mover of nature, her *driver*,—creates and demolishes mountains. Drawing toward the middle of the sea, the shores increase; and the inner, mediterranean seas gradually reveal their bottom, leaving merely the bed of a single river, which falls into the ocean. Thus Po, having made Lombardy dry, will subsequently do the same with all Adriatica. The Nile, having transformed the Mediterranean Sea into sand dunes and plains, resembling Egypt and Libya, would fall into the ocean beyond the Gibraltar.

"I am positive," concluded Leonardo, "that the study of petrified animals and plants, which has hitherto been despised by men of science, will give a beginning of a new science of the earth, of her past and her future."

His thoughts were so lucid and exact, and so full—despite his evident diffidence,—of an unshakable faith in knowledge; so dissimilar to the misty Pythagorean ravings of Paccioli, and to the dead scholastics of the learned doctors,—that, when he had ceased, a perplexity was evident on all faces. How was one to act? What was one to do? Was praise in order, or laughter? Was this a new science, or the self-satisfied babbling of an ignoramus?

"We would exceedingly desire, my Leonardo," said the Duke, with a condescending smile, such as grown-ups adopt in speaking to children, "we would exceedingly desire that thy prophecy be fulfilled; that the Adriatic Sea dry up, and the Venetians, our foes, be left in their lagoons, like lobsters on a shallow!"

All, deferentially, and at the same time exaggeratedly, laughed. The indication had been given,—and the court weather-vanes turned to the wind. The Rector of the University of Pavia, Gabriele Pirovano, a silvery-grey old man of benignant aspect, with the face of a majestic nonenity, proclaimed, his deferentially cautious, vapid smile reflecting the condescending jocularity of the Duke:

"The information you have imparted to us is exceedingly curious, Messer Leonardo. But I shall permit myself to remark: is it not more simple to explain the origin of these little shells by an accidental, amusing,—we may even say bewitching,—but entirely innocent play of nature, on which you desire to found an entire science; is it not a simpler matter, I say, to explain their origin,—even as it has been done ere now,—by the universal Deluge?"

"Yes, yes,—the Deluge!" Leonardo caught him up, by now already without any confusion, with an ease of manner which to many appeared entirely too free, even daring. "I know that all say: 'the Deluge.' Only, this explanation will not hold water. . . . Judge for yourself,—the level of the water during the Deluge, according to the words of him that measured it, was ten[32] cubits higher than the highest mountains. Consequently the shells, swirled by the tempestuous waves, should have fallen on the top, inevitably on the top, but not on the sides, nor at the pediments, of the mountains,—nor inside of subterranean caverns; and, to boot, they should have fallen in disorder, at the whim of the waves, but not at always the same level, nor in sequent strata, as we observe them. And do you but mark,—this is really curious!—those animals which go in colonies, such as molluscs, scuttle-fish, oysters, lie together, just as they should; while those of solitary habits lie apart, every jot as we can see even now on sea-shores. I myself have frequently observed the disposition of petrified shells in Tuscany, in Lombardy, in Piedmont. But if ye will say that they are not carried thither by the waves of the flood, but have risen of themselves, little by little, with the water, and in keeping with its rise, then even that objection is very easily overthrown, inasmuch as a shell-fish is an animal just as slow as a snail, or even slower. Never does it swim, but merely crawls over the sand and stones by the motion of its valves, and the greatest distance it can cover in a day's journey of this sort is three or four ells. How then, if ye will have the goodness to tell me,—how is it you expect, Messer Gabriele, that, during the forty days which the flood lasted, according to the testimony of Moses, it should crawl the two hundred and fifty miles, separating the knolls of Montferrato from the shores of the Adriatic? Only he that, despising experiment and observation, doth judge of nature by books, according to the concepts of chattering word-mongers, and who has never even once had the curiosity to look with his own eyes at that whereof he speaks, will durst to make such an assertion!"

An awkward silence fell. All felt that the rector's objection was weak, and that it was not he who should regard Leonardo as a master regards a pupil, but *vice versa*.

Finally, the court astrologer, a favourite of Moro's, Messer Ambrogio da Rosate, proposed, citing Pliny the Naturalist, another solution: the petrifications, having merely the appearance of sea animals, had been formed in the depths of the earth by the magical action of stars.

At the word "magical" the resigned, bored smile of scorn began to play on Leonardo's lips.

"But then, Messer Ambrogio," he retorted, "how do you explain the fact that the influence of the very same stars has, in the very same place, created animals not only of different kinds, but also of different ages; inasmuch as I have discovered that, by the cross-section of shells, as well as by the cross-sections of the horns of bulls and sheep, and the split trunks of trees, one can determine with exactitude not merely the number of the years of their life, but even the months? How would you explain that some of them are whole, others broken, others still filled with sand, silt, the claws of crabs, the bones and teeth of fish, and with large rubble, resembling that met with on seashores, made up of little pebbles rounded out by the waves? And what of the delicate imprints of leaves on the crags of the highest mountains? And what of the seaweeds, adhering to the shells, both petrified, congealed into one lump? Whence is all this? From the influence of the stars? But then, if we are to reason thus, signori, then, I suppose, you will not find in all nature a single phenomenon which could not be explained by the magical influence of stars,—and in that event all sciences are in vain, save that of astrology. . . ."

The old doctor of scholastics asked for the floor, and, when his request had been granted, remarked that the disputation was being carried on improperly, inasmuch as only one of two things was possible: either the problem of the excavated animals belonged to the lower, "mechanical" knowledge, foreign to metaphysics, in which case there was nothing to be said of it, inasmuch as they had not convened here to contend over subjects not related to philosophy; or else the problem was related to the true, higher knowledge,—to dialectics; in such case, it must even be discussed in accordance with the laws of dialectics, raising the concepts to pure mental contemplation.

"I know all that," remarked Leonardo, with a mien still more resigned and bored, "I know what you would say, messer. I also have given this matter much thought. Only all this is not so! . . ."

"Not so?" smiled the old man,—and he seemed to become swollen with venom. "But if it be not so, messer, then do enlighten us, if you will be so kind,—teach us what, according to you, is so?"

"Ah, no, I did not at all want to . . . I assure you. . . . I spoke merely of shells. . . . I, do you see, think that . . . In a word, there is no higher or lower knowledge, but one only, flowing out of experimentation. . . ."

"Out of experimentation? So that is how the matter stands! Well, then, if you will permit me to ask, what of the metaphysics of Aristotle, of Plato, of Plotinus,—all the ancient philosophers, who discoursed of God, of spirit, of essentials,—can it really be that all this . . ."

"Yes, all this is not science," calmly retorted Leonardo. "I acknowledge the greatness of the ancients, but not in this. In science they have taken the false path. They desired to fathom that which is inaccessible to knowledge, while that which was accessible they contemned. They have entangled themselves and others for many ages. For, in considering subjects not open to proof, men can not come to an agreement. Where there are no sensible deductions, their place is taken by loud shouts. But he that knoweth hath no need of shouting. The word of truth is unique, and when it is said, the shouts of the disputants must cease; but if they still continue, it means that there is no truth as yet. For do they argue in mathematics if two times three be six or five? Or whether the sum of the angles of a triangle be equal to two right angles or no? Does not every contradiction in this case disappear before the truth, so that its devotees may enjoy it in peace, which is never the case in the pseudo-metaphysical sciences?"

He was about to add something, but, having glanced at the face of his antagonist, grew silent.

"There, now, we have put our foot in it, Messer Leonardo!" the doctor of scholastics smiled with a still more caustic sneer. "However, I knew that you and I would come to understand one another. For I can not get it into my head,—you must pardon an old man like me. . . . How is this possible? Can it be that all our knowledge of the soul, of God, of life beyond the grave, all of which knowledge is not susceptible of experimentation, is 'not open to proof,' as you yourself were pleased to express it, though confirmed by the unfailing testimony of the Holy Scriptures?"

"I do not say that," Leonardo stopped him, with a frown. "I leave all God-inspired books out of the argument, inasmuch as they are verily the highest truth . . ."

He was not allowed to finish. Confusion sprang up. Some shouted, others laughed; still others, jumping up from their places, turned upon him with wrathful faces; a fourth group, shrugging their shoulders with contempt, turned their backs upon him.

"Enough! Enough!"—"Allow me to reply!"—"But what reply is needed here, if you please?"—"Nonsense!"—"May I have the floor?" —"Plato and Aristotle!"—"All this matter is not worth a tinker's damn! How do they permit it? The truths of our Mother Church! . . . Heresy, heresy! . . . Godlessness! . . ."

Leonardo maintained his silence. His face was calm and pensive. He perceived his isolation among these people, who deemed themselves servants of science; saw the uncrossable abyss that separated them from him, and felt vexed,—not with his antagonists, but himself, because he had not been able to stop speaking in time, had not declined the dispute; because once more, despite countless experiences, he had been tempted by the hope that it was sufficient to reveal the truth to men to have them accept it.

The Duke, with the grandees and the ladies of the court, all of whom had long since lost any comprehension of what was going on, still watched the dispute, with great pleasure.

"Splendid!" rejoiced Moro, rubbing his hands. "'Tis a real battle! Look ye, Madonna Cecilia,—they shall come to fisticuffs at any moment. There is that little old man, fairly jumping out of his skin, all a-quiver, threatening with his fists,—he has torn off his cap and is waving it about. And that little fellow in black,—that little fellow in black, now! He is foaming at his mouth! And what is it all about, now? On account of some petrified sea-shells or other. An amazing folk! A terrible lot, really. But what think ye of our Leonardo, though? Speak of your still waters running deep! . . ."

And they all laughed, admiring the contest of the learned as they would a cock-fight.

"Methinks I will go and rescue my Leonardo," remarked the Duke, "or else the red-caps will peck him to death with their beaks, like as not! . . ."

He entered the throng of frenzied combatants,—and they became quiet, making a path before him, as though a pacifying oil had been spilled on the tempestuous sea: Moro's mere smile sufficed to reconcile physics with metaphysics. In inviting guests to supper, he would graciously add:

"There, signori, you have had your argument,—let it suffice! One must fortify one's strength also. We would deem it a favour! Methinks my cooked animals from the Adriatic Sea,—'tis a boon 'tis not dried up yet,—will arouse less arguments than the petrified animals of Messer Leonardo."

VII

At supper Luca Paccioli, who was sitting next to Leonardo, whispered in his ear:

"Be not wroth, my friend, for that I kept my peace when they fell upon you,—they did not understand you aright; but in reality you could have come to an agreement with them, inasmuch as the one thing doth not interfere with the other,—but no extremities are ever necessary, and all things can be reconciled, all things can be affiliated. . . ."

"I am in perfect agreement with you, Fra Luca," said Leonardo.

"There, there, now! That is better! In peace and in harmony. For, if you please, why quarrel?—say I. Physics are good, and so are metaphysics. There is enough room for both. You scratch my back, and I will scratch yours. Is it not so, my dearest fellow?"

"Just so, Fra Luca."

"Well, that is splendid! It means that there can be no misunderstandings of any sort? You scratch my back and I will scratch yours. . . ."

"'More flies are taken with a drop of honey than a tun of vinegar,'" reflected the artist, glancing at the crafty, intelligent face and eyes full of a mouselike liveliness of the monk-mathematician, who had been able to reconcile Pythagoras with Thomas Aquinas.

"To your health, master!" Lifting his goblet and leaning toward him with the air of a fellow conspirator, Galeotto Sacrobosco the alchemist addressed him. "Certes, you caught them right deftly on the hook, the devil take it! A most exquisite allegory!"

"What allegory?"

"There, now, you are at it again! 'Tis not right, messer! Surely, 'tis of little use to use guile against me! Glory be to God, we are of the initiate,—we shall not betray one another . . ."

The old man gave him a sly wink.

"What allegory, you ask,—why, this: the dry land is sulphur; the sun, salt; the waters of the ocean, at one time covering the summits of the mountains,—quicksilver, the living moisture of Mercury. What? Is it not so?"

"So it is, Messer Galeotto,—precisely so!" Leonardo burst into laughter. "You have understood my allegory with amazing fidelity!"

"I have understood it, do you see? We, too, then, are knowing in a thing or two! As for the petrified sea-shells,—why, that is the Stone of the Wise Men, the great mystery of the alchemists, formed by the union of the sun,—the salt; the dry land,—the sulphur; and the moisture,—Mercury. The divine transmutation of metals!"

Elevating his index finger and his eyebrows, made scanty by age and scorched by the fire of alchemical furnaces, the old man burst into peals of most kindly, childlike laughter:

"But these scholars of ours, these red-caps, understood nothing, after all! There, let us drink to your health, Messer Leonardo, and to the flourishing of our mother—Alchemy!"

"With pleasure, Messer Galeotto! I can now see that I can really conceal nothing from you, and give you my word that in the future I shall never resort to guile."

After supper the guests dispersed. Only a small, choice gathering did the Duke invite into the cool, snug chamber, to which wine and fruits were brought.

"Ah, charming, charming!" Donzella Ermellina went into raptures. "I would never have believed that it could be so curious. I confess I thought 'twould be a bore. But there, it was better than any ball! I would be present with pleasure at every such learned encounter. How angry they got at Leonardo, how they took to shouting! What a pity they would not allow him to finish! I did so want him to tell us something of his sorcery, his necromancy. . . ."

"I know not, really, if it be true,—mayhap 'tis but gossip,—that Leonardo's mind has conceived such heretical thoughts, that he doth not believe in God, even. Giving himself up to natural sciences, he supposes that 'tis far better to be a philosopher than a Christian. . . ."

"Nonsense!" said the Duke firmly. "I know him. He hath a heart of gold. He is ferocious in words only, but in reality would not harm a flea. A dangerous man, they say. They have found someone to fear in good sooth! The Fathers Inquisitors may yelp to their hearts' content, but I shall let no one harm my Leonardo!"

"And posterity!" With a respectful bow spoke Baldassare Castiglione, the elegant grandee from the court of Urbino, who had come on a visit to Milan. "Posterity shall be grateful to Your Highness for having safeguarded such an extraordinary artist, one so unique in the whole world. But still, 'tis a pity that he neglects art, filling his mind with such strange fancies, such monstrous chimæras. . . ."

"You speak truly, Messer Baldassare," concurred Moro. "How many times have I told him 'Discard thy philosophy!' But then you know what sort of folk artists be. There is nothing to be done with them. One can not even make any demand upon them. Odd fish!"

"Your Grace has expressed it with absolute accuracy!" another noble chimed in,—he was the chief commissioner of salt revenues,—who had for a long while been itching to tell something about Leonardo. "Odd fish,—precisely! At times, do you know, they will think up such things that one can but give oneself up to wonder. I arrived at his work-room recently,—I wanted a little allegorical drawing for a wedding coffer. 'Is the master,' say I, 'at home, perchance?' 'Nay, he has gone away; he is very busy and does not accept any commissions.' 'And what,' I ask, 'is he busy with?' 'He is measuring the gravity of the air.' I thought at that time that they were making fun of me. But later I met Leonardo himself. 'Is it true, now, messer, that you are measuring the gravity of the air?' ''Tis true,' says he, and looked upon me as if *I* were a fool. The gravity of the air, indeed! How like you that, madonne? How many pounds, how many grains, in the zephyrs of spring! . . ."

"That is really naught!" remarked a young knight-of-the-chamber with a face of seemly dullness and self-satisfaction. "But I have heard, now, that he has invented a boat that goes against the current, without any oars!"

"Without oars? Of itself? . . ."

"Ay,—on wheels, by steam power."

"A boat on wheels! Probably you have thought it up yourself just now. . . ."

"I can assure you on my honour, Madonna Cecilia, that I heard it from Fra Luca Paccioli, who has seen the plan of the machine. Leonardo supposes that there is such power in steam that one can move with it not merely boats, but whole ships."

"There, now, you see,—did I not say that this is black magic,—necromancy!" exclaimed Donzella Ermellina.

"Well, he is an odd chap,—an odd chap, 'tis no use denying," concluded the Duke, with a good-natured, tolerant smile. "But still, I love him,—one feels joyous in his company, nor will one ever become bored!"

VIII

Returning home, Leonardo took a quiet street of the suburb near the Vercellina Gates. Goats nibbled grass on either side; a sunburned urchin in tatters was driving a flock of geese with a twig. It was a clear evening. Only in the north, over the invisible Alps, were piling up heavy clouds, that seemed to be of stone, rimmed with gold; and between them, in the pallid sky, flamed a solitary star.

Recalling the two combats of which he had been a witness,—the miraculous ordeal at Florence, and the Tourney of Knowledge at Milan,—Leonardo reflected on how they differed, and, at the same time, how alike they were,—like very doubles.

On a stone staircase, clinging to the outside of a decrepit little house, a little girl of six years sat eating a rye mill-cake with a baked onion. He stopped and beckoned her to him. She looked at him with fear; then, evidently entrusting herself to his smile, smiled herself and descended, walking softly with her brown little bare feet on the steps, littered with kitchen slops and egg- and lobster-shells. He took out of his pocket a bonbon, sugared and painstakingly wrapped in gilt paper,—one of those dainties which were served at court; he frequently took them from the table and carried them in his pocket, in order to give them to street gamins during his strolls.

"'Tis of gold!" said the little girl in a whisper. "A little gold ball!"

"'Tis not a ball, but an apple. Try it,—it is sweet inside."

Not daring to taste it, she was inspecting the sweet she had never seen before, in speechless rapture.

"What is thy name?" asked Leonardo.

"Maia."

"Well, dost thou know, Maia, how the rooster, the goat, and the ass went a-fishing?"

"Nay, I know not."

"Dost want me to tell thee?"

He stroked her matted, soft hair with his long, slender hand, as soft as that of a young girl.

"Well, let us go and sit down. Wait, though,—I had some anise drops also. For, as I can see, thou wilt not eat the golden apple."

He began rummaging in his pocket. A young woman appeared on the stoop. She glanced at Leonardo and Maia, and, nodding her head in amiable greeting, sat down at her spinning wheel. Her appearance was followed by that of a bent little old woman, with the same clear eyes as Maia's,—probably her grandmother. She also looked at Leonardo, —and suddenly, recognizing him, threw up her hands in horror, bent toward the spinner, and said something in her ear; the latter jumped up and cried out:

"Maia, Maia! Come here, quick! . . ."

The girl lingered.

"Be lively, now, thou little good-for-naught! There, just bide a while, I will make it hot for thee! . . ."

The frightened Maia ran up the steps. The grandmother snatched the golden apple from her and flung it over the wall into a neighbouring yard, where some pigs were grunting. The girl burst into tears. But the old woman whispered something to her, pointing to Leonardo. Maia instantly quieted down, gazing at him with eyes wide open and filled with horror.

Leonardo turned away, cast down his head, and, in silence, hurriedly passed by. He comprehended that the old woman knew his face, had heard that he was a wizard, and had thought that he might put the evil eye on Maia. He left them, as though he were running away, in such confusion that he continued rummaging in his pocket for the now useless anise drops, smiling a confused guilty smile.

Before these frightened, innocent eyes of a child he felt himself still lonelier than before a mob thirsting to kill him as an atheist; still lonelier than before the gathering of scholars, jeering at the truth as at the babbling of a madman; he felt himself just as aloof from men as the solitary evening star in the forlornly clear sky.

Having returned home, he entered his workroom. With its dusty books and scientific appliances it appeared to him as gloomy as a prison. He sat down at the table, lit a candle, picked up one of his note-books and plunged into his recently begun investigation of the laws of motion of bodies on inclined planes. Mathematics, as much as music, had the power of soothing him. And on this evening also it gave to his heart the wonted joyful peace. Having finished his calculation, he took his diary out of its secret drawer in the table, and with his left hand, in reverse script, which could be read only in front of a mirror, wrote down the thoughts inspired within him by the Tourney of the Learned:

"Bookworms and rhetoricians, disciples of Aristotle, jackdaws in peacock feathers, town criers and repeaters of the matters of other men, despise me, the inventor. But I could reply to them even as Marius did to the Roman patricians: 'Adorning yourselves with the matters of other men, ye do not wish to leave me the fruits of my own.'

"Among the investigators of nature and the imitators of the ancients, there is the same difference as between an object and its reflection in a mirror.

"They think that, not being a word-monger like to them, I have no right to write and to speak of science, inasmuch as I can not express my thoughts in a fitting manner. They know not that my strength lies not in words but in experience, the instructor of all those who have written well.

"Desiring not, nor being able, to refer to the books of the ancients, I shall refer to that which is more truthful than books,—to experience, the instructor of instructors."

The candle burned dimly. The sole friend of his sleepless nights, a tom-cat, jumping up on a chair, was caressing him indifferently as it purred. The solitary star, through the dusty panes of the window, seemed now still more distant, still more forlorn. He cast a look at it and recalled the eyes of Maia, fixed upon him with infinite horror, —but he did not become sad; again was he serene and assured in his loneliness.

Only in the most hidden depths of his heart, which he himself did not comprehend, like a warm spring under a crust of ice, there seethed an incomprehensible bitterness, like to remorse, as though he had in reality been in some fault before Maia,—he longed to win self-forgiveness, and could not.

IX

ON the following morning Leonardo was preparing to go to the monastery of Maria delle Grazie, to work on the countenance of the Lord. The mechanic Astro awaited him on the front steps, with note-books, brushes and the boxes of pigments. Walking out into the yard, the artist saw the hostler, Nastasio, who, standing under a shed, was zealously curry-combing a grey dappled mare.

"How is Giannino?" asked Leonardo,—Giannino was the name of one of his favourite horses.

"Why, there is nothing the matter with him," replied the hostler indifferently. "The piebald one has gone lame."

"The piebald!" queried Leonardo with vexation. "How long ago?"

"'Tis the fourth day."

Without looking at his master, in sullen silence, Nastasio continued to curry the horse's rump, with such force that it shifted from foot to foot. Leonardo evinced a desire to see the piebald, and Nastasio led him to the stable.

When Giovanni Beltraffio had gone out into the yard to wash himself with fresh water from the well, he heard that piercing, shrill, seemingly feminine voice which was Leonardo's whenever he would yell in his paroxysms of occasional anger,—momentary and deep, but which no one dreaded.

"Whoever asked thee, thou blockhead, thou drunken clout,—tell me, whoever asked thee to treat the horses at a farrier's?"

"Be reasonable, messer,—can one do otherwise than treat an ailing horse?"

"Treat! Dost thou think, thou ass's head, that it can be done with this stinking mixture?"

"Not a mixture, perhaps; but there is a sort of spell,—a charm. You do not understand this matter, that is why you are angry. . . ."

"Get thee to the devil with thy charms! Why, where does he, the ignoramus, the knacker, get the right to treat, when he knows nothing of the structure of a horse's body,—of its anatomy?"

Nastasio raised his bloated, indolent eyes, looked up from under his eyebrows at his master, and muttered with disdain:

"Anatomy!"

"Thou scoundrel! . . . Out, out of my house! . . ."

The hostler did not as much as wink an eye; by long experience he knew that when the flare-up of momentary wrath would pass, the master would be making up to him, just to have him stay, inasmuch as he valued in him a great connoisseur and lover of horses.

"I wanted to ask for my dismissal, anyway," said Nastasio. "There is three months' wages coming to me from Your Grace. But as far as the hay is concerned, 'tis no fault of mine. Marco does not give any money for oats."

"What is that,—something new? How dare he not give it when I have given him orders to? . . ."

The hostler shrugged his shoulders and turned away, indicating that he did not want to hold any further parley; he gave a business-like grunt, and again took to grooming the horse, but this time as if to vent his spleen upon it.

Giovanni listened, with a smile of amused curiosity, as he towelled his face, red from the cold water.

"Well, what say ye, master? . . . Shall we go, or not?" asked Astro, who had become bored with waiting.

"Bide a while," said Leonardo, "I must ask Marco about the oats, if this cheat be telling the truth or no."

He entered the house. Giovanni followed him.

Marco was at work in the atelier. As always, following the rules of the master with mathematical exactness, he was measuring the black paint for the shadows with a tiny, leaden spoon, constantly referring to a bit of paper covered over with figures. Drops of sweat stood out on his brow; the veins on his neck had swelled up. His breathing was heavy, just as if he were rolling a stone up-hill. His firmly-compressed lips, his hunched-up back, his red forelock, stubbornly sticking up, and his reddened hands, with gnarled, thick fingers,—everything seemed to say: Patience and labour will overcome all things.

"Ah, Messer Leonardo, you are not gone yet,—please, could you verify this calculation? Meseems I have botched it up . . ."

"All right, Marco. Later on. But here is what I wanted to speak with thee about. Is it true that thou dost not give any money for the horses' oats?"

"I do not."

"How is that, my friend? For have I not told thee," continued the artist, looking at the stern face of the majordomo with a gaze constantly more and more timid and wavering, "have I not told thee, Marco, to give money for the horses' oats, without fail? Dost thou not remember? . . ."

"I do remember. But there is no money."

"There, there, now, I knew it was so,—again no money! Be reasonable, Marco, judge for yourself,—can horses be left without oats? . . ."

Marco made no reply; merely threw his brush away angrily.

Giovanni watched the changes in their expressions; now the master looked the pupil, and the pupil the master.

"Hearken, master," said Marco, "you have asked me to take the management of the household upon myself and not to bother you. Then why do you begin upon this matter anew?"

"Marco!" exclaimed Leonardo reproachfully. "Why, Marco, I have given thee thirty florins but last week . . ."

"Thirty florins! Out of them count off four for the debt to Paccioli; two to this beggar Galeotto Sacrobosco; five for the hangman who steals corpses from the gallows for your anatomy; three for repairing the panes and the furnaces in the green-houses, where you keep reptiles and fishes; six whole florins for this striped devil . . ."

"For the giraffe, thou wouldst say?"

"Well, yes, for the giraffe. We have naught to eat ourselves, and yet we fatten this accursed creature! And yet it is all one,—no matter what you do with him, he will die anyway. . . ."

"'Tis naught, Marco, let him die," remarked Leonardo meekly; "then I shall perform an autopsy on it. It hath such curious vertebræ of the neck. . . ."

"Vertebræ of the neck! Eh, master, master, were it not for all these whims,—horses, corpses, giraffes, fishes, and other reptiles,—we would be living on the fat of the land, nor humbling ourselves before anybody. Is it not better to have a bit of daily bread? . . ."

"Daily bread! But then, am I demanding aught else for myself save daily bread? However, I know, Marco, that thou wouldst be right glad if all my animals, which I obtain at such cost and with such labour, whose necessity to me thou canst not even imagine, were to die. All that thou art after is to have thy way! . . ."

A helpless hurt began to sound in the voice of the master.

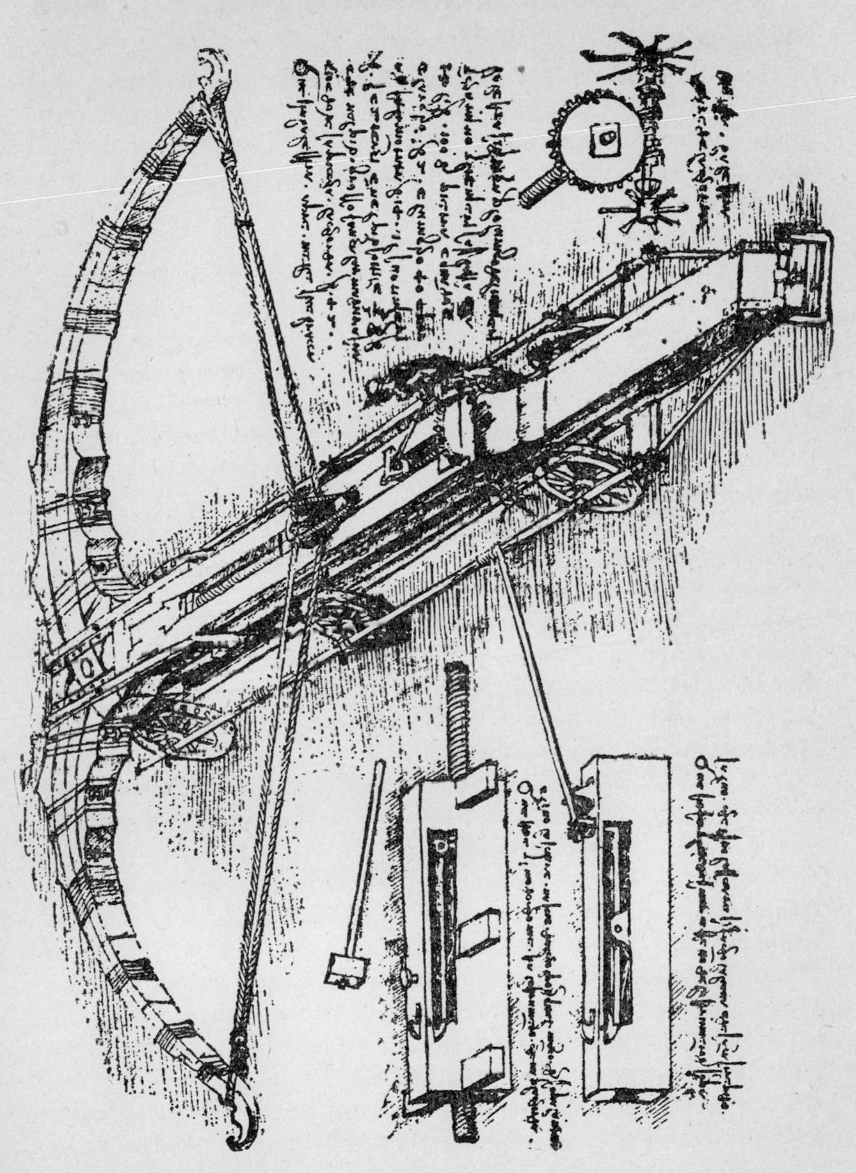

Marco kept a taciturn silence, his eyes downcast.

"What is to be, then?" continued Leonardo. "What, I say, Marco, is to become of us? No oats! What a sorry jest! So that is the pass we have come to! Matters have never come to such a pass with us yet! . . ."

"It has always been thus, and it always will be," retorted Marco. "And what can you expect? Here it is more than a year that we have not gotten as much as a groat from the Duke. Ambrogio da Ferrari makes you promises every day,—to-morrow and to-morrow, but one can plainly see that he is but mocking you. . . ."

"Mocking me!" exclaimed Leonardo. "Oh, no,—bide a while, I shall show him how to make mock of me! I shall complain to the Duke, that is what I will do! I shall knock this scoundrel Ambrogio into a cocked hat,—may the Lord send him an ill Easter-tide! . . ."

Marco merely made a gesture of hopelessness, as though he would say that, if anyone were to do any knocking into cocked hats, then, of course, it would not be Leonardo who would do it to the Duke's treasurer.

"Drop it, master, drop it,—do, now!" he said, and suddenly in the rugged, angular features of his face there flickered an expression kindly, tender and protective. "God is gracious, and we will yet find a way out somehow. If you really desire it, without fail,—well, I may contrive so that there be enough even for oats. . . ."

He knew that to do this he would have to take a part of his own money, which he used to send to his ailing old mother.

"'Tis no longer a matter of oats!" exclaimed Leonardo, and in exhaustion sank upon a chair.

His eyes began to blink, narrowing as if from a strong, cold wind.

"Hearken, Marco. I have not as yet told thee of this. I must, without fail, have eighty ducats the forthcoming month, because I,—dost thou see,—I have borrowed them. . . . Eh, look not at me so! . . ."

"Whom have you borrowed from?"

"From Arnoldo the money-changer."

Marco wrung his hands in despair; his red tuft simply shook.

"From Arnoldo the money-changer! There, I felicitate you; I must say you have done me a friendly turn! But do you know what a beast he is,—worse than any Jew or Moor? There is no cross upon him. Ah, master, master, what have you done! And how is it you never told me? . . ."

Leonardo dropped his head.

"I had to have the money,—the knife was at my throat. Be not thou angry at me, now. . . ."

And, after a short silence, he added with a timid and piteous air:

"Do thou bring the accounts, Marco. Mayhap we may even contrive something? . . ."

Marco was convinced that he would not contrive anything, but since there was no other way of pacifying the master save by exhausting to the last his sudden and momentary alarm, he went submissively for the accounts.

Seeing them from afar, Leonardo made a sickly wry face and glanced at the familiar thick book in its binding of green with an expression such as that of a man contemplating his own gaping wound.

He plunged into reckonings, in which the great mathematician made mistakes in addition and subtraction. At times, suddenly recalling a lost bill for several thousand ducats, he would search for it, rummaging in caskets, boxes, dusty piles of papers; but, instead, would find unnecessary, picayune accounts painstakingly written out in his own hand; for instance, one for Salaino's cape:

Cloth of silver....................	15 *lire*	4 *soldi*
Scarlet Velvet for trimming same....	9 "	——
Laces..........................	——	9 *soldi*
Buttons........................	——	12 "

Angrily he would tear up such accounts and throw the pieces under the table, swearing.

Giovanni watched the expression of human weakness on the master's face, and, recalling the words of one of the admirers of Leonardo: "The new god Hermes Trismegistus is united within him with the new titan Prometheus," he reflected with a smile:

"There he is,—neither a god nor a titan, but just such a man as all of us. And why have I ever feared him? O, the poor, dear fellow!"

X

Two days passed, and that which Marco had foreseen happened: Leonardo had forgotten money matters just as completely as if he had never given them a thought. Even on the following day he asked for three florins, for the purchase of an antediluvian fossil, with such a care-free air that Marco had not the heart to pain him with a refusal and gave him these three florins out of his own money, put by for his mother.

The treasurer, despite the supplications of Leonardo, had still not paid him his salary; at this time the Duke himself stood in need of money for the gigantic preparations for war with France. Leonardo borrowed from everybody he could,—even his own pupils. The Duke would not permit him to finish the Sforza monument even. The statue of clay, the form with the iron frame-work, the furnace for the molten metal, the forge, the smelting furnaces,—all stood in readiness. But when the artist presented his bill for the bronze, Moro became frightened,—even wrathful,—and refused him an audience.

Toward the end of November, in the year fourteen hundred and ninety-eight, brought to the last extremity by need, he wrote a letter to the Duke. Among the papers of Leonardo has been left a rough copy of this letter,—fragmentary, incoherent, resembling the mumbling of a man overcome by shame, unaccustomed to importune.

"Sire, knowing that the mind of Your Highness is engulfed by more important matters, but, at the same time, fearing lest my silence be the cause of the wrath of my Most Gracious Patron, I take the liberty of reminding you of my small needs, and of my arts, doomed to silence. . . .

". . . For two years I have not received any salary. . . .

". . . Other persons, in the service of Your Illustrious Highness, having outside incomes, are in a position to wait; whereas I, with my art,—which, however, I would fain abandon for something more profitable . . .

". . . My life is at the service of Your Highness, and I am in constant readiness to obey. . . .

". . . Of the monument I say naught, since I know how the times are. . . .

". . . 'Tis most grievous to me, that, owing to the necessity of earning my subsistence, I am compelled to interrupt my work and occupy myself with trifles. . . . I have had to feed six people for fifty-six months, yet I had but fifty ducats. . . .

". . . I am perplexed to what use I could put my abilities. . . .

". . . Should I consider glory, or daily bread? . . ."

XI

On a certain occasion in November, toward evening, after a day spent in solicitations at the magnanimous grandee's, Gaspare Visconti's; at Arnoldo's, the money-changer's; at the hangman's, who was demanding money for two cadavers of pregnant women, threatening to lodge information with the Most Holy Inquisition in the event of non-payment,—Leonardo, all tired out, returned home; he first passed into the kitchen, in order to dry his clothing; then, taking the key from Astro, set out toward the workshop; on approaching it, however, he heard the sound of voices behind the door.

"The doors are locked," he reflected. "What is the meaning of this, then? Can it be thieves, perhaps?"

He listened carefully, recognized the voices of his pupils, and surmised that they were looking over his secret papers, which he never showed to anyone. He was about to open the door, but suddenly there appeared before him a vision of their eyes, as they would look upon him, caught in the act, and he felt ashamed for them. Stealing away on tiptoes, blushing and looking over his shoulder, like one guilty, he went away from the door, and, passing through the workshop, from the other end of it, assuming a loud voice, so that they could not help but hear him, he called out:

"Astro! Astro! Give me a candle! Wherever have you all gone to? Andrea, Marco, Giovanni, Cesare!"

The voices in the workroom ceased. Something or other made a tinkling, ringing sound, like that of falling glass breaking. A window frame slammed. He was still listening intently, undecided as to whether he should go in. In his soul was neither malice nor grief,—but merely weariness of spirit and revulsion.

He had not been mistaken; having made their way into the room through the window from the yard, Giovanni and Cesare had rummaged in the drawers of his work-table, looking through his secret papers, his drawings and diaries.

Beltraffio with a pale face held a mirror. Cesare, stooping, had read by the reflection in the mirror the reverse script of Leonardo:

"'*Laude del Sole—Praise to the Sun.*

"'I can not but reproach Epicurus, who affirmed that the size of the sun was in reality such as it seems; I am amazed at Socrates, who, deprecating such a great luminary, did assert that it was but a stone at red-heat. And I would but that I had words strong enough for the reproach of those who prefer the deification of Man to the deification of the Sun. . . .'"

"Shall I skip?" asked Cesare.

"Nay, I beg of thee," answered Giovanni, "read on to the end."

"'Those that worship anthropomorphous gods,'" continued Cesare, "'are quite in error, inasmuch as man, be he even as the terrestrial globe in size, would appear smaller than the most insignificant planet, a scarcely perceptible dot in Creation. Moreover, all men are subject to corruption. . . .'"

"'Tis strange!" Cesare voiced his wonder. "How is that, then? He worships the sun, but as for Him that hath conquered death with death,—why He does not seem to have even existed! . . ."

He turned a page.

"But here is some more,—listen."

"'In all parts of Europe shall they bewail the death of a Man who died in Asia. . . .'"

"Dost understand?"

"Nay," Giovanni whispered.

"Good Friday," explained Cesare.

"'O, Mathematicians,'" he continued reading, "'do ye pour a flood of light upon this madness. Spirit can not be without the body, and where there is no flesh, nor blood, nor bones, nor tongue, nor muscles, there can be nor voice nor motion.' I can not make this passage out, —'tis blotted. But here is the ending: 'As for other definitions of the spirit, I leave that to the holy fathers, the instructors of the people, who know by an inspiration from above the mysteries of nature.'

"Hm, 'twould not be good for Messer Leonardo's health if these bits of paper were to fall into the hands of the Holy Fathers Inquisitors. . . . And here again is a prophecy:

"'Without doing aught, contemning poverty and labour, people shall live in luxury, in buildings resembling palaces, acquiring treasures visible for the price of those invisible, and asserting that this is the best means of being pleasing to God.'

"Indulgences!" Cesare unriddled it. "Why, this sounds like Savonarola! He is shying a stone in the Pope's garden. . . ."

"'Those who have died a thousand years ago shall feed the living.'

"Well, that is something I comprehend not. Must be something profound. And yet,—yes, yes, of course! 'Those who have died a thousand years ago,'—the martyrs and the saints, in whose names the monks gather money.

"'They shall hold converse with them that, having ears, hear not; they shall light holy lamps before them that, having eyes, see not.' —Icons.

"'Women shall confess to men all their lusts, all their secret shameful deeds.'—The Confessional.—How likest thou that, Giovanni? Eh? An amazing fellow! There, now, do thou but consider for whom he thinks up all these enigmas? And, to boot, there is no real malice about them. Just so,—a playing at sacrilege! . . ."

Having turned several more leaves, he read aloud:

"'Many, trading in seeming miracles, deceive the unthinking rabble, and execute those who expose their deceptions.'—This, probably, is about the Ordeal of Fire of Brother Girolamo, and about science, which demolishes belief in miracles."

He laid the note-book aside and glanced at Giovanni.

"Will that suffice, perhaps? What other proofs dost thou want? Which, precisely? . . ."

Beltraffio shook his head.

"Nay, Cesare, all this is still not the one precise thing. . . . Oh, if one could find but one such passage where he speaks definitely! . . ."

"Definitely? Oh, no, do not expect that, brother! Such is his nature, everything is equivocal; he is always being sly and shilly-shallying, like a woman. 'Tis not for naught he loves riddles. Go try and catch him! Why, he himself does not know himself. He is the greatest riddle to himself!"

"Cesare is right," reflected Giovanni. "Better is outright blasphemy than all these mockeries, this smile of Doubting Thomas, inserting his fingers in the wounds of the Lord."

Cesare pointed out to him a drawing in orange crayon upon blue paper,—a small drawing lost among the designs for machines and the calculations,—a drawing depicting the Virgin Mary with the Infant, lost in the desert; sitting on a stone, she draws triangles, circles and other figures: the Lord's Mother instructing the Son in geometry—the source of all knowledge.

Long did Giovanni contemplate this strange drawing. A desire arose within him to read the inscription under it. He drew the mirror nearer. Cesare glanced at the reflection and had barely time enough to make out the first three words: "Necessity—Eternal Instructress"—when Leonardo's voice was heard coming from the workshop:

"Astro! Astro! Give me a candle! Wherever have you all gone to? Andrea, Marco, Giovanni, Cesare!"

A shiver ran through Giovanni; he paled and let the mirror drop. It shattered.

"An ill omen!" smiled Cesare, scoffingly.

Like thieves caught in the act, they began to hurry, shoving the papers in a drawer, gathering up the fragments of the mirror; opening the window they jumped up on the window-ledge and climbed down into the yard, catching at the rain-spout and the thick branches of the grapevines entwining the house. Cesare lost his hold, fell, and almost sprained his leg.

XII

On this evening Leonardo could not find his usual peace of mind in mathematics. Now he would get up and pace the room; then he would sit down, begin a drawing, and immediately abandon it; within his soul was an indefinable disquiet, as though he had to decide something, and could not. His thoughts stubbornly recurred ever to the same thing.

He thought of how Giovanni Beltraffio had run away to Savonarola, then had again returned, and for a time had seemed to be gaining peace, having given himself up wholly to art. But, after the ill-fated Ordeal of Fire, and especially since the day that the news of the monk's downfall had come to Milan, he had become still more pitiful and lost.

The master saw how he was suffering; how Giovanni longed to leave him, and could not; surmised the struggle going on within the heart of his pupil, too profound not to suffer,—too weak to conquer its own inconsistencies. At times it seemed to Leonardo that he must repulse Giovanni, must drive him away, in order to save him,—but he had not enough courage to do this.

"If I did but know in which way to help him," pondered the artist.

He smiled with a bitter smile.

"I have put the evil eye upon him, have bewitched him! Probably men tell the truth, I have the evil eye. . . ."

Having ascended the steep steps of the dark stairs, he knocked at Giovanni's door, and, receiving no reply, opened it a trifle.

Murk reigned in the confined cell. One could hear the rain pattering on the roof, and the noise of the autumn wind. A holy lamp flickered in a corner before a Madonna; a black crucifix hung upon the white wall. Beltraffio was lying face down on the bed, fully dressed, awkwardly huddled up, as sick children huddle; his knees were bent up and he was hiding his face in the pillow.

"Art sleeping, Giovanni?" said the master.

Beltraffio jumped up, cried out faintly and looked at Leonardo with insane and widely open eyes, putting out his hands, with that expression of infinite horror which had shone in Maia's eyes.

"What ails thee, Giovanni? 'Tis I. . . ."

Beltraffio seemed to come to himself and slowly passed his hand over his eyes.

"Ah, 'tis you, Messer Leonardo. . . . But to me it seemed . . . I have had a terrible dream. . . ."

"So it is *you*,"—he looked at him from underneath his brows, intently, as though still mistrustful.

The master sat down at the edge of the bed and laid his hand on Giovanni's forehead:

"Thou hast fever. Thou art sick. Why hast thou not told me? . . ."

Giovanni was just turning away, but suddenly he again looked at Leonardo,—the corners of his mouth drooped, quivered, and, folding his hands in supplication, he said in a whisper:

"Master, drive me away! . . . For else I shall never go away myself, and yet stay with you I can not, inasmuch as I . . . Yes, yes. . . . I have behaved basely toward you. . . . I am a traitor! . . ."

Leonardo embraced and drew him close.

"Whatever art thou saying, lad? The Lord be with thee! For do I not see how thou art tormenting thyself? If thou dost but think that thou art guilty of aught before me, I do forgive thee all; mayhap thou, too, mayst some time forgive me. . . ."

Giovanni quietly raised his large, astonished eyes toward him, and suddenly, with an unrestrainable impulse, pressed closely to him, hiding his face on his breast, and in his beard, as soft as silk.

"If I shall ever," he babbled through his sobs, which shook his whole body, "go away from you, master, think not that I do not love you! I myself do not know what is the matter with me. . . . I have such strange thoughts,—as though I were going out of my mind. . . . God hath forsaken me. . . . Oh, but do not think otherwise,—nay, I love you more than anything in the world, more than my father, Fra Benedetto! None can love you as much as I! . . ."

Leonardo with a gentle smile was stroking his head, his cheeks, wet with tears, and consoling him, as one would a child:

"There, enough, enough,—cease! Do I not know that thou dost love me, my poor little, silly little lad? . . ."

"But, probably, it was Cesare that did again fill thee full of his talk?" he added. "And whatever dost thou hearken to him for? He is clever, and he too, the poor fellow, loves me, but thinks that he hates me. There is a great deal that he does not understand. . . ."

Giovanni suddenly grew quiet, ceased crying, glanced into the eyes of the master with an odd, searching gaze, and shook his head:

"Nay," he said slowly, as though utterance were difficult to him, "nay, 'tis not Cesare. 'Tis I, myself. . . . And not I, but *He*. . . ."

"Who is he?" asked the master.

Giovanni clung to him closer; his eyes again widened in horror.

"You must not," he managed to say, barely audibly, "you must not speak of *Him*. . . ."

Leonardo felt Giovanni trembling in his embrace.

"Listen, my child," he uttered in that strict, kindly (and a trifle dissembling) voice, which physicians adopt in speaking with sick persons, "I can see that thou hast something on thy heart. Thou must tell me all. I wish to know all, Giovanni,—dost thou hear? Then it will be easier for thee also."

And, after a short reflection, he added:

"Tell me, whom wert thou speaking of but now?"

Giovanni looked back in fear, put his lips to Leonardo's very ear, and spoke in a choking whisper:

"Of your double."

"Of my double? What meanest thou? Hast thou seen him in a dream?"

"Nay, in reality. . . ."

Leonardo looked at him intently, and for an instant it seemed to him that Giovanni was raving.

"For, Messer Leonardo, it was not you that came in here three days ago, on Tuesday, at night?"

"It was not. But dost thou not remember thyself?"

"Oh, no,—I do remember. . . . Well, then, you see, master, it was of a surety *He!* . . ."

"But wherever didst thou get it into thy head that I have a double? How did it happen?"

Leonardo felt that Giovanni himself wanted to tell, and hoped that the confession would relieve him.

"How did it happen? Why, in this fashion. *He* came to me the same way that you did to-day, at this very same hour, and also sat down at the edge of the bed, even as you are sitting now; and spoke and did everything as you are saying and doing; and his face is like your face, only as if it were in a mirror. He is not left-handed. And immediately it came into my mind that this was not you; and *He* knew that I thought so, but did not betray it,—he made believe that both of us knew naught of it. Only when he was departing did he turn around toward me, and said: 'But hast thou never, Giovanni, seen my double? If thou dost see him, have no fear.' Only then did I comprehend everything. . . ."

"And do you still believe, even now, Giovanni?"

"How can I but believe, when I have beheld *Him*, even as I behold you now? . . . *He*, too, spoke with me. . . ."

"Of what?"

Giovanni covered his face with his hands.

"'Tis best if thou wilt tell," encouraged Leonardo, "or else thou wilt keep brooding on it, and suffering."

"'Twas of naught good he spoke," said Giovanni, and glanced at Leonardo in hopeless supplication. "'Twas horrible! He spoke as if everything in the universe consisted solely of mechanics; as though everything were like this fearful spider, with revolving paws, which He . . . that is, not He, but you, invented. . . ."

"What spider? Ah, yes, yes—I recall. Thou hast seen the drawing of the war engine I have in my possession? . . ."

"Then too," Giovanni continued, "as though that which men call God is but eternal force, through which the fearful spider moves with his bloodied paws, paws of iron, and that everything is all one to Him,—truth or untruth, good or evil, life or death. And none can supplicate Him, inasmuch as He is like mathematics: two times two can not be five. . . ."

"There, there, now. Do not torture thyself. Enough of that. I already know. . . ."

"Nay, Messer Leonardo, wait,—you do not know all, yet. Do you but listen, master! *He* said that Christ, even, had come in vain,—Christ had died and had not risen again, had not conquered death with death,—had undergone corruption in the grave. And when he had said that, I fell to weeping. He took pity on me, and began to console me: 'Cry not,' said He, 'my poor, silly little lad; there is no Christ; but there is love; great love is the daughter of great knowledge; he that knoweth all, loveth all.' There, you see,—in your very words, all in your words! 'Before,' says he, 'there was love through weakness, from miracle, and through ignorance; but now,—through power, truth and knowledge, inasmuch as the Serpent did not lie: taste of the Tree of Knowledge, and ye shall be as the gods.' And after these words of His, I understood that He was from the devil and I cursed him, and He went away, but said that He would return. . . ."

Leonardo listened to him with the same curiosity as if these were no longer the ravings of a sick man. He felt how Giovanni's gaze, by now almost calm, revealing, was penetrating to the most secret depths of his heart.

"And most fearful of all," said the pupil in a whisper, slowly drawing away from the master, and looking at him pointblank with a fixed, piercing glance, "most repulsive of all was that He smiled while he was telling me all this,—well, yes, yes . . . altogether as you do now . . . like you! . . ."

Giovanni's face suddenly blanched, became distorted, and, pushing Leonardo away, he began screaming in a wild, insane scream:

"Thou . . . thou . . . again! . . . Thou hast dissembled. . . . In the name of God. . . . Perish, perish, disappear, thou accursed one! . . ."

The master got up and uttered, looking at him with a commanding gaze:

"God be with thee, Giovanni! I see that it really would be better if thou wert to go away from me. Dost remember, 'tis said in the Scriptures: 'He that feareth is not made perfect in love.'[33] If thou didst love me with a perfect love, then thou wouldst have had no fear; thou wouldst have understood that all this is delirium and madness; that I am not as men think me; that I have no double; that, perhaps, I believe in my Christ and Saviour more than those who style me a servant of Antichrist. Forgive me, Giovanni! May the Lord preserve thee. Fear not,—the double of Leonardo shall nevermore return to thee again. . . ."

His voice quivered and broke, from a sorrow infinite and devoid of all wrath. He arose, in order to go.

"Is that really so? Am I telling him the truth?" he reflected, and at this moment felt that if a lie were necessary to save Giovanni, he was ready to lie.

Beltraffio fell on his knees, kissing the master's hands.

"No more! No more! . . . I know that this is madness. . . . I believe you. . . . There, you will see, I will banish these fearful thoughts from me. . . . Only forgive, forgive, forgive me, Master; abandon me not! . . ."

Leonardo glanced at him with indescribable pity, and, stooping, kissed his head.

"Well, now, look thou, and remember, Giovanni,—thou hast promised me."

"And now," he added with his wontedly calm voice, "let us go down as quickly as we may. 'Tis cold. I shall not let thee stay here any more until thou hast gotten altogether well. Incidentally, I have some work that must be finished in time. Thou shalt assist me."

XIII

He led him into a bedroom adjoining the workshop; blew up the fire in the hearth, and, when the flames began to crackle, lighting up the room with a cozy glow, said that he had to prepare a panel for a picture. Leonardo hoped that this work would calm the sick man. And so it happened. Little by little Giovanni became engrossed. With an air of concentration, as though this were a curious and important matter, he assisted the master in impregnating the board with a poisonous solution to preserve it against worm-holes,—a solution of spirits, mixed with bisulphurous arsenic and corrosive sublimate. Next they began applying a primary layer of coating, filling in the unevenness and the cracks with alabaster, cypress lacquer, mastic; smoothing out the rough spots with a flat iron scraper. The work, as always, went at top speed, merrily, and seemed like play in the hands of Leonardo. At the same time he was giving counsels; instructions in the tying of brushes, beginning with the very thickest, and coarsest, made of pig bristles, set in lead, and ending with the finest and softest, made of squirrel hairs, inserted in a goose-quill; or how, in order that the poisonous proofing might dry more quickly, there should be added to it Venetian verdigris with red ferrous ochre.

Through the room spread a pleasant workmanlike odour, of turpentine and mastic. Giovanni with all his might rubbed hot flax oil into the panel with a bit of chamois rag. He began to feel hot; his chill passed off entirely.

Pausing for a minute's breathing spell, his face flushed, he looked over his shoulder at the master.

"Now, now,—a little faster!" Leonardo hurried him. "'Twill cool."

And, arching his back, spreading his feet far apart, his lips firmly set, Giovanni with new zeal went on with his work.

"Well, how dost thou feel?" asked Leonardo.

"I feel well," answered Giovanni with a merry smile.

Other pupils also gathered in this warm, light ingle-nook of the enormous Lombardian hearth of brick, covered with velvety-black soot; a pleasant thing it was to hear the howling wind and the patter of the rain as one sat by it. There arrived the benumbed, but, as always, care-free Andrea Salaino; the one-eyed cyclop blacksmith, Zoroastro da Peretola; Giacopo, and Marco d'Oggione. Only Cesare da Sesto was, as usual, missing from their friendly circle.

Putting the board aside, in order to give it an opportunity to dry thoroughly, Leonardo demonstrated to them the best means of obtaining pure oil for the pigments. A large earthen vessel was brought, wherein a dough made of nuts had been standing for some time, and the water of which had been changed six times. This dough had exuded a white juice, with a thick layer of amber-coloured grease which had come up to the surface. Taking some cotton paper and twisting it into long spills, on the manner of lamp-wicks, he put one end of each in the basin; the other ends he inserted in an iron funnel, set in the neck of a glass vessel. Soaking into the cotton paper, the oil ran down in aureately-transparent drops.

"Look, look!" Marco exclaimed in rapture. "Like a tear! Yet *I* always have turbid stuff, no matter how many times I filter it."

"Probably thou dost not take off the outer skin of the nuts," remarked Leonardo; "later on it comes out on the canvas, and the pigments become dark from it."

"Do you hear?" exulted Marco. "The greatest productions of art can perish from such trash,—from nut peels! And yet ye all laugh when I say that rules should be observed with mathematical precision. . . ."

The pupils, attentively watching the preparation of the oil, were, at the same time, chatting and sky-larking. Despite the late hour, no one felt sleepy, and, without paying any attention to the grumblings of Marco, who begrudged every billet of wood, they steadily kept on throwing in the fuel. A care-free gaiety had taken possession of all.

"Let us tell stories!" proposed Salaino, and started the ball rolling by acting out all the characters of the *novella* about the priest who, on Shrove Sabbath, went from house to house, and, having come into the house of a painter, had besprinkled his pictures with holy water. "Wherefore hast thou done this?" asked the artist. "Because I wish thee well, inasmuch as it is said: 'Ye shall be rewarded an hundredfold from above for your good work.'" The painter kept his silence; but, when the padre had gone, he lay in wait for him, threw a vat of cold water out of a window upon him, and called out: "Here is thy hundredfold from above for the good thou hast done me in spoiling my pictures!"

There came a downpour of *novella* upon *novella*, of conceit upon conceit,—each one more absurd than its predecessor. They all found unutterable delight in them, but Leonardo most of all. Giovanni was fond of observing how he laughed: his eyes would narrow, becoming like slits; his face assumed a childishly simple-hearted expression, and, moving his head, wiping away the tears that came into his eyes, he would go off into peals of high-pitched laughter, which seemed strange in contrast with his height and his mighty physique,—a laughter in which there sounded the same shrill feminine notes as in his cries of rage.

Toward midnight they felt hunger. Going to bed without a bite was not to be thought of, all the more so as they had supped but ill, since Marco treated them none too well. Astro brought everything there was in the pantry: the meagre remains of a ham, some cheese, some two score of olives, and the heel of a stale wheaten loaf; of wine there was none.

"Didst thou tilt the barrel well?" his comrades asked him.

"I tilted it over, have no fear,—I turned it on all sides,—but nary a drop."

"Ah, Marco, Marco, what art thou doing to us? How can one do without wine?"

"There you go, now,—'tis always 'Marco, Marco.' Wherein am I to blame if there be no money?"

"Money there is, and wine there shall be!" cried out Giacopo, tossing up a gold piece on his palm.

"Whence didst thou get it, thou imp? Hast thieved again? Wait, I shall yet tweak thy ears off!" Leonardo threatened him with his finger.

"Nay, nay, master, I have not stolen it,—honest to God! May I fall through on this spot, may my tongue wither,—if I won it not at dice!"

"Well, look thou, if it be thieves' wine that thou wilt regale us with . . ."

Having run to a little cellar nearby, The Green Eagle, not yet closed, since the Swiss mercenaries were celebrating the whole night through therein, Giacopo returned with two pewter mugs.

The wine made them still merrier. The boy poured it out, like to Ganymede, holding high the vessel, so that the red wine had a rosy foam; the white, an aureate one; and in his delight, at the thought that he was regaling them with his money, he played pranks, acted the tom-fool, jumped about, and in an unnaturally hoarse voice, in imitation of drunken merry-makers, would hum the brave catch of an unfrocked friar:

Devil seize cassock, cowl, and beads,
Ha, ha, ha! and he, he, he!
Oh, ye pretty wenches, needs
One much urge to sin with ye?

or the solemn hymn from the burlesque Latin *Mass to Bacchus*, composed by vagabond scholars:

They that watered wine do drink,
Shall soak for their evils;
Over fire on Hell's brink,
They'll be dried by devils.

Never, so it seemed to Giovanni, had he eaten or drunk of anything as delectable as this beggarly repast of Leonardo's, with the petrified cheese, the stale bread, and the suspicious, mayhap even stolen, wine of Giacopo.

They drank to the health of the master, to the glory of his atelier, to deliverance from poverty, and to each other.

In conclusion Leonardo, having surveyed his pupils, said with a smile:

"I have heard, my friends, that St. Francis of Assisi styled despondence the worst of vices, and did assert, that if one were desirous of pleasing God, one must always be gay. Let us, then, drink to the wisdom of St. Francis,—to eternal gaiety in God."

They were all a little surprised; but Giovanni surmised what the master wanted to say.

"Eh, master," Astro shook his head in reproach, "'gaiety,' says you; but what gaiety can there be, while we poor tumble-bugs crawl on the ground like grave maggots? Let others drink to what they will, but as for me,—I shall drink to human wings, to a flying machine! When winged men shall soar up to the very clouds,—only then shall true joy begin! And may the devil take all gravity,—all the laws of mechanics that hinder us. . . ."

"Oh, no, friend, thou wilt not fly far without mechanics!" the master stopped him.

When all had dispersed, Leonardo would not let Giovanni go upstairs; he helped him arrange a couch in his own bedroom, as near as possible to the grateful, expiring embers of the fireplace; and, having searched out a little drawing, made in coloured crayons, he handed it to his pupil.

The face of the youth portrayed on the drawing seemed so familiar to Giovanni that at first he took it for a portrait: there was a resemblance both with Brother Girolamo Savonarola,—but in the early years of his youth; and with the sixteen-year-old son of a rich Milanese usurer, hated of all,—the old Jew Barucco; the face was that of a sickly, dreamy adolescent, plunged in the secret wisdom of the Kabalas, a disciple of the rabbis; according to their words, the future luminary of the Synagogue.

But, when Beltraffio had looked intently upon this Hebrew lad, with thick, rufous hair, low brow, thick lips, he recognized Christ,—not as he is recognized in icons, but as though Giovanni himself had seen Him, had forgotten, and had now suddenly recalled Him.

In the head, drooping, like a flower on a too-frail stalk, in the gaze, as innocent as that of an infant, of the lowered eyes, there was a premonition of that last sorrow upon the Mount of Olives, when He, being in terror and longing, had said to His disciples: "My soul is exceeding sorrowful, even unto death."[34] . . . and he was withdrawn from them about a stone's cast[35] . . . and fell on his face and prayed, saying:[36] . . . "Abba, Father, all things are possible unto thee; take away this cup from me: nevertheless not what I will, but what thou wilt."[37] And a second time, and a third did he say: "O my Father, if this cup may not pass away from me, except I drink it, thy will be done."[38] And being in an agony he prayed more earnestly: and his sweat was as it were great drops of blood falling down to the ground.[39]

"What did He pray about?" reflected Giovanni. "How is it that He asked that there should not happen that could not but happen,—that which was of His own will,—that for which He had come into the Universe? Can it be that He, too, even as I, was tortured, and that He too struggled, until a bloody sweat came, with these fearful double-minded thoughts?"

"Well, how is it?" asked Leonardo, returning to the room, which he had left for a brief while. "But, meseems, thou art at thy old worries again?"

"Nay, nay, master! Oh, if you did but know how well and peaceful I feel. . . . It is all over now. . . ."

"Glory to God, Giovanni! For I told thee 'twould pass. See thou, then, that it never return again. . . ."

"'Twill not return, have no fear! Now I see," he pointed to the drawing, "I see that you love Him as doth no other among men. . . ."

"And should your double," he added, "come to me again, I know wherewith to drive him off: I shall but remind him of this drawing."

XIV

Giovanni heard from Cesare that Leonardo was finishing the Lord's countenance in The Last Supper, and he was desirous of seeing it. Many times did he ask the master for this privilege; the latter always promised, but put him off.

Finally, on a certain morning, he led him to the refectory of Maria delle Grazie, and, on the spot so familiar to him, which had remained vacant during sixteen years, between John and James, sons of Zebedee, in the rectangle of the open window, against the serene distance of the sky at night-fall and the hills of Sion he beheld the face of the Lord.

Several days later, toward evening, over deserted waste places, by the bank of the Catarana Canal, Giovanni was returning home from the alchemist Galeotto Sacrobosco,— the master had sent him thither after a rare book, a treatise on mathematics.

After the wind and the thaw it had become still and frosty. The puddles in the ruts of the road had become covered over with needles of fragile ice. The low clouds seemed to catch on the bare lilac tips of the larches, with their tattered jackdaws' nests. It was darkling rapidly. Only on the very edge of the sky did there stretch out a long, brassy-yellow furrow of the despondent sunset. The water in the unfrozen canal, still, heavy, as black as cast iron,—seemed bottomlessly deep.

Giovanni, although he did not confess these thoughts to himself, and drove them away with the last effort of his reason, was thinking of Leonardo's two depictions of the countenance of the Lord. He had but to shut his eyes to have them both appear before him, as though alive: one, near as one's own kin, filled with human weakness,—the face of Him who, on the Mount of Olives, did sorrow till bloody sweat came, and did pray a childlike prayer for a miracle; the other,—inhumanly calm, wise, strange and frightful.

And Giovanni reflected that perhaps, in their insolvable contradiction, they were both true. His thoughts were confused, as in a delirium. His head burned. He sank down on a stone over the water of the narrow, black canal in his exhaustion, and buried his head in his hands.

"Whatever art thou doing here? Just as if thou wert the shadow of a lover on the shores of Acheron," spoke a mocking voice. He felt a hand on his shoulder, shuddered, turned around, and beheld Cesare.

In the wintry twilight, which was dusty-grey, like a cobweb under the bare lilac-black larches with their bedraggled jackdaws' nests, Cesare—muffled up in his grey cape, lone, spare, with his long, sickly face of a pallid grey,—seemed a very phantom.

Giovanni arose, and they continued their way in silence,—save for the rustling of the dry leaves underfoot.

"Does he know that we were rummaging through his papers the other day?" Cesare finally asked.

"He knows," answered Giovanni.

"And, of course, feels no anger toward us. All-forgiveness!" Cesare burst into malevolent, forced laughter.

They again became silent. A crow, with a hoarse croak, flew over the canal.

"Cesare," pronounced Giovanni quietly, "hast thou seen the Lord's face in The Last Supper?"

"I have."

"Well, what dost thou think of it? How is it?"

Cesare quickly turned around to him.

"But what dost thou think of it thyself?"

"I know not. . . . Meseems . . ."

"Come right out with it,—dost thou mislike it, then?"

"It is not that. But the thought occurs to me, that, perhaps, this is—not Christ. . . ."

"Not Christ? Well, who else is it?"

Giovanni made no reply; he merely slowed down his pace and let his head sink.

"Listen," said he, in deep thought, "hast thou seen the other drawing, also for the head of Christ,—in coloured crayons, where He is drawn almost as a child?"

"I know,—a Hebrew lad, red-haired, thick-lipped, low of brow,—a face like that of this little Jew dog, the son of Barucco. Well, what about it? Does that one suit thee better?"

"Nay. . . . But still, I ponder of how dissimilar these two Christs be!"

"Dissimilar?" Cesare wondered. "Why, if thou wilt, these two are but the one face! In The Last Supper His is fifteen years older. . . ."

"However," added he, "it may even be that thou art right. But even if these be two Christs, they still resemble one another, like doubles. . . ."

"Doubles!" echoed Giovanni, and, with a shudder, halted. "What was it thou hast said, Cesare,—*doubles?*"

"Well, yes. What has frightened thee so? Why, hast thou not noticed it thyself?"

They again went on, in silence.

"Cesare!" Beltraffio exclaimed suddenly, with an unrestrainable impulse; "how is it thou dost not perceive? Can it be that he, the Omnipotent and Omniscient, whom the master has depicted in The Last Supper,—can it be possible that He was capable of grieving on the Mount of Olives, at a stone's throw, till the sweat fell as it were in bloody drops, and of praying our human prayer, even as children pray,—of praying for a miracle: 'Let not that happen for which I have come into the Universe; that which I know can not but be. Abba, Father . . . take away this cup from me.' But then, there is in this prayer everything,—everything, dost thou hear, Cesare?—and there is no Christ without it, and I would not barter it for any wisdom! He who would not pray thus would not have been human; would not have suffered, would not have died, even as we suffer and die! . . ."

"So that is what thou art thinking of," said Cesare slowly. "Well, now, there really is something in that. The other Christ,—the one in The Last Supper,—could not have prayed *thus*. . . ."

It grew absolutely dark. Giovanni distinguished with difficulty the face of his fellow traveller; it appeared to him strangely changed. Suddenly Cesare stopped, raised his arm, and pronounced in a stifled, solemn voice:

"Dost want to know whom he has portrayed,—if it be not He that prayed on the Mount of Olives, if it be not thy Christ? Listen: '. . . In the beginning was the Word, and the Word was with God, and the Word was God. The same was in the beginning with God. All things were made by him; and without him was not any thing made that was made.[40] . . . And the Word was made flesh. . . .'[41] Dost hear? —the Word, the reason of God, was made flesh. Among His disciples, who, hearing 'One of you shall betray me,'[42] are sorrowing, indignant, horrified,—He is calm, He is equally akin and a stranger to all,—to John, reclining on His breast; to Judas, betraying Him,—inasmuch as there is no longer for Him any good or evil, life or death, love or hate; there is but the will of the Father,—the Eternal Necessity: 'Not what I will, but what thou wilt,'[37]—why, this was said both by thy Christ, and by Him that prayed on the Mount of Olives, at a stone's throw, about an impossible miracle. Therefore do I say,—they be doubles. 'Emotions are of the earth; Reason is outside of emotions, when it contemplates,'—dost remember, these are Leonardo's words? In the faces and movements of the apostles, the greatest of men, he had depicted all the earthly emotions; but He who saith 'I have overcome the world,'[43] 'I and my Father are one,'[44]—is the Reason Contemplative, outside of emotions. Thou rememberest also these other words of Leonardo's about the laws of mechanics: 'O, Thy wondrous justice, Thou First Mover!' His Christ is the First Mover, Who, being the beginning and the central point of every motion, is immovable; his Christ is the Eternal Necessity, which has come to know and to love itself in man, as Divine Justice, as the will of the Father: 'O righteous Father, the world hath not known thee: but I have known thee. . . . And I have declared unto them thy name, and will declare it: that the love wherewith thou hast loved me may be in them. . . .'[45] Dost hear,—love comes from knowledge. 'Great love is the daughter of great knowledge.' Leonardo alone among men has comprehended this word of the Lord, and has embodied it in his Christ, Who 'loveth all because he knoweth all.'"

Cesare became silent,—and for a long time they went on in the breathless stillness of the frosty twilight.

"Dost remember, Cesare," Giovanni said at last, "how three years ago we were walking together, just as now, through this outskirt, and discussing The Last Supper? Thou didst then deride the master, saying that he was never to finish the countenance of the Lord, whereas I contradicted. Now thou art for him, and against me. Dost thou know, I would never have believed that thou—thou, precisely,—couldst speak of him thus! . . ."

Giovanni wanted to look into the face of his travelling companion, but Cesare hastily turned away.

"I am glad," concluded Beltraffio, "that thou dost love him,—yes, love him, Cesare; even more, perhaps, than I; thou wouldst hate him, yet canst not! . . ."

Cesare slowly turned his face upon him,—pale, distorted.

"And what didst thou think? I do love him! Who should, if not I? I fain would hate him, but am constrained to love, inasmuch as that which he has accomplished in The Last Supper, no one, not even he himself, perhaps, comprehends as I do,—I, his bitterest enemy! . . ."

And he again burst out into his forced laughter:

"But, now, when one thinks of it, is not the human heart strangely created? Since it has come to this, I may even tell thee the whole truth, Giovanni: I still mislike him,—mislike him still more than I did then! . . ."

"Wherefore?"

"Why, even for this, that I desire to be my own self,—dost hear? —my own self, the least of the least, but still neither an eye, nor an ear, nor a toe of his! The pupils of Leonardo are chicks in an eagle's eyrie! The rules of science, little spoons for measuring off colours, little tabulations of noses,—let Marco console himself with these! I fain would see how Leonardo himself, with all his rules, would have created the countenance of the Lord! Oh, of course, he instructeth us, his chicks, to fly in the way of eagles,—out of the goodness of his heart, for that he hath pity upon us, just as much as upon the blind puppies of the courtyard bitch, and the lame nag, and the criminal whom he escorts to his execution, in order to observe the last quiverings of his facial muscles, and the little grasshopper of autumn, with its tiny wings benumbed. . . . The overflow of his benevolence he poureth out on everything, like the sun. . . . Only, dost thou see, my friend, every man to his taste: one finds it pleasant to be a frozen little grasshopper, or a worm, whom the master, like to St. Francis, having lifted it up from the road, doth lay down on a green leaf, that the passers-by may not trample it underfoot. Well, but to another . . . dost know, Giovanni, 'twould be better if he were simply, without any sage pondering, to squash me! . . ."

"Cesare," said Giovanni, "if this be so, why do you not go away from him?"

"But why dost *thou* not go away from him? Thou hast singed thy wings, even as a moth on a candle, but still dost flutter about, thrusting thyself into the flame. Well, then, perhaps I, too, would fain be consumed in the same fire. But, however, who knows? I, too, have a hope . . ."

"What is it?"

"Oh, a most fatuous one,—even an insane one, if thou wilt! But still, willy-nilly, the thought will recur: what if there should come one dissimilar to him yet his equal,—neither Perugino, nor Borgognone, nor Botticelli—not even the great Mantegna,—for I know the master's true value: he hath nothing to fear from any of these,—but someone still unknown? I fain would merely look at the fame of another master, merely remind Messer Leonardo that even such insects as I, spared out of mercy from being crushed, are yet capable of preferring him to another, and thus hurt him,—for, despite his sheep's clothing, he still hath a devilish pride! . . ."

Cesare did not finish, stopping short, and Giovanni felt his arm seized by a trembling hand.

"I know," uttered Cesare, by now in a different voice, almost timid and imploring, "I know that this would never have come into thy head of itself,—who told thee that I love him?"

"He, himself," answered Beltraffio.

"Himself? So that is it!" murmured Cesare, in inexpressible confusion. "So, then, he thinks that . . ."

His voice broke.

They looked into each other's eyes, and suddenly they both comprehended that there was nothing more for them to talk about, that each one was too deeply plunged within his own thoughts and torments. In silence, without having said farewell to one another, they parted at the nearest crossing of the ways.

Giovanni kept on his way with faltering step, his head cast down, without seeing, without remembering his path; through deserted waste places, between the bare birches, along the bank of the straight, long canal, with its still, oppressive waters, as black as cast iron, wherein not a single star could see its reflection,—repeating, with an insanely fixed stare:

"Doubles . . . doubles. . . ."

XV

In the beginning of March, in the year fourteen hundred and ninety-nine, Leonardo unexpectedly received from the Ducal Treasury the salary which had been held back for two years. At that time rumours were current that Moro, apparently stricken by the news of the conclusion of a triple alliance hostile to him, between Venice, the Pope, and the King, intended, at the first appearance of the French army in Lombardy, to run off to the Emperor of Germany. Desirous of strengthening the loyalty of his subjects during his absence, the Duke lightened imposts and taxes, paid off his creditors, and showered those near him with presents.

A little while later, Leonardo won another mark of the Duke's favour: "Ludovicus Maria Sfortia, Duke of Mediolania, doth bestow upon Leonardus Quintius, a Florentine, and a most illustrious artist, sixteen perches of ground, together with a vineyard, acquired from the monastery of St. Victor, named the Suburban, which is near the Vercellina Gates," said the deed of gift.

The artist set out to thank the Duke. The audience was set for the evening. But it was necessary to wait till late at night, since Moro was snowed under with business. All day had he passed in dreary converse with treasurers and secretaries, in the checking of bills for military supplies, for cannon-balls, cannons, gunpowder; in the disentangling of old knots and the invention of new, in that endless net of deceptions and treacheries, which pleased him, when he was master of it, like a spider in its web, and in which he felt himself now a trapped fly.

Having concluded his business, he set out for the Galleria Bramante, over one of the moats of the Castle of Milan. The night was still,—save that, at times, one heard the sounds of a trumpet, the drawn-out cries of the sentries, the iron scraping of the rusty chains of the drawbridge. The page Ricciardetto brought two torches, placed them in the cast-iron candelabra set in the walls, and offered the Duke a small platter of gold, with finely cut bread thereon. Out from behind a corner of the moat, over the black mirror of the waters, attracted by the light of the torches, white swans swam forth. Leaning with his elbows on the balustrade, he cast pieces of bread in the water and admired the birds as they caught them, soundlessly cleaving the watery mirror with their breasts.

The Marchesa Isabella d'Este, sister of the late Beatrice, had sent as a present these swans out of Mantua, from the still, flat-shored creeks of Mincio, thickly grown with reeds and weeping willows,—a sanctuary for flocks of swans from of old. Moro had always loved these birds; but of late he had become still more passionately attached to them, and every evening fed them with his own hands, which for him was his sole respite from torturing thoughts about his affairs, about war, about politics, about his own treacheries and those of others. The swans recalled to him his childhood, when he was wont to feed them in the same way, on the slumbrous ponds of Vigevano, grown over with greenish scum, as if clothed with a cassock. But here, in the moat of a Castle of Milan, between the ominous turrets, towers, powder magazines, pyramids of cannon-shot, and the maws of cannon, they —silent, pure, white, in the silvery-blue haze of the moon,—seemed still more beautiful. The smooth surface of the water, which reflected the heavens above them, was almost invisible, and, swaying, filled with mystery, they glided, like apparitions, surrounded on all sides with stars, between two heavens,—a heaven above and a heaven below,—equally foreign and akin to both.

A little door behind the Duke creaked, and the head of the chamberlain Pusterla was thrust forth. Bowing respectfully, he approached Moro and handed him a paper.

"What is this?" asked the Duke.

"From the Chief Treasurer, Messer Borgonzio Botto,—a bill for military supplies, for gunpowder and cannon-shot. He apologizes muchly because he is compelled to disturb you. But the pack-train for Mortara sets out at dawn. . . ."

Moro seized the paper, crumpled it up, and threw it from him:

"How many times have I told thee not to be coming to me with any business matters after supper! Oh, Lord, it seems that soon they will give me no rest even in bed at night! . . ."

The chamberlain, without straightening his back, stepped backward to the door, saying in a whisper, so that the Duke might not hear, if he did not choose to:

"Messer Leonardo."

"Ah, yes, Leonardo. Why didst thou not remind me long ago? Ask him in."

And, turning to the swans anew, he reflected:

"Leonardo will not come amiss."

Upon Moro's yellow, bloated face, with its thin, crafty and feral lips, appeared a kindly smile. When the artist had entered the gallery, the Duke, continuing to toss pieces of bread, transferred upon him the same smile with which he had been contemplating the swans. Leonardo was about to bend his knee, but the Duke restrained him, and kissed his head.

"Greetings. 'Tis long since we have seen one another. What dost thou, friend?"

"I must thank Your Highness . . ."

"Eh, enough! Is it of such gifts that thou art worthy? There, now, do but give me time,—I shall know how to reward thee in commensuration with thy services!"

Having entered into conversation with the artist, he asked him about his latest works, inventions, and projects,—purposely picking out such as seemed to the Duke the most impossible, those tinged with the most fairy-tale flavour: the diving bell; the skis for walking on water as over dry land; the human wings. But when Leonardo would lead the talk around to matters of business,—the fortification of the Castle, the Canal of Martesana, the moulding of the monumental Steed,—the Duke would immediately avoid the conversation, with an air of squeamishness and ennui.

Suddenly, becoming engrossed in thought over something, which was a frequent occurrence with him of late, he grew silent, and let his head sink, with an air as far-away and withdrawn as if he had forgotten all about his companion.

Leonardo began saying farewell.

"Well, God be with thee, God be with thee!" the Duke nodded his head to him absent-mindedly. But, when the artist was already in the doorway, he called after him, approached him, laid both hands on his shoulders, and looked into his eyes with a long, sad gaze.

"Farewell," said he, and there was a break in his voice. "Farewell, my Leonardo! Who knows if we shall see each other alone again? . . ."

"Your Highness is leaving us?"

Moro heaved a profound sigh and made no reply.

"So that is how things stand, friend," continued he, after a silence.

"There, now, we have lived together for sixteen years, and never have I received aught but good from thee,—and thou too, 'twould seem, hast seen no ill from me. Let folks say what they will,—but in future ages, whoever shall name Leonardo, will also recall the name of Moro not unkindly!"

The artist, who was not fond of emotional outpourings, pronounced the only words which he stored in his memory against those occasions when courtly eloquence was demanded of him:

"Signor, I fain would have more than one life, that I might devote them all to the service of Your Highness."

"I believe thee," said Moro. "Sometime thou, too, shalt recall me, and feel sorry for me. . . ."

He did not finish, sobbed, embraced him hard, and kissed him.

"Well, God send thee weal, God send thee weal!"

When Leonardo had withdrawn, Moro continued to sit for a long while in the Galleria Bramante, admiring the swans, and within his soul was a feeling which he could not have expressed in any words. It seemed to him that in his shady,—even, perhaps, criminal,—life Leonardo was like to those white swans in the dark waters, in the moat of the Fortress of Milan, among the ominous barbicans, turrets, powder magazines, pyramids of cannon-shot and the maws of cannon,—just as impractical and beautiful, just as pure and virginal.

In the silence of the night one could hear only the slow fall of drops of pitch from the expiring torches. In their rosy light which blended with the light of the blue moon, the swans, like apparitions between two skies—one sky above, one sky below, equally foreign and akin to both,—filled with mystery, surrounded by stars, swaying statelily, dreamt on, with their doubles, in the dark mirror of the waters.

XVI

From the Duke, despite the late hour, Leonardo set out for the monastery of San Francisco, where his sick pupil, Giovanni Beltraffio, was. Four months ago, shortly after his conversation with Cesare about the two depictions of the Lord's countenance, he had been taken ill with brain fever.

That was toward the end of December, fourteen hundred and ninety-eight. Once, having visited his former master, Fra Benedetto, Giovanni had found with him a guest from Florence, the Dominican monk,

Fra Pagolo. At the request of Benedetto and Giovanni, he had told them of the death of Savonarola.

The execution had been set for the twenty-third of May of the same year, at nine o'clock in the morning, on the Piazza of the Signoria, before the Palazzo Vecchio,—the very same spot where the Bonfire of Vanities and the Ordeal of Fire had taken place.

At one end of a long scaffolding was piled up the bonfire; over it towered the gallows,—a thick log, driven into the ground, having a cross-beam, and three nooses and iron chains. Despite the exertions of the carpenters, who fussed for a long while with the cross-beam, now lengthening, now shortening it, the gallows had the form of the Cross.

Just as countless a mob as on the day of the Ordeal swarmed on the Piazza, in the windows, in the loggias, and upon the roofs of the houses. Out of the doors of the Palazzo came the condemned,—Girolamo Savonarola, Domenico Buonvicini, and Silvestro Maruffi. Having made a few steps upon the scaffold, they came to a stop before the tribunal of the Bishop of Bason, the envoy of Pope Alexander VI. The Bishop arose, took Brother Girolamo by the hand, and uttered the words of the excommunication with a faltering voice, without lifting up his eyes to those of the condemned man, who was gazing straight into his face. The concluding words he said incorrectly.

"*Separo te ab Ecclesia militante atque triumphante*. I cut thee off from the Church militant and triumphant."

"*Militante, non triumphante, hoc enim tuum non est*. From the militant, but not triumphant,—that is not within thy power," Savonarola corrected him.

The garments were torn off the excommunicants, leaving them half-naked, in their nether-shirts,—and they went on their way, stopping twice again before the tribune of the apostolic commissars, who read aloud the decision of the Ecclesiastic Court, and before the tribune of the Eight Citizens of the Florentine Republic, who, as representatives of the people, pronounced the sentence of death.

During this last procession, Fra Silvestro almost fell, having made a misstep; Domenico and Savonarola also stumbled; later it was found that the mischievous street gamins, the soldiers of the quondam Holy Army of Little Inquisitors, having made their way beneath the scaffolding, had thrust up stakes between the boards, in order to wound the feet of those going to their execution.

Fra Silvestro Maruffi, the innocent, was to be the first to go up on the scaffold. Preserving his insensible air, as though not realizing what was taking place with him, he clambered up the steps. But when the hangman had put the noose about his neck, he grasped the ladder, raised his eyes up to heaven, and exclaimed:

"Into Thy hands, O Lord, do I give up my spirit!"

Then, himself, without the aid of the hangman, with a reasoning, fearless motion, he jumped off the ladder.

Fra Domenico, awaiting his turn, shifted from foot to foot, in joyous impatience, and, when the sign was given him, darted for the ladder, with the smile of one going straight to Paradise.

Silvestro's corpse hung on one end of the cross-beam; Domenico's, at the other. The middle place awaited Savonarola.

Having ascended the ladder he paused, lowered his eyes, and glanced at the mob.

There fell a silence,—just such a silence as used to fall in the Cathedral of Maria del Fiore, in expectation of his sermon. But, when he had put his head through the noose, some voice cried out:

"Work a miracle, prophet!"

None comprehended whether this was a mockery, or the cry of an insane faith.

The hangman thrust him off the ladder.

The little old artisan, he of the meek, pious face, who had for several hours been watching near the bonfire, just as soon as Brother Girolamo hung limp, hastily crossed himself, and thrust a flaming torch into the faggots, with the very same words with which Savonarola had at one time ignited the Bonfire of Vanities and Anathemas:

"In the name of the Father, the Son, and the Holy Ghost!"

The flame flared up. But the wind blew it aside. The crowd swayed. Crushing one another, people started running, in the grasp of horror. Cries of "A miracle! A miracle! A miracle! They do not burn!" went up.

The wind died down. The flame again rose up and enveloped the corpses. The rope with which Savonarola's hands were tied was burned through,—they became loosened, fell down, seeming to stir in the fire,—and to many it appeared that, for the last time, he had blessed his people.

When the bonfire had died out, and there were left but the charred bones and the scraps of flesh upon the iron chains, the disciples of Savonarola made their way to the gallows through the crowd, being desirous of gathering up the remains of the martyrs. The guards drove them off, dumped the ashes into a cart, and carried them off to the Ponte Vecchio, in order to cast them into the river. But on the way the "snivellers" contrived to seize pinches of the ashes, and particles of the heart of Savonarola,—unconsumed of the fire, 'twould seem.

Having finished his story, Fra Pagolo showed to his auditors a scapulary with the ashes. Fra Benedetto kept on kissing it for a long time and watering it with his tears. Both monks went to the all-night mass. Giovanni was left alone. On their return they found him lying unconscious on the floor before the Crucifix; in his benumbed fingers he was clutching the scapulary.

For three months Giovanni hovered betwixt life and death. Fra Benedetto did not leave him for a minute. Frequently, in the silence of the nights, sitting at the head of the invalid's bed, and hearkening to his delirium, he was horrified. Giovanni raved about Savonarola, Leonardo da Vinci, and the Mother of God, who, drawing geometrical figures with her finger on the sand of the desert, instructed the Infant Christ in the laws of Eternal Necessity.

"What art thou praying about?" the sick man would repeat, with indescribable sadness. "Or dost thou not know, that there is no miracle, that this cup can not pass from thee, just as the straight line between two given points can not be anything but the shortest distance between them?"

He was tortured also by another apparition,—the two faces of the Lord, opposed and similar, like doubles: one, full of human suffering and frailty—the face of Him who, at the distance of a stone's cast, prayed for a miracle; the other face, that of the fearful, foreign, omnipotent and omniscient Word become flesh,—the First Mover. They were facing one another, as two eternal antagonists in single combat. And, even as Giovanni gazed at them intently,—the face of Him that was meek and sorrowful would grow dark, distorted, turning into the demon whom Leonardo had at one time depicted in a caricature of Savonarola, and, exposing his double, he styled him Antichrist . . .

Fra Benedetto saved Beltraffio's life. In the beginning of June in the year fourteen hundred and ninety-nine, when he had recovered to the extent of being able to walk, despite all the supplications and urgings of the monk, Giovanni returned to the atelier of Leonardo.

Toward the end of July of the same year, the army of the French King, Louis XII, under the command of the Seigneurs d'Aubigny, Louis of Luxembourg, and Gian-Giacomo Trivulzio, having crossed the Alps, entered Lombardy.

BOOK TEN

Still Waves

I

SMALL, IRON-BOUND DOOR IN THE NORTH-west tower of the Rocchetta led to a subterranean chamber, set about with oaken chests,—the strong-room of Duke Moro's treasury. Above this door, in the unfinished frescoes of Leonardo, was depicted the god Mercury, resembling an awesome angel. On the first of September, fourteen hundred and ninety-nine, at night, the court treasurer, Ambrogio da Ferrari, and the director of the ducal finances, Borgonzio Botto, were, with their assistants, taking out of this cellar moneys, pearls,—which, like grain, they scooped up with ladles,—and other valuables; putting them away in leathern sacks, and sealing them up; the servants brought them out into the garden and loaded them upon mules. Two hundred and forty bags had been filled; thirty mules had been loaded,—but still the guttering candle-ends lit up in the depths of the boxes heaps of gold pieces.

Moro sat at the entrance to the strong-room of the treasury at a writing stand, cluttered up with account books, and, paying no heed to the work of the treasurers, gazed at the flame of a candle with a meaningless stare.

Since the day when he had received the news of the flight of his chief commander, Signor Galeazzo Sanseverino, and of the approach of the French to Milan, he had become sunk in this strange lethargy.

When all the valuables had been carried out of the vaults, the treasurer asked him if he wished to take with him the gold and silver plate, or to leave it behind. Moro looked at him, frowning, as though making a mental effort to understand what he was saying; but immediately turned away, made a gesture of hopelessness, and again fixed his unmoving gaze on the candle-flame. When Messer Ambrogio repeated his question, the Duke did not hear him at all. The treasurers went away, having failed in eliciting any reply after all their efforts. Moro remained alone.

The old chamberlain, Mariolo Pusterla, announced the arrival of the new commandant of the fortress, Bernardino da Corte. Moro passed his hand over his face, arose, and said:

"Yes, yes, of course,—receive him!"

Cherishing a distrust toward scions of famous lines, he loved to create personalities out of nothing; to make the first last, the last first. Among his grandees were the offspring of stokers, of truck-gardeners, of cooks and muleteers. Bernardino, the son of a court lackey, subsequently the keeper of kitchen accounts, had himself in his youth worn the livery. Moro had elevated him to governmental duties of the first rank, and now bestowed upon him his greatest confidence, entrusting to him the defence of the Castle of Milan, the last stronghold of his power in Lombardy.

The Duke received the new prefect graciously; made him sit down; unrolled before him the plans of the Castle, and began to explain to him the military signals to be used between the contingent in the fortress and the inhabitants of the city: the necessity for quick assistance was designated, by day, by a crooked pruning hook,—at night by three flaming torches,—shown upon the main tower of the Castle; the treachery of the soldiers, by a white bed-sheet, hung out on the Bona of Savoy tower; a shortage of gunpowder, by a chair, let down on a rope from a barbican; a shortage of wine, by a skirt; of bread, by a pair of breeches of black fustian; the need of a doctor, by an earthen night-chamber. Moro had invented these signals himself, and simple-heartedly solaced himself with them, as though in them were now contained all his hope of deliverance.

"Remember, Bernardino," he concluded, "everything has been foreseen; thou hast a sufficiency of everything: money, powder, victuals, firearms; the three thousand mercenaries have been paid beforehand; thou hast in thy hands a fortress that could sustain a siege enduring for three years, but all I ask for is three months, and, if I do not return to deliver thee, do as thou deemest best. There, that is all, methinks. Farewell; May the Lord preserve thee, my son!"

He embraced him in parting.

When the prefect had gone, Moro ordered his page to make his camp bed, said his prayers, lay down, but could not fall asleep. He again lit the candle, took out of his travelling case a packet of papers, and picked out a poem of a rival of Bellincioni's, a certain Antonio Camelli da Pistoia, who had betrayed the Duke, his benevolent patron, and had deserted to the French. In the poem was depicted the war of Moro with France, under the guise of the Winged Serpent of the Sforzas with the ancient Gallic Cock:

I see the warring of the Cock and Serpent:
Beak and fang grappling, like a swirling whirlwind;
The Cock hath now plucked out the Dragon's eye;
The Serpent fain would coil, but can not.
The Cock's talons grasp the maw of the Serpent,
And the Snake squirms about in his pain.
The Reptile shall die, and the Gaul shall reign,—
And he that did himself above high heaven deem,
Shall be despised, not of men only,—the very beasts
Shall spurn him,—e'en the carrion-feeding crow.

Ever hast thou a caitiff been; but only in internecine squabbles,
Did the caitiff heart of thine full manly seem.
For that thou didst its foes into our land invite,
Didst usurp power, thy nephew having robbed,
O Moro, God doth thee with fortune ill pursue,
For which no other leech exists save death;
And when past happiness comes to thy mem'ry's view,
Fully wilt thou, Ludovico, sense,
How the anguish of those is intense
Who say: "We, too, once happiness knew!"

A mournful, and, at the same time, a well-nigh delectable feeling of being wronged, pervaded the heart of Moro. He recalled the recent, servilely fawning hymns of the selfsame Antonio Camelli da Pistoia:

He that beholds thy glory, Moro, turns to stone,
In sacred horror, as from Medusa's visage.—
Sovereign of peace and warring,
Thou dost conculcate heaven with one foot,
Earth with the other.
It doth suffice for thee, our Duke, a finger but to raise,
To make all of Creation turn;
Thou, after God, art first to guide,
The rudder of Creation, the wheel of Fortune.

It was past midnight. The flame of the expiring candle flickered, dying while the Duke still paced back and forth over the gloomy Tower of the Treasury. He meditated on his sufferings, on the injustice of fate, on the ingratitude of men.

"What have I done to them? Wherefore have they grown to hate me? I am a malefactor, a murderer, they say.—But at that rate even Romulus, that did his brother kill, and Cæsar, and Alexander,—all the heroes of antiquity,—are but murderers and malefactors. I was desirous of bestowing upon them a New Age of Gold, such as the nations had not seen since the times of Augustus, Trajan, and Antoninus. A little more,—and under my sovereignty, in a united Italy, the ancient laurels of Apollo, the olives of Pallas would have burst into bloom anew; there would have come a reign of eternal peace, a reign of the Divine Muses. The first among rulers, I sought greatness not in sanguinary exploits, but in the fruits of golden peace,—in enlightenment. Bramante, Paccioli, Caradosso, Leonardo, and how many others! Among most distant posterity, when the troublous din of arms shall have died down, their names shall ring coupled with the name of Sforza. Nor is that all I would have done,—to still a greater height would I, a new Pericles, have reared my new Athens, had it not been for this wild horde of Northern barbarians! Wherefore, O Lord, wherefore?"

His head sunk on his breast, he repeated the stanzas of the poet:

> Fully wilt thou, Ludovico, sense,
> How the anguish of those is intense
> Who say: "We, too, once happiness knew!"

The flame flared up for the last time, lit up the arched vaults of the tower, the god Mercury over the door of the treasury strong-room, —and went out. The Duke shuddered, inasmuch as the extinction of a candle-end was a bad omen. In the darkness, feeling his way, in order not to awaken Ricciardetto, he approached the bed, disrobed, lay down, and this time fell asleep at once.

He dreamt that he was standing on his knees before Madonna Beatrice, who, having just found out about her husband's assignation with Lucrezia, was upbraiding him and slapping his cheeks. He felt the pain, but was not offended; he felt joyous because she was again alive and hale. Submissively putting his face up to her strokes, he sought to catch her little swarthy hands, that he might cling to them with his lips, and he wept,—from love, from regret. But suddenly it was no longer Beatrice who stood before him, but the god Mercury instead,—the same Mercury depicted on Leonardo's fresco above the iron door of the treasure house, in the semblance of an awesome angel. The god had seized him by his hair and shouted: "Foolish fellow, foolish fellow! Wherein dost thou place thy trust? Dost think thy crafty shifts shall help thee,—shall save thee from the punishment of God, thou murderer?"

When he awoke, the light of morning glimmered in the windows. Knights, grandees, militaries, German mercenaries, who were to accompany him to Germany,—about three thousand mounted men, in all,—were waiting for the Duke's exit, on the main alley of the park, and on the highroad leading north,—toward the Alps.

Moro mounted a horse and set out for the monastery of Maria delle Grazie, to pray for the last time at the grave of his wife.

With the first rays of the sun the melancholy train started on its way.

II

Owing to autumnal inclemency, which had spoiled the roads, the journey was protracted for more than two weeks. On the eighteenth of September, late at night, on one of the last stages, the Duke, ailing and tired, decided to spend the night on the heights, in a cave that usually served as a shelter for shepherds. It would have been very difficult to find a more peaceful and convenient sanctuary, but he purposely chose this wild spot for a meeting with an envoy sent to him by the Emperor Maximilian.

The bonfire illuminated the stalactites in the low-hung vaults of the cave. On a camp turn-spit some pheasants were roasting for supper. The Duke was sitting on a travelling stool made out of straps; he was all muffled up, with a warming pan at his feet. At his side, as serene and quiet as always, with an air of domesticity, Madonna Lucrezia was preparing a wash against toothache, of her own invention,—of wine, pepper, cloves, and other strong spicery: the Duke had a toothache.

"Such is the posture of my affairs, Messer Odoardo," he was saying to the Emperor's envoy, consoling himself, not without a secret self-satisfaction, with the magnitude of his own tribulations. "Tell your liege lord where and in what state you met the lawful Duke of Lombardy!"

He was having one of those attacks of sudden talkativeness, which would now occasionally possess him after long silence and lethargy.

"'Foxes have holes, and the birds of the air have nests, but I have not where to lay my head'!"[46]

"Corio," he turned to the court chronicler, "when thou shalt be compiling thy chronicle, mention, also, this lodging in a shepherd's den,

—the last refuge of the descendant of the noble Sforzas, of the line of Anglus the Trojan the companion of Æneas!"

"Signor, your misfortunes deserve the pen of a new Tacitus!" remarked Odoardo.

Lucrezia handed the mouth wash to the Duke. He glanced at her and was lost in admiration. Pale, fresh, in the rosy reflected glow of the flame, with smooth black hair combed over the ears, with a brilliant on the thin thread of a *ferroniera* in the middle of her brow, she was regarding him with a smile of maternal tenderness, somewhat from under her brows, with her innocent eyes—attentive, stern and grave, like those of a child.

"O my darling! There is one that will not betray, will not be faithless," reflected the Duke, and, having finished gargling, commanded:

"Corio, write it down: 'In the furnace of great sufferings is true friendship proven, even as gold in fire.'"

Ianacci, the dwarf jester, approached Moro:

"Gossip dear,—oh, gossip dear!" he began speaking, settling down at the Duke's feet and slapping the latter's knee friendlily. "Prithee, why so downcast,—just like a mouse that hath a grievance against grain? Cast thy troubles from thee,—truly, do."

"There is a remedy for every ill, save death. Then, too, it must be said: 'tis better to be a living ass than a dead emperor.—Saddles!" he suddenly began to shout, pointing to a heap of harness, lying on the floor. "Look, now, gossip dear,—asses' saddles!"

"Whatever hast thou found to rejoice about in that?" asked the Duke.

"There is an ancient little fable, Moro! 'Twould not come amiss to mind thee of it. Dost want me to?—I shall tell it thee."

"Tell on, an it please thee."

The dwarf jumped up, till all the little bells upon him were a-jangle, and brandished his jester's wand, at the end of which hung a bladder filled with dried pease.

"Once upon a time there lived and had his being, at the court of King Alfonso of Naples, one Giotto, a painter. One day the sovereign ordered him to depict his reign on the wall of the castle. Giotto drew an ass, which, having on its back a saddle with a kingly device (a golden crown and sceptre), is sniffing another saddle, a new one, lying at its feet, with the same device. 'What doth this signify?' asked Alfonso. 'This is your people, sire,—not a day passeth but that they long for a new ruler,' the painter answered. And there thou hast my whole little fairy-tale, gossip dear. Though I be a fool, still mark thou my word: the French saddle, which the Milanese are now a-sniffing of, will gall their back right soon enough,—let but the little ass have his pleasure of it for a while, and the old shall again appear new; the new,—old."

"*Stultu aliquando sapientes*. The foolish are at times wise," said the Duke with a sad smile. "Corio, write it down—"

But this time he was not fated to utter any *memorabilia:* at the entrance to the cave the snorting of a horse was heard, the stamping of hoofs, and muffled voices. Mariolo Pusterla, the chamberlain, ran in with a frightened face, and whispered something in the ear of the chief secretary, Bartolomeo Calco.

"What has happened?" asked Moro.

All became quiet.

"Your Highness. . . ." the secretary essayed to speak, but his voice broke, and, without finishing, he turned away.

"Signor," said Luigi Marliani, approaching Moro, "may the Lord preserve Your Highness! Be prepared for all things,—bad news. . . ."

"Say on, say on!" exclaimed Moro, and suddenly blanched.

Near the mouth of the cavern, among the soldiers and courtiers, he beheld a man in tall leather boots, bespattered with mud. Everybody made way for him, in silence. The Duke pushed Messer Luigi away from him, darted toward the messenger, snatched the letter from his hands, opened it, ran it through, cried out, and fell straight back. Pusterla and Marliani barely managed to catch him in time.

Borgonzio Botto informed Moro that, on the seventeenth of September, on St. Satyr's day, the traitor Bernardino da Corte had surrendered the Castle of Milan to the French King's marshal, Gian-Giacomo Trivulzio.

The Duke was fond of, and had thoroughly mastered, swooning. At times he would resort to this device, as a bit of diplomatic craft. But on this occasion his swoon was not a pretended one.

For a long time they could not restore him to consciousness. Finally he opened his eyes, heaved a sigh, raised himself up, piously made the sign of the cross, and uttered:

"From Judas until our day there has never been a greater traitor than Bernardino da Corte!"

And on that day he uttered not another word.

Several days later, in the city of Innsbruck, where the Emperor Maximilian graciously received Moro, on a late hour at night, all alone with his chief secretary, Bartolomeo Calco, as he paced one of the chambers in the Palace of the Kaiser, the Duke was composing confidential epistles for the envoys whom he was despatching in secret to the Sultan of the Turks at Constantinople.

The old secretary's face bore no other expression save that of attention. The pen submissively scurried over the paper, barely keeping up with the rapid speech of the Duke.

"Remaining ever firm and steadfast in our good intentions and disposition toward Your Majesty, but especially so now, and putting our trust in the magnanimous aid of the Sovereign of the Ottoman Empire in the regaining of our realm, we have decided to despatch three couriers, by three different routes, in order that one of them at the least, may carry out our instructions."

Further on the Duke complained to the Sultan against Pope Alexander VI:

"The Pope, being by his very nature perfidious and evil . . ."

The dispassionate quill of the secretary came to a rest. His eyebrows arched, the skin of his forehead wrinkled up, as he made sure by asking, thinking that he had not heard aright:

"The Pope?"

"Well, yes, yes. Write as fast as thou canst."

The secretary bent his head still nearer to the paper, and the quill began to scrape anew:

"The Pope, as Your Highness knows, being by his very nature, perfidious and evil, has incited the King of France to undertake an expedition against Lombardy. . . ."

The victories of the French were described:

"Having received tidings thereof, we were seized with fear, and deemed it a blessing to withdraw to the Emperor Maximilian, in the expectation of Your Majesty's aid. All have betrayed and deceived us, but, most of all, Bernardino . . ."

At this name his voice began to tremble:

"Bernardino da Corte,—a viper warmed over our very heart, showered with our favours and generosities, who yet has sold us, like Judas. . . . However,—no, bide a while, say you naught of Judas," Moro stopped himself, remembering that he was writing to an infidel Turk.

Having depicted his misfortunes, he implored the Sultan to fall upon

Venice both by sea and by land, promising him certain victory and the annihilation of the age-old foe of the Ottoman Empire, the Republic of San Marco.

"And may it be known to Your Majesty," he concluded the epistle, "that in this war, as in every other enterprise, all that we possess belongeth to Your Majesty, who will scarce find in all Europe a more powerful and faithful ally."

He approached the table, was about to add something, but merely made a gesture of resignation and sank into an arm-chair.

Bartolomeo sprinkled the last page, not yet dry, with sand out of the sand-box. Suddenly he lifted up his eyes and looked at his sovereign: the Duke, having covered his face with his hands, was weeping. His back, his shoulders, his plump double-chin, his bluish clean-shaven jowls, his smooth hair-dress—the *zazzera*—were helplessly quivering from his sobs.

"Wherefore, wherefore? Where, then, is Thy Truth, O Lord?"

Turning toward the secretary his puckered-up face, at this moment resembling the face of a tearful old country-wife, he managed to babble out:

"Bartolomeo, I trust thee; tell me then,—tell me, according to thy conscience,—am I right or no?"

"Does Your Grace grasp the significance of the embassy to the Turks?"

Moro nodded his head. The old politician meditatively arched up his eyebrows, thrust out his lips, and again the skin on his forehead became wrinkled.

"Of course, on the one hand, when one is in Rome one must do as the Romans; but on the other. . . . May I venture to submit to Your Highness,—what if we were to wait?"

"Out of the question!" exclaimed Moro. "Long enough have I waited! I shall show them that they can not throw the Duke of Milan out of the game, like an unnecessary pawn; inasmuch as,—dost see, my friend?—when he that is in the right is wronged, even as I have been, who shall durst judge him if he turn for help not only to the Grand Turk, but to the very devil?"

"Your Highness," spoke the secretary ingratiatingly, "must we not apprehend that the invasion of Europe by the Turks may have unexpected consequences . . . for the Christian Church, for example?"

"Oh, Bartolomeo, dost thou really think that I have not foreseen this? I would far rather have agreed to die a thousand times than cause any harm to our Holy Mother the Church. God preserve me!

"Thou dost not yet know all my projects," he added, with his former crafty and feral smile. "Just thou bide thy time,—we shall cook such a mess of porridge, shall weave our enemies about with such nets, that they shall not be able to see God's light! One thing I will tell thee: the Grand Turk is but a tool in my hands. The time will come, —and we shall destroy him, shall eradicate the infidel sect of Mahomet, shall liberate the Sepulchre of the Lord from the yoke of the paynim!"

Making no reply, Bartolomeo despondently lowered his eyes.

"He is in a bad way," he reflected, "altogether in a bad way! He is sunk in dreams. What politics can there be here?"

On this night, with ardent faith and hope in the aid of the Grand Turk, the Duke prayed long before his favourite icon, the work of Leonardo da Vinci, wherein the Mother of God was portrayed in the guise of the beautiful concubine of Moro, the Countess Cecilia Bergamini.

III

Some ten days before the surrender of the Castle of Milan, Marshal Trivulzio, to the joyous shouts of the people: "France! France!" and to the pealing of bells, had ridden into Milan, as into a vanquished city.

The entry of the King was set for the sixth of October. The citizens were preparing a triumphant reception.

For the festal procession the trade syndics had gotten out of the cathedral sacristy two angels that, fifty years ago, even in the times of the Ambrosian Republic, had represented the geniuses of the people's liberty. The decrepit springs, which caused the gilded wings to move, had become weakened. The syndics gave them to be repaired to the erstwhile ducal mechanic, Leonardo da Vinci.

At this period Leonardo was occupied with the invention of a new flying machine. Early one morning, while it was still dark, he was sitting at his designs and mathematical calculations. The light, reed framework of the wings, drawn over with taffeta, resembling a membrane, did not recall a bat, like the former machine, but a gigantic swallow. One of the wings was ready, and slender, pointed, extraordinarily beautiful, reared from the floor to the ceiling, while below, in its shadow, Astro fussed with straightening out the broken springs in the wooden wings of the angels of the Milan Community.

This time Leonardo had resolved to follow as nearly as possible the structure of feathered bodies, in which Nature herself gives to man a model of a flying machine. He still had hopes of resolving the miracle of flight into the laws of mechanics. Evidently, all that it was possible to know, he knew, yet, notwithstanding, he felt that there was in flight a mystery unresolvable into any laws of mechanics. Again, as in his former attempts, he approached that which divides the creation of nature from the work of human hands, the structure of the living body from the dead machine, and it seemed to him that he strove toward the unattainable.

"Well, glory be to God, 'tis done!" exclaimed Astro, winding up the springs.

The angels began to wave their heavy wings. A breeze passed through the room,—and the thin, light wing of the gigantic swallow stirred, rustled, as though alive. The smith glanced at it with inexpressible tenderness.

"How much time, now, has been wasted upon these dummies!" he grumbled, indicating the angels. "Well, but now, do as ye will, master, I shall not step out of here till I finish the wings. The plan for the tail, please."

"'Tis not ready, Astro. Bide a while,—it must be mulled over."

"How is that, then, messer? You did promise it for the day before yesterday. . . ."

"No help for it, friend. Thou knowest, the tail of our bird is the rudder. Here, if there be even the tiniest error, everything is lost."

"Well, well, you know best. I shall wait, but in the meanwhile the second wing. . . ."

"Astro," said the master, "thou shouldst wait. Or else I fear me that there might be something else to be changed. . . ."

The smith made no reply. He cautiously lifted up and started turning the framework of reeds, drawn over with a network of cords made of ox sinews. Then, suddenly facing about toward Leonardo, he uttered in a stifled, trembling voice:

"Master, eh, master, do you not be angry with me, now, but should you, with your calculations, again arrive at the conclusion that with this machine also one can not fly,—I shall fly off anyway, in the teeth of your mechanics,—yea, yea,—I can endure it no more; I have no strength left! For I know,—if this time also . . ."

He did not finish and turned away. Leonardo looked attentively at his dull and obstinate face, with broad cheek-bones,—a face which bore the fixed expression of a single insane and all engulfing thought.

"Messer," concluded Astro, "better say straight off,—will we fly, or will we not?" There was such fear and such hope in his words, that Leonardo had not the spirit to tell him the truth.

"Of course," he answered, abashed, "one can not know without making an experiment; but methinks, Astro, that fly we will. . . ."

"Well, that sufficeth, that sufficeth!" the smith enraptured began to brandish his arms. "I want to hear naught more! If you, too, say so,—it means that we shall fly!" He wanted to restrain himself, but could not, and burst into happy, childlike laughter.

"What art thou laughing about?" Leonardo was curious.

"Forgive me, messer. I am always bothering you. Well, 'tis for the last time,—I shall not do it any more. . . . Would you believe it, whenever I think upon the Milanese, upon the French, upon Duke Moro, or the King,—well, then, I am touched, 'tis both funny and sad; they creep, the poor little mites, they fight, and they too, I will wager, think they are doing mighty things,—the crawling worms, the wingless pismires! And none of them knoweth what a miracle is preparing. . . . Just you imagine, master, how their eyes will pop, how their mouths will gape, when they shall behold the winged ones, flying through the air. For these shall be no wooden angels, that wave their wings for the amusement of the rabble! They shall behold, yet not believe their eyes, thinking them gods. Well, now, to be sure, they will not take *me* for a god,—a devil, sooner; but you, now, with wings, would verily be a god. Or, mayhap, they may say: 'Antichrist!' And they shall be awe-stricken, shall fall down and worship you. And you will do with them as you will. 'Tis my supposition, master, that there will be no more wars then, nor laws, nor masters, nor slaves,—all things shall change, all things new shall come,—such as we durst not even as much as think of now. And nations shall be united, and, soaring on wings, like to choirs of angels, shall chant forth the one hosanna. . . . Oh, Messer Leonardo! Lord, Lord! Can it really be true, now?"

He spoke as if in delirium.

"Poor fellow!" reflected Leonardo. "How he believes! Likely as not he may really go out of his head. Yet what am I to do with him? How tell him the truth?"

At this moment a loud knocking was heard at the outer door of the house; then voices, steps, and, finally, the same knocking at the locked doors of the workroom.

"Whomever does the foul one bring now? There is no perdition for them!" muttered the smith wrathfully. "Who is there? You can not see the master. He has left Milan."

"'Tis I, Astro! 'Tis I,—Luca Paccioli. For God's sake, open quick!"

The smith opened the door and let the monk enter.

"What ails you, Fra Luca?" asked the artist, scrutinizing the frightened face of Paccioli.

"There is naught the matter with me, Messer Leonardo,—however, with me also, but more of that later, but now . . . Oh, Messer Leonardo! . . . Your Colossus. . . . The Gascon halberdiers. . . . I am but come from the Castello, and have seen it with my own eyes,—the French are demolishing your Steed. . . . Let us run, let us run, quick!"

"Wherefore?" calmly retorted Leonardo,—save that his face paled slightly. "What could we do?"

"What mean you? Gracious! For you are not going to sit here with folded hands, the while your greatest creation is perishing! I have a way of reaching Ser de la Trémouille. We must pull wires. . . ."

"It is all the same,—we shall not get there in time," said the artist.

"We shall, we shall! We shall set out straight ahead, over the truck gardens, over the wattled fence. Only be quick!"

Dragged by the monk, Leonardo left the house, and they set off almost at a run to the Castle of Milan.

On the way Fra Luca told him of his own misfortune: the night before the *lands-knechte* had ransacked the cellar of the Canonica of San Simpliciano, where Paccioli dwelt,—had become blind drunk, started rioting, and, finding in one of the cells the crystal forms of geometrical bodies, had taken them for the devilish inventions of black magic, for "crystals of divination," and had smashed them to smithereens.

"Well, now, what harm," bewailed Paccioli, "what harm did my innocent little crystals do them?"

Entering the square of the Castle, they saw near the main South Gates, on the drawbridge of Battiponte, near the Torre di Filarete, a young French dandy, surrounded with a retinue.

"Maître Gilles!" exclaimed Fra Luca, and explained to Leonardo that this Maître Gilles was a fowler, a so-called "wood-hen caller," who instructed the siskins, crows, parrots, and black-birds of his most

Christian Majesty the King of the French, in singing, speaking, and other such arts,—a by no means unimportant personage at the court. Rumours were current that in France it was not only the crows that danced to the tune of Maître Gilles's pipe. Paccioli had already for long been thinking of presenting him with his works, *Divine Proportion* and *The Sum of Arithmetic*, in luxurious bindings.

"Please do not put yourself to any trouble over me, Fra Luca," said Leonardo. "Go you to Maître Gilles; I shall be able to do whatever is necessary by myself."

"Nay, I shall go to him later," said Paccioli, in confusion. "Or else, —know you what? I shall fly for an instant to Maître Gilles; I shall but enquire as to his destination, and come right back to you. But in the meanwhile do you go on straight to Ser de la Trémouille. . . ."

Picking up the skirts of his small brown cassock, the nimble monk's little bare feet twinkled, beating a fast tattoo with their *zoccoli*, and he started running and hopping after the Whistler to the King's Wood-hens.

Through the portcullis of the Battiponte Leonardo entered the Field of Mars,—the inner courtyard of the Castle of Milan.

IV

THE morning was foggy. The bonfires were dying out. The square and the buildings surrounding it, cluttered up with cannon, cannon-shot, camp impedimenta, sacks of oats, heaps of straw, piles of manure, —were all turned into one enormous barracks, stable, and inn. Around the camp shops and the kitchen rotisseries, about the kegs, empty and full, overturned, serving as gaming tables, was a hubbub of cries, laughter, oaths, polyglot profanity, blasphemies, and drunken songs. At times everything would become hushed, as the commanders passed by; the drum rolled, the trumpets of the Rhenish and the Suabian *lands-knechte* blared; the Alpine horns of the mercenaries from the free cantonments of Uri and Unterwalden went off into trills of melancholy shepherd strains. Making his way into the middle of the square, the artist beheld his Colossus, almost untouched. The Great Duke, the conqueror of Lombardy, Francesco Attendollo Sforza, with a bald head that resembled a Roman emperor's, with an expression of leonine power and vulpine cunning, sat as of yore on his steed, that reared up on its hind legs and trampled a fallen warrior with its hoofs.

Arquebusiers of Suabia, archers of Graubünden, slingmen of Picardy, arbalesters of Gascony were crowded around the statue and shouting, understanding one another but illy and supplementing their speech with bodily gestures, through which Leonardo surmised that their discussion dealt with the forthcoming contest of two marksmen, a Frenchman and a German. They were bound to shoot, in turn, at a distance of fifty paces, after drinking four mugs of strong wine. The wart on the cheek of the Colossus was to serve as a mark.

They paced off the distance, and threw lots as to which was to shoot first. A wench poured out the wine. The German drained off, without stopping for breath, one after the other, the four mugs agreed upon, drew apart, took aim, let fly,—and missed. The arrow scraped the cheek, knocking off the edge of the left ear, but leaving the birth-mark untouched.

The Frenchman had just put his arbalest up to his shoulder, when a commotion took place in the crowd. The soldiers drew apart, letting a train of gorgeous heralds, who accompanied a knight, pass through. He rode by, paying no attention to the pastime of the marksmen.

"Who is he?" Leonardo asked of a slingman standing beside him.

"Ser de la Trémouille."

"'Tis still not too late!" reflected the artist. "I ought to run after him and ask him to intercede. . . ."

Yet he remained stock-still, feeling such an inability to action, such an insuperable lethargy and weakening of the will, that it seemed to him, even if at that moment his life depended upon it, he would not have stirred a finger. Fear, shame, revulsion possessed him, at the mere thought of his having to jostle his way through a throng of lackeys, of hostlers,—and running after the noble, like Luca Paccioli.

The Gascon let fly. The arrow whizzed and sank into the birth-mark.

"*Bigorre! Bigorre! Montjoie Saint Denis!*" shouted the soldiers, waving their berets. "France has won!"

The marksmen surrounded the Colossus, and continued their contest. Leonardo would have gone away, but, frozen to the spot, as if in a frightful and absurd nightmare, he looked on resignedly at the destruction of the creation of the sixteen best years of his life,—perhaps the greatest work of sculpture since the times of Praxiteles and Phidias.

Under the hail of bullets, arrows and stones the clay was sifting down in fine sand and large lumps, and blew away into dust, exposing the tie-rods, just like the bones of an iron skeleton. The sun came out from behind the clouds. In the joyous spatter of glistening light the ruin of the Colossus seemed still more pitiful, with its beheaded trunk of the hero on a steed without legs, with a fragment of the regal sceptre held in a hand that had escaped destruction, and its inscription below, on the pediment: *Ecce Deus!*—Behold the God!

At this juncture the chief military commander of the French King, the old Marshal Gian-Giacomo Trivulzio, passed through the square. Glancing at the Colossus, he stopped in amazement; after another look, shielding his eyes from the sun with his hand, he turned around to those in his train and asked:

"What is all this?"

"Monseigneur," one of his lieutenants answered fawningly, "Captain George Cokeburn has given the arbalesters permission, on his own authority . . ."

"The monument of the Sforza!" exclaimed the marshal. "The creation of Leonardo da Vinci,—a target for Gascon marksmen! . . ."

He walked up to the throng of soldiers, who had become so engrossed with the shooting that they were oblivious to aught else, seized a Picardian slingman by the scruff of his neck, threw him down on the ground, and burst into infuriated cursing.

The old marshal's face turned purple; the sinews of his neck swelled up.

"Monseigneur!" mumbled the soldier, standing on his knees, his whole body quaking. "Monseigneur, we did not know. . . . Captain Cokeburn. . . ."

"You wait, you sons of dogs," Tribulzio shouted, "I will show you Captain Cokeburn; I'll truss up every one of you! . . ."

There was the flash of a sabre. He swung it back and would have struck, had not Leonardo with his own left hand seized the old man's a little above the wrist, with such force that the brazen hilt was crushed flat.

Vainly trying to free his hand, the marshal gave Leonardo a look of amazement.

"Who is this?" he asked.

"Leonardo da Vinci," the latter replied calmly.

"How dost thou dare!" the old man just began, in fury, but, meeting the serene gaze of the artist, became silent.

"So thou art Leonardo," he said, scrutinizing his face intently. "My hand,—let my hand go, now. Thou hast bent the hilt. There is strength for you! Well, comrade, i' faith thou art a brave fellow . . ."

"Monseigneur, I beseech you, be not wroth,—forgive them!" said the artist, respectfully.

The marshal looked into his face still more attentively, smiled, and shook his head:

"What a strange fellow! They have destroyed thy best creation,—and thou art interceding for them?"

"Your Excellency, even if you were to hang every man jack of them, what would that avail me or my creation? They know not what they do."

The old man pondered. Suddenly, his face cleared up; a kindly feeling sparkled in his small, intelligent eyes.

"Hearken, Leonardo, there is one thing I can make nor head nor tail of. How is it thou didst stand there and look on? Why didst thou not let us know, why didst thou not complain to me or to Ser de la Trémouille? By the bye, he must have just passed by here? . . ."

Leonardo cast down his eyes, and said, stammering and turning red, just as though he were at fault:

"I did not have time . . . I could not have recognized Ser de la Trémouille's face . . ."

"What a pity," concluded the old man, looking around at the ruin. "I would have sacrificed a hundred of my best men for thy Colossus!"

Returning home, and having crossed the bridge with the elegant loggia of Bramante, where the last meeting of Moro and Leonardo had taken place, the artist saw the French pages and hostlers amusing themselves with a hunt of the tame swans, the favourites of the Duke of Milan. The mischief-makers were shooting with bows and arrows. In the narrow moat completely enclosed with high walls, the swans darted about in wild terror. Among the white down and feathers, upon the black water, floated, swaying, their blood-stained bodies. One swan, just wounded, with a piercing, piteous cry, its long neck arched, was quivering with its enfeebled wings, as though it were trying to soar up before dying.

Leonardo turned away, and went past as fast as he could. It seemed to him that he himself resembled this swan.

V

On Sunday, the sixth of October, Louis XII, the King of France, rode into Milan through the Ticine Gates. In the retinue accompanying him was Cæsar Borgia, Duke of Valentino, the son of the Pope. During the procession from the Square of the Cathedral to the Castle, the angels of the commune of Milan duly waved their wings.

Since the day when the Colossus had been demolished, Leonardo had no more reverted to his work on the flying machine. Astro was finishing the appliance by himself. The artist had not the courage to tell him that these wings, also, were useless. Apparently avoiding the master, the smith also would not broach the subject of the forthcoming flight, —merely glancing at him occasionally with mute reproach in his single eye, in which burned a despondent, insane fire.

One morning, toward the end of the month, Paccioli came running to Leonardo with the tidings that the King demanded his presence at the Palace. The artist went unwillingly. Alarmed by the vanishing of the wings, he feared lest Astro, having gotten it into his head to fly at any cost, might come to grief.

When Leonardo entered the halls of the Rocchetta, so memorable to him, Louis XII was giving audience to the elders and syndics of Milan. The artist glanced at his future ruler, the King of France. There was nothing regal about his outward appearance,—a puny, weak body; narrow shoulders, a chest sunken in, a face with ugly wrinkles,—suffering, but not ennobled by suffering,—flat, everyday, with an expression of bourgeois virtue.

On the top step of the throne stood a young man of some twenty years, in a simple black garment devoid of any ornaments, save several pearls on the brim of his beret, and a golden chain made of the shells of the Order of Saint Archangel Michael; he had long, fair hair, a tiny beard, slightly parted, of dark auburn, an even pallor on his face, and dark blue, amiably intelligent eyes.

"Tell me, Fra Luca," whispered the artist in the ear of his companion, "who is this noble?"

"The son of the Pope," answered the monk, "Cæsar Borgia, the Duke of Valentino."

Leonardo had heard of the evil deeds of Cæsar. Although there were no palpable proofs, no one doubted that he had slain his brother, Giovanni Borgia, having wearied of being the younger, and desirous of casting off the cardinal's purple and inheriting the title of the Commander—Gonfaloniere—of the Church. There were rumours current still more unbelievable,—that, seemingly, the cause of this evil deed of Cain was the rivalry of the brothers not only in the matter of paternal favours, but also because of an incestuous lust for their own sister, Madonna Lucrezia.

"Impossible!" reflected Leonardo, regarding his calm face, his innocent eyes.

Having probably felt upon him the artist's intent gaze, Cæsar looked around; then, leaning toward an old man of benign mien standing beside him, in a long, dark garment,—probably his secretary,—he whispered something to him, indicating Leonardo, and, when the old man had answered him, bestowed an intent look on the artist. An exquisite smile, somewhat tinged with mockery, glided over the lips of Valentino. And, at the same instant, Leonardo sensed:

"Yes, it is possible,—everything is possible,—and things even worse than those reputed to him!"

The elder of the syndics, having ended his wearisome reading, approached the throne, got down on his knees, and offered up a petition to the King. Louis accidentally dropped the parchment roll. The elder began bustling, desirous of picking it up. But Cæsar, forestalling him, with a quick and dexterous movement picked up the roll and gave it to the King with a bow.

"The swine!" someone whispered maliciously behind Leonardo, in the throng of French grandees. "He is glad of the chance, and has thrust himself forward!"

"You speak truly, messer," another chimed in. "The son of the Pope fulfills excellently the post of a lackey. If you would but see how he, of a morning, waits on the King when His Majesty is dressing,—warming his shirt, and all. He would not balk at cleaning his stable, methinks?"

The artist noted the fawning action of Cæsar, but to him it appeared appalling rather than base,—like the treacherous caress of a feral animal.

All this time Paccioli was pulling wires, excited, pushing his companion by the elbow, but seeing that Leonardo, with his usual bashfulness, would, as lief as not, spend the whole day standing in the crowd, without finding an occasion to attract the attention of the King,—he took decisive measures, seized him by the hand, and, bending himself all up, with a rapid, unceasing whistling and sibilation of superlatives—*stupendissimo*, *prestantissimo*, *invicissimo*,—presented the artist to the King.

Louis began speaking of The Last Supper; he praised the depiction of the Apostles, but most of all was he enraptured by the perspective of the ceiling. Fra Luca expected the King at any minute to invite Leonardo to his service. But a page entered and handed to the King a letter just received from France. The King recognized the writing of his wife, his beloved Anne of Brittany,—the letter brought news of the Queen's confinement.

The nobles began to felicitate him. The throng pushed Leonardo and Paccioli away. The King did look at them, recalled them, was about to say something, but at once forgot again, graciously invited the ladies to drink with all speed to the health of the newly born girl, and went out into another hall.

Paccioli, seizing his companion by the hand, started dragging him in tow.

"Hasten! Hasten!"

"Nay, Fra Luca," calmly retorted Leonardo. "I thank you for your troubles; but I shall not remind him of myself: His Majesty hath no time for me now."

And he went out of the Castle.

On the drawbridge of Battiponte, in the South Gates of the Castello, Messer Agapito, the secretary of CæsarBorgia, caught up with him. He offered him, in the name of the Duke, the post of "Chief Architect,"—the same position that Leonardo had filled with Moro.

The artist promised to give him an answer in a few days.

Approaching his house, he noticed, still from afar, a crowd of people, and hastened his steps. Giovanni, Marco, Salaino and Cesare were carrying,—probably for lack of a litter,—on an enormous, rumpled, torn and broken wing of the new flying machine, that was like the wing of a gigantic swallow, their comrade, the smith Astro da Peretola, in torn, bloodied clothing, with a deathly pale face. That which the master had feared had happened: the smith had decided to test the wings, had flown off, made two or three flutters with the wings, had fallen, and would have been killed, had not one of the wings of the machine caught on the branches of a tree growing nearby.

Leonardo helped to carry the improvised litter into the house and carefully put the sick man into bed. When he bent over him, in order to inspect his wounds, Astro came to himself, and whispered, looking at Leonardo with infinite supplication:

"Forgive me, master!"

VI

In the beginning of November, after the magnificent festivals in honour of the newly born girl, Louis XII, having accepted from the Milanese the oath of allegiance and having appointed as his viceregent in Lombardy Marshal Trivulzio, departed for France.

A mass of thanksgiving to the Holy Ghost was said in the Cathedral. Quiet had been established in the city,—but merely an apparent quiet; the people hated Trivulzio for his cruelty and treacherousness. The partisans of Moro incited the rabble, spreading libellous letters. Those who had but recently accompanied his exile with jeers and curses now recalled him as the best of rulers.

Toward the end of January, a crowd near the Ticine Gates had wrecked the counters of the French collector of duties. On the very same day, at the Villa Laderago, near Pavia, a French soldier had attempted the honour of a young village girl of Lombardy. Defending herself, she struck the offender on the face with a besom. The soldier threatened her with an axe. In answer to her cries, her father had come running with a stick. The Frenchman killed the old man. A crowd gathered and put the Frenchman to death. The French fell upon the men of Lombardy, massacred a great number of the people, and devastated the little village. In Milan this news acted precisely as a spark falling in gunpowder. The people dammed up the squares, streets, marketplaces, with cries of fury;

"Down with the King! Down with the viceroy! Kill! Kill the French! Long live Moro!"

Trivulzio had far too few men to offer resistance to the population of a city of three hundred thousand. Putting cannon up in the tower which temporarily was serving as belfry for the Cathedral, he directed their mouths against the crowd, gave orders to shoot at the first sign, and, desirous of making a last attempt at peace, went out to the people. The rabble well-nigh killed him, drove him into the Town Hall, and here he would have perished, had not a division of Swiss mercenaries hastened to his succour from the fortress, led by their Captain, Coursainge.

There followed arsons, murders, robberies, tortures and punishments

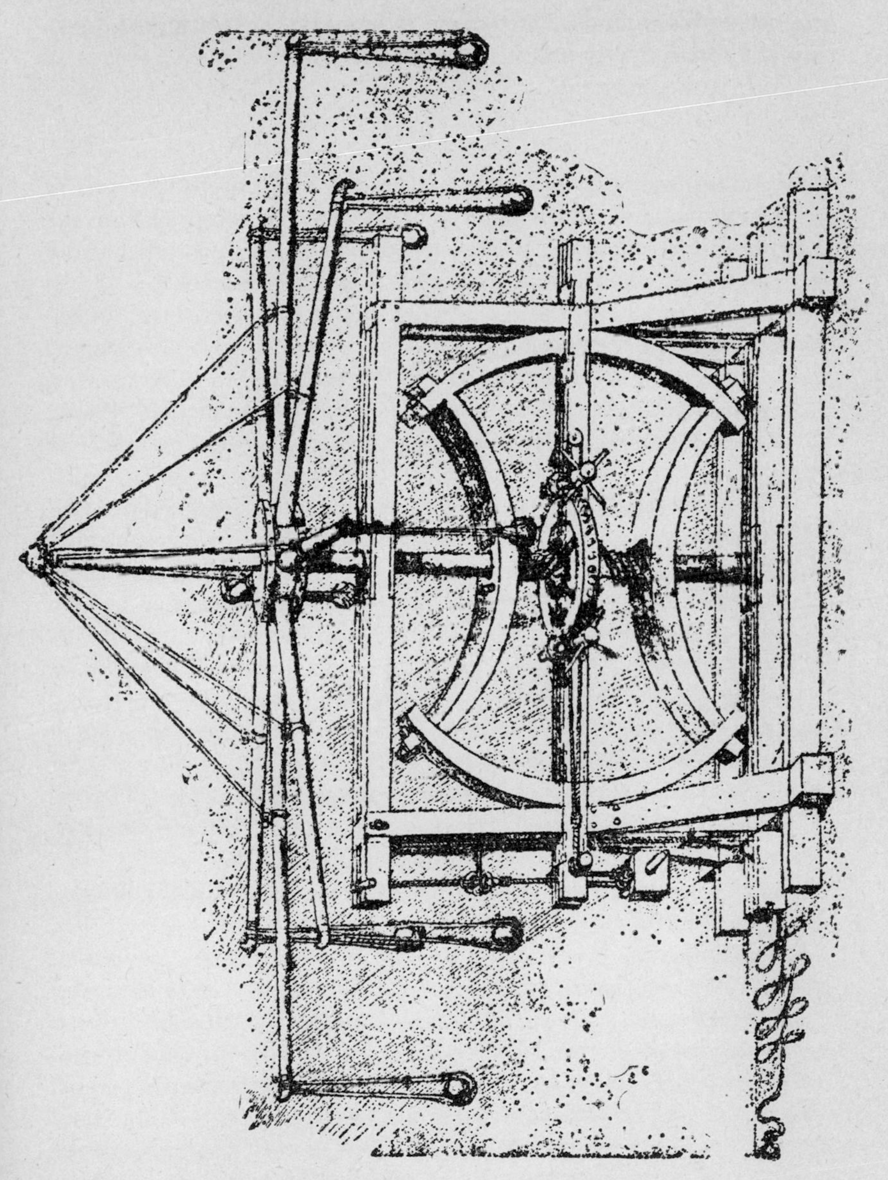

of all Frenchmen who fell into the clutches of the mob, and of those citizens who were suspected of sympathizing with the French. On the night of the first of February, Trivulzio secretly evacuated the fortress, leaving it under the protection of Captain D'Espi and of Codebecar. On the same night Moro, returning from Germany, was joyously received by the inhabitants of the city of Como. The citizens of Milan awaited him as a deliverer.

During the last days of the riot Leonardo, apprehensive of the cannon-shot, which had destroyed several neighbouring houses, had moved into his cellar, skillfully laying his chimneys through, building hearths and several living chambers. As if into a little fortress, everything of value in the house was carried over, paintings, drawings, manuscripts, books, scientific instruments.

At this period he resolved definitely to enter the service of Cæsar Borgia. But, before departing for Romagna (where, according to the conditions of the agreement entered into with Messer Agapito, Leonardo was supposed to arrive not later than the summer months of the year fifteen hundred), he intended to pay a flying visit to his old friend, Girolamo Melzi, at the latter's lonely Villa Vaprio near Milan, and bide his time till the parlous days of war and lawlessness would pass.

On the morning of the second of February, on Candlemas, Fra Luca Paccioli came running to the artist and announced that there was an inundation in the Castle, the Milanese Luigi da Porto, who had been in the service of the French, had deserted to the rebels and had at night opened the sluices of the canals which filled the moats of the fortress. The water had spread, had flooded the mill in the park beside the wall of the Rocchetta, had penetrated into the cellars, where the powder, oil, grain, wine and other supplies were kept; so that, had not the French succeeded after great difficulty in saving from the water a certain part of them, hunger would have compelled them to surrender the fortress, which was the very thing Messer Luigi had reckoned on. During the inundation the canals in the neighbourhood of the Castle in the low-lying suburbs of the Vercellina Gates had overflowed their banks and had flooded the swampy region where the monastery of Maria delle Grazie was located. Fra Luca imparted to the artist his fears of the water damaging The Last Supper, and proposed that they go to see if the painting be whole.

With an assumed indifference Leonardo retorted that he had no time just then, and that he had no fear for The Last Supper,—the picture, 'twould seem, was at such a height that the dampness could do it no hurt. But, just as soon as Paccioli was gone, Leonardo hastened to the monastery.

Entering the refectory, he beheld dirty puddles on the brick floor, —the traces of the inundation. There was a smell of dampness. One of the monks said that the water had risen to a quarter of an ell.

Leonardo went up to the wall containing The Last Supper.

The colours remained, apparently, clear.

Tender, transparent,—not water-colours, as is usual in mural paintings, but of oil, they were of his own invention. He had prepared the wall also in an especial manner: he had covered it over with a layer of clay and of juniper lacquer and drying oil; over the base first coating he had applied a second,—of mastic, pitch and gypsum. Painters of experience predicted the impermanence of oil colours upon a damp wall built up in a swampy lowland. But Leonardo with his usual passion for new experiments, for untried paths in art, persisted, paying no heed to counsels and warnings. From mural paintings in water-colours he was also repelled by the fact that working upon the newly prepared, damp white-wash required rapidity and surety,—precisely those qualities to which he was a stranger. "The painter of but few doubts attaineth but little," he would assert. These doubts, vacillations, corrections, these gropings, this endless slowness of work, all so necessary to him, were possible only in painting in oils.

Bending toward the wall, he inspected the surface of the picture through a magnifying glass. Suddenly, in the lower left corner, below the table-cover around which the Apostles were seated, he saw, near the feet of Bartholomew, a little crack, and, alongside, on the barely faded colours, a velvety white patch of exuding mould, that resembled hoar-frost.

He blanched. But immediately recovering, he continued his inspection still more closely. The first coating of clay had buckled up, as a consequence of the dampness, and had parted from the wall, lifting up the upper layer of gypsum with its fine crust of paints, and forming in it cracks imperceptible to the eye, through which cracks exuded the sweat of the nitrous dampness from the ancient, porous bricks.

The doom of The Last Supper was sealed; even if the artist were not fated to see the fading of the colours, which could be preserved for some forty (even fifty) years,—there was still no doubt of the fearful truth,—his greatest creation was lost.

Before leaving the refectory, he looked for the last time at the countenance of Christ, and,—as though he were now looking at it for the first time,—suddenly comprehended how dear this creation was to him. With the ruin of The Last Supper and the Colossus the last threads were being severed which bound him with the human life,—if not of those near to him in point of time, then the distant; now his isolation was becoming still more hopeless. The clay dust of the Colossus would be scattered by the wind; on the wall where the countenance of the Lord had been, the dull scale of the peeling colours would be covered with mould, and all wherein he had his life and being would vanish, like a shadow.

He returned home, descended to his underground quarters, and, passing through the room where Astro lay, halted for a minute. Beltraffio was applying a compress of cold water to the invalid.

"Fever again?" asked the master.

"Yes,—he is delirious."

Leonardo bent over in order to inspect the bandage and fell to listening to the rapid, incoherent babbling.

"Higher, higher. . . . Straight toward the sun. . . . If but the wings catch not afire. A little imp? Whence? What is thy name? Mechanics? Never yet have I heard any devil called Mechanics! . . . Why dost thou show all thy teeth a-grinning? . . . Well, drop it, now. . . . Thou hast had thy joke,—let that suffice. . . . He is dragging me,—dragging me. . . . I can not bide a while,—give me a chance to catch my breath. . . . Oh, 'tis the death of me! . . ."

A cry of horror escaped his breast. It seemed to him that he was plunging into an abyss. Then he again fell to muttering hurriedly:

"Nay, nay, laugh not at him! . . . 'Tis my fault. . . . He said that the wings were not ready. . . . 'Tis all over. . . . I have disgraced him,—disgraced the master! . . . Do ye hear? What is this? I know of him, now,—of the smallest one and yet the heaviest of devils,—I know of Mechanics! . . ."

"'Then the devil taketh him up into the holy city,'" the sick man continued in a chant, as one reads aloud in a church, "'and setteth him on a pinnacle of the temple. And saith unto him, If thou be the Son of God, cast thyself down: for it is written, He shall give his angels charge concerning thee: and in their hands they shall bear thee up, lest at any time thou dash thy foot against a stone! . . .'[47] But here I have gone and forgotten,—what was it he answered to the fiend of Mechanics? Dost thou not recall, Giovanni?"

He looked at Beltraffio with a gaze almost conscious. The latter kept silent, thinking the invalid still raving.

"Dost thou not recall?" persisted Astro.

In order to pacify him, Giovanni cited the twelfth verse of the fourth chapter of the Gospel according to St. Luke:

"'And Jesus answering said unto him, It is said, Thou shalt not tempt the Lord thy God.'"

"'Tempt not the Lord thy God!'" repeated the sick man with inexpressible feeling,—but immediately began raving again:

"Blue, blue,—nary a little cloud . . . There is no sun, nor shall there be,—both above and below there is but the blue sky. And there is no need of wings. Oh, if the master did but know how good, how soft it is to plunge into the heavens! . . ."

Leonardo gazed and pondered:

"Because of me,—he, too, because of me! I have tempted one of the little ones, I have put the evil eye upon him, even as upon Giovanni! . . ." He put his hand on the hot forehead of Astro. The sick man grew quiet by degrees and dozed off.

Leonardo entered his underground cell, lit a candle, and plunged into calculations.

For the avoidance of new errors in the construction of the wings he studied the mechanics of the wind, the currents of air, according to the mechanics of waves, the currents of water.

"If thou wilt cast two stones of equal size into calm water, at a certain distance from each other," he wrote in his diary, "two diverging circles will be made on the surface of the water thereupon. Query: when one of the circles, constantly widening, meets with the other, corresponding one, will the first enter the second, cleaving it, or will the impacts of the waves be refracted in the points of contact under equal angles?"

The simplicity with which nature had solved this problem in mechanics captivated him so that he added on the side-margin:

"*Questo a bellissimo, questo e sottile!*—Here is a most beautiful query, and a most subtle one!"

"I answer on the basis of an experiment," he continued. "The circles will cross one another, without blending, without mingling, and preserving as their constant central points both places where the stones fell."

Having made his calculation, he was convinced that mathematics, through laws of the internal necessity of reason, justify the natural necessity of mechanics.

Hour after hour passed unheeded. Evening came on. Having supped, and rested in conversing with his pupils, Leonardo again resumed his labours. By the familiar acuteness and clarity of his thoughts, he sensed beforehand that he was approaching a great discovery.

"Look how the wind in the field driveth the waves of rye, how they stream, one after the other, while their stalks, bending, yet remain unmoving. Thus do waves run over still water; this cat's-paw from a thrown stone, or from the wind, one should call the shivering of the water, rather than movement,—of which one can be convinced by throwing a bit of straw upon the spreading circles of the waves, and watching how it sways, without progression."

The experiment with the bit of straw recalled another one to his mind, similar to it, which he had already performed while studying the laws of the motions of sound. Having turned a few sheets, he read in his diary:

"The stroke of one bell is answered by a feeble quivering and ringing of another bell nearby; a string, sounding on a lute, compels to sound on another lute, nearby, the string of the same note, and, should you put a bit of straw upon it, you would see it quiver."

With inexpressible excitement he felt a connection between these two phenomena, so different, a whole undiscovered universe of knowledge between the two quivering bits of straw, one upon the cat's-paw of the waves, the other on the string, responsively resonant. And suddenly an unexpected blinding thought flashed like lightning through his mind:

"The law of mechanics is the same in both instances! As waves upon water from the thrown stone, so do the waves of sounds go through the air, crossing one another, without mingling, and preserving as their central point the place of origin of every sound.—And what of light? Even as echo is the reflection of sound, so the reflection of light in a mirror is the echo of light. There is but one sole law of mechanics in all the manifestations of force. There is but Thy sole will and justice, Thou First Mover: the angle of descent is equal to the angle of refraction!"

His face was pale, his eyes aflame. He felt that, anew, and this time so close as never before, he was peering into an abyss, into which none that had lived before had peered so closely. He knew that this discovery, if proven by experiment, was the greatest in mechanics since the time of Archimedes.

Two months before, having received from Messer Guido Berardi a letter with the news, just come to Europe, of the voyage of Vasco da Gama, who, having navigated two oceans and turned the South Cape of Africa, had found a new route to India, Leonardo had been envious. And now he had the right to say that he had made a greater discovery than Colombo and Vasco da Gama, that he had beheld greater vistas of a new heaven and a new earth.

A groan from the sick man came from the other side of the wall. The artist lent ear, and immediately recalled his failures,—the senseless destruction of the Colossus, the senseless perishing of The Last Supper,—the stupid and fearful fall of Astro.

"Can it be," he pondered, "that this discovery also will perish just as tracelessly, just as ingloriously, as everything that I do? Can it be that no one will ever hear my voice, and that I shall always be alone, even as now; in the murk, underground, as though buried alive,—with a dream of wings?"

But these thoughts did not stifle the joyousness within him.

"Let me be alone. Let me be in the murk, in silence, in oblivion. Let no one ever know. *I* know!"

Such a feeling of power and victory filled his soul as though those wings for which he had yearned all his life were already created and were raising him aloft.

He began to feel cramped in the underground quarters; he felt a desire for the sky and for spaciousness. Going out of his house, he set out in the direction of the piazza of the Cathedral.

VII

THE night was clear, moonlit. Over the roofs of the houses flared up smokily-purple reflections of conflagrations. The nearer one drew to the centre of the town, to the Piazza Broletto, the thicker did the crowd become. Now in the blue radiance of the moon, now in the red light of the torches, faces distorted by fury stood out; one caught glimpses of white banners with the scarlet crosses of the Milan Commune, and flashes of poles with lanthorns attached to them; of arquebuses, muskets, culverins, maces, staffs, spears, bear-spears, scythes, pitch-forks, staves. Like pismires the people swarmed, helping oxen to drag an enormous ancient bombard of barrel-staves, hooped with iron. The tocsin dinned; the cannon rumbled. The French mercenaries, entrenched in the fortress, were sending a hail of bullets upon the streets of Milan. The besieged boasted that, before surrendering, they would not leave one stone standing upon another. And with the din of the bells, with the rumbling of the cannon, was blended the unceasing wail of the people:

"Kill,—kill the French! Down with the King! Long live Moro!"

Everything that Leonardo saw resembled a strange and absurd dream.

Near the Eastern Gates, in Broletto, on the Piazza of the Fishmongers, they were hanging a Picardian drummer who had fallen into their hands,—a boy of sixteen. He stood on a ladder leaning against a wall. Mascarello, the broiderer in gold, and a most droll fellow, filled the post of hangman. Having put a rope around the boy's neck, and tapping his head lightly with the tips of his fingers, he declaimed with a buffoonesque solemnity:

"'This most humble French infantry-man of the Jump-the-Hedge Squad, called Monsoo Starve-Your-Belly-But-Clothe-Your-Back, is hereby given the accolade of the Order of the Knights of the Hempen Necklace. In the name of the Father, the Son, and the Holy Ghost!"

"Amen!" answered the mob.

The drummer, probably understanding but illy what was taking place with him, blinked his eyes with great frequency, as children about to cry do,—he shrank into himself and, twisting his thin neck, tried to ease the noose. An odd smile would not leave his lips. Suddenly, at the last instant, as though awaking from his stupor, he turned his astonished, comely little face, which had quickly blanched, and tried to make some utterance. Some request. But the mob began to roar. The boy made a feeble and submissive gesture of despair, took a little silver cross out of his bosom,—a gift from his mother or sister,—on a bit of narrow blue ribbon, and, having hurriedly kissed it, crossed himself. Mascarello pushed him off the ladder and called out gaily:

"Come, now, thou Knight of the Hempen Necklace, show us how they dance the French *gaillard!*"

And, amidst general laughter, the boy's body, hanging on the hook of a torch holder, quivered in its death agony, as though it were truly dancing.

Having gone a few steps farther, Leonardo saw an old crone, clad in tatters, who, standing in the street before a decrepit little house, just fallen in ruins from cannon-shot, among her heaped-up kitchen utensils and household goods, among feather beds and pillows, was stretching forth her arms and vociferating for help.

"What ails thee, aunty?" asked Còrbollo the cobbler.

"The boy,—they have crushed the boy under! He was lying in his crib. . . . The floor fell through. . . . He may be alive yet. . . . Oh, oh, oh, help me! . . ."

An iron cannon-shot, tearing through the air with squealing and whistling, plopped into the crooked roof of the little house. The beams crackled: the dust went up in a column. The roof tumbled, and the old woman became silent.

Leonardo approached the Town Hall. Opposite the Loggia degli Osii near the Lane of the Money Changers, a scholar, probably some student of the University of Pavia, standing upon a bench which served him as a cathedra, was delivering an oration about the greatness of the people, about the equality of the poor and the rich, about the overthrow of tyrants. The crowd listened mistrustfully.

"Citizens!" shrilled the scholar, waving about his knife, which in ordinary times served him for peaceful necessities,—mending goose quills, the slicing of *cervellata* (a white sausage from brains), the carving of arrow-transpierced hearts, with the names of tavern nymphs, upon the bark of the elms in suburban groves,—but which knife he now styled the Dagger of Nemesis. "Citizens, let us die for liberty. Let us wet the Dagger of Nemesis in the blood of tyrants! Long live the republic!"

"Whatever is he lying about?" voices were heard in the crowd. "We know what sort of liberty ye have in mind,—ye traitors, ye French spies! To the devil with the republic! Long live the Duke! Kill the traitor!"

When the orator began to clarify his idea with classical examples and citations of Cicero, Tacitus, Livy,—they dragged him down from his bench, threw him down, and they fell to drubbing him, to the refrain of:

"There is thy liberty, there is thy republic! That is the way, maties,

—give it him in the neck! Fiddlesticks, brother,—thou thinkest to fool us, but thou canst not! Thou wilt remember how to incite the people against their lawful Duke!"

Coming out upon the Piazza Arengo, Leonardo beheld the forest of white arrowy spires and towers of the Cathedral, resembling stalactites, in a double illumination,—a blue one, from the moon; a red, from the glow of the conflagrations.

Out of the crowd, which resembled a mound of piled up bodies, before the castle of the archbishop, came vociferations:

"What is up?" asked the artist of an old artisan, with a frightened, kindly, and melancholy face.

"Who can make them out? They know not themselves, likely as not. Giacopo Grotto, the master of the markets, is, so they say, a spy, bought over by the French. Fed the people with poisoned victuals, 'twould seem. Then, again, it may not even be he. They pummel the first one that falls into their hands. 'Tis a frightful business! O Lord Jesus Christ, have mercy upon us sinners!"

Out of the mound of bodies jumped up Gorgoglio, the glass-blower, flaunting, as though it were a trophy, a staff on the end of which was stuck a bloody head.

Farfanicchio, the street gamin, ran after him, hopping and squealing:

"A dog's death for a dog! Death to the traitors!"

The old man crossed himself piously and uttered the words of a prayer:

"*A furore populi libera nos, Domine!* From the wrath of the people deliver us, Lord!"

From the direction of the Castle were heard the sounds of trumpets, the beating of drums, the rattle of arquebus-fire, and the cries of the soldiers sallying out for a sortie. At the same instant there pealed forth from the bastions of the fortress a shot such as made the earth quake, and it seemed that the whole city was falling in ruins. This was a shot from the famous gigantic bombard, a brazen monster, called by the French *Margot la Folle*, and by the Germans *die Tolle Grete*,—Mad Margaret.

The shot hit a burning house beyond the Borgo Nuovo. A fiery pillar rose up to the night sky. The piazza was lit up by a red glow,—and the soft shining of the moon was dimmed. The people, like black shadows, darted hither and yon, scurrying about and dashing, possessed of horror. Leonardo contemplated these human phantoms.

Every time that he recalled his discovery,—in the glow of the fire, in the cries of the crowd, in the din of the tocsin, in the rumbling of the cannon, he thought he saw the soft waves of sounds and of light, that, swaying evenly, like a cat's-paw made on water by a fallen stone, spread through the air, crossing one another, without blending, and keeping as their centre the place of their origin. And a great joy filled his soul, at the thought that men could never, in any way, disturb this aimless play, this harmony of endless, unseen waves, and the law of mechanics, the law of justice, ruling over all, like the sole will of the Creator, the angle of descent equalling the angle of refraction.

The words which he had written down at one time in his diary rang in his soul:

"*O mirabile giustizia di te, primo Motore!* Oh, Thy wondrous justice, Thou First Mover! No force dost Thou deprive of the order and quality of its inevitable actions. Oh, Thou Divine Necessity, Thou compellest all effects to flow out of their causes in the shortest way."

In the midst of the rabble gone insane, in the heart of the artist was the eternal peace of contemplation, that was like to the serene light of the moon over the glow of the conflagrations.

On the morning of the fourth of February, in the year fifteen hundred, Moro entered Milan by the Porta Nuova.

On the evening before Leonardo had set out for the villa of Melzi, in Vaprio.

VIII

Girolamo Melzi had served at the court of the Sforzas. When, some years ago, his young wife had died, he had forsaken the court, settled down in the isolated villa at the foot of the Alps, at a five hours' ride to the northwest of Milan, and led a philosopher's life, far from the distractions of the world, delving his garden with his own hands and giving himself up to the study of the esoteric sciences and to music, of which he was passionately fond. They said that Messer Girolamo busied himself with black magic in order to summon from the world beyond the grave the shade of his dead wife.

Galeotto Sacrobosco the alchemist and Fra Luca Paccioli were not infrequent guests of his, passing whole nights in disputes about the secrets of Platonic Ideas, and the laws of Pythagorean Numbers, governing the music of the spheres. But it was Leonardo's visits which afforded the greatest joy to the host. Working on the construction of the Martesana Canal, the artist frequently visited this region, and had grown fond of the beautiful villa.

Vaprio was situated on the steep left bank of the river Adda. The canal was laid between the river and the garden. Here the swift current of the Adda was checked by rapids. One could hear the unceasing noise of the water, recalling the booming of sea surf. Between its steep banks of wind-beaten yellow sandstone the Adda rushed with its chill green waves,—boisterous, free; while alongside the placid canal, mirror-smooth, with the same green mountain waters as in the Adda, but calmed, tamed, slumbrously-heavy, glided silently between its strait banks. This contrast seemed to the artist full of a prophetic significance: he compared, and could not decide which was the more splendid,—the creation of intelligence and of human will, his own creation—the Martesana Canal, or its untamed sister of the mountains, the Adda; both currents were equally near and understandable to him.

From the upper terrace of the garden a vista of the green plain of Lombardy spread out, between Bergamo, Treviglio, Cremona, and Brescia. In the summer from the inundated fields, unencompassable by the eye, there arose a scent of hay. On the fertile fallow lands the boisterous rye and wheat screened to their very summits the fruit trees, joined with vines, so that the ears of grain kissed the pears, apples, plums,—and the whole plain seemed an enormous garden. Toward the North the mountains of the Como showed darkly; over them, in a semicircle, reared up the first ramifications of the Alps, and still higher, in the clouds, glowed their aureately-roseate snowy peaks.

Between the joyous campagna of Lombardy, where every nook of the soil was delved by the hand of man, and the wild, desolate, enormous crags of the Alps, Leonardo sensed the same contrast, filled with harmony, as between the placid Martesana Canal and the ominously-turbulent Adda.

Fra Luca Paccioli was also staying at the villa, as well as the alchemist Galeotto Sacrobosco, whose house near the Vercellina Gates had been demolished by the French. Leonardo, preferring solitude, held aloof from them. On the other hand, he soon became very friendly with Francesco, the host's little son.

Timid, as bashful as a girl, the boy for a long while fought shy of him. But once, entering the artist's room on an errand from his father, he saw the varicoloured glasses with the aid of which the artist was studying the laws of supplementary colours. Leonardo invited him to look through them; the amusement was to the boy's liking. Familiar objects took on a fairyland appearance now sombre, now joyous; now inimical, now kindly,—depending on whether he were looking through a yellow, a blue, a red, a lilac, or a green glass.

There was also another invention of Leonardo's which proved to be to his liking,—the camera obscura; when upon a sheet of white paper there would appear an animated picture, wherein one could distinctly see the wheels of a mill turning, a flock of daws wheeling above a church, the little grey ass of the woodchopper Peppo, loaded with faggots, picking its way over the muddy road, and the tips of the poplars bending before the wind,—Francesco could no longer contain himself and began clapping his hands.

But most of all was he captivated by the "rain-gauge," consisting of a brass ring with divisions, a little stick that resembled the shaft of a scale, and two little balls suspended therefrom,—one covered with wax, the other with absorbent paper; when the air was saturated with humidity, the cotton wool would absorb it; the little ball enveloped in it would sink, and, descending, would tip the beam of the scales for several divisions of the ring, by means of which one could with exactness measure the degree of humidity; whereas the wax ball remained impervious to it, and as light as before. In this manner the movements of the beam foretold the weather a day or two ahead. The boy constructed a rain-gauge of his own, and would rejoice when, to the amazement of the domestics, his predictions would be fulfilled.

In the village school of the old abbot of a neighbouring cloister, Don Lorenzo, Francesco studied but lazily,—he memorized Latin grammar with aversion; at the sight of the ink-smeared, green covers of his arithmetic his face would lengthen. But Leonardo's science was such that it seemed to the boy as interesting as a fairy-tale. The appliances of mechanics, of optics, of acoustics, of hydraulics, attracted him just as though they were living, magic toys. From morn till night he would not tire of listening to Leonardo's stories. With grown-ups the artist was secretive, inasmuch as he knew that every careless word might draw suspicions or a sneer upon his head. With Francesco he spoke of all things trustingly and simply; not only did he teach him, but, in his turn, learned from him. And, recalling the word of the Lord: "Verily I say unto you, Except ye be converted, and become as little children, ye shall not enter into the kingdom of heaven,"[48] he would add: "Nor shall ye enter into the kingdom of knowledge."

It was at this period that he was writing his *Book of Stars*.

On March nights, when the first breath of spring was already wafting upon the air, though cold had not yet departed from it, standing on the roof of the villa, together with Francesco, he observed the course of the stars; he drew the spots of the moon, so that, subsequently comparing them, he might learn whether they changed their outlines or no. On one occasion the boy asked him if it were true, as Paccioli said, of the stars, that they were like diamonds, set by God within the crystal spheres of the heavens, which, revolving, draw them along in their progress and produce music. The master explained that, according to the law of friction, the spheres, revolving for the duration of so many millennia, with unbelievable rapidity, would have fallen apart, their crystal edges would have been eroded, their music would have ceased, and the "irrepressible dancers" would have ceased moving.

Having pierced with a needle a sheet of paper, he allowed him to look through the opening. Francesco beheld the stars, devoid of their rays, resembling radiant, round, infinitely small dots or globules.

"These dots," said Leonardo, "are enormous; many of them worlds hundreds, thousands of times larger than ours; which, however, is by no means worse, nor more insignificant, than all the other heavenly bodies. The laws of mechanics,—mechanics, discovered by the intelligence of man, and sovereign on earth,—govern world and suns."

Thus did he establish the "nobility of our world."

"Just such an incorruptible star," said the master, "just such a radiant mote of dust, does the earth seem to the inhabitants of other planets, even as these worlds seem to us."

Much of what he said Francesco did not understand. But when, throwing back his head, he would contemplate the starry sky, he was overcome with awe.

"But what is *there*,—beyond the stars?" he would ask.

"Other worlds, Francesco, other stars, which we see not."

"And beyond them?"

"Still others."

"Yes, but in the end,—in the very end?"

"There is no end."

"There is no end?" repeated the boy, and Leonardo felt Francesco's hand tremble within his; in the light of the unmoving flame of a lamp burning on a little table in the midst of the astronomical instruments he saw that the child's face had become covered with sudden pallor.

"But where," asked he, slowly, with growing amazement, "where is paradise then, Messer Leonardo,—the angels, the martyrs, the Madonna, and God the Father, sitting on His throne,—and the Son, and the Holy Ghost?"

The master was about to retort that God is everywhere,—in all the grains of sand of the earth, as well as in the suns and the universes; but kept his peace, sparing the child's faith.

IX

When the trees had begun to open their buds, Leonardo and Francesco, passing whole days in the villa garden or in the neighbouring groves, would observe the resurgent life of the plants. At times the artist would sketch some tree or flower, trying to capture, as in a portrait, a living likeness,—that especial, unique aspect which would never be repeated again anywhere.

He explained to Francesco how to arrive at the years of a split tree trunk by the number of its rings; and, by the thickness of these rings, at the degree of moisture of the corresponding year; and at the direction in which the branches grew, inasmuch as the circles turned toward the north are thicker, whereas the pith of the tree trunk is always found toward the southern side of the tree, since that side is warmed by the sun, to which it is nearer than the side toward the north.

Leonardo spoke of nature with restraint, with a seeming coldness and asperity, caring only for scientific clarity. The tender details of the spring life of a plant he defined with dispassionate exactitude, as though the matter dealt with a dead machine: "The younger and thinner the branch, the more acute the angle of the branch and the trunk." He reduced to abstract mathematics the mysterious laws of conical disposition, with the regularity of crystals, of the needles on the firs, pines, and spruce-trees.

But meanwhile, beneath this dispassionateness and coldness, Francesco surmised the artist's love toward all living things: as well for the tiny leaf,—as pitiably wrinkled as the face of a new-born babe, which leaf nature had purposely placed under the sixth upper leaf, so that it might be the first to receive the light, so that a drop of rain, running down the stalk, might not be impeded by anything,—as for the ancient, mighty branches, which stretch forth from the shade toward the sun, like supplicating arms; or for the force of the vegetable sap, which hastens to the succour of a wounded spot, like living, seething blood.

At times, in the thickness of the forest, he would stop, and, smiling, gaze for long at a green shoot of grass struggling out from last year's withered leaves; at a bee, weak from its winter's sleep, crawling with difficulty into the unopened cup of a snow-drop. It was so quiet all around that Francesco heard the beating of his own heart. Timidly he would raise his eyes up to the master's. The sun, through the semi-translucent branches, illuminated the flaxen-fair hair, the long beard and the thick, jutting eyebrows of Leonardo, surrounding his head with an aura; calm was his face and splendid,—at such moments he resembled ancient Pan, who hearkens to the growing of the grass, the babbling of underground well-springs, the awakening of the mysterious forces of life.

To him all things were alive; the universe was one great body, even as the body of man was to him a universe in little. In a drop of dew he saw an image of the aqueous sphere embracing the earth. At the sluices in the little hamlet of Trezzo, near Vaprio, where the Martesana Canal commenced, he studied the river's waterfalls and whirlpools, which he likened to the waves of a woman's hair.

"Note," he would say, "how the hair follows two currents,—one straight, smooth, along which it is drawn by its own weight; the other, a return one, which weaves it into the ringlets of curls. Thus also in the movement of the water one part rushes downward, while the other forms whirlpools, the sinuosities of currents, resembling locks of hair."

The artist was attracted by these enigmatic resemblances, the consonancies of nature, like to voices calling to one another from different worlds.

Investigating the origin of the rainbow, he noted that the same plays of colour are met also in the wings of birds, and in stagnant water near rotting root, and in precious stones, and in grease a-top of water, and in old dulled glasses. In the designs of the hoar-frost on trees, in frozen windows, he found a similarity with living leaves, flowers and grasses,—as though in the world of icy crystals nature had prophetic dreams of vegetable life.

And at times he felt that he was drawing near to a great new world of knowledge, which, perhaps, would be revealed only to the coming ages. Thus, he wrote in his diary, anent the power of the magnet, and of amber, rubbed with cloth: "I can not see a means whereby the mind of man could explain this phenomenon. My supposition is that the force of the magnet is one of many forces unknown to man. The universe is full of innumerable possibilities, never yet bodied forth."

On one occasion Guidotto Prestinari, a poet living in Bergamo, near Vaprio, came to pay them a visit. At supper, growing offended at Leonardo, who had not lauded his stanzas sufficiently, he launched on a dispute about the advantages of poesy over painting. The artist kept his peace. But finally, the bitter feeling of the poet aroused amusement within him, and he took to contradicting him, half jestingly:

"Painting," said Leonardo, "is superior to poetry if only in that it depicts the works of God, rather than the conceptions of men, with which latter the poets content themselves,—at least those of the present day: they depict not, but merely describe, borrowing from others all that they have,—trafficking in the goods of others. They do but compose,—gathering the old rubbish of different sciences; well might they be compared with sellers of stolen goods. . . ."

Fra Luca, Melzi, and Galeotto began to refute him. Leonardo little by little became absorbed, and this time he spoke without any jesting:

"The eye giveth to man a more perfect knowledge of nature than doth the ear. That which is seen is more authentic than that which is heard. In verbal description there is but a series of separate images, following one another; whereas in a picture all images, all colours, appear simultaneously, blending into one, like to sounds in an accord, which makes possible in painting, as well as in music, a greater degree of harmony than in poesy. But, where there is no higher harmony, there is also no higher beauty.—Ask a lover which is the more delectable to him: a portrait of his beloved, or a description,—even if the latter be by the greatest of poets."

All involuntarily smiled at this argument.

"Here is something that happened to me once," continued Leonardo. "A certain youth of Florence was so taken with a feminine face in a picture of mine, that he purchased it, and wanted to destroy those signs which showed the picture of a sacred nature, in order that he might without fear kiss the beloved image. But conscience overcame the desires of love. He put the picture out of his house, since otherwise he had no peace. There, ye verse-makers, try, in describing the charm of woman, to arouse in man such a fervor of passion. Ay, signori, I will not say it of myself,—I know how much is lacking in me,—but of such an artist as has attained perfection; verily, through his power of contemplation, he is no longer merely a man. Whether he be spectator of heavenly splendour, or of images monstrous, laughable, pitiable, horrible,—he is a very potentate, like God!"

Fra Luca would chide the master for that he would not gather his works together, and commit them to print. The monk proposed to find a publisher. But Leonardo stubbornly refused. He remained true to himself to the very end: not a line of his was printed during his lifetime. But in the meanwhile he wrote his notes as if he were holding converse with his reader. At the beginning of one of his diaries he excuses himself for the disorder of his jottings, for their frequent repetitions: "Chide me not for this, reader, inasmuch as the subjects are countless, and my mind can not retain them so as to know what was, and what was not, spoken of in previous notes; all the more so since I write at great intervals, and at different years of my life."

Once, desiring to present the development of human spirit, he drew a row of cubes: the first, falling, knocks down the second; the second, a third, the third, a fourth, and so on, *ad infinitum*. Underneath he wrote: "One jolts the other." And he also added: "The cubes designate the generations of mankind and the stages of its knowledge." On another drawing he represented a plough, turning up the earth, with the inscription: "*Persistent Rigour.*"

He believed that his turn, too, would come in the row of falling cubes, —that at some time or other men would respond to his summons also.

He was like to a man who has awakened in the darkness, at too early an hour, when all others are still asleep. Lonely among those of his day he wrote his diaries in a cryptic script for some brother in the distant future; and for him, also, in the murk before the morn, a plougher of desert places, had he gone out into the field to make mystic furrows with his plough, in "persistent rigour."

X

In the last days of March, more and more alarming tidings began to arrive at the Villa Melzi. The troops of Louis XII, under the command of Ser de la Trémouille, had crossed the Alps. Moro declined battle, suspecting treason from his soldiers; and, tortured by superstitious premonitions, grew "more cowardly than a woman." Rumours of war and of politics reached like a faint, muffled rumbling to the villa at Vaprio.

Thinking neither of the French King, nor of the Duke, Leonardo and Francesco rambled over the neighbouring knolls, dales and groves. At times they climbed upward, following the current of the river, into the wooded hills. Here Leonardo would hire labourers and make excavations, searching for antediluvian sea-shells, and petrified marine animals and water plants.

On one occasion, returning from a ramble, they sat down to rest under an old linden-tree, on a cliff over the steep bank of the Adda. The endless plain, with its ranks of wayside poplars and elms, was spread out at their feet. The cheery little white houses of Bergamo could be seen in the glow of the evening sun. The enormous snowy masses of the Alps seemed to soar in the air. Only in the distance, almost on the very edge of the sky, between Treviglio, Castel Rozzone and Brignano, there was a swirling cloudlet of smoke.

"What is that?" asked Francesco.

"I know not," replied Leonardo. "A combat, perhaps. . . . There, dost see the little flames? Cannon-shots, 'twould seem. Can it be an encounter of the French and our men?"

Of late such chance exchanges of firing could be seen more and more frequently on the Lombardy plain, now on this spot, now on that.

They gazed for several instants at the cloudlet. Then, having forgotten it, they began to inspect the trophies of their latest excavations. The master picked up a large bone, as sharp as a needle, still encrusted with earth,—probably from the fin of some antediluvian fish.

"How many nations," he murmured meditatively, as though soliloquizing, his face irradiated by a serene smile, "how many kings has time turned to dust since this fish with its wondrous body structure fell asleep in the deep of the cavern where we found it to-day! How many millennia have passed over the universe, what overthrows have taken place, while it has lain in its secret place, shut in on all sides, propping up the heavy lumps of soil with the bare bones of its skeleton, demolished by patient time!"

He indicated the plain spreading out before them with an all-embracing gesture.

"All that you see here, Francesco, was at one time the bed of an ocean, covering a great part of Europe, Africa and Asia. The marine animals which we find in these mountains bear witness to those times when the summits of the Apennines were the islands of a great sea, and over the plains of Italy, where the birds soar now, the fishes were swimming. . . ."

He again looked at the distant cloudlet of smoke, with its sparks of cannon-shots. By now it appeared to him so small in the infinite distance, so tranquil and roseate in the evening sun, whose glow was like that of a holy lamp, that it was hard to believe a combat was raging there, and men were slaughtering one another.

A flock of birds flew across the sky. His gaze following them, Francesco tried to imagine the fish which had at one time been swimming here, in the waves of a great sea which had been just as deep and void as the sky.

They were silent. But at this instant both felt the one and the same thing: what did it matter which would vanquish the other,—the French the Lombardians, or the Lombardians the French; the King, or the Duke; one's own party, or the outlanders? The fatherland, politics, glory, war, the fall of kingdoms, the uprising of nations,—all that seems to men great or awesome,—does it not, amid the eternal serenity of nature, resemble that cloudlet, melting away in the light of evening?

XI

At the Villa Vaprio Leonardo finished a picture which he had begun many years ago, while yet in Florence.

The Mother of God, amid crags, in a cavern, with her right hand embraces the infant John the Baptist; with her left she blesses her Son, as though desiring to unite both,—the man and the God—in the one love. John, with hands piously folded, is on one knee before Jesus, Who is blessing him with the sign of two fingers. By the way the infant Saviour is sitting, naked on the naked earth, with one plump dimpled leg under the other, leaning upon a chubby little hand with its fingers spread out, it was evident that He was not yet able to walk,—only crawl. But in His face there is already perfect wisdom, which is at the same time also childish simplicity. A genuant angel, with one hand supporting the Lord, with the other indicating the Forerunner, turns to the spectator his face, filled with a grievous premonition, yet bearing a tender and strange smile. In the distance, among the crags, a humid sun shines through the haze of a shower upon the mistily blue, slender and pinnacled mountains, of an aspect extraordinary, unearthly, resembling stalactites. These crags, seemingly gnawed clean, worn down by briny surf, recall a dried-up sea-bed. And within the cavern reigns a deep gloom as under water. The eye barely distinguishes the subterranean well-spring, the round leaves of water plants, resembling web-feet, the feeble little cups of pale irises. One seems to hear the slow drops falling down from above, from the overhanging vaulted arch of the black-layered crags of dolomite, as the dampness penetrates between the roots of the creeping grasses, rushes and lycopodia. Only the face of the Madonna,—half childlike, half virginal, shines in the murk, like fine alabaster with a fire within it. The Queen of Heaven appears to men for the first time in the mysterious twilight, in the subterranean cavern,—mayhap the sanctuary of ancient Pan and the Nymphs, near the very heart of Nature, like a mystery of mysteries,—the Mother of the God-Man in the depths of Mother Earth.

This was the creation both of a great artist and a great scientist. The blending of shade and light, the laws of vegetable life, the structure of the human body, the structure of the earth, the mechanics of folds, the mechanics of feminine curls, which twist like the flowing of whirlpools, so that the angle of descent is equal to the angle of refraction, —all that the man of science had investigated with "austere rigour," had tested and measured with dispassionate exactness, had dissected, like a lifeless cadaver,—the artist had united anew into a divine whole, had transformed into living beauty, into mute music, into a mystic hymn to the Most Pure Virgin, the Mother of the Veritable One. With equal love and knowledge had he depicted the slender veins in the petals of the irises, and the dimple in the plump little elbow of the child, and the thousand-year-old cleft in the dolomite cliff, and the quivering of the deep water in the underground well-spring, and the quivering of deep sorrow in the smile of the angel.

All things did he know, and all things did he love, inasmuch as great love is the daughter of great knowledge.

XII

THE alchemist Galeotto Sacrobosco conceived the idea of making an experiment with the "Wand of Mercury." Thus were styled the sticks of myrtle, almond, tamarind, or some other "astrological" wood, which had, it would seem, an affinity with metals. These sticks were used to reveal copper-, gold- and silver-veins in mountains.

With this end in view he set out with Messer Girolamo to the eastern shore of Lake Lecco, where there were many diggings. Leonardo accompanied them, although he put but little trust in the Wand of Mercury and scoffed at it, as well as at the other maunderings of the alchemists.

Not far from the settlement of Mandello, near the foot of Monte Campione, there was an iron mine. The inhabitants thereabout related how several years before a landslide had buried within it a large number of workmen; how in its very lowest depth sulphurous fumes escape out of a crevice, and that a stone cast into it flies down with an unending, gradually diminishing rumble, without reaching bottom, inasmuch as the abyss has none. These tales had aroused the curiosity of the artist. He resolved that, while his companions were busy experimenting with the Wand of Mercury, he would investigate the abandoned mine. But the villagers, supposing that the Foul One dwelt therein, refused to accompany him. In the end one old miner consented.

A subterranean passage, steep, dark, resembling a well, with half-ruined slippery steps, descending in the direction of the lake, led to the shafts. The guide went on ahead with a lanthorn, Leonardo, bearing Francesco in his arms, followed him. The boy, despite the supplications of his father and the dissuasions of the master, had won his way after much imploring to be taken along.

The passage constantly grew narrower and steeper. They had counted up to two hundred steps, but the descent still continued, and it seemed as if it would never end. A stuffy dampness was wafted up from below. Leonardo was striking the walls with a pick-axe, listening to the sound, inspecting stones, the strata of the soil, the bright mica sparkles in the veins of granite.

"Afraid?" he asked with a kindly smile, feeling Francesco snuggling up to him.

"Nay, 'tis naught,—with you I am never afraid."

And, after a silence, he added quietly:

"Is it true, Messer Leonardo, what father says,—that you are going away soon?"

"Yes, Francesco."

"Whither?"

"To Romagna, to serve Cæsar, Duke of Valentino."

"To Romagna? Is that far?"

"'Tis several days' journey from here."

"Several days!" repeated Francesco. "That means we shall never see each other again?"

"Nay, why should that be? I shall come to you, just as soon as I can."

The boy grew pensive; then, with both arms, in impulsive tenderness, he embraced Leonardo's neck, snuggled up to him still closer, and said in a whisper:

"Oh, Messer Leonardo, take me,—take me with you!"

"Whatever art thou saying, lad? How can it be? A war is going on there. . . ."

"Let there be war! I tell you that I fear naught when I am with you! . . . I shall be your servant, I shall clean your clothes, sweep your rooms, give the horses their feed, and also, as you know, I can find sea-shells, and imprint plants on paper with charcoal. Why, you yourself were saying but the other day that I do it well. I shall do everything —everything that you may order me to do,—like a grown-up. Oh, do but take me, Messer Leonardo,—do not forsake me! . . ."

"But what of Messer Girolamo? Or dost thou think that he will let thee go with me?"

"He will let me go, he will! I shall wheedle it out of him. He is kind. He will not refuse me if I cry. . . . Well, if he will not let me go, then I shall slip away on the sly. . . . Only do you tell me that I may . . . Yes?"

"Nay, Francesco, I know that thou dost but say so; yet thou thyself wilt not leave thy father. He is old, poor fellow. . . ."

"Poor fellow, yes,—I am a poor fellow. . . . And yet you too. . . . Oh, Messer Leonardo, you do not know,—you think me a little fellow. But I know everything! Aunty Bonna says that you are a wizard, and the schoolmaster, Don Lorenzo, also says that you are wicked, and that I may send my soul to perdition with you. Once, when he spoke ill of you, I answered him so that he almost gave me a beating. And they all fear you. But I fear you not, because you are better than all of them, and I want to be with you always! . . ."

Leonardo stroked his head in silence; and, for some reason, there came back to him how several years ago he had been carrying in the very same way the little lad who had taken the part of the Golden Age at Moro's festival.

Suddenly the clear eyes of Francesco dimmed, the corners of his mouth drooped, and he whispered:

"Well, what can I do? Let it be so, then,—let it be! For I know why you do not want to take me with you. You love me not. . . . Whereas I . . ."

He burst into uncontrollable sobs.

"Cease, lad. Art thou not ashamed? Better listen to what I shall tell thee. When thou art grown up, I shall take thee as a pupil, and we shall live gloriously together, and shall never part again."

Francesco raised his eyes to him, with the tears still glistening on his long lashes, and looked at him with an intent, prolonged gaze.

"Is that true,—you will take me? Perhaps you do but say so, in order to console me, but will forget about it later? . . ."

"Nay, I promise thee, Francesco."

"You promise? But after how many years?"

"Well, in seven or eight, when thou shalt be fifteen. . . ."

"Seven. . . ." Francesco checked up on his fingers. "And we shall part no more?"

"Never, till very death."

"'Tis well, then, if it be for certain,—but only if it be for certain; in seven years?"

"Yes, for certain."

Francesco gave him a happy smile, caressing him with an especial caress he had invented,—which consisted of rubbing his cheek against Leonardo's face, as cats do.

"But do you know, Messer Leonardo,—'tis amazing! I had a dream once,—it seemed I was descending in darkness down long, long stairs, —just exactly as we are doing now; and it seemed as if I had always been doing so, and would always be doing it, and there was never an end to them. And someone whose face I could not see, was carrying me. But I knew that this person was my mother. And yet I do not remember her,—she died when I was very little. And here, now, is this dream, in reality. Only it is you, and not my mother. But with you I feel just as well as I did with her. Nor have I any fear. . . ."

Leonardo glanced at him with infinite tenderness.

In the darkness the child's eyes shone with a mysterious light. He offered his lips to Leonardo trustingly, as though really to a mother. The master kissed them,—and it seemed to him that in this kiss Francesco was surrendering his soul to him.

Feeling the heart of the child beating against his, firm of step, with insatiable inquisitiveness, following the dim lanthorn, down the fearful stairs of the iron mine, Leonardo descended lower and lower into the subterranean murk.

XIII

UPON returning home, the inmates of Vaprio were alarmed by the tidings of the approach of French troops.

The enraged King, in revenge for its uprising and treachery, was giving Milan up to the pillage of his mercenaries. All who could do so sought refuge in the mountains. Wains laden with household goods, with weeping women and children, wound along the roads. At night from the windows of the villa one could see "red roosters" on the plain, —the glow of conflagrations. From day to day a pitched battle was expected under the walls of Novara, which was to decide the fate of Lombardy. One day Fra Luca Paccioli, returning to the villa from the city, informed them of the latest fearful happenings. The battle had been set for the tenth of April. In the morning when the Duke, having left Novara, was putting his troops in battle array, by now in full view of the enemy, his chief forces, the Swiss hirelings, bribed by Marshal Trevulzio, refused to enter the conflict. The Duke implored them with tears not to ruin him, and swore, in the event of victory, to give them part of his lands. They remained implacable. Moro changed his clothes to those of a monk, and would have fled. But a certain Swiss from Lucerne, by the name of Schattenhalb, pointed him out to the French. The Duke was seized and led off to the Marshal, who paid the Swiss thirty thousand ducats,—"the thirty pieces of silver of Judas the betrayer."

Louis XII entrusted Ser de la Trémouille with the delivery of the captive to France. He who, according to the expression of the court poets, had been, "after God . . . the first to guide the rudder of creation, the wheel of Fortune," was trundled off on a cart, in a barred cage, like a trapped beast. The tale ran that the Duke, 'twould seem, had implored his gaolers, as a special favour, for permission to take with him to France the *Divine Comedy* of Dante.

The stay at the villa was becoming more dangerous with every day. The French were devastating Lomellina; the *lands-knechte*, Seprio; the Venetians, the Martesana region. Robber bands roamed round about Vaprio. Messer Girolamo with Francesco and Aunt Bonna was preparing to leave for Chiavenna.

Leonardo was passing his last night at the Villa Melzi. According to his wont, he was marking down in his diary all the curious things he had heard and seen during the day.

"When a bird hath a small tail," he wrote on that night, "but its wings are broad, it flaps them with greater force, turning so that the wind may blow directly under its wings and lift it upward,—as I have marked in the flight of a young kestrel over the cloister at Vaprio, to the left of the road to Bergamo, on the morning of the 14th of April, in the year 1500."

And alongside, on the same page:

"Moro has lost his kingdom, his possessions, his liberty, and all his works have come to naught."

Not a word more,—as though the fall of a man with whom he spent sixteen years, as though the overthrow of the great house of Sforza, were to him of lesser importance and interest than the empty flight of a bird of prey.

BOOK ELEVEN

There Shall Be Wings!

I

OT FAR FROM THE CITY OF EMPOLI, IN TUSCANY, between Pisa and Florence, on the southern slope of Monte Albano, was situated the hamlet of Vinci,—the native land of Leonardo.

Having arranged his affairs in Florence, the artist felt a desire, before his departure for Romagna, and entering the service of Cæsar Borgia, to visit this hamlet, where lived his aged uncle, Ser Francesco da Vinci, his father's brother, grown rich in the silk trade. He alone of all the family loved his nephew. The artist longed to see him, and, if it were possible, to place in the house of Ser Francesco his pupil, the mechanic Zoroastro da Peretola, who had not yet recovered fully from the consequences of his frightful fall. He stood in danger of being a cripple all life long. The mountain air, the quiet of the hamlet and its peace would, the master hoped, prove of greater help to the invalid than any medicine.

Leonardo departed from Florence, alone, on a mule, through the Al Prato Gates, following the downward current of the Arno. Near the city of Empoli, having abandoned the plain of the river with its highway to Pisa, he turned to the narrow rustic road, winding over the low, monotonous knolls.

The day was not a warm one, and was cloudy. The dully-white sun, sinking in the mist, with an aqueous, scattered light, foreboded a northern wind. The horizon on both sides of the road was widening. The knolls, imperceptibly and statelily, like waves, became higher. The mountains grew greater. One could feel the slow but constant ascent. The breath came easier. The traveller passed Sant' Ausano, Calistri, Lucardi, the *cappella* of San Giovanni.

It was growing dark. The clouds had scattered. Stars began to glimmer, winkingly. The wind freshened. This was the beginning of the piercingly-cold and sonorously-radiant northern wind from beyond the mountains,—the *tramontano*.

Suddenly, beyond the last steep turn, the hamlet of Vinci was revealed in its entirety. Here was hardly a level spot. The knolls had grown into hills; the plain, into knolls. And to one of these,—small, pointed,—clung the huddled hamlet of stone. Against the twilight sky, the black tower of an old fortress reared up, light and slender. Lights twinkled in the windows of the houses.

At the foot of a mountain, at the crossing of two roads, a little lamp in the niche of a wall lit up a clay image of the Mother of God, covered with shining white and blue glaze, a sculpture familiar to the artist since childhood. Before the Madonna knelt, bowed and with face covered with her palms, a woman in a poor dark dress,—probably a country woman.

"Caterina," Leonardo uttered in a whisper the name of his dead mother,—also a simple country girl of Vinci.

Having crossed the bridge over the rapid little mountain river, he turned to the right, up a narrow path between garden walls. It was altogether dark by now. A branch of a rose bush, hanging over a wall, brushed his cheek most softly, as though bestowing a kiss upon him in the dark, and wafted forth its fragrant freshness.

Before the ancient wooden gates in the wall he dismounted, lifted up a stone, and struck an iron brace. This was the house, at one time belonging to his grandfather, Antonio da Vinci, and now to his uncle Francesco, wherein Leonardo had spent the years of his childhood.

There was no response. In the silence one could hear the murmur of the Moline de Gatte current, at the bottom of the ravine. Above, in the hamlet, awakened by his knocking, the dogs began to bark. They were answered from the yard by the hoarse, cracked barking of what was probably an exceedingly senile hound. Finally, a hoary, bent old man came out with a lanthorn. He was hard of hearing, and for a long time could not make out who Leonardo was. But when he did recognize him, he burst into tears from joy, almost dropping his lanthorn, and fell to kissing the hands of the man whom he had, forty or more years ago, carried in his own arms,—and constantly kept on repeating through his tears: "Oh, signor, signor,—my Leonardo!" The watch dog, lazily,—evidently merely to humour his old master, —wagged his half-masted tail. Gian-Battista,—so was the old man called,—informed Leonardo that Ser Francesco had gone to his vineyard near the Madonna dell' Erta; thence he would be bound for Marcigliano, where a monk he knew was treating him for pain in his reins with a distillation of knapweed, and that he would return in two days. Leonardo decided to wait,—all the more so since on the following morning Zoroastro and Giovanni Beltraffio were supposed to arrive from Florence.

The old man led him into the house, which at this time was practically unoccupied,—Francesco's children living in Florence; he fell to bustling, summoned his pretty little sixteen-year-old, flaxen-haired granddaughter, and began ordering supper. But all Leonardo asked for was some wine of Vinci, bread, and some water from the well-spring, for which last his uncle's estate was famous. Ser Francesco, despite his prosperity, lived just as his father had lived, and his grandfather and great-grandfather before him, in a simplicity which might have seemed poverty to a man used to the conveniences of big cities.

The artist entered the lower chamber, so familiar to him,—a chamber which served both as reception hall and kitchen, with a few unwieldy chairs, and benches, and chests, of darkened turned wood, grown mirror-smooth from age; with its stand for the heavy pewter plate; with soot-covered beams along the whole length of its ceiling, with bundles of dried medicinal herbs hung up on them; with its bare white walls, its sooty hearth and brick floor. The sole innovation was the thick, turbidly-green, egg-shaped panes of glass in the windows. Leonardo remembered that in the years of his childhood the windows had been stretched over—as in all the houses of the inhabitants of Tuscan villages—with waxed cloth, so that the rooms were filled with twilight even in the daytime; while in the upper chambers, which served for bedrooms, the windows were closed only with wooden shutters, and not infrequently of mornings during the rigorous cold of winter, which was severe in these parts, the water in the wash-basins would freeze.

The gardener made a fire out of the fragrant mountain heather and juniper,—*ginepro*,—and lit a small lamp of clay with a long narrow neck and handle, resembling those which are found in ancient Etruscan tombs, which lamp hung within the fireplace on a small copper chain. His granddaughter's exquisite, tender visage seemed still more beautiful in the simple, humble room. Here, in this half-wild corner of Tuscany, in the blood, in the speech, in the household utensils, in the customs of the people, had been preserved imprints of immemorable antiquity,—the traces of the Etruscan tribe.

While the young girl was busying herself, putting on the table a round loaf of unleavened bread,—flat, resembling a pancake,—a platter of lettuce salad with vinegar, a jug of wine, and dried figs, Leonardo ascended the creaking staircase to the upper chambers. Here, too, everything was as of old. In the centre of the spacious, low chamber was the same enormous quadrangular bed, wherein a whole family could have found room and in which his good grandmother, Monna Lucia, the wife of Antonio da Vinci, had once slept with little Leonardo. Now the family couch, sacredly preserved, had descended by inheritance to Uncle Francesco. Just as of yore, on the wall at the head of the bed hung the crucifix, the little image of the Madonna, the sea-shell for holy water, a bundle of dried grey grass, called the "mist,"—*nebbia*, —and an ancient little sheet with a Latin prayer.

He returned below, sat down at the fire, drank some water and wine out of a round wooden bowl,—it smelt fragrantly of fresh olives, which also recalled to him his distant childhood,—and, being left alone, when Gian-Battista with his granddaughter had gone off to bed, sank into radiant, tranquil reveries.

II

He was thinking of his father, a notary of the Florentine Commune, Ser Pietro da Vinci, whom he had seen but a few days ago in Florence, in his own house, honourably acquired, on the lively Street of the Ghibellines,—an old man of seventy, still hale, full-blooded of face and with white curly hair. Leonardo had never, in all his life, met a man who loved life with such simple-hearted love as did Ser Pietro. In years past the notary had nurtured a fatherly tenderness for his illegitimate first-born. But when the two younger, lawful, sons—Antonio and Giuliano—had grown up, fearing that their father might set aside a part of their patrimony, they endeavoured to create a quarrel between father and son. During the last meeting he had felt himself a stranger in the family. Especial concern, in view of the rumours which were spreading at that time anent his impiety, was evinced by his brother Lorenzo, almost a boy in years, but already shrewd in matters of business, a "sniveller" and a disciple of Savonarola, a virtuous and avaricious shop-keeper of the guild of Florentine woolsters. Not infrequently he would let his conversation with the artist—in the presence of his father—turn upon Christian faith, upon the need for repentance, upon humility of thought, upon the heretical opinions of certain present day philosophers, and in parting had bestowed upon him a book, the *Salvation of the Soul*, of his own composition.

Now, sitting by the fireside of the old family chamber, Leonardo took out this book, written in the small, meticulous script of a shop-keeper:

"*A Book of Confession, Composed by one Lorenzo di Ser Pietro da Vinci, a Florentine; Sent to My Sister-in-Law, Nanna. Most Useful for them that be Desirous of Confessing their Sins. Take thou this Book, Reader, and Read Therein. When thou seest in the enumeration thy Sin, note it down; But that of which thou art Guiltless,—pass it by, It shall be of Benefit tc Others; inasmuch as, be* Thou *assured, of such Matter even a Thousand Tongues could not tell Enough.*"

There followed a detailed inventory of sins, compiled by the youthful woolster with a true shop-keeper's meticulousness; and another of the eight pious meditations, "Which every Christian should bear within his Soul, when approaching the Mystery of the Confession."

With a theological pompousness did Lorenzo discourse on whether it were a sin or no to wear cloths and other woolen goods on which no duty had been paid. "As concerning the Soul," he decided, "the wearing of Such Foreign weaves can cause no Harm, if the Duty be Unjust. And therefore let not your Conscience be Abashed, my Beloved Brethren and Sisters, but be ye of Good Cheer! . . ."

Leonardo turned his attention to the *Representations of the Four Christian Virtues*, wherein Lorenzo, probably not without a secret thought in his mind of his brother, the famous artist, advised painters how to represent the following allegories: Discretion—with three visages, to signify that it contemplates the present, the past, and the future; Justice,—with sword and scales; Fortitude,—leaning on a column; Temperance,—with compasses in one hand, with shears in the other, "Wherewith she cuts off and terminates every Excess."

There was wafted from the book upon Leonardo the familiar spirit of that bourgeois piety which had surrounded his childhood years and had reigned in the family, transmitted from generation to generation.

Even a hundred years before his birth the founders of the house of Vinci had been just such honest, parsimonious, and God-fearing clerks in the service of the Florentine Commune as his father, Ser Pietro. In the year 1339, in some business records, there was the first mention of the artist's great-great-grandfather's grandfather, a notary of the Signory, a certain Ser Guido di Ser Michele da Vinci.

His grandfather Antonio arose before him, as though he were alive. The worldly wisdom of the grandfather was every whit the same as the wisdom of his grandson, Lorenzo. He taught his children not to strive for anything great,—neither for glory, nor honour; neither for posts, governmental or military, nor for exceeding wealth, nor for exceeding learning.

"To hold to the mean in all things," he was wont to say, "is the surest way of all."

Leonardo remembered the calm and pompous voice of the old man, in which he instructed them in the corner-stone rule of life: "*Keep to the mean, in all things.*

"Oh, my children, take an example from the ants, that do take care to-day of the needs of the morrow. Be saving, be moderate. With whom shall I compare the goodly master of a household, the father of a family? With the spider shall I compare him, in the midst of his far-flung web, that, feeling the swaying of the thinnest thread, doth hasten to its aid."

He demanded that each evening, toward the angelus bells of the *Ave Maria*, all the members of the family be gathered together. He himself made the rounds of the house, locking the gates, carrying the keys up to the bed-chamber and hiding them under his pillow. Never a trifle in the household eluded his unslumbering eye: whether it was insufficient hay given to the oxen; whether the wick in the lamp were let too far out by a maid-servant, so that too much oil was consumed,—all things did he note, of all things did he take heed. But there was no niggardliness about him. He himself used the best of stuff for his clothes, and advised his children to choose likewise, without stinting money, inasmuch as it was sturdier,—there would be lesser need of change, and therefore clothing of good stuff was not only more respectable, but also cheaper.

The family, in the opinion of the grandfather, should live together, without parting, under the one roof, for, said he: "When all eat at the one table, one cloth sufficeth, and one candle; whereas at two tables, two cloths are needed, and two lights; when the one hearth warms all, one faggot of wood is enough; whereas two are needed for two hearths,—and thus in all things."

He looked down on women: "Their duty is to take care of the kitchen and the children, without mixing in the affairs of the husband; a man of folly is he that believeth in the reason of woman."

The wisdom of Ser Antonio was not devoid of craftiness.

"My children," he would reiterate, "be merciful, as is demanded of you by our Mother the Church; but still, prefer fortunate friends to unlucky ones, the rich to the poor. For therein doth the highest art of life consist,—while remaining benevolent, to out-cheat the cheater."

He taught them to plant fruit-trees on the boundary line of their field and that of another so that their shade be cast on the field of the neighbour; he taught them to refuse the request of a loan with graciousness.

"Herein the craftiness is two-fold," he would add, "you will both save your money, and have the pleasure of laughing at him that would cheat you. And if he that maketh the request be a clever man, he will comprehend you, and will begin to respect you still more for having been able to refuse him with decency. He is a knave that taketh; he is foolish that giveth. As for those of your kin and your household, assist them not only with moneys, but with sweat, blood, and honour as well,—with all that you possess,grudging not life itself for the welfare of the house; for remember, my beloved ones: 'tis of far greater glory and profit to a man to do good unto one's own, than unto strangers."

After an absence of thirty years, sitting under the roof of his fathers' house, hearkening to the prolonged howling of the wind, and watching the embers expiring on the hearth, the artist meditated of how his whole life had been one great infraction of his grandfather's thrifty, spider-and-ant wisdom, as ancient as the world,—had been that riotous usufruct, that lawless excess, which, in the opinion of his brother Lorenzo, the Goddess of Moderation was supposed to cut off with her shears of iron.

III

On the following day, early in the morning, he left the house, without awakening the gardener, and, passing through the humble hamlet of Vinci, with its high and narrow little houses, clinging in a huddle on the slope of the knoll around the old fortress, began to ascend toward the neighbouring little settlement of Anchiano, by a steep road that constantly went up-hill. Again, as yesterday, shone the mournful, pallid, seemingly wintry sun; the heavens were cloudless and chill, with edges of a turbid lilac, even thus early in the morning. The *tramontano* had gained strength during the night, but it did not blow by fits and starts, as yesterday, but steadily, directly from the north, as though falling from heaven, whistling monotonously in the ears.

Upon entering the little settlement of Anchiano, Leonardo halted, not recognizing the localities. He remembered that the ruins of the castle of Adimari had stood here on a time, and, in one of its towers, which had remained standing, there had been a little country ordinary. Now on this spot, on the so-called Campo della Torracchia, stood a new house with smoothly white-washed walls, in the midst of a vineyard. Behind the low stone enclosure a villager was digging around the vines with a pick-axe. He explained to the artist that the proprietor of the ordinary had died, while his heirs had sold the land to a wealthy sheep-raiser of Orbignano, who, having cleared the summit of the knoll, had cultivated upon it a vineyard and an olive grove.

It was not out of mere idle curiosity that Leonardo was making enquiries about the little inn at Anchiano: he had been born in it.

Here, at the very entrance to the poor little mountain settlement, above the highway, which, topping the Monte Albano, led from the plain of Nievole to Prato and Pistoia, in the sombre shell of the knightly tower of Adimari, fifty years ago there had nestled a gay country ordinary,—an *osteria*. A sign on creaking, rusty hinges, with the inscription of *Bottiglieria*,—Liquors at Retail,—the open door, showing tiers of kegs, and pewter mugs, and pot-bellied clay jugs; the two small, barred windows, unglazed, purblind, seeming to wink slyly, with their blackened shutters; and the steps of the little stoop, worn down to smoothness by the feet of the frequenters,—all these peeped out from beneath a fresh pent-roof of grape-vines, through which the sun filtered. The inhabitants of the settlements round about, on their way to the fair at San Miniato or Fucecchio; hunters of wild goats, muleteers, *doganieri*,—revenue guards of the Florentine border,—and other unpretentious folk would drop in here for a chat, or to drain a *fiasco* of the cheap, tart wine, or to have a game of draughts, of cards, of dice, of *zarro*, or *tarocca*.

The servant in this inn was a girl of sixteen, a total orphan, a poor *contadina*, a village maid, by the name of Caterina.

One day, in the spring of the year 1451, the young Florentine notary, Pietro di Ser Antonio da Vinci, having come from Florence, where he spent the greater part of the year on business, for a stay at his father's villa, was invited to Anchiano to conclude a long term lease of a sixth part of a stone olive-press. Having cemented the terms in legal order, the settlers invited the notary to wet the bargain in the neighbouring little inn on the Campo della Torracchia. Ser Pietro, a man simple, amiable, and courteous even with simple folk, willingly agreed.

They were served by Caterina. The young notary, as he himself subsequently confessed, fell in love with her at first sight. Under pretence of hunting quail, he put off his departure to Florence until autumn, and, having become a habitué at the tavern, he fell to courting Caterina, who proved to be a maid more inaccessible than he had presupposed. But it was not in vain that Ser Pietro was reputed a Lovelace. He was twenty-four; he dressed like a dandy; he was handsome, dextrous, strong, and possessed of a self-assured amatory eloquence, which simple women find so captivating. Caterina resisted for a long time, praying for help from the Most Pure Virgin Mary, but finally could not resist. Toward the time of year when the Tuscan quail, having grown fat on the juicy clusters of autumn, fly away from the vale of Nievole, —she was with child.

The rumour of Ser Pietro's *liaison* with the poor orphan, servant of the Anchiano ordinary, had reached Ser Antonio da Vinci. Threatening his son with a father's curse, he packed him off without delay to Florence, and in the winter of the same year, in order to make "the youngster settle down," married him off to Madonna Albiera di Ser Giovanni Amadori,—a girl neither young nor handsome, but coming of a respectable family and having a good dowry; as for Caterina, he married her off to a day-labourer of his, a poor villager of Vinci,—a certain Accattabrighe di Pietro del Vacca,—a man elderly, morose, of a heavy disposition, who, so it was said, had nailed his first wife into her coffin by beating her whenever he was drunk. Coveting the promised thirty florins and a tiny patch of an olive grove, Accattabrighe had not been queasy about covering up the sin of another with his honour. Caterina submitted without a murmur. But she sickened from sorrow, and well-nigh died after giving birth. Her breasts were dry; and, in order to nurture little Leonardo—thus was the infant christened,—a she-goat was procured from Monte Albano. Pietro, despite his love and sorrow for Caterina, also submitted; but begged his father into taking Leonardo into his house to be educated. In those days offspring from the wrong side of the blanket were not despised; they were almost always brought up as equals of the legitimate ones, and were not infrequently even shown the preference. The grandfather agreed, all the more so since his son's first marriage was without issue; and entrusted the little boy to the care of his wife, Monna Lucia di Pietro Zozzi da Baccaretto, Leonardo's kindly grandmother.

Thus did Leonardo, the son of the unsanctioned love of the twenty-four-year-old notary of Florence, and the seduced servant of the inn at Anchiano, enter the virtuous, God-fearing family of the da Vincis.

In the governmental archives of the city of Florence, in the census —*catasto*,—for 1457, was preserved a notation, written in the hand of his grandfather, Antonio da Vinci, notary:

"Leonardo, son of the above-mentioned Pietro, born out of wedlock, of him and of Caterina, now the wife of Accattabrighe di Pietro del Vacca, da Vinci."

Leonardo remembered his mother as in a dream,—especially her smile, tender, imperceptibly flitting, full of mystery, seeming somewhat sly and odd on her simple, sad face of an almost austere beauty. Once, in Florence, in the museum at San Marco, in the gardens of the Medici, he saw a statue which had been found in Arezzo, an olden city of Etruria,—a little copper Cybele, the immemorably ancient goddess of the Earth, with the same strange smile as that of the young village girl of Vinci,—his mother.

It was Caterina that the artist had in mind when he wrote in his *Book of Painting:* "Have you not noted how the mountain women, though clad in poor and coarse stuffs, surpass by their beauty those who are bedizened?"

Those who had known his mother when she had been young asserted that Leonardo resembled her. In particular did his slender, elongated hands, his long, gold-tinted curls, as soft as silk, and his smile, recall Caterina. From his father he had inherited his mighty physique, his health-begotten strength, his love of life; from his mother his feminine charm, which permeated his whole being.

The little house where Caterina dwelt with her husband was situated not far from the villa of Ser Antonio. At noonday, when his grandfather took his siesta, and Accattabrighe went off with his oxen to work in the field, the boy would thread his way through the vineyard, clamber over the wall, and run to his mother. She would be awaiting him, sitting on the front steps with a spindle in her hands. Seeing him from afar, she would stretch forth her arms. He would throw himself upon her, and she would cover with her kisses his face, his eyes, his lips, his hair.

Still more did he like the meetings at night. On holiday evenings old Accattabrighe would repair to the tavern, or to dice at his gossips'. In the night Leonardo would with exceeding caution arise from the wide family couch, where he slept beside his grandmother Lucia: half-dressed, he would noiselessly open the shutters, crawl out of the window, descend down the dry limbs of a spreading fig-tree to the ground, and run to Caterina. Sweet to him were the chill of the dewy grass, the cries of the night corn-crakes, the stinging of the nettles, the sharp stones that cut his bare feet; and the glimmer of the distant stars, and the fear lest his grandmother, awakening, miss him; and the mystery of the seemingly criminal embraces, when, having gotten into Caterina's bed, in the darkness, under the blanket, he would cling to her with all his body.

Monna Lucia loved and spoiled her grandson. He remembered her never-varying, dark-brown dress, the white kerchief framing her swarthy, kindly face, covered with wrinkles; her quiet lullabies, and the tempting odour of *berlingozzo*,—a rustic pasty with crust browned in cream, which she used to prepare.

But he and his grandfather did not get along. In the beginning Ser Antonio taught his grandson himself. The boy listened to the lessons unwillingly. When he had become seven, he entered the school attached to the Church of Santa Petronilla, adjacent to Vinci. Latinity also was wasted upon him.

Not infrequently, having left the house for school, he would make his way into a wild ravine, grown over with reeds, lie down on his back, and, whole hours through, follow the flight of the flocks of cranes, with an envy that was a torment. Or else, without plucking them, but merely unrolling the petals of flowers, painstakingly, so as not to damage them, he would marvel at their frail construction, their lowered stigmata, their stamens and anthers. When Ser Antonio would go to town on business, little Nardo, taking advantage of his grandmother's good nature, would run away to the mountains for days at a time, and, by craggy steeps, above precipices, by paths unknown to any, where only goats clambered, would scramble up to the barren summit of Monte Albano, whence he could see the unencompassable meadows, groves, fallow-lands, the marshy lake of Fucecchio, and Pistoia, Prato, Florence; the snowy Apuan Alps, and, in clear weather, the narrow, misty-blue streak of the Mediterranean. He would return home all scratched up, dusty, sun-burned, but so merry that Monna Lucia had not the heart to scold him, or to complain to his grandfather.

The boy led a lonely life. He saw but rarely his kindly Uncle Francesco, and his father, who gave him presents of citified sweets,—both men passed the greater part of the year in Florence; with his schoolmates he was not at all intimate. Their games were foreign to his nature. When they would tear off the wings of a butterfly, gloating in its crawling,—his face would become qualmishly distorted, and, paling, he would walk away. Seeing once the old housekeeper sticking in the cattle-yard a fatted suckling pig, which struggled and squealed piercingly, he long and stubbornly refused to eat meat, much to Ser Antonio's indignation.

On one occasion some schoolboys, under the leadership of a certain Rosso, a clever and malevolent mischief-maker, had captured a mole, and, having sated themselves with its sufferings, had tied it by one paw, half-alive, in order to give it up to the fangs of the sheep-dogs. Leonardo threw himself at the crowd of children, knocked down three boys,—being strong and nimble; taking advantage of their nonplussed stupefaction, since they were not expecting any such action from the habitually quiet Nardo, he seized the mole and dashed off into a field with all his might. Coming to their senses, his comrades started off after him, with shouts, laughter, whistling and cursing, throwing stones at him. The lanky Rosso,—he was Nardo's senior by five years,—clutched him by the hair, and a fracas was on. If his grandfather's gardener, Gian-Battista, had not hastened up, he would have received a cruel drubbing. But the boy attained his end,—during the rough-and-tumble the mole ran away, saving himself. In the heat of battle, defending himself from the attacking Rosso, Leonardo had blackened the latter's eye. The mischief-maker's father, a cook living in the adjacent villa of a noble, complained to his grandfather. Ser Antonio became so angry that he would have given his grandson a beating. His grandmother's intercession averted the punishment. Nardo was merely locked up for several days in a cubby-hole under the stairs.

Subsequently recalling this injustice, the first in an infinite sequence of others, which he was fated to undergo, he put this self-interrogation in his diary:

"If thou hast been imprisoned even in childhood, when thou didst act as thou shouldst—what will they do with thee now that thou art mature?"

Sitting in the dark cubby-hole, the boy watched a spider draining a fly in the heart of his web, which played like a rainbow in a ray of sunlight. The victim struggled in its paws, with a high, gradually expiring buzzing. Nardo could have saved it, even as he had saved the mole. But a dim, insuperable feeling restrained him: without hindering the spider from devouring its prey, he observed the greed of the monstrous insect, with the same dispassionate and innocent curiosity as he had the mysteries of the frail structure of flowers.

IV

Not far from Vinci was being erected a large villa for Signor Pandolfo Rucellai, by the Florentine architect Biagio da Ravenna, a pupil of the great Alberti. Leonardo, being frequently at the place where the building was going up, watched the labourers erecting the walls, the levelling of the laid stones with a square, the lifting of them with machines. On one occasion Signor Biagio, having started a conversation with the boy, was struck by his clear mind. At first *in passim*, half in jest, then later, having little-by-little become engrossed, he began to instruct him in the first basic principles of arithmetic, algebra, geometry, and mechanics. The ease with which the pupil caught everything, on the wing, as though he were recalling that which he had known before, seemed to the teacher incredible, well-nigh miraculous.

The grandfather looked askance at the whims of his grandson. He was displeased, also, by the fact that the latter was left-handed,—this was deemed an ill omen. It was supposed that people who made compacts with the devil, that wizards, and others who pore over books of black magic, were born left-handed. The inimical feeling toward the child was augmented in Ser Antonio, when a knowing woman, an experienced herb-doctor from Faltuniano, assured him that the old woman from Monte Albano, in the back-woods hamlet of Fornello, to whom the black she-goat, the wet-nurse of Nardo, had belonged, had been a witch. The sorceress might have, as easy as not, in order to please the devil, bewitched the milk of Nardo's she-goat.

"The truth is the truth," reflected the grandfather. "No matter how one pampers a wolf, it will still yearn for the forest. Well, 'tis the will of God, evidently! There is never a family without its freak."

Impatiently did the old man expect his favourite son Pietro to make him happy by the advent of a legitimate grandson and a worthy heir, inasmuch as Nardo somehow seemed like a chance foundling, and truly an "illegitimate" in this family.

The dwellers on Monte Albano told of a certain peculiarity of those regions, which was nowhere else met with,—the white colouration of many plants and animals,—he who was not an eye-witness would not credit these stories; yet the wayfarer roaming through the Albanian groves and meadows knows well that there one really does not infrequently come upon white violets, white strawberries, white sparrows, and even white fledglings in the nests of the black thrushes. That, aver the inhabitants of Vinci, is why this whole mountain has received, from antiquity immemorable, the name of the White,—Monte Albano.

Little Nardo was one of the marvels of the White Mountain, a sport in the worthy, every-day family of the Florentine notaries,—a white fledgling in a nest of black thrushes.

V

WHEN the boy had turned thirteen, his father took him from Vinci to his house in Florence. Since then Leonardo had visited his birthplace but rarely.

There has been preserved in one of the diaries of the artist, when he was in the service of the Duke of Milan, a brief and, as was his wont, an enigmatic entry: "Caterina arrived, on the 16th of July, 1493." One might think that the matter dealt with a servant, taken into the house for domestic needs. In reality this was the mother of Leonardo.

After the death of her husband, Accattabrighe di Pietro del Vacca, Caterina feeling that she, too, had not long to live, felt a desire to see her son before her death. Joining some pilgrim women who were setting out from Tuscany for Lombardy to worship at the relics of Sant' Ambrogio and the most unimpeachable Holy Nail, she had arrived at Milan. Leonardo received her with reverent tenderness. He felt himself in her presence, as hitherto, the little Nardo who used to come to her secretly in the night with his bare little feet, and, getting into her bed, beneath the blanket, cling closely to her.

The little old woman, after seeing her son, would have returned to her native hamlet; but he restrained her, hiring for her and arranging with great care a peaceful cell in the adjacent nunnery of Santa Chiara, near the Vercellina Gates. She fell ill and took to her bed, but stubbornly refused to move to his house, in order not to cause him any inconvenience. He placed her in the large Milan hospital, resembling a magnificent palace, built by Duke Francesco Sforza,—the Ospedale Maggiore,—and visited her every day. And yet none of his friends, or even his pupils, knew of Caterina's sojourn in Milan. He made practically no mention of her in his diaries,—save once, and then but casually, in reference to a curious face—as he put it, a "face out of a fairy-tale"—of a certain young girl, tortured with an excruciating ailment, whom he was observing at that time, also in the same hospital where his mother lay dying:

"*Giovannina—viso fantastico—sta, asca Caterina, all' ospedale.*— Giovannina—a face out of a fairy-tale,—ask Caterina, in the hospital."

When his lips touched for the last time her hand, growing cold, he felt that he was indebted to this poor *contadina* from Vinci, this humble dweller of the mountains, for all that he was and had. He honoured her with a magnificent funeral, as though Caterina had been not a lowly servant of a little tavern in Anchiano, but a woman of a high station. With the same exactness, inherited from his father the notary, with which he was wont to enter, without any need therefor, the prices of buttons, of silver trimmings and pink atlas for the new gala attire of Andrea Salaino, he entered the account of the funeral expenses as well.

Six years later, in Milan, already after the fall of Moro, packing his things before his departure for Florence, he found in one of his closets a small bundle, carefully tied. This was a rustic offering, which Caterina had brought him from Vinci, consisting of two shirts of coarse grey linen, woven with her own hands, and three pair of stockings, also made by her out of soft goat's-wool. He would not put them on, because he had become accustomed to fine linen. But now, suddenly seeing this little bundle, forgotten among scientific books, mathematical appliances and machines, he felt his heart well up with pity.

Subsequently, during the long years of his lonely and despondent wanderings from place to place, from city to city, he never forgot to take with him the unnecessary, lowly bundle of shirts and stockings, and every time, hiding it from all, he would shyly and painstakingly lay it away among those things which were especially dear to him.

VI

THESE recollections surged through the soul of Leonardo as he ascended Monte Albano by a steep little path, familiar to him since childhood. At a spot where the crag jutted out and the wind was less, he sat down on a stone to rest and to look about him. At his very feet

Anchiano glowed whitely in the sun. Farther down the dale, the small settlement of Vinci clung to its roundly-pointed knoll, looking like a wasps' nest, with the tower of its fortress just as pointed and black as the two cypresses on the Anchiano road. Nothing had changed; it seemed but yesterday that he had been clambering up these paths; and to-day, even as forty years ago, the plentiful *scopa* and whitish violets were growing here; the oaks rustled crisply with their wrinkled, dark-brown leaves; Monte Albano showed its sombre blue; and all things around were, as of yore, simple, unobtrusive, poor and bleak, recalling the North. And yet through this quiet and bleakness there seeped at times the exquisite, barely perceivable charm of the noblest land in the world, at one time ancient Etruria, now Tuscany, the eternally vernal Land of Resurgence,—a charm like to the strange tender smile on the austere, almost severely-beautiful face of the young village maid from Vinci, Leonardo's mother.

He arose and continued up the path that steeply ascended the mountain. The higher he went, the more cold and malevolent did the wind become.

Again memories thronged upon him,—but now they were of the first years of his youth.

VII

THE affairs of Ser Pietro da Vinci flourished. Adroit, merry, and good-natured, one of those for whom everything in life is a success, who live and let live, he knew how to get along with everybody. Especially was he favoured of those of the spiritual calling. Having become the trusted man of business of the rich monastery of the Most Holy Annunziata and many other pious institutions, Ser Pietro was rounding out his property, acquiring new tracts, houses, vineyards, all in the vicinity of Vinci, without changing his former unassuming mode of living, in accordance with the worldly wisdom of Ser Antonio. But he gave freely for the adornment of churches, and, taking thought of the honour of the house, laid a tomb-stone on the family vault of the Vincis in the Florentine Badia.

When Albiera Amadori, his first wife, died, quickly becoming consoled, the thirty-eight-year-old widower married an altogether young and exceedingly charming girl, almost a child,—Francesca di Ser Giovanni Lanfredini. But he had no offspring by his second wife either. At this period Leonardo was living with his father in Florence, in a house rented from a certain Michele Brandolini, on the Piazza San Firenze, near the Palazzo Vecchio. Ser Pietro intended to give his illegitimate first-born a good education, without stinting money, in order that he might subsequently, for lack of lawful issue, make him his heir,—also, of course, a Florentine notary, like all the eldest sons of the house of Vinci.

There was dwelling at this time in Florence a famous naturalist, mathematician, physicist and astronomer, Paolo dal Pozzo Toscanelli. It was he who addressed a letter to Cristoforo Colombo, wherein his deductions proved that the sea-route to India through the antipodes was not as distant as was supposed, encouraging him to undertake the voyage, and prophesying success. Without the aid and encouragement of Toscanelli, Colombo would not have encompassed his discovery,—the great navigator was but an apt implement in the hands of the unmoving contemplator,—he carried out that which was conceived and calculated in the lonely cell of the Florentine scholar. Away from the brilliant court of Lorenzo de' Medici, away from the elegant and sterile chattering of Neo-Platonists, and imitators of antiquity, Toscanelli "lived like a saint," to use an expression of his contemporaries,—a silent fellow, without any ulterior motives, and a keeper of fasts, who never partook of any flesh, and who was utterly continent. His face was hideous, almost repellent; but his radiant, serene eyes, as innocent as those of a babe, were beautiful.

When, on a certain night in 1470, a young stranger, almost a boy, knocked at the door of his house near the Palazzo Pitti, Toscanelli received him austerely and with coolness, suspecting his guest of the usual idle curiosity. But, having entered into conversation with Leonardo, he, just as Ser Biagio da Ravenna before him, was astounded by the youth's genius for mathematics. Ser Paolo became his teacher. On clear summer nights they would ascend a certain knoll near Florence, Poggio al Pino, covered with heather, fragrant juniper, and resinous, black pines, where a wooden shed, half-fallen to ruins from old age, served as an observatory for the great astronomer. He imparted to the disciple all that he himself knew of the laws of nature.

It was during these talks that Leonardo imbibed a faith in a new might of knowledge, as yet unknown to men.

His father did not hinder him; he merely advised him to choose some more lucrative occupation. Seeing that he was constantly either drawing or modelling, Ser Pietro carried off certain of these works to an old friend of his, a master goldsmith, painter, and sculptor,—Andrea del Verrocchio.

Shortly Leonardo entered his workshop for instruction.

VIII

VERROCCHIO, the son of a poor brick-maker, was Leonardo's senior by seventeen years. When, with spectacles on his nose and magnifying glass in hand, he sat behind the counter of his semi-dark workshop, —*bottega,*—not far from the Ponte Vecchio, in one of those ancient, leaning houses on rotted piles, whose walls are laved by the turbidly green waters of the Arno,—Ser Andrea resembled an ordinary Florentine shop-keeper, rather than a great artist. He had an immobile face, —flat, white, rounded and puffy, with a double chin; only in his thin, firmly pressed lips, and in the piercingly keen gaze of his tiny eyes could one see a reason cold, exact, and fearlessly inquisitive.

Andrea considered the ancient master, Paolo Uccello, his teacher. It was told of the latter that, taken up with abstract mathematics, which he compared with art, and with brain-racking problems of perspective, contemned and abandoned of all, Uccello had fallen into penury and had almost gone out of his head; he passed whole days without food, whole nights without sleep; at times, lying in bed, with wide-open eyes staring into the darkness, he would waken his wife by exclaiming:

"Oh, what a delectable thing is perspective!"

He died, bemocked and not understood.

Verrocchio, just as Uccello, supposed mathematics to be the common foundation of art and of science, and used to say that geometry, being a part of mathematics,—"the mother of all sciences"—was at the same time "the mother of drawing,—which is the father of all arts." Perfect knowledge and perfect enjoyment of beauty were to him one and the same thing. Whenever he came across a face rare either because of its hideousness or its charm or else some other part of the human body distinguished for either reason, he neither turned away with aversion, nor would he forget himself, lost in a dreamy languor, after the wont of such artists as Sandro Botticelli; he would, instead, study such cases, actually making anatomical casts of gypsum, which none of the masters had done before him. With infinite patience, he compared, measured, put to the test, sensing beforehand in the laws of beauty the laws of mathematical necessity. Still more indefatigably than Sandro, he sought for new surpassing charm,—but not in a miracle, not in a fairy-tale, not in the tempting gloaming, wherein Olympus blended with Golgotha, as Sandro sought,—but in such a penetration into the mysteries of Nature, as none had yet durst attempt, for to Verrocchio it was not the miracle that was the truth, but the truth was the miracle.

On the day when Ser Pietro da Vinci brought his eighteen-year-old son, the fate of both artists was decided. Andrea became not only the master, but the pupil as well, of his pupil, Leonardo.

In a picture which the monks of Vallombrosa had commissioned Verrocchio to do, depicting the baptism of the Saviour, Leonardo had painted a genuant angel. All that Verrocchio had had but a dim premonition of, and which he had sought for gropingly, like one blind, —Leonardo had perceived, found, and embodied in this image. Subsequently the legend ran that the master, brought to despair by the boy's having surpassed him, had forsaken painting. In reality, there was no enmity between them. They did but supplement one another: the pupil possessed that ease which Nature had not bestowed upon Verrocchio; the master, that concentrated perseverance which was lacking in the too versatile and inconstant Leonardo. Without envy and without rivalry, they were themselves frequently ignorant of which was the other's debtor.

At this period Verrocchio was executing, in copper, Christ and St. Thomas for the Or San Michele. In lieu of the paradisaical visions of Fra Beato, and the fairy-tale-like delirium of Botticelli, in his portrayal of Thomas inserting his fingers into the Lord's wounds there appeared before men for the first time the unprecedented daring of man before God, of judicial reason confronted with a miracle.

IX

LEONARDO's first production was a cartouche for a silken tapestry, woven with gold in Flanders,—the gift of the burghers of Florence to the King of Portugalia. The cartouche represented the fall into sin of Adam and Eve. The jointed trunk of one of the paradisaical palms was portrayed with such perfection that, according to the words of one eye-witness, "the mind grew darkened at the thought of any man's having so much patience." The muliebrile visage of the Serpent Demon breathed forth a seductive charm, and it seemed that one could hear his words: "Ye shall not surely die: for God doth know that in the day ye eat thereof, then your eyes shall be opened, and ye shall be as gods, knowing good and evil."[49] And the Woman was stretching forth her hands toward the Tree of Knowledge, with the same smile of daring curiosity with which Thomas the Doubter, in the statue of Verrocchio, was inserting his fingers into the wounds of the Crucified.

Once, at the request of a neighbour of his in Vinci, who extended him courtesies in angling and hunting, Ser Pietro asked his son to represent something on a round wooden shield, a so-called *rotella*. Such shields, with allegorical pictures and inscriptions, were used as decorations.

The artist conceived a representation of a monster which should inspire the spectator with horror, even as the head of Medusa did. Within a room, entry to which was denied to all save him, he gathered lizards, snakes, crickets, spiders, millipeds, nocturnal butterflies, scorpions, flitter-mice, and a multitude of other hideous animals. Selecting, unifying, exaggerating certain parts of their bodies, he formed a supernatural monster, non-existent yet actual,—gradually deducing that which is not out of that which is, with the same clarity that Euclid or Pythagoras deduce one theorem out of another. One could see the monster crawling out of a crevice in a cliff, and one seemed to hear its swish upon the ground with its jointed, slippery belly of glistening black. The gaping maw hawked forth its malodorous breath, the eyes darted forth flame, the nostrils smoke. But the most amazing thing of all was that the horror of the monster captivated and attracted, like to beauty.

Whole days and nights did Leonardo pass closeted in the room, where the unbearable fœtor of the dead vermin had infected the air so that it was difficult to breathe. But, at other times hyper-sensitive,—even to the verge of effeminacy,—to any bad odour, he did not notice it now. Finally, he informed his father that the picture was ready, and that he could take it. When Ser Pietro arrived Leonardo requested him to wait in another room, returned to his workroom, placed the picture on a wooden easel, surrounded it with a black cloth, closed the shutters so that but a single ray of the sun fell directly upon the *rotella*, and summoned Ser Pietro. The latter entered, gave one glance, cried out, and staggered back affrighted, he verily thought he was beholding a living monster. Watching, with an intense gaze, as amazement supplanted the horror upon his father's face, the artist uttered with a smile:

"The picture attains its end,—it has precisely the effect I desired. Take it,—'tis ready."

The second wife of Ser Pietro, Madonna Francesca, died while still young. His third marriage was to Margherita, daughter of Ser Francesco di Guglielmo, with a dowry of three hundred and sixty-five florins. His stepmother took a dislike to Leonardo, especially since she had made her husband happy with the birth of two sons, Antonio and Giuliano. Leonardo was extravagant. Ser Pietro helped him, although by no means munificently. Monna Margherita hounded her husband ceaselessly because he was taking his estate from his lawful heirs and "giving it away to a foundling, a step-son, the nursling of a witch's she-goat," as she styled Leonardo.

Among his companions, in the *bottega* of Verrocchio and in other workshops, he also had many enemies. One of them, referring to the unusual friendship between master and pupil, made up an anonymous complaint, wherein he accused them of sodomy. The slander attained a semblance of verity owing to the fact that Leonardo, while one of the handsomest youths in Florence, kept aloof from women. "In his entire appearance there was such a refulgence of beauty, that, upon beholding him, every grieving soul would brighten."

It was during the same year that, leaving the workroom of Verrocchio, he set up bachelor quarters. By that time there were already rumours current both anent the "heretical opinions" and the "godlessness" of Leonardo. Life in Florence was becoming onerous to him.

Ser Pietro procured for his son an advantageous commission from Lorenzo de' Medici. But Leonardo failed to please. From those about him Lorenzo demanded first of all a fawning adulation,—even though of the highest, most refined sort. People of exceeding courage or freedom he rather disliked.

The ennui of idleness was overcoming Leonardo. He even entered upon secret negotiations with a certain grandee—the Diodary of Syria,—through the embassy of the Sultan of Egypt, Kait Bey, which embassy had arrived in Florence, in order to enter the Diodary's service as his chief engineer,—although he knew that to do this he would have to forsake Christ and join the Mahommedan faith. It made no difference to him, as long as he would be able to leave Florence. He felt that he would perish if he were to remain.

Chance saved him. He invented a many-stringed lute of silver, which resembled a horse's skull. Lorenzo the Magnificent, a great amateur of music, liked the unusual appearance and sound of this lute. He proposed that its inventor journey to Milan, to bring it as a present to the Duke of Lombardy, Ludovico Sforza Moro.

In 1482, being thirty years of age, Leonardo forsook Florence and set out for Milan, not in the character of an artist or a savant, but merely that of court musician. Before departure, he wrote to Duke Moro:

"Most Illustrious Signor, having studied and weighed the works of present-day inventors of military engines, I have found that they contain nothing which would distinguish them from those to be found in general use. And therefore I am taking the liberty of addressing Your Highness, in order to discover to you the mysteries of my art."

And he enumerated his inventions: a new method of demolishing, without the aid of bombards, any fortress or castle, if but its foundations be not hewn out of stone; subterranean passages and minings, laid rapidly and noiselessly beneath moats and rivers; covered vehicles, impinging into the enemy's formation so that no power could resist them; bombards, cannons, mortars, *passe-volants*, of a new, "exceedingly splendid and useful construction"; battering rams to be used in sieges; gigantean catapulting devices, and other engines "amazing in action," and, for every separate contingency there was an invention of new machines; also, for naval combats, there was every possible device, for attack as well as for defence,—ships, whose sides could sustain shots of stone or iron; explosive compounds unknown to any.

"During times of peace," he concluded, "I hope to please Your Highness by architecture, by the erection of private and public edifices; by the construction of canals and aqueducts.

"Also in the art of carving, in marmor, copper, clay,—as well as in painting,—I can execute any required commissions, not inferior to any other, whoever he be.

"And I can also undertake the work of pouring out of bronze a Steed, which shall be to the eternal glory of the blessed memory of the Signor your Father, and of all the famed family of the House of Sforza.

"But should any of the above-mentioned inventions appear improbable, I propose to make an experiment in the Park of your Castle, or in any other place, suitably designated by Your Highness, to whose gracious attention entrusts himself Your Highness' most obedient servant,

"Leonardo da Vinci."

When he had for the first time beheld the snowy summits of the Alps above the green plain of Lombardy, he felt that a new life was beginning for him, and that this foreign land would be as a native one to him.

X

Thus, ascending Monte Albano, did Leonardo recall the half century of his life.

He was already near the peak of the White Mountain,—about to cross it. Now the little path rose straight ahead, without winding, between dry brush and the puny gnarled oaks with their last year's leaves. He ascended higher and higher, and there was a strange joy, familiar to him since childhood, in the effort of the climb, as though he were conquering the morose, frowning mountains, wind-flooded; with every step his view expanded, becoming clearer-cut and more unencompassable, for with every step the distance widened.

Spring no longer was; there was not a bud on the trees,—even the grass was barely green. One could not see the opposite plain,—in the direction where France lay. But the entire distance to Empoli, unencompassable to the eye, spread out before his gaze. And everywhere was spaciousness, a vast void, an airy expanse,—as though the narrow little path went away from underfoot, and slowly, with imperceptible smoothness, he were flying over these undulating, descending vistas upon gigantean wings. Here wings seemed natural, necessary, and the fact of their absence aroused wonder and fear in one's soul, as might be the case with a man suddenly deprived of his legs.

He recalled how, as a child, he had watched the flight of cranes, and when their barely perceptible honking would reach him,—which seemed like a summons: "Let us fly! Let us fly!"—he would weep for envy. He recalled how he freed on the sly the starlings and hedge-sparrows out of his grandfather's cages, admiring the joy of the liberated captives; how once his monkish school-teacher had told him of the son of Dædalus, Icarus, who had conceived the idea of flying on wings modelled of wax, and who had fallen and perished; and how, subsequently, in reply to his teacher's question as to who had been the greatest of the heroes of antiquity, he had made answer without hesitation: "Icarus, the son of Dædalus!" He also remembered his wonder and joy when, for the first time, on the Campanile—the belfry of the Cathedral of Maria del Fiore, in Florence,—he had seen among the bas-reliefs of Giotto, depicting all the arts and sciences, a droll, clumsy human figure,—Dædalus, the flying mechanic, covered from head to foot with bird feathers. He had also another recollection of his earliest childhood,—of those recollections which seem absurd to others, but, to him that keeps them hidden in his soul, filled with mystery, like prophetic dreams. "Probably 'tis my fate," he wrote anent this recollection in one of his diaries, "to write at length of the vulture, inasmuch as I can recall how once, in my early childhood, I dreamt that I lay in a cradle, and a certain Vulture had flown up to me, and did open my lips, and did pass his wings over them many times, as though to signify that all life long I would speak of wings."

The prophecy was fulfilled: Wings for Humanity became the ultimate aim of all his life. And here again, on the same slope of the White Mountain, did it appear to him, as to the child forty years ago, an unbearable grievance and an inconceivable thing that men were wingless.

"He that knows all things can do all things," he reflected.

"One has but to know—and there shall be wings!"

XI

On one of the last turns of the little path he felt someone seize him from the back by the edge of his garment,—he turned and beheld his pupil, Giovanni Beltraffio. His eyes puckered up, his head bent, clutching his hat, Giovanni was contending with the wind. Evidently he had been shouting and calling for a long while, but the wind had borne off his voice. But when the master turned around,—upon this desert, dead height, with his waving, long hair, with his long beard, which the wind had thrown over his shoulder, with an expression of unswerving, seemingly merciless will and thought in his eyes, in the deep wrinkles of his forehead, in his sternly contracted eyebrows,—his face appeared so unfamiliar and awesome that the pupil barely recognized him. The wide folds of his dark-red cape, beating in the wind, resembled the wings of a gigantic bird.

"I am but come from Florence," shouted Giovanni, but through the noise of the wind his shout sounded like a whisper, and one could distinguish only disjointed words: "A letter. . . . important. . . . ordered to give it to you. . . . immediately. . . ."

Leonardo comprehended that it was from Cæsar Borgia. Giovanni handed it over to the master. The artist recognized the writing of Messer Agapito, the Duke of Valentino's secretary.

"Go down!" he shouted, after a glance at Giovanni's face, turned blue from the cold. "I shall come right away. . . ."

Beltraffio began descending the steep, clutching at the branches of the bushes, slipping on stones, stooping, huddling,—so small, puny and weak, that it seemed as if the storm would lift him up at any moment and whirl him away, like a withered blade of grass.

Leonardo followed him with his eyes, and the piteous air of the pupil reminded the master of his own weakness,—the curse of impotence, which oppressed his whole life; the endless succession of failures: the senseless perishing of the Colossus, and of The Last Supper; the fall of Astro the mechanic; the ill-fortune of all those who loved him; the hatred of Cesare; the illness of Giovanni; the superstitious horror in the eyes of Maia; and his fearful, eternal solitude.

"Wings!" he reflected. "Can it be that this, too, will perish, just like everything that I do? . . ."

And there came to his memory the words which the ailing mechanic Astro had been whispering in his delirium,—the answer of the Son of Man to him who was tempting Him with the horror of the abyss and the rapture of flight: "Thou shalt not tempt the Lord thy God."[50]

He raised his head; closed his lips still more sternly, contracted his eyebrows, and began his ascent again, overcoming the wind and the mountain. The little path had vanished,—he was now walking on a way unbeaten, over bare rock, where probably none had trod before him. One more effort, one last step—and he stopped on the edge of the precipice. Farther progress was impossible,—one had need of wings. The crag had ended, abruptly, and on its farther side there opened up an abyss, hitherto unseen. Æthereal, murky, of a turbid lilac colour, did it yawn, as if below, underfoot, was no earth, but the same sky, the same void and infinitude, as above, overhead.

The wind had turned into a hurricane; it boomed and rumbled in one's ears, like to a deafening thunder,—as though invisible, fast, malevolent birds were flying past, swarm upon swarm, their gigantean wings fluttering and swishing. Leonardo bent over, glancing into the abyss,—and again, suddenly, but now with such force as never hitherto the feeling, familiar to him since childhood, of the natural necessity, of the inevitability of flying, took possession of him.

"There shall be," he said in a whisper, "there shall be wings! If not I, then some other,—'tis all one,—man *shall* fly. The spirit has not lied: those who have attained knowledge, the winged ones, shall be even as the gods!"

And there appeared before him the King of the Air, vanquisher of all limitations and gravities; the Son of Man, in all his glory and power, the Great Swan, flying on wings titanic, white, sparkling like snow against the azure of the heavens.

And his soul was filled with a joy that was akin to terror.

XII

WHEN he was descending Monte Albano, the sun was already near setting. The cypresses under its dense yellow rays seemed black, like coal; the receding mountains tender and transparent, like amethyst. The wind was abating.

He approached Anchiano. Suddenly from beyond a turn, below, in the deep, snug dale that resembled a cradle, there was revealed the little dark hamlet of Vinci,—a hornets' nest, with the tower of its fortress, as pointed as the dark cypresses. He halted, took out his memorandum book, and jotted down:

"From the Mountain which has received its name from the Conqueror,"—*Vinci vincere* signifies *to conquer*,—"shall the Great Bird take its first flight,—a man on the back of a great Swan, filling the universe with amazement, filling all books with its immortal name. —And may there be eternal glory to the nest where it was born!"

Glancing at his native hamlet at the foot of the White Mountain, he repeated:

"Eternal glory to the nest where the Great Swan was born!"

. . . .

Agapito's letter demanded the immediate arrival of the Duke's new mechanician in Cæsar's camp, for the construction of engines of siege for the forthcoming attack upon Faenza.

Two days later Leonardo left Florence for Romagna and Cæsar Borgia.

BOOK TWELVE

Aut Cæsar—aut Nihil

I

ESORTING TO DECEPTIONS AND MALEFACTIONS, committed under the supreme protection of the Roman Pontiff and of the Most Christian King of France, Cæsar Borgia was, at this period, subjugating the ancient Church State, supposedly received by the Popes as a gift from Emperor Constantine Palæologus. Having taken the City of Faenza away from its lawful ruler, the eighteen-year-old Astorre Manfredi, and the City of Forlì from Caterina Sforza, he cast the youth and the woman, both of whom had trusted to his knightly honour, into the prison of Sant' Angelo at Rome. He concluded an alliance with the Duke of Urbino, in order that, having disarmed him, he might fall upon him treacherously, as robbers do upon the highways, and plunder him.

In the autumn of fifteen hundred and two he conceived the idea of an expedition against Bentivoglio, the ruler of Bologna, in order that he might, having taken possession of this city, make it the capital of his own new kingdom. Horror fell upon the adjacent rulers when they understood that each one of them would, in his turn, sooner or later, fall a victim to Cæsar, and that his dream was, after having annihilated his rivals, to proclaim himself the sole sovereign potentate of Italy.

On the twenty-eighth of September the enemies of Valentino gathered in the city of Mugione, on the plain of Carpia, and concluded a secret alliance against Cæsar. Among other things taking place at this gathering, Vitellozzo Vitelli swore the oath of Hannibal,—to put to death, to immure, or to drive out of Italy the common foe within the year.

As soon as the news of the Mugione pact spread, it was joined by the countless rulers whom Cæsar had injured. The Duchy of Urbino revolted and fell away. His own troops were betraying him. The King of France tarried with assistance. Cæsar was on the verge of ruin. But, betrayed and forsaken, almost disarmed, he was still appalling. Having let slip in pusillanimous recriminations and vacillations the most fitting time for annihilating him, his foes entered into negotiations with him and concluded a truce. With crafty devices, with threats and promises, he seduced them, enmeshed and disrupted them. With a profound art of dissimulation, so natural to him, bewitching his new friends, he summoned them to the City of Sinigaglia, which had just capitulated, under the pretence that he would fain, no longer in words but in deeds, prove his devotion to them by means of an expedition in common.

Leonardo was one of the chief men near to Cæsar Borgia. At the latter's order, he adorned the vanquished cities with magnificent buildings, palaces, schools, libraries; he erected spacious barracks for Cæsar's troops on the site of the demolished fortress of the Castel Bolognesa; he dredged out the harbour of Porto Cesenatico, the best on the entire south shore of the Adriatic Sea; and joined it by a canal with the Cesena; he laid the foundations for the mighty fortress at Piombino, he constructed war engines, drew war maps, and, following the Duke everywhere, being on the spot wherever the bloody exploits of Cæsar took place,—in Urbino, Pesaro, Imola, Faenza, Cesena, Forlì,—he kept, as was his wont, a brief, exact diary. But not by a single word did he refer to Cæsar in these notes, as though not seeing, or not desiring to see, that which was going on all about him. He jotted down every trifle that he met with in his travels: the manner in which the agriculturists in Cesena joined their fruit-trees by means of climbing vines; the construction of the levers which set in motion the cathedral bells in Siena; the strange, low music of the cascading streams of the city fountain at Rimini. He made a sketch of the dove-cote and of the tower with the spiral staircase in the Castle of Urbino, whence the ill-fated Duke Guidobaldo had just made his escape, plundered by Cæsar, and, to use the expression of contemporaries, "only in his nether shift." He observed how, in Romagna, at the foot of the Apennines, the shepherds, in order to augment the sound of a horn, set its wide end in the narrow opening of some deep cavern,—and the thunder-like noise, filling the dale, repeated by the echo, becomes so strong that all the herds, even those feeding on the farthest mountains, hear it. Alone, on the shores of the desolate sea at Piombino, he watched, for days at a time, one wave topping another, now casting up, now sucking in rubble, chips of driftwood, stones and marine plants. "Thus do the waves combat for the plunder, which falls to the victor," wrote Leonardo. And, while all about him the laws of human justice were being violated,—without condemning, without excusing, he contemplated in the motion of the waves, apparently accidental and capricious, but in reality unchanging and regular, the uncontrovertible laws of divine justice,—of mechanics, founded by the First Mover.

On the ninth of June, fifteen hundred and two, in the Tiber, at Rome were found the dead bodies of the youthful ruler of Faenza, Astorre, and of his brother, both strangled, with ropes and stones about their necks, thrown into the river from the prison of Sant' Angelo. Their bodies,—according to the words of contemporaries, so beautiful that "their like was not to be found among a thousand,"—bore marks of an unnatural assault. Popular rumour attributed this evil deed to Cæsar.

And at this time Leonardo noted down in his diary:

"In Romagna they use carts on four wheels; the two fore wheels are small, the two rear ones large; an absurd construction, inasmuch as, according to the law of physics,—see paragraph five of my *Elements*, —all the weight bears upon the front wheels."

Thus, keeping silent about the greatest infractions of the laws of spiritual equilibrium, he waxed indignant at the infraction of the laws of mechanics in the construction of Romagna wains.

II

In the latter half of December of the same year, the Duke of Valentino with all his court and troops journeyed from Cesena to the city of Fano, where a meeting had been agreed upon with the erstwhile conspirators, Oliverotto da Fermo, Orsini, and Vitelli. Toward the end of the same month Leonardo left Pesaro to join Cæsar.

Setting out in the morning, he thought he would reach his destination at twilight. But a storm sprang up. The mountains were covered with impassable snow-drifts. The mules, their hoofs slipping on the ice-covered stones, were constantly stumbling. To the horror of the guide, his mule shied to one side, sensing a dead body swaying on the branch of an aspen.

It grew dark. They rode on at haphazard, with reins hanging, trusting to the intelligent animals. A little light sprang up, glimmering in the distance. The guide recognized the great inn at Novilara, exactly halfway between Fano and Pesaro. They were compelled to knock for a long while at the enormous doors, studded with iron nails, resembling the gates of a fortress. Finally a sleepy hostler with a lanthorn came out, and the master of the inn, next. He refused them lodging,

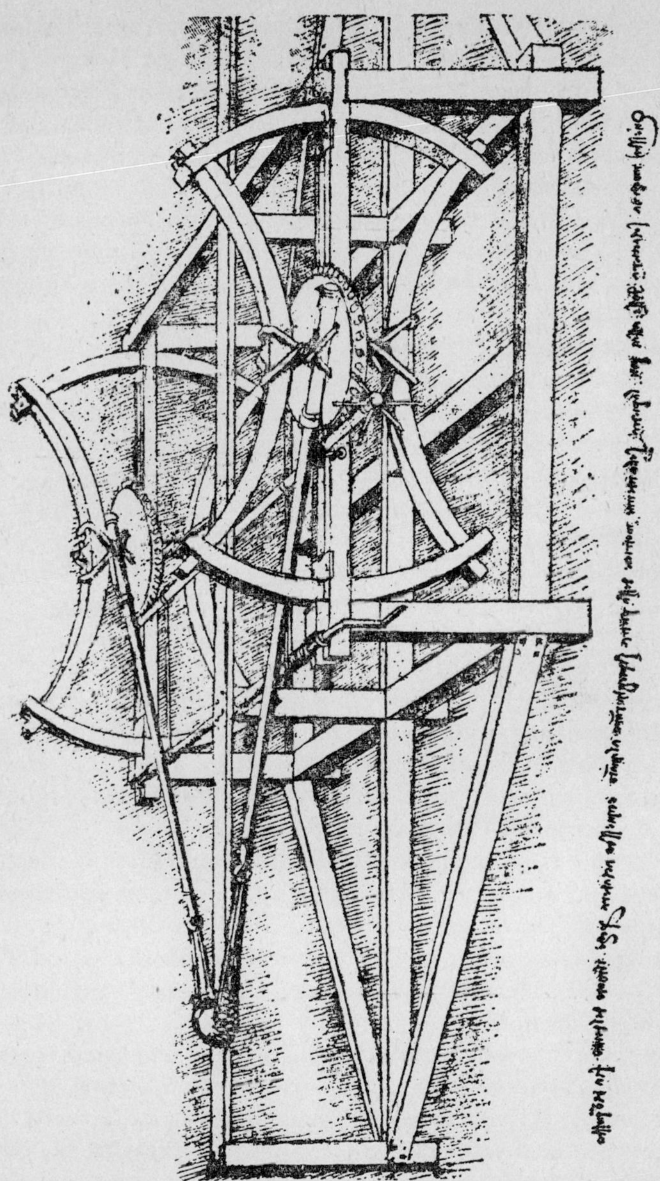

declaring not only all the rooms, but even the stables, to be filled to overflowing,—there was not, 'twould seem, a single cot which was not occupied that night by three or four people, and all of them people of high station,—warriors and courtiers from the retinue of the Duke.

When Leonardo gave his name and showed him his pass with the seal and the signature of the Duke, the landlord became exceedingly profuse of apologies, offered his own room, up to the present taken up only by three commanders of the French allied forces, who, having drunk themselves into a stupor, were sleeping the sleep of the dead, while he and his wife volunteered to make their own bed in a closet beside the smithy.

Leonardo entered the room which served both as refectory and kitchen, every jot the same as in all the hostelries in Romagna,—soot-covered, dirty, with spots of dampness on the bare, peeling walls, with chickens and guinea fowl slumbering on a roost right in the room, suckling pigs squealing in a wicket pen, and rows of aureate onions, of hams and blood sausages, hung up on the blackened beams of the ceiling. On the enormous hearth with its overhanging brick chimney blazed a fire, and a pig's carcass hissed on the turn-spit. In the reflected red glow of the fire the guests, seated at long tables, were eating, drinking, shouting, disputing, playing at sundry games including draughts and cards. Leonardo sat down by the fire to await the ordered supper.

At a neighbouring table, where among the auditors the artist recognized the old captain of the Duke's lancers, Baldassare Scipioni, the chief court treasurer, Alessandro Spanocchia, and the envoy from Ferrara, Pandolfo Colenuccio, an unknown man, waving his arms about, was speaking with unusual animation in a high, squeaky voice:

"By examples from modern and ancient history can I prove it, signori,—with mathematical exactness! Do you but recall the kingdoms that have attained military glory,—the Romans, the Lacedæmonians, the Athenians, the Ætolians, the Achaians, and a multiplicity of tribes on the other side of the Alps. All great conquerors gathered their troops from the citizens of their own nation: Ninus, from the Assyrians; Cyrus, from the Persians; Alexander, from among the Macedonians. . . . True, Pyrrhus and Hannibal obtained victories with hirelings; but in this instance it was all a matter of the unusual skill of the leaders, able to instill soldiers from other lands with the manhood and valour of native troops. In addition to that, forget not the chief position, the corner-stone, of the military science: in the infantry, say I, and only in the infantry, lies the deciding force of the army, and not in the cavalry, not in fire-arms and gunpowder, that absurd conceit of the new times! . . ."

"You are infatuated, Messer Niccolò," contradicted the captain of the lancers, with a polite smile. "Fire-arms are acquiring a greater significance with every day. Whatever you may say of the Spartans and the Romans, I will venture to assert the opinion that present-day troops are considerably better armed than those of ancient times. 'Tis not said to offend Your Honour,—but a squadron of French knights, or a division of artillery with thirty bombards, would overturn a cliff, let alone a division of your Roman infantry!"

"Sophisms! Sophisms!" fumed Messer Niccolò. "Signor, I recognize in your words a fatal error, whereby the best military men of our age pervert the truth. You wait,—some time or other the hordes of Northern barbarians will open the eyes of the Italians, and they shall perceive the pitiful helplessness of their hirelings; they shall be convinced that the cavalry and artillery are not worth a straw before the rocklike hardihood of well-regulated infantry. . . . And how is it that men argue against the self-evident? If you would merely reflect that with an insignificant division of infantry Lucullus scattered a hundred and fifty thousand of the cavalry of Tigranes, among which were the cohorts of horsemen, every bit like the squadrons of your present-day French knights! . . ."

Leonardo glanced with curiosity at this man, who spoke of the victories of Lucullus as if he had beheld them with his own eyes. The stranger had on a long garment of dark-red cloth, of a grandiose cut, with straight folds, such as were worn by the dignified governmental people of the Florentine Republic,—consular secretaries, among others. But the raiment had a worn look; here and there—true, on places none too conspicuous—there were spots; the sleeves were shiny. Judging by the edge of the shirt, which usually was let out in a narrow stripe on the neck from the closely buttoned collar, his linen was of a dubious freshness. His large, knotted hands,—with a callus on the middle finger of one, as is the case with people who write a great deal,—were ink-stained. There was little of the impressive, of that which would inspire people with respect, in the appearance of this man, still far from old, about forty, spare, narrow-shouldered, with amazingly animated eyes, and sharp, angular features, of extraordinary strangeness. Sometimes, during conversation, elevating his flat, long nose, just like a duck's bill, throwing his small head backward, narrowing his eyes, and pensively thrusting out his prominent lower lip, he would look over the head of his fellow speaker, as though he were gazing into the distance; on such occasions he resembled a sharp-sighted bird, gazing intently at a very distant object, all alert and with its thin long neck stretched out. In his uneasy movements, in the febrile glow upon his prominent, wide cheek-bones, on his swarthy and sunken clean-shaven cheeks, and especially in his large grey, ponderously intent eyes, one could sense an inner fire. These eyes would fain be malevolent; but at times, through the expression of cold bitterness, of a caustic mockery, there would flicker through them something timid and plaintive.

Messer Niccolò continued to develop his thought about the military strength of the infantry, and Leonardo wondered at the mixture of truth and falsehood, at the illimitable daring and the slavish adulation of the ancients, contained in the words of this man. Demonstrating the uselessness of fire-arms, he mentioned, among other things, how difficult the aiming of big cannon was, the shot of which are carried either too high over the heads of the foes, or too low, without reaching them. The artist put the true value on the shrewdness and aptness of this observation, knowing by his own experience the imperfections of the bombards of that day. But immediately after, having expressed the opinion that fortresses can not protect the realm, Niccolò cited the Romans, who built no fortresses, and also the dwellers of Lacedæmonia, who would not permit Sparta to be fortified, in order that they might have as a wall about them only the manhood of its citizens; and, as if everything that the ancients did and thought was truth incontrovertible, he cited the utterance of the Spartan anent the walls of Athens, famous in all the schools: "They would be useful, if all the dwellers in the city were only women."

Leonardo did not hear the conclusion of the dispute, because the landlord led him off to the room prepared for his lodging.

III

TOWARD morning the snow-storm was in full blast. The guide refused to travel, asserting that in such weather a good man would not put even a dog out of his house. The artist was forced to remain for another day. For lack of anything to do he began setting up in the kitchen hearth a self-turning spit of his own invention,—a large wheel with paddles set at an angle, brought into rotation by the draught of the warmed air in the chimney, and, in its turn, rotating the spit.

"With a contrivance like this," Leonardo explained to the wonder-struck spectators, "the cook need have no fear that his roast will burn, inasmuch as the degree of heat remains equable: when it increases, the spit quickens its motion, when the heat decreases, the spit slows down."

The artist constructed the perfect kitchen turn-spit with the same love and inspiration as the human wings.

In the same room Messer Niccolò was explaining to some youthful French sergeants of artillery, all desperate gamblers, a rule which, so it would seem, he had found in the laws of abstract mathematics, of winning infallibly at dice, overcoming the whims of "Fortune the strumpet," as he put it. With intelligence and eloquence he expounded this rule, but every time that he tried to prove it in practice, he would lose, to the no small wonder of himself and the malicious joy of his auditors,—consoling himself, however, with the fact that he had permitted an error in the application of a correct rule. The game ended with an explanation unpleasant to Messer Niccolò,—when the time came to pay, it came out that his purse was empty and that he was playing on credit.

Late in the evening there arrived, with an enormous quantity of bales and boxes, and with numerous servants, pages, hostlers, jesters, hounds, and all sorts of amusing animals, the noble Venetian courtesan, "the harlot magnificent,"—Lena Griffa, the same who had at one time in Florence almost undergone an attack of the Holy Army of the little inquisitors of Brother Girolamo Savonarola.

Two years ago, following the example of many of her sisterhood, Monna Lena had forsaken the world, turned into a repentant Magdalen, and had shorn her tresses to become a nun, in order that she might subsequently raise her price in the famous *Tariff of Courtesans, or Discourses for the Illustrious Stranger; in which are Designated the Prices and Qualities of all the Courtesans of Venice, together with the Names of their Bawds*. Out of the dark monastic chrysalis there had fluttered a scintillating butterfly. Lena Griffa rapidly made her upward way in the world: in accordance with the customs of the courtesans of the higher grade, the Venetian street *mammola*,—darling,—composed for herself a grandiose family tree, from which it was evident that she was neither more nor less than the daughter, on the wrong side of the blanket, of the brother of the Duke of Milan, the Cardinal Ascanio Sforza. At the same time she had become the chief concubine of a certain senile Cardinal, half out of his head from age, and incalculably rich. And it was to him that Lena was now journeying from Venice to the city of Fano, where Monsignor was awaiting her at the court of Cæsar Borgia.

Mine host was in a quandary: to refuse lodging to such an illustrious personage,—"Her Reverence,"—the Cardinal's concubine, he durst not, and yet of vacant rooms he had none. Finally, he managed to enter into an agreement with some merchants from Ancona, who, for a rebate promised them on their bill, transferred their lodging to the smithy, giving their room over to the retinue of the noble harlot. For their mistress herself he demanded the room of Messer Niccolò and his room-mates, the knights of Ives d'Allegra, offering them beds also in the smithy, with the merchants.

Niccolò became angry, and was just becoming heated, asking mine host if he were in his right mind, if he understood with whom he was dealing, allowing himself such impertinences with respectable persons on account of the first-come trollop. But here the landlady entered the lists,—a woman free of speech and belligerent, and who "was not in the habit of pawning her tongue with the Jew." She remarked to Messer Niccolò that, before bandying words and raising trouble, one should pay the reckoning for one's own provender, and that of his servant and three horses, and, by the way, return the four ducats which her man, out of the goodness of his heart, had lent him as far back as last Friday. And, as though to herself, but sufficiently loud so that all those present might hear, she wished an ill Easter to all those knaves and cheats who roam the highways, giving themselves out to be Lord knows what high and mighty personages, but really living without paying, and, to boot, turn up their noses before honest folk. Probably there must have been a modicum of truth in the words of this woman; at least, Niccolò unexpectedly quieted down, let his eyes drop before her divulging gaze, and was evidently considering how he might beat a decent retreat. The servants were already carrying his things out of the room, and a hideous little monkey, Madonna Lena's favourite, was making plaintive little grimaces, having hopped up on the table where lay the papers, quills, and books of Messer Niccolò, among which were the *Decades* of Titus Livius and the *Lives of Illustrious Men*, by Plutarch.

"Messer," Leonardo addressed him, "if you would be pleased to share my lodging with me, I should deem it a great honour to render Your Grace this inconsequential service."

Niccolò turned around to him with some wonder and became still more confused, but immediately recovered and thanked him with dignity. They passed into Leonardo's room, where the artist took care to give his new room-mate the best place. The more he observed him, the more attractive and curious did this queer fellow seem to him. The latter informed him of his name and title,—Niccolò Machiavelli, Secretary to the Council of Ten of the Republic of Florence.

Three months ago the crafty and wary Signoria had despatched Machiavelli for negotiations with Cæsar Borgia, whom it hoped to surpass in craftiness, replying to all his propositions of a defensive alliance against their common enemies, Bentivoglio, Orsini and Vitelli with Platonic and equivocal protestations of friendship. In reality the Republic, fearing the Duke, desired to have him neither for foe nor friend. To Messer Niccolò Machiavelli, deprived of all actual powers, was entrusted only the obtaining of a free passage for Florentine merchants through the Duke's possessions on the shores of the Adriatic Sea,—an affair, however, of no inconsiderable importance for trade, "this foster mother of the Republic," as the travelling instructions of the Signoria expressed it.

Leonardo also gave his name and his rank at the court of Valentino. They fell to talking, with a natural ease and confidence, peculiar to people of contrasting characters, yet lonely and contemplative.

"Messer," Niccolò immediately confessed, and this frankness pleased the artist, "I have heard, of course, that you are a great master. But I must warn you that I know nothing of painting, and even have no love for it, although I suppose that this art could make the same answer to me that Dante made to a certain wag who showed him a *fico* on the street: 'I would not give thee one of mine for an hundred of thine.' But I have also heard that the Duke of Valentino esteems you a great connoisseur of the military science, and that is what I would sometime like to discuss with Your Worship. It has always seemed to me that this was a subject all the more important and worthy of attention in that all the civic grandeur of a people is reared up on military might, upon the quantity and quality of its standing army, as I shall prove in my book concerning monarchies and republics, wherein the natural laws governing the life, growth, decline and death of every government shall be defined with the same exactitude with which the mathematician defines the laws of numbers, or the physicist the laws of physics and mechanics. For I must tell you that hitherto all those who have written of government . . ."

But here he paused and cut himself short with a good-natured smile:

"Pardon me, messer! I, 'twould seem, am imposing on your good nature: perhaps politics are of as little interest to you as painting is to me? . . ."

"No, no, on the contrary," said the artist. "Or, rather, I will speak with you as frankly as you have spoken with me, Messer Niccolò. I really do not relish the usual discussions about war and matters of government, because all of these discussions are false and vain. But your opinions are so dissimilar to the opinion of the majority, so new and unusual, that, believe me, I listen to them with the greatest of pleasure."

"Oh, take heed, Messer Leonardo!" Niccolò burst into laughter, still more good-naturedly. "You may yet have to repent,—you do not know me yet; why, this is my hobby-horse,—I shall mount it, and shall not let off until you yourself will command me to keep quiet! Feed me not with bread,—do but let me chat about politics with a man of intelligence! But there is the rub,—where will you find such men? Our Magnificent Signori want to know naught save the market prices of wool and of silk; whereas I," added he with a proud and bitter smile, "I, evidently, through the will of the Fates, having been born without the ability of discussing either losses or gains, or the wool industry or the silk, must choose one of two things: either to keep silent or to speak of governmental matters."

The artist once more reassured him, and, in order to renew the conversation, which did, in reality, appear interesting to him, he asked:

"You have just said, messer, that politics should be an exact science, the same as the natural sciences, founded on mathematics, deriving their authenticity from experience and the observation of nature. Have I understood you correctly?"

"Yes, yes!" answered Machiavelli, contracting his brows, narrowing his eyes, and gazing over Leonardo's head, all on his guard, and becoming like a keen-sighted bird which is gazing intently at a very distant object, its long, thin neck drawn out.

"Perhaps I may not be able to do this," he continued, "but I want to tell men that which has never yet been said of human affairs. Plato in his *Republic*, Aristotle in his *Politics*, St. Augustine in his *City of God*,—all who have written of government,—did not perceive the most important thing: the natural laws governing the life of every people, and placed outside of any human will, outside of good and evil. All have spoken of that which seems good and evil, noble and base, imagining unto themselves such governances as should be, but in reality are not and can not be. As for me, I do not desire either that which should be, nor that which seems, but only that which exists in reality. I would investigate the nature of the great bodies known as republics and monarchies,—without love and hatred, without praise and opprobrium,—even as a mathematician investigates the nature of numbers, or the anatomist the structure of the human body. That it is difficult and dangerous I know, inasmuch as in nothing else do men fear truth as much, and avenge it so, as in politics; but still shall I tell them the truth, even though they burn me after at the stake, like Brother Girolamo!"

With an involuntary smile Leonardo watched the expression of daring,—prophetic and at the same time flippant, like a school-boy's,—upon Niccolò's face, and in his eyes, glistening with a strange, almost an insane glitter; and the artist reflected.

"With what emotion he speaks about calm; with what a passion about dispassionateness!"

"Messer Niccolò," he said, "should you succeed in carrying out this project, your discoveries would have no lesser a significance than the geometry of Euclid, or the investigations of Archimedes in mechanics."

Leonardo was really struck by the novelty of that which he heard from Messer Niccolò. He recalled how, even thirteen years ago, upon finishing a book of drawings, picturing the inner organs of the human body, he had added on the side margin:

"May the All-Highest help me to learn the nature of men, their manners and customs, just as I am learning the inner structure of the human body."

IV

THEY conversed for long. Leonardo, among other things, asked him how he could, in his conversation yesterday with the captain of the lancers, deny all military significance to fortresses, gunpowder, and fire-arms. Was it not simply a jest?

"The ancient Spartans and Romans," retorted Niccolò, "irreproachable instructors of the military art, had no conception of gunpowder."

"But then, have not experience and a knowledge of nature," exclaimed the artist, "opened to us a great deal,—and do they not with every year open to us still more,—of that of which the ancients did not even dare to think?"

But Machiavelli stubbornly stood his ground:

"I think," he reiterated, "that in matters military and civic the new nations fall into errors by declining to imitate the ancients."

"Is such imitation possible, Messer Niccolò?"

"And why not? For have men and the elements changed; have the heavens and the sun changed their motions, their order and their power, —have they become other than they have been in the times of antiquity?"

And no arguments could shake his conviction. Leonardo perceived how, bold to daring in all things else, he suddenly became superstitious and timid, just like a pedant of the schools, the instant the subject of antiquity was broached.

"And in order that we may all the more worthily crown our conversation," said Niccolò, "allow me to read you a most beautiful passage from Livy; then listen to my elucidation."

He picked up a book from the table, drew the guttered end of the tallow candle nearer, put on his iron spectacles, broken but painstakingly tied with thread, with big round lenses, his face assuming an austere and devout expression, as though he were praying or officiating in church.

But, just as he had elevated his brows and his index finger, preparing to search for the chapter which makes evident that victories and the acquisitions gotten by conquest lead unstable governments to ruin rather than to greatness, and had uttered the first words of the solemn Livy, as canorous as bronze, the door opened very quietly, and there entered the room, stealthily, a wrinkled and bent little crone.

"Signori mine," she mumbled, bowing low, "forgive my disturbing you. My mistress, the most illustrious Madonna Lena Griffa, has had her pet little beastie escape,—a hare with a bit of blue ribbon about its neck. We are searching and searching, and have ransacked the whole house, till we are falling off our feet, and can never figure out where in the world it has gone to. . . ."

"There is never a hare here," Messer Niccolò interrupted her angrily, "get thee gone!"

And he arose, in order to put the old woman out,—but suddenly he looked at her closely through his spectacles; then, letting them down to the tip of his nose, gave another look over them, clapped his hands together, and ejaculated:

"Monna Alvigia! Is it thou, thou old hag? And here I was thinking that the fiends had long since with their hooks dragged off thy old carrion carcass into the infernal fire! . . ."

The crone narrowed her purblind, crafty eyes, and opened her mouth in a toothless grin, which made her still more hideous:

"Messer Niccolò! How many winters, how many summers, since I have seen you! There, I never guessed, I never knew, that God would grant us to meet once more! . . ."

Machiavelli made his excuses to the artist and invited Monna Alvigia to the kitchen for a chat, to recall the good old times. But Leonardo assured him that they did not disturb him; he picked up a book, and sat down at some distance. Niccolò summoned a servant and ordered him to fetch wine, with the same air as if he were the most esteemed guest in the house.

"And tell the cheat of a landlord, friend, that he should not dare to regale us with that sour stuff he served us the other day, inasmuch as Monna Alvigia and I relish not bad wine,—even as the priest Arlotto, who, so the story runs, would never kneel in front of the Holy Eucharist if the wine were bad, supposing that such stuff could not be transmuted into the blood of the Lord! . . ."

Monna Alvigia forgot the hare, just as Messer Niccolò had Titus Livius, and over the jug of wine they fell to chatting, like old friends. From their talk Leonardo gathered that the old woman had at one time been a courtesan herself; later, the keeper of a house of ill-fame in Florence; a go-between in Venice; and now served as chief housekeeper and wardrobe mistress to Madonna Lena Griffa. Machiavelli questioned her about common acquaintances,—about fifteen-year-old, blue-eyed Atalanta, who once, speaking of the love-sin, had exclaimed with an innocent smile: "Can this be a blasphemy against the Holy Ghost? The monks and the priests may preach what they please, but I shall never believe that 'tis a mortal sin to afford pleasure to poor mortals!"—about the beautiful Madonna Riccia, whose husband used to remark with the indifference of a philosopher, whenever he was informed of the infidelities of his spouse: "A wife in the house is like to a fire in the hearth: let your neighbours have as much as you will,—'twill not decrease." Also did they recall the stout, red-haired Marmillia, who, every time when she gave in to the supplications of her admirers, used devoutly to lower a curtain before the icon,—"That the Madonna might not see."

Niccolò, in all this gossip and bawdy talk, evidently felt in his element. Leonardo wondered at the transformation of this man of statecraft, a secretary of the Republic of Florence, and quiet and sage conversationalist, into the shiftless rake and habitué of dives. However, of real gaiety there was none in Machiavelli, and the artist sensed a secret bitterness in his cynical laughter.

"So it wags, my dear sir! The young grow up; the old age," concluded Alvigia, falling into an emotional mood and shaking her head, like an old Parca of love. "These be different times now. . . ."

"Thou liest, thou old witch, thou devil's chosen!" Niccolò gave her a sly wink. "Do not arouse the wrath of God, gossip mine. Whatever the lot of others be now, 'tis a carnival for your kind. Now the pretty little women have no jealous or poor husbands, and, having become friendly with such artful ladies as thou, they live in clover. The proudest of signore will yield for money,—all over Italy there is but wholesale sin and lewdness. 'Tis only by the yellow sign that one may know a loose woman from an honest one. . . ."

The yellow sign referred to was an especial head kerchief of a saffron colour which the law compelled the harlots to wear so that they might not, in a crowd, be confused with honest women.

"Oh, say not so, messer!" sighed the old woman heart-rendingly. "Where does the present day compare with the former? Why, just take this for instance: not so long ago we had not even as much as heard in Italy of the French sickness,—we lived as it were in Christ's bosom. Or, again, take this yellow sign,—oh, my God, 'tis simply a misfortune! Would you believe it, they almost put my mistress away in jail during the last carnival. Well, now, judge for yourself,—is it a fitting thing for Madonna Lena to be wearing the yellow sign?"

"And why should she not wear it?"

"My, my, whatever are you saying,—how can it be? Be reasonable! Why, is the most illustrious Madonna some street wench, of the sort that go traipsing around with any riff-raff? Does your worship know that the coverlet of her bed is more magnificent than the Papal vestments on the day of Holy Easter? And, as for her mind and learning,—there, I think, she can give pointers to all the doctors at the University of Bologna. You should but hear her discourse of Petrarca, of Laura, of the Infinity of Celestial Love. . . ."

"Of course," grinned Niccolò, "who else should know of the infinity of love if not she! . . ."

"Oh, you may laugh,—you may laugh, messer, but, honest to God, may I never arise from this spot: the other day, when she was reading to me her epistle—in verse—to a certain poor youth, whom she advises to turn to the practice of virtues, I just listened and listened, and then went and burst into tears; well, it gets into one's very soul so,—just as it used to be the case in Santa Maria del Fiore, when Brother Girolamo,—may he rest in heaven,—was wont to preach. Truly is she a new Tully Cicero! And then, too, it must be said: 'tis not for naught that the most illustrious personages pay her as much—or perhaps two or three ducats less,—merely for her conversation about the mysteries of Platonic Love, as they pay others for a whole night. And yet you speak of the yellow sign, forsooth!"

In conclusion Monna Alvigia told of her own youth. She, too, had been beautiful, and she, too, had been courted; all her whims were fulfilled,—and what only did she not do! Once, in the city of Padua, in the vestry of the cathedral, she had taken a bishop's mitre off and had put it on her female slave's head. But with the years her beauty had faded; her admirers had scattered; and she had had to live by renting out rooms and taking in washing. And then, to boot, she was taken ill, and had fallen to such poverty that she was fain to beg for alms on the church steps in order that she might purchase poison and commit suicide. But the Most Pure Virgin saved her from death; through the open-handed generosity of a certain old abbot, who had fallen in love with her neighbour, a blacksmith's wife, Monna Alvigia entered upon a thorny path, taking up a more profitable trade than that of washing.

Having told of the miraculous aid of the Lord's Mother, her especial Intercessor, she was interrupted by a servant of Madonna Lena, who had come running to tell her that her mistress was asking the housekeeper for the little vial with the ointment for the little monkey, whose paw was frost-bitten, and for the *Decameron* of Boccaccio, which the noble whore read before falling asleep, and which she hid under her pillow, together with her prayer-book.

When the old woman had left, Niccolò took out some paper, fixed his quill, and began composing a report to the Magnificent Signoria of Florence, about the projects and actions of the Duke of Valentino,—an epistle filled with civic wisdom, despite its easy, semi-jocose style.

"Messer," said he suddenly, lifting up his eyes and glancing at the artist, "do confess, now,—you were astonished that I had passed so suddenly from conversation about grand and serious subjects, about the virtues of the ancient Spartans and the Romans, to small talk with a bawd about wenches? But do not judge me too severely; and remember, my dear sir, that we are taught this diversity by nature herself, with all her contrasts and transformations. For the most important thing is to follow nature fearlessly in all things! Then, too, why pretend? We are all men, all human. Do you know the old fable of how the philosopher Aristotle, at the whim of a wanton woman, with whom he was hopelessly in love, did, in the presence of his pupil, Alexander the Great, get down on all fours and put her on his back,—and, all naked and shameless, she did ride the sage, even as one rides a mule? Of course, 'tis but a fable, but it hath a profound meaning. For if Aristotle himself did venture upon such folly for the sake of a comely wench,—how are we ordinary sinners to resist? . . ."

The hour was late. Everybody had long been asleep. All was quiet, save for a cricket singing in a corner, and the sound of Monna Alvigia behind a wooden partition in the next room mumbling and muttering something as she rubbed the monkey's frost-bitten paw with the medicinal ointment. Leonardo lay down but could not fall asleep for a long time, and watched Machiavelli, diligently bent over his work, with the spattering goose-quill in his hand. The flame of the candle-end cast on the wall an enormous shadow of his head, with sharp, angular lines,—the nether lip out-thrust, the thin neck disproportionately long, the nose long, like a beak. Having finished his reports of Cæsar's politics, and sealed the outer cover with wax, writing the usual injunction on important despatches: *cito, citissime, celerrime!* (urgent, most urgent, urgent to the last degree!)—he opened his Titus Livius, and plunged into his beloved labour of many years,—the compilation of expository comments on the *Decades*.

Leonardo watched the strange black shadow on the white wall dancing and making shameless grimaces in the light of the expiring candle-end, whereas the face of the secretary of the Republic of Florence preserved a grave calm, just like a reflection of the grandeur that was Rome. Only in the very depth of his eyes, as well as in the corners of his sinuous lips, there lurked at times an equivocal, craftv, bitterly mocking expression, almost as cynical as at the time of his conversation about wenches with the bawd.

V

On the next morning the storm abated. The sun sparkled in the hostelry's hoar-frost-covered small panes of turbid green, as through pale emeralds. The snow-covered fields and knolls glistened, as soft as down, blindingly white beneath the blue heavens.

When Leonardo awoke, his fellow lodger was no longer in the room. The artist descended to the kitchen. A large blaze was flaming on the hearth, and a roast hissing on the self-turning spit. Mine host could not have his fill of admiring contemplation of Leonardo's contrivance, while an ancient little old woman, who had come from a far-away mountain settlement, gazed with popping eyes, in a superstitious horror, at the carcass of mutton browning of itself, moving as if it were alive and turning its sides so as not to burn.

Leonardo ordered his guide to saddle the mules, and sat down at table, to have a snack against the forthcoming journey. Alongside of him Messer Niccolò was conversing, in an exceeding temper, with two new arrivals. One of them was a courier from Florence; the other a young man of irreproachable worldly appearance, whose face was that of the common run, neither foolish nor intelligent, neither evil nor good, —the unrememberable face of the crowd; he was a certain Messer Lucio, as Leonardo subsequently found out; a grand-nephew of Francesco Vettori, an illustrious citizen, who had extensive connections and was friendlily disposed toward Machiavelli, and who was directly related to Pietro Soderini, Gonfaloniere. Setting out for Ancona on family affairs, Lucio had undertaken to search out Niccolò in Romagna, and to transmit to him the letters of his Florentine friends. He had arrived together with the courier.

"You are pleased to be excited in vain, Messer Niccolò," Lucio was saying. "Mine uncle Francesco assures me that the money will be sent out soon. 'Twas promised him even last Thursday but the Signoria. . . ."

"My dear sir," Machiavelli maliciously cut him short, "I have two servants and three horses, which can not be fed by the promises of the Magnificent Signori! In Imola I received sixty ducats,—and paid seventy for debts. If it were not for the compassion of kindly folk, the Secretary of the Florentine Republic would have died from starvation. I must say the Signoria take good care of the honour of their city when they compel a trusted personage to importune in a foreign court for two or three ducats, on the plea of poverty!"

He knew that his complaints were in vain, but it made no difference to him, so that he might but vent the bitterness seething within him. The kitchen was almost empty; they could speak freely.

"Your compatriot, Messer Leonardo da Vinci,—the Gonfaloniere must know him,—" Machiavelli continued, indicating the artist, to whom Lucio made a polite bow, "was witness but yesterday to the insults to which I am subjected. . . . I demand,—do you hear, I do not request, but demand,—my resignation!" he concluded, growing still more heated, and evidently picturing to himself the entire Magnificent Signoria in the person of the young Florentine. "I am a poor man. My affairs are in disorder. Finally, I am a sick man. If things will go on at their present rate, I shall be carried home in a coffin! In addition to that, all that could be accomplished with the instructions given me I have already accomplished. But to protract the negotiations, to beat about the bush, to take a step forward and two steps back,—to dally with thistles,—your humble servant declines! I deem the Duke too clever for such puerile politics. However, I have written to your uncle. . . ."

"My uncle will, of course, do everything for you that lies in his power, —but here is the rub: the Council of Ten esteems your reports so necessary for the good of the Republic, and shedding such light on the matters here, that none would even hear of your resignation. 'We would be glad to, now, but there is none to replace him with.' A unique man a man of gold, say they, the eye and ear of the Republic. I can assure you, Messer Niccolò, your letters have such success in Florence that you yourself could not wish a greater. All are enraptured with the inimitable elegance and the felicity of your style. Uncle was telling me that the other day, in the hall of the Council, when they were reading one of your jocose epistles, the Signori were simply convulsed with laughter. . . ."

"Ah, so that is how matters stand!" exclaimed Machiavelli, and his face gave a sudden twitch. "Well, now I comprehend everything: my letters have struck the fancy of the Signori. Glory be to God, Messer Niccolò has proven of some use, after all! They are convulsed with laughter over there, d'you see, appreciating the elegance of my style, while I lead a dog's life here, freezing, starving, shivering from fever, enduring humiliations, beating about like an ice-bound fish,—all for the weal of the Republic, may the devil seize it, with the Gonfaloniere to boot, the tearful old woman that he is! May ye all lie uncoffined and unshrouded! . . ."

He burst into street vituperation. He was filled with his habitual impotent indignation at the thought of these leaders of the people, whom he despised and whose chore he did. Desiring to change the conversation, Lucio handed him a letter from his young wife, Monna Marietta. Machiavelli ran his eye over a few lines, scrawled in a large childish hand on grey paper:

"I have heard," wrote Marietta, among other things, "that in those regions where you now are there are fevers raging and other illnesses. You can imagine the state of my soul. Thoughts of you give me no rest nor day nor night.—The boy, thanks be to God, is well. He is becoming amazingly like you. His little face is as white as snow, while his little head is thickly covered with darling black hair, all black,—oh, so black,—every whit like that of Your Worship. He seems beautiful to me, because he resembles you. And he is so lively, so merry, as though he were already a year old. Would you believe it, the minute he was born, he opened his little eyes, and yelled all over the house.—But do you not forget us, and I beg you, very, very much, come as quickly as you can, because I can not, and will not, wait any longer. Come, for God's sake! And in the meanwhile, may the Lord preserve you, and may also the Most Pure Virgin, and the all-powerful Messer Antonio, to whom I pray without cease for the welfare of Your Worship."

Leonardo remarked that during the reading of this letter Machiavelli's face was illumined by a kindly smile, unexpected from his sharp, angular features, as though from behind them had peeped out the face of another man. But it disappeared at once. Making a shrug of contempt, he crumpled up the letter, thrust it in his pocket, and grumbled sullenly:

"And whoever had to go and blab about my illness?"

"It was impossible to conceal it," retorted Lucio. "Every day Monna Marietta comes to some one of your friends, or member of the Council of Ten, questioning, worming out, where you are, and what is going on with you. . . ."

"Yes, I know, I know, do not tell me,—I know how she can be!"

He made an impatient gesture, and added:

"Matters of government should be entrusted to unmarried men. One of two things,—either wife or politics!"

And, in turning away a little, he continued in a high-pitched voice:

"Perhaps you have intentions of marrying, young man?"

"Not as yet," answered Lucio.

"Never, then,—do you hear, never,—commit this folly. May God preserve you! To marry, my dear sir, is just the same as to seek an eel in a bag of snakes! Married life is a burden for the back of Atlas, and not an ordinary mortal. Is it not so, Messer Leonardo?"

Leonardo looked at him and surmised that he loved Monna Marietta with profound tenderness, but, being ashamed of this love, was concealing it behind a mask of cynical impudicity.

The hostelry became empty. The guests, having risen early, had gone their ways. Leonardo, too, got ready for the journey. He invited Machiavelli to travel with him. But the latter sadly shook his head, and answered that he would have to wait for money from Florence in order to pay his reckoning with the host and to hire horses. Of the recent assumed ease of manner there was not even a trace left. He had suddenly drooped, had sunk; he seemed unhappy and ill. The ennui of immobility, of a too-long stay on the self-same spot, was murderous to him. It was not in vain that in a certain letter the members of the Council of Ten reproached him with his too frequent and causeless migrations, which gave rise to confusion in government matters: "Thou seest, Niccolò, to what a pass thy restless spirit, so avid for change of place, brings us."

Leonardo took him by the hand, led him aside, and offered to lend him some money. Niccolò declined.

"Do not offend me, my friend," said the artist. "Recall what you yourself said yesterday,—what a rare conjunction of stars is necessary to have two such people as we meet. Why, then, do you deprive yourself and me of this benevolence of fate? And do you not feel that it is you who would be rendering a sincere service to me, rather than I to you? . . ."

In the artist's face and voice there was such kindliness that Niccolò had not the heart to cause him sorrow, and he took thirty ducats, which he promised to return as soon as he would receive money from Florence. He immediately paid his reckoning in the hostelry with the generosity of a grandee.

VI

THEY took their departure. The morning was quiet, serene, with an almost vernal warmth and thawing in the sun, with fragrantly-frosty freshness in the shade. The deep snow with its blue shadows crunched under the hoofs. Between the white knolls sparkled the pale-green wintry sea, and the yellow, slanting sails, resembling the wings of aureate butterflies, flickered here and there upon it. Niccolò chattered, jested, and laughed. Every trifle elicited from him unexpectedly amusing or sad ideas.

Riding past a poor fishing hamlet on the shores of the sea and the mountain stream of Arcilla, the travellers beheld on a piazzetta before the church some fat, jolly monks in the midst of a throng of young women of the village, who were buying little crosses, beads, holy relics, pebbles from the House of the Mother of God at Loretto, and little feathers from the wings of the Archangel Michael.

"What are you gaping for?" Niccolò cried to the husbands and brothers of the women, who were also standing nearby on the square. "Let not the monks nigh women! Do ye not know how easily fat takes fire, and how the holy fathers love not only to have the beauties merely call them fathers, but actually make them so?"

Having started a conversation with his fellow traveller anent the Church of Rome, he began to prove how it had been the ruin of Italy.

"I swear by Bacchus," he exclaimed, and his eyes flared up with indignation, "I would love as myself him that would compel all this riff-raff,—the popes and the monks,—to renounce either their power or their libertinage!"

Leonardo asked him what he thought of Savonarola. Niccolò confessed that at one time he had been a vehement adherent, had hoped that he would save Italy, but had soon understood the impotence of the prophet.

"I am sick to vomiting of all this bigots' shop-keeping. I do not want to recall it even. Well, the devil take them!" he concluded, with aversion.

VII

ABOUT noon they entered the gates of the city of Fano. All the houses were filled to overflowing with the soldiers, commanders, and retinue of Cæsar. Leonardo, in his capacity of court architect, was assigned two rooms near the palace on the square. He offered one of them to his fellow traveller, since it would have been difficult to get other quarters.

Machiavelli went off to the palace and returned with important news: the Duke's chief viceroy, Don Ramiro di Lorqua had been executed. On Christmas morning, the people had beheld on the Piazzetta, between the Castello and the Rocca Cesena, a beheaded corpse wallowing in a puddle of blood; alongside of it was an axe, and, on a spear stuck into the ground, Ramiro's chopped-off head.

"None knows the cause of the decollation," concluded Niccolò. "But 'tis all the people speak of now all over the city. And what most curious opinions! I have purposely come to fetch you. Truly, 'twould be a sin to neglect such a chance of studying an experiment in the natural laws of politics!"

Before the ancient Cathedral of Santo Fortunato the crowd was awaiting the appearance of the Duke. He had to pass through for an inspection of his troops. The talk was all of the execution of the viceroy. Leonardo and Machiavelli mingled with the crowd.

"How now, maties? I can not get it into my head," a young artisan, good-natured and rather stupid of face, was earnestly asking, "how is it they were saying that the Duke loved and favoured him above all the other nobles, now?"

"That is why he sought him out for a reckoning,—for that he loved him," sententiously uttered a merchant of benign mien, in a pelisse of squirrel fur. "Don Ramiro was deceiving the Duke. He oppressed the people in the name of the Duke, put them to death in prisons and through tortures, and practiced extortions. Yet before the King he played the lamb. Thought he had all the ends hid,—but no such thing! His hour struck; the measure of the ruler's long patience was overfilled, and he spared not his first noble for the weal of the people; without waiting for a verdict did he chop off his head on the block, even as he might that of the least of evil-doers, so that others might find evil-doing not to their liking. Now, never fear, all those that have down upon their chops have tucked their tails between their legs,—they see that fearful is his wrath, and just his judgment. Gracious is he to the meek; he pulleth down the arrogant!"

"*Regat eos in virga ferrea*," a monk cited the words of Revelation. "And he shall rule them with a rod of iron."[51]

"Verily, verily,—they should taste of the rod of iron, the sons of dogs, torturers of the people!"

"He knoweth how to punish,—and knoweth how to spare!"

"There never was a better ruler!"

"'Tis verily so!" said an old villager. "The Lord has evidently taken pity on Romagna. Before they used to flay the skin off the quick and the dead, ruining folk with taxes. There is naught to eat as it is, but here they take the last pair of oxen out of your yard for non-payment. 'Twas only when the Duke Valentino came into power that we were able to catch our breath,—may the Lord send him health!"

"Take the courts, too," continued the merchant. "They used to drag one on and on,—just pulling your whole soul out of you. But now they decide in an instant,—one could not wish for greater despatch!"

"He hath protected the orphan and consoled the widow," added the monk.

"He pities the people, that he does; there is no gainsaying it!"

"He will let none be wronged!"

"Oh, Lord, Lord!" an ancient little beggar woman began to babble, slobbering from emotion. "Our father, thou, our benefactor, our provider, may the Queen Mother of Heaven preserve thee, our little radiant sun! . . ."

"You hear? You hear?" Machiavelli whispered in his companion's ear. "The voice of the people is the voice of God! I have always said that one must be on a plain to see the mountains,—one must be with the people to know the ruler. This is where I would bring those who deem the Duke a monster! He has concealed all this from the wisest, and revealed it to the simple."

There came sounds of martial music. The crowd stirred excitedly.

"'Tis he. . . . 'Tis he. . . . He comes. . . . Look. . . ."

They raised themselves on tiptoe, craning their necks. Curious heads were thrust out of windows. Young maidens and girls, love in their eyes, ran out on the balconies and loggias that they might behold the hero,—"*Cesare biondo e bello*"—"Cæsar the beautiful, he of the flaxen curls." This was a rare bit of good fortune, inasmuch as the Duke almost never showed himself to the people.

The musicians marched in front with a deafeningly reverberant rataplan of kettle-drums, in time to the heavy tramping of the soldiers. Behind them came the Duke's Romagnola guards,—all picked, handsome lads, with halberds three ells long, in helmets and breast-plates of iron, in a livery of two colours,—the right half yellow, the left red. Niccolò could not have his fill of admiring the truly ancient, Roman alignment of this division, created by Cæsar. Behind the guards strode the pages and equerries, in garments of a luxury never yet seen,—short vests of cloth of gold, in mantelets of scarlet velvet, with leaves of the bracken woven in gold thereon; the scabbards and the belts for their swords were of snake-skin, with buckles showing the seven heads of a viper, darting its venom toward the sky,—the device of the Borgias. The name of Cæsar was woven over their breasts in silver upon black silk. Farther on were the body-guards of the Duke,—Albanian *stradioti* in green Turkish turbans, with crooked yataghans. Bartolomeo Capranico, the *Maestro del Campo*, or chief of the field forces, bore, raised aloft, the bared sword of the Banner Carrier of the Church of Rome. Behind him, on a black Barbary stallion, with a diamond sun in its forelock, rode the sovereign of Romagna himself, in a mantle of pale azure silk, with the lilies of France done in pearls thereon, in a mirror-smooth cuirass of bronze, with a gaping lion's maw on the breast-plate, and a helmet representing a sea monster, or dragon, with prickly feathers, wings, and fins of fine hammered brass, sonorously quivering at every move.

The face of Valentino,—he was twenty-six,—had grown thin and sunken since Leonardo's first sight of him at the court of Louis XII in Milan. His features had become sharper; his eyes, with their black-blue glitter of chilled steel, had become harder and more impenetrable. His flaxen hair, still profuse, and his little bi-forked beard, had turned darker. His nose had grown thinner, reminding one of the beak of a bird of prey. But a perfect serenity, as before, reigned upon this dispassionate face. Only now there was upon it an expression of still more impulsive daring and of an appalling keenness, like that of a bared, sharpened blade.

The Duke was followed by the artillery, the best in all Italy,—fine brazen culverins, falconets, *cerbottane*, and thick mortars of cast iron, which fired stone shots. Harnessed to oxen, they rolled along with a dull, shattering rumbling and chattering, which blended with the sounds of the trumpets and the kettle-drums. In the purple rays of the setting sun the cannons, armour, helmets and lances would flare up with lightning flashes, and it seemed that Cæsar was riding in the regal purple of a winter evening, like a triumphator, directly toward this enormous, low, and sanguinary sun.

The crowd gazed at the hero in silence, with bated breath, desiring to greet him with cries and daring not, in a reverent awe akin to horror. Tears were rolling down the cheeks of the old beggar woman.

"The holy saints! . . . Most Pure Mother!" she was babbling, crossing herself. "The Lord hath finally permitted me to behold thy dear radiant face, thou dear red sun of ours! . . ."

And the sparkling sword, entrusted by the Pope to Cæsar for the protection of the Church of the Lord, seemed to her the sword of fire of the Archangel Michael himself.

Leonardo smiled involuntarily, noting the same expression of simple-hearted rapture on the face of Niccolò and on that of the half-witted beggar woman.

VIII

Upon returning home, the artist found an order, signed by the Duke's chief secretary, Agapito, to appear on the following day before His Highness.

Lucio, who, while continuing on his way to Ancona, had halted for a rest at Fano, and would have to make his departure in the morning, had come to them to bid farewell. Niccolò began speaking of the execution of Ramiro di Lorqua. Lucio asked him his opinion of the real cause of this execution.

"To surmise the causes of the actions of such a ruler as Cæsar is difficult,—well-nigh impossible," retorted Machiavelli. "But if it pleases you to know what I think, you are welcome. Before its conquest by the Duke, Romagna, as you know, being under the yoke of a multitude of individual insignificant tyrants, was filled with uprisings, robberies, and deeds of violence. Cæsar, in order to put an immediate end to them, appointed as his chief viceroy his intelligent and faithful servant, Don Ramiro di Lorqua. By cruel executions, which awoke in the people a salutary fear of the law, he ended disorder in a brief space of time, and established perfect quiet in the land. But when the ruler perceived that the end was attained, he thereupon resolved to destroy the implement of his cruelty,—he ordered the viceroy to be seized, using the latter's extortions as a pretext, executed, and his body to be exposed in the square. This horrible spectacle simultaneously satisfied and overwhelmed the people. As for the Duke, he derived three gains from the action, full of a wisdom profound and worthy of imitation, firstly, he tore out by the roots the tares of discord, sown in Romagna by its former weak tyrants; secondly, by having made the people believe that whatever cruelties had been committed were without the knowledge of their ruler, he washed his hands of everything and threw the onus of responsibility upon the head of the viceroy, at the same time taking advantage of the good fruits of the latter's ferocity; thirdly, having offered his favourite servant as a sacrifice to the people, he presented the example of lofty and incorruptible justice."

Machiavelli spoke in a calm, quiet voice, preserving a dispassionate immobility on his face, as though he were expounding the deductions of abstract mathematics; only in the very depths of his eyes there flickered, now sinking low, now flaring high, a spark of mischievous gaiety, almost as provocative as that of a school-boy.

"A fine justice, I must say!" exclaimed Lucio. "Why, from your words, Messer Niccolò, one can deduce that this would-be justice is the greatest baseness!"

The secretary of Florence cast down his eyes, trying to extinguish their sprightly fire.

"That may be," he added coldly; "that may very well be, messer; but what of it?"

"Why, what mean you by 'what of it'? Can it be that you deem baseness worthy of imitation,—deem it civic wisdom?"

Machiavelli shrugged his shoulders.

"Young man, when you have acquired some degree of experience in politics, you will see for yourself that there is a difference between how men act, and how they ought to act, such that to forget it means sentencing oneself to certain perdition, inasmuch as all men are by their nature evil and corrupt, if benefit or fear compel them not to virtue. That is why I say, that a ruler, in order to avoid perdition, must first of all learn the art of appearing virtuous; but to be or not to be so, depending upon necessity, without fearing pricks of conscience for those secret vices without which the preservation of power is impossible, inasmuch as, when one investigates the nature of good and evil, one arrives at the conclusion that much which seems valorous virtue destroys the might of rulers, while that which seems like vice exalts it."

"Good heavens, Messer Niccolò!" Lucio became indignant at last. "Why, then, if one is to reason so, all things are permissible,—there is never a malefaction or baseness which may not be justified. . . ."

"Yes,—all things are permissible," said Niccolò, still more quietly and coldly, and, as though intensifying the significance of his words, he raised his arm and repeated: "All things are permissible to him who can and would reign!"

"One's hair stands up on end from what you say, Messer Niccolò!" Lucio voiced his horror; and, since his worldly intuition prompted him that to jest was the most seemly way out, he added, essaying a smile:

"However, be it as you will, I still can not imagine that you really think thus. To me it seems unbelievable. . . ."

"Perfect truth almost always seems unbelievable," Machiavelli cut him short, dryly.

Leonardo, who had been listening attentively, had long since noticed that, while pretending indifference, Niccolò had been stealthily casting searching glances at his companion, as though desirous of measuring the force of the impression which his ideas were producing: did their novelty and oddity astound, did they frighten? There was self-vanity in these secret, uncertain glances. The artist felt that Machiavelli was not sure of himself, and that his mind, with all its keenness and finesse, did not possess a calm, conquering force. From his aversion for thinking as all men did, from his hatred for commonplaces, he fell into the opposite extreme, into exaggeration, into the pursuit of rare truths,—even though incomplete, yet, at any cost, overwhelming. With fearless dexterity he played with unheard-of combinations of contradictory words,—for example, *virtue* and *ferocity*,—as a mountebank plays with bared swords. He had a whole arsenal of these sharpened, glittering, tempting and fearful half-truths, which he let fly, like to envenomed darts at his enemies, such as Messer Lucio,—people of the herd, with their bourgeois decency and their common sense. He vented his vengeance upon them for their triumphant vulgarity, for his unperceived superiority; he pricked them, he stingingly hurt them, —but he did not kill, nor even draw blood.

And the artist suddenly recalled his own monster, which he had at one time imaged forth on the wooden shield, the *rotella*, at the order of Ser Pietro da Vinci, creating it from different parts of repulsive vermin. Had not Messer Niccolò, too, formed just as aimlessly and disinterestedly his godlike monstrous tyrant, his non-existent and impossible Prince,—an unnatural and captivating monster, a Medusa head,—to frighten the mob?

But, with all that, under this insouciant whim and mischievousness of imagination, under this dispassionateness of the artist, Leonardo surmised within him a veritable great suffering,—as though the mountebank, playing with the swords, were purposely cutting himself till the blood came: in his glorification of the cruelty of others there was cruelty to his own self.

"Perhaps he is one of those pitiable sick men who seek a satiation of their pain by irritating their own wounds?" reflected Leonardo.

And still he did not know the ultimate secret of this dark, intricate heart, so near to him, yet foreign.

While he was gazing at Machiavelli with deep curiosity, Messer Lucio was helplessly, as in an absurd dream, struggling with the phantasmagoric Medusa head.

"Oh, well, I shall not dispute," he was beating a retreat into the last stronghold of common sense. "Perhaps there is a certain moiety of truth in what you say. . . . I, at least, think that everybody will agree with me also."

"Oh, of course, everybody will agree with you!" Niccolò cut him short, now probably losing his self-possession. "Only that is far from being proof, Messer Lucio. Truth dwelleth not on the high roads, upon which all travel. But in order to end our dispute, here is my last word. In observing the actions of Cæsar, I find them perfect, and my preposition is that he may be shown as the best example for emulation to those who acquire power through arms and good fortune. Within him are united such ferocity with such virtue, such is his ability to caress and destroy men, so firm are the foundations of his power, laid down by him within such a brief space of time,—that even now he is a sovereign unique in all Italy,—perhaps in all Europe; as for that which awaits him in the future,—why, that is difficult even to imagine. . . ."

His voice quavered. Spots of red stood out on his sunken cheeks; his eyes burned, as in a fever. He resembled a clairvoyant. From beneath the mocking mask of the cynic peered out the face of a quondam disciple of Savonarola.

But just as soon as Lucio, fatigued with the dispute, proposed to seal a truce with two or three bottles at a little wine-cellar nearby,—the clairvoyant vanished.

"Do you know what?" Niccolò retorted. "Let us better go to another little place. My scent for such things is as keen as a hound's! Methinks there must now be here some of the prettiest little lasses. . . ."

"Oh, what sort of lasses can they have in this miserable little town?" Lucio voiced his doubts.

"Hearken, young man," the secretary of Florence stopped him with pompousness, "never be you squeamish and pass by these miserable little cities. God save you from that! In these same filthy little suburban holes, in dark little by-lanes, you can at times bring to light such things as will make you lick your fingers! . . ."

Lucio patted Machiavelli on the shoulder with an easy familiarity, and called him a mad-cap.

"'Tis dark," he sought for excuses, "and cold, to boot!—we shall freeze. . . ."

"We shall take lanthorns," Niccolò insisted, "put on fur-coats, and muffle up our faces. At least, none shall recognize us. On such expeditions the more mystery, the more pleasure.—Messer Leonardo, are you going with us?"

The artist declined. He disliked the usual coarse masculine talk about women; he shunned it with a feeling of insurmountable shame. This man of fifty years, the intrepid investigator of the mysteries of nature, who accompanied men to executions that he might watch the expression of the last horror on their faces, would at times be nonplussed by a light-minded jest, not knowing how to hide his eyes, and blushing like a boy.

Niccolò drew Messer Lucio along with him.

IX

On the next day a chamberlain came from the palace early in the morning to find if the Chief Engineer of the Duke were satisfied with the quarters assigned him, whether he were affected by any shortage in the city, filled with such a multitude of strangers, and transmitted to him, with the greetings of the Duke, a present, consisting, as was the hospitable custom of those times, of household provender,—a sack of flour, a keg of wine, a carcass of mutton, eight brace of capons and chickens, three packets of wax candles, and two boxes of confetti. Seeing Cæsar's attentiveness toward Leonardo, Niccolò begged the latter to put in a good word for him with the Duke,—to obtain an audience for him.

At eleven o'clock at night—Cæsar's usual time for reception—they set out for the castle.

The Duke's mode of life was a strange one. When the envoys from Ferrara had once complained to the Pope that they could not obtain a reception from Cæsar, His Holiness had answered them that he himself was dissatisfied with the conduct of his son, who turned day into night, and who put off business audiences for two or three months at a time.

His time was divided as follows: summer and winter he lay down to sleep at four or five o'clock in the morning; three in the afternoon was to him merely the dawn breaking; at four the sun arose; at five in the evening Cæsar dressed and immediately breakfasted, at times while lying in bed; during the meal, and after, he was occupied with business. He surrounded all his existence with a mystery impenetrable, not only through a secretiveness natural to him, but through calculation. He rarely left the castle, and almost always masked. To the people he showed himself only on days of high solemnities; to his troops, at moments of extreme danger. But then, every one of his appearances was overwhelming, like the appearance of a demi-god: he loved, and knew how, to astonish.

Of his generosity there were current incredible rumours. The gold which flowed incessantly into the treasury of St. Peter from all Christendom did not suffice for the maintenance of the Chief Captain of the Church. The envoys assured their sovereigns that he was reputed to spend no less than eighteen hundred ducats per day. Whenever Cæsar rode through the streets of cities, the crowd ran after him, knowing that he shod his horses with special, easily shed silver shoes, that he might purposely lose them on his way, as a gift to his people.

Wonders were told of his bodily prowess also; once in Rome,—so the story ran,—during a bull fight, the youthful Cæsar, at that time the Cardinal of Valencia, had cloven the skull of a bull with one blow of a falchion. During the last few years the French sickness had merely shaken, but not wrecked, his health. With the fingers of his beautiful, femininely slender hand he bent horse-shoes, twisted rods of iron, and tore ship cables. Inaccessible to his own nobles and the envoys of great potentates, he could be seen on the knolls in the environs of Cesena, lending his presence to the bare fist fights of the half-wild mountain shepherds of Romagna. At times he even took part himself in these games.

At the same time, he was the perfect cavalier, the arbiter of fashions in the *beau monde*. Once, at night, on the wedding day of his sister, Madonna Lucrezia, leaving the siege of a fortress, straight from camp, he galloped up to the castle of the groom, Alfonso d'Este, the Duke of Ferrara; unrecognized of any, all in black velvet, in a black mask, he passed through the throng of guests, made a bow, and, when they had made way before him, he began a solo dance to the sounds of music, and made a few circles through the hall with such elegance that immediately all present recognized him. "Cæsar! Cæsar! The Unique Cæsar!" enraptured whispers arose in the throng. Paying no attention either to guests or hosts, he led the bride to one side, and, bending over, began whispering something in her ear. Lucrezia cast down her eyes, flared up in a blush, then blanched, like linen, and became still more beautiful,—all tender, pale, like a pearl; innocent, perhaps, but weak, infinitely submissive to the fearful will of her brother,—submissive, so it was asserted, even unto incest.

He took care of but one thing,—that there might be no evident proof. Perhaps rumour exaggerated the evil deeds of the Duke; perhaps reality was still more horrible than rumour. At any rate, he knew how to cover his tracks.

X

The ancient Gothic city hall of Fano served His Highness for a palace.

Passing through a large, gloomy and cold hall,— the common reception room for the less important visitors,— Leonardo and Machiavelli entered a small, inner chamber, which had probably been a belfry at one time, with coloured panes in the crenellated windows, and high seats in the church choir stall, where, in fine oak carving, were depicted the twelve Apostles and the early preceptors of the first ages of Christianity. In the faded fresco on the ceiling, among the clouds and angels, soared the Dove of the Holy Spirit. Here those near to the Duke were to be found. They spoke in half-whispers: the presence of the sovereign could be felt through the walls.

A bald-headed little ancient, the ill-fated envoy of Rimini, awaiting an audience with the Duke already for the third month, evidently fatigued from many sleepless nights, sat dozing in a corner upon a church seat. At times the door would open; Agapito, the secretary, with an absorbed air, his spectacles on his nose and with a quill behind his ear, would poke his head out and invite some one of those present to His Highness. At his every appearance the envoy of Rimini would make a painful start, and arise; but, seeing that it was not his turn, would sigh deeply and again sink into a doze, lulled by the sound of an apothecary's pestle in a copper mortar.

For lack of other convenient quarters in the cramped city hall, this oratory had been turned into a camp pharmacy. Before the window, where the altar had once stood, upon a table cluttered up with the bottles, cucurbits and jars of the medicinal laboratory, the Bishop of Santa Giusta, Gaspare Torella, the *archiartos*, or chief leech, of His Holiness the Pope and of Cæsar, was preparing a remedy, recently come into fashion, for the French sickness—syphilis: a distillation from the so-called Holy Wood,—*Guaiacum*,—brought from the meridian isles, newly discovered by Colombo. Triturating in his shapely hands the pungently smelling, saffron yellow pith of the *Guaiacum*, which he kneaded together into unctuous lumps, the episcopal leech was expounding with an amiable smile the nature and properties of the healing tree. Everybody listened to him with interest: many of those present knew the frightful malady through experience.

"And where on earth did it ever come from?" The Cardinal Santa Balbina was shaking his head in grievous puzzlement.

"The Spanish Jews and the Moors, so they say, have brought it over," said the Bishop of Elna. "Now, since they have issued a law against the blasphemers, it has abated somewhat, glory be to God. But some five or six years ago, not only human beings, but even animals,—horses, swine, dogs,—used to get sick; even trees, and the grain in the fields."

The physician evinced his doubts as to whether wheat or oats could become sick with the French sickness.

"God hath punished us," sighed profoundly the Bishop of Trana, "for our sins hath He sent us this scourge of His wrath!"

The speakers became silent. Only the measured ring of the pestle in the mortar could be heard, and it seemed that the preceptors of the first ages of Christianity, depicted on the walls of the choir stall, were listening with wonder to the strange conversation of these new pastors of the Lord's Church. In the chapel, illumined by the flickering little apothecary's lamp, where the stifling camphor odour of the medicinal tree mingled with the barely perceptible fragrance of the erstwhile incense, the gathering of Roman prelates seemed to be performing a mystic religious service.

"Monsignor,"—the ducal astrologer, Valgulio, turned toward the physician,—"is it true, now, that this disease is transmitted through the air?"

The physician shrugged his shoulders in doubt.

"Of course, through the air!" Machiavelli confirmed him with a sly grin. "How else could it spread not only in the men's quarters, but in the women's as well?"

Everybody smiled.

One of the court poets, Battista Orphino, solemnly, as though it were a prayer, read aloud a dedication to the Duke of a new book by the Bishop of Torella about the French sickness, wherein the author, asserting among other things that Cæsar had with his virtues apparently eclipsed the great men of antiquity,—Brutus in justice, Decius in constancy, Scipio in moderation, Marcus Regulus in fidelity, and Paulus Emilius in magnanimity,—also glorified the Gonfaloniere of the Church of Rome as the founder of mercurization.

During this conversation the secretary of Florence, taking aside now this courtier, now that, was dexterously questioning them about the future policy of Cæsar; he investigated, watched and sniffed the air, like a blood-hound. He approached Leonardo also, and, letting his head sink on his breast, laid his index finger on his lips, looking at the artist from underneath his brows, and repeated several times in deep pensiveness:

"I shall eat the artichoke. . . . I shall eat the artichoke. . . ."

"What artichoke?" the artist wondered.

"That is the whole trick,—what *is* the artichoke? . . . Recently the Duke put a riddle to the envoy of Ferrara, Pandolfo Colenuccio: I, said he, shall eat the artichoke, leaf by leaf. Perhaps this signifies the union of his enemies, whom he, having disrupted, will destroy, —and then, again, it may be altogether something else. I have been racking my head over it for a whole hour now!"

And, bending toward Leonardo, he said in a whisper:

"Here everything is in riddles and catches! They chatter of all sorts of fiddle-faddle, but the minute one broaches business, they grow as mute as fish, or monks at a meal. Well, they shall not take me in! I can sense that they are preparing something. But what, precisely?

What? Would you believe it, messer,—I would pawn my soul to the Devil to know what, precisely!"

And his eyes took on a glitter, like a desperate gambler's.

Out of the slightly opened door Agapito's head was thrust. He beckoned to the artist.

Through a long, half-dark passage, occupied by the body-guards—the Albanian *stradioti*—Leonardo entered the Duke's dortoir, a snug chamber whose walls were hung with silken rugs upon which was woven the chase of the unicorn, and with bas-relief work on the ceiling, depicting the loves of Queen Pasiphaë and her bull. This bull, the scarlet or golden calf, was the heraldic beast of the House of the Borgias; it was repeated in all the ornamentations of the room, together with the Papal three-crowned tiara and the keys of St. Peter.

The room was very hot: the physicians advised those afflicted to avoid a draught after anointment with mercury, and to warm themselves in the sun or at a fire. In the marble fireplace blazed fragrant juniper; in the lamps burned an oil with an admixture of violet perfume; Cæsar was fond of aromatic odours.

As was his wont, he was reclining, fully clad, on a low couch without any baldaquin, which stood in the middle of the room. Only two positions of the body were habitual with him,—either in bed, or on horse-back. Immobile, dispassionate, his elbows resting on pillows, he was watching two of his courtiers playing chess on a little jasper table beside the bed, and was listening to the report of his secretary,—Cæsar possessed the faculty of dividing his attention among several objects at once. Plunged in pensiveness, he was rolling, with a slow monotonous motion, a golden pomander filled with fragrant scents, from one hand to the other, from which pomander, as well as from his damascene dagger, he never parted.

XI

He received Leonardo with the charming amiability natural to him. Without allowing him to bend his knee, he squeezed the artist's hand friendlily, and seated him in an arm-chair. He had invited him for a consultation about the plans of Bramante for a new monastery in the city of Imola, the so-called *Valentina*, with a rich chapel, hospital, and a hostelry for strangers. Cæsar was desirous of making these philanthropic institutions a memorial of his Christian compassion. After the designs of Bramante, he showed him the newly cut specimens of letters for the press of Geronimo Soncino, in the city of Fano, of which press he was a patron, since he was solicitous for the flowering of arts and sciences in Romagna.

Agapito presented to the potentate a collection of laudatory hymns of the poet laureate, Francesco Uberti. His Highness benignly accepted them and gave orders to reward the poet generously. Then, since he demanded that he be presented not merely with encomia, but satires as well, the secretary presented to him the epigram of a Neapolitan poet, caught at Rome and put into the prison of Sant' Angelo,—a sonnet, full of harsh upbraiding, wherein Cæsar was dubbed a mule, the offspring of a strumpet and the Pope, who sat upon a throne once possessed by Christ, but now by Satan; Cæsar was also dubbed a Turk, a circumcised one, an unfrocked cardinal, a practicer of incest, a fratricide and one fallen away from God. "Wherefore dost Thou wait, O patient God," exclaimed the poet, "or seest Thou not that he hath turned the Holy Church into a stall for mules and into a house of ill-fame?"

"What are your orders for disposing of this scoundrel, Your Highness?" asked Agapito.

"Leave him till my return," said the Duke quietly. "I myself will attend to him." Then he added, still more quietly: "I shall be able to teach politeness to writers."

The method whereby Cæsar "taught politeness to writers" was well known,—for the less offensive affronts he lopped off their hands and pierced their tongues with red-hot iron.

Having ended his report, the secretary withdrew.

The chief court astrologue, Valgulio, approached Cæsar with a new horoscope. The Duke heard him out attentively, well-nigh reverently, inasmuch as he believed in the ineluctability of fate, in the potency of the stars. Among other things, Valgulio explained that the Duke's last attack of the French malaise had depended upon the malign influence of the arid planet Mars, which had entered the sign of the humid Scorpion; but, as soon as Mars would be in conjunction with Venus, with Taurus in the ascendant, the disease would pass of itself.

Having with a wave of his hand dismissed the astrologer, he again turned to the court architect. Leonardo spread out before him his military plans and maps. These were not merely the investigations of a scientist, explanatory of the formation of the soil, the current of the waters, the barriers formed by mountain chains, the deltas of rivers revealed by plains,—but they were also the creations of a great artist,—bird's-eye pictures of localities. The sea was marked in a dark blue colour, the mountains were in brown, the rivers in a light blue, the cities in a dark red, the meadows in a light green; and with an infinite perfection every detail was executed,—the squares, the streets, the turrets of the cities, so that they might be instantly recognized, without reading their names, added on the margin. One seemed to be flying over the earth and from a vertiginous height beholding the unencompassable distance at one's feet. With especial attention did Cæsar scrutinize the map of the region bounded on the south by the Lake of Bolsena; on the north by the Vald'Eme, the river of which fell into the Arno; on the west by Arezzo and Perugia, and on the east by Siena and the maritime district. This was the heart of Italy, the native country of Leonardo, the land of Florence, of which the Duke had long been dreaming, as of a most dainty tid-bit to acquire.

Sunk in contemplation, Cæsar delighted in this feeling of flying. He would not have been able to express in words that which he was experiencing, but it seemed to him that he and Leonardo understood one another,—that they were working together. He dimly surmised the great new might over people which science could bestow, and desired this might for himself, these wings of victorious soaring. Finally, he looked up at the artist and squeezed his hand with a bewitchingly amiable smile:

"I thank thee, my Leonardo! Serve me as thou hast up to now served me, and I shall know how to reward thee."

"Art thou comfortable?" he added solicitously. "Art satisfied with thy salary? Perhaps thou hast some other wish? Thou knowest I am glad to fulfill every request of thine."

Leonardo, embracing the opportunity, put in a word for Messer Niccolò,—asking for him an audience with the Duke.

Cæsar shrugged his shoulders with a good-natured smile.

"A strange fellow, this Messer Niccolò! He strives for audiences, but, when I receive him, we have nothing to talk about. And whatever did they send this queer chap to me for?"

After a silence, he asked Leonardo for his opinion of Machiavelli.

"I think, Your Highness, that he is one of the most intelligent men that I have met in all my life."

"Yes, he is intelligent," concurred the Duke; "I may even grant that he knows a thing or two of affairs of state. But still. . . . One can not place any reliance in him. He is a dreamer, a weather-vane. He knows no limits in anything. However, I have always wished him weal; but now, since I have found out that he is thy friend, all the more so. For he is really a kind-hearted fellow! There is no guile in him, even though he imagines himself the craftiest of men, and tries to hoodwink me, as though I were an enemy of your Republic. However, I am not wroth: I comprehend that he acts thus because he loves his native land more than his very soul.—Ah, well, let him come, then, if he desires it so greatly. . . . Tell him I will see him gladly.—And, by the bye,—who was it I heard from, just the other day, that Messer Niccolò seems to have conceived in his mind a book about politics or the military science,—something of that sort? . . ."

Cæsar again smiled his soft smile, as though he had recalled something of an amusing nature.

"Has he told thee of his Macedonian phalanx? No? Listen, then. One day Niccolò explained from this book of his about military science, to Bartolomeo Capranico my *Maestro del Campo*, and to other captains, the rule for the disposition of the troops in an order that resembled the ancient Macedonian phalanx, with such eloquence that all wanted to see it tried out. They went out into the field before the camp, and Niccolò began to issue commands. He struggled and struggled with two thousand soldiers; kept them for three hours out in the cold, in the wind and rain, but could not form his much lauded phalanx. Finally Bartolomeo lost patience, also stepped out before the troops, and, although he has read never a book about the military science in all his born days, in the wink of an eye, to the sound of a tambourine, he disposed the infantry into splendid fighting formation. And it was then that all were convinced once more what a great difference there is between the deed and the word.—Only look thou, Leonardo, tell him naught of this,—Niccolò dislikes being reminded of the Macedonian phalanx!"

It was late,—about three in the morning. A light supper was brought to the Duke,—a platter of vegetables, a trout, a little white wine: he was distinguished for his moderation in food,—the moderation of a true Spaniard.

The artist made his farewell. Cæsar once more, with a captivating amiability, thanked him for the military charts, and ordered three pages to escort him with torches, as a mark of honour.

Leonardo told Machiavelli of his meeting with the Duke. Hearing of the charts of the environs of Florence which he had made for Cæsar, Niccolò was horrified.

"What? You, a citizen of the Republic, have done this for the bitterest foe of your native land? . . ."

"I supposed," retorted the artist, "that Cæsar was reputed an ally of ours. . . ."

"Reputed!" exclaimed the secretary of Florence, and indignation flashed in his eyes. "But do you know, messer, that if this should but come to the knowledge of the Magnificent Signori, you are open to an accusation of treason? . . ."

"Really?" Leonardo voiced his simple-hearted wonder. "However, do not think aught of it, Niccolò; I really understand nothing of politics,—like one blind. . . ."

They stared silently into each other's eyes, and suddenly both felt that in this they forever differed, down to the heart's very core; they were strangers to one another in this respect, and would never agree: for one there seemed to be no native land at all; the other loved it, as Cæsar expressed it, "more than his very soul."

XII

THAT night Niccolò went away, leaving no word of his reason for going or of his destination. He returned the following day, in the afternoon,—fatigued, chilled; entering Leonardo's room, he carefully closed the door, announced that he had long been wanting to talk over a certain matter with him, which required great secrecy, and began to lead up to it circuitously.

One day, three years ago, at twilight, in a desolate region of Romagna, between the cities of Cervia and Porto Cesenatico, armed horsemen in masks had fallen upon a detachment of horse, which was escorting from Urbino to Venice the wife of Battista Caracciolo, a captain of infantry of the Most Serene Republic, Madonna Dorotea; driving off the guard, they had separated her, as well as her cousin, Maria, a fifteen-year-old novice in the nunnery at Urbino, who was travelling with her; had seated them on horses and galloped away. Since that day Dorotea and Maria had vanished without a trace.

The Council and the Senate of Venice held the Republic to be insulted in the person of its captain, and turned to Louis XII, to the

King of Spain, and to the Pope, with complaints against the Duke of Romagna, accusing him of the abduction of Dorotea. But proofs there were none, and Cæsar replied with a mocking scorn that, since he felt no shortage of women, he had no need to seize them in battle on the high roads. Rumours were current that Madonna Dorotea had quickly found consolation, following the hero in all his expeditions and not grieving too much over her husband.

Maria had a brother, Messer Dionigio, a young captain in the service of Florence, in the field against the Pisans. When all the suits of the Florentine Signoria proved just as useless as the complaints of the Most Serene Republic, Dionigio resolved to try his own luck; he had arrived in Romagna under another name, presented himself to the Duke, earned his confidence, penetrated into the tower of the Fortress of Cesena, and escaped with Maria, who was disguised as a boy. But on the boundary of Perugia the pursuit overtook them. The brother was slain,—Maria brought back to prison.

Machiavelli, as the Secretary of the Republic of Florence, had taken part in this affair. Messer Dionigio had become friendly with him, entrusted him with the secret of this weighty enterprise, and told him all that he had been able to find out from the turnkeys, who deemed Maria a saint and asserted she wrought cures, that she prophesied; and that, —so it seemed,—her hands and feet were impressed with sanguinary crucificial wounds, like the stigmata of St. Catherine of Siena.

When Dorotea had palled upon Cæsar, he turned his attention to Maria. A notorious seducer of women, knowing himself to possess a charm which the most chaste could not resist, he felt certain that, sooner or later, Maria would prove as submissive as all the others. But he was mistaken. His will met, in the heart of this child, an unconquerable resistance. Rumour said that latterly the Duke frequently visited her prison cell, that he remained alone with her for long periods, but what transpired at these meetings was a mystery to all. In conclusion Machiavelli declared that he intended to liberate Maria.

"If you, Messer Leonardo," he added, "would agree to help me, I would conduct this affair so that none would find out aught of your participation. However, all I wanted to ask of you was certain bits of information concerning the inner plan and construction of the fortress of San Michele, wherein Maria is. To you, as court engineer, it would be easier to make your way inside and find out."

Leonardo gazed at him in silence, with wonder, and under this searching gaze Niccolò suddenly burst into unnatural, harsh, and almost malignant laughter.

"I dare hope," he exclaimed, "that you will not suspect me of excessive sentimentalism or chivalric magnanimity! Whether the Duke seduce this girl or not is, of course, all one to me. Why, then, do I go to all this trouble, you want to know? Why, even if it be only to prove to the Magnificent Signoria that I can be of some use besides playing the buffoon. But the main thing is that one must have something to amuse oneself with. The life of man is such that if one does not permit himself occasional follies one will expire from boredom. I am weary of chattering, of dicing, of frequenting bordellos and writing useless reports to the Florentine woolsters! And so I have thought of this affair,—not merely words, after all, but an affair! And besides 'twould be a pity to let the chance slip. The whole plan is ready, with the most wondrous artifices! . . ."

He spoke hurriedly, as though he were justifying some fault. But Leonardo had already comprehended that Niccolò felt an excruciating shame for his kindliness, and that, as usual, he was hiding it under a mask of cynicism.

"Messer," the artist stopped him, "I beg you to rely upon me as upon yourself in this affair,—with one condition: that, in the event of failure, I shall be held as liable as yourself."

Niccolò, evidently touched, responded to the pressure of Leonardo's hand and at once laid the Machiavellian plan before him. Leonardo made no objections, although in the depth of his soul he doubted whether this plan, which smacked somewhat of excessive finesse and craftiness, but did not resemble reality, would prove quite as easy in actuality as in words.

Maria's liberation was set for the thirtieth of December,—the date of the Duke's departure from Fano. Two days before the date, late in the evening, one of the bribed turnkeys came running to them to forewarn them of an impending accusation. Niccolò was not at home. Leonardo set out to search for him through the city. After much seeking he found the secretary of Florence in a gambling hell, where a band of scoundrels, Spaniards serving in Cæsar's army for the most part, were plucking inexperienced players.

In a circle of young revellers and libertines Machiavelli was elucidating Petrarca's famous sonnet beginning:

Ferito in mezzo di core di Laura—
Stricken by Laura to my very heart's core—

revealing an unseemly meaning in every word, and proving that Laura had infected Petrarca with the French malaise. His auditors were rolling about from laughter.

From an adjacent room came the sounds of men yelling, of women squealing, of falling chairs crashing, the clatter of swords, bottles breaking and money scattering—a sharper had been caught. Niccolò's companions darted off in the direction of all the noise. Leonardo whispered to him that he had a bit of important news concerning the Maria matter. They walked out.

The night was still and starry. The virginal, newly fallen snow crunched underfoot. After the closeness of the gambling den Leonardo breathed in with enjoyment the frosty air, which seemed fragrant.

Hearing of the accusation, Niccolò decided with unexpected insouciance that as yet there was nothing to worry about.

"Were you puzzled, seeing me in this den?" he turned to his companion. "The Secretary of the Florentine Republic, well-nigh filling the post of buffoon to the court riff-raff! But what is one to do? Hunger prances, and hunger dances,—hunger sings gay little songs. . . . They, even though they be base knaves, are still more generous than our Magnificent Signori! . . ."

There was such cruelty to his own self in these words of Niccolò, that Leonardo could not contain himself and stopped him.

"'Tis not true! Why do you speak thus of yourself, Niccolò? Why, know you not that I am your friend and do not judge you as the common run does? . . ."

Machiavelli turned away, and, after a short silence, continued in a low, changed voice:

"I know. . . . Be not wroth with me, Leonardo! At times, when my heart is too heavy, I jest and laugh instead of crying. . . ."

His voice broke, and, with head downcast, he said still more quietly:

"Such is my lot! I was born under an unlucky star. The while people of my age, men of the utmost insignificance, enjoy the highest degree of success in everything, and are living amid wealth, and honours, acquiring money and power, I alone am left behind all, obliterated by dolts. They deem me a light-minded fellow. Perhaps they are right. Oh, I have no fear of great efforts, deprivations, dangers. But to suffer all my life petty and base affronts, to be making ends meet, to tremble over every copper,—really, that I can not. Eh, what avails it to talk! . . ." He made a hopeless gesture, and tears quivered in his voice.

"An accursed life! If God doth not take pity upon me, methinks I will abandon everything,—my affairs, Monna Marietta, my boy,—why, I am but a burden to them; let them think that I have died. I shall escape to the end of the world, hide myself in some hole or other, where none knows me; I shall hire myself out to a *podestà* as a clerk, or something of the sort, or shall teach children their alphabet in some village school, that I may not perish of hunger,—until I become dulled, or lose consciousness; for, the most horrible thing of all, my friend, is to realize that one has powers, that one might accomplish something, yet never will,—that one will perish senselessly! . . ."

XIII

TIME passed, and, in proportion with the approach of the day of Maria's liberation, Leonardo noticed that Niccolò, despite his self-assurance, was weakening, losing his presence of spirit,—now carelessly procrastinating, now bustling about without any sense. By his own experience the artist surmised what was taking place in Machiavelli's soul. This was no cowardice, but that incomprehensible weakness, indecisiveness, of men not created for action,—that momentary treachery of the will at the last minute, when one must decide without doubt or vacillation,—all of which feelings were so familiar to Leonardo himself.

On the eve of the fatal day Niccolò set out for the little suburb adjacent to the tower of San Michele, in order to make all final preparations for Maria's escape. Leonardo also was to arrive there in the morning. Left alone, he awaited from minute to minute grievous news, by now no longer doubting that the matter would end with a foolish failure like a school-boy's prank.

The breaking of a dull winter morning was making pale the window-panes. There came a knock at the door. The artist opened it. Niccolò, pale and confused, entered.

"'Tis over!" he muttered, sinking on a chair in utter fatigue.

"I knew it was so," said Leonardo, without any wonder. "I told you, Niccolò, that we would be caught."

Machiavelli glanced at him, absently.

"Nay, 'tis not that," he continued. "We were not caught, you see,—but the bird has flown the cage. We were too late. . . ."

"Flown,—how?"

"Why, just so. To-day, before dawn, Maria was found on the floor of the prison with her throat slit."

"Who is the murderer?" asked the artist.

"It is not known; but, judging by the wounds, 'tis scarcely the Duke. Whatever else they be, the Duke and his headsmen are masters in this sort of thing: they would know how to slit a child's throat. She died a virgin, they say. She killed herself, I think. . . ."

"It is impossible! A girl like Maria,—why, was she not esteemed a saint? . . ."

"Everything is possible," continued Niccolò, "you do not know them yet! This monster. . . ."

He stopped and turned pale, but concluded with an unrestrainable impulse:

"This monster is capable of everything! Probably he was able to make even a saint lay hands on herself. . . ."

"Before," he added, "when she was not so closely guarded, I saw her twice. Very thin, very slender, like a blade of grass; with a child's face. Her hair was thin, and light, like flax, just like Filippino Lippi's Madonna, in the Badia of Florence, who appeared to San Bernardo. Then, too, she was not remarkable for any special beauty,—whatever did the Duke find to entice him. . . . Oh, Messer Leonardo, if you did but know what a pitiful and charming child this was! . . ."

Niccolò turned away, and it seemed to the artist that tears glistened on his eyelashes. But, immediately recovering himself, he concluded in a grating, high-pitched voice:

"I have always said it,—an honest man in court is like a fish in the frying pan. I have had my fill of it! I was not made to be the servant of tyrants. I shall finally manage to have the Signoria send me to another embassy,—it makes no difference where, so long as it be as far as possible from here!"

Leonardo felt sorry for Maria, and it seemed to him that he would have stopped at no sacrifice to have saved her; but, at the same time, in the deepest recess of his heart there was a sense of relief, of liberation, at the thought that there was no further need of action. And he surmised that Niccolò was experiencing the same feeling.

XIV

On the thirtieth of December, at dawn, the chief war forces of Valentino,—about ten thousand infantry and two thousand cavalry,—left the town of Fano, and pitched their camp on the way to Sinigaglia, on the shore of the river Metauro, to await the Duke, who was to leave Fano on the following day, designated by the astronomer Valgulio.

Having concluded a peace with Cæsar, the conspirators of Mugione had, by agreement with him, undertaken a common expedition against Sinigaglia. The city had surrendered, but the castellan had declared that he would give the keys up to none else save the Duke. His erstwhile foes, but present allies, having a premonition of evil at the last minute, were evasive of meeting him. But Cæsar gulled them once more and set them at rest,—as Machiavelli subsequently expressed it, "charming them with kindnesses, like to the basilisk, which enticeth its victim with sweet singing."

Niccolò, burning up with curiosity, did not want to wait for Leonardo, and set out immediately after the Duke. Several hours later the artist left by himself.

The way led to the south, just as from Pesaro, on the very edge of the sea, with mountains to the right. Their promontories at times approached so near to the shore that there was barely a narrow space for the road. The day was grey, calm. The breathless air was enchained with a languid dreaminess. The croaking of the ravens foreboded a thaw. The early dusk was falling together with the drops of finely drizzling rain and thawing snow.

The dark-red brick towers of Sinigaglia came in view. The town, squeezed in between the two barriers,—the water and the mountains,—like a veritable trap, was situated at the distance of a mile from the flat seashore, and at the distance of a long-bow shot from the foot of the Apennines. Upon reaching the river Misa, the road took a sharp turn to the left. Here a bridge was built obliquely across the river, and, opposite it, were the gates of the city. In front of them lay a small square, with the low houses of a suburb,—for the most part the warehouses of the merchants of Venice. At that time Sinigaglia was an expansive, half-Asiatic mart, where the merchants of Italy exchanged their wares with Turks, Armenians, Greeks, Persians, and Slavs from Montenegro and Albania. But when the artist beheld it, even its most populous streets were empty. Leonardo came across nothing but soldiers. Here and there, among the arched sheds of warehouses and *fondachi* stretching monotonously and without end along both sides of each street, he noted signs of pillage,—shattered window-panes, broken padlocks and bolts, doors wrenched off, bales of goods strewn about. There was a smell of fire. Half-burned foundations still smoked, and at the corners of the old brick palaces, from the stout rings of the torch-holders, swung the bodies of hanged men. It was growing dark when, on the chief square of the city, between the Palazzo Ducale and the round, squat fortress of Sinigaglia, with its ominous barbicans and surrounding deep moat, Leonardo beheld Cæsar in the midst of his troops, in the light of torches. He was meting out punishment to the soldiers guilty of pillage. Messer Agapito was reading the sentence. At a sign from Cæsar, the condemned were led away to the gallows. While the eyes of the artist sought someone in the throng of courtiers whom he might interrogate concerning what had taken place here, he caught sight of the secretary of Florence.

"Do you know? Have you heard?" Niccolò turned to him.

"Nay, I know naught, and am glad to have met you. Tell me all about it."

Machiavelli led him into a nearby street, then, through several cramped and dark alleys, buried under snow-drifts, into a forsaken suburb near the seashore, where, near the wharf, in a lonely little hovel, leaning all awry, owned by the widow of a shipmaster, he had that morning succeeded in finding the only vacant lodging in the town,—two tiny closets, one for himself and the other for Leonardo. Silently and hurriedly Niccolò lit a candle, extracted out of a travelling cellarette a bottle of wine, blew up the brands on the hearth, and seated himself opposite his companion, fixing him with his burning gaze:

"So you know naught yet?" he asked exultingly. "Hearken! 'Tis an event extraordinary and memorable! Cæsar has avenged himself upon his enemies. The conspirators have been seized,—Oliverotto, Ursini, and Vitelli await their death."

He threw himself back in his chair, and looked at Leonardo in silence, enjoying the latter's amazement. Then, controlling himself through an effort, that he might appear calm and dispassionate, like a chronicler setting forth the events of ancient times, or a man of science describing the phenomena of nature,—he began the story of the famous "Trap of Sinigaglia."

The allies, Vitellozzo Vitelli, Gravina, and Pagolo Orsini, mounted on mules, had gone to meet Cæsar, accompanied by a large number of horsemen. As though having a premonition of his ruin, Vitellozzo seemed so woebegone that those who knew his former happiness and valour wondered at him. Subsequently it was told that before his departure for Sinigaglia he had bidden farewell to all his household, as though foreseeing that he was going to his death.

The allies dismounted, doffed their *berrette*, and greeted the Duke. He also got off his horse, and at first gave his hand in turn to each, then embraced and kissed them, calling them "Beloved Cousins." In the meanwhile the commanders of Cæsar, as had been previously agreed upon, surrounded Orsini and Vitelli so that each found himself between two of the Duke's courtiers; Cæsar, noting the absence of Oliverotto, made a sign to his captain, Don Miguel Corella, who galloped ahead and found the missing man at Borgo. Oliverotto joined the train, and the entire gathering, amiably conversing on matters military, set out in the direction of the castle, which was located in front of the fortress. At the portals the allies would have fain made their farewell, but the Duke, still with the same captivating urbanity, detained them and invited them within the castle. The minute they had stepped into the reception hall, the doors were locked, eight armed men threw themselves upon the four, two to each, seizing and binding them. The bewildered amazement of the unfortunate captives was such that they made almost no resistance. The rumour ran rife that the Duke intended to put an end to his enemies that very night, by strangling them in the secret recesses of the castle.

"Oh, Messer Leonardo," Machiavelli concluded his narration, "if you had but seen how he did embrace them, how he did buss them! One wavering look, one movement, might have betrayed him. But there was such sincerity in his face that,—would you believe it,—to the last minute I suspected naught; I would have wagered my arm that he was not dissembling. I think that of all the deception perpetrated in the world since politics have existed, this is the most splendid!"

Leonardo smiled.

"Of course," he said, "one can not deny the Duke possesses valour and craft, but still I must confess, Niccolò, I am so little initiated into the mysteries of politics that I do not comprehend,—just what, precisely, are you enraptured over in this betrayal?"

"Betrayal?" Machiavelli stopped him. "When the matter, messer, touches the saving of the fatherland, one can not speak of betrayal and loyalty, of evil and good, of mercy and cruelty,—but all means are alike, if but the end be attained."

"But wherein is it a matter of saving the fatherland in this case, Niccolò? It seems to me that the Duke was thinking but of his own gain. . . ."

"What! And you—you, too—do not comprehend? Why, 'tis as plain as day! Cæsar is the future unifier and sovereign of Italy. Can you not see it? . . . There has never yet been so auspicious a time for the advent of a hero as now. If Israel had had to languish in bondage in Egypt, that a Moses might arise; and the Persians under the yoke of the Medes, that Cyrus might be exalted; and the Athenians perish in internecine strife, that Theseus might gain glory,—so, precisely, has it been necessary in our day that Italy sink to such ignominy as is hers to-day, that she experience a bondage worse than that of the Hebrews, a heavier yoke than the Persians endured, greater discords than the Athenians had, without a chief, without a leader, without rule, devastated and trampled upon by barbarians, having borne all the tribulations that any nation may bear,—so that a new hero, the saviour of the fatherland, might arise! And even though in the days that are past some hope may have glimmered for her occasionally in men who seemed to be the chosen ones of God, Fate did every time betray such men at the very height of their greatness, before the fulfillment of their grand exploit. And, half-dead, well-nigh without the breath of life, she is still awaiting him who shall heal her wounds,—terminating the oppressions in Lombardy, the robberies and extortions in Tuscany and Naples; making whole these malodorous cankers, suppurating from time. Day and night doth she call aloud to God, supplicating Him for a Deliverer. . . ."

His voice took on a ringing sound, like a chord drawn too taut—and broke. He was pale, all of a tremble,—his eyes were ablaze. But at the same time, there was in this sudden effort something convulsive and impotent, resembling a fit. Leonardo recalled how a few days ago, referring to the death of Maria, he had called Cæsar a "monster." The artist did not point out to him this inconsistency, knowing that he would now repudiate this pity for Maria as an ignominious weakness.

"Time will tell, Niccolò," said Leonardo. "Only here is something I would fain ask you,—why is it to-day, precisely, that you have apparently become firmly convinced of the Divine choice of Cæsar? Or has the Trap of Sinigaglia convinced you, with greater clarity than all his other actions, that he is a hero?"

"Yes," answered Niccolò, by now having gained complete control of himself and again feigning dispassionateness. "The perfection of this deception, more than all the other actions of the Duke, indicates that he possesses that combination, so rare among men, of great and opposed qualities. Mark you, I do not praise, I do not condemn,—I do but investigate. And here is my idea. For the attainment of any ends at all there exist two modes of action,—the lawful and the violent. The first is human; the second, bestial. He who would govern must be master of both modes,—the ability to be, at his will and choice, either a man or a beast. Such is the esoteric meaning of the ancient fable of how King Achilles and the other heroes were nurtured by Chiron the Centaur, half-god, half-beast. Kings, the foster-children of the Centaur, just as he, unite in themselves the two natures,—the bestial and the divine. Ordinary men can not endure liberty, dreading it more than death, and, upon committing a crime, fall under the onus of remorse. Only the Hero, the Chosen One of Fate, has the fortitude to endure liberty,—he transgresses the law without fear, without a twinge of conscience, remaining as innocent in evil as beasts and gods. To-day for the first time have I beheld in Cæsar this ultimate liberty,—the seal of his being chosen!"

"Ay, now I understand you, Niccolò," said the artist, deeply pensive. "Only it seems to me that the free man is not he who, like Cæsar, dares all because he knows naught and loves naught, but, rather, he who dares because he knows and loves. Only through such freedom shall men conquer evil and good, the height and the depth; all earthly obstacles and bounds, all its burdens, becoming even as the gods,—and shall fly."

"Fly?" said Niccolò, perplexed.

"When perfect knowledge shall be theirs, they shall create wings, shall invent a machine that shall enable them to fly. I have pondered upon this a great deal. Perhaps naught will come of it; 'tis all one,—if not I, then some other shall achieve it,—but there shall be wings for mankind."

"Well, I felicitate you!" Niccolò burst into laughter. "We have talked ourselves into wingéd men. A fine Prince shall mine be,—half-god, half-beast,—with the wings of a bird. There is a veritable Chimæra for you!"

He listened intently to the hours striking in a nearby belfry, and, jumping up, began to hurry. He had to get to the castle in time, in order to find out about the impending execution of the conspirators.

XV

THE sovereigns of Italy felicitated Cæsar with the "Most Exquisite Gull." Louis XII, hearing of the Trap of Sinigaglia, styled it "A deed befitting an ancient Roman." Isabella Gonzaga, Marchesa of Mantua, sent Cæsar as a present for the forthcoming carnival a hundred silk masks of different colours.

"Most Illustrious Signora, Our Most Beloved Gossip and Dear Cousin," the Duke wrote in acknowledgment, "We have received the hundred masks sent Us by Your Excellency as a present, and they are most pleasing to Us, by reason of their rare elegancy and diversity; and especially because they have come most apt as to time and place,—better could not have been chosen,—as though Your Signora had surmised beforehand the significance and order of our actions, inasmuch as We have, by the grace of God, gained possession in one day of the land and city of Sinigaglia, with all the fortresses, have meted out just execution to all Our guileful traitors and enemies; have set Castello, Fermo, Cisterna, Montone and Perugia free from the yoke of tyrants and brought them into proper obedience to Our Most Holy Father, the Pontiff of Christ. But all the more are these false faces pleasing to Our heart, as the open-faced evidence of the good disposition of Your Highness, toward us,—as that of a sister to a brother."

Niccolò, laughing, asserted that one could not even think of a better gift to the master of all dissimulations and visages,—to Fox Borgia from Vixen Gonzaga,—than this hundred masks.

XVI

IN the beginning of March, fifteen hundred and three, Cæsar returned to Rome. The Pope had proposed to the Cardinals to reward the hero with the mark of the highest distinction the Church could bestow upon her defenders,—The Rose of Gold. The Cardinals had agreed, and the ceremony was set for two days later.

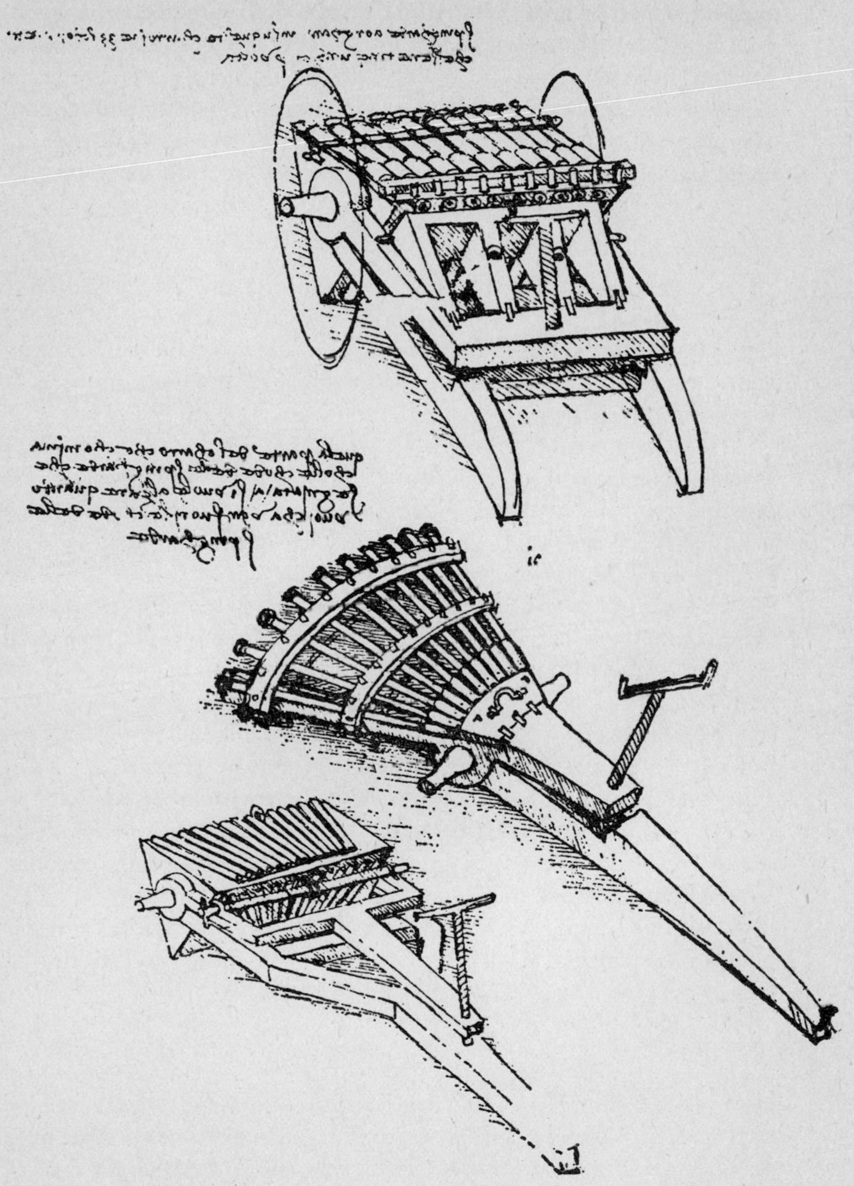

TWELVE · Leonardo da Vinci

On the first tier of the Vatican, in the Hall of the Pontiffs, whose windows looked out on the Court of the Belvedere, the Roman Curia and the envoys of great sovereigns gathered. Glittering with the precious stones of his pluvial, in a tiara of three crowns, fanned by peacock flabella, a corpulent but hale old man of seventy mounted the steps of the throne, kindly-majestic and benign of mien,—Pope Alexander VI.

The trumpets of the heralds blared forth, and, at a sign from the chief *cerimoniere*, Johannes Burckhardt, there entered armour-bearers, pages, courtiers, and body-guards of the Duke, and his Master of Camp, Bartolomeo Capranico, holding, point up, the bared sword of the Standard Bearer of the Church. The lower third of the sword had been gilt, and upon it were etched exquisite designs: the Goddess of Loyalty seated upon her throne,—the inscription reading *Loyalty Is Mightier Than Arms;* Julius Cæsar, as Triumphator, upon a chariot, the inscription reading: *Either Cæsar, Or Naught;* the Passing of the Rubicon, with the words: *The Die Is Cast;* and, finally, the bringing of a sacrifice to the Bull, or Apis, of the House of Borgia, with naked young priestesses burning incense over a human victim; upon the altar was the inscription: *Deo Optimo Maximo Hostia—A Sacrifice For God The All-Benevolent; The All-Powerful.* And, below, was another: *In nomine Cæsaris omen—The Name of Cæsar Is The Good Fortune of Cæsar.* The human sacrifice to the God-Beast attained a significance all the more horrible inasmuch as these designs and inscriptions had been ordered at the time when Cæsar had been contemplating the assassination of his brother, Giovanni Borgia, in order to inherit the Sword of the Captain and the Standard Bearer of the Church of Rome.

The hero himself followed the sword. On his head was the high ducal *berretta*, shaded by the wings of the Dove of the Holy Ghost, made out of pearls. Cæsar drew near to the Pope, doffed his *berretta*, got down on his knees, and kissed the ruby cross on the slipper of the Pontiff. Cardinal Monreale handed to His Holiness the Rose of Gold,—a miracle of the jeweller's art; a tiny vessel, hidden within the golden petals of the main central flower, exuded myrrh, and diffused all around a veritable semblance of the breath of countless roses. The Pope arose and spoke in a voice trembling from emotion:

"Receive, thou my beloved offspring, this Rose, which signifieth the joy of the two Jerusalems, the earthly and the heavenly, of the Church Militant and Triumphant; the flower beyond utterance, the joyance of the righteous, the beauty of incorruptible garlands; so that thy virtue, too, may bloom in Christ, like to the Rose dwelling on the shore of many waters. Amen!"

Cæsar took from the hands of his father the mystic Rose. The Pope could not restrain himself; "His flesh overcame him," to use the words of an eye-witness; infringing, to the indignation of the finicky Burckhardt, the routine of the ceremony, he leaned over, stretched out his trembling arms toward his son, and his face wrinkled up, his whole corpulent body began to sway. Thrusting out his thick lips and splutteringly gasping, he babbled in a senile voice:

"My child. . . . Cæsar. . . . Cæsar! . . ."

The Duke had to hand the Rose to the Cardinal of St. Clement, who was standing next to him. The Pope impulsively embraced his son and pressed him to his bosom, laughing and crying. The trumpets of the heralds blared anew; the bell of St. Peter's boomed forth,—and was answered by the bells of all the other churches of Rome, and by the rumbling of cannon-fire from the fortress of Sant' Angelo.

"Long live Cæsar!" yelled the Romagna guards from the Court of the Belvedere. The Duke appeared before his troops on the balcony.

Under the blue skies, in the shining of the morning sun, in the purple and gold of his regal vestments, with the pearl Dove of the Holy Ghost above his head, with the mystic Rose in his hands,—the joy of both Jerusalems,—he seemed to the crowd not a mortal but a god.

XVII

At night a magnificent masked procession, according to the design on Valentino's sword, was arranged.—The Triumph of Julius Cæsar.

On the chariot, with the inscription of *Divine Cæsar*, the Duke of Romagna sat in state, his hands holding a palm branch, his head entwined with laurels. The chariot was surrounded by soldiers, dressed to look like the legionaries of ancient Rome, with iron eagles and *fasces*. Everything had been done meticulously, according to books, monuments, bas-reliefs, and medals.

In front of the chariot paced a man in the long white raiment of an Egyptian hierophant holding a sacred gonfalon with the heraldic Scarlet Bull of the Borgias, gilt with virgin red gold,—Apis, the patron divinity of Pope Alexander VI. Youths in silver tunics chanted, accompanying themselves with tympani:

TWELVE · Leonardo da Vinci

Vive diu Bos! Vive diu Bos! Borgia vive!
Glory to the Bull! Glory to the Bull! To the Borgias, glory!

And high above the throng, against the starry sky and illuminated by the flickering of torches, the Beast idol swayed, fiery red, like to the sun rising.

In the throng was Leonardo's pupil, Giovanni Beltraffio, who had just come to his master at Rome from Florence. He contemplated the Scarlet Beast, and recalled the words of the Apocalypse:

"And they worshipped the beast, saying, Who is like unto the beast? Who is able to make war with him? . . .

"And I saw a woman sit upon a scarlet coloured beast, full of names of blasphemy, having seven heads and ten horns.

"And upon her forehead was a name written, MYSTERY, BABYLON THE GREAT, THE MOTHER OF HARLOTS AND ABOMINATIONS OF THE EARTH."[52]

And even as he who had written the words had wondered on a time, Giovanni, gazing at the Beast, also "wondered with a great wonder."[53]

BOOK THIRTEEN

The Scarlet Beast

I

INEYARDS CAN PRODUCE VEXATIONS AS WELL as grapes. Leonardo had a vineyard near Florence, on the knoll of Fiesole. A neighbour of his, desiring to appropriate a bit of his land, embarked on a law-suit. Being in Romagna, the artist entrusted this matter to Giovanni Beltraffio; toward the end of March, fifteen hundred and three, Leonardo summoned him to Rome.

On his way Giovanni turned aside into Orvieto, to have a look at the celebrated, recently completed frescoes of Luca Signorelli in the Cathedral. One of the frescoes pictured the advent of Antichrist. Giovanni was struck by the face of Antichrist. At first it appeared to him malignant, but when he had scrutinized it more closely he saw that it was not malignant, but only filled with infinite suffering. In the clear eyes, with their heavy, meek gaze, was reflected the ultimate despair of a wisdom that had rejected God. Despite the freakish ears of a satyr, the twisted fingers recalling the claws of a beast, he was beautiful. And before Giovanni, from behind this face, there appeared, just as once in his delirium, another, divine Face, similar to the first to the verge of horror,—a face he longed for yet dared not recognize.

To the left, in the same picture, was portrayed the destruction of Antichrist. Having flown up to the skies on invisible wings, in order to prove to men that he was the Son of Man, coming on the clouds to judge the quick and the dead, the Enemy of the Lord was falling into an abyss, stricken by an Angel. This unsuccessful flight, these human wings, awoke in Giovanni familiar, fearful thoughts about Leonardo.

II

LEONARDO was taken up with anatomy in the hospital at San Spirito. Giovanni assisted him. On one occasion, noting Giovanni's constant melancholy, and desiring to divert him in some way, he proposed that they go together to the Pope's palace.

At this time the Portuguese and the Spaniards had turned to Alexander VI for a decision of moot questions as to the possession of new lands and islands recently discovered by Cristoforo Colombo. The Pope was to consecrate, definitely, the boundary line which divided the terrestrial globe, a line he had laid ten years ago, at the first tidings of the discovery of America. Leonardo had been invited with the other savants, whom the Pope desired to consult.

Giovanni at first declined; but then curiosity overcame him,—he was fain to see him of whom he had heard so much. On the following morning they set out for the Vatican, and, traversing the large Hall of the Pontiffs,—the same wherein Alexander VI had bestowed the Rose of Gold upon Cæsar,—they entered the inner chambers, the so-called Hall of Christ and the Mother of God,—the reception room; then, the study of the Pope. The vaults and the semicircular lunettes on the walls between the arches were decorated with the frescoes of Pinturicchio,—scenes from the New Testament and hagiology. Side by side, on the very same vaults, the artist had depicted pagan mysteries. The Son of Jupiter,—Osiris, God of the Sun,—descends from heaven and espouses the Goddess of the Earth, Isis. He instructs men in the delving of the soil, in the gathering of fruit, in the planting of the vine. Men slay him. He comes to life again, emerges out of the ground, and appears anew under the guise of a white bull, the immaculate Apis.

However strange here, in the chambers of the Roman Pontiff, may have been this propinquity of scenes from the New Testament with the deification of the Golden Bull of the House of Borgia, in the guise of Apis, the same all-pervading joy of life reconciled both mysteries, —that of the Son of Jehovah and that of the Son of Jupiter; slender young cypresses bent to the wind amid inviting knolls, resembling the knolls of lonely Umbria, and in the heavens the soaring birds played their vernal games of love; next to Sant' Elisabetta, embracing the Mother of God with the salutation: "Blessed is the fruit of thy womb,"[54] a mite of a page was teaching a little dog to serve on its hind legs, while in the Espousal of Osiris and Isis just such another madcap was riding, naked, astride a goose meant for the sacrifice,—everything breathed forth the same joyousness; in all the decorations, amid the garlands of flowers, amid the angels with the crosses and censers, amid the ægipedal dancing fauns with thyrsi and baskets of fruit, appeared the mystic Bull, the Aureately-Scarlet Beast,—and from him did this joyousness seem to emanate.

"What is this?" reflected Giovanni. "Sacrilege, or childlike innocence? Does not the same holy emotion appear on the face of Elisabetta, in whose womb the babe leaped, and in the face of Isis, weeping over the rent limbs of the god Osiris? Does not the same rapture of prayer appear on the face of Alexander VI, bending his knee before the Lord coming out of His Sepulchre, and on the faces of the Egyptian priests, receiving the God of the Sun, slain of men and resurgent under the guise of Apis?"

And this god, before whom men fall prostrate on their faces, to whom they chant pæans, and burn incense upon altars, this heraldic beast of the House of Borgia, the transformed Golden Calf, was none other than the Roman Pontiff himself, deified by the poets.

Cæsare magna fuit, nunc Roma est maxima: Sextus
Regnat Alexander, ille vir, iste: Deus.

Great was Rome at the time of Cæsar, but now is it greatest;
Alexander now reigns there; the first was a mortal, the latter God is.

And more fearful than any contradiction did this carefree reconciliation of God and Beast seem to Giovanni.

As he inspected the paintings, he also lent an ear to the conversation of the grandees and the prelates who thronged the halls as they awaited the Pope.

"Whence come you, Beltrando?" the Cardinal Arborea was asking the envoy from Ferrara.

"From the Cathedral, Monsignor."

"Well, and how was His Holiness? Did he grow wearied?"

"Not in the least. One could not have wished for a Mass better said. Majesty, sanctity, benignancy like that of the angels! It seemed to me that I was not on earth but in heaven, among the holy chosen ones of God! And not I alone,—many did weep when the Pope elevated the chalice with the Holy Communion. . . ."

"And what may have been the malaise from which the Cardinal Michiele passed away?" the French envoy, recently arrived, voiced his curiosity.

"From food, or drink, which proved harmful to his stomach," answered the datary, Don Juan Lopez, a Spaniard by birth, like the majority of those attached to Alexander VI.

"They do say," said Beltrando, "that on Friday, now, just on the very next day after the death of Michiele, His Holiness refused to receive the Spanish envoy, whom he had been awaiting with such impatience,—giving the grief and the care occasioned him by the death of the Cardinal as an excuse."

In this conversation, beyond the obvious, there was a secret meaning: thus, the indisposition and the cares which the death of Cardinal Michiele had occasioned the Pope consisted of his counting over all that day long the moneys of the deceased; the food, harmful to the stomach of His Reverence, had been the celebrated poison of the Borgias,—a sweet white powder, which killed gradually, within any period of time designated beforehand, or else an infusion of dried Spanish flies, triturated through a sieve. The Pope had invented this rapid and easy means of obtaining moneys: keeping an accurate surveillance of the incomes of the Cardinals, in the event of the need arising he despatched to the other world the first one whom he deemed grown sufficiently wealthy, and declared himself the heir. 'Twas said that he fattened them even as swine are fattened for slaughter. Johannes Burckhardt, the German master of ceremonies, had exceedingly frequent occasions to mark off in his diary, with imperturbable brevity, amid descriptions of churchly pomps, the sudden demise of this prelate or that:

"*Biberat calicem.*—He hath drained the chalice."

"But is it true, Monsignori," asked Pedro Carranza, a chamberlain, —another Spaniard,—"is it true, as they say, that Cardinal Monreale has been taken ill this night?"

"Really?" exclaimed Arborea. "But what is the matter with him?"

"I know not of a certainty. They speak of nausea, of vomiting. . . ."

"Oh, Lord, Lord!" sighed Arborea heavily, and told them over on his fingers: "The Cardinals Orsini, Ferrari, Michiele, Monreale. . . ."

"Is it, perhaps, the air here, or the water of the Tiber, that hath such harmful properties for the healths of Your Reverences?" Beltrando put in slyly.

"One after the other! One after the other!" whispered Arborea, blanching. "A man is alive this day, but on the morrow . . ."

A hush fell upon them all.

A new throng of grandees, knights, body-guards (under the command of the Pope's grandson-nephew, Don Rodriguez Borgia), chamberlains, cubicularies, dataries, and other dignitaries of the Apostolic Curia, surged into the chambers from the vast adjacent halls of Papagallo.

"The Holy Father! The Holy Father!" the reverent susurration arose, and died away.

The throng swayed, undulating and parting, the portals were flung open,—and Pope Borgia, Alexander VI, made his entry into the reception hall.

III

HE had been handsome of person in his youth. It was asserted that it sufficed for him to look at a woman to inflame her with passion, as though there were a power in his eyes which drew women to him, even as a magnet draws iron. Even now his features, although they had spread from excessive corpulency, still retained a majestically benign mien. His face was swarthy in colour; his skull bare, with remnants of grey hair at the nape of his neck; he had a large aquiline nose, a dewlap, small, quick-darting eyes, filled with an unusual liveliness, fleshy, soft lips, jutting forward, with a concupiscent, crafty expression, which yet was at the same time almost childishly naïve.

In vain did Giovanni search for anything awful or cruel in the appearance of this man. Alexander Borgia was possessed in the highest degree of the gift of worldly amenities—an innate exquisiteness. No matter what he said or did, it seemed that just so must one speak or do,—that nothing else was possible. "The Pope is seventy," wrote one envoy, "but with every day he grows younger; his most oppressive griefs last for but a day; he is of a gay disposition by nature; all that he doth undertake serves for his benefit; but then, by the bye, he never does think of aught else save the glory and happiness of his children."

The Borgias traced their lineage from the Castilian Moors who had come from Africa,—and truly, to judge by the swarthy colour of the skin, the thick lips, the fiery gaze of Alexander VI, there must have been African blood flowing through his veins.

"One can not conceive," reflected Giovanni, "of a better aureole for him than these frescoes of Pinturicchio, depicting the glory of the ancient Apis, the Bull born of the Sun."

Old Borgia himself, despite his seventy years, as hale and stalwart as a stud bull, seemed a descendant of his heraldic Beast, the Aureately-Scarlet Bull, the God of the Sun, of Joyousness, of Lust and Fertility.

Alexander VI entered the hall conversing with a Hebrew, one Salomone da Sesso, a master goldsmith,—the same that had depicted the

Triumph of Julius Cæsar on the sword of Valentino. He had gained the especial favour of His Holiness in engraving on a flat, large emerald, in imitation of ancient stones, the Venus Callipygos;[55] she had so pleased the Pope that he had ordered this stone to be set in the cross wherewith he blessed the people on solemn Masses in the Cathedral of St. Peter; and, in this fashion, kissing the Crucifix he also kissed the beautiful goddess. He was not, however, godless: not only did he observe all the outward rites of the Church, but within the secret places of his heart he was pious; especially did he reverence the Most Pure Virgin Mary and deemed her his particular Mediatrix, his constant, ardent supplicant before God.

The holy lamp which he was now ordering from Salomone, the Jew, was a gift promised to Maria del Popolo for Madonna Lucrezia's recovery from illness. Sitting by the window, the Pope was inspecting precious stones. His love for them amounted to passion. With the long, slender fingers of his shapely hand he touched them softly, choosing them, his thick lips thrust out with a gormandizing and concupiscent expression. Especially was he pleased with a large chrysoprase, darker than an emerald, with mysterious sparks of gold and purple. He ordered to be brought to him, out of his own treasury, the coffer of pearls. Every time he opened it he recalled his beloved daughter Lucrezia, who resembled a pale pearl. Having sought out in the throng of grandees the envoy of his son-in-law, Alfonso d'Este, the Duke of Ferrara, he beckoned to him to approach.

"Look you, Beltrando, forget not the little present for Madonna Lucrezia. 'Twould not be seemly for thee to return from her uncle empty-handed."

He styled himself "uncle," inasmuch as in official documents Madonna Lucrezia was styled not as the daughter but as the niece of His Holiness: the Roman Pontiff could not have legitimate children.

He rummaged in the casket, drew out an enormous, elongated, roseate Indian pearl,—it was as big as a hazel nut and beyond all value; raising it up to light, he became lost in admiration: he pictured it within the deep incision of a black dress against the even white of Madonna Lucrezia's bosom, and he experienced an indecision as to which he should bestow it upon,—the Duchess of Ferrara, or the Virgin Mary? But immediately, recalling that 'twere sinful to take away from the Queen of Heaven the gift promised to her, he handed the pearl to the Hebrew, and ordered it to be set in the most prominent place,—between the chrysoprase and the carbuncle, which latter was the gift of the Sultan.

"Beltrando," he turned again to the envoy, "when thou shalt see the Duchess, tell her from me to remain in health and to pray more assiduously to the Queen of Heaven. As for us, as thou seest, we remain, through the grace of the Lord and the Most Virgin Mary, who is ever our Intercessor, in perfect health, and do send her our Apostolic blessing.—As for our bit of a present, it shall be delivered at your quarters this very evening."

The Spanish envoy, having approached the casket, exclaimed reverently:

"Never have I seen such a great quantity of pearls! They would equal, at the least, seven measures of wheat?"

"Eight and a half!" the Pope corrected him with pride. "Ay, I may write it down as an added honour,—'tis a decent little lot of pearls! I have been hoarding them for twenty years. For have I not a daughter who is a great hand for pearls? . . ."

And, puckering up his left eye, he burst into low, queer laughter.

"She knows, the little knave, what is becoming to her. My desire is," he added, solemnly, "that after my death Lucrezia have the best pearls in all Italy!"

Plunging both his hands into the pearls, he scooped them up in handfuls and let them run through his fingers, admiring the tenderly dim grains as they trickled down, swishing, and emitting an even white sheen.

"All, all is for her, our beloved daughter!" he kept repeating, spluttering and gasping.

And suddenly something flashed within the Pope's flaming eyes which made the chill of horror dart through the heart of Giovanni,—and he recalled the rumours of the monstrous lust of old Borgia for his own daughter.

IV

CÆSAR was announced to His Holiness.

The Pope had invited him on important business: the French King, expressing through his envoy at the Vatican his displeasure against the inimical projects of the Duke of Valentino against the Republic of Florence, which was under the high protection of France, accused Alexander VI of lending his support to his son in these projects.

When the arrival of his son was announced, the Pope bestowed a glance by stealth at the French envoy; approaching him, he took him under the arm and saying something in his ear led him, as though by chance, to the door of the room where he expected Cæsar; next, entering it, he left the door ajar,—probably also by chance, so that whatever was said in the adjacent chamber might be heard by those standing near the door within the first,—the French consul among their number.

Soon the infuriated shouts of the Pope were heard issuing therefrom. Cæsar, at first, began to contradict him, calmly and respectfully. But the old man took to stamping his feet and screamed in an uncontrollable rage:

"Get thee gone out of my sight! Mayest thou strangle, thou son of a dog, thou offspring of a whore!"

"Ah, God! Do you hear that?" whispered the French envoy to the man next to him, the *oratore* of Venice, Antonio Giustiniani. "They shall come to blows; His Holiness will beat him up!"

Giustiniani merely shrugged his shoulders,—he knew that if any one were to do any beating, it would be rather the son who would beat the father than the father the son. Ever since the murder of Cæsar's brother, the Duke of Candia, the Pope trembled before Cæsar, even though he had come to love him with a tenderness still greater than before, in which a superstitious horror mingled with pride. All remembered how the chamberlain Perotte, a mere boy, who had aroused the Duke's wrath had, after seeking sanctuary under the raiment of the Pope, been stabbed on His Holiness' breast by Cæsar, so that the boy's blood had squirted into the Pope's face. Giustiniani surmised also that their present quarrel was but a by-play: they desired to throw the French envoy completely off the track, by proving to him that even if the Duke had any intentions at all against the Republic, the Pope took absolutely no part in them,—Giustiniani was always saying that they worked hand in hand: the father never did that of which he spoke; the son never spoke of that which he did. Having sent after the departing Duke the threat of a father's curse and of excommunication, the Pope returned to the Reception Hall, all a-tremble with fury, gasping for breath and wiping the sweat from his face, which had grown scarlet. Only, in the very depth of his eyes, there lurked a merry sparkle. Approaching the French envoy, he again led him aside, this time within the recess made by the door which led to the Court of the Belvedere.

"Your Holiness," the polite Frenchman essayed to apologize, "I would not wish to be the cause of your wrath. . . ."

"Why, did you overhear us?" the Pope was ingenuously amazed, and, without giving him time to recover, with a gesture of paternal kindliness took him by the chin with two fingers—a mark of especial favour—and rapidly, gracefully, with an irresistible impulse, began to speak of his loyalty to the King and of the blamelessness of the Duke's intentions.

The envoy listened, befogged, bewildered; and, although he had proofs almost incontrovertible of the Duke's treachery, would rather have distrusted his own eyes than the expression of the Pope's eyes, face, and voice.

Old Borgia lied naturally. He never meditated over his lies beforehand,—they formed on his lips of themselves, just as guilelessly, almost without his will, as with women in matters of love. All life long had he developed this ability of his through exercise, and had finally attained such perfection that, although all knew that he was lying, and that, to use an expression of Machiavelli's, "the less desire the Pope had to fulfill anything, the more oaths did he give,"—all believed him, inasmuch as the secret of success of this lying consisted in that he believed it himself.

V

Having finished his conversation with the envoy, Alexander VI turned to his chief secretary, Francesco Remolino da Ilerda, Cardinal of Perugia, who had at one time been present at the judgment and execution of Brother Girolamo Savonarola. The Cardinal was waiting, with a Bull about the establishment of a Spiritual Censorship, ready for the signature. The Pope had himself given it much thought and had composed it:

"Recognizing," it read, among other things, "the usefulness of the printing press, an invention which preserves truth for all time and makes it accessible to all, but desirous of guarding against and averting any evil which may ensue to the Church from latitudinarian and seductive works, we do hereby forbid the printing of any book whatsoever, without the permission of spiritual authority,—the local vicar or bishop."

Having heard the Bull to the end, the Pope looked over the Cardinals with his eyes, putting the usual question:

"*Quod videtur?* How see you the matter?"

"Besides books printed," suggested Arborea, "ought we not to take some measures also against works of the same nature in manuscript, —such as the nameless epistle to Paolo Savelli?"

"I know," the Pope interrupted him. "Ilerda has shown it me."

"If it be already known to Your Holiness . . ."

The Pope looked the Cardinal straight in the eyes. The latter was abashed.

"Thou wouldst say: How is it I have not instigated a search, have not endeavoured to bring the guilty one to light? Oh, my son, wherefore should I take to persecuting my accuser, when there is naught in his words save truth?"

"Holy Father!" Arborea was horrified.

"Ay," continued Alexander VI, in a moved and solemn voice, "my accuser is right! The least of the sinners am I,—a thief, and an extortioner, and a lecher, and a homicide! I tremble and know not where I may hide my face from the judgment of man,—how then shall it be on the last day of the fearful judgment of Christ, when even the just may hardly justify themselves? . . . But if not only men, but even Angels, Powers, Virtues, and Dominions of Heaven condemn and reject me, I shall not still my voice, I shall not cease to cry out to my Mediatrix, to the Most Pure Virgin, and I know that she will take compassion upon me,—I know! . . ."

With a stifled sob which shook his whole corpulent body, he extended his arms to the Mother of God in Pinturicchio's picture over the door of the Hall. Many thought that in this fresco, at the desire of the Pope, the artist had given the Madonna a resemblance of Giulia Farnese, the beautiful Roman, a concubine of His Holiness', the mother of Cæsar and Lucrezia. Giovanni looked on, listened, and wondered: was this a buffoonade, or faith? Or was it, perhaps, both the one and the other, combined?

"One more thing will I say, my friends," continued the Pope, "not in vindication of myself, but to the glory of the Lord. The writer of the epistle to Paolo Savelli styles me an heretic. I call the living God to witness,—of this am I blameless! Ye yourselves,—but, no, ye would not tell me the truth to my face; well, take thee, Ilerda: I know that thou alone dost love me and dost see my heart; no flatterer art thou, —tell me then, Francesco, do tell me, before God,—am I guilty of heresy?"

"Holy Father," answered the Cardinal with deep emotion, "is it for me to judge thee? Thy bitterest foes, were they to read the creation of Alexander VI, *The Shield of the Holy Church of Rome*, must acknowledge that of heresy thou art blameless."

"You hear? You hear?" exclaimed the Pope, pointing to Ilerda and exulting like a child. "If he hath vindicated me, it means that God will vindicate me also. Whatever else may be the case, but of free thought, of the mutinous love of the wisdom of this age, of heresy, —I am blameless! Not by a single thought, nor by a doubt against God, have I ever polluted my soul. Pure and unshakable is our faith. And may this Bull of Spiritual Censorship be a new adamant shield for the Church of the Lord!"

He took a quill, and in a large, childishly clumsy but majestic script, he traced on the parchment:

"*Fiat*,—So Be It. *Alexander Sextus episcopus servus servorum Dei.* Alexander the Sixth, Bishop, the Servant of the Servants of the Lord."

Two monks, Cistercians, from the Apostolic College of Seals,—*piombature*,—hung from the bull on a silken cord, let through the thickness of the parchment, a leaden ball, and flattened it out with iron pincers into a flat seal, with a cross and the name of the Pope imprinted thereon.

"Now dost thou release thy servant!" exclaimed Ilerda in a whisper, raising toward heaven his sunken eyes, blazing with the fire of an insane zeal. He did really believe that if one were to place in one dish of a scale all the malefactions of Borgia, and in the other this Bull anent Spiritual Censorship, that the latter would outweigh the first.

VI

A CONFIDENTIAL cubiculary approached the Pope and said something in his ear. Borgia, with a preoccupied air, passed into the next room, and, through a little door, hidden by wall hangings, into a narrow vaulted passage, lit up by a hanging lanthorn; here the cook of the poisoned Cardinal Monreale was waiting forhim. Rumours had reached Alexander VI that the quantity of poison had proven insufficient, and that the sick man was recovering. Having interrogated the cook in detail, the Pope was convinced that, despite the temporary improvement, the Cardinal would die within two or three months. This was still more advantageous, inasmuch as it diverted suspicions.

"But still," he mused, "one feels sorry for the old man! A merry soul he was, a man most circumspect, and a good son of the Church."

Moved, he sighed, cast down his head, his plump, soft lips good-naturedly stuck out. He was not lying,—he really felt sorry for the Cardinal, and had it been possible to take his money away without causing him harm, he would have been happy. As he was returning to the reception hall, he caught sight, in the Hall of the Liberal Arts, which at times served as a refectory for cozy friendly luncheons, a covered board, and felt hunger. The division of the terrestrial globe was put over until after dinner. His Holiness invited the guests to the refectory.

The table was decorated with living white lilies in crystal vessels,—the flowers of the Holy Annunciation, of which the Pope was especially fond, because their virginal beauty reminded him of Lucrezia. The courses were not luxurious: Alexander VI was noted for his temperance in food and drink.

As he stood in the throng of chamberlains, Giovanni lent an attentive ear to the conversation around the board. Don Juan Lopez, the datary, led the conversation around to to-day's quarrel between His Holiness and Cæsar; and, as though not suspecting that it was assumed, began zealously to vindicate the Duke. All present joined him, proclaiming the virtues of Cæsar.

"Ah, nay, nay,—say naught of it!" the Pope shook his head with a grumbling tenderness. "Ye know not, my friends, what a man this is! Every day I am on tenter hooks as to what his next prank may be. Mark you my words,—he will bring us all to grief and will break his own neck to boot. . . ."

His eyes took on a sparkle of paternal pride.

"And whomever does he take after, when you come to think of it? You know yourselves,—I am a man simple and without guile. Whatever is on my mind is on the tip of my tongue also. But Cæsar,—the Lord only knows what he is up to; he is forever silent, and forever secretive. Would you believe it, signori,—I may be yelling at him, upbraiding him, and yet I myself am afraid of him; yea, yea,—afraid of my own son, because he is most courteous, even exceedingly courteous; yet when he gives you a sudden glance,—'tis exactly as if you received a knife stroke through your heart. . . ."

The guests fell to defending the Duke still more strenuously.

The room was becoming stuffy. The Pope's head swam a little, not so much from wine as from intoxicating visions of the greatness of his son. The company walked out on the *ringhiera*,—the stone balcony overlooking the Court of the Belvedere. Below the Papal hostlers were bringing mares and stallions out of their stables.

"Alonzo, what sayst thou,—let them go?" the Pope called out to the head hostler. The latter grasped his meaning and issued an order: the coupling of stallions and mares was one of the favourite amusements of His Holiness. The gates of the stable were flung open; the whips began to crack; happy neighing was heard, and a whole drove scattered over the court; the stallions pursued and covered the mares.

Surrounded by his Cardinals and grandees the Pope savoured this sight for a long while. But little by little his face became overcast: he recalled how, several years agone, he had been enjoying the same amusement with Madonna Lucrezia. The image of his daughter rose up before him, as if it were alive,—flaxen-haired, blue-eyed, her sensuous lips somewhat thick, taking after her father; all fresh and tender, like a pearl; infinitely submissive, calm, knowing not evil though in the midst of evil; in the ultimate horror of sin without corruption or passion. Also did he recall, with indignation and hatred, her present husband, the Duke of Ferrara, Alfonso d'Este. Why had he ever given her up, why had he ever given his consent to this marriage? . . .

Heaving a deep sigh, and letting his head droop, as though he had suddenly felt the weight of his years upon his shoulders, the Pope returned to the reception hall.

VII

HERE the spheres, charts, the compasses,—the draftsman's and the mariner's,—were all in readiness for the laying down of the great meridian, which was to pass three hundred and seventy Portuguese leagues to the south of the Azores, and the Cape Verde. This point had been chosen because precisely there, as Colombo asserted, the navel of the world was situated; the sprout of the pearlike globe, resembling the nipple of a woman's breast,—a mountain reaching to the lunar sphere of the heavens, of the existence of which mountain he had become convinced by the deviation of the magnetized needle of his compass during his first voyage.

From the extreme western point of Portugal on the one side, and from the shores of Brazil on the other, equal distances were marked off to the meridian. Later on master mariners and astronomers were to determine with greater exactness these distances in terms of days of sailing. The Pope offered up a prayer, blessed the terrestrial sphere with the same cross in which was set the emerald with the Venus Callipygos, and, having dipped a brush in red ink, drew over the Atlantic Ocean, from the North Pole to the South, a great pacificatory line: all the islands and lands discovered, or to be discovered, to the east of this line belonged to Spain; those to the west of it, to Portugal. Thus, with a single motion of his hand, he cut the globe of the earth in half, like an apple, and divided it between Christian nations. At this moment, it seemed to Giovanni, Alexander VI, venerable and solemn, filled with a consciousness of his power, resembled the Cæsar-Pope he had prophesied, the unifier of the two worlds,—the terrestrial and the celestial, of this world and yet not of it.

On the evening of the same day Cæsar, in his chambers at the Vatican, was giving a feast for His Holiness and for the Cardinals, at which were present fifty of the most beautiful of the Roman "noble whores" —*meretrices honestæ*. After supper the windows were closed with shutters, the doors were locked, the enormous silver candelabra were taken off the tables and set upon the floor. Cæsar, the Pope, and the guests tossed roasted chestnuts to the strumpets, and the latter would pick them up, crawling about on all fours, absolutely naked, between the innumerable host of wax candles. They fought, laughed, squealed and tumbled; soon, on the floor, at the feet of His Holiness, was a whole squirming mound of swarthy, white and pink bodies, in the bright glow flung upward from the guttering candles.

The seventy-year-old Pope was amusing himself like a child, tossing the chestnuts in handfuls and clapping his palms, calling the courtesans his "little *wagtail* birdlets." But little by little his face became overcast with the same shadow as after the luncheon on the Ringhiera Belvedere,—he recalled how, in the year of fifteen hundred and one, on the eve of All Saints' Day, he had been admiring, with Madonna Lucrezia, his beloved daughter, this same game of the chestnuts.

As a conclusion of the festa, the guests descended to the private chambers of His Holiness, to the Hall of the Lord and the Mother of God. Here was arranged a love contest between the courtesans and the most stalwart of the Duke's Romagna body-guards; rewards were bestowed upon the victors.

Thus was celebrated at the Vatican the day so memorable to the

Church of Rome, marked by the division of the terrestrial globe and the establishment of spiritual censorship.

Leonardo had been present at this supper and a witness of all that had taken place. Invitations to such celebrations were esteemed a great mark of favour, which it was impossible to decline. On the same night, upon his return home, he wrote down in his diary:

"Seneca speaks truly: within every man is a god and a beast, chained together."

And further, next to an anatomical drawing:

"It seems to me that men with base souls, with despicable passions, are unworthy of the same beautiful and intricate bodily structure as men of great intelligence and contemplation: for them would suffice a mere sack with two openings,—one for receiving food, the other for casting it out, inasmuch as they are truly no more than a mere passage for food, no more than fillers of cess-pools. Only in face and voice do they resemble men; whereas in all things else they be worse than the brute beasts."

VIII

SUMMER came on. Putrid fever of the Pontine marshes,—the malaria,—was raging throughout the city. Toward the end of July and the beginning of August not a day passed without some one of those attached to the Pope dying. Of late he seemed disquieted and sad. It was not the fear of death, however, that gnawed at him, but another yearning, a yearning of old,—yearning for Madonna Lucrezia. Formerly, too, he had had such attacks of unbearably frantic desires, blind and deaf, like to madness, and he feared them: it seemed to him that if he were not to satisfy them immediately, they would strangle him. He wrote to her, imploring her to come, were it but for a few days, trusting to detain her thereafter by force. She replied that her husband would not allow her to come. Before no evil deed would old Borgia have held back that he might extirpate this last son-in-law of his, the most hated of all, just as he had extirpated all the other husbands of Lucrezia. But 'twas an ill matter to jest with the Duke of Ferrara,—his was the best artillery in all Italy.

On the fifth of August the Pope set out for the suburban villa of Cardinal Adrian. At supper, despite the warnings of his leeches, he ate his favourite, highly-spiced dishes, washing them down with heavy Sicilian wine, and enjoyed for a long while the dangerous freshness of the Roman evening. On the following morning he felt unwell. Subsequently it was told that, having approached an open window, the Pope had caught sight of two funeral processions at the same time,—that of one of his own chamberlains, and of Messer Guglielmo Raymondo. Both of the departed had been corpulent.

"'Tis a dangerous time of the year for us fat folk," the Pope was reputed to have said. And, no sooner had he said this, than a turtle-dove flew in at the window, struck against the wall, and, stunned, fell at the feet of His Holiness.

"An ill-omen! An ill-omen!" he had uttered in a whisper, blanching, and had at once withdrawn to his dortoir. That night he had nausea and vomiting.

The leeches differed in their diagnoses of the Pope's illness: some called it the tertian fever; others, the spreading of the gall; others still, "a sanguinary stroke." Rumours ran through the city that the Pope had been poisoned. He grew weaker with every hour. On the sixteenth of August it was decided to have recourse to the last remedy,—a medicament of brayed precious stones. It made the sick man still worse.

Once, in the night-time, awakening out of his stupor, he began groping over his bosom, under his shirt. During many years Alexander VI had carried on his person a tiny casket of gold, a reliquary to be worn next the flesh, in the form of a pomander, with particles of the Blood and Flesh of the Lord. Astrologers had foretold him that he would not die while he had it upon him. Whether he had lost it himself, or whether some one of those about him had stolen it, desiring his death, has remained a mystery. Learning that it was nowhere to be found, he closed his eyes in hopeless resignation, and said:

"This means I die. 'Tis the end!"

On the morning of the seventeenth, feeling the faintness of death upon him, he ordered all out of the room, and beckoning to the Bishop of Vanosa, his favourite leech, reminded him of a treatment, invented by a certain Hebrew, leech to Innocent VIII, who, so it was told, had transfused into the veins of the dying Pope the blood of three infants.

"Your Holiness," retorted the Bishop, "do you know the upshot of that experiment?"

"I know, I know," babbled the Pope. "But, perhaps, it did not succeed because the children were seven or eight years of age, whereas, so they say, the youngest, infants at the breast, are needed. . . ."

The Bishop made no reply. The eyes of the sick man dimmed. He was already delirious:

"Ay, ay, the very smallest . . . the whitest . . . little ones. . . . Their blood is pure, scarlet. . . . I love little children. *Sinite parvulos ad me venire*. Suffer little children to come unto me, and forbid them not. . . ."[56]

This raving from the lips of the dying Vicar of Christ went against the grain of even the imperturbable Bishop, who was inured to everything.

With a monotonous, helpless, convulsively-hurried motion of his hand, like that of one drowning, the Pope still groped, still felt for, still sought on his bosom the vanished reliquary with the Flesh and Blood of the Lord.

During his illness he had not thought once of his children. Hearing that Cæsar also was at death's door, he remained apathetic. And when he was asked if he did not desire to have his last wishes transmitted to his son or daughter, he turned away in silence, as though those whom he had loved all life long with such a vehement love were no longer existent for him.

On Friday, August eighteenth, in the morning, he confessed to his confessor, Pietro Gamboa, Bishop of Carinola, and received communion. Toward vespers the prayers for the dying were begun. Several times the dying man made efforts to say something, or to make a sign with his hand. Cardinal Ilerda bent toward him, and through the feeble sounds his lips emitted gathered that the Pope was saying:

"Quick. . . . Quick. . . . Read the prayer to my Mediatrix. . . ."

Although, according to the ritual of the Church, this prayer was not supposed to be read over the dying, Ilerda fulfilled the last request of his friend and chanted the *Stabat Mater Dolorosa*.

An inexpressible emotion gleamed in the eyes of Alexander VI as though he already beheld his Mediatrix before him. With a last effort he stretched forth his hands; his entire body gave a flutter of life, he raised himself up a little, repeated, with a tongue growing numb: "Reject me not, O Holy Virgin!"—fell back on his pillows,—and was no more.

IX

AT the same time Cæsar, also, was hovering betwixt life and death. His leech, the Bishop Gaspare Torella, put him through an unusual treatment:—he ordered a mule's belly to be slit, and the sick man, shaken by an ague, to be dipped within the bloody, steaming entrails; after that he was plunged into icy water. Not so much through this treatment as through an incredible effort of the will, Cæsar conquered his illness. In these fearful days he preserved a perfect calm; he watched the transpiring events, listened to reports, dictated letters, issued orders. When the news of the Pope's death came, he ordered himself to be carried by a secret passage from the Vatican to the fortress of Sant' Angelo.

All sorts of legends anent the death of Alexander VI ran rife through the city. The ambassador from Venice, Marino Sanuto, reported to his Republic that the dying man had—so it was said—seen an ape, which teased him, hopping about the room, and when one of the Cardinals offered to catch it, had exclaimed in horror: "Let it be, let it be,—'tis the Devil!" Others told that the Pope had kept on repeating: "I am coming, I am coming; only do thou bide a wee bit longer!" and explained this by saying that Rodrigo Borgia, the future Alexander VI, while at the conclave which was choosing the Pope after the decease of Innocent VIII, had concluded a compact with the Devil, having sold him his soul for twelve years of Papacy. It was also asserted that, a minute before his death, seven fiends had appeared at the head of his bed; and that, the moment he had died, his body had begun to decompose, to seethe, throwing up foam from the mouth, just like a cauldron on a fire, growing in the middle, swelling up like a mountain, losing all human semblance; and that it had become denigrated, "like coal, or the darkest of cloth, while the face became like the face of an Æthiopian."

According to custom, before the burial of a Roman Pontiff, requiems had to be said for nine days in the Cathedral of St. Peter. But such was the horror inspired by the remains of the Pope that no one wanted to officiate. No candles were around the body, nor incense, nor lectors, nor guards, nor men praying. For a long while no grave diggers could be found. Finally six gallows-birds were unearthed, ready to undertake anything for a tumbler of wine. The coffin proved not of the right size. Thereupon the tiara of three crowns was taken off the Pope's head; a rug with holes was thrown over him, in lieu of a pall, and, somehow or other, with many thrusts, the body was squeezed into the box which was too short and too narrow. Others asserted that, without honouring him with even a coffin, he had been dragged into a pit by his heels, which were tied to a cord, like carrion or the corpse of a plague victim.

But even after his body had been earthed, there was no rest for him: the superstitious horror among the people kept on increasing. It seemed that in the very air of Rome, to the death-laden breath of malaria had been joined a new, unknown stench, still more loathsome and ominous. In the Cathedral of St. Peter a black dog began to appear, which ran about with unbelievable speed, in regularly spreading circles. The inhabitants of Borgo durst not step out of their houses with the coming of dusk. And many were firmly convinced that Pope Alexander VI had not died a real death; that he would arise again, take his seat on the throne anew,—and that then the reign of Antichrist would commence.

X

In the meanwhile Leonardo, withdrawn from all, was tranquilly working on a picture which he had begun long ago on a commission from the Servite monks for their church, Santa Maria dell' Annunziata at Florence, and later, being in the service of Cæsar Borgia, had carried on with his usual dilatoriness. The picture represented St. Anne and the Virgin Mary.

At the same time Leonardo was making designs for all sorts of machines,—gigantic lift-cranes, water-pumps, wire-rollers, saws for the hardest stone, machines for turning iron rods; weaving looms, contrivances for shrinking wool, for weaving ropes, for making pottery. And Giovanni wondered why the master carried on these two labours —upon the machines and upon the picture—together. But this conjunction was not a chance one.

"I affirm," he wrote in his *First Principles of Mechanics*, "that force is something spiritual and unseen; spiritual, because it hath in it a life unembodied; unseen, because the body wherein force is born does not change either its weight or its appearance."

The fate of Leonardo was being decided with the fate of Cæsar. Despite the calm and valour preserved by Cæsar—"that great connoisseur of fate," to use an expression of Machiavelli's,—he felt that fortune had averted her face from him. Hearing of the death of the Pope and the Duke's illness, his foes united and seized the lands of the Roman Campagna. Prospero Colonna was advancing to the gates of the City; Vitelli was moving upon Citta di Castello; Gian-Paolo Baglioni upon Perugia;

Urbino revolted; Camerino, Cagli, Piombino were falling away, one after the other; the conclave, convened for the election of a new Pope, demanded the Duke's withdrawal from Rome. Everything was betraying him, everything was tumbling about his ears. And those who had but recently trembled before him, now mocked him and welcomed his downfall,—kicking the expiring lion with their asses' hoofs. Poets composed epigrams:

"'Cæsar or Naught!' Find we not both in thee?
Cæsar wert thou before; soon naught shalt thou be!"

Once, at the Vatican, conversing with the Venetian envoy, Antonio Giustiniani,—the same who, in the days of the Duke's greatness, had predicted that "he would be consumed, like a fire of straw,"—Leonardo began speaking of Messer Niccolò Machiavelli.

"Has he told you of his work on the science of government?"

"Of course; we have conversed of it more than once. Messer Niccolò is pleased to jest, naturally. Never will he let this book see the light. For can such subjects be written about? To give counsels to sovereigns; to unveil the secrets of power before the people; to prove that every government is naught else save violence, covered with the mask of justice,—why, this is just the same as instructing hens in the wiles of foxes, or the setting of wolf-fangs in the jaws of sheep! May God preserve us from such politics!"

"Then you think that Messer Niccolò is deluded, and will change his ideas?"

"Not at all. I am in perfect agreement with him. One must do as he says,—but not say it. However, even if he does give this book to the world, no one shall suffer, save himself. God is gracious,—the sheep and the hens shall believe—even as they have believed hitherto—their lawful rulers, the wolves and the foxes, who shall accuse him of diabolical politics,—of vulpine craftiness, of lupine ferocity. And everything shall remain as it has ever been. At least, there shall be enough fools left to last our life-time!"

XI

In the autumn of fifteen hundred and three, the Gonfaloniere of the Florentine Republic, Pietro Soderini, who held the office for the term of his life, invited Leonardo to join his service, intending to send him as a military engineer to the Pisan camp, to construct engines to be used in the siege.

The artist's stay in Rome was drawing to an end.

One evening he was roaming over the Palatine Hill. There, where on a time the palaces of the Emperors—of Augustus, of Caligula, of Septimius Severus—had reared up, was now only the wind soughing through the ruins; and among the grey olives one heard but the bleating of the sheep and the stridulation of grass-hoppers. Judging by the multiplicity of the fragments of white marble the sculptures of gods of an unknown beauty reposed in the earth, like dead men awaiting their resurrection. The evening was clear. The brick skeletons of the arches and walls, lit up by the sun, glowed a rich scarlet against the dark-blue sky. And more regal than purple and gold, which had at one time adorned these dwelling places of the Roman Emperors, were the purple and gold of the autumnal leaves.

On the northern slope of the knoll, not far from the gardens of Capronica, Leonardo, kneeling, was parting the grasses and attentively examining a splinter of ancient marble with an exquisite design. Out of the bushes, from a narrow path, stepped a man. Leonardo glanced at him, arose, gave him another glance, approached him, and exclaimed:

"Can it be you, Messer Niccolò?" And, without waiting for an answer, he embraced and kissed him, as one would a brother.

The raiment of the Secretary of Florence seemed still older and poorer than it had been in Romagna,—it was evident that the rulers of Florence, as of yore, were not spoiling him, and keeping him in but a sorry state. He had grown thinner; his clean-shaven cheeks had sunk in; his long, thin neck had stretched out; his flat, ducklike bill stuck out still more, and his eyes burned more brightly with a febrile glitter. Leonardo began to question him as to whether he would be in Rome for long, and what his mission was. When the artist mentioned Cæsar, Niccolò turned away, avoiding his glances and shrugging his shoulders, and answered coldly, with an assumed ease:

"At the will of the fates, I have been a witness to such events that nothing amazes me any more. . . ."

And, evidently desiring to change the conversation, he asked in his turn how Leonardo's affairs stood. Hearing that the artist had entered the service of the Florentine Republic, Machiavelli could only make a gesture of hopelessness:

"You will have no cause to rejoice! God alone knoweth which is better,—the malefactions of such a hero as Cæsar or the benefactions of such a pismire hill as our Republic. However, the one is as precious as the other. Do but ask me,—for do I not know the beauties of popular government!" he smiled his bitterly scoffing smile.

Leonardo imparted to him the words of Antonio Giustiniani about the vulpine craftiness which he, Machiavelli, was evidently preparing to teach to the hens, about the fangs of wolves which he desired to bestow upon the sheep.

"What is true is true!" Niccolò burst into good-natured laughter. "I shall irritate the geese,—hence I can see how honest folk will be ready to burn me at the stake for that I was the first to speak of that which all do. The tyrants shall declare me an inciter of the people; the people, an instrument of the tyrants; the bigots,—an infidel; the godly—evil, while the evil ones shall grow to hate me for that I shall seem to them still more evil than themselves."

And he added, with a quiet sorrow:

"Do you remember our conversations in Romagna, Messer Leonardo? I frequently think upon them, and it seems to me that you and I have a destiny in common. The discovery of new truths has always been, and always will be, fraught with as much danger as the discovery of new lands. In the presence of tyrants and the mob, of the little and the great, you and I are everywhere strangers, superfluities; homeless vagrants, eternal exiles. He who does not resemble all, is alone against all, inasmuch as the universe is created for the rabble, and it holds naught save the rabble. So goes it, my friend," he went on, still more quietly and pensively, "'tis a weary thing, say I, to live in this world; and, perhaps, the most abominable thing in life is not cares, nor maladies, nor poverty, nor grief,—but tedium. . . ."

In silence they descended the western slope of the Palatino, and through a narrow, dirty street came out at the foot of the Capitol, near the ruins of the temple of Saturn,—the spot where once the Roman Forum had been.

XII

On both sides of the ancient Via Sacra,—the Sacred Way,—from the arch of Septimius Severus to the amphitheatre of Flavius, clustered sorry little ancient houses. The foundations of many of them were reputed to have been built from the fragments of precious sculptures, from the limbs of Olympian gods,—for the duration of centuries the Forum had served as a quarry. In the ruins of pagan temples dismally and timidly snuggled the Christian churches. The strata of street rubbish, dust, manure, had raised the level of the ground more than ten ells. But still here and there reared up ancient columns with architraves threatening to topple down. Niccolò pointed out to his companion the site of the Roman Senate, the Quira, now called the Cows' Common. It had become a cattle market.

The sun, penetrating under the Arch from the direction of the Capitol, illumined the triumphal procession of an emperor with its last purple rays, through bluish, malodorous kitchen-fumes, resembling clouds of incense. And the heart of Niccolò contracted painfully when, for the last time, having looked back at the Forum, he beheld the roseate reflection of the evening light upon the three solitary columns of white marble before the church of Maria Liberatrice. The despondent, senile babbling of pealing bells, the even song of *Ave Maria*, seemed a funereal lament for the Roman Forum.

They entered the Coliseum.

"Ay," said Niccolò, contemplating the titanic blocks of stone in the walls of the amphitheatre, "they who were able to erect such edifices were not our kind. Only here, in Rome, does one feel what a difference there is between us and the ancients. What chance have we of rivalling them! We can not even imagine what men they were! . . ."

"It seems to me," retorted Leonardo slowly, as though with an effort, coming out of his pensive trance, "it seems to me, Niccolò, that you are not right. The men of the present age have a no smaller soul than the ancients had, but of a different nature. . . ."

"Is it Christian resignation you are speaking of, perchance?"

"Yes,—resignation. . . "

"Perhaps," agreed Machiavelli coldly.

They sat down to rest on the half-ruined bottom step of the amphitheatre.

"I maintain," continued Niccolò, with a sudden outburst, "I maintain that men should either accept or reject Christ. We have done neither the one nor the other. We are neither Christians nor pagans. We have shoved off one shore, but have not beached on the other. To be righteous we have not sufficient strength; to be evil we are afraid. We are not white nor black,—merely drab; not cold, not hot,—merely tepid. We have lied ourselves out so, have grown so pusillanimous, shilly-shallying, limping with both legs between Christ and Belial, that now even we ourselves do not know what we want, whither we are going. The ancients,—they, at least, knew and did everything to the end,—they did not dissemble, did not offer their right cheek when their left was smitten. But, ever since men have come to believe that for the sake of bliss in heaven it is necessary to bear every sort of injustice on earth, a great and safe field has been opened up for knaves. And, in reality, what if not this new teaching has made the world impotent, and given it up as a victim to abominable miscreants? . . ."

His voice quavered; his eyes flamed with a hatred almost insane; his face became distorted, as though from insufferable pain.

Leonardo kept silent. Through his soul passed radiant, childlike thoughts, so simple that he would not have been able to express them: he gazed at the blue sky, shining through the crevices in the walls of the Coliseum, and reflected that nowhere else does the azure of the heavens seem as youthfully radiant and joyous as through the cracks of half-ruined buildings.

He did not contradict Machiavelli, sensing that the latter would not comprehend him, inasmuch as that which was joyance to him, Leonardo, was sorrowing to Niccolò; Leonardo's honey was Niccolò's gall, great hatred the daughter of great knowledge.

"But do you know, Messer Leonardo," said Machiavelli, desiring, as was his wont, to wind up the conversation with a jest, "'tis only now that I have perceived how greatly mistaken those are who deem you an heretic and a godless man. Remember my words: on the day of the Last Judgment, when they shall separate us, the sheep from the goats, you will surely be with the meek lambs of Christ,—you will surely be in paradise with the holy saints!"

"But with you, Messer Niccolò!" the artist caught him up, laughing. "If I should ever get into paradise, then you, surely, would not escape."

"Oh, no,—not for your humble servant! I yield my place beforehand to all who may desire it. The tedium of this world sufficeth me. . . ." And his face became suddenly illuminated by a good-natured merriment.

"Hearken, my friend,—here is the sort of dream I had once: It seemed to me they had brought me to a gathering of hungry and dirty tatterdemalions, monks, whores, slaves, cripples, feeble-minded,—and had proclaimed that these were the very ones of whom it is said: 'Blessed are the poor in spirit: for their's is the kingdom of heaven.'[57] Then they led me to another place, where I beheld a host of majestic men, —a host like to the ancient Senate; here were military leaders, emperors, popes, law-givers, philosophers,—Homer, Alexander the Great, Plato, Marcus Aurelius; they conversed on science, on art, on statecraft. And they told me that this was hell, and these the souls of the damned, rejected of God for that they had come to love the wisdom of this age, which wisdom is madness before the Lord. And they asked me whither I would go, to hell or to paradise? 'To hell!' I cried out, 'To hell, by all means,—to the sages and heroes!' "

"Well, if it really be as you have dreamt it," Leonardo retorted, "then I, too, may not be averse . . ."

"Oh, no, 'tis too late! Now you can no more squirm your way out. They will drag you off by force. For Christian virtues they shall reward you even with the Christian Paradise."

When they left the Coliseum it had grown dark. The enormous yellow cresent moon floated out from behind the dark vaults of the Basilica of Constantine, cleaving the layers of cloud that were as translucent as nacre. Through the smoky, dove-grey murk spreading from the arch of Titus Vespasian to the Capitol, the three solitary pallid columns before the Church of Maria Liberatrice, resembling apparitions, seemed in the glow of the moon still more beautiful. And the senilely babbling bell, the twilight Angelus, sounded over the Roman Forum still more despondently, like a dirge, like a keen.

BOOK FOURTEEN

Monna Lisa Gioconda

I

EONARDO WROTE IN HIS *Book of Painting:* "For portraits thou shouldst have a special studio,—a court, like an oblong quadrangle, ten ells wide, twenty long; the walls should be painted black, with a sheltering projection and a canvas awning, the latter arranged so that, folding or unfolding, as required, it may serve for protection from the sun. If you have not attached the awning, paint only before twilight, or when it be cloudy and hazy. Such light is perfect."

Such a courtyard for portraiture he had arranged in the house of his landlord, a noble citizen of Florence, the Commissary of the Signoria,— Ser Pietro di Batto Martelli; a lover of mathematics, a man of intelligence, and friendlily disposed to Leonardo.

The time was a calm, warm and hazy day toward the end of the spring of fifteen hundred and five. The sun shone through the humid haze of the clouds, with a dull, seemingly subaqueous light, with soft shadows, that melted away like smoke,—the light Leonardo liked best, and which, as he asserted, bestowed an especial charm to feminine faces.

"Is it possible that she will not come?" he mused upon her whose portrait he had been painting for almost three years, with a steadfastness and diligence unusual to him.

He was preparing the studio for her reception. Giovanni Beltraffio watched him on the sly and wondered at the perturbation of his expectancy, almost impatience, which was inappropriate in the usually calm master. Leonardo arranged in order upon their shelf sundry brushes, palettes, little pots with paints, which had congealed, becoming covered, as though with ice, by a light film of glue; he took off the canvas cover from the portrait, which stood on a movable three-legged easel, or *leggio;* he turned on the fountain erected for her amusement, whose jets in falling struck against glass hemispheres, turning them and producing low, strange music; around the fountain grew her favourite flowers,—irises,—planted and carefully cultivated by his own hand; he brought some sliced bread in a basket for the tame doe, who was wandering through this yard, and which she used to feed out of her hand; he adjusted the deep-piled rug in front of her chair of smooth dark oak, with back and arms done in lattice-work. Upon this rug, his accustomed place, a white tom-cat of a rare breed, brought from Asia and bought also for her amusement, with eyes of different colours,—the right yellow, like topaz, the left blue, like sapphire,—was already curled up and purring.

Andrea Salaino brought notes and began tuning his viol. There arrived also another musician,—one Atalante. Leonardo had known him while still in Milan, at the Court of Duke Moro. He played especially well upon a silvern lute, which the artist had invented, and which bore a resemblance to a horse's skull. The best of musicians, singers, story-tellers, and poets, the wittiest of conversationalists, did the artist invite to his studio, that they might divert her, and obviate the ennui which is usual on the faces of sitters for portraits. He studied her face for the play of thoughts and emotions aroused by the conversations, stories, and music.

Subsequently the gatherings had become less frequent, he knew that they were no longer necessary; that she would not grow bored even without them. Only the music was not discontinued, since it helped both of them to work,—for *she*, too, took part in the labour of her portrait.

All was in readiness, but still she came not.

"Is it possible that she will not come?" he reflected. "To-day the light and shade seem to be created especially for her. Should I send after her, perchance? But then, she knows how expectant I am. She must come."

And Giovanni saw how his impatient disquiet increased. Suddenly a slight breath of air swayed the jet of the fountain to one side; the glass tinkled, the white petals of the irises quivered under the watery dust. The sensitive doe, stretching out its neck, was poised in expectation. Leonardo listened attentively. And Giovanni, although he himself heard nothing as yet, understood by his face that it was *she*.

First, with a meek bow, there entered Sister Camilla, a convertite nun, who lived in her house and accompanied her on every occasion to the studio of the artist; she had the ability of obliterating herself and becoming invisible, modestly taking her seat in a corner with prayer book in hand, without lifting up her eyes or saying a word, so that for the three years she and her mistress had been visiting him Leonardo had almost never heard her voice.

FOURTEEN · Leonardo da Vinci

After Camilla came in she whom all had been expecting,—a woman of thirty, in a simple dark dress, with a transparently dark, smoky coif coming half down her forehead,—Monna Lisa Gioconda.

Beltraffio knew that she was a Napoletana, of an ancient family, the daughter of Antonio Gerardini, a grandee who had at one time been wealthy, but who had become ruined during the French invasion of 1495; and the wife of the Florentine citizen, Francesco dell Giocondo, who had married Monna Lisa after being twice a widower. When Leonardo was painting her portrait, the artist was past fifty, while Monna Lisa's spouse, Messer Giocondo, was forty-five. He had been chosen one of the twelve *Banuomini*, and was slated to become prior soon. This was an ordinary man, such as always and everywhere abound,—not too bad, not too good; businesslike, prudent, plunged in his duties and the affairs of his agricultural estate. The exquisite, youthful woman seemed to him the seemliest ornament of his house. But the charm of Monna Lisa was to him less comprehensible than the merits of a new breed of Sicilian bullocks, or the benefit of customs duties on undressed sheep-skins. It was said that she had married him not out of love, but only at the will of her father, and that the bridegroom she had chosen first had found a voluntary death on the battlefield. There were also rumours current (perhaps they were but gossip) about other adorers of hers,—passionate, persistent, but whose suit was always vain. However, evil tongues—and of such there were not a few in Florence—could say nothing bad of La Gioconda. Quiet, demure, pious, strictly observant of all the rites of the Church, compassionate toward the poor, she was a good housewife, a faithful spouse, and not so much the stepmother as the tender mother to her twelve-year-old stepdaughter, Dianora.

And that was all that Giovanni knew of her. But the Monna Lisa who came to the studio of Leonardo seemed to him altogether another woman. For three years—time did not exhaust, but, on the contrary, deepened this strange feeling—he experienced a wonder, resembling fear, at her every appearance, as before something phantasmal. At times he explained this feeling by his having become accustomed to seeing her face on the portrait, and the master's art being so great, that the living Monna Lisa seemed to him less actual than the one portrayed on the canvas. But there was something besides, still more mysterious.

He knew that Leonardo had the opportunity of seeing her only during his work, in the presence of others, at times of many invited persons, at times only of Sister Camilla, inseparable from her,—and never alone; and yet Giovanni sensed that they possessed a secret which drew them together and set them apart from all. He also knew that this was not a secret of love,—or, at least, not of that which men are wont to style love.

He had heard Leonardo discourse how all artists were inclined to copy their own bodies and faces in the bodies and faces they portrayed. The reason for this, as the master saw it, lay in the fact that the human soul, being the creator of its body, strove, every time that it was confronted with the necessity of inventing a new body, to repeat in the latter that which it had already at one time created,—and so potent is this inclination that at times even in portraits, through the outward semblance of that which is portrayed, there glimmers at least the soul, if not the actual face, of the artist.

That which was taking place before the eyes of Giovanni was still more striking: it seemed to him that not only she who was depicted on the portrait, but even the living Monna Lisa herself, was coming to resemble Leonardo more and more, as is sometimes the case with people who live together uninterruptedly for many years. However, the chief force of the growing resemblance did not consist so much of the features themselves—although even here also it occasionally amazed him of late—as much as in the expression of the eyes, and in the smile. He recalled, with inexplicable wonder, that this same smile he had seen in the case of Thomas the Doubter, inserting his fingers into the Lord's wounds, in the sculpture of Verrocchio, for which the youthful Leonardo had served as model; and in the case of Our Mother Eve before the Tree of Knowledge in the master's first picture; and in the Angel shown in The Virgin of the Rocks, and in Leda and the Swan, and in many other feminine faces which the master had painted, drawn and modelled, still before he had known Monna Lisa, as though all his life, in all his creations, he had been seeking a reflection of his own charm, and had, finally, found it in the face of Gioconda.

At times, when Giovanni would contemplate for long this common smile of theirs, he would feel eerie, almost afraid, as before a miracle: the reality seemed a dream, the dream—reality, as though Monna Lisa were not a living being, the wife of a Florentine citizen, one Messer Giocondo, the most ordinary of mortals, but that she was a being resembling phantoms, and evoked by the will of the master,—a changeling, a feminine double of Leonardo himself.

Gioconda stroked her favourite, the white cat, which had jumped up on her lap; and invisible sparks ran through the white fur with a barely audible crackling, under her soft, slender fingers. Leonardo began working. But suddenly he abandoned his brush, scrutinizing her face attentively; not the least shadow or change upon this face could elude him.

"Madonna," asked he, "are you perturbed by aught to-day?"

Giovanni also felt that she did not look like her portrait as much as usually.

Lisa raised her calm gaze to Leonardo.

"Yes, a little," she replied. "Dianora is not altogether well. I have not slept all night."

"Mayhap you are tired, and are not much inclined for my portrait? Would it not be better to postpone the sitting? . . ."

"Nay, 'tis naught. Would you not regret losing such a day? Look, what tender shadows, what a humid sun: 'tis my day!"

"I knew," she added, after a silence, "that you were expecting me. I would have come sooner, but was detained,—Madonna Sophonisba . . ."

"Who? Ah, yes, I know. . . . A voice like that of a street huckstress, and smelling like a perfumer's shop. . . ."

Gioconda smiled.

"Madonna Sophonisba must needs tell me, without fail, of yesterday's celebration at the Palazzo Vecchio held by the most illustrious Signora Argentina, wife of the Gonfaloniere, and what, precisely, was served at supper, and what dresses were worn, and who was attentive to whom. . . ."

"'Tis just as I thought, then! 'Tis not Dianora's illness that had upset you, but the small talk of this chatter-box.—How queer it is! Have you ever noticed, madonna, that at times some nonsense or other, which we may hear from a mere acquaintance, and which nonsense we have no concern with,—common worldly folly or vulgarity,—will suddenly cast a gloom upon the soul, and upset us more than powerful grief?"

She inclined her head in silence,—it was evident that they had long since grown to understand one another, almost without words, at a mere hint.

He again made an attempt to resume work.

"Tell me some story," said Monna Lisa.

"Which shall it be?"

After a little thought, she said:

"Tell me of the Realm of Venus."

He had several stories which were her favourites, for the greater part from the recollections of himself or others, or from his travels, observations of nature, projects for pictures. He narrated them almost always in the same words,—simple, half childlike, to the sounds of soft music. Leonardo made a sign, and when Andrea Salaino on his viol, and Atalante on his silvern lute that resembled a horse's skull, struck up that music which had been chosen beforehand and which invariably accompanied *The Realm of Venus*, he began in his high, feminine voice, as one would an olden fairy-tale or a lullaby:

"Mariners, dwelling on the shores of Cilicia, aver that those who are fated to perish in the waves, at times during the most fearful storms, chance to behold the Island of Cyprus, the realm of the goddess of love. Around it beat tempestuous waves, whirlwinds, and waterspouts; and many mariners, drawn by the beauty of the island, have shivered their ships against the cliffs surrounded by whirlpools. Oh, how many of them have been dashed to pieces, how many have sunk! There, upon the shore, are still to be seen their pitiful skeletons, half-covered with the sand, entwined with sea-grasses,—some thrust forth their prows, others, their sterns; some, the gaping beams of their sides, like to the ribs of half-rotted corpses; others, the splinters of their rudders. And so great is their number, that this scene is like the Day of Resurrection, when the sea shall give up all the ships that have perished within it. But, above the isle itself there is a sky eternally blue, and the shining of the sun upon its knolls, flower-decked; and in the air there is a calm, such that the high flame of the censers upon the steps in front of the temple stretches toward the sky, just as straight, as immovable, as the white columns, the black cypresses, reflected in a mirror-smooth lake. No sound is there, save for the sweet murmur of the jets of the fountains, as they flow over the edge and fall from one porphyry bowl into another. And those drowning in the sea behold a-near this placid lake; the wind bringeth to them the fragrance of the myrtle groves,—and the more fearful the tempest, the profounder the peace in the realm of Cyprida."

He lapsed into silence; the strings of the lute and the viol were stilled and there fell a silence, which is more beautiful than all sounds,—the silence after music. Only the jets of the fountain murmured, striking against the hemispheres of glass.

And, as though lulled by the music, walled off from actual life by the silence,—radiant, a stranger to everything save the will of the master,—Monna Lisa gazed straight into his eyes with a smile that was filled with mystery, like still waters, perfectly clear, but so deep that no matter how much the gaze plunged within them, no matter how it probed, it could not see the bottom,—she was smiling upon him with his own smile.

And it seemed to Giovanni that now Leonardo and Monna Lisa were like two mirrors, which, reflecting themselves in one another, were deepening to infinity.

II

On the following morning the artist was working in the Palazzo Vecchio on his Battle of Anghiari.

In 1503, upon his arrival in Florence from Rome, he had received this commission from the supreme ruler of the Republic, Pietro Soderini the Gonfaloniere, who held the office for the term of his life, to depict some memorable battle on the wall of the new Council Hall, in the palace of the Signoria, the Palazzo Vecchio. The artist had chosen the famous victory of the Florentines at Anghiari, in fourteen hundred and forty, over Niccolò Piccinino, the commander of the Duke of Lombardy, Filippo Maria Visconti.

The wall of the Council Hall was already covered with a part of the picture: four horsemen have come to grips and are fighting for the battle flag; a tatter flutters at the tip of a long pole, its shaft broken. Five hands have seized it and are furiously dragging it in different directions. Sabres are crossed in the air. By the way in which the mouths are distended one can perceive that unbearable screams are issuing therefrom. The distorted human faces are no less fearful than the bestial maws of the mythical monsters on their cuirasses. The men have infected the horses with their madness; they have reared up on their hind legs; their front ones are entangled, and with ears drawn back, their insanely crossed pupils flashing, their teeth bared, they are biting one another, like feral beasts. Below, in the bloody mire, under their hoofs, one man is slaying another, having seized him by the hair, pounding his head against the ground, and not noticing that both may at any instant be trampled to death.

This was war in all its horror, a senseless slaughter, "*pazzia bestialissima*," to use an expression of Leonardo's, "which leaves no level spot upon the earth without its blood-filled footprints."

No sooner had he begun work when steps were heard upon the resounding brick floor of the deserted hall. He recognized them, and, without turning around, made a wry face. The new arrival was Pietro Soderini, one of those people of whom Niccolò Machiavelli had said that they were neither hot nor cold,—only tepid; neither black nor white,—only drab. The noble citizens of Florence, descendants of shopkeepers who had grown wealthy, having in their turn clambered up to the status of nobility, had chosen him for one of the leaders of the Republic, as the equal of all, as a perfect mediocrity, immaterial and innocuous to all, trusting that he would be their obedient tool. But they had erred. Soderini proved to be a friend of the poor, a defender of the people. However, no one attributed much importance to this. He was, despite everything, still too insignificant; in lieu of able statecraft, he had the diligence of a government clerk; instead of an intellect, prudence; in lieu of virtue, good nature. Everybody knew that his spouse, the haughty and inaccessible Madonna Argentina, who did not conceal her contempt for her husband, was wont to style him "my rat." And, truly, Messer Pietro brought to mind an old, respectable rat that haunts the under-boards of some chancellery. He did not possess even that adroitness, that vulgarity, which is as necessary to rulers as axle-grease is for the wheels of a machine. In his Republican honour he was stiff,—as firm, straight, and flat as a board; so incorruptible and immaculate that, to use an expression of Machiavelli's "he reeked of soap, like newly-washed linen." Desiring to create amity between all, he simply irritated. The rich he had failed to please; the poor he had failed to help. He always sat down between two stools; always got in between cross-fires. He was a martyr to the golden mean. On one occasion Machiavelli, whose patron Soderini was, composed an epigram upon him, in the form of an epitaph:

> The night that Pietro Soderini died
> His soul did venture into Hades:
> "Whither, thou silly one?" old Pluto cried,—
> "Go to the middle circle, for little lads and ladies!"

In accepting the commission, Leonardo had had to sign an exceedingly binding agreement, with a forfeit in case of the least delay. The Magnificent Signori defended their points like shop-keepers. A great lover of red tape, Soderini made life miserable for him with demands of particularity as to every groat issued by the treasury,—for the erection of scaffolding, for the purchase of lacquer, of soda, lime, colours, flaxseed oil, and other trifles. Never, in the service of "tyrants," as the Gonfaloniere contemptuously termed them, had Leonardo experienced such servitude as in the service of the people, in a free Republic, in the realm of the equality of the commonalty. But the worst of all was that, like the majority of people who are ignorant and not gifted, in matters of art, Messer Pietro had a passion for giving counsel to artists.

Soderini addressed Leonardo with a question concerning the moneys given out for the purchase of thirty-five pounds of Alexandrine white, and not entered into the account. The artist confessed that he had not bought any white, that he had forgotten what he had spent the money for, and offered to return it to the treasury.

"Why, why! Whatever are you saying, Messer Leonardo! I do but remind you of it just so, for the sake of order and exactness. Do not be too hard upon us,—we be humble folk and small. Mayhap, by comparison with the munificence of such magnificent princes as Sforza and Borgia our thriftiness may seem niggardliness. But what would you? We must needs cut the cloth to suit the purse. No sovereigns are we, but merely the servants of the people, and are liable and accountable to them for every soldi; for, as you know yourself, the moneys of the treasury are a sacred trust; you have there the widow's mite, and the drops of sweat of the honest toiler, and the blood of the soldier. The Prince is alone,—whereas we be many, and all of us are equal before the law. So wags it, Messer Leonardo! The tyrants have paid you in gold, whereas we pay but in copper; but is not the copper of liberty better than the gold of bondage, and is not a quiet conscience above all reward? . . ."

The artist listened in silence, feigning agreement. He waited for Soderini's speech to end, with a despondent submissiveness, even as a traveller on a highway, who, being overtaken by a whirlwind of dust, waits, with head bowed and eyes shut. In these ordinary thoughts of ordinary men Leonardo felt a blind, deaf, implacable force, resembling the forces of nature, with which one can not contend; and although at first sight such thoughts appeared to him merely flat, when he came to ponder upon them more deeply he experienced the same sensation as if he were glancing into a fearful void, into a vertiginous abyss.

Soderini was carried away. He would fain have drawn his opponent into a dispute. That he might flick him on the raw, he began speaking of art. Putting on his round, silver spectacles, with the pompous air of a connoisseur he fell to scrutinizing the finished portion of the picture.

"Splendid! Amazing! What moulding of the muscles, what knowledge of perspective! Look at those horses, now,—do look at those horses! Just as if they were alive!"

Then he glanced at the artist over his spectacles, good-naturedly and sternly, as a schoolmaster might upon an apt but insufficiently diligent pupil:

"But still, I will say even this time that which I have said many times: if you will finish as you have begun, the effect of the picture will be too heavy, too depressing; and do not be wroth with me, most respected sir, for my frankness, for I always tell people the truth to their faces,—this was not what we were looking forward to. . . ."

"What was it, then, that you were looking forward to?" asked the artist with a timorous curiosity.

"Why, this,—that you would perpetuate for posterity the military glory of the Republic, would depict the memorable exploits of our heroes; something—if you know what I mean—that would, while it elevated the soul of man, also give him a good example of love for the fatherland and of civic virtues. Let us say that war actually is as you have depicted it. But why, I ask you, Messer Leonardo,—why not ennoble it, why not adorn it, or, at the least, soften certain extremes, inasmuch as moderation is necessary in all things? I may be mistaken, perhaps,—but it appears to me that the true purpose of the artist consists precisely of this: that, while guiding and instructing, he benefit the people. . . ."

Having broached the subject of the weal of the people, he could no longer stop. His eyes sparkled with the inspiration of common sense; in the monotonous sound of his words was the persistence of the drop which wears away a stone.

The artist listened in silence, in stupefaction; and only occasionally, upon coming to, and trying to imagine what, precisely, this virtuous man thought of art, he would feel eerie, as though he were entering a confined, dark chamber, filled to overflowing with people, with such a stuffy atmosphere that one could not stay an instant in it without suffocation.

"Art that brings no benefit to the people," Messer Pietro was saying, "is the amusement of idle men, the vainglorious whim of the rich, or the luxury of tyrants. Is it not so, most respected sir?"

"Of course, you are right," concurred Leonardo, and added, with a barely perceptible smile in his eyes:

"But do you know what, signor? This is what we ought to do, in order to terminate this long-standing dispute of ours: in this very Council Hall, at a gathering of the people, let the citizens of the Florentine Republic decide, by means of the majority of votes, cast by white and black balls, whether my picture can, or can not, bring any benefit to the people. Here the gain would be two-fold: Firstly, the certainty is mathematical,—you have but to count the votes to know the truth. Secondly, every well-informed and intelligent man, if he be alone, is apt to fall into error; whereas ten or twenty thousand fools and ignorami, convened together, can not make any mistake, inasmuch as the voice of the people is the voice of God."

Soderini did not immediately comprehend him. Such was his reverence before the sacred rites of white and black ballots, that it did not even enter his head that someone might permit himself to scoff against this mystery. But when he comprehended, he fixed his gaze upon the artist with dull amazement, almost with fright, and his little purblind, roundish eyes began to leap, to dart, like a rat that senses a cat. However, he rapidly recovered. Through an innate tendency of his mind, the Gonfaloniere regarded all artists in general as fellows devoid of common sense, and therefore was not offended at Leonardo's jests. But Messer Pietro grew sad,—he deemed himself a benefactor of this man, inasmuch as, despite the rumours concerning Leonardo's betrayal of the government, concerning the war-maps of the environs of Florence, which he was said to have made for Cæsar Borgia, the enemy of the fatherland, Soderini had magnanimously taken him into the service of the Republic, trusting in his own good influence and the penitence of the artist.

Changing the conversation, Messer Pietro, this time with a business-like, bureaucratical air, informed him, *in passim*, that Michelangelo Buonarotti had been commissioned to execute a war-painting on the opposite wall of the same Council Hall; he dryly made his farewell, and departed. The artist followed him with his eyes. A little grey-haired old man, a little drab old man, bandy-legged, round-backed; from a distance he reminded one more than ever of a rat.

III

COMING out of the Palazzo Vecchio, Leonardo stopped in the square, before the David of Michelangelo. Here, at the gates of the Town Hall of Florence, stood he, this Titan of marble, in relief against the dark stone of the grim and graceful tower. The naked, adolescent body is spare. The right arm, with the sling, is lowered, so that the veins stand out; the left, raised in front of his breast, holds a stone. His eyebrows are contracted, and his gaze is fixed upon the distance, as with a man taking aim. The curls are entwined over his low forehead, like a garland. On this square where Savonarola had been burned at the stake the David of Michelangelo seemed to be that Prophet whom Savonarola had been so vainly calling,—that Hero whom Machiavelli awaited.

In this creation of his rival Leonardo sensed a soul that was, perhaps, the equal of his soul, but in eternal contrast to his, even as action is contrary to contemplation, passion to dispassionateness, the tempest to the calm. And this force so foreign to him attracted him, aroused in him a curiosity and a desire to approach it, in order that he might come to know it to the end.

In the warehouses for building materials in the Florentine Cathedral of Maria del Fiore there had lain an enormous block of white marble, spoiled by an unskilled sculptor,—the best of masters had refused it, deeming it no longer fit for anything. When Leonardo had arrived from Rome, it was offered to him. But while, with his accustomed dilatoriness, he was pondering over it, and measuring, and calculating, and vacillating, another artist, younger than he by three and twenty years, one Michelangelo Buonarotti, snatched the commission away from him, and with incredible speed, working not only in the daytime but also at night, by artificial light, finished his Titan in five and twenty months. For sixteen years had Leonardo wrought on his monument to Sforza, the Colossus of Clay,—and he durst not even think of how much time he would have needed for a marble piece the size of David.

The Florentines declared Michelangelo to be Leonardo's rival in sculpture; and Buonarotti unhesitatingly accepted the challenge. Now, approaching the war picture in the Council Hall, although he had practically never held a brush in his hand, with a bravado which may have appeared unreasoning he was embarking upon a contest with Leonardo in painting as well.

The greater the meekness and good will that Buonarotti encountered in a rival, the more merciless did his hatred wax. Leonardo's calm seemed to him contempt. With a hyper-sensitive self-consciousness he lent an attentive ear to gossip, sought for excuses for quarrels, took advantage of every opportunity to hurt the feelings of his foe.

With feverish haste did Michelangelo commence his picture in the Council Hall, desirous of catching up with his rival,—which, however, was no difficult matter. The incident he had chosen was from the war with the Pisans. On a hot July day some Florentine soldiers are bathing in the Arno. The alarm has been sounded,—the enemy has appeared; the soldiers are hurrying for shore, crawling out of the water, in the coolness of which their tired bodies had been luxuriating, and, submitting to duty, are donning their sweaty, dusty raiment, putting on their brazen armour and coats-of-mail, made red-hot by the sun.

Thus, protesting against the picture of Leonardo, Michelangelo depicted war not as a senseless slaughter,—"the most bestial of madnesses"—but as a manly exploit, the fulfillment of an eternal duty,—the struggle of heroes for the glory and greatness of their fatherland.

The Florentines watched this duel between Leonardo and Michelangelo, with the curiosity natural to the mob confronted by a seductive spectacle. And since everything that was devoid of politics seemed to them flat, like a dish unseasoned by pepper and salt, they hastened to announce that Michelangelo stood for the Republic against the Medici, and Leonardo,—for the Medici against the Republic. And the contest, having become comprehensible to all, blazed forth with renewed force, was transferred from the houses into the streets, into the squares, and even those who had nothing to do with art participated in it. The productions of Leonardo and Michelangelo became the battle banners of two warring camps. Matters reached such a stage that some men,—no one knew who they were,—took to throwing stones at the David of nights. The noble citizens accused the people; the leaders of the people,—the noble citizens; artists,—the pupils of Perugino, who had recently opened his studio in Florence; while Buonarotti, in the presence of the Gonfaloniere, declared that Leonardo had bribed the scoundrels who had thrown stones at his David. And many believed him,—or, at least, pretended to believe.

Once, while working on Gioconda's portrait,—there being no others in the studio, save Giovanni and Salaino,—when the conversation veered upon Michelangelo, Leonardo said to Monna Lisa:

"It seems to me, at times, that if I could but talk to him for a while, face to face, everything would explain itself, and there would not be a trace left of this foolish quarrel; he would understand that I am no enemy of his, and that there is never a man who could come to love him as I . . ."

Monna Lisa shook her head:

"Come, is it really thus, Messer Leonardo? Would he truly understand?"

"He would!" exclaimed the artist. "It is impossible for such a man not to understand! The sad part of the whole thing is that he is too shy, and is not sure of himself. He torments himself, feels jealousy and fear, because he does not yet know himself. 'Tis but delirium and madness! I would tell him everything, and he would be calmed. Why, is it for him to fear *me?* Do you know, madonna,—the other day, when I beheld his cartoon for The Bathing Warriors, I could not believe my eyes. No one can imagine who he is, and what he will be. I feel that, even now, he is not only equal to me, but stronger than I,—yes, yes, I feel it,—he is stronger than I! . . ."

She looked at him with that gaze which, so it seemed to Giovanni, reflected the gaze of Leonardo within it, as in a mirror, and smiled her calm, strange smile.

"Messer," she said, "do you recall that passage in Holy Writ wherein God saith to the Prophet Elijah, who had fled from the unrighteous King Ahab, into the desert, unto Horeb, the mount of God: 'Go forth, and stand upon the mount before the Lord. And, behold, the Lord passed by, and a great and strong wind rent the mountains, and brake in pieces the rocks before the Lord; but the Lord was not in the wind: and after the wind an earthquake; but the Lord was not in the earthquake: and after the earthquake a fire; but the Lord was not in the fire: and after the fire a still small voice. And it was so, when Elijah heard it, that he wrapped his face in his mantle. . . .'[58] Messer Buonarotti may be as strong as the wind rending the mountains and breaking in pieces the rocks before the Lord. But he hath not the still small voice, the calm, wherein the Lord dwells. And he knows this, and hates you for that you are stronger than he,—even as the calm is more potent than the tempest."

FOURTEEN · Leonardo da Vinci

In the Brancacci Chapel, in the old church beyond the river, the Maria del Carmine, where the famous frescoes of Tommaso Masaccio were,—the school for all the great masters of Italy,—Leonardo, too, had studied from them on a time,—he beheld on one occasion a youth unknown to him, almost a boy, who was studying and copying these frescoes. He had on an old black short jacket bedaubed with paint; his linen was clean, but coarse,—probably home-made. He was graceful, sinuous, with a slender neck, unusually white, soft and long, like that of an anæmic girl; there was a somewhat demure and sweetish charm about his face, as oval as a small egg and transparently pale, with large dark eyes, like that of the village women of Umbria, whom Perugino had drawn his Madonnas from,—eyes that were strangers to profound thought, and as deep and void as the skies.

Some time later he met this youth anew in the monastery of Maria Novella, in the Papal Hall, where the cartoon of the Battle of Anghiari was on exhibition. He was studying and copying it just as assiduously as the frescoes of Masaccio. This time, probably knowing Leonardo's face, the youth eagerly fixed him with his eyes, evidently desiring, yet not daring, to begin a conversation with him. Noting this, Leonardo approached him. Hurriedly, excited and blushing, with an ingratiation the least trifle importunate, yet of a childlike innocence, the young man informed Leonardo that he deemed the latter his master, the greatest of all the artists of Italy, and that Michelangelo was unworthy to untie the shoe straps of the creator of The Last Supper.

Several times more did Leonardo come upon this youth, and would hold long conversations with him, and look over his drawings; and, the more he came to know him, the more did he become convinced that this was a great master of the future.

On one occasion a saying escaped him which amazed,—almost frightened,—Leonardo by its profundity:

"I have noticed that when one draws, there is no need of thought, —the result is better."

It seemed as if this boy with all his being were telling him that that unity, that perfect harmony of emotion and reason, of love and knowledge, which Leonardo sought, did not exist at all, nor was it possible.

And before this youth's meek, care-free, meaningless tranquillity, Leonardo experienced greater doubts, greater fear for the coming destinies of art, for the work of all his life, than he experienced before the indignation and hatred of Buonarotti.

"Whence come you, my son?" Leonardo had asked him on one of the first meetings. "Who was thy father, and what is thy name?"

"I was born in Urbino," answered the youth, with his kindly smile, which was just a bit mawkish. "My father is Giovanni Sanzio, the painter. My name is Raphael."

IV

At this time Leonardo was compelled to leave Florence on an important matter.

Since times immemorable the Republic had been waging war with the neighbouring city of Pisa,—a war endless, merciless, exhausting to both cities. Once, in a conversation with Machiavelli, the artist imparted to him a military project,—to direct the waters of the Arno from their old bed into a new; to divert them from Pisa into the Livorno swamp by means of canals, so that, after cutting off the besieged city from communication with the sea, and putting to a stop the delivery of food supplies, it might be compelled to surrender. Niccolò, with the passion for the unusual so habitual to him, was captivated with this project and imparted it to the Gonfaloniere; he partially convinced the latter and infatuated him with his eloquence, having deftly touched the self-love of Messer Pietro, to whose ineptitude many attributed at present all the failures of the Pisan war, and partially deceived him, concealing the actual expenditures and difficulties of the project. When the Gonfaloniere proposed it to the Council of Ten, he was almost laughed at to his face. Soderini became offended, resolved to prove that he was not possessed of less common sense than anyone else, and began to act with such stubbornness that he got his way, thanks to the zealous aid of his enemies, who lent their votes for the proposal, which seemed to them the height of absurdity,—so that they might bring about the downfall of Messer Pietro. Machiavelli concealed his crafty subterfuges from Leonardo for the time being, relying on subsequently drawing the Gonfaloniere into the affair definitely, when he would use the latter like a pawn, and attain everything that they needed.

The commencement of the work boded well. The water level of the river decreased. But soon the difficulties were revealed, which commanded constantly increasing expenditures, whereas the thrifty Signori chaffered over every groat.

In the summer of fifteen hundred and five, the river, having overflowed its banks, after a great cloudburst, ruined part of the dam. Leonardo was summoned to the scene of operations.

On the day before his departure, returning from the other side of the Arno, after discussing this affair with Machiavelli, the artist was crossing the bridge of Santa Trinità, bound in the direction of the Strada Tornabuoni. The time was late; passers-by were few. Only the noise of the water at the mill-dam beyond the Ponte allà Caraia disturbed the quiet. The day had been sultry, but, before evening, some rain had fallen and freshened the air.

The view of Florence showed in sharp outlines against the clear sky, like an initial illumination upon the dulled gold of ancient books,—a view unique in the world, as familiar to him as the face of a living being,—all of Florence, in the double light of the evening and the moon, seemed like a single enormous silvery-dark flower. Leonardo had noted that every city, just as every human being, has its own odour; the odour of Florence was like that of moist dust,—such as irises have,—mingled with a barely perceptible odour of lacquer and the pigments of very old pictures.

He was musing upon Gioconda.

He knew almost as little of her life as did Giovanni. He was not offended, he was not amazed, by the fact that she had a husband, one Messer Francesco; thin, tall, with a mole on his left cheek, and with shaggy eyebrows; a trustworthy man, who loved to discourse of the excellencies of the Sicilian breed of bullocks, and the new duty on the hides of rams. There were moments when Leonardo rejoiced over her spectral charm,—aloof, distant, non-existent,—and more actual than all existing things; but there were also other moments when he felt her living beauty.

Monna Lisa was not one of those women who in those days were styled "Heroines of Learning." Never did she flaunt her bookish knowledge. Only by chance did he find out that she read Latin and Greek. She carried herself and spoke with such simplicity that many discounted her intellect. But, in reality, it seemed to him that she had that which was deeper than intellect, especially the feminine intellect,—an oraculary wisdom. She had sayings which would suddenly make her akin to him, near to him,—nearer than all those he knew, his sole and eternal companion and sister. At these moments he was fain to cross over the charmed circle which separated contemplation from life. But he would immediately repress this desire within him, and every time that he killed this living beauty of Monna Lisa, the spectral image of her upon the canvas,—an image he had evoked,—would become still more imbued with life, still more actual.

And it seemed to him that she knew this and submitted, helping him; that she brought herself as a sacrifice to her own spectre; rendering her soul up to him, and rejoicing. Was that which united them love? Nothing save tedium or laughter was aroused within him by the Platonic maunderings of that day, by the languishing sighs of celestial lovers, the mawkish sonnets *à la* Petrarca. No less foreign to him was also that which the majority of people style love. Just as he did not eat meat, not because he deemed it forbidden, but because it aroused aversion, so did he refrain from women also, inasmuch as all carnal possession,—it made no difference whether in marriage or in fornication,—he deemed not sinful, but gross. "The act of copulation," he wrote in his anatomical notes, "and the organs that serve therein, are distinguished by such hideousness, that, were it not for the charm of faces, the ornaments of the participants, and the power of lust,—humankind would cease." And he held himself aloof from this "hideousness," from the lecherous struggles of males and females, just as from the sanguinary carnage of the devourers and the devoured, without indignation, without condemnation, and without justification, acknowledging the law of natural necessity in the struggles of love and hunger, but without any desire to participate in either, submitting to another law—that of love and continence.

But even if he had loved her, could he have desired a more perfect union with his beloved than in these profound and mystic caresses,—in the bringing forth of an immortal image, of a new being, which was being conceived, being born of them both, even as a child is born of its father and mother,—and was both Leonardo and Lisa?

And yet at the same time he felt that even in this so uncorrupt a union there was a danger, a greater, perhaps, than in the union of the usual carnal love. They were both treading the edge of an abyss, where none had ever yet trod, conquering the temptation and the attraction of the abyss. There were between them elusive, transparent words, through which their secret penetrated, even as the sun penetrates through humid mist. And at times he would reflect: What if the mist were to dissipate, and the blindingly dazzling sun were to flash forth, under which mysteries and spectres expire? What if he or she were to find endurance beyond them, were to transgress the line,—and contemplation were to become life? Had he the right to probe a living soul with the same dispassionate inquisitiveness as he did the laws of mechanics, of mathematics, or the life of a plant envenomed with poisons, or the structure of a dissected cadaver,—the only soul near to him, that of his eternal companion and sister? Would she not wax indignant, would she not repulse him with hatred and contempt, as every other woman would have repulsed him?

And it seemed to him at times that he was executing her with a fearful, slow execution. And he was horrified by her submissiveness, which was even as boundless as his own tender and merciless inquisitiveness.

Only of late had he come to feel within him this limitation, had comprehended that, sooner or later, he must decide which she was to him,—a living being or only a mere spectre,—the reflection of his own soul in a mirror of muliebrile charm. He still cherished a hope that the separation would put off for a time the inevitability of a decision, and he almost rejoiced because he was leaving Florence. But now, when the separation was approaching, he understood that he had erred; that it would not only not put off, but would bring the decision nearer.

Plunged in these thoughts he did not notice how he entered a blind alley, and, when he looked about him, did not recognize immediately where he was. Judging by the marble campanile of Giotto, visible above the roofs of the houses, he was not far from the Cathedral. One side of the narrow, long street was in impenetrably-black shadow; the other, in bright, almost white, moonlight. A little flame glowed red in the distance. Yonder, before the corner balcony, with its sloping tiled pent roof, with semicircular arches upon graceful pillars,—a Florentine *loggia*,—men in black masks and capes were singing a serenade, to the sounds of a lute. He listened.

It was an olden song of Love, composed by Lorenzo de' Medici, the Magnificent, a one-time accompaniment for the carnival procession of the god Bacchus and of Ariadne,—an infinitely joyous and despondent song of love, which Leonardo loved, having heard it often in his youth:

Youth is wondrous, but how fleeting!
Sing, and laugh, and banish sorrow;
Give to happiness good greeting,—
Place thy hope not on the morrow. . . .

The last line found an echo of dark foreboding in his heart.

Was fate sending him now, on the threshold of old age, into his subterranean murk and loneliness, a near, living soul? Would he thrust it from him, would he reject life for contemplation, as he had so many times rejected it; would he sacrifice anew the near for the distant, the actual for the non-existent and the beautifully unique? Which would he choose,—the living or the immortal Gioconda? He knew that, having chosen one, he would lose the other, and both were equally dear to him; also did he know that he had to choose, that he could no longer protract and continue this execution. But his will was impotent. And he did not want to, and could not, decide which was better: to put to death the living one for the immortal one, or the immortal one for the living,—that which was actual, or that which would always be on the canvas of the picture.

Having passed through two more streets, he approached the house of Martelli, his host. The doors were locked; the lights were out. He raised up the hammer, and struck an iron cramp. The gate-keeper did not respond,—probably he was asleep or had gone away. The strokes, repeated by the reverberating vaults of the stone staircase, died away and silence fell; the light of the moon seemed to intensify it.

Suddenly ponderous, slow-measured brazen sounds pealed forth,—the striking of hours on a nearby belfry. Their voice spoke of the mute and ominous flight of time; of gloomy, lonely old age; of the irretrievability of the past. And for a long while their last sound, now weakening, now augmenting, quavered and swayed through the moonlit stillness in spreading waves of sound, as though repeating:

Place thy hope not on the morrow. . . .

V

On the following day Monna Lisa came to his studio at the usual time, for the first time alone, without her perpetual companion, Sister Camilla. Gioconda knew that this was their last meeting.

The day was sunny, blindingly bright. Leonardo drew the canvas awning to,—and in the court with black walls there reigned that soft, murky light, that translucent, seemingly subaqueous shade, which called forth upon her face its utmost charm.

They were alone. He worked in silence, in concentration, in a perfect calm, having forgotten his thoughts of yesterday about the parting, about the inevitable choice, as though for him there existed neither the past nor the future, and time stood still,—as though she had ever sat thus before him and would ever sit, with her quiet, strange smile. And that which he could not do in life, he did in contemplation: blended the two images into one, united the actuality and the reflection,—the living and the immortal. And this bestowed upon him the joy of a great liberation. Now he neither pitied nor feared her. And he knew that she would be submissive to him unto the end,—would accept all things, would endure all things; would die, and not wax rebellious. And at times he regarded her with the same inquisitiveness as he regarded those condemned men whom he had accompanied to their execution, in order that he might watch the last quivers of pain on their faces.

Suddenly it appeared to him that an extraneous shadow of a living thought, not of his inspiration, and unwanted, had flitted across her face, like the misty trace of a living breath upon the surface of a mirror. In order to encompass her about again,—in order to draw her anew within his spectral circle, to banish this living shadow, he began to tell her in a chanting and compelling voice, such as a sorcerer might use to work his incantations, one of those mysterious fables, like enigmas, which at times he wrote down in his diaries:

"Not having the strength to resist my desire of beholding new forms, unknown of men, created by the art of nature, and pursuing my journey for long amid barren, sombre crags, I did finally attain the Cavern, and halted at its mouth, in perplexity. But, coming to a decision and lowering my head, bending my back, putting the palm of my left hand on the knee of my right leg, and with my right hand shielding my eyes, that I might become accustomed to the darkness, I did enter and take a few steps. With eyebrows contracted and eyes puckered, straining my sight, I frequently changed my direction and blundered in the murk, groping, now here, now there, endeavouring to see. But the murk was too profound. And when I had been some time therein, two emotions arose and began to contend within me,—fear and curiosity; fear before the exploration of the dark Cavern, and curiosity as to whether there were not some wondrous mystery within it. . . ."

He fell silent. The extraneous shadow still would not vanish from her face.

"Which of the two emotions conquered, then?" asked she.

"Curiosity."

"And did you come to know the mystery of the Cavern?"

"I came to know that which it was possible to know."

"And will you impart it to men?"

"One can not impart all, and I would not know how to do it. But I would fain instill within them such strong curiosity that it may always conquer fear."

"But what if curiosity alone prove insufficient, Messer Leonardo?" she said, her glance flashing unexpectedly. "What if some other greater thing be needed to penetrate the last, and, perhaps, the most wondrous mysteries of the Cavern?"

And she looked into his eyes with a mocking smile such as he had never yet seen her use.

"What else is needed, then?" he asked.

She kept silent.

Here a thin and piercing ray of dazzling sunlight penetrated through a crack between two lengths of canvas in the awning. The subaqueous twilight was illuminated. And upon her face the enchantment of tender, light shades and "dark light," which were like to distant music, was disturbed.

"You are going away to-morrow?" asked Gioconda.

"Nay,—this evening."

"I, too, am going away soon."

He glanced at her intently, was about to add something, but let it pass in silence,—he surmised that she was going away in order not to stay in Florence without him.

"Messer Francesco," continued Monna Lisa, "is journeying on business to Calabria, for about three months, until autumn; I have managed to persuade him into taking me along."

He turned away, and, in vexation, frowning, glanced at the sharp, malignant and truthful ray of sunlight. The spray of the fountain, until now of one colour, lifelessly and transparently white, now, in this refracting, living ray, flared up in the contrasting and diverse colours of the rainbow,—the colours of life.

And suddenly he felt that he was coming back into life,—he, the timid, the weak, the pitiful and pitying.

"'Tis naught," said Monna Lisa. "Draw the awning to. 'Tis still early. I am not fatigued."

"Nay, no matter. 'Tis enough," said he, and cast away his brush.

"You will never finish the portrait?"

"Why so?" he retorted hastily, as though frightened. "Are you not going to come to me any more, when you return?"

"I shall come. But, perhaps, after three months I shall be altogether another person, and you will not recognize me. For you yourself have said that human faces, especially those of women, change rapidly. . . ."

"I fain would finish it," said he slowly, as though to himself. "But I do not know. It seems to me at times that that which I desire is impossible of accomplishment. . . ."

"Impossible?" she wondered. "However, I have heard that you never finish, because you strive for the impossible. . . ."

In these words there sounded,—it may be that he only imagined it,—an infinitely submissive, plaintive reproach.

"There it is,—that which I dreaded," he reflected,—and a fear descended upon him.

She arose, and said simply, as always:

"Well, 'tis time.—Farewell, Messer Leonardo. Godspeed on your travels."

He raised his eyes to her,—and again he imagined upon her face a last forlorn reproach and supplication. He knew that this moment was for them both irretrievable and eternal, like death. But the more he exerted his will, to find the resolve and the word, the more did he feel his impotence, and the impassable abyss growing deeper and deeper between them. But Monna Lisa was smiling upon him with her former quiet and radiant smile. Yet now it seemed to him that this quiet and radiance were like to those which are in the smile of the dead.

His heart was transpierced by an infinite, unbearable pity, and it made him still more impotent. Monna Lisa held out her hand to him, and in silence he kissed this hand, for the first time since they had known one another,—and at the same instant he felt how, rapidly bending over him, she touched his hair with her lips.

"May God preserve you," said she, still with the same simplicity.

When he fully recovered himself, she was no longer there. Around him was the quiet of the dead summer noon, more ominous than the quiet of the most profound, dark midnight.

And exactly as last night, but still more ominously and solemnly, slow-measured brazen sounds pealed forth,—the striking of the hours on a nearby belfry. They spoke of the mute and fearful flight of time, of gloomy, lonely old age, of the irretrievability of the past. And for a long while their last sound quavered, dying away, and seeming to repeat:

Place thy hope not on the morrow. . . .

VI

In agreeing to take part in the work of diverting the Arno from Pisa, Leonardo felt almost certain that this military enterprise would draw in its wake, sooner or later, another more pacific and important. Even in his youth had he dreamed of the construction of a canal which would make the Arno navigable from Florence to the sea of Pisa, and, having irrigated the fields with a network of nurturing veins of water and increased the fertility of the land, would transform Tuscany into one great flourishing garden.

It seemed to Leonardo that now, before old age, fate was giving him what was perhaps his last chance to fulfill in the service of the people that which he had not succeeded in doing in the service of princes,—to demonstrate to men the might of science over nature. When Machiavelli confessed to him his deceptionof Soderini, his concealment of the actual difficulties of the project, having assured him that, apparently, thirty or forty thousand working days would suffice,—Leonardo, not wishing to take any responsibilities upon himself, decided to impart to the Gonfaloniere the entire truth, and presented his estimate.

The Signori were horrified. Accusations rained down upon Soderini from all sides,—they wondered how such absurdity could ever have entered his head. But Niccolò still kept on hoping; he pulled wires, he resorted to all sorts of guile; he deceived; he penned eloquent missives, asseverating the undoubted success of the work begun. But, despite the enormous expenditures, increasing with every day, matters fared from bad to worse.

It seemed as if an evil spell had been put upon Messer Niccolò,—all that he laid his hand to turned treacherous, crumbling and melting in his hands, changing into words, into abstract thoughts, into malignant jests, which harmed him most of all. And involuntarily the artist recalled Machiavelli's steady losses while he was explaining his rule of infallibly winning; his unsuccessful liberation of Maria; his ill-fated Macedonian phalanx. In this queer fellow, unquenchably thirsting for action and absolutely unfit for it, mighty in thought, impotent in life, like to a swan on dry land, Leonardo recognized himself.

In his report to the Gonfaloniere and the Signoria he advised them either to reject the enterprise at once, or to end it, without stopping before any expense. But the directors of the Republic preferred, according to their wont, the middle road. They decided to utilize the canals already dug as moats which should serve as a barrier to the movements of the Pisan troops, and, since the too daring projects of Leonardo did not inspire trust in anybody, they invited from Ferrara other engineers familiar with canals and excavations. But the while they were disputing in Florence, exposing one another, discussing the question in all sorts of public places, in meetings and councils, according to the majority of votes, and white balls and black, their enemies, without waiting for them, destroyed with cannon shots that which had already been done.

All this enterprise had finally become so repugnant to the artist that he could not hear of it without revulsion. Affairs long since permitted him to return to Florence. But, finding out by chance that Messer Giocondo was returning from Calabria in the beginning of October, Leonardo decided to come ten days later, that he might find Monna Lisa in Florence for a certainty.

He counted the days. Now, at the thought that the separation might be protracted, such a superstitious fear and yearning would contract his heart that he tried not to think of it, would not speak with anyone or put questions, apprehensive lest he be told that she would not return on time.

He arrived in Florence early in the morning. Autumnal, dim, humid, it seemed to him especially dear and near, recalling Gioconda. And the day was *her* day,—misty, quiet, with a humidly dim, seemingly subaqueous sun, which gave to the faces of women an especial charm.

No longer did he ask himself how they would meet, what he would say to her, what he would do that they might no more be parted, that the spouse of Messer Francesco might become his sole eternal companion. He knew that all things would arrange themselves, that the difficult would become easy, the impossible possible,—if they were but to meet, to see one another.

"The main thing is not to indulge in thought,—then the result is better," he kept on repeating Raphael's words. "I shall ask her, and this time she will tell me that which she had not had time to tell me then,—what is necessary, besides curiosity, to penetrate into the last, perhaps the most wondrous mysteries of the Cavern?"

And such joy filled his soul, as though he was not five-and-fifty, but sixteen, as though all life were before him. Only in the very depth of his heart, where not a single ray of consciousness penetrated, beneath this joyousness, was an ominous foreboding.

He set out to see Messer Niccolò, in order to give him certain business papers and plans of the excavating work. He proposed to drop in at Messer Giocondo's on the next morning; but he could not restrain himself, and decided that on the same evening, when returning from Machiavelli and passing by the house of Giocondo on the Lung' Arno delle Grazie, he would enquire of the hostler, the gate-keeper, or some servant if the master and mistress had returned, and if all were well with them.

Leonardo was going down the Strada Tornabuoni toward the bridge,—the same route, but in an opposite direction, to that which he had taken on the last night before his departure. The weather had suddenly changed toward evening, as is frequently the case in Florence in the fall. From the ravine of Mugnone a strong northern wind had begun to blow,—piercing, as though it were a draft. And the summits of the Mugello had suddenly grown white, from hoar-frost, as though they had turned silver-haired. It was drizzling. Suddenly, below, from under the canopy of clouds,—a canopy that seemed sharply cut and that left above the horizon only a streak of clear sky,—the sun spurted out and illumined the miry, wet streets, the sheen of roofs, and the faces of people, with a copper-yellow light, chill and coarse. The rain turned to copper dust. And here and there, afar off, window-panes began to sparkle, like embers at red-heat.

Opposite the church of Santa Trinità, near the bridge, at the corner of the wharf and the Strada Tornabuoni, reared the enormous Palazzo Spini, of roughly quarried brownish-grey stones, with latticed windows and with crenellations, recalling a mediæval fortress. Below, along its walls, as is the case with many old Florentine castles, stretched long stone benches, upon which the burghers of all ages and callings were accustomed to loll, playing at dice or draughts, listening to the news, discussing their affairs, warming themselves in the sun in winter, resting in the shade in summer. From that side of the palace which looked upon the Arno, over the bench had been built a pent roof of tiles with little pillars, on the manner of a *loggia*. Passing by, Leonardo saw a gathering of people he was vaguely acquainted with,—some sitting, others standing. They were conversing with such animation that they did not remark the wind and rain.

"Messer,—Messer Leonardo!" they called after him. "Come hither, an you please; do decide our dispute."

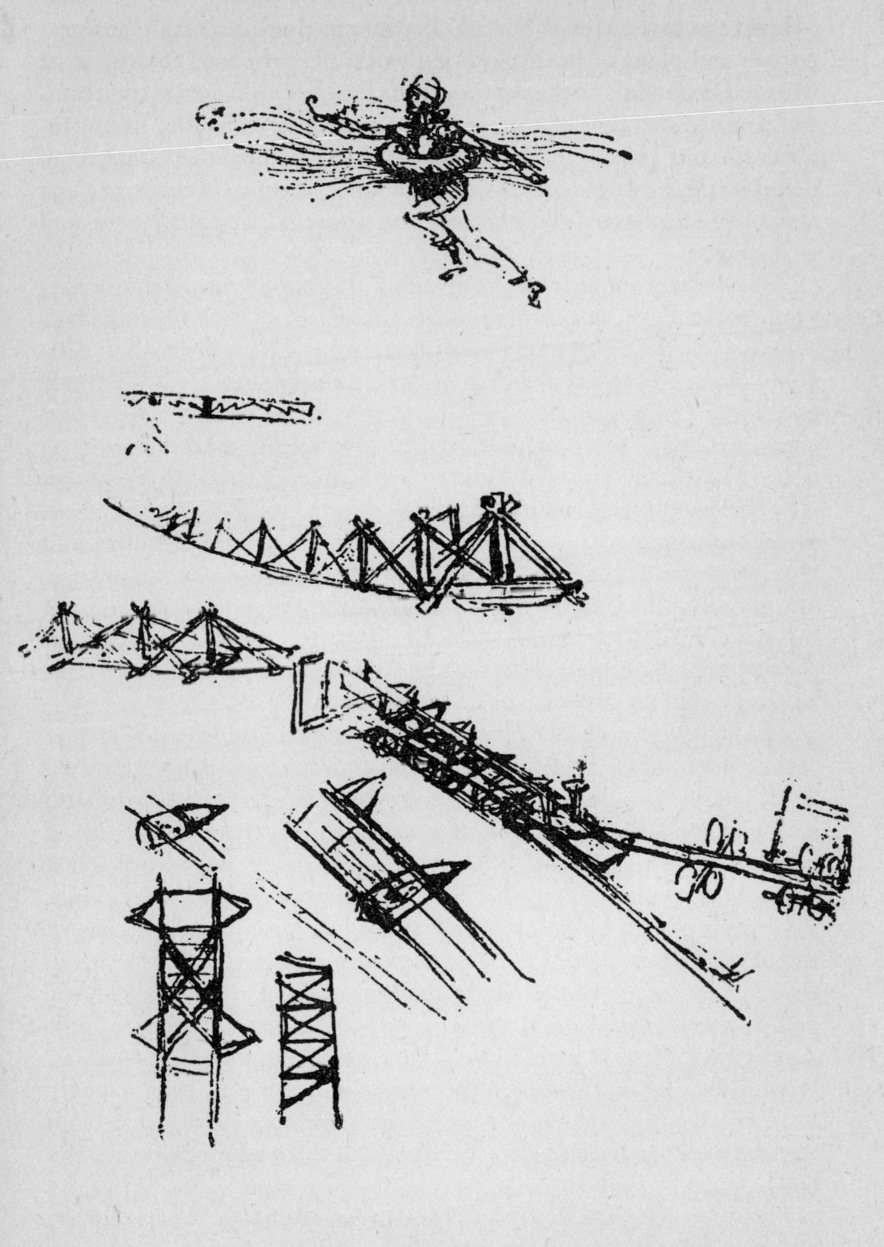

He paused. The discussion dealt with several enigmatic stanzas of the *Divine Comedy* in the thirty-fourth canto of the *Inferno*.

The more they disputed the more unsolvable did the secret of the poet become.

While an old wealthy woolster was explaining the subject of the dispute to the artist, Leonardo, his eyes puckering somewhat from the wind, was gazing into the distance, in the direction of the Lung' Arno Acchiaioli, where a man was walking along the wharf, with a heavy ungainly, ursine gait, carelessly and poorly clad; squat, bony, with a large head, black, coarse, curly hair and a sparse and matted goatee; his ears stuck out, and his flat face had broad cheek-bones. This was Michelangelo Buonarotti. Especial, almost repellent, ugliness was imparted to his face by his nose, broken and flattened by the blow of a fist in his early youth, during a fight with a rival sculptor, whom he had aroused to fury by his malicious jests. The pupils of his little yellow eyes played at times with a strange dark-red glitter. His inflamed eyelids, practically devoid of lashes, were red, inasmuch as, not content with the day, he must needs labour at night also, fastening a round little lanthorn to his forehead, which made him resemble a Cyclop with a fiery eye stirring about in underground darkness, and with a muffled ursine growling and the iron clangour of his iron mallet furiouslycontending with the stone.

"What say you, messer?" the disputants addressed Leonardo.

Leonardo had always hoped that his quarrel with Buonarotti would end amicably. He had hardly thought of this quarrel during his absence from Florence and had almost forgotten it. There was such calm and radiance in his soul at this minute, and he was ready to address his rival with such kind words, that Michelangelo, he thought, could not but understand.

"Messer Buonarotti is deeply versed in Alighieri," answered Leonardo with a polite, calm smile, indicating Michelangelo. "He will explain this passage to you better than I."

Michelangelo was walking, as was his wont, with his head lowered, looking to neither side, and had not noticed the gathering. Hearing his name coming from the lips of Leonardo, he halted and lifted up his eyes. Shy and wary to the verge of savagery, the gaze of men was onerous to him, inasmuch as he never forgot his ugliness, and was tormented for shame of it,—it seemed to him that everybody was laughing at him.

Caught off his guard, he was at first at a loss; he glanced suspiciously from under his brows at everybody with his little yellowish-brown eyes, helplessly winking his inflamed eyelids, painfully blinking from the sun and the gaze of men.

But when he beheld the radiant smile of his rival, and his penetrating gaze directed down upon him from above involuntarily, inasmuch as Leonardo was taller in stature than Michelangelo,—his wariness, as was often the case with him,—was momently turned into fury. For a long space he could not utter a word. His face now paled, now flushed, in irregular splotches. Finally, with an effort, he uttered in a dull, stifled voice:

"Explain it thyself! For art thou not handy with books, O wisest of men, who didst put thy trust in the Lombardian capons, fussing about for sixteen years with thy clay Colossus, and couldst not mould it in bronze,—having to abandon everything in ignominy! . . ."

He felt that he was not saying that which he wanted to say; he sought and could not find words offensive enough to wound his rival. All present became quiet, turning curious eyes upon them. Leonardo kept silent. And for a few moments each looked into the eyes of the other,—the one with his former meek smile, which was now full of wonder and hurt, the other with a smile of scoffing contempt, which he did not quite carry off, merely distorting his face convulsively, making it still more ugly. Before the furious force of Buonarotti, the feminine charm of Leonardo seemed infinite weakness.

Leonardo had a drawing depicting the struggle of two monsters,—the Dragon and the Lion: the winged serpent, sovereign of the air, was vanquishing the wingless sovereign of the earth. That which was now taking place between them, despite their consciousness and will, resembled this struggle. And Leonardo sensed that Monna Lisa was right,—never would his rival forgive Leonardo his "calm, which was stronger than the tempest."

Michelangelo wanted to add something, but merely made a gesture of hopelessness, turned away rapidly, and continued his journey in his uncouth, ursine gait, with dull indistinct muttering, with head lowered and back bent, as though an immeasurable weight were oppressing his shoulders. And he was soon lost to view, as though he had dissolved in the turbid, fiery-copper dust of the rain and the ominous sun. Leonardo also continued on his way.

Upon the bridge he was overtaken by one of those who had been among the gathering near the Palazzo Spini,—a spry and meanly insignificant homunculus, who looked like a Hebrew, despite his being a pure-blooded Florentine. The artist could not recall who this homunculus might be, nor what his name was,—he merely knew that he was a malicious scandal-monger. The wind blew stronger on the bridge; it whistled in the ears and pricked the face with icy needles. The waves of the river, receding into the distance toward the sun that lay under a sky that was low and dark, as though it were of stone, seemed a subterranean current of molten copper. Leonardo walked along a narrow, dry space, paying no heed to his fellow wayfarer, who was keeping pace with him, splashing through the mire, hopping and skipping, running ahead of him occasionally, like a little dog, trying to catch his eye and to start a conversation about Michelangelo. He evidently longed to seize upon some word or other of Leonardo's, in order that he might instantly transmit it to his rival and bruit it about the town. But Leonardo kept silent.

"Tell me, messer," persisted the annoying mannikin, "you have not, of course, finished the portrait of Gioconda as yet?"

"I have not finished it," answered the artist, and frowned. "But what concern is that of yours?"

"Nay, I meant naught,—I was simply curious. Why, when one comes to think of it, you have been struggling with this one picture for three whole years, and have not finished it yet. But to us, who are not of the initiate, it seems even now so perfect that a greater we could not even imagine! . . ."

And he smiled fawningly. Leonardo glanced at him with aversion. This meanly insignificant mannikin suddenly became so hateful to him that it seemed, if he were to give free rein to his feelings, he would seize him by the nape of his neck and throw him in the river.

"However, what is the future fate of this picture?" continued his irrepressible companion. "Or have you not heard yet, Messer Leonardo? . . ."

He was, evidently, drawing the thing out and beating about the bush with a purpose, having something in the back of his mind. And, suddenly, through his aversion, the artist felt a brute fear of the speaker,—as though his body were slimy and moving in segments, like the body of an insect. The latter, too, must have sensed something. He now resembled a Jew more than ever; his hands began to shake, his eyes to dance.

"Ah, my God,—truly, you have arrived but this morning, and know not as yet. Imagine, what a misfortune! Poor Messer Giocondo! He is a widower for the third time. It is now already a month since Madonna Lisa has departed, by the will of God. . . ."

Everything grew dark before Leonardo's eyes. For an instant it seemed to him that he would fall. The mannikin was greedily piercing him with his sharp little eyes. But the artist made an incredible effort,—and his face, save for a slight pallor, remained impenetrable; at least his companion did not notice anything. Completely disappointed, and having become stuck in the mire up to his shanks on the Piazza Frescobaldi, he fell behind.

Leonardo's first thought upon recovering was that the scandal-monger had lied, had purposely invented this news in order to see what impression it would make on him, and afterwards retail it everywhere, supplying new food for the rumours already long current concerning a liaison between Leonardo and Gioconda.

The veritability of death, as it always is at the first moment, seemed unbelievable.

But that same evening he learned everything; on her return journey from Calabria, where Messer Francesco had arranged his affairs advantageously,—among other things, supplying Florence with raw hides of rams,—in the dull little town of Lagonegro, Monna Lisa had died; some said of swamp fever, others, from an infectious disease of the throat.

VII

THE affair of the canal, which was to divert the Arno from Pisa, ended in ignominious failure. During the autumnal increase of waters an inundation had destroyed the work begun, and had transformed the blooming lowland into a putrid quagmire, where the workers died from infection. The enormous labour, the money and the human lives,—all had perished for naught.

The canal builders from Ferrara were casting the blame upon Soderini, Machiavelli and Leonardo. Their acquaintance turned away from them on the street and avoided bowing to them. Niccolò fell ill from shame and grief.

Two years before Leonardo's father had died. "On the 9th of July, in the year of 1504, of a Wednesday, at eight in the night," he wrote down with his customary brevity, "expired my father, Ser

Pietro da Vinci, a notary at the palace of the Podestà. He was eighty. He has left ten children of the male sex, and two of the female."

Ser Pietro had, on more than one occasion, in the presence of witnesses, expressed his intention of willing to Leonardo, his illegitimate first-born, a share of the estate equal to that of each of his other children. Whether he had himself changed this intention before his death, or whether his sons did not want to carry out the wishes of the departed, there remains the fact of their announcement that, in his status of a natural son, Leonardo was not to participate in the division of the estate. Thereupon an adroit Hebrew, one of the usurers from whom the artist was accustomed to borrow moneys under the security of his expected patrimony, offered to buy up his rights in the litigation with his brothers. Greatly as Leonardo dreaded family and legal squabbles, his financial affairs were so involved at that period that he agreed nevertheless. There began a litigation over three hundred florins which was destined to drag along for six years. His brothers, taking advantage of the general irritation against Leonardo, poured oil upon the flame, accusing him of impiety, of governmental treason while in the service of Cæsar Borgia, of sorcery, of profanation of Christian graves while digging up corpses for anatomical dissections,—they even resurrected the slander which had been buried twenty-five years ago, concerning his unnatural vices; they dishonoured the memory of his dead mother, Caterina Accattabrighe.

To all these unpleasantnesses was joined his failure with the picture in the Council Hall. So strong was Leonardo's habit of dilatoriness, permissible in mural painting by the use of oil-colours, and so strong his aversion to the rapidity required by water-colours, that, despite his warning experience with the Mystic Supper, he decided to paint the Battle of Anghiari in the same way,—even though with different pigments, which he thought perfected, but in oils nevertheless. When his work was half-completed, he made a large fire on iron braziers before the picture, so as to hasten the absorption of the colours by the white-wash, according to a new method invented by him; but he was soon convinced that the heat affected only the lower part of the picture, while the colours and varnish on the upper part, withdrawn from the heat, were not drying. After many vain efforts he understood definitely that his second experiment with mural painting in oils was just as unsuccessful as the first; the Battle at Anghiari would perish even as The Last Supper; and again, to use an expression of Buonarotti's, he had to "abandon everything in ignominy."

The picture in the Council Hall became more distasteful to him than the affair of the Pisan Canal and the litigation with his brothers. Soderini tormented him with demands of a bureaucratical accuracy in the execution of the commission, hurried him to finish the work by the time set, threatened him with the forfeit, and, seeing that naught availed, took to accusing him openly of dishonesty, of appropriating the treasury's money. But when Leonardo, having borrowed the money from his friends, wanted to give him back all that he had received from the treasury, Messer Pietro refused to accept it; and yet there was a letter being passed from hand to hand in Florence, disseminated by the friends of Buonarotti,—it was from the Gonfaloniere to the confidential Florentine envoy at Milan, who was exerting himself to obtain the artist's release to the French King's Viceroy in Lombardy, Seigneur Charles d'Amboise:

"The actions of Messer Leonardo are most unworthy," said this letter, among other things. "Having taken a large sum in advance, and scarcely begun work, he has dropped everything, and has behaved in this matter like a traitor to the Republic."

One winter night Leonardo was sitting alone in his workroom. The storm howled in the hearth-chimney. The walls of the house shook from its fitful attacks; the flame of the candle wavered; a stuffed bird with moth-eaten wings, suspended from a cross-beam in a contrivance for the study of flight, swung, as though preparing to soar upward; and in a corner, over a shelf that held the tomes of Pliny the Naturalist, a familiar spider was uneasily darting through his web. Drops of rain and of thawing snow struck against the window-panes, as though someone were most gently tapping for entrance.

After the day passed in worldly cares Leonardo felt fatigued and prostrated, as after a night passed in delirium. He at first made an attempt at his old work,—the investigation of the laws of motion of bodies upon an inclined plane; then at a caricature of the little old crone, with a pug nose like a wart, with porcine little eyes and monstrous upper lip drawn downward; he tried to read,—but everything dropped from his hands. Yet he did not feel sleepy, with the whole night before him.

He glanced at the heaps of old, dusty books, at the cucurbits, retorts, the jars with pale little monstrous marasmi in alcohol, at the brass quadrants, the globes, the different devices of mechanics, astronomy, physics, hydraulics, optics, anatomy,—and an inexplicable aversion filled his soul.

Was he not himself like to this old spider in the dark corner over the books smelling of mildew, over the bones of human skeletons and the dead parts of dead machines? What did life hold in store for him, what separated him from a Lethean fate save a few small leaves of paper, which he would cover with small symbols of letters comprehensible to none?

And he recalled how, in his childhood, on the Monte Albano, as he heard the calls of the flocks of cranes in flight and, inhaling the odour of resinous grasses, gazed upon Florence,—transparently lilac in the smoky haze of the sun, like to an amethyst, so small that it was all contained between two aureate blooming twigs of the young wood that covers the slopes of these mountains in the spring,—he had been happy, knowing naught, thinking naught.

Could it be that all the labour of his life was but a delusion,—and that great love was not the daughter of great knowledge?

He hearkened closely to the howling of the storm, to its screeching and rumbling. And Machiavelli's words came to his mind: "The most fearful thing in life is not cares, nor poverty, nor grief, nor disease, nor even death itself,—but tedium."

The inhuman voices of the night wind spoke of that which was comprehensible to the heart of man, innate to it and inevitable,—of the ultimate loneliness in the midst of fearful, blind darkness, in the bosom of the father of all being,—ancient Chaos; of the infinite tedium of this world.

He arose, took a candle, unlocked an adjacent room, entered it, and approached a picture standing on a three-legged easel, hung with a cloth in heavy folds, like to a winding sheet,—which he flung back.

It was the portrait of Monna Lisa Gioconda.

He had not uncovered it since the day he had been working upon it for the last time, at their last meeting. Now it seemed to him that he was beholding it for the first time. And such a force of life did he feel upon this face, that he felt eerie before his own creation. He recalled superstitious stories of magical portraits, which, being transpierced with a needle, cause the death of the portrayed. Here, he reflected, it was just the contrary; he had taken her life from the living woman to bestow it upon the unliving.

Everything about her was distinct, exact,—to the last crease of her raiment, to the cross stitching upon the fine embroidery framing the opening of her dark dress against her pale bosom. It seemed that, if one looked intently and long, one could see her bosom breathing, the blood pulsing in the dimple beneath her throat, her expression changing. And yet, at the same time, she was spectral, distant, a stranger, more ancient in her immortal youth than the primeval crags of basalt perceptible in the background of the picture,—æthereally blue mountains, like stalactites, of some other world, long since dead. The curves of the currents flowing among the crags reminded one of the curves of her lips with their eternal smile. And the waves of her hair cascaded down from under her transparently-dark coif in accordance with the same laws of divine mechanics as the waves of water.

Only now—as though death had opened his eyes—did he comprehend that the charm of Monna Lisa was all that which he had been seeking in nature with such insatiable inquisitiveness, only now did he comprehend that the mystery of the universe was the mystery of Monna Lisa. Save that now it was no longer he who was probing her soul, but she who was probing his. What meant the gaze of these eyes, which reflected his soul, eyes that plunged farther and farther within its depths, as in a mirror,—unto infinity? Was she repeating that which she had not finished saying at their last meeting,—that more than curiosity was needed to penetrate to the deepest, and, perhaps, the most wonderful, mysteries of the Cavern? Or was this the imperturbable smile of omniscience, wherewith the dead look upon the living?

He knew that her death was not an accidental event: he could have saved her, had he wanted to. Never yet, so it seemed to him, had he looked so directly and closely into the face of death. Under the chill and caressing gaze of Gioconda an unbearable terror was turning his soul to ice.

And, for the first time in his life he retreated before the abyss, daring not to look within it,—not desiring to know. With a hasty, stealthy movement he let fall the cover with heavy folds, that was like a winding sheet, over her face.

In the spring, at the request of Charles d'Amboise, the French Viceroy, Leonardo received a leave of absence from Florence for three months, and set out for Milan. He was as glad to leave behind him his native land, and beheld the snowy masses of the Alps over the green plain of Lombardy, as shelterless an exile, as he had been five and twenty years ago.

BOOK FIFTEEN

The Most Holy Inquisition

I

URING HIS FIRST STAY IN MILAN, WHILE IN the service of Duke Moro, Leonardo had studied anatomy in the company of a certain scholar of eighteen,—young, but already celebrated, one Marc Antonio, of an ancient line of Veronese patricians, the della Torre, whose love of learning was hereditary. The father of Marc Antonio taught medicine in Padua; his brothers, also, were savants. He had consecrated himself to the service of science when scarcely a youth, even as on a time the scions of doughty families consecrated themselves in knightly service to the lady of their heart and to God. Neither the games of childhood nor the passions of youth diverted him from this strict service. He had come to love a maiden; but, deciding that it was impossible to serve two masters—love and science—had given up his bride and definitely forsaken the world. Even in his childhood he had impaired his health with excessive studies. His thin, pale face, like that of an ascetic anchorite, but still beautiful, recalled the face of Raphael, save that its expression was one of deep thought and sadness.

When still an adolescent, two celebrated universities of northern Italy,—that of Padua and of Pavia,—had contended over him. And when Leonardo returned to Milan, the twenty-five-year-old Marc Antonio was deemed one of the first savants of Europe.

They had evidently the same strivings in science,—both supplanted the scholastic anatomy of the mediæval Arabian expounder of Hippocrates and Galen by experimentation upon, and observation of, nature; by the investigation of the structure of the living body; but, under this exterior similarity, there was concealed a deep differentiation as well.

At the last outposts of knowledge the artist sensed a mystery, which, throughout all the manifestations of the universe, drew him to it, just as a magnet draws iron, even through cloth.

Marc Antonio also sensed a mystery in the manifestations of nature, but did not grow submissive before this mystery, and, being able neither to reject nor to conquer it, struggled with it and feared it. The learning of Leonardo was directed toward God, the learning of Marc Antonio was directed against God, and his lost faith he was fain to supplant with a new—a faith in the reason of man.

He was compassionate. Not infrequently, refusing the rich, he visited the poor, treating them gratis, assisting them with money, and was ready to give away to them all that he possessed. His was the goodness native to those not of this world and those plunged in meditation. But when the talk would touch upon the ignorance of monks and churchmen, the foes of science, his face would become distorted, his eyes would flash with untamable wrath, and Leonardo felt that this compassionate man, were he to be given power, would send men to be burned at the stake in the name of reason, even as his enemies the monks and the churchmen burned them in the name of God.

Leonardo was just as lonely in science as in art; Marc Antonio was surrounded by disciples. He drew the crowd after him; he inflamed hearts like a prophet; he worked miracles, reviving the sick not so much by medicaments as by faith. And the youths who heard him, like all disciples, carried the thoughts of their master to extremity. They no longer struggled, but with never a care denied the mystery of the universe, thinking that if not to-day then to-morrow science would conquer everything, leaving not one stone standing upon another of the ancient edifice of faith. They boasted of their absence of faith, as children boast of new wearables; they rioted like schoolboys,—and their triumphantly victorious boisterousness reminded one of the yelping boisterousness of puppies. For the artist the fanaticism of these pseudo-servants of knowledge was just as repugnant as the fanaticism of the pseudo-servants of God.

"When science shall conquer," he reflected sadly, "and the rabble shall enter its holy place, will it not defile with its allegiance even science, as it has defiled the Church, and will the knowledge of the mob be any the less vulgar than the faith of the mob?"

At that time the procuring of cadavers for anatomical dissections, which were forbidden by Pope Boniface VIII's Bull of *Extravagantes*, was a matter difficult and hazardous. Two hundred years ago Mundini dei Luzzi had been the first of the scientists to dare perform an anatomical dissection of two cadavers before all the world, in the University of Bologna. He had chosen women, as being "the nearer to animal nature." Yet, nevertheless, according to his own confession, his conscience tormented him so much that to anatomize the head, "the dwelling place of spirit and reason," he had not dared.

Times had changed. The auditors of Marc Antonio were less timid. Without stopping before any hazards and even crimes, they procured fresh cadavers,—not only did they buy them for big sums from the headsmen and hospital grave diggers, but even took them by force, stole them from the gallows, dug them out of churchyard graves, and, had the master permitted them, would have killed travellers at night in the deserted environs.

The abundance of cadavers made his work with della Torre especially important and precious to the artist. He was preparing a whole series of anatomical drawings in pen and red crayon, with marginal explanations and remarks. Here, in their investigative technique, the contrast of the investigators told still more. The one was only a scholar, the other both a scholar and an artist. Leonardo knew and loved,—and his love deepened his full knowledge. His drawings were so exact, and at the same time so beautiful, that it was difficult to decide where art ended and science began: the one entered into the other, blending together into one indivisible whole.

"To him who would retort to me," he wrote in this marginalia, "that it is better to study anatomy upon a cadaver than through my drawings, I would retort: That would be so if thou wert able to see in a single dissection all that one of my drawings depicts; but no matter what thy penetration may be, thou wouldst come to see and to recognize but a few veins. Whereas I, in order to obtain complete knowledge, did perform the dissection of ten human bodies of different ages, disintegrating all members, taking off, to the last particles, all the flesh surrounding the veins, without spilling any blood, unless one take into reckoning barely perceptible drops from the capillary vessels. And when one body would prove insufficient, because it would decompose during the investigation, I would dissect as many cadavers as were required for a perfect knowledge of the subject, and would twice begin the same investigation, in order to see the variations. Multiplying drawings, I give such a representation of each member and organ as if thou wert holding them in thy hands, and, turning them about, wert inspecting them from all sides,—from within and from without, from above and from below."

The clairvoyance of the artist bestowed upon the eye and hand of the scientist the precision of a mathematical instrument. The divisions of the veins, known to none, concealed in the connecting tissues or in mucous membranes, the finest of blood-carrying vessels and nerves, branching out into the sinews and muscles, his hand did feel through the scalpel and reveal,—a hand so strong that it could bend horseshoes, a hand so tender that it captured the secret of muliebrile charm in the smile of Gioconda.

And Marc Antonio, who did not wish to believe in anything save reason, would at times experience confusion, well-nigh fear, before this fatidical knowledge, as before a miracle.

At times the artist would say to himself: "This is as it should be; this is seemly." And when, upon investigation, he would be convinced that it was actually so, the will of the Creating One seemed to answer to the will of the contemplating one: beauty was truth, truth,—beauty.

"Even as, before me, Ptolemy did describe the universe in his *Cosmography*, I do describe the human body,—this universe in little, this universe within a universe."

He had a presentiment that his labours, if they were to become known and understood of men, would create the greatest upheaval in science; he waited for "followers," for "successors," who would be able to appreciate in his drawings, "the benefaction which he did extend to mankind."

II

At the solicitation of the viceroy, Charles d'Amboise, and the King of France, the artist received from the Florentine Signoria leave of absence for an indefinite period, and in the following year—fifteen hundred and seven—having finally gone over to the service of Louis XII, he settled down in Milan, and only rarely visited Florence on matters of business.

Four years passed. Toward the end of fifteen hundred and eleven Giovanni Beltraffio, who was by this time already accounted a skilled master, was working upon a mural painting in the new church of San Maurizio, belonging to the old nunnery of Maggiore, which latter was built upon the ruins of an ancient Roman circus and a temple of Jupiter. Next to it, behind a high wall, facing the Strada della Vigni, was located a neglected garden and a castle, at one time magnificent but now abandoned and half-ruined, belonging to the family of Carmagnola.

The nuns let this ground and house to Galeotto Sacrobosco the alchemist, and his niece, Monna Cassandra, the daughter of Galeotto's brother, Messer Luigi, the famous collector of antiquities; both had recently returned to Milan.

Shortly after the first invasion of the French and the sacking of the little house of Monna Sidonia near the Catarana Canal beyond the Vercellina Gates, they had left Lombardy and had passed nine years in wandering through the Orient,—Greece, the Islands of the Archipelago, Asia Minor, Palestine, Syria. There were strange rumours current concerning them: some asserted that the alchemist must have found the Philosopher's Stone, which transmuted lead into gold; others, that he must have enticed enormous sums out of the Diodary for experiments, and, having appropriated them, had fled; a third group, that Monna Cassandra, through a compact with the Devil and a manuscript of her father's, had dug up an ancient treasure trove, buried on the site of an ancient Phœnician temple of Astarte; a fourth group, finally, that she had in Constantinople robbed a certain old, incalculably rich merchant of Smyrna, whom she had bewitched and made drunken with magic herbs. Whatever may have been the case, having left Milan beggars, they returned rich.

The former witch, pupil of Demetrios Chalcondylos, foster child of the old witch Sidonia, Cassandra became, or, at least, pretended to become, a pious daughter of the Church; she paid strict observance to all the rites and fasts, attended masses, and by her generous donations attained the special protection not only of the sisters of the nunnery of Maggiore, who had given her shelter on their land, but of their spiritual superior himself, the Archbishop of Milan. Evil tongues asserted, however (perhaps only through envy for sudden riches, natural to human beings), that she had returned from her distant wanderings a still greater pagan; that the witch and the alchemist had found it necessary to flee from Rome, to save themselves from the Most Holy Inquisition, and that, sooner or later, they would not escape the stake and the faggots.

Galeotto was still as reverent as ever before Leonardo, and deemed him his teacher,—the possessor of the "secret wisdom of Hermes Trismegistus, the Thrice Great."

The alchemist had brought with him from his travels many rare books, for the greater part those of the Alexandrian scholars of the time of the Ptolemies, dealing with the mathematical sciences. The artist would borrow these books, usually sending Giovanni, who was working in the neighbourhood in the Church of San Maurizio. After some time Beltraffio, according to his habit of old, began to drop in on them with increasing frequency, under any likely pretext, but in reality only to see Cassandra.

The girl, during their first meetings, was on her guard against him, acting the repentant sinner, speaking of her desire to take the veil; but little by little, becoming convinced that there was naught to fear, became more trusting. They recalled their conversations of ten years ago, when they had both been little more than children, in the deserted little suburb beyond the Catarana dam, near the monastery of Santa Redegonda; they recalled the evening of the pallid heat-lightnings, with the stifling odour of the summer waters of the canal, the dull mutterings of the thunder, that seemed to come from underground; and also how she had foretold him the resurrection of the Olympian gods, and how she had called him to the Witches' Sabbath.

Now she lived like a hermit; she was, or seemed, ailing, and almost all her time free from church services she passed in a sequestered chamber, allowing none to enter, in one of those portions of the old castle which had survived time, a gloomy hall with ogive windows looking out on the garden, growing wild, where the cypresses reared up as a silent bulwark, and the vivid moist moss covered the trunks of hollow elms. The furnishings of this room reminded one of a museum and book ambry. Here were to be found the antiquities she had brought back from the Orient,—fragments of Hellenic statues; dog-headed deities of Egypt in smooth black granite; engraved stones of the Gnostics bearing the magic word *Abraxas*,—representing the three hundred and sixty-five celestial firmaments; Byzantine parchments, as hard as ivory, with fragments of the productions, lost forever, of Greek poesy; clay shards with cuneiform Assyrian inscriptions; books of the Persian magi, bound in iron; and Memphian papyri, as thinly-transparent as the petals of flowers.

She told him of her wanderings, of wonders seen, of the desolate grandeur of temples of white marble, upon black cliffs gnawed by the sea, amid the eternally blue Ionian waves, fragrant of the brine, as with the freshness of the nude body of Venus Anadyomene; told him of her immeasurable toil, tribulations, dangers. And once, when he asked what she had sought in these wanderings, why she had been collecting these antiquities, enduring so many sufferings,—she answered him in the words of her father, Messer Luigi Sacrobosco:

"That I might bring the dead to life!"

And there sprang up a fire in her eyes which made him recognize the witch Cassandra of yore.

She had changed but little. She had the same face, devoid of sorrow and joy, immobile, like the face of ancient sculptures,—a broad, low brow; straight, narrow eyebrows; sternly-pressed lips, on which one could not imagine a smile; and eyes like amber, transparently yellow. But now this face, refined by ill-health or by a single, exceedingly keen thought, expressed still more clearly a severe calm, and, at the same time, a childlike helplessness,—especially the lower part, which was too narrow, small, with a somewhat prominent lower lip. Her dry, bushy hair, alive, more alive than her face, as though it were endowed with a separate life, like the snakes of Medusa, surrounded her pallid face with a black aureole, which made it seem still more pallid and immobile, her scarlet lips still more vivid, her yellow eyes still more transparent. And still more irresistibly than ten years ago was Giovanni drawn by the charm of this girl, who aroused within him curiosity, fear, and pity.

During her travels in Greece, Cassandra had visited the native place of her mother, where had died the last of the teachers of Hellenic Wisdom, Gemistos Pletho.

"More than half a century has passed since the death of Pletho," Giovanni argued, "but still his prophecy remains unfulfilled. Can it be that you still believe, Monna Cassandra? . . ."

"The perfect truth," she uttered calmly, "was not in Pletho's possession. He was led astray in many things, inasmuch as there were many things he had no knowledge of."

"Of what?" asked Giovanni, and suddenly, under her deep, intense gaze, felt his heart sink within him.

Instead of answering, she took down from a shelf an olden parchment,—a tragedy by Æschylos, *Prometheus Bound*, and read aloud for him a few verses. Giovanni understood Greek a little, and that which he did not understand she explained to him.

Having enumerated his gifts to men: oblivion in death; hope; fire purloined from heaven,—gifts which would sooner or later make men the equals of gods,—the Titan foretold the fall of Zeus.

"What thinkest thou, Giovanni?" asked Cassandra, shutting the book.

Giovanni made no reply; it seemed to him that an abyss was opening up before him, as if in the light of a sudden flash of lightning. But Monna Cassandra continued to gaze upon him as fixedly as before, with her clear, transparent eyes; at this instant she did really resemble the ill-fated captive of Agamemnon, Cassandra the clairvoyant virgin.

"Giovanni," she added, after a short silence, "hast thou ever heard of a certain man who, more than ten centuries ago, had dreamt of resurrecting the gods who had died, even as Pletho dreamt,—one Emperor Flavius Claudius Julian?"

"Julian the Apostate?"

"Yes,—he who did, alas, appear an Apostate to his enemies the Galileans and to himself, but dared not be one, inasmuch as he did pour new wine into old wine-skins; the Hellenes, as well as the Christians, might have styled him Apostate. . . ."

She paused, as though hesitating to finish what she was saying, and then added quietly:

"If thou didst but know, Giovanni,—if I could but tell thee all, to the very end! . . . But nay, the time is not come yet. For the nonce I will say but this: there is one god among the Olympian gods, who is nearest of all to his subterranean brethren, a god radiant and dark, like the murk at break of morn; as merciless as death; who has come down to earth and did bestow upon mortals a forgetfulness of death, a new flame from the flame of Prometheus—in his own blood, in the intoxicating juice of the grape-vines. And who among men, O my brother, shall understand and proclaim to the universe, wherein the Wisdom of the One Crowned with Clusters of Grapes is like to the wisdom of the One Crowned with Thorns,—of him who has said: 'I am the true vine'?[59] And that He, even as the god Dionysos, doth intoxicate the world with His blood? Hast thou comprehended whereof I speak, Giovanni? If thou hast not, keep silent, and ask me not, inasmuch as there is a mystery herein, which may not be spoken of yet. . . ."

Latterly a daring of thought, hitherto unknown, had appeared in Giovanni. He feared naught, for that he had naught to lose. He knew that neither the faith of Fra Benedetto nor the knowledge of Leonardo would allay his torment, resolve the contradictions from which his soul was dying. Only in the dark prophecies of Cassandra did there seem to him to be probably the most fearful, yet the sole, way to reconciling them, and upon this last way he walked after her with the valour of despair.

They were drawing nearer to one another.

On one occasion he asked her why she was dissembling and hiding from men that which she deemed the truth.

"Not all things are for all men," retorted Cassandra. "The confession of martyrs, as well as the miracle and the portent, are necessary only to the mob, inasmuch as only those who do not believe to the ultimate end die for their faith, that they may prove it to themselves and others. But perfect faith is perfect knowledge. Dost thou think, for instance, that the death of Pythagoras would have proved the truths of geometry he had discovered? Perfect faith is mute, and the truth of it is above confession, even as the master hath said: 'Know ye all men, but be ye known of none.'"

"What master?" asked Giovanni, and reflected: "This might have been said by Leonardo,—he, too, knoweth all men, but is known of none."

"The Egyptian Gnostic, Basilides," answered Cassandra, and explained that the great teachers of the first ages of Christianity, for whom perfect faith and perfect knowledge were identical, were called *Gnostics,—the Knowers*. And she imparted to him strange, at times monstrous, legends that resembled delirium.

Thus, in all ages and among all nations,—in the tragedies of Æschylos, in the legends of the Gnostics, in the life of Emperor Julian the Apostate, in the teaching of Pletho the Sage,—he found distant echoes of a great discord and struggle, kindred to those which filled his own heart. His sorrow deepened, and was quieted by the consciousness that even ten centuries ago men were already suffering, struggling with the same "double-minded thoughts," perishing from the same contradictions and temptations, as he.

At this time there arrived in Milan a famous Doctor of Theology, the inquisitor Fra Giorgio da Casale. Pope Julius II, alarmed by the rumours of the unprecedented spread of witchcraft in Lombardy, had despatched him thither with threat-laden Bulls. The sisters of the nunnery of Maggiore, and Monna Cassandra's protectors in the palace of the archbishop, forewarned her of her danger. Fra Giorgio was the same member of the Inquisition whom Monna Cassandra and Messer Galeotto had barely managed to escape in Rome. They knew that if they were to fall into his clutches once more no protection would avail to deliver them, and decided to hide themselves in France, and, if need be, farther away,—even in England, or Scotland.

In the morning, two days before their departure, Giovanni was conversing with Monna Cassandra, in her studio, as was their custom, —in the secluded chamber in the Palazzo Carmagnola. The sun, penetrating into the windows through the thick, black branches of the cypresses, seemed pallid, like moonlight; the face of the girl appeared especially beautiful and immobile. Only now, before their separation, did Giovanni understand how near she was to him. He asked if they would see one another again, and if she would reveal to him that ultimate mystery of which she had so often spoken.

Cassandra bestowed a glance upon him, and in silence took out of a casket a flat, quadrangular, transparently green stone. This was the famous *Tabula Smaragdina*, or emerald tablet, reputed to have been found in a cavern near the city of Memphis, in the hands of the mummy of a certain sacrificator, who had been, according to the legend, a reincarnation of Hermes Trismegistus, of the Egyptian Horus, the god of the boundary line, the guide of the dead into the realm of shades. On one side of the emerald were cut in Coptic, on the other in ancient Hellenic characters, four lines:

> Heaven above,—heaven below,
> Stars above,—stars below,
> All that is above is also below,—
> If thou comprehendest, weal betide thee.

"What means this?" asked Giovanni.

"Come to me to-night," she said quietly and solemnly. "I shall tell thee all that I myself know; dost hear,—everything to the end. But now, as is the custom before parting, let us drain a last fraternal cup."

She took out a small round vessel of clay, sealed with wax, such as are used in the Far East; poured out some wine, as thick as oil, of a strange odour, of an aureate rose colour, into an ancient goblet of chrysolite, carved along its edges with a representation of the god Dionysos and bacchantes, and, approaching the window, raised up the cup, as though for a votive libation. In the ray of the pallid sun the naked bodies of the bacchantes on its transparent sides took on the rosy living glow of the wine, as though it were their blood, as they danced to the glory of the god crowned with clusters of grapes.

"There was a time, Giovanni," she uttered still more quietly and solemnly, "when I thought thy master Leonardo possessed of the last mystery, inasmuch as his face is as beautiful as if in him an Olympian god were joined with a subterranean Titan. But now I perceive that he does but strive yet does not attain, that he seeketh but findeth not, that he knoweth but doth not realize. He is a forerunner for him that cometh after him, and who is greater than he.—Let us, then, drink together, brother of mine, this farewell goblet to the Unknown, whom we are both summoning,—to the ultimate Reconciler!"

And reverently, as though performing a great mysterious rite, she drank half the cup and gave it over to Giovanni.

"Fear not," she said, "there are no forbidden charms in it. This wine is without sin and holy: it is from the vines growing on the knolls of Nazareth. 'Tis the purest blood of Dionysos—the Galilean."

When he had drunk, she, placing her hands on his shoulders with a trusting caress, said in a rapid, stealthy whisper:

"Come, then, if thou wouldst know all; come, I shall tell thee the secret which I have never told anyone,—I shall reveal the last torment and joy, in which we shall be together forever, as brother and sister, as bride and groom!"

And within a ray of the sun, penetrating through the thick branches of the cypresses, a ray as pallid as though of the moon,— even as on that memorable ominous night on the Catarana dam, in the flashing of the pallid heat-lightnings,—she drew close to him her immobile, ominous face, as white as the marble of sculptures, in its aureole of black, bushy hair, as living as the snakes of Medusa, with lips as scarlet as blood, with eyes as yellow as amber.

The chill of a familiar horror darted through the heart of Giovanni, and he thought:

"The White She-Demon!"

III

At the hour agreed upon he was standing before the wicket in the deserted lane of della Vigni, before the garden wall surrounding the castle of Carmagnola. The door was locked. He knocked for a long while; no one opened. He approached from another side, from the street of Sant' Agnese, the gates of the adjacent nunnery of Maggiore, and learned from the portress the dreadful news: the Inquisitor of Pope Julius II, Fra Giorgio da Casale, had made a sudden appearance in Milan, and had ordered Galeotto Sacrobosco the alchemist to be seized forthwith, as well as his niece, Monna Cassandra, as persons under greatest suspicion of black magic. Galeotto had managed to flee. Monna Cassandra was within the walls of the Most Holy Inquisition.

Learning of this, Leonardo turned with requests and petitions for the misfortunate girl to his well wishers, Florimond Roberte, chief treasurer of Louis XII, and to the viceroy of the French King in Milan, —Charles d'Amboise. Giovanni also exerted himself, running about, carrying the master's letters, and making enquiries at the Judgment Hall of the Inquisition, situated near the Cathedral, in the palace of the Archbishop.

Here he became acquainted with the chief clerk of Fra Giorgio, one Fra Michele da Valverde, a Magister of Theology, who had written a book concerning black magic,—*The Newest Flail for Witches*, wherein, among other things, it was proved that the so-called Nocturnal Goat, —*Hyrcus Nocturnus*, the chief of the Sabbath,—was the nearest possible kin to the goat which on a time the Hellenes used to offer in sacrifice to the god Dionysos, amidst voluptuous dances and chorals, whence tragedy was subsequently derived.—Fra Michele was insinuatingly amiable to Beltraffio. He took,—or pretended to take,—the liveliest concern for the fate of Cassandra, and believed in her innocence; and, at the same time, dissembling as an ardent admirer of Leonardo, "the greatest of the Christian masters," as he expressed himself, questioned the pupil of the life, habits, occupations and thoughts of the master. But, the moment the conversation touched upon Leonardo, Giovanni would be on his guard, and would rather have died than betray the master with a single word. Becoming convinced that trickeries were in vain, Fra Michele took occasion to announce one day that, despite the short term of their acquaintance, he had come to love Giovanni as a brother, and that he deemed it his duty to forewarn him of the danger threatening him from Messer da Vinci, suspected of sorcery and black magic.

"'Tis a lie!" exclaimed Giovanni. "He never occupied himself with black magic, and even . . ."

Beltraffio did not finish. The inquisitor gave him a prolonged look.

"What would you say, Messer Giovanni?"

"Nay,—'tis naught."

"You do not want to be frank with me, my friend. For I know,—you would say: 'Messer Leonardo even does not believe in the possibility of black magic.'"

"The Devil," the monk retorted with a quiet smile, "is a most excellent logician. At times he nonplusses his most experienced opponents.

From a certain witch we recently learned his speech at the Sabbath. 'My children,' he had said, 'rejoice and make merry, inasmuch as with the aid of our new allies, the men of science who, denying the might of the devil, do by that very thing dull the sword of the Most Holy Inquisition, we shall within a short time sustain a perfect victory, and shall spread our realm throughout all creation.'"

Calmly and assuredly did Fra Michele speak of the most incredible actions of the Unclean Power; for instance, of the signs whereby are distinguishable the changeling infants, born of fiends and witches: while always remaining small, they are considerably heavier than normal infants at breast, weighing from eighty to a hundred pounds, constantly caterwauling and sucking dry the milk of five or six wet-nurses. With mathematical precision he knew the number of the chief rulers of Hades,—572; as for the subjects, the junior fiends of different ranks, their number was 7, 405, 926.

But Giovanni was especially struck by his learning concerning the Incubi and Succubi,—bisexual demons, who took on, at will, the shape either of man or woman, in order that, by tempting people, they might enter into carnal congress with them. The monk explained how the fiends, now solidifying the air, now purloining corpses from the gallows, did form bodies for their lust,—which bodies, however, during the most fiery caresses remain cold, like dead bodies. He was citing the words of St. Augustine, who denied the existence of the Antipodes as a blasphemous heresy, and had no doubt of the existence of Incubi and Succubi; these, on a time,—so it seemed,—had been revered by pagans under the appellation of fauns, satyrs, nymphs, hamadryads, and other deities, dwelling in trees, water and air.

"Even as in antiquity," Fra Michele added on his own authority, "the unclean gods and goddesses would descend to mortals for their abominable miscegenation, so even now, in precisely the same way, not only the younger, but even the mightiest of demons,—as, for instance, Apollo and Bacchus,—can appear as Incubi; or Diana and Venus as Succubi."

From these words Giovanni could conclude that the White She-Demon, who had been haunting him all his life, was the Succubus Aphrodite.

Sometimes Fra Michele would invite him into the Judgment Hall during an inquest,—probably still hoping, sooner or later, to find in him a confederate and informer, knowing by experience the fascination of the horrors of the Inquisition. Overcoming his fear and aversion, Giovanni did not refuse to be present at the interrogations and tortures, because he, in his turn, had hopes, if not of lightening the fate of Cassandra, at least of learning something about her. Partly in the Judgment Hall, partly from the stories of the inquisitor, Giovanni learned almost incredible instances, in which the ludicrous was united with the horrible.

One witch, an altogether young little girl, having repented and returned to the bosom of the Church, blessed her torturers for that they did save her from the claws of Satan, enduring all tortures with infinite fortitude and meekness, joyously and quietly waiting for death, believing that the temporary fire would deliver her from the eternal; the only thing she implored from her judges was to cut the devil out of her hand, who had apparently entered in the guise of a sharp spindle. The Holy Fathers called in an experienced chirurgeon. But, despite the large sum offered him, the leech refused to cut out the devil, fearing lest the fiend wring his neck during the operation.

Another witch, the wife of a bread-baker, a hale and handsome woman, was accused of begetting several changelings during her liaison of eighteen years' duration with the devil. This unfortunate creature, during the most fearful tortures, would, by turns, pray, bark like a dog, or turn numb from pain, losing speech and consciousness, so that they had to open her mouth by force with a special wooden contrivance, to compel her to speak; finally, tearing herself out of the hands of her executioners, she fell upon her judges, with a frenzied scream: "I have given my soul up to the devil, and shall belong to him forever!"—and fell down lifeless.

Monna Sidonia, Cassandra's reputed aunt, who had also been seized, had, in order to escape the tortures, set fire to the straw litter on which she lay in prison, one night, and suffocated from the smoke.

A half-witted huckstress of rags, a little crone, was proven to have gone to the Sabbath every night astride her own daughter, whose arms and legs were maimed, and which the devils, now, used to shoe with horseshoes. Good-naturedly and slyly winking to the judges, as though they were her confidants in a prearranged prank, the little old woman willingly agreed with all the accusations brought against her. She felt very chill. "The little fire! The little fire!" she mumbled in her joy, spluttering from laughter as very little children do, and rubbing her hands, as she was led up to the flaming bonfire, in order to be burned.

"God send you health, my dear little ones,—at last I shall warm myself!"

A girl, of some ten years, without shame or fear told the judges how one evening, in the cattle yard, her mistress, a dairy-woman, had given her a piece of bread and butter, sprinkled over with something sour-sweet,—very tasty. This was a devil. When she had eaten the bread, a tom-cat with eyes blazing like coals ran up to her, and began rubbing up against her, purring and arching his back. She went with him into a hay-rick and here, on the straw, gave herself up to him, and many times, in mischievous play, without thinking it any evil, permitted him all he desired. The dairy-woman had said: "See, what a bride-groom thou hast!" And after that she gave birth to a great white worm with a black head, the size of an infant at breast. She buried it in some manure. But the tom-cat came to her, scratched her all up, and in a human voice bade her nurture the child, the greedy worm, with milk fresh from the cow.—The girl told this with such exactness and detail, gazing at her inquisitors with such innocent eyes, that it was hard to decide whether she was lying with a strange aimless mendacity, at times natural to children, or whether she was delirious.

But an especial, unforgettable horror was aroused in Giovanni by a sixteen-year-old witch, of an unusual beauty, who to all the questions and admonitions of her judges replied with ever the same obstinate, undeviatingly imploring cry: "Burn me up! Burn me!" She asserted that the devil was "leisurely walking through her body, as though in his own house," and that when "he was scampering, rolling within her spine, just like a rat under the floor," there was such an eerie, such a languorous feeling in her heart, that, if her hands had not been held back or if she had not been tied up with ropes at such times, she would have shattered her head against a wall. Of repentance and forgiveness she would not hear, inasmuch as she deemed herself pregnant by the devil, irretrievably lost, condemned even in life by the Eternal Judgment, and implored that she be burned before the monster was born. She was an orphan, and very rich. After her death her enormous estate was to pass into the hands of a distant relative, a miserly old man. The Holy Fathers knew that if the unfortunate remained among the living, she would donate all her riches for the work of the Inquisition, and therefore endeavoured to save her, but in vain. Finally they sent to her a priest who was famed for his skill in softening the hearts of obdurate sinners. When he began assuring her that there was not, nor could be, any sin whatsoever which the Lord had not redeemed with His Blood, and that He would forgive all, she answered with her fearful cry: "He will not forgive,—He will not forgive,—I know! Burn me, or I shall lay hands on myself!" As Fra Michele expressed it, "Her soul thirsted after the holy fire, even as a wounded hart thirsteth after the spring of waters."

The Chief Inquisitor, Fra Giorgio da Casale, was a bowed little old man, with a peaked, pale little face, kindly, calm and simple, recalling the face of St. Francis. According to the words of those who knew him intimately, he was "the meekest of men on earth," most disinterested, a keeper of fasts, like one who had taken a vow of silence, and absolutely continent. At times, when Giovanni would contemplate his face closely, it seemed to him that there really was no malice or guile in him, that he suffered more than his victims, and tortured and burned them out of compassion, because he believed it impossible to save them otherwise from the eternal fire. But at times, especially during the most refined tortures and monstrous confessions, there would suddenly glimmer in the eyes of Fra Giorgio an expression such that Giovanni could not decide which was more dreadful, more insane,—the judges or the judged.

On one occasion an old witch, a midwife, told the inquisitors how, with a pressure of her thumb, she was wont to crush in the crown of new-born babes, and had by this means done to death more than two hundred infants, without any aim, merely because she liked the way the soft little skulls of the children crunched, like to egg-shells. Describing this amusement, she laughed with such laughter that a chill ran down Giovanni's back.—And suddenly it appeared to him that the old inquisitor's eyes were burning with the same voluptuous fire as the witch's. And although at the next instant he thought that he had merely imagined this, still the impression of an unspeakable horror persisted in his soul.

Another time, with humble remorse, Fra Giorgio confessed that, more than by all his other sins, he was tormented by his conscience for that many years ago, "out of a criminal compassion, inspired by the devil," he had ordered some seven-year-old children, suspected of lustful congress with Incubi and Succubi, instead of being burned, to be merely flogged with twigs on the square before the fires wherein their fathers and mothers were burning.

The madness which reigned within the walls of the Inquisition among the victims and executioners spread through the town. People of common sense believed in that which they laughed at as silly tales during the ordinary times. Denunciations multiplied. Servants pointed out their masters, children their parents. One old crone was burned merely because she had said: "May the Devil help me, God will not!" Another was declared a witch, because her cow, in the opinion of her neighbours, was giving three times as much milk as she should have been.

A devil, in the shape of a dog, got in the habit of coming, well-nigh every day after the *Ave Maria*, into the nunnery of Santa Maria della Scala, and did defile in turn all the nuns, from the sixteen-year-old novice to the decrepit abbess, not only in their cells, but in the church proper, during services. The sisters at Santa Maria became so habituated to the devil that they no longer feared him and were not ashamed before him. And this had endured for eight years.

In the mountainous settlements near Bergamo had been found one and forty cannibal-witches, who sucked the blood and devoured the flesh of unchristened babes. In Milan itself were convicted thirty priests, who did baptize children "not in the name of the Father, the Son, and the Holy Ghost, but in the name of the Devil"; women who dedicated their unborn children to Satan; girls and boys from three to six, who, tempted of the devil, had given themselves up to unspeakable lechery,—experienced inquisitors recognized these children by a particular glitter in their eyes, by their languishing smile, and their moist, exceedingly red lips. There was no way of saving them, save through fire.

And most fearful of all seemed the fact that, in proportion to the growing zeal of the Fathers Inquisitors, the fiends not only did not cease, but, on the contrary, multiplied their afflictions, as though they were getting into the way of relishing the thing and were playful.

In the abandoned laboratory of Messer Galeotto Sacrobosco was found an unusually fat, shaggy devil,—some asserted it had been found alive, others that it had just died, but had been exceedingly well-preserved,—imprisoned, so it was told, within a lentil-shaped crystal; and although, upon investigation, it proved to be no devil at all but a flea, which the alchemist had been studying through a magnifying glass, many still retained their conviction that this was a veritable devil, but that he had metamorphosed himself into a flea in the hands of the inquisitors, in order to mock them.

All things seemed possible; the dividing boundary line between reality and delirium was disappearing. There were rumours current that Fra Giorgio had discovered in Lombardy the compact of twelve thousand witches and wizards, who had sworn to bring about within three years such bad crops through all Italy that people would be compelled to devour one another like beasts.

The Chief Inquisitor himself, an experienced commander in the Army of Christ, who had made a study of the devices of the foe, experienced bewilderment, almost fear, before this aggressive advance of the Satanic cohorts.

"I know not wherein this will end," Fra Michele had once said in a frank discussion with Giovanni. "The more of them we burn the more new ones spring up out of their ashes."

The usual tortures,—Spanish boots; iron stocks, gradually constricted by screws, so that the bones of the victims crunched; the tearing out of nails with red-hot pincers,—all seemed child's play in comparison with the new refined tortures invented by the "meekest of men," Fra Giorgio; for instance, the torture by sleeplessness,—*tormentum insomnia*,—consisting of driving the accused through the passages of the prison, for several days and nights, without allowing them to fall asleep, till their feet were full of sores and the unfortunates went mad. But even at these tortures did the Enemy laugh, inasmuch as He was to such a degree stronger than hunger, sleep, thirst, iron, and fire, as the spirit is stronger than the flesh.

In vain did the judges have recourse to guiles: leading the witches within the walls backwards, that their gaze might not bewitch the judge nor inspire him with a criminal pity; stripping, before torture, the women and children to the skin and shaving them without leaving a hair on their bodies, in order that the inquisitor might the easier search for the "seal of the devil,"—*stigma diabolicum*,—which, hiding under the skin or in the hair, made the witch insensible to pain; giving them holy water to drink and sprinkling them with it; keeping the instruments of torture in the fumes of incense and consecrating them with particles of the Offertory of the Consecrated Wafer and of the bodies of saints; putting about the waist of each witch a belt of cloth the length of the Lord's body, and hanging thereto scraps of paper on which were marked the words uttered on the Cross by the Saviour. Naught availed: the Enemy triumphed over all these sanctities.

The nuns, who were repentant of their lustful cohabitation with the devil, averred that he had gone into them between two *Ave Marias*, and that, even while having the Holy Communion in their mouths, they felt their accursed lover defiling them with the most shameless of caresses. Sobbing, the unfortunates confessed that "their bodies belonged to him together with their souls."

Through the lips of the witches in the Judgment Hall the Wily One derided the inquisitors, uttering such blasphemies that the most intrepid felt their hair stand up on end, and he nonplussed the doctors and Magisters of Theology with a most cunningly woven web of sophisms, the most refined theological contradictions, or else exposed them with questions, full of such a clairvoyance of their hearts, that the judges were transformed into the judged, the accusers became the accused.

The despondence of the citizens reached its extreme when the rumour spread of the denunciation supposed to have been received by the Pope, with incontrovertible proofs, that the wolf in sheep's clothing, who had penetrated into the fold of the Pastor; that the servant of the devil, who pretended to be his persecutor, in order the more surely to send to perdition the flock of Christ, that the head of the Satanic cohorts,—was none other than the Grand Inquisitor of Julius II, Fra Giorgio da Casale.

Judging by the words and actions of the judges, Beltraffio could conclude that the power of the Devil seemed to them equal to the power of God, and that it was not at all known which would prove the victor in this single combat. He wondered how these two teachings—that of the inquisitor, Fra Giorgio, and of the witch Cassandra—met in their extremes, inasmuch as for both of them the sky above was equal to the sky below, the meaning of human life consisted of the struggle of two abysses in the heart of man,—with but this difference that the witch was still seeking perhaps an unattainable reconcilement, whereas the inquisitor was fanning the fire of this enmity and intensifying its hopelessness.

And in the image of the Devil, with whom Fra Giorgio was so hopelessly contending, in the image of the Serpentine One, the Reptilian, the Sly, Giovanni recognized the image—dimmed, as though in a tarnished, distorting mirror—of the Beneficent Serpent, the Winged One, the Ophiomorphos, Son of the Superior Liberating Wisdom, the Light-Carrier, like to Lucifer the Morning Star, or Prometheus the Titan.

The impotent hatred of his enemies, the sorry servants of Ialdabaoth, seemed a new pæan of victory for the Invincible One.

At this time Fra Giorgio announced to the people a magnificent festa,—designated to take place in a few days, for the joy of the faithful children of the Church of Christ,—the Auto-da-fé on the Piazza Broletto of one hundred and thirty-nine wizards and witches. Hearing of this from Fra Michele, Giovanni uttered, blanching:

"And Monna Cassandra?"

Despite the hypocritical communicativeness of the monk, Giovanni knew naught about her to that very day.

"Monna Cassandra," answered the Dominican, "has been condemned together with the others, although she merits the worst of punishment. Fra Giorgio deems her the most powerful of the witches he has ever encountered. So insuperable are the charms of insensibility which gird her about during tortures, that, to say naught of confession or repentance, we have not, after all, succeeded in getting a single word nor a moan out of her,—we have not heard as much as the sound of her voice."

And, having said this, he looked into the eyes of Giovanni with a penetrating gaze, as though expectant. A thought flashed through Beltraffio's mind to end everything at once,—to inform against himself, to confess that he was a confederate of Cassandra's, that he might perish with her. He did not do so not out of fear, but out of indifference,—a strange lethargy which possessed him more and more during the last days, and resembling the "charms of insensibility" which had encompassed the witch during her tortures. He was as calm as the dead are calm.

IV

On the following day Beltraffio did not leave his room. He felt unwell since morning, and his head ached. He lay in bed till evening, in a half-daze, thinking of naught.

When it had grown dark, there was heard over the city an unusual clangour of bells, calling to one another,—a clangour that was both funereal and festal,—and through the air spread a faint but persistent and repulsive odour of burning. This odour made his head ache still worse, and he felt nausea. He went out into the street.

The day had been sultry, with the air raw and warm, as in a bath,—one of those days which occur in Lombardy during the sirocco, in late summer and early autumn. There was no rain, yet moisture was dripping from the roofs and trees. The brick pavement glistened. And under the open sky, in the turbidly-yellow viscid fog the malodorous smell of burning was still stronger. Despite the late hour, the streets were thickly peopled. Everybody was coming from one direction,—the Piazza Broletto. When he scrutinized their faces, it seemed to him that all whom he met were in the same half-daze as he,—they wanted to awake, and could not.

The crowd hummed with an indistinct low rumble. Suddenly, by fragmentary words which reached him by chance,—concerning the one hundred and thirty-nine wizards and witches just burned, concerning Monna Cassandra,—he understood the reason for the fearful odour which was pursuing him: it was the stench of charred human bodies.

He did not remember how he made his way to the cloister of San Francesco and entered the cell of Fra Benedetto. The monks admitted him; Fra Benedetto was away,—he had gone to Bergamo. Giovanni locked the door, lit a candle, and fell on the bed in exhaustion. In this peaceful abode, so familiar to him, all things preserved their former atmosphere of calm and sanctity. He breathed more freely; the fearful evil stench was absent,—the odour peculiar to monasteries prevailed.

At the head of the cot, on the smooth white wall, hung a black Crucifix, and, above it, the gift of Giovanni,—a dried little garland of scarlet poppies and dark violets, gathered on that memorable morning in the grove of cypresses on the heights of Fiesole, at the feet of Savonarola, when the brethren of San Marco had been chanting, playing on viols, and dancing around the master, like little children or cherubim.

He raised his eyes to the Crucifix. The Saviour still spread out His nailed hands as of yore, as though calling the Universe to His embraces: "Come unto me, all *ye* that labour and are heavy laden."[60] "Is this not the sole, the perfect truth?" reflected Giovanni. "Shall I not fall at His feet, shall I not cry out: Yea, Lord, I believe,—help me Thou in my unbelief!"

But prayer died away on his lips. And he felt that though eternal perdition were impending for him, he would not be able to lie, to be unknowing of that which he knew,—would be able neither to deny nor to reconcile the two truths which were contending in his heart. In his former quiet despair he turned away from the Crucifix,—and at the same instant it seemed to him that the malodorous fog, the frightful smell of burning, was penetrating even within here, within this last refuge. He covered his face with his hands.

And before him appeared that which he had beheld recently,—although he could not have told whether it had been in a dream or in reality: in the depth of the recess in the wall, in the reflection of a red flame, amidst the implements of tortures and the executioners, amid bloody human bodies, he saw the denuded body of Cassandra, guarded by the spells of the Beneficent Serpent, the Liberator; insensible under the implements of torture, under iron, fire, and the eyes of the torturers,—incorruptible, invulnerable, like the virginally pure and firm marble of carved sculptures.

Regaining his senses, he understood, from the guttering candle and by counting the strokes of the bell on an adjacent belfry, that several hours had passed in oblivion, and that now it was already past midnight. Everything was still. The fog must have dispersed. The evil odour was no more, but the air had grown still sultrier. Pale blue heat-lightnings flashed through the windows, and, as on that memorable, ominous night near the Catarana dam, one could hear the dull rumbling of thunder, seeming to come from underground.

His head was spinning; his mouth felt parched; he was tortured by thirst. He remembered that a pitcher of water stood in the corner. Getting up, holding on to the wall with one hand, he dragged himself up to the pitcher, took a few gulps, wet his head, and was about to return to the cot, when he felt some presence in the cell,—he turned around, and saw someone sitting on Fra Benedetto's cot, beneath the black Crucifix, in a black monastic garment that reached to the ground, with a pointed cowl, like those of the Battuti brethren, which covered the face. Giovanni wondered, inasmuch as he knew that the door was locked, but did not become frightened. He felt, rather, a relief, as though only now, after long efforts, he had become awake. His head immediately ceased to ache.

He approached the sitter and began a close scrutiny. The latter got up,—the cowl fell back. And Giovanni beheld the face,—immobile, pallid, like the marble of carved sculptures, with lips as scarlet as blood, with eyes as yellow as amber, surrounded by an aureole of black hair, more alive than the very face, as though endowed with a separate life, like the snakes of Medusa.

And, slowly and solemnly, as though for an incantation, Cassandra —for it was she—lifted up her arms. Reverberations of thunder were heard, by now near, and it seemed to him that the voice of the thunder was repeating her words:

Heaven above,—heaven below,
Stars above,—stars below,
All that is above is also below,—
If thou comprehendest, weal betide thee.

The black garments, winding, fell to her feet,—and he saw the refulgent candour of her body, incorruptible, like that of Aphrodite, come out of her tomb of a thousand years,—like that of Venus Anadyomene of Sandro Botticelli, with the face of the Most Pure Virgin Mary, with unearthly sorrow in her eyes,—like that of the voluptuous Leda on the flaming bonfire of Savonarola.

Giovanni cast a last look at the Crucifix, a last horror-filled thought flashed through his mind: "The White She-Demon!"—and the curtain of life seemed to be rent asunder before his eyes, revealing the ultimate mystery of an ultimate reconcilement.

She approached him, seized him in her arms, and folded him in her embrace. A blinding flash of lightning united heaven and earth. They sank on the humble couch of the monk. And with all his body Giovanni felt the virginal chill of her body, which was as delectable and as fearful to him as death.

V

Zoroastro da Peretola had not died from the consequences of his fall at his unsuccessful attempt with wings, but neither had he gotten over them completely,—he remained a cripple for all life. He forgot how to talk, merely muttering incomprehensible words, so that none save the master could understand him. He would roam through the house, without finding a place for himself, limping on his crutches, enormous, ungainly, with rumpled hair, like a sick bird; or he would listen intently to what people were saying, as though trying to understand something; or sitting in a corner, with his legs tucked in under him, without paying any attention to anybody, would rapidly wind a broad ribbon of cloth upon a round spool,—an occupation gotten up for him by the master, since the hands of the mechanic retained their former skill and necessity for action; he whittled sticks out of wood, sawed out small blocks for skittles, carved out spinning tops; or else, for hours at a time, in a half-daze, with a senseless smile, swaying, and waving his arms as though they were wings, purred under his nose a never-varying song:

> Birds cry, birds cry;
> Cranes fly, eagles fly,
> Midst the sun's haze on high
> Where no earth meets the eye;
> Cranes fly, cranes fly;
> Birds cry, birds cry. . . .

Then, looking at the master with his only eye, he would suddenly begin to weep. At such moments he was so piteous that Leonardo would turn away as quickly as he could, or go away. But to put the sick man away entirely he had not the heart. Never, in all his wanderings, did he abandon him, taking care of him, sending him money, and, as soon as he himself was settled in any place, would take him into his own house. Thus years passed, and this cripple was a sort of living reproach, an eternal mockery at Leonardo's life-long effort,—the creation of human wings.

Not less was his pity for another pupil of his,—perhaps the one who was closest to his heart,—Cesare da Sesto. Not content with imitation, Cesare was fain to be himself. But the master annihilated him, absorbed him, transformed him into a part of his own personality. Not sufficiently weak to submit, nor sufficiently strong to conquer, Cesare could but endure inescapable torture, growing malevolent, and unable to find either complete salvation or complete perdition. Like to Giovanni and Astro, he was a cripple,—neither dead nor alive, one of those whom Leonardo had put under his "evil eye," whom he had "spoiled."

Andrea Salaino informed Leonardo of the secret correspondence of Cesare with the pupils of Raphael Sanzio, who was working for Pope Julius II in Rome on the frescoes in the chambers of the Vatican. Many predicted that in the rays of this new luminary the glory of Leonardo was fated to grow dim. At times it seemed to the master that Cesare was contemplating treachery.

But the loyalty of the artist's friends was probably worse than the treachery of his foes.

Under the name of the Academy of Leonardo there had been formed in Milan a school of young Lombardian painters, partly consisting of his former pupils, partly of newcomers beyond number, who multiplied, crowding about him, imagining that they were following in his footsteps, and assuring others to that effect. From a distance he followed the bustling activity of these innocent traitors, who knew not themselves what they wrought. And at times there would arise in him a feeling of squeamishness, as he beheld how all that was holy and great in his life was becoming the property of the rabble,—the countenance of the Lord in The Last Supper being transmitted to posterity in copies which reconciled it with churchly vulgarity; the smile of Gioconda, shamelessly exposed, becoming lecherous, or else, transmuted in reveries of Platonic love, growing benign and foolish.

In the winter of fifteen hundred and twelve, in the little town of Riva di Trento, on the shore of the Lake of Garda, died Marc Antonio della Torre, thirty-one years of age, after contracting putrid fever from some poor people he had been treating. Leonardo was losing in him the last one of those who, even though they were not near to him, were strangers in a lesser degree than others.

One winter night Leonardo was sitting in his chamber, hearkening to the howling of the tempest, just as on the night of that day when he had learned of the death of Gioconda. The inhuman voices of the night wind spoke of that which was understandable to the human heart, of that which was kindred and inevitable to it: of the last loneliness in the fearful, blind darkness, in the bosom of ancient Chaos, the Father of all being; of the boundless tedium of this world. He pondered upon death, and this thought, which now came to him more and more frequently, mingled with the thought of Gioconda.

Suddenly there came a knocking at the door. He arose and unlocked it. An unknown youth walked into the room, with merry and kindly eyes, with the glow of the frost on his fresh face; stars of snow were melting in his dark red curls.

"Messer Leonardo!" exclaimed the youth. "Do you not recognize me?"

Leonardo looked at him attentively, and recognized his little friend, Francesco Melzi, the eight-year-old boy with whom he had taken rambles through the vernal groves of Vaprio. He embraced him with fatherly tenderness. Francesco told him that he was come from Bologna, whither his father had gone shortly after the French invasion in the year fifteen hundred, not desiring to see the disgrace and tribulations of his native land, and where he had become seriously ill, which illness had lasted for many long years; recently he had died, and young Melzi had hastened to Leonardo, remembering the latter's promise.

"What promise?" asked the master.

"What? Have you forgot? And here was silly me, hoping! . . . But do you really not remember? . . . It was during the last days before our parting, in the settlement of Mandello, near the lake of Lecco, at the foot of Monte Campione. We were descending into an abandoned mine, and you were carrying me in your arms, lest I fall; and when you told me that you were departing for Romagna, to enter the service of Cæsar Borgia, I fell to crying and would have run away with you from my father, but you would not have this, and gave me your word that in seven years, when I would grow up . . ."

"I remember, I remember!" the master interrupted him joyously.

"Well, now! I know, Messer Leonardo, that you need me not. But then, I will not be in the way, either. Indeed, drive me not away. However, even if you were to do so, 'tis no matter,—I would not go away under any circumstances. . . . As you will, master, do with me what you want, but I will nevermore leave you. . . ."

"My dear little lad!—" murmured Leonardo, and his voice quavered. He embraced him anew, kissing his head, and Francesco clave to his bosom with the same trusting tenderness as the little boy whom Leonardo had carried in his arms into the iron mine, descending lower and lower into the subterranean murk, down the slippery, fearful stairs.

VI

SINCE the artist's abandonment of Florence in fifteen hundred and seven, he had ranked as the court painter in the service of the French King, Louis XII. But, not receiving any salary, he was compelled to depend upon favours. Frequently he was forgotten altogether, whereas he did not know how to bring himself to notice by his productions, because with the passing of the years he worked less and more slowly. As formerly, being in constant need and becoming more and more involved in monetary matters, he borrowed from all he could,—even his own pupils; and, without settling his old debts, contracted new ones. He wrote the same sort of shamefaced, awkward and degrading requests to the French viceroy, Charles d'Amboise, and to Florimond Roberte, that he had at one time written to Duke Moro.

In the anterooms of nobles, amid the other petitioners, he would resignedly await his turn, although, with oncoming old age, more and more steep did the stairs of strangers become, and more and more bitter the taste of strangers' bread. He felt himself just as superfluous in the service of princes as he had on a time felt himself in the service of the people,—always, everywhere the stranger. While Raphael, availing himself of the generosity of the Pope, had from a half-beggar become a rich man, a Roman patrician; while Michelangelo was hoarding his soldi against a rainy day,—Leonardo, as before, remained a homeless wanderer, knowing not where he would lay down his head at his death.

He had decided to forsake Milan and go over to the service of the Medicis.

Pope Julius II died. Giovanni de' Medici was chosen as his successor, under the name of Leo X. The new Pope designated his brother Giuliano as the Chief Captain and Standard-Bearer of the Church of Rome, —a post filled at one time by Cæsar Borgia. Giuliano set out for Rome. Leonardo was to follow him thither in the autumn.

A few days before his departure from Milan, at sunrise after the night when the hundred and thirty-nine wizards and witches had been burned on the Piazza Broletto, the monks in the cloister of San Francesco had found in the cell of Fra Benedetto Leonardo's pupil, Giovanni Beltraffio, lying insensible on the floor. Evidently, this was an attack of the same ailment as that of fifteen years ago, after the story of Fra Pagolo concerning the death of Savonarola. But this time Giovanni recovered rapidly. Only occasionally, in his apathetic eyes, in his strangely immobile, seemingly dead face, there would flash an expression which inspired Leonardo with a greater fear for him than his former serious illness. Still cherishing a hope of saving him by putting him away from himself, from his "evil eye," the master advised him to remain in Milan with Fra Benedetto, until complete recovery. But Giovanni implored not to be abandoned, with such unshakable obstinacy, with such quiet despair, that Leonardo had not the heart to refuse.

The French troops were approaching Milan. The rabble was turbulent. Procrastination was out of the question. And, even as he had once departed from Lorenzo de' Medici to Moro, from Moro to Cæsar, from Cæsar to Soderini, from Soderini to Louis XII, Leonardo, the eternal wanderer, continuing his hopeless travels with a sad resignation, was now departing to his new patron, Giuliano de' Medici.

"On the 23rd of September, in the year 1513," he noted in his diary with his wonted brevity, "I set out from Milan for Rome, with Francesco Melzi, Salaino, Cesare, Astro, and Giovanni."

BOOK SIXTEEN

Leonardo, Michelangelo, and Raphael

I

OPE LEO X, FAITHFUL TO THE TRADITIONS OF the House of Medici, was able to attain the celebrity of a great Mæcenas of the arts and sciences. Learning of his elevation, he said to his brother, Giuliano de' Medici:

"Let us have our fill of delight of Papal sovereignty, since God hath granted it to us!"

And his favourite fool, the monk Fra Mariano, added with philosophical pompousness:

"We shall live, Holy Father, for our pleasure,—for all else is but nonsense!"

And the Pope surrounded himself with poets, musicians, artists, savants. Anyone who could compose prolific verses, which could even be mediocre, as long as they were polished, could reckon upon a fat prebend, upon a snug post from His Holiness. An Age of Gold was inaugurated for imitative rhetoricians, who had a single unshaken faith,—in the unattainable perfection of the prose of Cicero and the verses of Vergil. "The mere thought," they would say, "that the new poets can surpass the ancient is the root of all impiety."

These pastors of Christian souls avoided mentioning Christ by name in their sermons, since this word did not exist in the orations of Cicero; the nuns they styled vestals, the Holy Ghost the Breath of Supreme Jupiter, and petitioned the Pope for permission to add Plato to the number of Saints.

The composer of *Azolani*, a dialogue of a love not of this earth, and of *Priapus*, a poem of unbelievable impudicity, a future Cardinal, Pietro Bembo, confessed that he did not read the epistles of Paul the Apostle, "lest he corrupt his own style."

When Francis I, after his victory over the Pope, demanded from him as a gift the recently discovered Laocoön, Leo X declared that he would sooner part with the head of Peter the Apostle—the sacred remains of which were preserved in Rome—than with the Laocoön.

The Pope liked his savants and his artists, but hardly more than he did his fools. The notorious poetaster, glutton and drunkard, Querno, who had received the rank of Archpoet, he laureated in a festal triumph with a garland of red cabbage and had showered him with the same munificent gifts as he had Raphael Sanzio. On his magnificent feasts for men of learning he spent the enormous revenues from the Marco of Ancona, from Spoleto and Romagna; but was himself noted for his moderation, inasmuch as the stomach of His Holiness digested but poorly. This Epicurean suffered from an incurable complaint,—a putrid fistula. And his soul, even as his body, was consumed by a secret canker,—ennui. He imported for his bestiarium rare animals from far lands; for his collection of fools,—amusing cripples, monsters, and madmen out of hospitals. But neither animals nor humans could divert him. On holidays and feasts, amidst the merriest pranks, an expression of ennui and squeamishness would not leave his face. Only in politics did he show his true nature: he was just as cruel and perjurious as Borgia.

When Leo X was lying on his death-bed, abandoned of all, the monk Fra Mariano, his favourite fool, possibly his sole friend, and who had remained faithful to him to the end,—a man kindly and pious,—seeing that the Pope was dying like a pagan, did implore him with tears: "Recall God, Holy Father,—recall God!" This was an unintentional, but at the same time the most malicious mockery at the eternal mocker.

A few days after his arrival in Rome, in the reception room of the Pope, in the palace of the Vatican, Leonardo was awaiting his turn, since to attain an audience with the Pope was an exceedingly difficult matter even for those whom the Pope had expressed a desire to see. Leonardo was listening to the talk of the courtiers, concerning the proposed triumphal procession of the Papal favourite, the monstrous dwarf Baraballo, who was to be led about the streets upon an elephant recently sent from India. They also related the new exploits of Fra Mariano,—of how the other day, at supper, in the presence of the Pope, jumping up on a table, he had started running about, amid general laughter, slamming the Cardinals and Bishops over the head, throwing and catching fried capons from one end of the table to the other, so that the sauces ran in streams over the garments and faces of Their Reverences.

While Leonardo was listening to the story, from behind the doors of the reception room came the sounds of music and singing. Upon the faces made haggard by expectancy there appeared a still greater despondence. The Pope was a poor but a passionate musician. The concerts, in which he always took part, lasted endlessly, so that those who came to him upon business would fall into despair at the sound of music.

"Do you know, messer," the man who was sitting next to Leonardo —an unrecognized poet, with a hungry visage, who had been vainly awaiting his turn for three months—said in Leonardo's ear, "do you know the means of obtaining an audience with His Holiness? Declare yourself a jester. My old friend, the famous scholar Marco Masuro, seeing that one can do naught with learning here, ordered the Papal chamberlain to announce him as a new Baraballo,—and he was at once received, and obtained all that he desired."

Leonardo did not follow the good counsel, and once again, having waited in vain, took his departure. Latterly he had been experiencing strange premonitions. They seemed to him baseless. Worldly cares, his ill-successes at the court of Leo X and Giuliano de' Medici, did not disquiet him,—he had long since grown used to them. But nevertheless his ominous disquiet increased. And especially on this refulgent autumnal evening, as he was returning home from the palace, did his heart dully ache, as before a nearing evil.

During his second stay in Rome he was living in the same place he had lived in before, when Alexander VI had been alive,—a few steps away from the Vatican, behind the Cathedral of St. Peter, in a narrow lane, in one of the small, isolated buildings of the Papal Mint.

He entered a spacious, vaulted chamber, with spiderlike cracks upon the peeling walls, with windows abutting on the wall of an adjacent house, so that, despite the early, clear evening, it was already dark here. In a corner, with his legs tucked in under him, sat the ailing mechanic Astro, whittling some sticks or other, and, as was his wont, purring the despondent little song under his breath as he swayed:

Birds cry, birds cry;
Cranes fly, eagles fly,
Midst the sun's haze on high
Where no earth meets the eye;
Cranes fly, cranes fly;
Birds cry, birds cry. . . .

Leonardo's heart throbbed still more from the dull ache of his prophetic sadness.

"What is it, Astro?" he asked kindly, laying his hand on the mechanic's head.

"'Tis naught," answered the other, and looked at the master intently, almost intelligently,—even slyly. "There is naught the matter with me. But Giovanni, now. . . . Oh, well, he is better off as it is. . . . He has taken wing. . . ."

"What art thou saying, Astro? Where is Giovanni?" asked Leonardo,—and suddenly understood that the prophetic sadness wherewith his heart dully ached was for him,—for Giovanni.

Paying no further attention to the master, the invalid fell to whittling anew.

"Astro," Leonardo approached him, and took his hand, "I beg of thee, my friend, recall what thou wouldst have said. Where is Giovanni? Dost hear, Astro,—I have urgent need of seeing him at once! . . . Where is he? What is the matter with him?"

"Why, do you not know yet?" uttered the invalid. "He is there, above. His thirst he did allay. . . . He has gone away. . . ."

He was evidently seeking and could not find the necessary sound, which slipped his memory. This was of frequent occurrence with him. He confused individual sounds and even entire words, using one in place of another.

"You do not know?" he added, calmly. "Well, let us go. I will show you. Only be not afraid. 'Tis for the best. . . ."

He arose, and unwieldily shifting his weight on his crutches, led him up a creaking staircase. They entered the garret. It was sultry here from the tiled roof heated by the sun; there was a smell of bird-droppings and straw. Through a dormer window penetrated an oblique, dusty, red ray of the sun. When they entered, a flock of pigeons, frightened, fluttered up with a rustling of wings and flew off.

"There," uttered Astro, with his former calmness, pointing to the interior of the garret, where it was dark.

And Leonardo saw, below one of the transverse, thick beams, Giovanni standing erect,—immovably, strangely drawn out and seemingly staring straight at him with his widely open eyes.

"Giovanni!" cried out the master, and suddenly blanched, his voice breaking.

He ran toward him, beheld the fearfully distorted face, and touched his hand; it was cold. The body gave a lurch; it was hanging upon a strong silken cord,—one of those the master used for his flying machine, tied to a new iron hook, evidently recently screwed into the beam. A piece of soap was also lying near, with which the suicide must have soaped the noose.

Astro, again becoming lost in musing, approached the dormer window and looked out.

The building stood on a little knoll. From this height there opened up a vista of the tile roofs, the turrets, the belfries of Rome; of the turbidly green plain of the Campagna, undulating like a sea, and bathed in the rays of the setting sun, with the long, black, occasionally torn threads of the Roman aqueducts; the mountains of Albano, Frascati, Rocca di Papa, and the clear sky, where swallows were darting. He looked, and with a beatific smile, swaying, waved his arms as though they were wings:

Birds cry, birds cry;
Cranes fly, eagles fly. . . .

Leonardo wanted to run, to summon help, but could not stir, and stood in the catalepsy of horror, between his two pupils,—the dead and the insane. . . .

A few days after, going through the papers of the deceased, the master found a diary among them. He read it attentively. Those contradictions from which Giovanni had perished Leonardo did not comprehend; he only came to feel, more clearly than ever before, that he had been the cause of this perishing,—he had "put the evil eye upon him," had "spoiled" him, had poisoned him with the fruits of the Tree of Knowledge. Especially was he struck by the last lines of the diary, —written, judging by the differences in the colour of the ink and in the handwriting, after an interval of many years:

"The other day, in the cloister of Fra Benedetto, a monk who had come from Athos was showing me in an ancient parchment roll, in a coloured drawing for a heading, John the Winged Precursor. Such representations do not exist in Italy; it was taken from Greek icons. His limbs are thin and long. His body, covered with a shaggy garment of camel hair, seems feathered, like a bird's. 'Behold, I will send My Angel, and he shall prepare the way before Me: and the Lord, whom ye seek, shall suddenly come to his temple, even the Angel of the covenant, whom ye delight in: behold, he shall come.'[61] But this is no angel, no spirit, but a man with gigantean wings."

There followed fragmentary words, crossed out in many places, penned with an evidently trembling hand:

"The resemblance of Christ and Antichrist is a perfect resemblance. The visage of Antichrist in the visage of Christ, the visage of Christ in the visage of Antichrist. Who shall distinguish them? Who shall resist their temptation? The ultimate mystery is an ultimate sorrow, whose like has never yet been in this universe.

"In the Cathedral of Orvieto, in the picture of Luca Signorelli, are wind-blown folds in the raiment of Antichrist falling into an abyss. And just such folds, resembling the wings of a gigantean bird, were at Leonardo's shoulders, as he stood on the edge of the precipice, on the summit of Monte Albano, above the hamlet of Vinci."

On the last page, in a still different handwriting, probably after another long interval, was written:

"The White She-Demon is everywhere, always. May she be accursed! The ultimate mystery: two are one. Christ and Antichrist are one. Heaven above and heaven below. Nay, may this never be,—may this never be! Better death. I render up my life into Thy hands, my God! Judge Thou me."

The diary concluded with these words. And Leonardo understood that they had been written on the eve, or on the very day, of his suicide.

II

IN one of the reception halls of the Vatican, in the so-called Stanza della Segnatura, with the recently completed mural painting of Raphael, under the fresco depicting the god Apollo, amidst the muses on Parnassus, sat Pope Leo X, surrounded by dignitaries of the Church of Rome, savants, poets, *zauberkünstler*, dwarfs, buffoons.

His enormous body,—white, puffy, like those of old women afflicted with dropsy, and his face,—bloated, round, pale, with whitish frog-like eyes bulging out,—were hideous; he was practically blind in one eye, with the other he saw but badly, and whenever he had to scrutinize anything, he used, instead of a magnifying glass, a monocle or *occhialino*, of a beryl with many facets; in his seeing eye there shone an intelligence, cold, clear, hopelessly wearied. The Pope's pride was his hands,—which were really beautiful; he displayed them at every opportune occasion, and vaunted them, as well as his pleasing voice.

After a business reception, the Holy Father was resting, conversing with those near to his person about two new poems. These were written in impeccably elegant Latin verses, in imitation of Vergil's *Æneid*. One bore the title of *The Christiad*,—a periphrasis of the Evangel, with a confusion, fashionable in that day, of Christian and pagan figures and images: thus, the Holy Communion was called the "Divine Food, hidden from the weak vision of men under the guise of Ceres and Bacchus,"—*i.e.*, bread and wine; Diana, Thetis and Æolus extended services to the Mother of God; when the Archangel Gabriel was announcing the good tidings in Nazareth, Mercury eavesdropped at the door and transmitted the tidings to the gathering of the Olympians, counselling them to take decisive measures.

The other poem, also by Fracastor, entitled *Siphilis*, dedicated to the future Cardinal, Pietro Bembo,—the same who shunned reading the Epistles of Paul the Apostle, "lest he corrupt his own style,"—hymned forth in lines just as irreproachably elegant as the first, and also after Vergil, the French malaise and the modes of treatment by sulphur baths and mercury ointment. The origin of the disease was explained, *in passim*, by the fable of a certain shepherd of ancient times by the name of Siphilus, who had aroused the ire of the god of the Sun with his mockeries; the god did punish him with a malady which would not yield to any treatment, until the Nymph America did initiate him into her mysteries and did lead him to a grove of the healing Guaiacum trees, a sulphur spring, and a lake of mercury. Subsequently Spanish travellers, having sailed across the ocean and discovered the New Lands, wherein the nymph America dwelt, did also offend the god of the Sun, having shot in the chase the birds sacred to him, of which one did prophesy in a human voice that for this sacrilege Apollo would send them the French malaise.

The Pope declaimed from memory several fragments from both poems. He had particular success with the Speech of Mercury before the gods of Olympus, concerning the Good Tidings brought by the Archangel, and the Love Plaint of the Shepherd Siphilus, addressed to the Nymph America.

When he had finished, to the whispering of enraptured praises and respectfully restrained plaudits, which seemed to have escaped involuntarily, Michelangelo,—recently arrived from Florence,—was announced. The Pope frowned slightly, but immediately ordered him to be received.

The sombre Buonarotti inspired in Leo X a feeling akin to fear. He preferred Raphael,—the gay, the amenable to reason, the "good fellow." The Pope received Michelangelo with his unchanging bored amiability. But, when the artist began speaking of a matter in which he deemed himself mortally offended,—of the commission for the new marble façade of the Florentine church of San Lorenzo, a commission given to him and suddenly withdrawn,—the Holy Father managed to stifle this conversation, and, with a habitual movement inserting the beryl monocle into his seeing eye, looked upon him with a good nature in which lurked a mocking slyness, and uttered:

"Messer Michelangelo, we have one little matter in which we would fain know thy opinion,—our brother, the Duke Giuliano, adviseth us to utilize for some work thy fellow countryman, the Florentine Leonardo da Vinci. Tell us, as a favour, what thou thinkest of this idea, and what work would be most fit to be put in the hands of this artist?"

With his eyes sullenly cast down, and, as was his wont, tortured under the eyes fixed upon him, from his insuperable shyness and the consciousness of his ugliness, Michelangelo remained silent. But the Pope was looking at him intently through his beryl monocle, awaiting an answer.

"It may probably not be known to Your Holiness," Buonarotti finally spoke, "that many deem me an enemy of Messer da Vinci. Whether this be true or no, I assume that for me it is least seemly to be an arbiter in this matter, or to express any opinion at all, bad or good."

"I swear by Bacchus," exclaimed the Pope, becoming animated, and evidently preparing something amusing, "that even if this were really so, we would all the more wish to know thy opinion of Messer Leonardo; for, no matter what may be the case with another, we do not deem thee capable of prejudice, and do not doubt that in judging thy enemy thou wilt be able to evince no less nobility than in judging a friend. But still, never have I believed, nor will I believe, that you are in reality enemies. Come, now! Such artists as he and thou can not but be above vanity. And what is there for you to divide, what is there to be rivals about? But even if there has been aught between you,—why bring it up? Is it not better to dwell in peace? 'Tis said: in accord the small increaseth, in discord the great decreaseth. And is it possible, my son, that if I, thy father, would desire to join your hands,—is it possible that thou wouldst refuse me, wouldst not extend thy hand?"

Buonarotti's eyes flashed,—as was frequently the case with him, timidity was momently transformed into fury.

"I do not extend my hand to traitors!" he uttered dully and impetuously, barely retaining control of himself.

"Traitors?" the Pope caught him up, becoming still more animated.

"'Tis a grave accusation, Michelangelo; 'tis grave, and we feel certain thou wouldst not venture to voice it without having proof . . ."

"Of proofs I have none, nor are any needed! I speak but what everyone knows. For fifteen years has he been a toad-eating hanger-on of the Duke Moro,—him that did first bring barbarians upon Italy and did betray the fatherland to them. But when God did punish the tyrant with deserved punishment, and he did perish, Leonardo went over to the service of a still greater scoundrel, Cæsar Borgia, and, being a citizen of Florence, made military charts of Tuscany, to make the conquest of his own native land easier for the enemy."

"Judge not, lest ye be judged," said the Pope, with a quiet mockery. "Thou dost forget, my friend, that Messer Leonardo is no warrior, nor a statesman, but solely an artist. Have not the servants of the untrammelled Camenæ a right to a greater freedom than other mortals? . . ."

"Pardon me, Your Holiness," Michelangelo interrupted him, almost rudely. "I am a simple man, not given to rhetorics,—I understand not philosophical refinements. I have become accustomed to calling white white, and black black. And the most despicable of scoundrels does he seem to me who reveres not his mother, who denies his native land. Messer Leonardo, I know, deems himself above all human laws. But by what right? He is forever promising, ever preparing to astound the world with his miracles. Is it not high time to get to work? Where are they,—these miracles of his and the portents? . . ."

The Pope, fixing Michelangelo with his light, froglike eyes, was observing him, calmly and coldly, and meditating upon the vanity of all earthly things, upon the vanity of vanities, contemplating the debasement of the proud, the insignificance of the great. He was already visioning how he might bring together these two rivals, egging them on one another, arranging a spectacle yet unseen, a sort of cock-fight of gigantean proportions,—a philosophic diversion, which he, the amateur of everything rare and monstrous, would enjoy with the same Epicurean curiosity, a trifle squeamish and bored, as the fighting of his buffoons,—his cripples, innocents, apes, and dwarfs.

"My son," he finally said, with a quiet, sad sigh, "I see now that the enmity, in which we hitherto did not want to believe, really does exist between you, and am amazed,—aye, I confess, I am amazed, and saddened, by thy opinion of Messer Leonardo. Pray, how is this, then, Michelangelo? We have heard of him so much good: to say naught of his great art and learning, his heart, so they say, is so kindly, that not only human beings does he feel for, but even the dumb brutes, even plants, he does not permit to be harmed in any way, by any man, —like to the Hindu sages, called the gymnosophists, of whom the travellers tell us so many wondrous things. . . ."

Michelangelo kept silent, having turned away. At times his face would be distorted by a spasm of malice. He felt that the Pope was making mock of him. Pietro Bembo, who was standing nearby and attentively following the conversation, understood that the jest might have an ill ending: Buonarotti was unsuitable for the game begun by the Pope. The adroit courtier intervened all the more willingly because he himself did not have any too much love for Leonardo, by hearsay, on account of his jeers at the rhetoricians, the "imitators of antiquity," "the daws in peacock feathers."

"Your Holiness," said he, "there may be a moiety of truth in the words of Messer Michelangelo; at any rate, there are such contradictory rumours current about Messer Leonardo, that, really, one does not know at times what to believe. He spares dumb creatures, 'tis said, partaking not of flesh,—yet at the same time invents death-dealing engines for the extermination of mankind, and is fond of escorting criminals to execution, observing the expression of the last horror upon their faces. I have also heard that his pupils and those of Marc Antonio not only purloined cadavers from hospitals for anatomical dissections, but dug them up out of the ground in Christian cemeteries. However, 'twould seem that during all times great savants were prone to extraordinary eccentricities. . . ."

"Be silent, be silent, Pietro! The power of the Lord be with us!" the Pope stopped him in unassumed perturbation.

He did not go on, and piously crossed himself. His whole corpulent, bloated body was agitated. Being a sceptic, Leo X was at the same time as superstitious as an old woman. But especially did he dread black magic. Rewarding with one hand the composers of such poems as *Siphilis* and *Priapus*, with the other he affirmed the plenipotences of the Grand Inquisitor, Fra Giorgio da Casale, for his fight with the wizards and witches.

The Pope's horror, however, did not last for long,—upon the departure of Michelangelo a concert was arranged, at which His Holiness was particularly successful with a difficult aria,—such successes always put him in a well-disposed humour; then, during the luncheon, presiding at a council of his buffoons as to the order of the triumphal procession of the dwarf Baraballo on an elephant, he was completely diverted, and forgot about Leonardo.

But on the following day the prior of San Spirito,—where, in the monastery hospital, the artist was occupied with anatomical studies, —received the strictest injunction not to give him any cadavers, nor to allow him within the premises of the hospital, together with a reminder as to the Bull of Boniface VIII, *De sepulturis*, which forbade, under pain of excommunication, the autopsy of human bodies without the knowledge of the Apostolic Curia.

III

After the death of Giovanni, Leonardo began to find his stay in Rome oppressive. Uncertainty, expectancy, compulsory inactivity, had tired him out. His customary occupations,—books, machines, experiments, painting,—had become repugnant to him.

Whenever during the long autumnal evenings, alone with the demented Astro and the shade of Giovanni in the house which had become still more dismal, he got into an unbearably eerie state, he would go off for a visit to Messer Francesco Vettori, the Florentine ambassador, who corresponded with Niccolò Machiavelli, and would talk of him and give Leonardo Machiavelli's letters to read.

Fate persecuted Niccolò as of yore. The dream of all his life—the popular militia he had created, from which he expected the salvation of Italy—proved utterly worthless,—at the siege of Prato, in fifteen hundred and twelve, under the first Spanish shots, it scattered in all directions before his eyes, like a flock of rams. Upon the return of the Medicis, Niccolò was relieved of his post, "demoted, deposed, deprived of everything." Soon after that a conspiracy for the re-establishment of the Republic and the overthrow of the tyrants was disclosed. Niccolò had taken part in it. He was seized, tried, tortured,—being jerked upon a strappado on four different occasions. He bore the tortures with a manliness which, according to his own confession, "was unexpected to himself." Being released on bail, he was left under surveillance and forbidden for a year to cross the boundary of Tuscany. He fell into such penury that he was compelled to abandon Florence and settle down on a little bit of hereditary land in a mountain settlement some ten miles from the city on the Roman Road. But even here, after all the misfortunes he had experienced, he did not abate: from a fiery republican he turned into just as ardent a friend of the tyrants, with a sincerity habitual to him in such sudden metamorphoses, in his transitions from one extremity to another. Even during his session in prison he addressed the Medicis with repentant and laudatory epistles in verse. In his book, *The Prince*, dedicated to Lorenzo the Magnificent, the nephew of Giuliano, he offered, as the highest exemplar of princely wisdom, Cæsar Borgia, who had but recently died in exile, and whom he had at one time so harshly uncrowned, and now did newly surround with an aureole of almost superhuman grandeur, and add to the number of immortal heroes. In his heart of hearts Machiavelli felt that he was deluding himself: the bourgeois autocracy of the Medicis was just as repulsive to him as the bourgeois republic of Soderini; but, no longer having the strength to deny himself this last dream, he clutched at it as a drowning man does at a straw. Ill, lonely, with unhealed wales on his hands and feet from the ropes wherewith he had been jerked up on the strappado, he implored Vettori to negotiate for him with the Pope, with Giuliano, to obtain for him "any little post at all, inasmuch as inactivity was more fearful than very death to him; if he might but be taken into service again,—he was ready for any work at all,—if it were but turning stones."

In order not to bore his patron with his perpetual supplication and complaints, Niccolò at times tried to amuse him with jests and with stories of his amatory adventures. At fifty, the father of a starving family, he was—or pretended to be—as deeply in love as a schoolboy. "I have laid aside all sage, all important thoughts: neither legends of the great deeds of antiquity, nor discourses upon contemporary politics amuse me: I am in love!"

Whenever Leonardo would read these playful epistles, there would occur to him the words which Niccolò had once uttered in Romagna, upon coming out of a gambling hell, where he had been playing the zany before the Spanish riff-raff: "Hunger danceth, hunger pranceth, hunger sings gay little songs." At times in these letters also, amid Epicurean counsels, amatory effusions, and the cynical laughter at his own expense, there would escape a cry of despair:

"Can it be that not a single living soul will recall me? If you still bear me any love, Messer Francesco, as you did once upon a time, you would not be able to witness without indignation that ignominious life which I now lead."

IV

READING these letters, Leonardo felt how near, despite all his contrast, Niccolò was to him. He recalled the latter's prophecy, that their fate was identical, that they would both remain forever homeless wanderers in this world, where "naught exists, save the rabble." And truly, Leonardo's life in Rome was just as ignominious as Niccolò's life in his God-forsaken hamlet: the same tedium; the same loneliness; the same forced inactivity, which was more dreadful than any torture, the same realization of one's powers,—and superfluity to mankind. Even as Niccolò, he permitted fate to trample him underfoot, to have its will of him, only with a resignation still greater, not even curious as to whether there were any bound to its impudicity, inasmuch as he had long since become convinced that there was no such bound.

Leo X, occupied with the triumph of Baraballo the buffoon, still had not found the leisure to receive Leonardo, and, in order to get rid of him, entrusted him with the perfection of the minting machine in the Papal Mint. Not despising, according to his wont, any work, even the most modest, the artist carried out the commission to perfection,—he invented a machine such that the coins, formerly with uneven, jagged edges, now came out irreproachably round.

At this period his affairs, in consequence of his former debts, were in such disorder that the greater part of his salary went to pay the interest. Had it not been for the help of Francesco Melzi, who had come into his patrimony, Leonardo would have endured extreme need.

In the summer of fifteen hundred and fourteen he contracted Roman malaria. This was the first serious illness of his life. He took no medicines, nor would let any leeches nigh him. Francesco alone tended him, and with every day Leonardo grew more and more attached to him, appreciating his simple love, and it seemed to the master that God had sent him in this boy his last friend, a guardian angel, the staff of his homeless old age.

The artist felt that he was being forgotten and at times made vain efforts to bring himself to notice. Ill, he wrote congratulatory epistles to his patron, Giuliano de' Medici, with the courtly amiability so usual in those days,—in which amiability he succeeded but illy:

"When I learned of Your greatly desired recovery, my Most Illustrious Sire, my joy was so great that it did even cure me, reviving me from the dead as if by miracle."

Toward autumn his malaria passed. But ill-health and weakness still remained. During the few months after the death of Giovanni, Leonardo had stooped and grown old, as though over a period of many years. A strange pusillanimity, a sadness that was like deathly fatigue, would possess him more and more frequently. With apparent fervour he would occasionally approach some favourite work,—mathematics, anatomy, painting, the flying machine,—but would immediately abandon it; he would begin on something else,—only to abandon that also with aversion.

On his blackest days he would suddenly become engrossed with childish amusements.

The painstakingly washed and dried guts of rams, so soft and thin that they could all be held in the hollow of one's hand, he would join through a wall with a smith's bellows, hidden in an adjacent room, and, when they would be blown up into such gigantean bubbles that the frightened spectator had to retreat and hug a corner, he would compare them with virtue, which also seems small in the beginning, and insignificant, but, gradually growing, fills the entire world.

An enormous lizard, found in the Garden of the Belvedere, he pasted over with beautiful scales of fishes and serpents; he attached to it horns, a beard, eyes, and wings filled with quicksilver, which quivered at the creature's every move; he placed it in a box, tamed it, and began to show it to his visitors, who, taking this monster for a devil, would shrink away from it in horror.

Or out of wax he would mould little supernatural monsters, with wings filled with heated air, which made them so light that they would rise up and soar, while Leonardo, enjoying the amazement or the superstitious fear of the spectators, exulted, and in the grim wrinkles of his face, in his dim, sad eyes, there would suddenly glimmer something so good-natured, childishly merry, but, at the same time, so pitiable in this old, tired face, that Francesco's heart would be rent.

Once the latter accidentally overheard Cesare da Sesto saying, as he showed the guests out, after the master had gone out of the room:

"So goes it, signori. That is the sort of little playthings we amuse ourselves with now. What is the use of hiding our sin? Our little old man has fallen into dotage, has gotten into his second childhood, the poor little fellow. He started off with human wings, and ended with little flying dolls of wax. The mountain hath brought forth a mouse!"

And he added, bursting into his malignant, forced laughter:

"I am really amazed at the Pope, whatever else may be said of him, he surely knows what is what when it comes to zanies and innocents. Messer Leonardo is a veritable treasure trove for him. They seem to have been created for each other. Truly, now, signori, do exert yourselves for the master, that the Holy Father may take him into his service. Have no fear, His Holiness will remain satisfied; our old man will be able to divert him better than Fra Mariano himself, or even the dwarf Baraballo!"

This jest was nearer the truth than might have been thought: when rumours of these tricks of Messer Leonardo reached Leo X, he felt such a desire to see them that he was ready to forget even the fear inspired by the sorcery and godlessness of Leonardo. Adroit courtiers gave the artist to understand that the time to act had come: fate was sending him an opportunity to become a rival not only of Raphael, but of Baraballo himself, in the good graces of His Holiness. But once again Leonardo, as so many times before in his life, did not heed the counsel of worldly wisdom,—was not able to utilize the opportunity and seize the wheel of fortune in time.

Surmising intuitively that Cesare was Leonardo's enemy, Francesco forewarned the master; but the latter would not believe.

"Leave him alone,—touch him not," he would defend Cesare. "Thou dost not know how he loves me, even though he would fain hate me. He is just as unfortunate,—more unfortunate,—than . . ."

Leonardo did not finish. But Melzi conjectured that he would have said: More unfortunate than Giovanni Beltraffio.

"And is it for me to judge him?" continued the master. "I, perhaps, am myself at fault before him. . . ."

"You,—before Cesare?" Francesco was amazed.

"Yes, my friend. Thou wouldst not understand this. But to me it at times seems that I have put the evil eye upon him, have spoiled him; for dost thou see, little lad of mine, I really must have the evil eye. . . ."

And, after a short reflection, he added with a quiet, kindly smile:

"Let him be, Francesco, and have no fear,—he will not do me any evil, and will never leave me, never betray. But that he has waxed rebellious and doth struggle with me,—why, that is for his soul, his freedom, because he seeks to find himself, is fain to be himself. Aye, let him! May the Lord help him,—for I know that when he shall conquer he will return to me, will forgive me, will understand how I love him, and then I shall give him all that I have,—will reveal to him all the secrets of art and knowledge, that he may, after my death, expound it to men. For, if he will not, who will? . . ."

Even in summer, during Leonardo's illness, Cesare would disappear from the house for weeks at a time. In the autumn he disappeared entirely and did not return any more. Noting his absence, Leonardo asked Francesco about him. The latter cast down his eyes in confusion and answered that Cesare had gone to Siena to execute an expeditious commission. Francesco was afraid that Leonardo might begin questioning him in detail as to why Cesare had gone away without saying farewell. But, believing—or pretending to believe—the unskilled lie, the master began speaking of something else. Only the corners of his lips quivered and drooped with that expression of bitter squeamishness which had of late begun to appear on his face with increasing frequency.

V

The autumn was rainy. But towards the end of November came sunny days, radiantly clear, which are nowhere else as beautiful as in Rome; the gorgeous fading of autumn was akin to the desolate grandeur of the Eternal City.

Leonardo had long been preparing to visit the Sistine Chapel, to see the fescoes of Michelangelo. But he kept on putting the matter off, as though he were afraid. Finally one morning he left the house accompanied by Francesco, and set out for the Chapel.

This was a narrow, long building, very high, with bare walls and ogive windows. On the ceiling and walls were the recently finished frescoes of Michelangelo.

Leonardo looked upon them,—and was rooted to the spot. No matter what his apprehensions had been, he still had not expected that which he beheld. Before these Titanic forms, that seemed to be the visions of delirium,—before all these creations of his rival, Leonardo did not judge, did not measure, did not compare,—he did but feel himself annihilated. In his mind he went over his own productions: the perishing Last Supper, the perished Colossus, the Battle of Anghiari, the countless multitude of other unfinished works,—a succession of vain efforts, of ludicrous failures, of ignominious defeats. All his life he had been but beginning, preparing, getting ready, but up to the present had not accomplished anything, and—why deceive one's self?—now it was too late; never would he accomplish anything. Despite all the incredible toil of his life, was he not like to the wicked and slothful servant that had digged in the earth and hid his talent?

And, at the same time, he realized that he had striven for greater, for higher things than Buonarotti,—to that union, to that ultimate harmony, which the latter knew not and did not desire to know in his infinite turbulence, indignation, rebelliousness and chaos. Leonardo recalled Monna Lisa's words about Michelangelo,—that his strength was like to a tempestuous wind, rending mountains, and breaking in pieces the rocks before the Lord; and that he, Leonardo, was stronger than Michelangelo, even as the calm is stronger than the tempest, inasmuch as the Lord is in the still small voice, in the calm, and not in the tempest. Now it was clearer to him than ever that Monna Lisa had not been mistaken, for sooner or later the human spirit would return to the path indicated by him, Leonardo, from chaos to harmony, from division to unity, from tempest to calm. But still, how was one to know for how long the victory would remain with Buonarotti, how many generations he would draw after him? And the consciousness of his own integrity in contemplation made still more tormenting for him the consciousness of his impotence in action.

They left the Chapel in silence. Francesco surmised that which was taking place in the master's heart, and did not dare to question him. But, when he glanced at his face, it appeared to him that Leonardo had stooped a little more, as though he had aged many years, had grown decrepit, within the hour they had passed in the Sistine Chapel.

Having crossed the square of San Pietro, they went along the street of Borgo Nuovo toward the bridge of Sant' Angelo. Now the master was thinking of another rival, perhaps no less than Buonarotti to be apprehended by him,—Raphael Sanzio. Leonardo had seen his recently completed frescoes in the upper reception halls of the Vatican, the so-called Stanze, and could not decide which was predominant in them,—grandeur in execution or insignificance in conception; inimitable perfection, recalling the lightest and most radiant creations of the ancients, or servile ingratiation to the great ones of this earth.

This upstart from Urbino, a dreamy adolescent, with the face of an Immaculate Madonna, seeming an angel who had flown down to earth, arranged his affairs in a way that could not be bettered: he decorated the stables of the Roman banker, Agostino Quidgi, prepared designs for his plate,—golden platters and dishes, which the banker, after entertaining the Pope, would cast into the Tiber, that they might no more be used of any. "The fortunate lad"—*fortunato garzon*, as Francia called him,—attained glory, riches, honours, as though in play. He disarmed his bitterest enemies and enviers with his amiability.

The workshop of Raphael became an enormous factory, where adroit men of business, such as Giulio Romano, turned canvas and pigments into ringing coin, with unbelievable speed, with the brazenness of the market-place. As for himself, he no longer cared for perfection, contenting himself with mediocrity. He served the rabble,—and the rabble served him, accepted him as its chosen one, as its favorite child, the flesh of its flesh and the blood of its blood, born of its own spirit. Report proclaimed him the greatest artist of all ages and all nations: Raphael became the god of painting.

And, worst of all was the fact that in his fall he was still great, seductively-splendid, not only to the mob but to the chosen spirits. Accepting the glittering toys from the Goddess of Luck, with a simple-hearted insouciance, he yet remained pure and innocent, like a child. "The fortunate lad" did not know himself what he did.

And more deadly for future art than the discord and chaos of Michelangelo was this lissome harmony of Raphael, this academically lifeless, false reconcilement. Leonardo had a presentiment that beyond these two summits, beyond Michelangelo and Raphael, there were no paths to the future,—farther on was an abyss, a void. And at the same time he realized how much both owed to him,—they had taken from him the science of shade and light, of anatomy, of perspective; a full knowledge of nature, of man,—and, having derived from him, had annihilated him. Plunged in these thoughts he went on as before, as though in a trance, his eyes cast down, his head bent. Francesco tried to start a conversation with him, but his words died away every time that, looking at the face of the master, he saw on the pale aged lips an expression of quiet, infinite qualmishness.

Approaching the bridge of Sant' Angelo, they had to stand aside, making way for a crowd of some sixty men, on foot and on horseback, in sumptuous garments, moving toward them through the narrow street of Borgo Nuovo. Leonardo glanced at them at first absentmindedly, thinking this the train of some Roman grandee, cardinal, or ambassador. But he was struck by the face of one young man, arrayed more sumptuously than the others, mounted on a white Arabian horse in gilt trappings studded with precious stones. Somewhere, it seemed to him, he had already seen this face. Suddenly he recalled the puny, pale lad in a black jacket stained with paints and out at the elbows, who had been saying, eight years ago in Florence, with a timid ecstasy: "Michelangelo is not worthy of loosening the strap of your shoon, Messer Leonardo!" This was he, the present rival of Leonardo and Michelangelo,—"the god of painting"—Raphael Sanzio. His face, although as childlike as ever, innocent and devoid of profound thought, now resembled somewhat less than formerly the face of a cherub,—it had grown fuller, heavier, and bloated to a barely perceptible degree. He was journeying from his palazzo in the Borgo to an audience with the Pope at the Vatican, accompanied, as usual, by his friends, pupils and admirers,—he never happened to leave his house without having about him a guard of honour of some fifty men, so that every one of these excursions recalled a triumphal procession.

Raphael recognized Leonardo, blushed just the least trifle, and with a hurried, exaggerated respectfulness, doffing his *berretta*, he bowed to him. Certain of his pupils, not knowing Leonardo's face, turned around to look with amazement at this old man, to whom the "Divine One" was making such a low obeisance,—modestly, almost poorly dressed, hugging the wall to make way for them.

Paying no attention to anybody, Leonardo fixed with his eyes a man who was walking beside Raphael, among his nearest pupils, and scrutinized him with amazement, as though not believing his eyes: this man was Cesare da Sesto. And he suddenly understood everything,—the absence of Cesare, his own fatidical disquiet, the clumsy deception of Francesco: his last pupil had betrayed him.

Cesare bore the gaze of Leonardo and looked into his eyes with a mocking smile, impudent and at the same time pitiful, from which his face became painfully distorted, becoming appalling, like the face of a madman.

And it was not he, but Leonardo, who cast down his eyes.

The train passed on. The master and the pupil also went on their way. Leonardo leaned on the arm of his companion; his face was pale and calm.

Having crossed the bridge of Sant' Angelo, through the street of Dei Coronari they came out on the Piazza Navone, where a bird mart was located. Leonardo bought up a great number of birds,—crows, siskins, warblers, pigeons, a hunting hawk, and a young wild swan. He gave away all the money he had upon him, and even borrowed from

Francesco. Slung from head to foot with cages, in which the birds were jargoning, these two men, the old and the young, drew the attention of all. Passers-by turned around with curiosity; street gamins ran after them.

Having crossed all Rome, past the Pantheon and the Forum of Trajan, they came upon the Esquiline knoll, and, through the gates of Maggiore, passed out of the city, by the ancient Roman Road, the Via Lavicana. Then they turned up the narrow deserted path into the field. Before them spread the still and pallid Campagna, unencompassable to the eye.

They chose a spot on one of the little hummocks, took off their cages, put them on the ground, and Leonardo began to liberate the birds. This was a pastime of his, beloved from childhood. As they flew off with joyous fluttering and swishing of wings, he followed them with a kindly gaze. His face was illumined by a soft smile. At this moment, having forgotten all his bitter griefs, he seemed as happy as an infant.

There were only the hunting hawk and the wild swan left in the cages, —the master was saving them for the last. He sat down to rest and took out of his travelling wallet a bundle with his humble supper,—bread, roasted chestnuts, dried figs, a flask of Orvieto wine, with its covering of woven straw, and two kinds of cheese,—knowing that Francesco did not like goat cheese, he had purposely taken cream cheese along for him. The master invited the pupil to share the meal with him, and began his snack, looking with pleasure at the birds, which, sensing freedom in their cages, were beating their wings; he liked to celebrate the liberation of the winged captives with such little feasts in the fields, under the open sky.

Francesco contemplated him,—and a familiar feeling of pity was taking possession of him.

Thus, now, as he watched how the master, sitting on the grass among the empty cages, and giving an occasional glance at the remaining birds, was slicing with an old folding knife—with a broken bone handle—the bread and the thin slices of cheese, putting them into his mouth and carefully, with an effort, masticating them, as old men masticate with enfeebled gums, so that the skin on their cheek-bones moves, —he suddenly felt welling up in his heart that familiar, burning pity. And it was all the more unbearable because it was united with reverence. He wanted to cast himself down at the feet of Leonardo, to embrace them, sobbing, to tell him that even if the master were rejected and despised of all men, there was still in this ingloriousness a greater glory than in the triumph of Raphael and Michelangelo.

But he did not do this,—he had not the courage, and continued to contemplate the master in silence, holding back the tears which contracted his throat, and with difficulty swallowing the pieces of cream cheese and bread.

Having ended his supper, Leonardo arose, released the hunting hawk, then opened the last and largest cage, which held the swan. The enormous white bird fluttered out, noisily and joyously waved its wings, turned roseate in the rays of sunset, and flew off straight toward the sun. Leonardo followed it with a prolonged gaze, filled with infinite sorrow and longing.

Francesco comprehended that this sorrow of the master was for the dream of all his life,—of human wings, of the "Great Bird," which he had on a time foretold in his diary:

"Man will undertake his first flight on the back of an enormous Swan."

VI

THE Pope, yielding to the requests of his brother, Giuliano de' Medici, commissioned Leonardo to do a small painting. Dallying, as was his wont, and putting off from day to day beginning the work, the artist busied himself with preparatory experiments, the perfection of pigments, the invention of a new lacquer for the forthcoming picture. Learning this, Leo X exclaimed with feigned despair:

"This queer fellow will never accomplish aught, inasmuch as he considers the end, without attacking the beginning!"

The courtiers seized this jest and spread it through the town. Leonardo's fate was decided. Leo X, the greatest connoisseur and appreciator of art, had pronounced sentence upon him: henceforth Pietro Bembo and Raphael, the dwarf Baraballo and Michelangelo, could rest unperturbed on their laurels,—their rival had been annihilated. And all, spontaneously, as though they had conspired, averted their faces from him; they forgot about him, as the dead are forgotten. But the reflection of the Pope was, nevertheless, transmitted to him. Leonardo heard it out with the same apathy as though he had foreseen it long ago, and had not expected any other. On the night of the same day, left alone, he wrote in his diary:

SIXTEEN · Leonardo da Vinci

"Patience for the insulted is the same as clothing is for the chilled. In proportion as the cold increaseth, dress thyself warmer, and thou shalt not feel the cold. Just so, during great injustices, increase thy patience,—and the injustice shall not touch thy soul."

On the first of January, in the year fifteen hundred and fifteen, died Louis XII, King of France. Since he had no sons, he was succeeded by his next of kin, his son-in-law, Claude de France, son of Louise of Savoy, Duke of Angoulême, François de Valois,—under the name of Francis I.

Immediately upon ascending the throne, the youthful King undertook an expedition to win back Lombardy; with unbelievable speed he crossed the Alps, passed through the strait passes of d'Argentière, made a sudden appearance in Italy, obtained a victory at Marignano, deposed Moretto, and entered Milan a triumphator.

At this stage Giuliano de' Medici had gone off to Savoy. Seeing that there was nothing to be done in Rome, Leonardo decided to seek his fortune with the new king, and in the fall of the same year set out for Pavia, to the court of Francis I. Here the conquered were giving festas in honour of the conquerors. Leonardo, as a mechanic, was invited to take part in arranging them, for old memory's sake, a memory preserved about him in Lombardy since the time of Moro.

He contrived a lion that moved of itself,—this lion, at one of the festas, traversed the entire hall, halted before the King, reared up on its hind legs and opened its bosom, out of which the white lilies of France showered down at the feet of His Majesty.

This toy served the fame of Leonardo more than all his other works, inventions and discoveries.

Francis I was inviting to his service the Italian savants and artists. The Pope would not release Raphael and Michelangelo. The King extended an invitation to Leonardo, offered him a salary of eight hundred *écus* a year, and the small castle of Du Cloux in Touraine, near the city of Amboise, between Tours and Blois.

The artist agreed, and in the sixty-fourth year of his life, the eternal wanderer, abandoning his native land sans hope and sans regret, left Milan for France, with his old servant Villanisso, the female servant Maturina, Francesco Melzi, and Astro da Peretola, in the beginning of the year fifteen hundred and sixteen.

VII

THE road, especially at this time of the year, was difficult.

They left the little hamlet of Bardonecchia early in the morning, while it was still dark, in order to make their way to the crossing of the mountains while it was yet light. The mules for riding and the pack mules, their hoofs clattering and their bells jingling, clambered up the narrow path at the edge of the precipice.

At one of the turns Leonardo dismounted,—he wanted to have a nearer view of the mountains. Learning from the guides that a side path for pedestrians, still narrower and more difficult, led to the same place as the one for the mules, he, with Francesco, began clambering up it to a neighbouring crag, which afforded a view of the mountains.

When the jingling bells had died away, a quiet fell such as is to be found only in high mountains. The travellers heard the beatings of their hearts, and the occasional prolonged rumbling of an avalanche, that was like to the rumbling of thunder, repeated by many-voiced echoes. They clambered higher and higher.

Leonardo leaned upon Francesco's arm. And the pupil recalled how, many years ago, in the village of Mandello, near the foot of the mountain of Campione, the two of them had been descending into the iron mine by a slippery, fearful staircase into the subterranean abyss,—at that time Leonardo had been carrying him in his arms, now Francesco supported the master. And there, underground, there had reigned the same stillness as here on the height.

"Look, look, Messer Leonardo!" exclaimed Francesco, indicating the precipice that had suddenly opened up at their feet, "again the valley of Doria Riparia! This is probably for the last time. We are coming to the crossing of the mountains right away, and we shall see it no more."

"There,—there are Lombardy, Italy," he added in a low voice. His eyes flashed with joy and sadness. He repeated, in a still lower voice: "For the last time. . . ."

The master glanced in the direction indicated by Francesco, where lay his native land,—and his face remained indifferent. He silently turned away, and again forged ahead,—there, where radiantly glowed the eternal snows and glaciers of Mont Tabora, Mont Senisa, Roccio-Melone.

Heeding not fatigue, he was now walking so fast that Francesco, who had lagged below, at the edge of the precipice, bidding farewell to Italy, had fallen behind him.

"Whither are you going, whither are you going, master?" he shouted to him from a distance. "Do you not see that the path is coming to an end? One can not go higher! There is a precipice there! Be careful!"

But Leonardo, not listening to him, went up higher and higher, with a firm, youthfully light step, that seemed to be winged, above the vertiginous chasms.

And in the pallid heavens the icy masses glowed radiantly, rearing up, like a veritable Titanic wall raised up by God between two universes. They enticed him and drew him on, as though beyond them lay the ultimate mystery,—the only one that could slake his curiosity. Akin, desired, though they were divided off from him by uncrossable abysses, they seemed near, as though it sufficed but to extend one's hand to touch them; and they gazed upon him as the dead gaze upon one living, with an eternal smile, that was like to the eternal smile of Gioconda.

The pallid face of Leonardo was illumined by their pallid reflection. He smiled even with the same smile as they. And, gazing upon these masses of radiant ice, against the chill heavens, as radiant as the ice, —he thought of Gioconda and of death as of one identical thing.

BOOK SEVENTEEN

Death — The Winged Precursor

I

IGH ABOVE THE RIVER LOIRE, AT AMBOISE, in the very heart of France, the King had a castle. At eve, when the sunset expired, illumined by a pallid green light that seemed subaqueous, and with the yellowish white stone of Touraine of which it was built reflected in the desolate river, the castle appeared spectrally light, like a cloud.

When the King arrived in Amboise for the chase, the little town would come to life,—the streets resounded deafeningly to the baying of the hounds, the trampling of horses, the blowing of horns; it was motley with the raiment of the courtiers; music was heard of nights coming from the castle, and its white walls, seeming clouds, were lit up with the red glow of torches.

But the King departed—and once more the little town was plunged into silence; save that of Sundays the good wives of the burghers, in white caps of lace, woven by long needles of straw, wended their way to mass; but on weekdays the whole city seemed to have died,—with never a sound of human step or voice,—only the cries of the swallows, darting between the white towers of the castle, or the hum of the revolving wheel in a turner's shop; or, of spring evenings, when the freshness of poplars was wafted on the air from the gardens about the town, the boys and girls, at decorous play, like grown-ups, would gather in a circle, and, taking one another by the hand, would dance and sing an olden little song about St. Denis, the patron saint of France. And, in the transparent twilight, the apple-trees from behind their stone walls, dropped their whitely roseate petals on the heads of the children. But when the song died away, the same hush would resume its reign: throughout all the town there was heard but the measured brazen striking of the hours above the gates of the tower of Horloge, and the cries of the wild swans in the shallows of the Loire, smooth as a mirror, reflecting the pale-green sky.

To the south-east of the castle, some ten minutes' walk away, on the road to the mill of Saint-Thomas, was situated another small castle, Du Cloux, which had at one time belonged to the seneschal and armour bearer of Louis XI.

It was in this castle Francis settled Leonardo da Vinci.

II

The King received the artist with kindness; conversed with him for long about his previous and future works, respectfully styling him his "Father" and "Master." Leonardo proposed to rebuild the castle of Amboise and to construct an enormous canal, which was bound to transform the adjacent swampy region of Sologne, a barren desert infected with fevers, into a blooming garden, connect the Loire with the bed of the Saône at Mâcon, and join the heart of France, Touraine, through the province of Lyons, with Italy, and thus open up a new way from Northern Europe to the shores of the Mediterranean Sea. Thus did Leonardo dream of benefiting a strange land with those gifts of knowledge which his native land had rejected.

The King gave his consent for the construction of the canal, and, almost immediately after his arrival in Amboise, the artist set off to study the region. While Francis hunted, Leonardo studied the structure of the soil of Sologne at Pomorantin, the current of the sources of the Loire and Cher, measured the level of the waters, and prepared draughts and charts.

Travelling through this region, he on one occasion entered Loches, a little town to the south of Amboise, on the bank of the river Indre, amid the far-flung Tourainian meadows and forests. Here was an old castle belonging to the King, with a prison tower, where Ludovico Moro, Duke of Lombardy, after languishing in captivity for eight years, had died. The old turnkey told Leonardo how Moro had attempted to escape, having concealed himself in a wain beneath rye straw; but, not knowing the road, he had lost his way in a nearby forest; on the following morning he had been overtaken by his pursuers, and the hunting hounds had found him in some bushes.

According to the turnkey, a few months before his death Moro had invented an odd amusement for himself: he had obtained, after much supplication, brushes and colours, and took to painting upon the walls and vaults of his dungeon. On the white-wash, peeling in from the dampness, Leonardo found traces here and there of this painting,—intricate designs, stripes, little sticks and crosses, and stars,—red ones upon a field of white, yellow ones on a blue, and, among them, the head of a Roman warrior in a helmet,—probably an unsuccessful self-portrait of the Duke, with an inscription in broken French:

"My device in captivity and sufferings: My Arms Are My Patience."

Another inscription, still more illiterate, sprawled over the entire ceiling, at first in enormous letters three ells high, in yellow characters of an old, clerkly script:

"*Celui qui*—"

Then, since space did not suffice, in small, cramped letters:

"—*n'est pas contan*." "He who is unhappy."

Reading these piteous plaints, regarding the ungainly drawings, reminiscent of those scribblings with which school-boys disfigure their note-books, the artist recalled how, many years ago, Moro had been admiring, with a kindly smile, the swans in the moat of the fortress at Milan.

"Who knows?" reflected Leonardo. "Was there not, perhaps, in the soul of this man a love for the beautiful, which vindicates him before the tribunal of the Most High?"

Also did he recall that which he had heard on a time, from a traveller arrived from Spain, of the fall of another patron of his, Cæsar Borgia.

The successor of Alexander VI, Pope Julius II, had traitorously given Cæsar up to his enemies. He was carried off to Castile and immured in the tower of Medina del Campo. He escaped, with a skill and daring unbelievable, letting himself down a rope out of the window of his prison, from a vertiginous height. His gaolers managed to cut the rope. He fell, hurting himself, but preserved enough presence of spirit to crawl, upon recovering his senses, up to the horses held in readiness by his confederates, and to gallop off. He appeared in Pampeluna at the court of his father-in-law, the King of Navarre, and entered his service as a *condottiere*. At the news of Cæsar's escape, horror spread throughout Italy. The Pope trembled. Ten thousand ducats' reward was set aside for Cæsar's head.

On a certain winter evening, in fifteen hundred and seven, in an encounter with the French hirelings of Beaumont, under the walls of Vienne, having mowed his way into the ranks of the enemy, Cæsar was abandoned by his own men, driven into a ravine,—the dried-up bed of a river,—and here, like a beast at bay, defending himself to the last with a desperate courage, he fell, transpierced by more than twenty strokes. The hirelings of Beaumont, having succumbed to the temptation of the magnificence of his accoutrements and raiment, tore them off the dead man, and left the naked corpse at the bottom of the ravine. At night, having made a sortie from their fortress, the Navarrese found him and for a long while could not make certain of his identity. Finally the little page Juanico recognized his master, threw himself upon his dead body, embraced it, and burst into sobs, for he had loved Cæsar.

The face of the dead man, turned up to the sky, was beautiful; it seemed that he had died even as he had lived,—without fear and without repentance.

The Duchess of Ferrara, Madonna Lucrezia Borgia, mourned her brother all her life. When she died a hair-shirt was found next her body.

The Duke's subjects in Romagna, the half-wild shepherds and tillers of the soil in the ravines of the Apennines, also preserved a grateful memory of him. For long they would not believe in his death, biding his coming as a deliverer, as a god, and hoping that sooner or later he would return to them, would establish justice anew in the world, would overthrow the tyrants and defend his people. Mendicant singers throughout the towns and hamlets chanted "The Tearful Lament of Duke Valentino," in which occurred the line:

> *Fe cose estreme, ma sensa misura.*
> Criminal his deeds, but great beyond measure.

Comparing the lives of these two men, Moro and Cæsar, filled with great action, yet which had flickered by without a trace, like a shadow, with his, which was filled with great contemplation, Leonardo found his own less barren and did not murmur against fate.

III

THE rebuilding of the castle of Amboise, the construction of the canal of Sologne, terminated as had almost all his undertakings,—in naught. Assured by counsellors of common sense of the impossibility of carrying out the too-daring projects of Leonardo, the King little by little cooled toward them, became disenchanted, and soon forgot all about them. The artist comprehended that from Francis I, despite all his graciousness, he ought not to expect any more than from Moro, Cæsar, Soderini, Medici, or Leo X. His last hope of being understood,—of giving to men at least a small part of that which he had hoarded for them all his life,—had betrayed him; and he resolved to withdraw, now irretrievably, into his solitude,—to reject all activity.

In the spring of fifteen hundred and seventeen he returned to the Castle of Du Cloux,—ill, exhausted by the fever he had contracted in the swamps of Sologne. Toward summer he felt better. But perfect health never returned to him again.

It was during these days that the artist began a strange picture.

Under projecting, overhanging crags, in humid shade, amid ripening grasses in the stillness of a breathless noon, filled with greater mystery than the profoundest midnight, a god, crowned with clusters of grapes,—long-tressed, muliebrile, with face pale and languishing, with the dappled skin of a doe about his loins, a thyrsus in his hand, sat cross-legged, and, as though hearkening intently, had bent his head forward; he was all curiosity, all impatience; with an induplicable smile he indicated with his finger the spot whence came a sound,—probably the song of mænads, or the rumbling of distant thunder, or the voice of the great god Pan: a deafening cry, from which all living things flee in a supernatural panic.

In the coffer of the deceased Beltraffio, Leonardo had found a carved amethyst,—probably the gift of Monna Cassandra,—with a representation of Bacchus. In the same chest were loose leaves with verses from the *Bacchantes* of Euripides, translated from the Greek and written down by Giovanni. Leonardo read them over.

In this tragedy Bacchus, the most youthful of the gods of Olympus, son of the Thunderer and of Semele, appears to men in the guise of a muliebrile, seductively beautiful youth, a newcomer from India. The King of Thebes, Pentheus, orders him to be seized, that he may be put to death, because, under the pretext of a new Bacchic wisdom, he preached to men barbaric secret rites, the frenzy of sanguinary and orgiastic sacrifices.

"O outlander," says Pentheus scoffingly to the unrecognized god, "thou art beautiful and art possest of all that is needed to seduce women, —thy long locks, filled with languor, fall down thy cheeks; thou dost hide thyself from the sun, like a maiden, and dost preserve in the shade the whiteness of thy face, in order to captivate Aphrodite."

The Chorus of Bacchantes, in controversion of the impious one, chants of Bacchus,—"the most fearful and merciful of the gods, bestowing upon mortals, through inebriation, perfect joy."

On the same leaves, alongside the stanzas of Euripides, were extracts from the Holy Scripture, made by the hand of Giovanni Beltraffio.

From the Song of Songs:

"Drink, yea, drink abundantly, O beloved."[62]

From the Evangel:

"I will drink no more of the fruit of the vine, until that day that I drink it new in the kingdom of God."[63]

"I am the true vine, and my Father is the husbandman."[64]

"My blood is drink indeed."[65]

"Whoso . . . drinketh my blood hath eternal life."[66]

"If any man thirst, let him come unto me, and drink."[67]

Leaving his Bacchus unfinished, Leonardo began another picture, still more strange,—that of John the Precursor. He worked upon it with a persistence and haste most unusual in him, as if he had a premonition that his days were numbered, that he had not much strength left, and that it was decreasing with every day, and hurried to express in this, his last creation, his most cherished secret,—that which he had kept in life-long silence, not only from all men, but even from himself. Within a few months the work progressed to such a degree that one could grasp the artist's conception.

The background of the picture recalled the murk of that Cavern which aroused fear and curiosity, of which he had once told Monna Lisa. But this murk, seeming at first impenetrable, became transparent, as the gaze penetrated it, so that the blackest shadows, while preserving all their mystery, blended with the most pallid light, gliding and melting within it like smoke, like the sounds of distant music. And beyond the shadow, beyond the light, appeared that which was nor light nor shade, but something in the nature of "light shadow," or "dark light," as Leonardo expressed it. And, like a miracle, but more actual than all that exists, like to a spectre, but more alive than life itself, there stood forth out of this light murk, the face and nude body of a muliebrile Youth, seductively beautiful, recalling the words of Pentheus:

"Thy long locks, filled with languor, fall down thy cheeks; thou dost hide thyself from the sun, like a maiden, and dost preserve in the shade the whiteness of thy face, in order to captivate Aphrodite."

But, if this were Bacchus, wherefore, instead of the nebris, the dappled skin of a doe, were his loins enveloped in a garment of camel hair? Wherefore, in lieu of the thyrsus of Bacchic orgies, did he hold in his hand a cross made of a desert reed, the prototype of the Cross of Golgotha? And wherefore, inclining his head, as though hearkening, all expectancy, all curiosity, was he indicating the cross with one hand, with a smile that had in it something of sadness and of mockery, and himself with the other hand, as though he were saying:

"There cometh one mightier than I after me, the latchet of whose shoes I am not worthy to stoop down and unloose."[68]

IV

FRANCIS was a great lover of women. In all his expeditions, together with his chief dignitaries, buffoons, dwarfs, astrologues, chefs, negroes, minions, masters of hounds and priests, the King was followed by "gay girls," under the patronage of the "venerable lady," Johanna Lignier. In all celebrations, and even in religious processions, did they take part. The court blended with this travelling house of ill fame, so that it was difficult to decide where the one ended and the other began: the "gay girls" were demi-ladies-of-honour; the ladies-of-honour, through their loose depravity, earned for their husbands the golden necklace of St. Michael the Archangel. The King's extravagance on women was boundless. The taxes and assessments increased with every day, but still there was not sufficient money. When it was no longer possible to take anything from the people, Francis began taking away from his nobles their precious table services, and on one occasion minted into coin the silver lattice work from the grave of the great saint of France, Martin de la Tours,—not out of impiety, however, but out of need, inasmuch as he deemed himself a faithful son of the Church of Rome, and persecuted all heresy and godlessness as an affront to his own majesty.

Since the time of Louis the Holy there had been preserved among the people a legend of the healing force reputed to issue from the kings of the House of Valois,—by the touch of a hand they made whole the scabby and the strumous; toward Easter, Christmas, Trinity Sunday, and other holy days, those who desired to be made whole gathered not only from all the ends of France, but even from Spain, Italy, Savoy.

During the festivities on the occasion of the betrothal of Lorenzo de' Medici and the christening of the Dauphin, a multitude of the sick had gathered at Amboise. On a designated day they were admitted into the courtyard of the King's castle. Formerly, when faith had been stronger, His Majesty, going the round of the sick, making the sign of the cross over each and touching each one with his finger, would pronounce: "The King hath touched thee, God will heal thee." Faith had weakened, healings became rarer, and now the words of the rite were uttered in the form of a wish: "May God heal thee,—the King hath touched thee."

At the conclusion of the rite, a ewer was brought, with three towels, soaked with vinegar, clean water, and orange perfume. The King washed himself, and wiped his hands, face and neck. After the sight of human poverty, hideousness, and disease, he was fain to divert his soul and rest his eyes with something beautiful. He remembered that he had long been preparing to visit the workshop of Leonardo, and with a few of his attendants set out for the Castle of Du Cloux.

All day, disregarding his weakness and ill health, the artist had been zealously working on John the Precursor. The oblique rays of the sun penetrated through the semi-ogive windows of the workshop,—a large cold room with a brick floor and a ceiling of oak beams. Taking advantage of the last light of the day, he was hurrying to finish the raised right hand, which indicated the Cross.

Sounds of voices and steps were heard beneath the window.

"Receive nobody," said the master, turning around to Francesco Melzi, "dost hear,—receive nobody. Say I am ill, or not at home."

The pupil went out into the entry, in order to stop the uninvited guests; but, beholding the King, bowed respectfully and opened the doors before him. Leonardo had barely time to cover the portrait of Gioconda, which stood next to John the Precursor,—he did this always, because he did not like to have it seen by strangers.

The King entered the workroom.

Leonardo, in accordance with the custom at court, was about to make a genuflection before Francis. But the latter restrained him, made a genuflection himself, and embraced him respectfully.

"'Tis a long while since we have seen one another, Maître Léonar'," he uttered with kindness. "How is thy health? Dost paint much? Hast any new pictures?"

"I am ever ailing, Your Highness," answered Leonardo, and took the portrait of Gioconda, in order to put it to one side.

"What is this?" asked the King, indicating the picture.

"An old portrait, Sire. Your Majesty has already been pleased to see it . . ."

"No matter,—show it to me. Thy pictures are such, that the more one sees of them the more one likes them."

Seeing that the artist was delaying, one of the courtiers approached, and, snatching away the cloth, revealed Gioconda.

Leonardo frowned. The King sank into a chair and for a long time contemplated her in silence.

"'Tis amazing!" he said at last, as though coming out of his pensive trance. "Here is the most beautiful woman that I have ever beheld! Who is she?"

"Madonna Lisa, the wife of the Florentine citizen Giocondo," replied Leonardo.

"Didst paint it long ago?"

"Ten years ago."

"Is she just as beautiful now?"

"She died, Your Majesty."

"Maître Léonar' dë Vensi," spoke the court poet Saint-Gelais, distorting the artist's name after the French fashion, "worked upon this picture for five years, and has not finished it,—thus, at least, does he himself affirm."

"Did not finish it?" the King voiced his amazement. "What else can one wish for, pray? She seems to live, save that she speaks not. . . ."

"Well, I must confess," he turned anew to the artist, "thou art truly to be envied, Maître Léonar'. Five years with a woman like that! Thou canst not complain of fate: thou wast fortunate, old man. And where were the husband's eyes? If she had not died, thou wouldst perhaps not have finished the picture to this day!" And he burst into laughter, narrowing his small glistening eyes, his resemblance to a faun becoming still greater: the thought that Monna Lisa may have remained a faithful wife did not even enter his head.

"Aye, my friend," he added, smiling, "thou art a connoisseur of women. What shoulders, what a bosom! But that which is invisible, must probably be still more beautiful. . . ."

Leonardo went aside, making believe that he wanted to shift an easel with another picture nearer the light.

"I know not if it be the truth, Your Majesty," said Saint-Gelais in a half-whisper, bending toward the ear of the King so that Leonardo could not hear, "I have been assured, now, that Lisa Gioconda is no exception,—that this queer chap has never loved any woman in all his life, and that he is apparently absolutely continent. . . ."

And, still more quietly, with a playful smile, he added something, probably very immodest, about Socratic love, about the unusual beauty of certain pupils of Leonardo, about the free manners of Florentine masters. Francis was amazed, but shrugged his shoulders with the complaisant smile of a clever man of the world, devoid of prejudices, who lives and lets live, comprehending that in matters of this sort it was a case of every man to his taste.

After Gioconda he turned his attention to an unfinished cartoon which stood beside it.

"And what is this?"

"Judging by the clusters of grapes and the thyrsus, it must be Bacchus," conjectured the poet.

"And this?" the King indicated a picture next to it.

"Another Bacchus?" conjectured the poet hesitatingly.

"Strange!" wondered Francis. "The hair, the bosom, the face, are altogether like those of a girl. He resembles Monna Lisa,—the smile is the same."

"Androgyne, perhaps?" remarked the poet; and when the King, who was not distinguished for his scholarly attainments, asked him what the word meant, Saint-Gelais reminded him of the ancient fable of Plato concerning bisexual beings, men-women, more perfect and beautiful than human beings,—children of the Sun and the Earth, in whom were united both beginnings, the male and the female; so strong and proud that, like to the Titans, they had conceived a rebellion against the gods and their overthrow from Olympus. Zeus, quelling the rebels, but not wishing to extirpate them entirely, lest he be deprived of prayers and sacrificial offerings, clave them in half with his lightning, "Even as country-women, it is said by Plato, slice eggs with a thread or a hair when salting them for preservation. And since that time, both halves, men and women, yearning, are drawn to one another, with insatiable desire, which is love, recalling to mortals the primordial unity of the sexes."

"Mayhap," the poet concluded, "Maître Léonar' in this creation of his dream, was trying to resurrect that which no longer exists in nature, wishing to unite the beginnings severed by the gods,—the male and the female."

Listening to this explanation, Francis regarded this picture as well with the same shameless, stripping gaze as he had regarded Monna Lisa.

"Resolve our doubts, master," he addressed Leonardo. "Who is this: Bacchus or Androgyne?"

"Neither the one nor the other, Your Majesty," spoke Leonardo, blushing as though he were at fault. "This is John the Precursor."

"The Precursor? Impossible! Whatever art thou saying, pray? . . ."

But, having scrutinized the painting more closely, he noticed in the dark background the thin cross of reed, and, puzzled, shook his head. This confusion of the sacred and the sinful seemed to him sacrilegious, and, at the same time, was pleasing to him. However, he immediately decided that no significance should be attached to this: could one ever know what ideas artists got into their heads?

"Maître Léonar', I am buying both pictures: Bacchus—John, that is,—and Lisa Gioconda. What dost thou want for them?"

"Your Majesty," the artist began timidly, "they are still unfinished. I proposed . . ."

"Nonsense!" Francis interrupted him. "John, if thou wilt, thou mayst even finish,—I will wait, if needs must. But dare thou not even touch Gioconda. 'Tis all one, thou wilt not make it any better. I would have it with me at once,—dost hear? Name the price, then; have no fear: I shall not chaffer with thee."

Leonardo felt that he must find an excuse, a pretext for a refusal. But what could he say to this man, who transformed all he touched into vulgarity or indecency? How could he explain what the portrait of Gioconda was to him, and why, for no sum, could he agree to part with it?

Francis thought that Leonardo kept silent for fear of letting the pictures go too cheaply.

"Well, there is no help for it,—if thou dost not want to do it thyself, I shall even set my own price upon it."

He looked at Monna Lisa, and said:

"Three thousand *écus*. Too little? . . . Three and a half thousand?"

"Sire," began the artist anew, with a voice that quavered, "I can assure you . . ." And he stopped; his face again paled slightly.

"Well, so be it,—four thousand, Maître Léonar'. Enough, methinks?"

A murmur of amazement ran through the courtiers; never had any patron of the arts, not even Lorenzo de' Medici himself, set such prices for pictures.

Leonardo raised his eyes to Francis in inexpressible confusion. He was ready to fall at his feet, to supplicate him as one supplicates for one's life, that he take not Gioconda away from him. Francis took this confusion as an impulse of gratitude, arose, preparing for departure, and in farewell again embraced him.

"Well, then, it means the bargain is struck? Four thousand. Thou canst receive the money whenever thou wilt. To-morrow I shall send for Gioconda. Rest assured, I shall pick a place for her thou wilt be content with. I know her value, and shall be able to preserve her for posterity."

When the King was gone, Leonardo sank into a chair. He gazed at Gioconda, with a forlorn gaze, still not believing that which had happened. Incongruous, puerile plans occurred to him: to hide her so that none might find her, and not give her up, even though threatened with death; or to send her off to Italy with Francesco Melzi; to run away with her himself.

Twilight came on. Several times Francesco had looked into the workroom, but had not ventured to speak with the master. Leonardo still sat before Gioconda; his face seemed in the darkness pallid and immobile, like that of a dead man.

At night he entered the room of Francesco, who had already lain down, but could not fall asleep.

"Get up. Let us to the castle. I must see the King."

"'Tis late, master. You have become fatigued to-day. You will fall ill again. Why, you are unwell right now! Truly, would it not be better to-morrow? . . ."

"Nay,—right now. Light a lanthorn; escort me.—However, it does not matter; if thou dost not want to, I shall go alone."

No longer contradicting, Francesco arose, dressed, and they set out for the castle.

V

THERE was a ten minutes' walk to the castle,—but the road was steep, badly paved. Leonardo walked slowly, leaning on Francesco's arm.

The starless night was sultry and black, as though underground. The wind blew in gusts.

The King was supping amid a small chosen circle, amusing himself with an antic of which he was especially fond: out of a large silver goblet, with skillful carving along its edge and base, representing indecencies, he was compelling the youthful ladies and maids-of-honour to drink, in the presence of all, observing how some laughed, others blushed and cried from shame, others still grew angry, while a fourth group closed their eyes, in order not to see, and a fifth pretended that they saw but did not understand.

Among the ladies was the King's own sister, the Princess Marguerite, —the "Pearl of Pearls," as she was styled. The art of pleasing was to her "more of a need than her daily bread." But, captivating all, she remained indifferent to all; only her brother did she love with a strange, excessive love: his weaknesses seemed to her perfections, his vices, virtues, the face of a faun, the face of Apollo. For him, at any moment of her life, she was ready not only, as she expressed it, "to scatter her ashes on the wind, but even give up her immortal soul." There were rumours afloat that she loved him more than it was permitted for a sister to love a brother. But, at any rate, Francis abused this love; he availed himself of her services not only in his hardships, illnesses, dangers, but also in all his amatory adventures.

On that evening a new guest was to drink out of the obscene goblet, an altogether young girl, almost a child, the heiress of an ancient family, searched out somewhere in the wilds of the Bretagne by Marguerite, presented at court, and now beginning to please His Majesty. The girl had no need of dissembling: she really did not comprehend the indecent depictions; she merely blushed the least trifle from the curious and mocking glances concentrated upon her. The King was in an exceedingly merry mood.

The arrival of Leonardo was announced to him. Francis ordered him to be received, and, together with Marguerite, went to meet him.

As the artist, in confusion, with eyes downcast, was passing through the illuminated halls, through the ranks of the ladies and knights of the court, the glances which followed him had in them something of amazement and of mockery,—from this tall old man with grey hair, with grim visage, with a glance timid to the verge of wildness, there was wafted upon the most insouciant and frivolous-minded a breath from another, foreign world, even as cold is wafted from a man who enters a room directly from the frost.

"Ah, Maître Léonar'!" the King greeted him, and, as was his custom, respectfully embraced him. "A rare guest! What shall I regale thee with? I know thou dost not eat meat,—vegetables, mayhap, or fruits?"

"I thank you, Your Majesty. . . . I crave your pardon,—I fain would have a word or two with you. . . ."

The King looked at him closely.

"What ails thee, friend? Art ill, perhaps?"

He led him aside, and asked, indicating his sister:

"She will not be in the way?"

"Oh, nay," retorted the artist, and made a genuflection before Marguerite, "I dare hope that Her Highness, too, will intercede for me . . ."

"Speak on. Thou knowest I am aye glad to hear thee."

"I am come about the same thing still, Sire,—the picture which you desired to purchase,—about the portrait of Monna Lisa . . ."

"What? Again? Why didst thou not tell me at once? What an odd fellow! I thought we had come together on the price."

"I am not speaking of money, Your Majesty . . ."

"Of what then?"

And Leonardo again felt, under the apathetically kind gaze of Francis, the impossibility of speaking about Gioconda.

"Sire," he uttered at last, making an effort, "Sire, be merciful, do not deprive me of this portrait! 'Tis yours, anyway, nor have I need of the money: do but leave it with me for but a space,—until my death. . . ."

He became confused, did not finish, and with a despairing supplication looked at Marguerite. The King, shrugging his shoulders, frowned.

"Sire," interceded the girl, "fulfill the request of Maître Léonar'. He has deserved it,—be gracious!"

"And you are for him also,—and you too? Why, this is a veritable conspiracy!"

She laid a hand upon her brother's shoulder and whispered in his ear:

"How is it you do not perceive? He loveth her to this very day . . ."

"But she hath died!"

"What of it? Doth one not love the dead? For have you not said yourself that she is alive in this portrait? Be kind, dear little brother, leave him the last memory of his past, make not an old man grieve. . . ."

Something stirred in Francis' mind,—something half-forgotten, scholastic, bookish,—anent the eternal union of souls, of knightly fidelity: he felt a desire to be magnanimous.

"God be with thee, Maître Léonar'," said he with a slightly mocking smile. "'Tis evident one can not get the better of thee in obstinacy. Thou didst know how to choose thy petitioner. Be at rest, I shall fulfill thy wish. Only remember: the picture belongs to me, and thou shalt receive the money for it in advance." And he patted his shoulder.

"Fear not, my friend: I pledge thee my word,—none shall separate thee from thy Lisa!"

Tears sprang to Marguerite's eyes; with a soft smile she gave her hand to the artist, and the latter kissed it in silence.

The music struck up; the ball commenced; pairs began circling the hall.

And no longer did anyone recall the strange, foreign guest, who had passed among them, like a shade, and had disappeared anew in the murk of the starless night, as black as though it were underground.

VI

JUST as soon as the King had departed, the usual quiet and desolation reigned again over Amboise.

Leonardo worked as before upon John the Precursor. But the work, in proportion as it advanced, became constantly more difficult, more slow. At times it seemed to Francesco that the master desired the impossible. With the same daring as, on a time, in the case of the mystery of the life of Monna Lisa, he now experienced, in the case of John, who pointed to the Cross of Golgotha, that in which life and death blend into a single, still greater mystery.

At times, at dusk, Leonardo, having taken the cover off Gioconda, would for long gaze upon her, and upon John, standing beside her, as though comparing them. And then it seemed to his pupil, perhaps from the play of the uncertain light and shade, that the expression on the faces of both, the Youth and the Woman, was changing; that they were stepping out of the canvas, like spectres, under the intense gaze of the artist, becoming alive with a life supernatural, and that John was coming to resemble Monna Lisa, and even Leonardo himself in his youth,—even as a son resembles his father and mother.

The health of the master was failing. In vain did Melzi supplicate him to rest, to leave his work,—Leonardo would not hear of rest.

On one occasion, in the autumn of the year fifteen hundred and eighteen, he felt especially unwell. But, overcoming illness and fatigue, he worked through the whole day; he merely finished earlier than usual, and requested Francesco to escort him upstairs, to his bed-chamber,—the spiral staircase was steep; in consequence of his frequent attacks of dizziness, he did not venture during the last few days to go up it without someone's aid.

This time, too, Francesco was supporting the master. Leonardo walked slowly, with difficulty, pausing every two or three steps, to catch his breath. Suddenly he swayed, leaning upon his pupil with the entire weight of his body. The latter understood that the master was faint, and, fearing that he would not be able to hold him up alone, called the old servant, Battista Villanisso. The two of them caught up Leonardo, who sank into their arms; they began calling for help, and, when two more servants hastened up, carried the sick man into his bedchamber.

Refusing, as was his wont, all treatment, he lay in bed for six weeks. The right side of his body was stricken with paralysis; he had lost the use of his right arm. Toward the beginning of winter he became better. But he mended with difficulty and slowly.

During all his life, Leonardo had equal mastery of both his right and his left hand, and he needed both for his work: with his left he drew, with his right he painted; that which one hand did, the other could not have done; in this union of two opposed powers consisted, as he affirmed, his superiority over other artists. But now when, in consequence of paralysis, the fingers of his right hand had grown numb, so that he was deprived—or almost so—of their use, Leonardo feared that painting would become impossible for him.

During the first days of December he got up from his bed; he began walking only in the upper chambers at first; later on he ventured down to the workroom. But he did not return to his work.

Once, during the quietest hour of the day, when all were having their siesta after the noon meal, Francesco, desiring to ask the master something, and not finding him in the upper chambers, went down to the workroom, cautiously opened the door, and looked in. Of late Leonardo, more sombre and unsocial than he had ever been, liked to remain alone for long periods, not allowing anyone to enter without permission, as though afraid that he was being spied upon.

Through the slightly open door he saw that Leonardo was standing before John and attempting to paint with his stricken hand: his face was distorted with the spasmodic agony of a desperate effort; the corners of his compressed lips drooped, his eyebrows contracted; grey locks of hair stuck to his brow, bedewed with perspiration. His benumbed fingers would not obey him: the brush trembled in the hand of the great master, as in the hand of an inexperienced pupil.

In horror, not daring to stir, Francesco looked upon this last struggle of the living spirit with the dying flesh.

VII

The winter of this year was severe. Birds of passage fell down dead. One morning, coming out on the front steps, Francesco found on the snow a half-frozen swallow and brought it to the master. The latter brought it to with his own breath, and built a nest for it in a warm nook behind the hearth, that he might liberate it in the spring.

He no longer attempted to work: the unfinished John, together with other pictures, drawings, brushes, and colours, he hid in the farthest corner of the workroom.

The days passed in idleness. At times they were visited by Maître Guillaume, the notary.

Fra Guglielmo, a Franciscan monk, the spiritual father of Francesco Melzi,—born in Italy, but long settled in Amboise,—would also drop in on them; he was a simple little old man, gay and kindly; he told excellently the olden *novelle* concerning Florentine mischief-makers and madcaps. Leonardo, as he listened to him, would laugh the same kindly laughter as he. During the long winter evenings they played at draughts, jack-straws, and cards.

The early dusk would come on; a leaden light poured in at the windows; the guests would depart. Then for hours at a time Leonardo would pace the room to and fro, occasionally glancing at the mechanic Astro da Peretola. Now, more than ever before, this cripple was a living reproach, a mockery of the life-long striving of the master,—the creation of human wings.

Finally, it would grow entirely dark. Quiet would fall throughout the house. And outside the windows howled the storm; the bare boughs of old trees would swish noisily, and this noise resembled the talk of malignant ogres. To the howling of the wind was joined another, still more grievous,—probably the howling of wolves on the outskirts of the forest. Francesco would make a fire in the hearth, and Leonardo would sit down by it.

Melzi played well on the lute, and had a pleasant voice. At times he would try to disperse the gloomy thoughts of the master with music. Once he sang for him an olden song, composed by Lorenzo de' Medici, accompanying the so-called *tionfo*,—a carnival procession of Bacchus and Ariadne; it was an infinitely joyous and despondent song of love, which Leonardo loved because he had frequently heard it in his youth:

Youth is wondrous but how fleeting!
Sing, and laugh, and banish sorrow;
Give to happiness good greeting,—
Place thy hopes not on the morrow. . . .

The master listened, with head downcast: there came to his mind a summer night, shadows as black as coal, vivid moonlight, almost white, on a deserted street, the sounds of a lute before a marble *loggia*, and thoughts of Gioconda.

The last sound quivered, dying away, blending with the rumbling and rattling of the storm. Francesco, sitting at the feet of the master, lifted his eyes up to him, and saw tears coursing down the face of the old man.

At times, reading over his diaries, Leonardo would write in them new thoughts of that which now engrossed him more than aught else,—death.

Thus, with his reason, he justified in death the divine necessity,—the will of the Prime Mover. Yet, at the same time, in the depth of his heart something waxed indignant, could not and would not submit to reason.

Once he dreamt that he came to, in a coffin, underground, buried alive, and that with a desperate effort, as he stifled, he was pushing against the lid of the coffin.—On the following morning he reminded Francesco of his wish not to be buried until the first marks of decomposition appeared.

Of winter nights, to the moans of the storm, gazing at the embers on the hearth drawn over with a thin veil of ashes, he would recall the years of his childhood in the settlement of Vinci: the infinitely joyous cry of the cranes, that seemed a summons: "Let us fly! Let us fly!"—the resinous, mountain odour of heather; the view of Florence on the sunny plain, transparently lilac, so small that it was encompassed between two aureate branches of the young wood that covered the slopes of Monte Albano.—And then he would feel that he still loved life, that, though half-dead, he still clung to it and feared death as a black pit, wherein, if not to-day then to-morrow, he would fall with a cry of a last horror. And such sad yearning would constrict his heart, that he wanted to cry as little children cry. All the consolations of reason, all the words about Divine Necessity, about the Will of the Prime Mover, seemed false, scattering like smoke before this senseless horror. Dark eternity, the mysteries of the world beyond this, he would have given away for a single ray of the sun, for a single breath of the spring wind, laden with the fragrance of unfolding leaves, for a single branch with the aureately-yellow flowers of the young wood covering the slopes of Monte Albano.

VIII

On certain mornings, upon arising, he would look through the frozen windows at the snow-drifts, at the leaden sky, at the trees covered with hoar-frost,—and it would seem to him that winter would never end.

But in the beginning of February there came a breath of warmth; on the sunny side of houses, from the pendent icicles, resounding drops began to drip; the sparrows chirped up; the trunks of trees were surrounded with dark circles of thawing snow; buds burgeoned; and through the rarefied vapour of clouds there gleamed a pale blue sky.

In the morning, when the sun penetrated into the workroom in oblique rays, Francesco would place the chair of the master where they fell, and for hours at a stretch the old man would sit immovably, sunning himself, his head downcast, his emaciated hands placed on his knees. And in these hands, and in the face with its half-closed lids, there was an expression of infinite weariness.

The swallow, that had spent the winter in the workroom, tamed by Leonardo, now flew, circling the room, perching on his shoulder or hand, permitting itself to be taken and kissed on its little head; then, again fluttering up, would take to soaring, with impatient cries, as though sensing the spring. With an attentive gaze he followed every turn of its little body, every move of its wings,—and the thought of human wings was again awakening within him.

Once, having unlocked a large chest, which stood in a corner of the workroom, he began rummaging among the piles of papers, note-books, and countless loose leaves, with designs of machines, with fragmentary notations from the two hundred *Books of Nature* he had composed. All his life he had been intending to put in order this chaos, to connect in a general thought the fragments, to unite them in one harmonious whole, into one great *Book of the Universe*,—but had always put the matter off. He knew that here were discoveries which would shorten by several ages the labour of knowledge, would change the destinies of mankind and lead it along new paths. And, at the same time, he knew that this was not to be: now it was too late,—everything would perish, just as fruitlessly, just as senselessly, as The Last Supper, the monument of the Sforzas, the Battle of Anghiari, because in science also he did but desire with a wingless desire, did but begin and not finish, did accomplish naught and would naught accomplish as though mocking fate punished him for the immeasurability of that which he desired by the insignificance of that which he had accomplished. He foresaw that men would be seeking that which he had found already, would discover that which he had already discovered,—would travel his path, following his tracks, but would pass him by, forgetting about him, as though he had never been.

Having found a small note-book, turned yellow with age, entitled *Birds*, he laid it to one side.

Of late years he almost never occupied himself with the flying machine, but he constantly thought of it. Watching the flight of the tamed swallow, and feeling that a new project had come to final maturity within him, he decided to approach a last experiment, with a last hope, perhaps insane, that by the creation of human wings the labour of all his life would be saved and vindicated.

He attacked this work with the same obstinacy, with the same feverish haste, as he had John the Precursor,—thinking not of death, conquering his weakness and illness, forgetting sleep and food, sitting through whole days and nights over his draughts and calculations. At times it seemed to Francesco that this was not work, but the delirium of a madman. With growing sadness and fear did the pupil look at the face of the master, distorted by the convulsion of a desperate, seemingly frenzied, effort of the will,—the desire for the impossible, that which it is not given to men to desire with impunity.

A week went by. Melzi did not leave him, did not sleep of nights. —Once, after a third sleepless night, a deathly fatigue overcame Francesco. He snuggled down in a chair by the dead hearth and dozed off.

Morning was greying in the windows. The awakened swallow was chirping. Leonardo sat at a small table, quill in hand, bent forward, his head bowed over the paper scrawled with figures.

Suddenly he swayed,—gently and strangely; the quill fell out of his fingers; his head began to droop more and more. He made an effort to rise; he wanted to call Francesco,—but the barely audible cry died away on his lips; and awkwardly and ponderously falling with all his weight on the table, he overturned it. The guttering candle fell. Melzi, awakened by the noise, jumped up. In the murky light of morning, next to the overturned table, the extinguished candle, and the scattered leaves he saw the master, lying on the floor. The frightened swallow was circling through the room, striking the ceiling and the walls with her swishing wings.

Francesco understood that this was the second stroke.

The sick man lay for several days without consciousness, continuing his mathematical calculations in his delirium. Recovering his senses, he immediately demanded the designs of the flying machine.

"Never, master, no matter what you do!" exclaimed Francesco. "I would rather die than allow you to begin working before you get altogether better . . ."

"Where didst thou put them?" asked the sick man with vexation.

"No matter where I put them, have no fear,—they will be safe. I will return everything to you when you get up . . ."

"Where didst thou put them?" Leonardo persisted.

"I brought them up to the garret and locked them up."

"Where is the key?"

"I have it."

"Give it to me."

"Pray, messer, what do you want them for?"

"Give it to me,—give it to me, quick!"

Francesco delayed. The sick man's eyes flared up in wrath. Not to irritate him, Melzi gave up the key. Leonardo hid it under his pillow and grew calm.

He began to mend sooner than Francesco expected.

In the beginning of April, he passed a whole day peacefully; he had played draughts with Fra Guglielmo. In the evening Francesco, tired out by many sleepless nights, had dozed off as he sat on a bench at the feet of the master, leaning his head against the bed. Suddenly he woke up, as though from a sudden jolt. He listened and could not hear the breathing of the sick man. The night light had gone out. He lit it, and saw that the bed was empty; he made the round of all the upper chambers, aroused Battista Villanisso,—the latter had not seen Leonardo either.

Francesco was already preparing to go down to the workroom, when he recalled the papers hidden in the garret. He ran thither, opened the unlocked door, and saw Leonardo, half-dressed, sitting on the floor before an overturned old box, which served him as a table; by the light of a tallow candle-end, he was writing,—probably making calculations for his machine,—rapidly muttering something under his breath, as in delirium. And this muttering, and the burning eyes, and the rumpled white hair, and the bristling eyebrows, contracted with a seemingly superhuman effort of thought, and the corners of the sunken mouth,—its corners drooping in an expression of senile feebleness, and the whole face, which seemed like that of a stranger, unfamiliar, as though he had never seen it before,—all these were so frightful that Francesco halted in the doorway, not daring to enter.

Suddenly Leonardo seized his crayon, and crossed out the page covered over with figures, so that the point of it broke; then, turning around he saw his pupil and got up, pale, swaying. Francesco darted toward him, to sustain him.

"I have told thee," with a soft strange mocking smile said the master, "I have told thee, Francesco, that I would finish soon. Well, now, I have finished,—finished everything. Now thou needst fear no longer, —I will do no more. Enough! Old have I grown,—old and foolish; more foolish than Astro. Naught do I know. That which I have known, I have forgot. What right have I to wings? . . . The devil take it all,—the devil take it! . . ."

And seizing the leaves from the improvised table, he ferociously crumpled and tore them.

From that day on he grew worse. Melzi had a premonition that this time he would never get up again. Occasionally the sick man would fall into a coma that was like a faint, lasting for days at a time.

Francesco was pious. He believed with simplicity in all that the Church taught. He alone had not come under the influence of those ruinous spells—the "evil eye"—of Leonardo, which were felt by almost everybody who had become attached to him. Knowing that the master did not observe the rites of the Church, he still sensed, through the intuition of love, that Leonardo was not a godless man. And further on he did not penetrate, did not feel any curiosity. But now the thought that he might die without confession horrified him. He would have given his soul to have saved the master, but he dared not broach this matter to him.

One evening, sitting at the head of the sick-bed, he was looking at him with this same horrifying thought:

"What art thou thinking of?" asked Leonardo.

"Fra Guglielmo dropped in this morning," replied Francesco, a trifle abashed, "wanting to see you. I told him he could not. . . ."

The master looked straight into his eyes, filled with supplication, fear, and hope.

"'Twas not that thou wast thinking of, Francesco. Why dost thou not wish to tell me?"

The pupil kept silent, abashed. And Leonardo comprehended everything. He turned away and frowned.—Always had he wished to die as he had lived,—in freedom and in truth. But he felt sorry for Francesco,—could it be that even now, in the last moments before death, he would disturb the peaceful faith, would seduce one of these "little ones"?

He again glanced at his pupil, put his emaciated hand upon Francesco's, and uttered with a soft smile:

"My son, send for Fra Guglielmo,—ask him to come to-morrow. I would confess and take communion. Invite Maître Guillaume also."

Francesco made no reply,—he merely kissed the hand of the master, with infinite gratitude.

IX

On the following morning, the twenty-third of April, on the Saturday of Passion Week, when Maître Guillaume, the notary, arrived, Leonardo communicated to him his last will: the four hundred florins, given for safe-keeping to the camerlingo of the Church of Santa Maria Nuova in the city of Florence, he bequeathed to his brothers, with whom he had been carrying on a law-suit, as a mark of complete reconciliation; to his pupil, Francesco Melzi, his books, scientific appliances, machines, manuscripts, and the remainder of the salary due from the King's treasury; to his servant, Battista Villanisso, all the household goods in the castle of Du Cloux, and half the vineyard outside the walls of Milan, near the Vercellina Gates, while the other half was to go to his pupil Andrea Salaino. As for the funeral rites, and so forth, he requested the notary to apply to Francesco Melzi, whom he appointed his executor.

Francesco with Maître Guillaume arranged with care a funeral which would make evident that Leonardo, despite popular rumour, had died a faithful son of the Church. The sick man approved of everything, and, wishing to show that he was taking an interest in Francesco's solicitude for the seemliness of the funeral, designated that, instead of the proposed eight pounds of candles during the requiem, ten be used; that instead of fifty, seventy Tourainian *sous* go for distribution to the poor.

When the will was ready, and there remained but to make it valid with the signatures of witnesses, Leonardo remembered about his old servant, the cook Maturina; Maître Guillaume had to add a new clause, whereby she received a dress of good black cloth, a head-dress lined with fur, also of cloth, and two ducats in gold, for her many years of faithful service. This consideration of the dying man for his poor servant filled Francesco's heart with the familiar feeling of unbearable pity.

Fra Guglielmo entered the room with the Holy Communion, and everybody withdrew. When he left the sick man, the monk set Francesco's mind at rest by informing him that Leonardo had fulfilled the rites of the Church with humility and submission to the will of God.

"Whatever people may say of him, my son," concluded Fra Guglielmo, "he is made innocent, according to the word of the Lord: 'Blessed are the pure in heart: for they shall see God.'"[69]

At night the sick man had attacks of asthma. Melzi feared that he would die in his arms. Toward morning,—this was on the twenty-fourth of April, Easter Sunday,—he felt relief. But since he was still asthmatic, and it was hot in the room, Francesco opened a window. White pigeons were soaring in the blue sky, and with the fluttering swish of their wings was blended the pealing of paschal bells. But the dying man no longer saw and no longer heard aught.

It seemed to him that unbelievable weights, like to enormous bowlders, were falling, tumbling upon him, crushing him; he wanted to rise up, to throw himself off,—and suddenly, with a final effort, he freed himself, flying off on gigantean wings; but again the stones tumbled down, piling up, crushing him; again he struggled, came off victorious, flew off,—and so on, without end. And every time the weight was more and more fearful, the effort more and more unbelievable. Finally he felt that he could no longer contend, and, with a cry of final despair: "My God! My God! Why hast thou forsaken me?" he submitted. And, as soon as he had submitted, he comprehended that the stones and the wings, the pressing of the weight and the striving for flight, the height and the depth, were one and the same; to fly or fall —'twas all the same. And he flew and fell, no longer knowing whether he was being lulled by the quiet waves of perpetual motion, or whether his mother was rocking him in her arms, to a lullaby.

For several days more his body still seemed alive to those about him; but he did not recover consciousness again. Finally, one morning,—this was on the second of May,—Francesco and Fra Guglielmo noted that his breath was failing. The monk began saying the prayer for the dying. After some time the pupil, placing his hand against the master's heart, felt that it no longer beat. He closed his eyes.

The face of the dead man changed but little. Upon it was the expression which it had frequently borne when alive,—that of a profound and quiet attention.

While Francesco with Battista Villanisso and the old servant Maturina were washing the body, the windows were wide open. At this moment, from below, from the workroom, the tamed swallow, which had been forgotten during the last few days, sensing liberty, flew up the well of the staircase and through the upper chambers, into the room where the dead man lay. Having circled above him, amid the funeral candles, burning with a dull flame in the light of the sunny morning, it swooped down, perhaps through old habit, upon the hands of Leonardo. Then, suddenly fluttering, it soared up, and through the open window flew off into the heavens, with a happy cry. And Francesco reflected that the master had for the last time done that which he had so loved to do,—given its freedom to a winged captive.

In accordance with the wish of the deceased, his body lay for three days; but in no charnel house, however,—Francesco had opposed this, —but in the same room where he had died. During the funeral, everything mentioned in the will was punctiliously carried out.

He was buried in the monastery of St. Florentine. But, since his quickly forgotten grave was soon level with the earth, and the memory of him vanished without a trace in Amboise, the place where Leonardo's ashes rest has remained unknown to the following generations.

Informing Leonardo's brothers in Florence of the death of the master, Francesco wrote:

"The grief occasioned within me by the death of him who was for me more than a father, I can not express. But, while I live, I shall mourn for him, inasmuch as he did love me with a great and tender love. But everyone, I think, should mourn the loss of such a man, whose like nature can not create.—Almighty God, send him now eternal rest."

X

On the day of Leonardo's death, Francis had been hunting in the forest of Saint-Germain. Learning of the demise of the artist, he ordered his workroom to be sealed till his arrival, since he wished to choose the best pictures for himself. However, Francis had at that time cares more important to him than art.

At this period one of the two Russian envoys in Rome, Dmitri Gerasimov, had returned to Moscow, the other, Nikita Karachiyarov, remained in Rome. Learning of the forthcoming election of the Kaiser, and the subsequent negotiations of Francis with his sovereign's bitterest foe, King Sigismund, Nikita, to obtain fuller and more exact data, set out for France together with the Papal envoy, and, even as during his first journey, took with him his old clerk Iliya Potapich Kopylo, the interpreter Vlassiy, and two junior clerks, Fedor Ignatievich Rudometov—"Fedka the Roasted,"—and Eutychus Paisevich Gagarov.[70]

Eutychus, as was the custom of many Russian travellers of that day, kept a brief record of his travels, wherein he noted down all that he had seen or heard of the curious.

Francis I, from Saint-Germain, journeyed to the hunting castle of Fontainebleau; thence to Amboise.

Immediately upon his arrival the King inspected the studio of Leonardo. On the evening of the same day the Princess Marguerite, with the envoy of the Kurfürst of Brandenburg and other foreign grandees, Nikita Karachiyarov of their number, set out for the Castle of Du Cloux. Getting wind of this, Fedka the Roasted advised his uncle, Iliya Potapich Kopylo, and Eutychus Gargarov, also to visit "Duclov," assuring them that they could see much that was curious in the house "of such a praiseworthy master as Leonardus, a man of wondrous reasoning, kind-hearted, in bookly knowledge well versed, in the science of language very rhetor, deeply learned in natural sciences, and possessed of a quick intelligence." Iliya Potapich and Eutychus, accompanied by Vlassiy the interpreter, followed him to the castle of Du Cloux.

When they arrived, Marguerite and the other guests, having already finished their tour of inspection, were then preparing to depart. Nevertheless, Francesco received the new guests with the unvarying courtesy which he extended to all visitors from foreign lands to the house of the master; he led them to the workroom, and began showing them everything therein.

As Eutychus was looking at the pictures, he paused in wonder before John the Precursor. At first he took him for a woman, and was incredulous when Vlassiy, according to Francesco's words, said that this was the Baptist; but, scrutinizing it more closely, he saw the reed cross,—"the cruciform staff,"—precisely the same as that with which the Russian icon-makers painted John the Precursor; he noted, moreover, the raiment of camel hair.—He was abashed. But, despite all the contrast of this Wingless Precursor with the winged, to whom Eutychus had become accustomed, the more he gazed upon him the more was he captivated by the foreign charm of the muliebrile Youth, and his smile, filled with mystery, with which he pointed to the Cross of Golgotha. In a daze, like one under a spell, he stood before this picture, thinking of naught, only feeling his heart constantly increase its beat from inexplicable emotion.

Iliya Potapich could not restrain himself,—he spat ferociously and swore:

"'Tis the impiety of the devil! The ignorance of the learned! This lewd one, like to a harlot, all denuded, having neither beard nor moustache,—is *he* the Forerunner? If he be a forerunner, then 'tis not of Christ, but rather of Antichrist. . . . Let us go, Eutychus, let us go, speedily, my child; befoul not thy een,—to us of the Orthodox Faith 'tis not even befitting to gaze upon such icons of theirs,—impious, pleasing to the fiend,—may they be accursed!"

And, taking Eutychus by the hand, he dragged him away from the picture almost by force, and for a long time after leaving Leonardo's house he would not be calmed.

Eutychus listened to him without comprehending. He was thinking of something else,—of "the icon pleasing to the fiend"; he was fain to forget it, and could not,—the mysterious visage of the Muliebrile, of the Wingless, floated before his eyes, frightening and captivating him, pursuing him like to a possession.

XI

SINCE, on this second arrival of Karachiyarov, the influx of foreigners into Amboise was not so great, their landlord had set aside for the Russian embassy quarters in the lower chambers of his house, more commodious and convenient. But Eutychus, preferring privacy, settled himself in the same room he had occupied two years ago,—under the very roof of the house, next to the dove cote; and, as before, arranged his tiny workroom in the niche of the dormer window.

Returning home from the castle of Du Cloux, and desiring to banish temptation, he began working on a new, almost completed image: John the Winged Precursor stood against the blue heavens, on a yellow sandy mountain, parched in the sun, half-round, as though it were on the edge of the world, surrounded by a dark-blue, almost black ocean. He had two heads,—one, the living, on his shoulders; the other in a vessel, which he held in his hand, as if to signify that only by having mortified everything mortal within him could man attain the winged, superhuman state; his visage was strange and appalling, the gaze of his wide-open eyes resembled the gaze of an eagle, staring at the sun; his shaggy cassock of camel hair reminded one of the feathers of a bird; his beard and hair floated in the air, as though from the strong wind of flight; the bones of his thin, emaciated hands and feet, unbelievably long, like those of a crane, barely covered by the skin, seemed supernaturally light, as though hollow within, like the ligaments and bones of the feathered folk; from his shoulders depended two gigantean wings, wide-spread against the azure sky, above the tawny earth and the black ocean, white as snow outside, scarlet-gold within, like flame, like to the wings of an enormous swan.

Eutychus had before him the task of finishing the gilding of the inner side of the wings.

But the work did not impart to him the usual oblivion: the wings of the Precursor reminded him now of the wings of Dædalus the Mechanic, now of the wings of Leonardo's flying machine. And the visage of the mysterious Youth-Virgin, the visage of the Wingless, would arise before him, obscuring the Winged, luring and frightening him, pursuing him like to a possession.

Hour after hour went by. He was thrown alternately into fever and chills. In the murk, lit up by the flares of heat lightnings, he lay with open eyes, listening to the stillness, in which he thought he heard strange swishings, whisperings, rustlings,—fatidical sounds, the omens of ancient Russian bookmen: "Ear-Ringing, Wall-Crackling, Mouse-Squeaking."

The second crowing of roosters was heard,—and he recalled the ancient legend of how, in the middle of the night, when the angels, taking the sun from the Throne of God, do bear it toward the east, the Cherubim strike their wings, and on earth every fowl flutters for joy, and the cock, taking his head from under his wing, awakes and beats his wings, prophesying light for the universe.

And again, and again, incongruous thoughts, that were like delirium, lagged upon each other's heels, broke off and, like rotted threads, tangled. In vain did he offer up prayers, holding his breath, as admonished by Nil Sorsky, the Russian saint,—naught availed: the visions became more and more vivid, more and more persistent.

Suddenly out of the murk there floated forth and stood out before him, as though alive, full of diabolical beauty, the visage of the Muliebrile, the Youth-Virgin, who, pointing to the Cross of Golgotha, with a tender and mocking smile gazed straight into the eyes of Eutychus with such an intense, caressing gaze, that his heart died within him from horror, and a cold sweat came out upon his brow.

He lit a candle; deciding to pass the remainder of the night without sleep, he took a book down from a shelf and began reading. This was an ancient Russian relation, *Of the Kingdom of Babylon.*

Having laid this book aside, Eutychus took another book,—the legend of *The White Hood.*

The relation *Of the Kingdom of Babylon* foretold the earthly, the legend of the *The White Hood* the heavenly, grandeur of the Land of Russia. Every time that Eutychus read these legends, his soul was filled with a dim emotion, which was incomprehensible even to him, akin to a boundless hope, from which his heart beat fast and his breath stopped short, as before a chasm.

No matter how bleak and humble his native land may have seemed to him in comparison with foreign lands, he believed in these prophecies of the coming grandeur of the Third Rome, of "Jerusalem, the New-begun City," of the ray of the rising sun on the seventy cupolas of the universal Russian temple of Sophia of the Wisdom of God.

He felt that there was a great mystery, and that, if he were to go deep within it, visions more fearful than those which had but now left him would beset him anew.

Trying not to think, he extinguished the candle and lay down on the bed.

XII

AND he dreamt a dream:

With a fiery face, with fiery wings, in glittering chasubles, a Woman was standing on a sickle-shaped moon in the midst of clouds, under a seven-pillared tabernacle with the inscription: "Wisdom hath builded her house";[71] prophets, saints, patriarchs, angels bearing gifts, Powers, Thrones, Dominions, Princedoms surrounded her, and among the host of the prophets, at the very pediment of Wisdom stood John the Precursor, with the same thin, crane-like arms and legs, with the same white gigantean wings as in the icon, but with another face: by the exposed brow with its obdurate creases, by the bristling eyebrows, the long white beard and grey hair, Eutychus recognized the face graven on his memory, of the old man resembling Elijah the Prophet, who, two years ago, had come to his workroom,—the face of Leonardo da Vinci, the inventor of human wings.—Beneath, under the clouds on which the Woman stood, blazed, like hot flames, against the blue sky, the golden cupolas and domes of churches; one could see black, newly-ploughed fields, blue groves, radiant rivers and an infinite vista,—in the last he recognized the Land of Russia.

Bells boomed forth in triumphal pealing; the Many-Eyed Ones began chanting a conquering pæan, an Alleluia; the Six-Winged Ones, covering in awe their faces with their wings, cried out: "*Let all mortal flesh be silent, and stand with fear and trembling*";[72] and the Seven Archangels beat their wings; and the seven thunders spake. And above the Woman with eyes of fire, above St. Sophia of the Wisdom of God, the heavens opened, and an object appeared,—white, sunlike, appalling. And Eutychus understood that this was the *White Hood*, the Crown of Christ over the Land of Russia.

The scroll which the Precursor held in his hand unrolled, and Eutychus read: "Behold, I shall send My Angel, and he shall prepare the way before me: and the Lord, whom ye seek, shall suddenly come to his temple, even the Angel of the covenant, whom ye delight in: behold, he shall come."

The voices of the thunders, the beating of the angels' wings, the conquering chant of the Alleluia, blended into a single pæan of praise for St. Sophia of the Wisdom of God.

And all the fallow-fields, the groves, rivers, mountains, and infinite vistas of the Land of Russia, echoed back in answer.

Eutychus awoke.

It was early morning, and grey. He arose and opened the window. The fragrant freshness of leaves and grasses laved by rain was wafted up to him,—a thunderstorm had passed in the night. The sun had not yet risen. But, at the edge of the sky, above the dark woods, beyond the river, where it was to rise, the huddled clouds glowed with purple and gold. The streets of the city slumbered in their murk; the slender white belfry of Saint-Hubert alone was illumined by a pale-green, seemingly subaqueous light. The silence was absolute, filled with great expectancy,—save that, on the sandy shallows of the desolate Loire, the wild swans were calling to one another.

From behind the dark woods, like a glowing ember, appeared the rim of the sun, and something that was like music was wafted over earth and heaven.

The white pigeons fluttered up from under the projection of the roof and rustled their wings.

A ray penetrated into the workroom of Eutychus, falling on the icon of John the Precursor, and his gilded wings,—scarlet-gold on the inner side, like flame, white on the outer, like snow, wide-spread against the azure sky, above the tawny earth and the black ocean, like to the wings of a gigantean swan,—suddenly glittered, sparkling in the purple of the sun, as though they had become animated with a supernatural life.

Eutychus recalled his dream, took up a brush, and, having dipped it in scarlet ink, wrote on the white scroll of the Winged Precursor:

Behold, I will send My Angel, and he shall prepare the way before me: and the Lord, whom ye seek, shall suddenly come to his temple, even the Angel of the covenant, whom ye delight in: behold, he shall come. . . .

FINIS

TRANSLATOR'S NOTES

1. Revelation XX,—2, 3.
2. Psalm LV,—1, 2, 4.
3. St. John XV,—1.
4. Genesis VI,—17.
5. Zechariah II,—7. "Deliver thyself, O Zion, that dwellest with the daughter of Babylon."
6. St. John XIII,—1, 2, 21–27.
7. St. John XIII,—37.
8. St. John XVII,—21.
9. Genesis II,—16, 17.
10. Lorenzo de' Medici, 1492.
11. Zechariah XIV,—20.
12. Psalm LXVIII,—1, 2.
13. St. John VIII,—12.
14. St. Matthew X,—16.
15. I Corinthians VIII,—11.
16. Genesis II,—17.
17. I John II,—18.
18. James I,—8.
19. I Corinthians X,—21.
20. St. Luke II,—32.
21. St. Matthew XXI,—16.
22. St. Matthew XVIII,—3.
23. I Corinthians I,—19.
24. Probably in Book I, Epigram XXXVII. The best—and only complete—version is Mitchell S. Buck's.

24[a]. This conceit occurs in Rabelais, *Baron Munchausen*, *Paul Bunyan*, and also, if I remember rightly, in Lucian and Montaigne.

24[b]. *Paradise*, XV, 106. I am indebted for this translation (a far better one than Cary's) to Frances Winwar, the novelist.

24[c]. *Paradise*, XVI, 96.

25. One of the prodigies of the good Gutefundus. Frank R. Stockton retells his adventures in his scarce *Tales out of School.*
26. In every-day Russian, the French Sickness means syphilis; the German Sickness is gonorrhœa. In present-day German, the French Sickness means the latter disease.
27. Deut. VI,—16.
28. St. Matthew XVII,—20.
29. St. Mark XIII,—26.
30. Psalm LXVIII,—34–35.
31. St. Mark XI,—9.
32. Genesis VII,—20. "Fifteen cubits upward did the waters prevail."
33. I John IV,—18.
34. St. Matthew XXVI,—38.

35. St. Luke XXII,—41.
36. St. Matthew XXVI,—39.
37. St. Mark XIV,—36.
38. St. Matthew XXVI,—42.
39. St. Luke XXII,—44.
40. St. John I,—1, 2, 3.
41. St. John I,—14.
42. St. John XIII,—21.
43. St. John XVI,—33.
44. St. John X,—30.
45. St. John XVII,—25, 26.
46. Moro is adapting to his own needs Matthew VIII,—20, and Luke IX, —58.
47. St. Matthew IV,—5, 6.
48. St. Matthew XVIII,—3.
49. Genesis III,—4, 5.
50. St. Matthew IV,—7.
51. Revelation II,—27.
52. Revelation XIII,—4; XVII,—3, 5.
53. Revelation XVII,—6 reads "wondered with great admiration." The word is used in its archaic sense of wonder, surprise or astonishment.
54. St. Luke I,—42.
55. Venus of the Beautiful Buttocks.
56. St. Luke XVIII,—16.
57. St. Matthew V,—3.
58. I Kings XIX,—11, 12, 13.
59. St. John XV,—1.
60. St. Matthew XI,—28.
61. Malachi III,— 1. — I have adhered, in view of its significance, to the Russian version. The King James version reads "messenger" for "Angel."
62. Song of Songs V,—1.
63. St. Mark XIV,—25.
64. St. John XVI,—1.
65. St. John VI,—55.
66. St. John VI,—54.
67. St. John VII,—37.
68. St. Mark I,—7.
69. St. Matthew V,—8.
70. I have preferred not to use the nearest English equivalent: Eutychus [Prosper] is the young man who fell asleep—and also from a third floor window—at one of Paul's apostolic sermons,—showing the superiority of modern pews (Acts XX,—9 to 12 inclusive).
71. Proverbs IX,—1.
72. "The Cherubic Hymn" from the liturgy of St. James. I am greatly indebted to Arthur W. Johnson, Esq., of Ipswich, Mass., for help in locating and correcting this quotation.